D0378270

BY HARRY TURTLEDOVE

The Guns of the South

THE WORLDWAR SAGA

Worldwar: In the Balance

Worldwar: Tilting the Balance

Worldwar: Upsetting the Balance

Worldwar: Striking the Balance

Homeward Bound

THE VIDESSOS CYCLE

The Misplaced Legion

An Emperor for the Legion

The Legion of Videssos

Swords of the Legion

THE TALE OF KRISPOS

Krispos Rising

Krispos of Videssos

Krispos the Emperor

THE TIME OF TROUBLES SERIES

The Stolen Throne

Hammer and Anvil

The Thousand Cities

Videssos Besieged

A World of Difference

Departures

How Few Remain

THE GREAT WAR

The Great War: American Front

The Great War: Walk in Hell

The Great War: Breakthroughs

AMERICAN EMPIRE

American Empire: Blood and Iron

American Empire: The Center Cannot Hold

American Empire: The Victorious Opposition

SETTLING ACCOUNTS

Settling Accounts: Return Engagement

Settling Accounts: Drive to the East

Settling Accounts: The Grapple

Settling Accounts: In at the Death

Every Inch a King

The Man with the Iron Heart

THE WAR THAT CAME EARLY

The War That Came Early: Hitler's War

The War That Came Early: West and East

The War That Came Early: The Big Switch

The War That Came Early: Coup d'Etat

The War That Came Early: Two Fronts

VIDESSOS CYCLE

Volume One

Volume Two

VIDESSOS CYCLE

VOLUME TWO

2013 Del Rey Books Trade Paperback Edition

Published in the United States by Del Rey, an imprint of The Random House Publishing Group, a division of Random House, Inc., New York.

Del Rey is a registered trademark and the Del Rey colophon is a trademark of Random House, Inc.

The Legion of Videssos and *Swords of the Legion* were both published in paperback in 1987 by Del Rey, an imprint of the Random House Publishing Group, a division of Random House, Inc.

ISBN: 978-0-345-54259-5
eBook ISBN: 978-0-345-54570-1

Printed in the United States of America

www.delreybooks.com

Maps by Shelly Shapiro

2 4 6 8 9 7 5 3 1

VIDESSOS CYCLE

VOLUME TWO

THE LEGION OF VIDESSOS
SWORDS OF THE LEGION

Harry Turtledove

Ballantine Books
New York

VIDESSOS CYCLE

VOLUME TWO

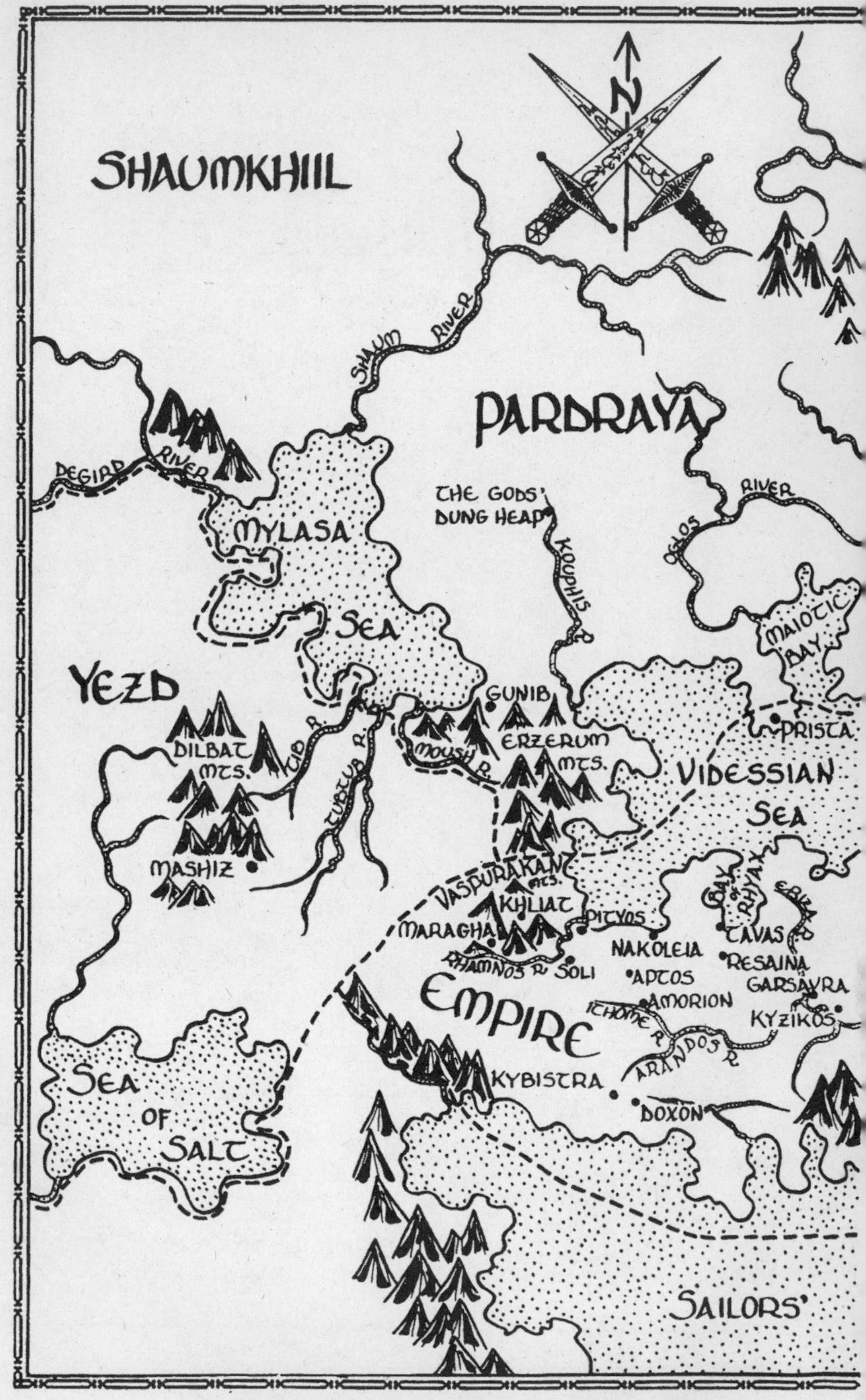
N
SHAUMKHIIL
SHAUM RIVER
PARDRAYA
DEGIRD RIVER
MYLASA
SEA
THE GODS' DUNG HEAP
KOUPHIS R.
OGLOS RIVER
MAIOTIC BAY
YEZD
DILBAT MTS.
TIB R.
TUTUB R.
MASHIZ
GUNIB
MOUSH R.
ERZERUM MTS.
PRISTA
VIDESSIAN SEA
VASPURAKAN MTS.
KHLIAT
MARAGHA
PITYOS
RHAMNOS R.
SOLI
NAKOLEIA
APTOS
AMORION
BAY OF RHYAX
ERIZA R.
TAVAS
RESAINA
GARSAVRA
KYZIKOS
EMPIRE
ICHOME R.
ARANDOS R.
KYBISTRA
DOXON
SEA OF SALT
SAILORS'

HALOGA
NORTHERN
SEA
BAY OF
HALOGA
AGDER
KINGDOM
OF
AGDER
THATAGUSH
KHATRISH
ASTRIS RIVER
DUCHY
NUSTAD
OF
SOTEVAG
NAMDALEN
METEPONT
IMBROS
VIDESSOS
KYPAS
THE
KEY
OPSIKION
VIDESSOS
OF
SEA
SHELLY SHAPIRO '86

THE LEGION OF VIDESSOS

For Kevin, Marcella, Tom, and Kathy

WHAT HAS GONE BEFORE:

THREE COHORTS OF A ROMAN LEGION, LED BY MILITARY TRIBUNE Marcus Aemilius Scaurus and senior centurion Gaius Philippus, were trying to rejoin Caesar's main army when they were ambushed by Gauls. The Gallic leader Viridovix challenged Marcus to single combat. Both bore druids' swords as battle spoil. When the blades crossed, a dome of light surrounded Viridovix and the Romans. Suddenly they were in the world of the Empire of Videssos, a land where priests of the god Phos could work real magic. There they were hired as mercenaries by the Empire.

In Videssos the city, capital of the Empire, Marcus met the soldier-Emperor Mavrikios Gavras and the prime minister, Vardanes Sphrantzes, a bureaucrat whose enmity Marcus incurred. At a banquet for the Romans, he met Alypia, Mavrikios' daughter, and the sorcerer Avshar. Avshar forced a duel on him; but when the druid's sword neutralized Avshar's spells, Marcus won. Avshar sought revenge by magic. It failed, and Avshar fled to Yezd, western enemy of Videssos. Videssos declared formal war on Yezd.

As native and mercenary troops flooded into the capital, tension broke out between Videssians and the troops from the island kingdom of Namdalen over a small religious difference, with each declaring the other to be heretics. The Videssian patriarch Balsamon preached tolerance, but fanatic monks stirred the trouble into rioting. Marcus led the Romans to control the riots. As those were ending, Marcus saved the Namdalener woman Helvis. They made love, and she and her young son soon joined him in the Roman barracks.

Finally the unwieldy army marched west against Yezd, accompanied by women and dependents. Marcus was pleased to learn Helvis was pregnant, but shocked to discover the left wing was commanded by Sphrantzes' young and wholly inexperienced nephew, Ortaias.

Two Vaspurakaners, Senpat Sviodo and his wife Nevrat, acted as guides to the Romans. Gagik Bagratouni, a Vaspurakaner noble, joined the army. When a fanatic priest, Zemarkhos, cursed him, Bagratouni threw the priest in a sack with his dog and beat the sack. But Marcus, fearing a pogrom, interceded for the priest.

At last the two armies met, with Avshar commanding the Yezda. Battle seemed a draw, until a spell from Avshar panicked Ortaias, who fled. Mavrikios Gavras was killed as the left wing collapsed, and the army of Videssos was routed.

The Romans retreated in order, collecting their womenfolk. They rescued Nepos, a priest and teacher of sorcery, and were joined by Laon Pakhymer and a band of mounted Khatrishers, giving them cavalry support. They marched eastward, harried by the Yezda.

They wintered in the friendly town of Aptos. Marcus learned that Ortaias, calling himself Emperor, had married Alypia. But Mavrikios Gavras' brother Thorisin had retreated with twenty-five hundred troops to a nearby city. In the spring, Marcus joined him to march toward Videssos the city. Cloaked under a spell by Nepos, they crossed the narrow strip of water to the city, but found the gates slammed in their faces. No army had ever penetrated the city's walls.

Days passed futilely, until a desperate band inside the city managed to throw open the gates. Then they drove the city forces under Ortaias' commander Rhavas back to the palace. There Rhavas—Avshar in disguise—resorted to foul magic. But the swords of Marcus and Viridovix overcame the spell. Avshar retreated to where Vardanes and Ortaias Sphrantzes held Alypia hostage. But under pressure, Vardanes attacked Avshar, who killed him and then fled to a small chamber—and suddenly vanished.

Crowned as Emperor, Thorisin annulled Alypia's marriage and banished Ortaias to serve as a humble monk.

But there were still troubles. Tax receipts were far too low, and ships from the island called the Key prevented supplies from reaching the city. Thorisin appointed Marcus to supervise the tax collectors. Marcus soon discovered that rich landowners never paid properly; the worst offender was general Baanes Onomagoulos, an old friend of Mavrikios Gavras. Learning this, Thorisin sent a force of Namdaleners under count Drax to deal with Onomagoulos. Marcus persuaded the Emperor to free a prisoner, Taron Leimmokheir, and give him command of the puny naval forces. By trickery, Leimmokheir managed to defeat the ships of the Key.

Meanwhile, Thorisin was sending a party to far north Arshaum for help. Gorgidas, Greek physician of the legion and close friend of Marcus, decided to go along. And at the last minute, Viridovix, escaping the wrath of Thorisin's mistress, joined Gorgidas.

In a temple ceremony, Thorisin announced that count Drax had won a battle against Onomagoulos, who was now dead. Next—Yezd!

I

"Too hot and sticky," Marcus Aemilius Scaurus complained, wiping his sweaty forehead with the heel of his hand. In late afternoon Videssos' towering walls shaded the practice field just outside them, but it was morning now, and their gray stone reflected heat in waves. The military tribune sheathed his sword. "I've had enough."

"You northerners don't know good weather," Gaius Philippus said. The senior centurion was sweating as hard as his superior, but he reveled in it. Like most Romans, he enjoyed the Empire's climate.

But Marcus sprang from Mediolanum, a north Italian town founded by the Celts, and it was plain some of their blood ran in his veins. "Aye, I'm blond. I can't help it, you know," he said wearily; Gaius Philippus had teased him for his un-Roman looks as long as they had known each other.

The centurion could have been the portrait on a denarius himself, with his wide, squarish face, strong nose and chin, and short cap of graying hair. And like nearly all his countrymen, Scaurus included, he kept on shaving even after two and a half years in Videssos, a bearded land. The Romans were stubborn folk.

"Look at the sun," Marcus suggested.

Gaius Philippus gauged it with a quick, experienced glance. He whistled in surprise. "Have we been at it that long? I was enjoying myself." He turned to the exercising legionaries, shouting, "All right, knock off! Form up for parade to barracks!"

The soldiers, original Romans and the Videssians, Vaspurakaners, and others who had joined their ranks since they came to the Empire, laid down their double-weight wicker swords and heavy practice shields with groans of relief. Gaius Philippus, who was past fifty, had more stamina than most men twenty and thirty years his junior; Scaurus had envied it many times.

"They're looking quite good," he said.

"It could be worse," Gaius Philippus allowed. Coming from the veteran, it was highest praise. A thoroughgoing professional, he would never be truly satisfied by anything short of perfection—or, at least, would never admit it if he was.

He grumbled as he rammed his sword into its bronze scabbard. "I don't like this polluted blade. It's not a proper *gladius;* it's too long, Videssian iron is too springy, and the grip feels wrong in my hand. I should have given it to Gorgidas and kept my good one; the fool Greek wouldn't have known the difference."

"Plenty of legionaries would be happy to trade with you," Marcus said. As he'd known it would, that made the veteran clap a protective hand to the hilt of the sword, which was in fact a fine sample of the swordsmith's art. "As for Gorgidas, you miss him as much as I do, I'd say—and Viridovix, too."

"Nonsense to the one and double nonsense to the other. A sly little Greekling and a wild Gaul? The sun must have addled your wits."

The tribune knew insincerity when he heard it. "You're not happy without something to grouse over."

"Nor are you, unless you're picking at my brains."

Marcus smiled wryly; there was some truth in the charge. Gaius Philippus was a more typical Roman than he in more ways than looks, being practical, straightforward, and inclined to distrust anything that smacked of theory.

They made a formidable pair, with the veteran as shrewd tactician and Scaurus, whose Stoic training and political background gave him a breadth of view Gaius Philippus could never match, as strategist devising the legionaries' best course. Before the tribune's druid-enchanted sword met Viridovix' and propelled the Romans to Videssos, he had not planned on a military career, but any rising young man needed to be able to point to some army time. Now, as mercenary captain in the faction-filled Empire, he needed all his political skill merely to survive among soldiers and courtiers who had been double-dealing, he sometimes thought, since before they left their mothers' breasts.

"You there, Flaccus! Straighten it up!" Gaius Philippus shouted. The Roman shifted his feet an inch or two, then looked back inquiringly. Gaius Philippus glared at him, more from habit than anger. His gaze raked the rest of the soldiers. "All right, move out!" he said grudgingly. The buccinators' cornets and trumpets echoed his command, a metallic blare.

The Videssian guardsmen at the Silver Gate saluted Marcus as they would one of their own officers, with bowed heads and right fists clenched over their hearts. He nodded back, but eyed the great iron-faced gates and spiked portcullis with scant liking; too many irreplaceable Romans had fallen trying unsuccessfully to force them the previous summer. Only rebellion inside the city had let Thorisin Gavras make good his claim to the Empire against Ortaias Sphrantzes, though Ortaias was no leader. With works like the capital's, a defense did not need much leadership.

The legionaries tramped through the gloom of the walled passageway between the city's outer and inner walls, and suddenly Videssos brawled around them. Entering the city was always like taking a big swig of strong wine. The newcomer breathed deeply, opened his eyes a little wider, and braced himself for the next pull.

Middle Street, Videssos' chief thoroughfare, was one Marcus knew well. The Romans had paraded down it the day they first entered the capital, made a desperate dash to the palace complex when Ortaias was toppled from the throne, and marched along it countless times on their way back and forth between barracks and practice field.

It was a slow march today; as usual, Middle Street was packed tight with people. The tribune wished for a herald like that one he'd had the first day in Videssos, to clear the traffic ahead of him, but that was a luxury he no longer enjoyed. The legionaries were just behind a pair of huge, creaking wagons, both full of sand-yellow limestone for some building project or other. A dozen horses hauled each one, but at a snail's pace.

Vendors swarmed like flies round the dawdling soldiers, shouting out the virtues of their wares: sausages and fried fish, which had flies of their own; wine; flavored ices—a favorite winter treat, but brought in by runner in warm weather, and so too expensive for most troopers' wallets—goods of leather, or wicker, or bronze; and aphrodisiacs. "Make you good for seven rounds a night!" the peddler announced dramatically. "Here, you, sir, care to try it?"

He thrust a vial toward Sextus Minucius, newly promoted underofficer. Minucius was tall, handsome, and young, with a perpetual blue-black stubble on his cheeks and chin. In crested helmet and highly polished mail shirt, he cut an impressively masculine figure.

He took the little jar from the Videssian's skinny hand, tossed it up and down as if considering, and gave it back. "No, you keep it," he said. "What do I want with a potion to slow me down?" The legionaries bayed laughter, not least at the sight of one of Videssos' glib hucksters at a loss for words.

Every block or two, it seemed, they passed one of Phos' temples; there were hundreds of them in the city. Blue-robed priests and monks, their shaved heads gleaming almost as brightly as the golden globes atop the temples' spires, were no small part of the street traffic. They drew the circular sun-sign of their faith as they passed Marcus' troopers. Enough men, Videssians and Romans who had come to follow the Empire's god, returned it to hold their ever-ready suspicions of heresay at bay.

The legionaries marched through the plaza of Stavrakios with its gilded statue of that great, conquering Emperor; through the din of the coppersmiths' district, where Middle Street bent to run straight west to the Imperial Palaces; through the plaza called, for no reason Marcus had even been able to learn, the forum of the Ox; past the sprawling red-granite edifice that held Videssos' archives—and its felons as well—and into the plaza of Palamas, the greatest of the imperial capital's fora.

If Videssos the city was a microcosm of Videssos the empire, the plaza of Palamas was Videssos the city in small. Nobles wearing their traditional brocaded robes rubbed shoulders with street toughs in puffed-sleeve tunics and garish hose. Here a drunken whore lolled against a wall, her legs splayed open; there a Namdalener mercenary, the back of his head shaved so it would fit his helmet better, haggled with a fat Videssian jeweler over the price of a ring for his lady; there a monk and a prosperous-looking baker passed the time of day arguing some theological point, both smiling at their sport.

Seeing the mercenary made Scaurus glance at the Milestone, an obelisk of the same ruddy granite as the archives building, from which all distances in the Empire were reckoned. A huge placard at its base lauded the great count Drax, whose regiment of Namdaleni had crushed the revolt Baanes Onomagoulos had raised in the westlands. Onomagoulos' head, just fetched to the city, was displayed above the placard. The late rebel was nearly bald, so instead of being hung by the hair, the head was suspended from a cord tied round its ears. Only a few Videssians paid any attention; in the past couple of generations, unsuccessful rebels had become too common to attract much notice.

Gaius Philippus followed Marcus' eye. "Whoreson had it coming," he said.

The tribune nodded. "After Mavrikios Gavras was killed, he thought the Empire should be his by right. He never could think of Thorisin as anything but Mavrikios' worthless little brother, and if there's any worse mistake to make, I can't think of it offhand."

"Nor I." Gaius Philippus had a soldier's respect for the Avtokrator of the Videssians, one which Thorisin Gavras returned.

The palace compound's calm, uncrowded beauty always came as something of a shock after the ferment of the plaza of Palamas. Marcus was never sure how he would react to the transition; sometimes it soothed him, but about as often he felt he was withdrawing from life itself. Today, he decided, the plaza had been a little too strident for his taste. A quiet afternoon at the barracks doing nothing would suit him down to the ground.

"Sir?" the sentry said hesitantly.

"Eh? What is it, Fostulus?" Marcus looked up from the troops' pay-sheet listings, looked down again so he would remember where he was, then looked up once more.

"There's a baldy outside, sir, says he needs to talk with you."

"A baldy?" The tribune blinked. "You mean, a priest?"

"What else?" Fostulus said, grinning; he was not one of the Romans who followed Phos. "Big fat fellow, must be rising fifty from the gray in his beard. He's got a mean mouth," the sentry added.

Marcus scratched his head. He knew several priests, but the description did not sound like any of them. Still, it would not do to offend Videssos' religious hierarchy; in some ways it was more powerful than the Emperor himself. He sighed and rolled up the account parchment, tying it shut with a ribbon. "Bring him in, I suppose."

"Yes, sir." Fostulus saluted—Roman-style, with outthrust arm—then spun smartly on his heel and hurried back to the doorway. The hobnails in the soles of his *caligae* clicked on the slate floor.

"Took you long enough," Scaurus heard the man grumbling as Fostulus led him back to the little table in the rear corner of the barracks hall that the tribune used as a makeshift office. Marcus rose to greet him as he approached.

Fostulus had been right; the priest was nearly of a height with Scaurus, whose northern blood gave him more inches than most Romans or Videssians enjoyed. And when they clasped hands, the fellow's firm, dry grip showed considerable strength. "You can go now, Fostulus," the tribune said. With another salute, the sentry returned to his station.

The priest flung himself into a chair, which creaked under his weight. Sweat darkened the armpits of his blue robe and sprayed from his shaved pate; Marcus was glad he had closed the account roll. "Phos' light, standing there in the sun is hot work," the Videssian said accusingly, his voice a rumbling bass. "D'you have any wine for a thirsty man?"

"Well, yes," the tribune said, disconcerted by such brusqueness; most Videssians were smoother spoken. He found a jug and a couple of earthenware cups, poured, handed one cup to the priest, and raised the other in salute. "Your health, ah—" he paused, not knowing the man's name.

"Styppes," the priest said curtly; like all Videssian clerics, he had abandoned his surname, a symbol of his dedication to Phos alone.

Before he tasted the wine, he raised both hands to the sky, murmuring his faith's basic creed: "We bless thee, Phos, Lord with the great and good mind, by thy grace our protector, watchful beforehand that the great test of life may be decided in our favor." Then he spat on the floor in rejection of Skotos, Phos' evil opponent in the Empire's dualistic religion.

He waited for a moment for the Roman to join him in the ritual, but

Scaurus, although he respected Videssos' customs, did not ape the ones he failed to share. Styppes gave him a disdainful glance. "Heathen," he muttered. Marcus saw what Fostulus had meant about his mouth; its narrow, bloodless lips barely covered strong yellow teeth.

Then Styppes drank, and the tribune had to fight to keep contempt from his face in turn. The Videssian drained his cup at a draught, filled it without asking Scaurus' leave, emptied it once more, refilled, and swallowed a third while Marcus' lips were hardly wet. Styppes started to pour again, but the jug gave out with his cup half-empty. He snorted in annoyance and tossed it off.

"Will the wine do you, or was there something else you wanted?" Scaurus asked sharply. He was immediately ashamed of himself; had Stoicism not taught him to accept each man as he was, good and bad together? If this Styppes loved the grape too well, despising him for it would hardly change him.

Marcus tried again, this time without sarcasm. "How can I, or perhaps my men, help you?"

"I doubt it would be possible," Styppes answered, raising the tribune's hackles afresh. "But I have been told to help you." His sour expression did not speak well for his pleasure at the undertaking.

The priest was a veteran drinker. His speech did not slur, and he moved with perfect assurance. Only a slight flush to what had been a rather pallid complexion betrayed the wine he had on board.

Sipping from his own cup, Scaurus took hold of his temper with both hands. "Ah? Told by whom?" he asked, making a game stab at sounding interested. The sooner this sponge in a blue robe left, the better. He wondered whether his priestly friend Nepos or Balsamon the patriarch had sent him and, if so, what they had against the Romans.

But Styppes surprised him, saying, "Mertikes Zigabenos informs me you have lost your healer."

"That's so," Scaurus admitted; he wondered how Gorgidas was faring on the Pardrayan steppe. Zigabenos was commander of the imperial bodyguard, and a very competent young man indeed. If this priest had his favor, perhaps there was something to him after all. "What of it?"

"He suggested I offer you my services. I have been trained in Phos' healing arts, and it is not right for any unit of his Majesty's army to be without such aid—even one full of pagans, as is yours," Styppes ended disparagingly.

Marcus ignored that. "You're a healer-priest? And assigned to us?" It was all he could do to keep from shouting with glee. Using themselves as channels of Phos' energies, some priests could work cures on men Gorgidas had given up for dead; as much as anything, his failure to learn their methods had driven him to the plains. Nepos had healed his share, even though he was no specialist in the art. To have a man who was could prove more precious than rubies, Scaurus thought. "Assigned to us?" he repeated, wanting to hear Styppes say it again.

"Aye." The priest still seemed far from overjoyed; as he was familiar with it, his talent was much less wonderful to him than to the Roman. He looked at the bedrolls neatly checkering the barracks floor. "You'll have quarters for me here, then?"

"Certainly; whatever you like."

"What I'd like is more wine."

Not wanting to antagonize him or seem mean, Marcus struck the seal from another jug and handed it to him. "Care for any?" Styppes asked. When the tribune shook his head, the priest, disdaining his cup, drank the jar dry. Scaurus' worries returned.

"Ahhh," Styppes said when he was done, a long exhalation of pleasure. He rose—and lurched somewhat; so much neat wine downed so fast would have sozzled a demigod. "Be back," he said, and now the drink was in his speech, too. "Got to get m'gear from the mon'stery, fetch it here." Moving with the carefully steady strides of a man used to walking wine-soaked, he started toward the doorway.

He had only taken a couple of steps when he turned back to Marcus. He studied him with owlish intensity for nearly a minute, then left just as Scaurus was about to ask him what was on his mind. Frustrated, the Roman went back to his paysheets.

That evening, Helvis asked him, "So, how do you like this Styppes?"

"Like him? That has nothing to do with anything—what choice have I? Any healer is better than none." Wondering how frank he should be with her, Marcus leaned back against a thin wood partition; two of the four barracks halls the legionaries used were divided up to give partnered soldiers and their women and children some privacy.

She frowned, sensing his hesitation, but before she could frame her question, her five-year-old son Malric threw aside the wooden cart he had been playing with and started to sing a bawdy Videssian marching song at the top of his lungs: "Little bird with a yellow bill—"

She rolled her eyes, blue like those of many Namdaleni. "Enough of that, young man. Time for bed." He ignored her, singing on until she grabbed his ankles and lifted him. He hung upside down, shrieking laughter. His tunic fell down over his head; he thrashed his way out of it. Helvis caught Marcus' eye. "There's half the battle won."

The tribune smiled, watching as she peeled his stepson's trousers off. Even in such inelegant activity, she was a pleasure to look at. Her skin was fairer and her features less aquiline than the Videssian norm, but strong cheekbones and a generous mouth gave her face a beauty of its own. And her figure was opulent, its rich curves filling her long skirt and lace-bodiced blouse of maroon linen in a way that caught any man's eye. As yet her early pregnancy had not begun to swell her belly.

She swatted Malric lightly on his bare bottom. "Go on, kiss Marcus goodnight, use the pot, and go to sleep." Her voice was a smooth contralto.

Malric complained and fussed to see if she was serious; the next swat had more authority behind it. "All right, Mama, I'm going," he said, and trotted over to Scaurus. "Goodnight, Papa." He had spoken Namdalener patois with Helvis, but used Latin with the tribune; he had picked up the Roman tongue with a child's ease in the nearly two years Marcus and Helvis had been together.

"Good night, son. Sleep well." Scaurus ruffled the boy's shock of blond hair, so like that of his dead father Hemond. Malric piddled, then slid under the blanket and closed his eyes. Marcus' own son Dosti, not quite a year old, was asleep in a crib close by the sleeping mats. He whimpered, but quieted as soon as Helvis pulled the coverlet up over him. Some nights now, the tribune thought hopefully, he slept all the way through.

When Helvis was sure Malric was asleep, too, she turned back to Scaurus. "What's wrong with the healer-priest?"

At the blunt question, Marcus' hesitation disappeared. "Not much," he said, but before she could do more than begin to raise her eyebrows, he went on, "except that he's an arrogant, greedy, ill-tempered sot—at the moment he's passed out on the floor in one of the bachelor halls, snoring like a sawmill. I doubt he could fix a fleabite, let alone really heal."

Helvis laughed nervously, half amused at Styppes' shortcomings, half scandalized by Scaurus' open contempt for him. She was a zealous follower of Phos, and hearing a priest of any sect maligned made her ill at ease; still, as a Namdalener she reckoned the Videssians heretics and so, in a way, fair game. The ambiguity confused her.

A splinter gouged Marcus' shoulder through his shirt. As he dug it out with a thumbnail, he thought that ambiguity was something he, too, had come to know with Helvis. They were too different to be wholly comfortable with one another, each of them too strong-willed to yield easily. Religion, policy, love-making . . . sometimes it seemed there were few things over which they did not quarrel.

But when things went well, he said to himself with an inward smile, they went very well indeed. Still rubbing his shoulder, he stood and kissed her. She looked at him quizzically. "What was that for?"

"No real reason."

Her face lit. "That's the best reason of all." She pressed herself against him. Her chin fit nicely on his shoulder; she was tall for a woman, as tall, in fact, as many Videssian men. He kissed her again, this time thoroughly. Afterward, he never was sure which one of them blew out the lamp.

Scaurus was spooning up his breakfast porridge—barley flavored with bits of beef and onion—when Junius Blaesus came up to him. The junior centurion looked unhappy. "Mglmpf?" the tribune said, and then, after he had swallowed, "What's the matter?" From Blaesus' hangdog air, he had a fair idea.

The Roman's long face grew glummer yet. A veteran *optio,* or under-officer, he was newly promoted to centurion's rank and did not like to admit there were problems in his maniple that he had trouble handling.

Marcus cocked an eyebrow at him and waited; pushing would only make him more sensitive than he was.

At last Blaesus blurted out, "It's Pullo and Vorenus, sir."

The tribune nodded, unsurprised. "Again?" he said. He took a deliberate swig of wine; like almost all Videssian vintages, it was too sweet for his taste. He went on, "Glabrio had nothing but trouble with them. What are they squabbling about now?"

"Which of them threw the *pilum* better at practice yesterday. Pullo swung at Vorenus last night, but they got pulled apart before they could mix it." Relief was flowering on the junior centurion; Quintus Glabrio, whose unit he now led, had been a truly outstanding officer. If, before his death, he had not been able to control the two fractious legionaries, then Blaesus could hardly be blamed for having problems with them.

"Swung on him, you say? We can't have that." Scaurus finished his porridge, wiped off the bone spoon, and put it back in his belt-pouch. He rose. "I'll have a word or two with them. Set your mind at ease, Junius; it won't be the first time."

"Yes, sir." Blaesus saluted and hurried off on other business, relieved to have survived the interview. Marcus watched him go, not quite satisfied. Quintus Glabrio, he thought, would have come with him, instead of being content to have passed the problem on. It seemed an evasion of responsibility, a grave flaw by Scaurus' Stoic-tinged standards. Well, he thought, that must be why Blaesus stayed an *optio* so long.

Titus Pullo sprang to attention when he saw the tribune walking toward him, a fair sign of a guilty conscience. So, interestingly, did Lucius Vorenus. Except for their feud with each other, they were excellent soldiers, probably the two finest in the maniple. Both were in their late twenties, Pullo a bit stockier, Vorenus perhaps a trifle quicker.

Scaurus glared at them, doing his best to project an image of stern reproach. "We've been through all this before," he said. "Docking your pay doesn't do much good, does it?"

"Sir—" Pullo said, and Vorenus said, "Sir, he—"

"Shut up," the tribune snapped. "Both of you are confined to barracks for the next two weeks—and that includes staying here when your mates go out to exercise. Since you're so fond of arguing over your practices, maybe you'll learn to keep your tempers if you have nothing to argue about."

"But, sir," Vorenus protested, "without practice we'll lose our edge." Pullo nodded vigorously; here, at least, was something upon which the two Romans could agree. Both were filled with the pride that marked the best fighting men.

"You should have thought of that before you wrangled," Marcus pointed out. "You won't go soft, not in two weeks' time—cleaning details will see to that. Dismissed!" he said sharply. But as they turned, shamefaced, to go, he had an afterthought. "One thing more: don't make the mistake of keeping this foolish quarrel alive. If there is a next time, I'll make whichever one of you is guilty the other's servant. Think on that before you squabble."

To judge from their faces, neither found the prospect appetizing. Pleased at his ingenuity, the tribune started off to get ready for practice. He wished he could order himself to take a couple of weeks off. The day gave every promise of being another scorcher.

"And how did you handle your battling troopers?" Senpat Sviodo asked him; as usual, the Vaspurankaner's resonant tenor voice held an amused edge.

"You must have heard me," Marcus answered, but then realized that while Senpat might have heard him, he had not understood. Among themselves the Romans clung to their Latin, one of the few reminders they had of their lost homeland. Their comrades understood the strange speech but haltingly, lacking Malric's childish facility for learning new tongues. The tribune explained.

The smile that was never far from the young Vaspurakaner noble's handsome features came into the open. He had a good smile, white teeth flashing against his olive skin, framed by the beard he wore close-trimmed in the Videssian style. "You Romans are a strange folk," he said, only a trace of his throaty native tongue coloring his Videssian. "Who else would punish someone by taking work away from him?"

Marcus snorted. Senpat had enjoyed twitting the legionaries since the day he met them almost two years before, but if there was a better mounted scout than he, it had to be his wife. "Your lady Nevrat would understand," the tribune said.

"So she might," Senpat admitted, chuckling. "But then she enjoys such things, where I merely endure them." He gave a theatrical grimace to indicate his disgust at any and all types of work. "Now I suppose you expect me to bake myself in the broiling sun for the sake of hitting the target a hairsbreadth closer to the center."

"What better way to chastise you for your endless heckling?"

"Oh, what we Firstborn suffer in the cause of truth." The Vaspurakaners traced their ancestry back to an eponymous hero, Vaspur—in their theology, the first man created by Phos. Not surprisingly, the Videssians did not share this view.

Senpat pulled his Vaspurakaner cap rakishly over one eye. On most of his countrymen the three-peaked headgear looked strange and lumpy, but he wore it with such a jaunty air that he carried it off quite well. He tossed his head. The brightly dyed ribbons that hung down from the back of the cap's floppy brim flew round his head.

"Since there's no help for it," he sighed, "I suppose I'll fetch my bow." He started to leave.

"If you carped any more, you'd grow scales," Marcus said. Senpat looked briefly blank; the wordplay did not work in Vaspurakaner. Then he winced, looking back suspiciously in case the tribune had more puns lying in wait for him. Scaurus did not, but he was grinning at managing one in a language not his own . . . and a bad one at that.

"Hold it up a little higher, would you, Gongyles?" Thorisin Gavras said.

Gongyles was a very junior lieutenant, his beard fuzzy; his sudden flush was visible through the straggly growth on his cheeks. "I'm sorry, your Imperial Majesty," he stammered, awed that the Avtokrator of the Videssians would speak to him for any reason. He raised the map of the Empire's westlands so all the officers gathered in the Hall of the Nineteen Couches could see it.

The hall held no couches, nor had it for centuries, but tradition died hard in Videssos. Scaurus, sitting on a plain wooden chair in front of a table that wobbled because one leg was too short, smiled at the homage on the callow soldier's face. He whispered to Gaius Philippus, "Remember when Mavrikios kept Ortaias Sphrantzes standing there for hours holding that damned map? His arms must have been ready to fall off."

The senior centurion laughed softly. "It would've served him right if they had," he said; his scorn for Ortaias was boundless. His face hardened. "Then he wouldn't have come along with us to Maragha, and Mavrikios might be alive. Bloody turntail coward; we had a draw till he ran."

In his contempt, he did not bother to lower his voice much. Thorisin, who stood by the map, looked a question at him, not understanding the veteran's Latin. It was Gaius Philippus' turn to go red, though the color hardly showed under his deep tan. "Nothing, sir," he muttered.

"All right, then." The Emperor shrugged. Mavrikios Gavras had used a wooden pointer to guide his officers' eyes across the map of the westlands in that council a couple of years before. His younger brother was a less patient man. He drew his saber from its well-scuffed leather sheath and pointed his way with that.

For all his impatience, his term as Emperor was beginning to leave its mark on him. The lines on either side of his mouth and proud nose were carved deep into his cheeks, though he was but a few years older than Scaurus. There were lines round his eyes, lines that had not been there before he came to the throne. His hair was thinning, too; what had once been a widow's peak was becoming a forelock.

But he had the active stride of a younger man, and it took but a single glance at his strong mouth and determined eyes to see that he was yet a man of great vigor and bearing up well under the heavy hands of duty and time. "This is what we'll have to do," he said, and his marshals leaned forward as one to listen.

He tapped at the parchment with his sword before he began to speak, mustering his thoughts. As always, the wide peninsula that held the Empire's western provinces reminded Marcus of a knobby thumb. From marching and countermarching through a good part of the westlands, he knew the map was more accurate than anything Rome could have produced. Discouragingly, it also accurately showed the land the Yezda had taken since Maragha. Most of the high central plateau was lost; the nomads were beginning to settle there and pushing eastward toward the fertile plains that ran to the Sailors' Sea.

The Emperor ran his blade west along the Arandos River, which flowed down from the highlands through the broad coastal plain. "The whoresons are using the Arandos valley to come right down our throats. It runs both ways, though. Drax' Namdaleni will plug the gap at Garsavra until we reinforce them. After that, it's our turn to push west again and reclaim what's ours. . . . Yes, this time you have something to say to me, Roman?"

"Aye, or ask you, rather." Gaius Philippus pointed toward the red-filled circle that marked Garsavra. "Your great count Drax may be a canny enough soldier, but how does he propose to hold a town with no putrid wall?"

Hardly any cities in the westlands were walled. Until the Yezda came, the westerners had lived for hundreds of years without fear of invasion. Such fortifications as had once existed were centuries gone, torn down for the building stone they yielded. To Marcus' way of thinking, a land free of walls was Videssos' finest achievement. It told of a security far greater than any his Rome could give its subjects. Even in Italy, an unwalled town would have been as unnatural as a white crow. It had only been fifty years since the Cimbri and Teutones swarmed over the Alps, asking Marius' legionaries if they had any messages for the barbarians to take to their wives.

"Never fear, outlander, t'ey'll hold it," Utprand son of Dagober said from down the table, his Namdalener accent thick enough to slice. "Drax is a poor excuse for a Namdalener, but his men, t'ey'll hold." The great count had taken on too many Videssian ways for his countryman's liking. They had some old rivalry between them as well; Scaurus was hazy on the details.

"You Romans are good at overnight fieldworks, but we know a few tricks, too," Soteric Dosti's son said, supporting his captain. Helvis' brother had served in the Empire longer than Utprand and lost most of his island accent. He went on, "Give a regiment of ours ten days in one place, and they have a motte-and-bailey up that'll hold 'em all. Garsavra may not have walls, but it won't lack for a strongpoint."

My brother-in-law, Marcus thought—not for the first time—talks too much. Mertikes Zigabenos scowled at Soteric, as did several other Videssian officers. Nor, plainly, was Thorisin overjoyed at the prospect of

Namdalener-held castles going up in his land, however necessary they might be for the moment.

The Videssians hired Namdalener mercenaries, but they did not trust them. Namdalen had been a province of the Empire before it fell to Haloga corsairs a couple of centuries ago. The mixed folk that sprang from the conquest combined Videssos' imperial traditions with the ambition and barbaric love of battle the northerners brought. The Dukes of Namdalen dreamed one day of ruling from the imperial capital, a dream that was nightmare to the Videssians.

Zigabenos said to Utprand, "With your heavy cavalry, you islanders shouldn't be reduced to garrison duty. When our main force reaches Garsavra, we'll surely put less valuable troops in whatever fortresses Drax may have built."

"Isn't he slick, now?" Gaius Philippus whispered admiringly. Marcus nodded; what better way to ease the islanders out of positions that could be dangerous to the Empire than to make that easing appear a compliment to their fighting skills? Zigabenos had to an unusual degree the Videssian talent for mixing politics and war; he was the man who had set off the riots in the city that overthrew Ortaias Sphrantzes and won Thorisin Gavras the Empire.

But Utprand had not risen to lead his regiment solely by the strength of his right arm. He was impatient with any sort of subtlety, but there was a considerable wit behind his cold blue eyes. With a shrug he said, "Time will show w'at it shows," a thought that could have come from his pagan Haloga ancestors.

The talk shifted to lines of march, supply centers, and all the other minutiae that went into a major campaign. Despite his travels in the westlands, Marcus listened carefully. Attention to detail was never wasted.

On the other hand, a couple of the Khamorth chieftains looked actively bored. The nomads made fine scouts and raiders, being as mobile as their distant cousins from Yezd. But they were not interested in anything but the fight itself: preparing for it seemed to them a waste of time. One plainsman snored until his seatmate, a Videssian, kicked him in the ankle under the table. He woke with a start, sputtering guttural curses.

However rude they were in manner, the nomads had a firm grip on the realities of the mercenary's trade. One of them caught Thorisin

Gavras' eye during a lull in the planning. Thinking he had some point to make, the Emperor asked, "What is it, Sarbaraz?"

"You not run out of money halfway through fight?" Sarbaraz asked anxiously. "We fight for your Ort'iash, he give us more promises than gold, and his gold not much good either." That was true enough; Ortaias Sphrantzes had debased Videssos' coinage until what was styled a goldpiece was less than one-third gold.

"You'll be paid, never fear," Gavras said. His eyes narrowed in annoyance. "And you know I don't coin trash, either."

"True, true—in city. We get away from city, from—how you say?—treasury, then what? Then maybe you run out of money, like I say. My boys not happy if that happen—maybe make up missing pay off countryside." Sarbaraz grinned insolently, exposing crooked teeth. The Khamorth had no use for farmers, except as prey.

"By Phos, I said you'd be paid!" Thorisin shouted, really angry now. "And if your bandits start plundering, we'll set the rest of the army on you and see how you like that!"

He took a deep breath and then another, trying to calm himself; before he became Emperor, Marcus thought approvingly, he would have let his temper run away with him. When he spoke again, it was with studied reason: "There will be plenty of coin along for the army's needs. And even if the campaign should run longer than we expect, we won't have to send back to the city for more goldpieces, just to the local mint at, at—" He snapped his fingers in irritation, unable to remember the town's name. By inclination he was a soldier, not a financier; he found taxes and revenues as dull as the Khamorth did grain supply and encampment sites.

"Kyzikos," Alypia Gavra supplied. As was her way, the Emperor's niece had sat quietly through most of the council, occasionally scribbling a note for the history she was composing. Most of the officers took no notice of her; they were used to her silent presence.

For his part, Marcus felt the same mixture of longing, guilt, and a touch of fear Alypia always raised in him. He was more than fond of her, which did nothing to help his sometimes-stormy life with Helvis. Moreover, he knew his feelings were returned, at least in part. The fear came there. If a mercenary could not hope to hold a castle in Videssos, what would befall one who held a princess?

"The mint at Kyzikos is not far southeast of Garsavra," she was explaining to Sarbaraz. "In fact, it was first established as a paycenter for our troops in a war against Makuran . . . let me see." Her green eyes grew thoughtful. ". . . Not quite six hundred years ago."

The nomad had not been happy at having to listen to any woman, even one of the imperial family. At her last words he stared, frankly unbelieving. "All right, you have mint, we get money. No need to mock me—who could remember six five-twenties of years?"

He translated his own people's number-system into Videssian. Scaurus wondered what Gorgidas would make of that; he'd probably say it harked back to a time when the Khamorth could not count past their fingers and toes. But then, Gorgidas was seeing Khamorth aplenty himself.

"Skotos take the rude barbarian," the tribune heard one Videssian officer whisper to another. "Does he doubt the princess' words?"

But Alypia told Sarbaraz, "I did not mean to mock you," as courteously as if apologizing to a great noble. She was without the hot Gavras temper that plagued Thorisin and had sometimes flared in her father Mavrikios as well. Nor were her features as sharply sculptured as those of the male Gavrai, though she shared their rather narrow oval face.

Marcus wondered what her mother had looked like; Mavrikios' wife had died years before he became Avtokrator. Very few Videssians had green eyes, which must have come from that side of the family.

"When do you plan to start the season's fighting?" someone asked Thorisin.

"Weeks ago," the Emperor snapped. "May Onomagoulos rot in Skotos' hell for robbing me of them—aye, and of all the good men his rebellion killed. Civil war costs a country twice, for winners and losers both are its own."

"Too true," Gaius Philippus muttered, remembering his own young manhood and the fight between Sulla and the backers of Marius—to say nothing of the Social War that had matched Rome against its Italian allies. He raised his voice to speak to Gavras. "We can't get ready for weeks ago, you know."

"Not even you Romans?" the Emperor said with a smile. There was honest respect in his voice; the legionaries had taught Videssos more than it ever knew of instant readiness. Thorisin rubbed his chin as he considered. "Eight days' time," he said at last.

Groans came from several officers; one of the Namdaleni, Clozart Leatherbreeches, growled, "Ask for the moon while you're about it!" But Utprand silenced him with a glare. When the Emperor looked a question at the dour mercenary chief, he got a nod back. He returned it, satisfied; Utprand's word on such things was good.

Gavras did not bother checking with the Romans. Scaurus and Gaius Philippus exchanged smug grins. They could have been ready in half Thorisin's eight days and knew it. It was gratifying to see the Emperor did, too.

As the meeting broke up, Marcus hoped for a few words with Alypia Gavra; in ceremony-ridden Videssos such chances came too seldom. But Mertikes Zigabenos buttonholed him as they walked out through the brightly polished bronze doors of the Hall of the Nineteen Couches. The Videssian officer said, "I hope you're pleased with the healer-priest I got for you."

Under most circumstances Scaurus would have passed it off with a polite compliment. After all, Zigabenos had been trying to do him and his men a favor. The sight of Alypia heading off with her uncle toward the imperial family's private chambers, though, left him irritated enough for candor. "Couldn't you have found one who doesn't drink so much?" he asked.

Zigabenos' handsome face froze. "Your pardon, I am sure," he said. "Now if you will excuse me—" With a bow calculated to the fraction of an inch, he stalked off.

Gaius Philippus came up. "How did you step on *his* corns?" he asked, watching the stiff-backed departure. "Don't tell me you gave him a straight answer?"

"I'm afraid so," the tribune admitted. There were times, he thought, when you could make no worse mistake with the Videssians.

The bustle of preparing to move out did not keep the legionaries from their mornings at the practice field. As they were returning one day, Marcus found the barracks halls a good deal grimier and more untidy than even moving's dislocation could have let him put up with. Annoyed, he went looking for Pullo and Vorenus. It was not like them to let down on any job, even one as menial as a housekeeping detail.

He found them standing side by side in the sun behind one of the bachelor halls. They came out of their rather stiff stance as soon as he came round the corner. He filled his lungs for an angry shout.

But Styppes, who was comfortable under the shadow of one of the citrus trees that surrounded the Romans' quarters, anticipated him. "What are you doing breaking your poses, miserable barbarians? Come back this instant—my sketches are hardly begun!"

Scaurus had not noticed the priest in the shade. He rounded on Styppes, ignoring the two legionaries. "Who, sirrah, gave you the authority to take my men away from the duties I assigned them?"

Styppes squinted as he stepped into the sunshine, several sheets of parchment and a charcoal stick in his hand. "Which has the greater weight," he demanded, "the trivial concerns of this existence or Phos' undying glory, which endures forever?"

"This existence is the only one I know," the tribune retorted. Styppes gave back a place in horror, as if confronted by a wild beast. He made the sun-sign of his god on his breast, gabbling out a quick prayer against Marcus' blasphemy. Scaurus realized he had gone too far; in theology-crazed Videssos, an answer like his could launch a riot. He backtracked. "Neither of these soldiers follows Phos, to my knowledge." He glanced at Vorenus and Pullo, who nodded nervously, caught between Styppes and their commander. Marcus turned back to the priest. "What is your concern with them, then?"

"A proper question," Styppes said grudgingly, though he eyed the tribune with scant liking. "While Skotos will doubtless drag their heathen souls down to the eternal ice below, still in body they are images worth commemorating. I sought their likenesses for icons of Phos' holy men Akakios and Gourias, both of whom are to be depicted as young beardless men."

"You paint icons?" Marcus said, hoping he was keeping the skepticism out of his voice. Next, he thought, the fat tosspot would claim he could lay eggs.

Styppes, though, seemed to be taking him seriously. "Aye," he said, offering his parchment scraps to the Roman. "You will understand these are but rough sketches, and poor ones at that. The charcoal is wrong, too; the fools at the monastery use hazelwood, but myrtle gives a finer line and smudges less."

The tribune hardly heard the priest's complaints. He shuffled rapidly through the pieces of parchment, his eyes growing larger at every one. Styppes was an artist, whatever else he was. In a few deft strokes his charcoal picked out the two Romans' salient features: Pullo's strong nose and angular cheekbones, Vorenus' thoughtful mouth beneath heavy eyebrows, the scar that creased his chin.

Pullo was scarred, too, but Styppes' drawing did not show his battle marks. Used to Roman portraiture, which could be brutally realistic, Marcus asked, "Why have you shown one man's wounds, but not the other's?"

"The holy Gourias was a soldier who suffered martyrdom defending an altar of Phos against the Khamorth pagans, and is to be portrayed with a warrior's tokens. Akakios Klimakos, though, gained fame for his charity and had no experience of war."

"But Pullo here is scarred," the tribune protested.

"What of it? I care nothing for your barbarians for their own sakes; why should I? But as representatives of those who were found worthy of Phos, they gain some small importance. Where their features fail to conform to the ideal, am I to betray the ideal for them? My interest is in the holy Klimakos and Gourias, not your Pullus and Voreno, or whatever their names may be." Styppes laughed at the idea.

His theory of art was opposed to everything Scaurus took for granted, but the tribune was too nettled by his scorn to care about that. "You will, in that case, do me the favor of not distracting my men from the tasks assigned them. *My* interest is in seeing those carried out."

Styppes' nostrils flared. "Impudent pagan!"

"Not at all," the tribune said, wary of making him an open enemy. "But just as you have your concerns, I have mine. Your Gourias would understand the duty a soldier owes his commander—and the harm that can come from weakening it."

The healer-priest looked startled. "That is not an argument I would have looked for from an unbeliever." His eyes were red-veined, but also shrewd.

Marcus spread his hands. Anything that works, he said, but only to himself.

"All right, then," the priest finally said. "Perhaps I was hasty."

"What the men do in their free time is their own affair. If they care to pose for you then, I certainly would not mind," the tribune said, relieved he had smoothed things over.

Calculation grew on Styppes' fat face. "And what of you?" he asked.

"Me?"

"Indeed. When I first set eyes on you, I knew you would make a fine model for portraying the holy Kveldulf the Haloga."

"The holy who?" Marcus said in surprise. The Halogai lived in the cold lands far to the north of Videssos. Some served the Empire as mercenaries, but more often they were raiders and pirates. As far as Scaurus knew, they followed their own grim gods, not Phos. "How did a Haloga become a Videssian holy man?"

"Kveldulf exalted the true faith in the reign of Stavrakios of revered memory." Styppes made the sign of the sun over his heart. "He preached it to his kinsmen in their icebound fjords, but they would not hear him. They would have bound him to a tree to spear him to death, but he stood still for their weapons, choosing to die in a way that served Phos' glory."

No wonder the Halogai had not accepted Kveldulf, the tribune thought. Stavrakios had conquered their province of Agder from them, and they must have seen Kveldulf as a stalking-horse for greater encroachment; Videssos often used religion to further political goals. Scaurus did not share that line of reasoning with Styppes. Instead he said, "Why me? I don't really look like a Haloga."

"True; feature for feature you might almost be a Videssian. All the better. You are blond like the northern savages, and through you I can depict the holy Kveldulf so as to make his origin clear even to unlettered worshipers, but symbolically represent his acceptance of the Empire's true faith."

"Oh." Marcus started to scratch his head, then stopped in mid-gesture, unwilling to show his confusion to the healer-priest. He wished Gorgidas was at his side to make sense of Styppes' prototypes and symbols; if anyone could, it would be a Greek. To the hardheaded Romans, a portrait was a portrait, to be judged by how closely it resembled its original.

Still bemused, he nodded vaguely when Styppes again pressed him to pose, and gave Vorenus and Pullo only a quarter of the blistering they deserved. Hardly believing their luck, they saluted and disappeared before he stopped woolgathering.

If Kveldulf preached like Styppes, he thought, his fellow barbarians had another good reason for martyring him.

Despite Styppes' interference, the legionaries' preparations went forward smoothly enough. The surviving Romans were old hands at breaking winter quarters and, under their watchful eyes, the recruits who had joined them since they came to Videssos performed well. The spirit that ran through Scaurus' men was powerful; the newcomers wanted to meet the standards the Romans set.

Their performance satisfied even Gaius Philippus, who chivvied them no worse than he did men who sprang from Latium or Apulia. The senior centurion had a different problem to drive him to distraction, one not so easily dealt with as an unruly trooper.

Three days before the Videssian army was due to leave the capital, the veteran came up to Marcus and brought himself to rigid attention. That was a danger sign in itself; he did not bother with such formality unless he was going to say something he did not think Scaurus would want to hear. When the tribune saw the bruise he carried under one eye, his apprehension doubled—had some soldier been stupid enough to swing at Gaius Philippus? If so, the centurion might be about to report a dead legionary.

"Well?" Scaurus said when Gaius Philippus stayed mute.

"Sir," Gaius Philippus acknowledged, and paused so long again Marcus feared his first hasty guess was right. Then, as if some dam inside the senior centurion went down, he burst out, "Sir, is there any way we can leave the damned tarts behind? The men'll be better soldiers for it, really they will, not thinking about the futtering they'll get tonight or whether their brats spit up dinner."

"I'm sorry, but no," Scaurus answered immediately. He knew Gaius Philippus had never truly accepted the Romans taking partners. It went against every tradition of the legions, and also against the veteran's nature. His only use for women was quick pleasure; anything beyond that seemed beyond his comprehension as well.

But Videssos' customs differed from Rome's. Mercenary companies that served the Avtokrators routinely brought their wives and lemans with them on campaign; Marcus had felt unable to deny his men a privilege the rest of the army enjoyed.

"What went wrong?" the tribune asked.

"Wrong?" Gaius Philippus cried, fairly howling the word in his frustration. "Not a bloody fornicating thing goes right with those idiot women; and when it does, they botch it again just for the fun of it. Scaurus, you should have seen what the slut who gave me this—" He gingerly touched his cheek. "—was up to."

"Tell me." Marcus knew the senior centurion had to work the anger out of his system somehow and was willing to be a handy ear.

"By one of Jove's special miracles, this bitch named Myrrha—she's Publius Flaccus' woman, if you don't know—managed—in five days, mind you—to pack up her gear in three sacks, each of 'em big enough to rupture any donkey ever born. But that's as may be; at least she was packed.

"And then her little darling started whining for a sweet, and may the gods shrivel my balls if she didn't dump every bit of her trash on the floor till she found a honeydrop. I was watching all this, you know. It must have taken a good quarter of an hour—and I let her have it. That's when I picked up my shiner here."

Gaius Philippus' parade-ground bellow could peel whitewash off walls; Myrrha, Scaurus decided, had to be a strong-spirited girl to stand up under it. Used to the harsh discipline of the legions, the senior centurion had long forgotten softer ways. Worse, he was furious at being defied without a chance for revenge.

"Come on, enough of this," Marcus said. He put his arm round the older man's shoulder. "You were doing your duty, which was right. Is it worth letting someone who is misled and ignorant of what is proper distract you?"

"Bet your arse it is," Gaius Philippus growled. Scaurus winced; so much for the soothing power of Stoicism.

Despite the veteran's fit of temper—and largely because of his hard work—the legionaries were ready well before Thorisin's deadline. It came and went, though, without the army sailing. Not only were some detachments—mostly Khamorth mercenaries, but a few Videssian units as well—unprepared, but shipping was still inadequate to transport them, despite the best efforts of the drungarios of the fleet, Taron Leimmokheir. Onomagoulos' revolt had split the Videssian fleet down the middle; here, too, its aftereffects were still being felt.

"Leimmokheir's trying for jail again." Senpat Sviodo laughed, but there was truth behind the joke. The drungarios had spent months in prison when Thorisin Gavras wrongly thought him involved in an assassination plot. If he truly failed the irascible Emperor, he might well return.

Ships of all sizes and descriptions, from great, beamy transports that normally shipped grain to little lateen-rigged fishing smacks, gathered in Videssos' harbors. It seemed the capital held as many sailors as soldiers. The seamen, Videssians all, swarmed into the city's taverns and eateries. They brawled with the mercenaries, sometimes in sport, sometimes for blood.

Marcus thought of Viridovix and wondered how he'd fared sailing to Prista. If the gusty Celt knew what he was missing, he'd likely head back if he had to swim; he had never been known to back away from a tavern row.

With Videssos' docks jammed with ships berthed gunwale to gunwale, the arrival of one more merchantman out of Kypas in the westlands should have made no difference. But it carried more in its hold than a cargo of wine; the news it bore raced through the capital with the speed of fire. In Videssos, what two men knew, everyone knew.

Phostis Apokavkos brought the word to the legionaries' barracks. He was well connected, having scratched out a living in the thieves' quarter of the city before Scaurus adopted him as a Roman. Now he came rushing in, his long face working with anger. "Curse the filthy foreigners!" he shouted.

Heads jerked up and hands reached instinctively for swords. Videssos was cosmopolitan and xenophobic at the same time; a cry like that too often was the rallying call for a mob. The troopers relaxed when they saw it was only Apokavkos and swore at him for startling them.

"Are you including us, Phostis?" Scaurus asked mildly.

"What? Oh, no, sir!" Apokavkos said, shocked. His hand came up in a smart legionary-style salute. There were times, the tribune thought, when he was more Roman than the Romans. They had given him the chance he'd never had on his farm in the far west or in the capital, and won his total allegiance in return. These days he shaved his face like a Roman, cursed in accented Latin, and, alone among all the recruits who had joined Marcus' men in Videssos, had his hand branded with the legionary mark.

"It's the Phos-detested Namdalener heretics, sir," he started to explain. In some ways he was a Videssian still.

"Utprand's men?" Scaurus' alertness returned, as did his troopers'. The Romans had done riot duty before, holding the city rabble and the men of the Duchy apart. It was soldiering of a kind to turn any man's stomach.

But Apokavkos shook his head. "No, not them buggers—there's enough honest men about to keep 'em in line." He spat on the floor in disgust. "I'm talkin' 'bout Drax' crew."

"What do you mean?" "Let it out, man!" legionaries called to Apokavkos, but Marcus felt his heart sink. He had a horrid feeling he knew what was coming.

"The whoreson pirate," Apokavkos was saying. "Send him over the Cattle-Crossing to put down a rebel, and he thinks he's a king. The dung-chewing Skotos' spawn's stolen the westlands from us!"

II

"LAND!" THE LOOKOUT CALLED FROM HIS PERCH HIGH ON THE *CONqueror*'s mast.

"Och, the gods be praised!" Viridovix croaked. "I thought them after forgetting the word." The Gaul's normally ruddy face was sallow and drawn; cold sweat slicked his red hair and long, sweeping mustaches. He clutched the *Conqueror*'s starboard rail, waiting for the next spasm of seasickness to rack him.

He did not wait long. A puff of breeze brought the stink of hot oil and frying fish from the ship's galley astern. It set him retching again. Tears ran down his cheeks. "Three days now! A dead corp I'd be if it was a week."

In his anguish he spoke Celtic, which no one on board—no one in this entire world—understood. That, though, was not why the crew and the diplomats he accompanied eyed him with curiosity and pity. The waters of the Videssian Sea were almost glassy calm; it was a wonder anyone could be taken sick in such fine weather. Viridovix cursed his feeble stomach, then broke off when it took its revenge.

Gorgidas emerged from the galley with a steaming bowl of beef broth. The Greek might claim to renounce medicine for history, but he was still a physician at heart. Viridovix' misery alarmed him, the more so since he did not share and could not understand the strapping Gaul's frailty.

"Here, soak this up," he said.

"Take it away!" Viridovix said. "I dinna want it."

Gorgidas glared at him. If anything could be counted on to kindle his wrath, it was a deliberately foolish patient. "Would you sooner have the dry heaves instead? You'll keep spewing till we reach port—give yourself something to spew."

“Sure and the sea is a hateful place,” the Gaul said, but under Gorgidas’ implacable stare he slurped the broth down. A few minutes later he gave most of it back. “A pox! Bad cess to the evil kern who thought of boats. The shame of it, me being on one on account of a woman.”

“What do you expect, when you fall foul of the Emperor’s mistress?” Gorgidas asked rhetorically—Viridovix’ foolishness annoyed him. Komitta Rhangavve had a temper fit to roast meat, and when Viridovix refused to abandon his other women for her, she threatened to go to Thorisin Gavras with a tale of rape; thus the Celt’s sudden departure from Videssos.

“Aye, belike you’re right, teacher; you’ve no need to lecture me on it.” Viridovix’ green eyes measured Gorgidas. “At least it’s not myself I’m running from.”

The doctor grunted. Viridovix’ remark had too much truth in it for comfort—he was a barbarian, but far from stupid. After Quintus Glabrio died under Gorgidas’ hands, his lifelong art came to look futile and empty. What good was it, he thought bitterly, if it could not save a lover? History gave some hope for usefulness without involvement.

He doubted he could explain that to the Gaul and did not much want to. In any case, Viridovix’ one sentence summed up his rationalizations too well.

Arigh Arghun’s son strolled across the deck to them and saved him from his dilemma. Even the nomad from the far steppe beyond the River Shaum had no trouble with his sea legs. “How is he?” he asked Gorgidas, his Videssian sharp and clipped with the accent of his people.

“Not very well,” the Greek answered candidly, “but if land’s in sight we’ll make Prista this afternoon. That should cure him.”

Arigh’s flat, swarthy face was impassive as usual, but mischief danced in his slanted eyes. He said, “A horse goes up and down, too, you know, V’rid’rix. Do you get horsesick? There’s lots of riding ahead of us.”

“Nay, I willna be horsesick, snake of an Arshaum,” Viridovix said. He swore at his friend with all the vigor in his weakened frame. “Now begone with you, before I puke on your fancy sheepskin boots.” Chuckling, Arigh departed.

“Horsesick,” Viridovix muttered. “There’s a notion to send shudders into the marrow of a man. Epona and her mare’d not allow it.”

“That’s your Celtic horse-goddess?” Gorgidas asked, always interested in such tidbits of lore.

“The same. I’ve sacrificed to her often enough, though not since I came to the Empire.” The Gaul looked guilty. “Sure and it might be wise to make amends for that at Prista, am I live to reach it.”

Prista was a town of contrasts, an outpost of empire at the edge of an endless sea of grass. It held fewer than ten thousand souls, yet boasted fortification stouter than any in Videssos save the capital’s. For the Empire it was a watchpost on the steppe from which the wandering Khamorth tribes could be played off against each other or cajoled into imperial service. The plainsmen needed it to trade their tallow, their honey, their wax, their furs and slaves for wheat, salt, wine, silk, and incense from Videssos, but many a nomad khagan had coveted it for his own—and so the stonework. Walls were not always enough to hold them at bay; Prista’s past was stormy.

Every sort of building could be found inside those walls. Stately homes of the local gray-brown shale in classical Videssian courtyard style stood next to rough-timbered shacks and houses built of slabs of sod from the plain. On unused ground, nomads’ tents of hides or brightly dyed felt sprang up like toadstools.

Though Prista held a Videssian governor and garrison, much of its population was of plains blood. The loungers on the dock were squat, heavy-set men with unkempt beards. Most of them wore linen tunics and trousers instead of the steppe’s furs and leathers, but almost all affected the low-crowned fur caps the Khamorth wore in cold weather and hot. And when Pikridios Goudeles asked one of them to help carry his gear to an inn, the fellow sat unmoving.

Goudeles raised an eyebrow in annoyance. “My luck to pick a deaf-mute,” he said and turned to another idler, this one baring his broad hairy chest to the sun. The man ignored him. “Dear me, is this the country of the deaf?” the bureaucrat asked, beginning to sound angry; in Videssos he was used to being heeded.

“I’ll make them listen, the spirits fry me if I don’t,” Arigh said, stepping toward the knot of men. They glowered at him; there was no love lost between Arshaum and Khamorth.

Lankinos Skylitzes touched Arigh's arm. The officer was a man of few words and had no liking for Goudeles. He was quite willing to watch the pen-pusher make an ass of himself. But Arigh could cause riot, not embarrassment, and that Skylitzes would not brook.

"Let me," he said, striding forward in Arigh's place. The dock-rats watched him, not much impressed. He was a large man with a soldier's solid frame, but there were enough of them to deal with him and his comrades, too . . . and he kept company with an Arshaum. But their scowls turned to startled grins when he addressed them in their own speech. After a few seconds of chaffering, four of them jumped up to shoulder the envoys' kits. Only Arigh carried his own—and seemed content to do so.

"What a rare useful thing it must be, to be able to bespeak the people wherever you go," Viridovix said admiringly to Skylitzes. The Gaul was already becoming his usual exuberant self once more. Like the giant Antaios in the myth, Gorgidas thought, he drew strength from contact with the earth.

Economical even in gestures, Skylitzes gave a single nod.

That seemed to frustrate Viridovix, who turned to the Greek. "With your history and all, Gorgidas dear, would you no like to have these folk talk your own tongue so you could be asking them all the questions lurking in your head?"

Gorgidas ignored the sarcasm; Viridovix' question touched a deep hurt in him. "By the gods, Gaul, it would give me pleasure if anyone in this abandoned world spoke my tongue, even you. Here the two of us are as closest kin, but I can no more use Hellenic speech with you than you your Celtic with me. Does it not grate you, too, ever speaking Latin and Videssian?"

"It does that," Viridovix said at once. "Even the Romans are better off than we, for they have themselves to jabber with and keep their speech alive. I tried teaching my lassies the Celtic, but they had no thought for sic things. I fear I chose 'em only for their liveliness under a blanket."

And so were you sated but alone, Gorgidas thought. As if to confirm his guess, the Gaul suddenly burst into a torrent of verse in his native tongue. Arigh and the Videssians gaped at him. The local bearers had been stealing glances at him all along, curious at his fair, freckled skin and fiery hair. Now they shrank back, perhaps afraid he was reciting some spell.

Viridovix rolled on for what might have been five or six stanzas. Then he stumbled to a halt, cursing in Celtic, Videssian, and Latin all mixed together.

"Beshrew me, I've forgotten the rest," he mourned and hung his head in shame.

After the imperial capital's broad straight streets paved with cobblestones or flags and its efficient underground drainage system, Prista came as something of a shock. The main thoroughfare was hard-packed dirt. It zigzagged like an alley and was hardly wider than one. Sewage flowed in a channel down the center. Gorgidas saw a nomad undo his trousers and urinate in the channel; no one paid him any mind.

The Greek shook his head. In Elis, where he had grown up, such things were commonplace. The cry of "*Exito!* Here it comes!" warned pedestrians that a fresh load of slops was about to be thrown out. But the Romans had better notions of sanitation, and in their greater cities the Videssians did, too. Here on the frontier they did not bother—and surely paid the price in disease.

Well, what of it? Gorgidas thought; they have healer-priests to set things right. Then he wondered even about that. By the look of things, many of the Pristans kept their plains customs and probably did not follow Phos. He glanced toward the Videssian god's temple. Its discolored stones and weather-softened lines proclaimed it one of the oldest buildings in the town, but streaks of tarnish ran down the gilded dome atop it. Skylitzes saw that, too, and frowned.

If Pikridios Goudeles felt any dismay at the temple's shabby condition, he hid it well. But he grew voluble when he saw the inside of the inn the natives, through Skylitzes, had assured him was the best Prista offered. "What a bloody hole! I've seen stockyards with better-run pens."

Two of the Pristans scowled; Gorgidas had thought they understood Videssian. In truth, the Greek was with Goudeles. The taproom was small, poorly furnished, and decades overdue for cleaning. Caked-on soot blackened the wall above each torch bracket. The place smelled of smoke, stale liquor, and staler sweat.

Nor was the clientele more prepossessing. Two or three tables were filled by loafers who might have been blood-brothers to the idlers on the docks. Half a dozen Videssians drank at another. Though most of them were in their middle years, they wore gaudy, baggy-sleeved tunics like so many young street ruffians; each looked to have a fortune in gold on his fingers and round his neck. Their voices were loud and sharp, their speech filled with the capital's slang.

In Latin, Viridovix murmured, "Dinna be gambling with these outen your own dice."

"I know thieves when I see them," Gorgidas answered in the same language, "even rich thieves."

If the taverner was one such, he spent his money elsewhere. A short, fat man, his sullen mouth and suspicious eyes belied all the old saws about jolly plump folk. The upstairs room he grudgingly yielded to the embassy was hardly big enough to hold the five straw-stuffed mattresses a servant fetched in.

Goudeles tipped the men with the party's equipment. Once they had gone, he fell down onto a mattress—the thickest one, Gorgidas noted—and burst out laughing. At his companions' curious stares, he said, "I was just thinking: if this is the best Prista has to offer, Phos preserve me from the worst."

"Enjoy it while you may," Skylitzes advised.

"No, the pudgy one is right," Arigh said. Goudeles, unpacking a fresh robe, did not seem overjoyed at his support, if that was what it was. The Arshaum went on, "Even the finest of towns is a prison; only on the plains can a man breathe free."

Someone rapped politely on the door—a soldier. He had the half-Khamorth look of most folk here, being wide-shouldered, dark, and bushy-bearded. But he wore chain mail, instead of the boiled leather of the plains, and spoke good Videssian. "You are the gentlemen from the *Conqueror,* the envoys to the Arshaum?"

He bowed when they admitted it. "His excellency the *hypepoptes* Methodios Sivas greets you, then, and bids you join him at sunset tonight. I will come back then to guide you to his residence." He dipped his head again, sketched a salute, and left as abruptly as he had come. His boots thumped on the narrow stone stairway.

"Is the *hyp*—whatever—a wizard, to be after knowing we're here almost before we are?" Viridovix exclaimed. He had seen enough sorcery in the Empire to mean the question seriously.

"Not a bit of it," Goudeles replied, chuckling at his naïveté. "Surely as Phos' sun rises in the east, one of the leisured gentlemen of the harbor is in his pay."

More sophisticated than the Gaul at governors' wiles, Gorgidas had reasoned that out for himself, but he was not displeased to have it confirmed. This Sivas' main function was to watch the plains for the Empire. If he kept them as closely surveyed as he did his own city, Videssos was well served.

Methodios Sivas was a surprisingly young man, not far past thirty. His outsized nose gave him an air of engaging homeliness, and he was boisterous enough to fit his frontier surroundings. He pounded Arigh on the back, shouting, "Arghun's son, is it? Will you make me put sentries at the wells again?"

Arigh giggled, a startling sound from him. "No need. I'll be good."

"You'd better." Making sure each of his guests had a full wine cup, Sivas explained, "When this demon's sprig came through here on his way to the city, he threw a handful of frogs into every well in town."

Lankinos Skylitzes looked shocked and then guffawed; Goudeles, Viridovix, and Gorgidas were mystified. "Don't you see?" Sivas said, and then answered himself, "No, of course you don't. Why should you? You don't deal with the barbarians every day—sometimes I forget it's me on the edge of nowhere, not the rest of the Empire. Here's the long and short of it, then: all Khamorth are deathly afraid of frogs. They wouldn't drink our water for three days!"

"Hee, hee!" Arigh said, laughing afresh at the memory of his practical joke. "That's not all, and you know it. They had to pay a Videssian to hunt down all the little beasts, and then sacrifice a black lamb over each well to drive away the pollution. And your priest of Phos tried to stop *that,* quacking about heathen rites. It was glorious."

"It was ghastly," Sivas retorted. "One clan packed up an easy five thousand goldpieces' worth of skins and went back to the steppe with 'em. The merchants howled for months."

"Frogs, is it?" Gorgidas said, scribbling a note on a scrap of parchment. The *hypepoptes* noticed and asked him why. Rather hesitantly, he explained about his history. Sivas surprised him with a thoughtful nod and several intelligent questions; sharp wits hid beneath his rough exterior.

The governor had other interests hardly to be expected from a frontiersman. Though his residence, with its thick walls, slit windows, and iron-banded oak doors, could double as a fortress, the garden that bloomed in the courtyard was a riot of colors. Mallows and roses bloomed in neat rows. So did yellow and lavender adder's-tongues, which told Gorgidas of Sivas' skill. The low plants, their leaves mottled green and brown, belonged in moist forests or on the mountainside, not here at the edge of the steppe.

As was only natural, Sivas, isolated from events in the capital, was eager to hear the news the embassy brought with it. He exclaimed in satisfaction when he learned how Thorisin Gavras had regained control of the sea from the rebel forces led by Baanes Onomagoulos and Elissaios Bouraphos. "Damn the traitors anyway," he said. "I've been sending messages with every ship that sailed for the capital for the last two months; they must have sunk them all. That's too long, with Avshar running loose."

"Are you sure it's himself?" Viridovix asked. The name of the wizard-prince was enough to distract him from his flirtation with one of the *hypepotes*' serving girls. A bachelor, Sivas had several comely women in his employ, even if their mixed blood made them too stocky to conform to the Videssian ideal of beauty.

He did not seem put out by the Celt's trifling. Viridovix had obviously intrigued him from the moment he set eyes on him; men of the Gaul's stature and coloring were rare among the peoples the Videssians knew, and his musical accent was altogether strange.

Now Sivas answered, "Who but shrouds himself in robes so his very eyes are unseen? Who but stirs discord in his wake as the wind stirs waves on the sea? And who but rides a great black charger in a land of ponies? On the plains, that were enough to name him without the other two."

"Sure and it's the spalpeen, all right," Viridovix agreed. "Still and all, my good Celtic blade should do to let the mischief out of him." Methodios Sivas raised a politely skeptical eyebrow, but Gorgidas knew Viridovix was not idly boasting. His sword was twin to the one Scaurus bore, both of them forged and spell-wrapped by Gallic druids and both uncannily mighty in this land where magic flourished.

"Yet another matter has reached me since my last dispatches to Videssos," Sivas said. By his voice, it was one he would rather not have heard. He paused for a moment before going on: "You will understand this is rumor alone, and unsupported, but it's said Varatesh has thrown in his lot with your cursed wizard."

Again Gorgidas was conscious of something important slipping past him; again Viridovix and Goudeles were as mystified. Even Arigh seemed unsure of the name. But Lankinos Skylitzes knew it. "The outlaw," he said, and it was not a question.

"It's but a voice on the breeze, you understand," Sivas repeated.

"Phos grant it stay such," Skylitzes answered, and drew the sun-sign on his breast. Seeing his comrades' incomprehension, he said, "The man is dangerous and wily, and his riders are no bargain. A great clan against us would be worse, but not much."

His obvious concern reached Gorgidas, who did not think Skylitzes one to alarm himself over trifles. Arigh was less impressed. "A Khamorth," he said contemptuously. "Next you'll have me hiding from baby partridges in the grass."

"He's one to be reckoned with, and growing stronger," Sivas said. "You may not know it, but this winter when the rivers froze he raided west over the Shaum."

Arigh gaped, then hissed a curse in his own language. The Arshaum were convinced of their superiority to the Khamorth, and with justice; had they not driven the bushy-beards east over the river? It had been decades since Khamorth, even outlaws, dared strike back.

Sivas shrugged. "He's a ready-for-aught, you see." Arigh was still stormy, so the *hypepoptes* called to his serving maid, "Filennar, why don't you detach yourself from your brick-whiskered friend and fetch us a full skin?"

She swayed away, Viridovix following her hungrily with his eyes.

"A skin?" Arigh said eagerly. He forgot his anger. "Kavass? By the three wolf tails of my clan, it's five years since I set tongue to it. You benighted farmer-folk make do with wine and ale."

"A new tipple?" That was Pikridios Goudeles, sounding intrigued. Gorgidas remembered the Arshaum boasting of the plains drink before, but had forgotten what the nomads brewed it from. Viridovix, a toper born, no longer seemed so dismayed over Filennar's disappearance.

She soon returned, carrying a bulging horsehide with the hair still on the outside. At Sivas' gesture, she handed it to Arigh, who took it as tenderly as he might an infant. He undid the rawhide lace that held the drinking-mouth, raised the skin to his face. He drank noisily; it was good manners on the plains to advertise one's enjoyment.

"Ahhh!" he said at last, pinching the mouth closed after a draught so long his face had begun to darken.

"There's dying scarlet!" Viridovix exclaimed—city slang for drinking deep. He raised the skin for a swig of his own, but at the first taste his anticipation was replaced by a surprised grimace. He spat a large mouthful out on the floor. "Fauggh! What a foul brew! What goes into the making of it, now?"

"Fermented mares' milk," Arigh answered.

Viridovix made a face. "Sure and it tastes like the inside of a dead snail." The Arshaum glowered at him, irritated at hearing his beloved drink maligned.

Lankinos Skylitzes and Methodios Sivas, both long familiar with the steppe brew, showed no qualms at drinking and smacked their lips in best nomad style. When the skin came to Goudeles he swallowed enough for politeness' sake, but did not seem sorry to pass it on to Gorgidas.

"Get used to it, Pikridios," Skylitzes said, amusement just below the surface of his voice.

"That is a phrase with which I could easily grow bored," the bureaucrat said tartly. More than a little warmed by all he'd drunk, Skylitzes chuckled.

Gorgidas gave a suspicious sniff as he hefted the horsehide, now half empty. He expected a sour, cheesy odor, but the kavass smelled much more like a light, clear ale. He drank. Actually, he thought, it had surprisingly little flavor of any kind, but it put a quick warm glow in his belly. For potency it matched any wine he knew.

"It's not bad, Viridovix. Try it again," he urged. "If you were looking for something as sweet as wine it's no wonder you were startled, but surely you've had worse."

"Aye, and better, too," the Gaul retorted. He reached for a flagon of wine. "On the steppe I'll have no choice, but the now I do and I'm for the grape, begging your pardon, Arigh. Pass him his snail-squeezings, Greek, sith he's so fond of 'em and all." Viridovix' larynx bobbed as he swallowed.

Sivas gave the embassy a token guard of ten men. "Enough to show you're under the Empire's protection," he explained. "Prista's whole garrison wouldn't be enough to save you from real trouble, and if I did send them out, every clan on the plains would unite to burn the town round my ears. They find us useful, but only so long as we don't seem dangerous to them."

The *hypepoptes* did let the envoys choose horses and remounts from the garrison's stables. His generosity saved them from the mercies of their fellow guests at the inn, who had proved to be horse traders. True to Viridovix' prediction, they were also gamblers. Gorgidas sensibly declined to game with them; Arigh and Pikiridios Goudeles were less cautious. The Arshaum lost heavily, but Goudeles held his own.

When Skylitzes heard that he smiled a rare smile, observing, "Seal-stampers are bigger bandits than mere horse copers dream of being."

"To the ice with you, my friend," Goudeles said. Gold clinked in his belt-pouch.

In another area the bureaucrat was wise enough to take expert advice. Like Gorgidas and Viridovix, he asked Arigh to choose a string of horses for him. Only Skylitzes trusted his own judgment enough to pick his beasts, and did so well that the plainsman looked at him with new respect. "There's a couple there I wouldn't mind having for myself," he said.

"Och, how can he be telling that?" Viridovix complained. "I know summat o' horseflesh, at least as we Celts and the Videssians reckon it, and such a grand lot of garrons I've never seen before, like as so many beans in the pod."

With its Gallic flavor, the word was an apt one to describe the rough-coated steppe ponies. They were small, sturdy beasts, unlovely and not very tame—nothing like the highbred steeds the Videssians prized. But Arigh said, "Who needs a big horse? The plains beasts'll run twice as long and find forage where one of those oat-burners would starve. Isn't that right, my lovely?" He stroked one of his horses on the muzzle, then jerked his hand away as the beast snapped at him.

Gorgidas laughed with the rest, but nervously. He was at best an indifferent horseman, having practiced the art only rarely. Well, then, you can't help getting better, he told himself; but Arigh's promise of months in the saddle made his legs twinge in anticipation.

A week after the *Conqueror* put into Prista, the embassy and its accompanying guards rode out the town's north gate. Though the party numbered only fifteen, from any distance it looked far larger. In steppe fashion, each man rode at the head of five to seven horses, some carrying gear and iron rations, the rest unloaded. The nomad custom was to ride a different animal each day so as not to wear down any of them.

The morning sun shone silver off the Maiotic Bay. The pinched-off arm of the Videssian Sea was several miles to the east, but there were no hills to screen it from view. Beyond the bay a darkness marked another promontory of land jutting south into the ocean. That horizon line, too, was low, flat, and smooth, another portion of the steppe that rolled west—how far? No man knew.

Gorgidas gave such things irregular thought. Most of his attention rested on staying aboard his horse; as beasts will, the cursed animal sensed his inexperience and seemed to take a perverse pleasure in missteps that almost threw him from the saddle. That, luckily, was of the style both Videssians and plainsfolk favored: high-cantled, with pommels before and behind, and with that marvelous invention, stirrups. Without such aids the Greek would have been tossed more than once.

All the improvements, though, did nothing to dull the growing ache in his thighs. He was in good hard shape, able to keep up with the Roman legionaries on march, but riding plainly made different demands. His discomfort was only made worse by the short stirrup leathers the nomads used, which made him draw his knees up and cramped his legs the more.

"Why keep them so short?" he asked the squad leader heading the embassy's guardsmen.

The underofficer shrugged. "Most things in Prista we do Khamorth-style," he said. "They like to stand tall in the saddle for archery." He was a Videssian himself, a lean dark man with heavily muscled forearms. His name was Agathias Psoes. Three or four of his men also looked to have come from across the sea. The rest, like the soldier who had greeted the ambassadors, were obviously locals. Among themselves all the troopers spoke a strange jargon, so thickly laced with Khamorth phrases and turns of syntax that Gorgidas could hardly follow it.

"I have some longer strips," Arigh said. "We Arshaum don't need to get up to know what we're shooting at." He won scowls from his escorts, but ignored them. So did Gorgidas. He took the leathers gratefully. They helped—somewhat.

The Greek's distress was nothing compared to that of Pikridios Goudeles. The seal-stamper was an influential man, but not one who had ever been required to push his body much. When the day's ride ended and he awkwardly scrambled down from his horse, he tottered about like a man of ninety. His hands were soft, too, and chafed from holding the reins. Collapsing to the ground with a groan, he said, "Now I understand Gavras' ploy in making me a legate; he expects my exhausted corpse to be buried on these plains, and may well get his wish."

"He might have wanted you to see the price the Empire pays for your comforts in the city," Lankinos Skylitzes said.

"Hrmmp. Without comforts, what's the point of civilization? When you're in Videssos, my sober friend, you sleep in a bed, too, not rolled in your blanket on the street." Goudeles' bones might ache, but his tongue was still sharp. Skylitzes grunted and went off to help the cavalrymen gather brush for the night's watchfire.

It blazed hot and bright, the only light as far as the eye could reach. Gorgidas felt naked and alone on the vast empty plain. He missed the comforting earthworks and ditches the Romans threw up wherever they went; a whole army could be skulking in the darkness just beyond the sentries' vigilance. He jumped as a nightjar flashed briefly into sight, drawn by the insects the fire lured.

Breakfast the next morning was smoked mutton, hard cheese, and thin, flat wheatcakes one of the troopers cooked on a portable griddle. The nomads seldom ate bread. Ovens were too bulky for a people ever on the move. The cakes were chewy and all but flavorless; Gorgidas was sure he would grow mightily tired of them in short order. Well, he thought, with such fare you need hardly fear a flux of the bowels—more likely the opposite. The climate spoke for that, too—folk in lands with harsh winters and a prevailing north wind tended to constipation, or so Hippokrates taught.

His medical musings annoyed him—that should be over and done. To set his conscience at ease, he jotted a note on the soldier's cooking methods.

Viridovix had been unusually quiet on the first day's journey out of Prista. He was again as the embassy left camp behind. He rode near the rear of the company and kept looking about in all directions, now left, now right, now back over his shoulder. "There's nothing there," Gorgidas said, thinking he was worried they were being followed.

"How right you are, and what a great whacking lot of nothing it is, too!" the Celt exclaimed. "I'm feeling like a wee bug on a plate, the which is no pleasure at all. In the forests of Gaul it was easy to see where the world stopped, if you take my meaning. But here there's no end to it; on and on it goes forever."

The Greek dipped his head, feeling some of the same unhappiness; he, too, had come to manhood in a narrow land. The plains showed a man his insignificance in the world.

Arigh thought them both daft. "I only feel alive on the steppe," he said, repeating his words back in Prista. "When I first came to Videssos I hardly dared walk down the street for fear the buildings would fall on me. How folk cramp themselves in cities all their lives is past me."

"As Pindar says, convention rules all," Gorgidas said. "Give us time, Arigh, and we'll grow used to your endless spaces."

"Aye, I suppose we will," Viridovix said, "but I'm hanged if I'll like 'em." The Arshaum's shrug showed his indifference.

In one way the broad horizon worked to the traveler's advantage: game was visible at an extraordinary distance. Frightened by the horses, a flock of gray partridges leaped into the air. They flew fast and low, coasting, flapping frantically, coasting again. Several troopers nocked arrows and spurred their mounts after the fleeing birds. Their double-curved bows, strengthened with horn, sent arrows darting faster than any hawk.

"We should have nets," Skylitzes said as he watched three shafts in quick succession miss one dodging bird, but the horsemen were archers trained from childhood, and not every shot went wide. They bagged eight partridges; Gorgidas' mouth watered at the thought of the dark, tender meat.

"Good shooting," Viridovix said to one of Agathias Psoes' men. The soldier, from his looks almost pure Khamorth, held two birds by the feet. He grinned at the Celt. Viridovix went on, "It's a fine flat path your shafts have, too. What's the pull on your bow?"

The trooper passed it to him. Next to the long yew bows the Celts favored, it was small and light, but Viridovix grunted in surprise as he tugged on the sinew bowstring. His arm muscles bunched before the bow began to bend. "Not a bit of a toy, is it?" he said, handing it back.

Pleased at his reaction, the soldier smiled slyly. "Your shield, give him here," he said, his Videssian as accented as the Celt's. Viridovix, who wore it slung over his back when combat was not near, undid its strap and gave it to the horseman. It was a typical Gallic noble's shield: oblong, bronze-faced, with raised spirals of metal emphasized by enameling in bright red and green. Viridovix kept it in good repair; he was fastidious about his arms and armor.

"Pretty," the trooper remarked, propping it upright against a bush. He walked his horse back until he was perhaps a hundred yards from it. With a savage yell he spurred the animal forward, let fly at point-blank range. The shield went spinning, but when Viridovix recovered it there was no shaft stuck in it.

"Sure and the beast kicked it ov—" the Celt began. He stopped in amazement. High in the upper right-hand corner of the shield, a neat hole punched through bronze and wood alike. "By my enemies' heads," he said softly, shaking his own.

The guardsman picked up his arrow, which had flown another ten or twelve feet after piercing the shield. He put it back in his quiver, saying, "A good buckler you have. Through mine it would farther have gone." His own shield was a small round target of wood and leather, good for knocking a sword aside, but not much more.

Viridovix said, "And I was after thinking the plainsmen were light-armored on account of the scrawny little cobs they rode, the which couldna carry the weight o' metal."

"Why else?" Gorgidas said.

"Use your eyes, clodpoll of a Greek," the Celt replied, waving his shield in Gorgidas' face. "Wi' sic bows you're a pincushion with or without ironmongery, so where's the good in muffling up?"

To Viridovix' irritated surprise, Gorgidas burst out laughing. "Where's the jape?"

"Your pardon," the Greek said, jotting a note. "The idea of a weapon so strong as to make defense unprofitable never occurred to me. This steppe bow isn't one, you know; in their mail and plate the Namdaleni stood up to it quite well. But the abstract concept is fascinating."

Trying to poke his little finger through the arrowhole, Viridovix muttered, "The pox take your abstract concepts."

The moving brown smudge in the distance slowly resolved itself into a herd of cattle, their horns pricking up like bare branches from a winter forest. With them were their herders, perhaps a score of Khamorth. Most of them abandoned the herd and came riding up when they spied the approaching envoys.

Their leader shouted several phrases in his own tongue, then, seeing imperials among the newcomers, added in horrible Videssian, "Who you? What here you do?"

He did not wait for an answer. His swarthy face darkened with anger when he noticed Arigh. "Arshaum!" he cried, and his men snarled and grabbed for swords and bows. "What you do with Arshaum?" he asked Goudeles, choosing the bureaucrat perhaps because he was most splendidly dressed. "Arshaum make all Khamorth clans—how you say?—

suffer. Your Emperor eat pig guts to deal with them. I, Olbiop son of Vorishtan, say this and I true speak."

"We kill!" one of Olbiop's men cried. The guardsmen were reaching for their weapons, too, and Arigh had an arrow ready to nock. Viridovix and Lankinos Skylitzes both sat warily, each with hand on sword hilt. Gorgidas' Roman blade was still buried in his gear; he waited for whatever fortune might bring.

It was then that Pikridios Goudeles showed his worth. "Stop, O noble Olbiop Vorishtan's son, lest you fall unwittingly into error!" he said dramatically, his voice booming forth with a rhetor's well-trained intonations. Gorgidas doubted if the nomad caught more than his own name, but that was enough to make his head swivel to Goudeles.

"Translate for me, old man, that's a good fellow," the bureaucrat whispered to Skylitzes beside him.

At the soldier's nod he struck a pose and launched into florid Videssian oratory: "O leader of the Khamorth, our being slain by you would be a matter more difficult, grievous, and deadly than death itself. Its—"

"I couldn't repeat that, let alone translate it," Skylitzes said, eyes widening.

"Shut up," Goudeles hissed, and then resumed with a gesture no less graceful for being made atop a scruffy horse rather than in a chamber of the imperial palace. Skylitzes followed gamely as the rhetoric poured out.

"Its defamation would live on to remain among all men; this thing has never been done, but will have been invented by you. There will be clear testimony to your deed, that you killed men on an embassy; and the report's fearfulness will be shown still more fearful by the deed."

The translation was plainly a poor copy of the original, without its sudden reversals, its alliteration, its twisting tenses. It did not matter; Goudeles had the nomads under his spell whether or not they understood him. Like most unlettered folk, they set great stock in oratory, and the seal-stamper was a master in an older school than theirs.

He went on, "I pray I might know my end by your swords today, now that I have heard my Avtokrator greeted with false words. Let me persist, though, in entreating you, first, to look upon us more gently and to slacken your anger and soften your quick choler with charity; and, second, to be persuaded by the common custom of ambassadors. For we are the shapers of peace and have been established as the dispensers of its holy calm.

"Therefore remember that until the present our relations have been incorruptibly tranquil—surely we shall continue to enjoy the same kindness. I know well that your affairs would not otherwise be secure. For understanding most properly offered to those who are near—understanding, of course, which does not turn aside from that which is suitable—will not be evilly influenced by the yet-unrevealed exchange of fortune."

He bowed to the Khamorth. They nodded back, dazed by his eloquence. "What was all o' that meaning?" Viridovix asked Gorgidas.

"Don't kill us."

"Ah," the Celt said, satisfied. "I thought that's what the omadhaun said, but I wasna sure."

"Don't trouble yourself. Neither were the nomads." The turgid Videssian oratory, awash in rhetorical tricks, never failed to oppress Gorgidas. He was used to a cleaner, sparer style. The height of Videssian eloquence was to say nothing and take hours doing it. Still, Goudeles' harangue had served its purpose; the Khamorth lapped up every gaudy phrase.

"Ha, Silvertongue!" Olbiop was saying to Goudeles. "You come to village with us, eat, spend night, be happy." He leaned forward and planted a kiss on the Videssian's cheek. Goudeles accepted it without change of expression, but, when Olbiop turned to bawl orders to his followers, the pen-pusher gave his comrades a stricken look.

"There are exigencies in the diplomat's art I never anticipated," he murmured plaintively. "Do they never bathe on the plains?" He surreptitiously rubbed at the spot, then wiped his hand on his robe over and over again.

Most of the Khamorth rode back to their herd. A handful stayed with Olbiop to escort the embassy. "Come with me you," the leader said. Agathias Psoes looked a question at Skylitzes, who nodded.

"How do the barbarians come by villages?" Gorgidas asked, Olbiop being safely out of earshot. "I thought they were all nomads, forever following their flocks."

Skylitzes shrugged. "Once Videssos held more of the steppe than Prista alone, and planted colonies of farmers on it. Some linger, as serfs to the plainsmen. In time, I suppose, they will die out or become wanderers themselves. Already most of them have forgotten Phos."

They reached the farming village not long before sunset. Olbiop led them straight through its unkempt fields, trampling the green young wheatstalks with lordly indifference. Gorgidas saw other similar swathes and wondered how the villagers raised enough of their crop to live.

Yapping dogs met the incomers at the edge of the village. Already they had passed crumbling buildings which said it had once been larger. One of the Khamorth shot an arrow at a particularly noisy hound. He grazed it in the leg. It fled, yelping shrilly, while the plainsman's comrades shouted at him. "They mock him for nearly missing," Skylitzes explained, anticipating Gorgidas' question.

"Headman!" Olbiop bellowed in Videssian as he rode down the grass-filled central street. He followed it with a stream of abuse in his own language.

An elderly man in rough, colorless homespun emerged from one of the dilapidated houses. The rest of the villagers stayed out of sight, from long experience with their overlords. The headman went down to his belly on the ground before Olbiop, as a citizen of the Empire might to Thorisin Gavras. Skylitzes' mouth tightened at such homage rendered a barbarian of no high rank, but he said nothing.

"We need food, sleep-place, how you say—comfort against cold," Olbiop ordered, ticking off the points on his fingers. A colloquy in the nomads' tongue followed. At length the Khamorth asked a question of Psoes, who nodded easily. Gorgidas resolved to learn the plains speech; he missed too much by depending on his companions to interpret.

Psoes was still chuckling. "As if the boys'd rust, spending another night in the open. You toffs enjoy yourselves, now." The underofficer spoke briefly to his men, who began to make camp in the village square. At their leader's word, Olbiop's followers joined them. The chieftain stayed with the legates.

The headman bowed to the Videssian party. "An it please you, this way," he said. His accent was plains-roughened, his phrasing archaic; the village was long sundered from living currents of speech in the Empire.

The building he led them to had been a temple once. A wooden spire still topped its roof, though Phos' golden globe had fallen from it. The roof itself was patched with thatch; hunks of sod chinked the walls, which were of rudely cut local stone. There was no door—a leather curtain hung in the entranceway.

"Well, 'tis the guesting house. Climb you down and go in," the village headman said, not understanding the hesitation of some of his visitors. "Your beasts will be seen to. Make free with the fire—there's plenty to burn. I go to ready your victuals and other, ah, comforts. How many be ye?" He counted them twice. "Six, is it? Aye, well," he sighed.

"For your hospitality you have our heartfelt gratitude," Goudeles said courteously, dismounting with obvious relief. "Should we need some trifling assistance, how may we address you?"

The headman gave him a wary glance. Bluster and threats he was used to; what danger lurked behind these honeyed words? Finding none, he grudgingly answered, "I'm called Plinthas."

"Splendid, good Plinthas. Again, we thank you." More suspicious than ever, the villager led their horses away. "Phos, what an ugly name," Goudeles exclaimed as soon as he was gone. The seal-stamper went on, "Let's see what we have here." He sounded as if he expected the worst.

The one-time temple had a musty smell; guests seemed few and far between. The benches that had once surrounded the central worship area were long gone—on the plains, wood was too precious to sit idle in an unused building. Nor had it known an altar for many years; in place of that centerpiece was a fire pit. Skylitzes was right, Gorgidas thought. Not even a memory of Phos remained here.

The Videssian officer drew flint and steel from his pouch and deftly lit the central fire. The envoys stretched out at full length on the hard-packed dirt floor. Goudeles sighed with bliss. As the party's poorest horseman, he was the most saddlesore. His soft hands were no longer merely chafed, but blistered. "Have you a salve for these?" he asked Gorgidas, displaying them.

"I fear I packed few medicines," the Greek replied, not caring to explain to Goudeles his reasons for abandoning the physician's art. Seeing the Videssian's pain though, he added, "A salve of grease and honey would soothe you, I think—you could ask this Plinthas for them."

"Thanks; I'll do that when he comes back."

The fire suddenly flared as a fresh bundle of tight-packed straw caught. Gorgidas glimpsed a hand-sized splotch of blue paint high up on one wall. He walked over for a closer look. It was the last remnant of a religious fresco that probably once covered all the walls of the temple. Neglect, mold, soot, and time had allied to efface the rest—like the nameless village itself, the shabby ruin of a brighter dream.

The leather curtain twitched aside; Goudeles opened his mouth to make his request of Plinthas. But it was not the headman who entered the shrine-turned-serai. Half a dozen young women came in, some carrying food, others cooking tools and soft sleeping mats, the last almost staggering under the weight of several skins of what Gorgidas was sure would be either kavass or beer.

Olbiop gave a roar of approval. He leaped to his feet and grabbed at one of the women, kissing her noisily and folding her into a bear hug. She barely had time to pass the skillet and saucepan she bore to a companion before his hands were greedy on her, squeezing her rump and reaching inside her loose tunic.

"The Khamorth is a pig, aye, but no need for such horror on your face," Skylitzes said softly to Gorgidas. "Giving guests women is a plains courtesy; the unforgivable rudeness is to decline."

The Greek was still dismayed, but for a reason different from the one Skylitzes might have guessed. He could not remember how many years it had been since he last coupled with a woman—fifteen at least, and that final time had been anything but a success. Now it seemed he had no choice—refusal, the Videssian had made clear, was impossible. He tried not to think about the price failure would cost him in the eyes of his fellows.

Viridovix, on the other hand, shouted gleefully when he overheard Skylitzes. He swung one of the girls into his arms; choosier than Olbiop, he picked the prettiest of the six. She was short and slim, with wavy brown hair and large eyes. Unlike the rest, she wore a brooch of polished jet near the neck of her blouse. "And what might your name be now, my fine colleen?" the Celt asked, smiling down at her; he was almost a foot taller than she.

"Evanthia, Plinthas' daughter," she answered shyly.

"You mean himself outside? The headman?" At her nod Viridovix chuckled. "Then it must be your mother you look like, for he's no beauty."

She bobbed in a curtsey, smiling back at him now. Gorgidas had seen him weave that spell before; few were immune to it. Evanthia said, "I never knew there were men with hair the color of rust. Your speech rings strangely, too; what far land are you from?"

With that invitation Viridovix was off, launching into his tale like a man diving into the sea. He paused a few seconds later to take a mat from Evanthia and spread it on the ground. "Here, sit by me, my darling, the which'll make it more comfortable for you to listen." He winked at Gorgidas over her shoulder.

The other partnerings were quickly made. The girls from the village did not seem upset at the arrangement—save perhaps Olbiop's chosen, for he pawed her unceasingly. On reflection, Gorgidas found no reason why they should be. They were but following their people's longtime custom, a practice he had extolled not long before.

His own companion was named Spasia. She was not as well-favored as Viridovix' lady; she was plump and had a faint fuzz above her upper lip. But her voice was pleasant, and Gorgidas soon saw she was not stupid, though she had no more idea of the world around her than any villager would. Her eyes kept flicking to the Greek's face. "Is something wrong?" he asked her, wondering if she could sense she did not rouse him.

But her reply was altogether artless: "Are you what they call a eunuch? Your cheeks are so smooth."

"No," he said, trying not to laugh. "My folk have the custom of shaving their faces, and I follow it even here." He reached into his pack to show her the leaf-shaped razor he used.

She felt the edge. "Why keep such a painful custom?" she asked. He did laugh then, for he had no ready answer.

The women readied the food they had brought: chickens, ducks, rabbits, fresh-baked loaves of bread—real bread, for, being settled, they could have a permanent oven—several kinds of berry tarts, and various herbs and leafy vegetables mixed together into a salad. Roasting meat's welcome smell filled the former temple.

Pleasantly full from a good dinner, his head buzzing a little after several draughts of potent kavass, Gorgidas leaned back on his mat and scratched his belly. With the Videssians and Viridovix, he had laughed at Olbiop and Arigh for refusing the salad; to the nomads, greens were cattle fodder, not food fit for men. "Don't be egging 'em on, now," Viridovix had said. "All the more for the rest of us." The Greek had gone along; some of the vegetables, including a white radish strong enough to bring tears to his eyes, were new to him, while a tasty dressing of spiced vinegar and oil added savor to the serving.

If the plainsmen had no yen for lettuces and cucumbers, they made up for it with their drinking, downing the fermented mare's milk in great gulps. They smacked their lips and belched enormously with the good manners of the steppe. Olbiop's companion kept a kavass skin in his hand as often as she could; Gorgidas wondered if she hoped he would swill himself into insensibility.

If so, she was disappointed. The Khamorth was no inexperienced stripling, to pass out when there were other pleasures yet to enjoy. He pulled the girl to him, worked his hands under her tunic once more, and pulled it off inside out over her head. She yielded with no great enthusiasm; her air was that of someone who had tried a ploy, seen it fail, and now was left with the consequences.

Gorgidas had thought the Khamorth would take the woman out into the night, but he pulled down her skirt, stripped off his own fur jacket, trousers, and boots, and fell to with a will, as if the two of them were alone. The Greek looked away; Pikridios Goudeles pretended not to see, never missing a syllable in the story he was telling his companion; Arigh and Skylitzes, used to steppe ways, were themselves not far behind the Khamorth. Viridovix gaped a moment or two, surprise and rut both on his face, before he grinned and gathered Evanthia in. Her arms tightened around him.

Goudeles caught Gorgidas' eye above the recumbent couples. "When you come to Videssos, you eat fish," he said, and sank down on his sleeping-mat with his partner.

"Push more than your pen, there!" Skylitzes called; the bureaucrat gave back an obscene gesture.

Gorgidas still did not lay a hand on Spasia. The orgy all around raised no lust in him, nor mirth either. With the physician's detachment he could not seem to lose, he watched bodies move, joining and separating, listened to sighs and hard breathing and now and again a gasp of pleasure or a wild fragment of laughter.

He felt Spasia's gaze on him. "I do not please you," she said. It did not sound like a question.

"It's only that I—" he began, but Olbiop's hoarse yell interrupted him.

The Khamorth was leaning on an elbow, waiting for his tool to regain its proper temper. "No stones, woman-face?" he called tauntingly. "Why I get you woman? No good she do you."

Even with the fire playing on them, Gorgidas felt his cheeks grow hot. The thing would have to be essayed, he realized. Spasia's eyes held quiet pity as he slid his arm around her and brought her face toward his. She was kind; maybe that would help.

The very feel of her mouth, soft and small, was strange to him, and the firm pressure of her breasts between them seemed a distraction. He was used to a different kind of embrace, a shared hardness. Awkwardly, still conscious of watching eyes, he helped her out of blouse and skirt. His own clothing slid off easily. His body was slim, stringily muscled, and stronger than it looked. He was one-and-forty; it had looked much the same at twenty-one and would yet if he reached sixty-one. Kissing Spasia again, he pushed her gently down to the soft felt. Her lips were pleasant, her warmth against him comforting, but he remained unstirred.

Viridovix hooted and pointed and shouted to Olbiop: "Will you look at that, Khamorth dear? Silvertongue you were after calling himself this afternoon past; sure and he's earning the name the now!" Plainsman and Gaul cheered Goudeles on.

For a moment Gorgidas hoped it had been the watchers that balked him, but he had no success even after their stares traveled elsewhere. "Your pardon, I beg," he said softly to Spasia. "It's not yourself—"

"May I help you, then? You are gracious to a stranger you will never see again; that deserves some reward."

Startled, the Greek began to toss his head in his nation's no, but stopped. "Maybe you can," he said, and touched the nape of her neck.

Perhaps it was the familiarity of the caress; whatever the reason, he almost shouted when he felt himself respond to it. He lifted her face away from him. Smiling, she rolled invitingly onto her back. "There," she whispered, a half sigh.

Soon her breath came short and fast, her mouth now seeking his, her arms round his back trying to pull him ever closer. He laughed quietly to himself as she quivered in release beneath him; he had come to the steppe to break with his past, but hardly like this.

Even though he had accomplished it, however, it still seemed strange and not a little perverse, nothing he really cared to make a habit of. And, ironically, because he was not truly kindled he was able to go on long after his companions flagged. Spasia's mouth was half-open, her eyes glazed with pleasure; now Olbiop, Viridovix, and Arigh were applauding the Greek's stamina. When he was done at last, the Khamorth came over and slapped his sweaty back. "I wrong," he said, no small admission from one of the overweening plainsmen.

The debauch went on far into the night, with partners shifting kaleidoscopically. Having established his credit—even if in counterfeit coin, he thought—Gorgidas felt free to abstain, and Spasia wanted no other. Lying side by side, they talked quietly of his wanderings and her life in the village until sleep overtook them.

The last thing she said was, "I hope you gave me a son." That brought the Greek back to wakefulness, but the only answer she gave his low-voiced question was a snore. He moved closer to her and drifted off himself.

The next morning Olbiop woke them all with a loud groan. Holding his head in both hands as if afraid it might fall off, the Khamorth shoved the leather curtain aside and, still naked, staggered to the village well. Gorgidas heard him curse the creaking windlass as he drew a bucket of water. He poured it over his pounding head, the other Khamorth laughing at his sorry state.

The nomad returned, his greasy hair dripping. The drenching was his first bath in a very long time; despite it he smelled powerfully of horses and endless years of sweat. He shuddered at the thought of breakfast, but swigged kavass.

"The scales of the snake that stung him," Spasia said, reheating a rabbit leg for Gorgidas. Clothed again, she seemed once more a stranger. The Greek fumbled in his kit, wishing his packing had been less functional. He finally came across a small silver box of powdered ink, an image of Phos on its lid. Spasia tried to refuse it, saying, “You gave of yourself last night. That was enough.”

“That was fair exchange,” he replied. “Take it, for broadening my horizons if nothing else.” She looked at him, uncomprehending, but he did not explain. At last she accepted it with a murmured word of thanks.

Other farewells were going on around them. “Nay, lass, you canna be coming with us. ’Twas but the meeting of a night,” Viridovix said patiently, over and over, until Evanthia understood. The Gaul had said many goodbyes in his time, and did not hurry them. For all his ferociousness in battle, for all his delight in strife of any kind, he was not a cruel man.

Along with the rest of the travelers, Gorgidas slung his kit on a packhorse’s back, checking to make sure the leather lashings were secure. When he was satisfied, he swung himself up into the saddle of the pony he would ride that day. Skylitzes gestured. Flanked by the squad from Prista and Olbiop’s nomads, the embassy rode out of the village. A scrawny yellow dog followed until one of the Khamorth made as if to ride it down. It fled, peering fearfully back over its shoulder. Distance swallowed people, buildings, streets, the hamlet itself.

The plainsmen did not stay with the imperial party long; the herds awaited their return. Olbiop traded gibes with Agathias Psoes and his troopers, boasting of his own prowess. “And then are this one,” he said, jabbing a thumb toward Gorgidas. “He futter good, for no-balls man.”

“And to the crows with you,” the Greek muttered, but in his own language.

Olbiop took no notice in any case. “You careful now, Psoes. We catch you no guard—how you say?—embassies, we kill you.”

“Pick your place,” the underofficer replied in the same bantering tone, but he and the nomad both knew a day might come when they were not joking. With a last wave, Olbiop and his men turned back toward the south.

“Let’s travel,” Skylitzes said.

“A moment, please.” Gorgidas dismounted and unstrapped his kit from the packhorse, which had begun to graze during the halt. The others watched curiously as he rummaged. When he came upon his razor, he threw it far out onto the steppe. He remounted, dipped his head to Skylitzes. “Very good. Let’s travel.”

III

A RIPE STRAWBERRY WHIZZED PAST MARCUS' HEAD AND SQUASHED against the barracks wall behind him. "For heaven's sake, Pakhymer," he said wearily, "put your damned toy catapult away and pay attention, will you?"

"I was just checking it," Laon Pakhymer replied innocently. For all his pockmarks and thick beard, he wore a small-boy grin. He led a mercenary regiment of light cavalry from Khatrish, the small Khaganate on Videssos' eastern border. Like all the Khatrishers Scaurus knew, he had trouble taking anything seriously. No *gravitas,* the tribune thought.

Even so, he was glad Pakhymer had chosen to come to the legionary officers' meeting. Though not properly part of Scaurus' command, his horsemen worked well with the Roman infantry.

As if the flying berry had been some strange signal, the tribune's lieutenants left off chattering among themselves and looked toward him to hear what he had to tell them. He rose from his seat at the head of the table and took a couple of paces back and forth to put his thoughts in order. The splash of juice on the clean white plaster behind him was distracting.

"All bets are off—again," he said at last. "Sometimes I think we'll never fight the Yezda. First the civil war with Ortaias Sphrantzes, then Onomagoulos, and now the great—" He loaded the word with irony, "—count Drax."

"What's the latest?" Sextus Minucius asked hesitantly. He was attending his first council as underofficer and seemed sure everyone else was better informed than he.

Scaurus wished it were so. "You know as much as the rest of us, I fear. It's like Apokavkos said when he brought us the news yesterday.

When Drax beat Onomagoulos in the westlands, he found himself left with the only real army there. Appears he's decided to set up on his own."

"But the westlands—Garsavra, Kypas, Kyzikos—they've been ours forever," Zeprin the Red protested, his florid face angry. He was no Videssian, despite that "ours," but a Haloga mercenary who had served the Empire so long he had made it his own, as Phostis Apokavkos had the Romans. Before Maragha, he had held high rank in the Imperial Guards. A lot of things had been different before Maragha.

"Namdalen used to be Videssian, too," the tribune said. Zeprin grunted, nodded ruefully. Marcus went on, "And speaking of that, Drax is making the islanders' old dream of a new Namdalen on the Empire's soil come true. When news of it gets back to the Duchy, we'll see land-hungry barons sailing west to carve out their own little domains while the carving's good. The only way I can see to keep that from happening is to break Drax fast."

Gagik Bagratouni, the *nakharar* who headed the Vaspurakaners in Scaurus' force, raised a hand. "There are—how you say?—more Namdaleni closer to Drax than in the Duchy." His broad, hook-nosed face showed concentration as he spoke; Videssian did not come easily to him. "Utprand plenty of them has, and here. What does—*is*—Thorisin about them going to do?"

"Get that one right and you win the goldpiece," Gaius Philippus muttered. Bagratouni lifted his thick eyebrows, not quite understanding.

"I see three choices, all risky," Marcus said. He ticked them off on his fingers: "He can separate them from the rest of his army and send them, say, toward the Khatrish border. They'd be out of the way there, but who would hold them in check if they decided to imitate Drax?

"Or he can leave them behind, here in the capital, with the same danger. And if they seize Videssos the city, Videssos the Empire is dead." The tribune remembered Soteric talking lovingly of the prospect.

Bagratouni gave a running, low-voiced translation of Scaurus' words to his lieutenant Mesrop Anhoghin. Where his Videssian stumbled, his aide had next to none. The lanky Anhoghin was even more heavily bearded than the *nakharar.*

Marcus finished, "Or he can keep them with the rest of us and hope they don't go over to Drax the first chance they get. I hope so, too," he added, and got a laugh.

"Aye, wouldn't that be just what we needed?" Gaius Philippus said. "Facing the damned Namdalener heavy horse is bad enough head-on. My blood runs cold to think of being taken in flank by treachery."

"I've heard Drax and Utprand are rivals," Minucius said. "Is it so?"

"It's true, I think, though I don't know the why of it," Marcus answered. He looked up and down the table. "Does anyone?"

"I do," Laon Pakhymer said promptly. Somehow Scaurus was unsurprised. Khatrishers, inquisitive as sparrows, were made for gossip. Pakhymer explained, "They were friends and allies once, and joined up to besiege some noble's keep. The place was on a lake; Utprand took the landward side while Drax covered the water. They sat there and sat there, starving this fellow out. He kept fighting, even though it was hopeless—didn't want to surrender to Utprand, I think."

Remembering the Namdalener captain's wintry eyes, Scaurus decided he could not blame the hapless noble.

Pakhymer continued, "So he didn't. He opened the gates on the lakeshore and yielded himself and his castle up to Drax—and Drax only. When Utprand asked for his first share of the spoil, the great count—" He was as sarcastic as Marcus had been. "—told him where to head in. Since then, for some reason they haven't gotten on well." Pakhymer had an infectious grin.

"That is a fair reason," Zeprin the Red rumbled. "The gods spit on the oath-breaking man." For all the holy Kveldulf's labors, the Halogai were pagans yet, worshiping their own band of gloomy deities.

Pakhymer's tale somewhat reassured Marcus; there did seem to be a true and lasting enmity between the two Namdalener leaders. That was the sort of thing Videssos' wily politicians could use to good effect.

The tribune also wondered briefly how loyal Bagratouni and his Vaspurakaners would prove. True, the Yezda had driven them from their homeland into Videssos, but they had suffered worse from a pogrom led by a fanatic Videssian priest. Might they not see Drax and his Namdaleni as allies now instead of foes, even band together with them as fellow heretics? One more thing to worry about, he decided, and filed it away.

The meeting ended soon; there was not enough information to plan further. As the officers wandered away, Scaurus called Gaius Philippus to his side. "What would you do, were you Thorisin?" he asked, thinking the veteran's keen sense of the practical might let him guess what the Emperor intended.

"Me?" The senior centurion scratched at his scarred cheek as he thought. At last he gave the ghost of a chuckle. "I think I'd find another line of work."

"Come on, in you go," sailors urged over and over as the legionaries jumped down into the transports that would take them over the narrow strait the Videssians called the Cattle-Crossing and into the westlands. One of the more considerate ones added, "Mind your feet, you lubbers. The gangplank's bloody slippery in this rain."

"Tell me more," Gaius Philippus said, his cloak wrapped tight around him to protect his armor from the wet. Marcus wished they were embarking from the Neorhesian harbor on the city's northern edge rather than the southern harbor of Kontoskalion. The storm was blowing out of the south, and he had no protection against it here.

Every so often he heard a thump and a volley of curses as a soldier missed a step and tumbled into the waist of a ship. Further down the docks, horses whinnied nervously as their Khatrisher or Namdalener masters coaxed them on board.

Senpat Sviodo landed clumsily beside Scaurus. The strings of the pandoura slung across his back jangled as he staggered to keep his balance. "Graceful as a cat," he declared.

"A drunken, three-legged cat, maybe," Gaius Philippus said. Not a bit put out, Senpat made a face at him.

The young noble's wife leaped down a moment later. She did not need the arm he put out to steady her; her landing truly was cat-smooth. Nevrat Sviodo, Marcus thought, was a remarkable woman for many reasons. To begin with, she was beautiful in the swarthy, strong-featured Vaspurakaner way. Now her finest feature, her wavy, luxuriantly black hair, hung limp and sodden under a bright silk kerchief.

But there was more to Nevrat than her beauty. She wore tunic and baggy trousers like her husband; a slim saber hung at her belt and it had seen use. Moreover, she was a fine horsewoman, with courage any man might envy. No ordinary spirit would have ridden out after Maragha from the safety of the fortress of Khliat, seeking her husband and the legionaries with no idea whether or not they lived—and finding them.

And as if that was not enough, she and Senpat enjoyed a love that seemed to have no room in it for ill. There were times Scaurus had to fight down jealousy.

More women were coming aboard now, and their children as well. Minucius' companion Erene landed nearly as well as Nevrat had, then caught two of her girls as they jumped into her arms. Helvis handed down Erene's third daughter, who was only a few months older than Dosti.

Malric leaped down on his own, laughing as he tumbled and rolled on the ship's rough planking. Helvis started to follow him; Marcus and Nevrat jumped forward together to break her fall. "That was an idiot thing to do," Nevrat said sharply, her brown eyes snapping with anger.

Helvis stared at her. "Who are you to scold me for such trifles?" she replied, not caring for the rebuke. "You've done more dangerous things than hopping off a gangplank."

Nevrat frowned, sadness touching her. "Ah, but I would not, had Phos granted me a child to carry." Her voice was very low; Helvis, suddenly understanding, hugged her.

"That's my job," Senpat said, and attended to it. Merriment danced in his eyes. "We have to keep practicing, that's all, until we do it right." Nevrat poked him in the ribs. He yelped and poked her back.

Thorisin Gavras, his mistress Komitta Rhangavve at his side, came strolling down the docks to watch his army embark. The Emperor still worried about Utprand's Namdaleni, even after deciding to hazard using them. He studied every boarding mercenary, as if seeking treason in the heft of a duffel or the patches on a surcoat.

He relaxed somewhat when he reached the legionaries, giving Marcus a self-mocking smile. "I should have listened, when you warned me of Drax," he said, shaking his head. "Is all well here?"

"Looks to be," the tribune answered, pleased Gavras had remembered, and without anger. "Things are helter-skelter right now."

"They always are, when you're setting out." The Emperor smacked his fist into the palm of his hand. "Phos' light, I wish I were coming with you, instead of Zigabenos! This waiting business is hard on the nerves, but I don't dare leave the city until I'm sure the Duchy won't land on my back. It wouldn't do to get stuck inland and then have to try to scramble back east to face maybe Tomond the Duke on ground of his choosing."

A couple of years ago, Marcus thought, Thorisin would have charged blindly at the first foe to show himself. He was more cautious now. The capital was Videssos' central focus as well as its greatest city. It sat astride travel routes by land and sea, and from it all the Empire's holdings could be quickly reached.

Komitta Rhangavve sniffed at such trifles. "You could have stopped all this before it ever began if you'd heeded me," she said to Thorisin. "If you'd made a proper example of Ortaias Sphrantzes, this cursed Drax would have been too afraid to think of rebelling—and Onomagoulos before him, too, for that matter."

"Be quiet, Komitta," the Emperor growled, not caring to hear his fiery paramour take him to task in public.

Her eyes sparked dangerously; her thin, pale face had the fierce loveliness of a bird of prey. "I will not! You cannot speak to me so; I am an aristocrat, though you grant me no decent marriage—" And so you sleep with a Gallic mercenary, Marcus thought, appalled at the line she was taking. Komitta seemed to realize its danger, too, for she returned to her first complaint. "You should have dragged Sphrantzes to the Forum of the Ox and burned him alive, as usurpers deserve. That—"

But Thorisin had heard enough. He could make himself hold his temper for affairs of state, but not for his own. "I should have taken a paddle to your bloodthirsty aristocratic backside the first time you started your 'I-told-you-so's,'" he roared. "You'd see a happier man here today."

"You vain, hulking pisspot!" Komitta screeched, and they were off, standing there in the rain cursing each other like fishmongers. Seamen and soldiers listened, first in shock and then with growing awe. Marcus saw a grizzled sailor, a man with a lifetime of inventive profanity behind him, frowning and nodding every few seconds as he tried to memorize some of the choicer oaths.

"Whew!" Senpat Sviodo said as Gavras, fists clenched, wheeled and stamped away. "Lucky for that lady that she shares his bed. She'd answer for lèse majesté if she didn't."

"She should anyway," Helvis said. Though a Namdalener, she shared the Videssians' venerant attitude toward the imperial dignity. "I can't imagine why he tolerates her."

But Scaurus had seen Thorisin and his mistress row before and come to his own conclusions. He said, "She's like a sluice gate on a dam: she lets him loose all the spleen inside him."

"Aye, and gives it back in double measure," Gaius Philippus said.

"Maybe so," Marcus said, "but without her, he might fall over from a fit of apoplexy."

Gaius Philippus rolled his eyes. "He might anyway."

"And if he did," Senpat Sviodo said, "she'd say it was to spite her."

He looked up in surprise at the crash of the gangplank being hauled on board. Sailors, nearly naked in the warm rain, stowed it under a deck tarpaulin. "Hello! We're really going to sail in this, are we?" Sviodo said.

"Why not? It's only over the Cattle-Crossing, and the wind doesn't seem too bad," Marcus answered. He was no more nautical than most Romans, but felt like a fount of knowledge next to the Vaspurakaner, whose homeland was landlocked. Showing off, he continued, "They say wetting sails actually helps them, for less air slips through their fabric."

His seeming expertise impressed Senpat, but Helvis, from a nation of true seafarers, laughed out loud. "If that were so, dear, this would be the fastest ship afloat right now. It's like salt in cooking: a little is fine, but too much is worse than none."

Ropes hissed across the wet deck as the sailors wound them into snaky coils. A donkey brayed a few ships away. Two mates and the captain cursed—not half so spendidly as Thorisin and Komitta had—because the big square sail bore Helvis out by hanging from the yardarm like a limp, clinging sheet on a clothesline.

At last a fresh gust filled it; it came away from the mast with a wet sigh. The captain swore again, this time at the man on the steering oar for being slow—whether with reason, Scaurus could not tell. The ship slid away from the dock.

Soteric Dosti's son rode up alongside the marching column of legionaries. Troopers in the front ranks grumbled at the dust his horse kicked up; those further back were already eating their comrades' dust. The Namdalener reined in beside Marcus and shed his conical helmet with a groan of relief. Sweat ran in little clean rills through the dirt on his face. "Whew!" he said. "Hot work, this."

"No argument there," the tribune answered, doubting that his brother-in-law had ridden over to complain about the weather.

Whatever his point was, he seemed in no hurry to make it. "Fine country we're passing through."

Again Scaurus had to agree. The lowlands of the Empire's western provinces were as fertile as any he had known. The rich black soil bore abundantly; the entire countryside seemed clothed in vibrant shades of green. Farmers went out each morning from their villages to the fields and orchards surrounding them to tend their wheat and barley and beans and peas, their vines, their olives, mulberries, peaches, and figs, their nut-trees, and sweet-smelling citruses. A few of the peasants cheered as the army tramped past them to fight the Namdalener heretics. More did their best to give soldiers on any side a wide berth.

The western plain was the breadbasket for Videssos the city, shipping its produce on the barges that constantly plied the rivers running eastward to the sea. It also fed the army as it marched southwest from the suburbs across the strait from the capital. This close to the Cattle-Crossing, the Empire's governors still held the land; with the bureaucratic efficiency Videssos was capable of at its best, they had markets ready to resupply the imperial forces. Marcus wondered how long it would be before the first of Drax'—what was it Soteric had called them?—motte-and-bailey castles would stand by the roadside to block their way. Not long now, he thought.

"Fine country," Soteric repeated. "Too muggy in summer to be perfect, but the land's fruitful enough to grow feathers on an egg. I can see what was in Drax' mind when he decided to take it for his own." He paused a moment, ran his fingers through his light-brown hair, almost the same color as Helvis'. Unlike many of his countrymen, he had a full head; he did not crop the back of his skull. "By the Wager, I wouldn't mind settling here myself one day."

He looked down at Scaurus from horseback, studying him. His eyes might be the same blue as his sister's, the tribune thought, but they had none of her warmth. His high-arched nose put an imperious cast on all his features.

"No?" the Roman said, watching his brother-in-law as closely as he was being watched. Picking his words with care, he went on, "You don't want to go back to the Duchy? Would you sooner take a farm here when your time with the Empire is done?"

"Aye, when my time is done," Soteric said, chuckling silently. He kept scanning the tribune's face. "That may not be so long now."

Marcus did his best to hold a mask of bland innocence. "Really? I thought you'd taken service for a good many years—as I have." He looked the Namdalener in the eye.

Soteric grimaced; his mouth thinned in irritation. "Well, I may be wrong," he said. He jabbed his spurs into his horse's flank so roughly that it started and tried to rear. He fought it down. Wheeling sharply, he trotted away. The tribune watched him go, full of misgivings. He wondered whether Utprand could hold the younger man in check—or whether he intended to try.

Sunset painted the western sky with blood. Somewhere in a nearby copse an owl, awake too soon, hooted mournfully. The army came to a halt and made camp. Confident they were still in friendly country, the Videssians and Namdaleni built sketchy palisades and ran up their tents higgledy-piggledy inside them. The Khamorth outriders were even less orderly; they stopped where they chose, to rejoin their comrades in the morning.

The legionaries' camp, by contrast, was the usual Roman field fortification, made as automatically in safe territory as when an enemy was on their heels. Gaius Philippus chose a defensible spot with good water; after that the troopers carried on for themselves. Each man had his assigned duty, which never varied. Some dug out a protective ditch in the shape of a square; others piled the excavated dirt into a rampart; still others planted on the earthwork sharp stakes they carried along for that reason. Inside the campground, the legionaries' eight-man tents went up in neat blocks, maniple by maniple, leaving wide streets between them.

No one grumbled at the work that went into a camp, even though it might only be used once and then abandoned forever. To the Romans, such fieldworks were second nature. The men who filled their ranks, for their part, had seen the legionary encampment's value too many times to care to risk getting by with less.

So, for that matter, had Laon Pakhymer and his Khatrishers. Marcus was glad to invite them to share the campsite; they had done so often enough after Maragha. Moreover, they helped cheerfully with the work of setting up. Although not as practiced as the legionaries, they did not shirk.

"They're a sloppy lot," Gaius Philippus said, watching two Khatrisher privates get into a noisy argument with one of their officers. The shouting match, though, did not keep the three of them from filling a shield with dirt and hauling it to the rampart, then trotting back to do it again. The senior centurion scratched his head. "I don't see how they get the job done, but they do."

Khatrisher sentries kept small boys away from their strings of cantankerous little horses. Scaurus was not overjoyed at the presence of women and children in the camp, nor had he ever been. He was more adaptable than Gaius Philippus, but even to him it seemed almost too un-Roman to endure. Two summers before, he had excluded them as the legionaries marched west against the Yezda. But after Maragha's disaster, safety counted for more than Roman custom. And it was little harder to turn cheese back into milk than to revoke a privilege once granted.

The tribune's tent was on the main camp road, the *via principalis,* halfway between the eastern and western gates. Outside it, as Scaurus got there, Malric was playing with a small striped lizard he had caught. He seemed to be enjoying the sport more than the lizard did. "Hello, Papa," he said, looking up. The lizard scuttled away and was gone before he thought about it again. He promptly began to cry and kept right on even after Marcus picked him up and spun him in the air. "I want my lizard back!"

As if in sympathy, Dosti started crying inside the tent. Helvis emerged, looking vexed. "What are you wail—" she began angrily, then stopped in surprise when she saw the tribune. "Hello, darling; I didn't hear you come up. What's the fuss about?"

Marcus explained the tragedy. "Come here, son," she said, taking

Malric from him. "I can't give you your lizard," she said, adding parenthetically, "Phos be praised." Malric did not hear that; he was crying louder than ever. Helvis went on, "Would you rather have a candied plum, or even two?"

Malric thought it over. A year ago, Scaurus knew, he would have screeched "No!" and kept howling. But after a few seconds he said, "All right," punctuating it with a hiccup.

"That's a good boy," Helvis said, drying his face on her skirt. "They're inside; come with me." She sighed. "Then I'll see if I can quiet Dosti down." Cheerful again, Malric darted into the tent. Helvis and Marcus followed.

Though commander, Marcus did not carry luxuries on campaign. Apart from sleeping-mats, the only furniture in the tent was Dosti's crib, a collapsible table, and a folding chair made out of canvas and sticks. Helvis' portable altar to Phos sat on the grass, as did the little pine chest that held her private tidbits. Scaurus', of darker wood, was beside it.

Helvis opened her chest to get Malric his sweets, then rocked Dosti in her arms and sang him to sleep. Her rich voice was smooth and gentle in a lullaby. "That wasn't so bad," she said in relief as she carefully put the baby back in the crib. Scaurus lit a clay olive-oil lamp with flint and steel and marked the day's march on the sketch-map he carried with him.

After Malric had gone to sleep, Helvis said, "My brother told me he talked with you today."

"Did he?" the tribune said without inflection. He wrote a note on the map, first in Latin and then, more slowly, in Videssian. So Soteric had ridden back to the women, had he?

"Aye." Helvis watched him with an odd mixture of excitement, hope, and apprehension. "He said I should remind you of the promise you made me in Videssos last year."

"Did he?" Scaurus said again. He winced; he could not help it. When Gavras' siege of the city looked to be failing, he had been on the point of joining the Namdaleni in abandoning the Emperor and traveling back to the Duchy. Only Zigabenos' coup against Ortaias kept the stroke from coming off. Helvis, he knew, had been more disappointed than not when, after unexpected victory, the Namdaleni and Romans stayed in imperial service.

"Yes, he did." Determination thinned her full lips until her mouth was as hard as her brother's. "I was a soldier's woman before you, too, Marcus; I knew you could not do what you planned—" Scaurus grimaced again; it had not been his plan. "—once Thorisin sat the throne. Too often we do what we must, not what we want. But here is the chance come again, finer than before!"

"What chance is that?"

Her eyes glowed with anger. "You are no witling, dear, and you play one poorly. The chance to be our own again, at the call of no foreign heretic master. And better yet, the chance to take a new realm, like the founding heroes in the minstrels' songs."

She had it, too, the tribune thought, the Namdalener lust for Videssian land. "I don't know why you're so eager to pick the Empire's bones," he said. "It's brought peace and safety to a great stretch of this world for so many years I grow dizzy thinking of them. It's base to leap on its back when it's wounded, like a wildcat onto a deer with a broken leg. Tell me, would you islanders do better?"

"Maybe not," she said, and Scaurus had to admire her honesty. "But by the Wager, we deserve the chance to try! Videssos' blood runs thin and cold; only her skill at trickery has kept us from what's ours by right for so long."

"By what right?"

She stepped forward, her right arm moving. Marcus raised his hands to catch a blow, but she seized his sword hilt instead. "By this one!" she said fiercely.

"The same argument the Yezda use," he said; her fingers came away from the blade as if it had burned her. He hitched it away; he did not want anyone but himself touching this sword. "And how would you deal with *them*, here in your new Namdalen?"

In his mind's eye he saw ceaseless petty wars: islander against Yezda, Videssians against nomads, two against one, alliances, betrayals, ambushes, surprise attacks, and the guiltless, prosperous farmers and townsmen of the westlands ground to powder under the iron horseshoes of endlessly marching armies. The picture revolted him, but Avshar, he knew, would laugh at it in chill delight.

He said that and watched Helvis flinch. "The trouble with your brother, and what makes him deadly dangerous," he went on, "is that he has enough imagination to be ruthless, but not enough to see the ruin his ruthlessness will cause." Seeing her outrage, he went on quickly, "This is all quarreling over the reflection of a bone anyhow. It's not Soteric who heads the Namdaleni, but Utprand."

"Utprand? Talk of cold, will you? Utprand eats ice and breathes fog." Her scorn weakened but could not destroy the aptness of the image. A startled laugh jerked from Scaurus.

Helvis was still watching him, with the air of someone studying a waterclock that had once worked but now refused to run. "Tell me one thing," she said. "How is it, if you love this Empire so much—" The scorn was there in her voice again. "—that you would have gone to Namdalen last year?"

Marcus remembered his Stoic teacher, a consumptive Greek named Timanor, wheezing, "If it's not right, boy, don't do it; if it's not true, don't say it." Timanor or no, he wished he had a lie handy.

Because he did not, he sighed and followed his master's advice. "Because then I thought my staying would make the war between Thorisin and Ortaias longer and worse, and help tear Videssos to pieces."

Even in the lamplight he saw the color fade from her cheeks. "Because it would tear Videssos—?" she whispered, as if the words were in some language she did not understand well. "Videssos?" Her voice rose like the tide. "Videssos? Not a thought for me, not a thought for the children, but this moldy, threadbare Empire?"

She was almost screaming; Dosti and Malric both woke, frightened, and began to cry. "Go away, get out!" she shouted at Scaurus. "I don't want to look at you, you flint-hearted, scheming marplot!"

"Out? This is my tent," the tribune said reasonably, but Helvis was furious far past reason.

"Get out!" she screamed again, and this time she did swing at him. He threw up his arms; her nails clawed his wrist. He swore, grabbed her hands, and tried to hold her still, but it was like holding a lioness. He pushed her away and strode into the night.

Few legionaries met his eye as he walked past the row of officers' tents. The same thing had happened to some of them, but they did not have a commander's dignity to protect.

Gaius Philippus was talking with a couple of sentries at the palisade. "Thought you'd turned in," he said when he saw the tribune.

"Argument."

"So I see." The senior centurion whistled softly, spying the deep scratches on Marcus' arm. "You can doss with me tonight, if you care to."

"Thanks. Later, maybe." Marcus was too keyed up from the fight to want to sleep.

"I hope you flattened her?"

The tribune knew his lieutenant was trying to show sympathy, but the rough advice did not help. "No," he answered, "it was my fault at least as much as hers."

Gaius Philippus snorted, unbelieving, but Scaurus tasted his own words' bitter truth. He went off to pace round the perimeter of the camp. He knew his past actions had let Helvis—and Soteric with her—believe he would take the islanders' side against the Empire. Saying otherwise would only have touched off a quarrel, and he had thought the question would never arise.

And now he had question and quarrel both, both of them worse for his tacit untruth. He laughed without mirth. Old Timanor proved no donkey after all.

"You snore," the tribune accused Gaius Philippus the next morning.

"Do I?" The veteran bit into an onion. "Well, who's to care?"

Sandy-eyed, Scaurus watched the legionaries break camp, watched their women, chattering with each other, make their way back to their place in the center of the army's line of march. Helvis was already gone; his tent had seemed strangely deserted when he knocked it down. He wondered if she would be back or choose to stay with Soteric and her own people.

It was good to forget such worries as his soldiers shook themselves out into traveling order. Straightforward questions yielded straightforward answers: Blaesus' maniple should march in front of Bagratouni's Vaspurakaners, not behind them; this road looked better than that one; Quintus Eprius should lose three days' pay for gambling with loaded dice.

A Khamorth scout came trotting back past the legionaries toward Mertikes Zigabenos, whose Videssians brought up the rear of the column. In a few minutes another rode by. Wondering if something was in the wind, Marcus called after him. The nomad ignored his hail. "Bastard," Gaius Philippus said.

"We'll find out soon enough, anyway."

"I know," the senior centurion answered gloomily.

An hour or so later, he squinted down the road and said, "Hello! I don't remember passing *that* the last time we were on our way to Garsavra." The veteran's scowl deepened with every forward step he took. "It's a bloody fornicating fortress, that's what it is."

The castle sat athwart the main road south; if the imperial army was to go any farther, it would have to be dealt with. As the legionaries approached, Scaurus watched Namdalener defenders running about on the palisade, and others atop the tower inside. Thin in the distance, he heard the islanders shouting to each other.

Seen at close range, it was easy to understand how Drax' men had thrown up their fortification so quickly. A ditch surrounded the work, a great gash in the green-covered land around it. The Namdaleni used some of the dirt to form an earthen rampart enclosing a good-sized court—the bailey. In that, at least, thought the tribune, the keep was made like a Roman camp, although here the trench was far deeper and wider and the protecting wall no mere breastwork, but taller than a man.

Inside the bailey, though, the men of the Duchy had heaped the rest of the dirt from their digging into a high mound. And on that motte stood a wooden tower, built in such haste that most of its logs did not have the bark trimmed off them. Archers shooting from atop that tower could command the field. They were already sniping at the imperials' Khatrisher and Khamorth outriders. The nomads shot back, but even their powerful bows could not reach so high.

Zigabenos called a brief council of war. "Just as they want, we'll have to stop and take them out," he declared. "We can't leave a couple of hundred full-armored horsemen on our flank, and I dare not split up my forces to mask the place. Phos alone knows how many more of these pestholes we'll see."

"But starving it out will take forever, and I'd not care to storm it, by the Wager," Soteric said. He seemed so proud of the fieldwork his fellow Namdaleni under Drax had built that even Utprand looked at him in annoyance.

Zigabenos, however, remained suave. "There are ways."

"So there are." Gaius Philippus laughed, understanding him perfectly. He turned to Soteric. "Your toy yonder—" He jerked his chin at the castle. "—is a wonder against hill-bandits or barbarians like the Yezda. But those lads inside are fools to think to hold it when they're facing professionals."

The young Namdalener flushed. "They're professionals, too."

"Aye, belike," Gaius Philippus nodded, still good-humored. "They'll be warm ones, too, bye and bye."

The army's siege train unlimbered that afternoon, at ranges beyond reply from the tower. Soldiers chopped wood to give frameworks to the engines, whose mechanical parts and cordage had been hauled from the capital. Roman engineers worked side by side with their Videssian counterparts.

They sweated together through the night by torchlight. Common troopers cut brush and tied it into bundles to fling into the trench when the time came to storm the castle. Everywhere men were checking blades and armor, shields and shoes, knowing their lives could ride on their precautions.

Marcus was too busy seeing to the legionaries' needs to worry much about Helvis. He could do nothing tonight in any case. With fighting near, the women's camp was at a safe distance behind the army's lines.

Sometime after midnight the drumming of hooves came loud from the Namdalener castle. The men inside had laid planks over their ditch and sent riders pounding out to warn their comrades of the imperials' coming. Whooping, Khamorth and Khatrishers gave chase. They soon ran down two of the messengers, but a third eluded them in the darkness. "Ordure," Gaius Philippus said when the nomads brought that word back.

"Ah, well," Marcus said, trying to make the best of it, "it's not as if Drax didn't know we were moving on him." The senior centurion merely grunted.

Dawn came too early for the tribune's liking, the sun dyeing the clouds first crimson, then golden as the stars faded. A Videssian herald, carrying a white-painted helmet on a spearshaft as a sign of truce, walked up to the very edge of the castle's ditch and called on the Namdaleni to surrender. The islanders yelled obscenities back in their own dialect. An arrow dug into the turf a few feet from the herald. The shot was deliberately wide, but lent his retreat speed, if not dignity.

Zigabenos barked an order. Dart-throwers bucked and crashed. Javelins whizzed at the palisade, making Drax' men keep their heads down. The Namdaleni would pop up, fire at whatever they thought they could hit, and duck behind their earthwork again.

Stone-flingers went into action a few minutes later, hurling rocks as heavy as a man against the tower. They scarred it, and now and then a timber cracked, but it showed no signs of collapse. The islanders had built well. Engineers winched their weapons' twisted gut cords back over and over; oaths filled the air whenever one snapped.

But the machines that hurled darts and stones were only a side show, as were the arrows the Videssians and Khamorth sent flying into the bailey. The Videssian engineers began loading some of their catapults with thin wooden casks full of an incendiary mixture and lobbing them at the tower on the motte.

In their siege warfare the Romans often flung burning pitch or tallow at wooden works. The Empire's fire-brew was deadlier yet. It was compounded of sulfur, quicklime, and a black, foul-smelling oil that seeped up from the ground here and there in imperial territory. As the casks smashed against the tower, sheets of liquid fire dripped down its sides.

The archers inside screamed in terror as the flames took hold. Namdaleni leaped down from the palisade and dashed across the bailey to fight the fire. Marcus heard their dismayed cries as the first buckets of water splashed onto the blaze. Thanks to the quicklime, it burned as enthusiastically wet as dry.

The catapults kept firing; as their cords stretched, the barrels of incendiary they hurled began falling short. Several burst at the top of the motte, splattering flame over the islanders battling the burning tower. Men ran shrieking, blazing like so many torches. The liquid fire dripped under mail shirts and clung to flesh, to hair, to eyes, burning and burning. A Namdalener plunged his sword into a comrade writhing on the ground beside him, afire from head to knees. Thick, black, greasy smoke rose straight into the sky, as sure a message to Drax as any his riders might bring.

Trumpets blared outside the doomed castle. Covered by archery, the legionaries rushed forward, hurling their bundles of brush into the ditch; whether or not he trusted them, Zigabenos held his own islanders out of this first fight with their countrymen. Though no battle-lover, Marcus was glad to run forward at the head of his men. Standing by while Drax' soldiers burned was harder than fighting.

Almost no one was left on the earthwork to hold the legionaries at bay. A spear hurtled past the tribune, but then his *caligae* were chewing at the soft dirt of the palisade's outer face. Shouting at the top of their lungs, the rest of the storming party were close behind.

The Namdalener who had thrown the spear stood at the top of the rampart to engage Scaurus, a big, beefy man with gray stubble on his face. He swung his heavy sword two-handed. Marcus took the blow on his shield. He grunted at the impact and almost slid down the slope. The islander easily parried his awkward counterthrust, then raised his blade for another swipe.

A *pilum* bit into his neck. The sword flew from his hands. They clutched for a moment at the Roman spear's long iron shank, then slid limply away as his knees buckled and he began to topple. Scaurus charged over his body; already legionaries were dropping down into the bailey.

Only a handful of islanders fell at the rampart. Once it was lost, they wasted little time in dropping swords and helmets in token of surrender. Longtime mercenaries, they saw no point in fighting to the death in a hopeless cause. "Think the Emperor'll take us on again, maybe on the Astris to watch the plainsmen?" one of their officers asked Marcus seriously, not a bit abashed by his revolt.

The tribune could only spread his hands in front of him. Strapped for men, Thorisin might do just that.

"Look out! Heads up!" Namdaleni and Romans cried together. The tower on the motte came crashing down, scattering charred timbers and red-hot embers in all directions. A legionary gasped and swore as a blazing chunk of wood seared his leg; one islander was crushed beneath a falling log. He had already been hideously burned; perhaps, Marcus thought, it was for the best.

A Namdalener healer-priest did what he could for the victims of the rain of fire. That was not much; no healer-priest could call the dead back to life. The islanders' clerics stood out less than their Videssian counterparts. Unlike the Empire's priests, they wore armor and fought alongside other soldiers, a gross barbarism in the imperials' eyes.

Marcus climbed to the top of the earthwork once more. An arrow whistled over his head; he glared out, trying without success to spot the overeager archer who'd loosed it. "Hold up! The place is ours!" he shouted, and gave the thumbs-up signal of the gladiatorial games. The Videssians did not use it, but they understood. The soldiers cheered. Zigabenos waved to the tribune, who returned the salute.

Inside the fortress, islanders recovered their fallen comrades' swords to pass on to their kin, a melancholy ceremony Scaurus knew only too well: he had brought Hemond's sword to Helvis after Avshar's magic killed the islander. Fourteen Namdaleni had died here, most from burns. To the tribune's relief, no legionaries were lost, and only a couple hurt.

As they led their prisoners out of the castle, troopers on both sides were exchanging names and bits of military lore. The legionaries were becoming as much mercenaries as the men of the Duchy, plying their trade with skill but without animosity. And ever since they came to Videssos, the Romans had gotten on well with the Namdaleni, sometimes to the alarm of the Videssians themselves.

When Drax' men saw the Namdaleni in the imperial army, though, they showered abuse on them: "Turncoats! Cowards! You scum are on the wrong side!" The officer who had talked to Scaurus—his name, the tribune had learned, was Stillion of Sotevag—spied a captain he knew and shouted, "Turgot, you should be ashamed!" Turgot looked sheepish and did not answer.

Then Utprand strode forward; his icy glare froze the ragging to silence. "Turncoats you speak of?" he said, not loud but very clear. "T'ose as follow Drax know the word, yes, very well." He turned his back on them, calm and contemptuous.

Mertikes Zigabenos sent the captured rebels back to the capital with a guard of Videssian horsemen. "Very nicely done," he complimented

Marcus. "So much for the vaunted Namdalener fortress; taken without losing a man. Yes, nicely done."

"Aye, so much indeed," Gaius Philippus said when Zigabenos had gone off to get the army moving once more. "It held us up for a day and cost us whatever surprise we had. I'd say Drax made a fair bargain."

Styppes dealt capably with one of the Roman casualties, a trooper with a badly gashed calf. As always, the act of healing awed Scaurus. The priest held the cut closed with his hands. Murmuring prayers to focus his concentration, he brought all his will to bear on the wound. The tribune, watching, felt the air—thicken? congeal? Latin lacked the concept, let alone the word—around it as the healing current passed through the priest. And when Styppes drew away his hands, the gaping cut was no more than a thin white scar on the soldier's leg.

"Much obliged, your honor," the legionary said, getting to his feet. He walked with no trace of a limp.

For the second seriously injured soldier, a Vaspurakaner whose skull had been broken by a falling timber when the tower collapsed, Styppes had less to offer. After examining the man, the priest said only, "He will live or die as Phos wills; he is beyond my power to cure." Though disappointed, Marcus did not think he was slacking. Gorgidas could not have helped the luckless trooper, either.

The tribune came up to Styppes, who was—inevitably, Scaurus thought—refreshing himself from a wineskin. In fairness, his craft was exhausting; Scaurus had seen healer-priests fall asleep on their feet.

Styppes wiped his mouth and then his sweat-beaded forehead on the sleeve of his robe. "You took hurt in the fighting, too?" he asked the tribune. "I see no blood."

"Er, no," Scaurus said hesitantly. He held out his wrist to the healer-priest. Helvis' nails had dug deep; the gouges were red and angry-looking. "Our former physician would have given me some salve or other for these. I was hoping you might—"

"What?" Styppes roared, furious. "You want me to squander the substance of my strength on your doxy's claw marks? Get you gone—

Phos' service is not to be demeaned by such fribblings, nor do healers waste their time over trifles."

"The poor Vaspurakaner is too much for you, and I too little, eh?" the tribune snapped back, angry in return. Styppes unfailingly found a way to grate on him. "What good are you, then?"

"Ask your Roman," the healer-priest retorted. "If your cursed scratches mortify, I'll see to them. Otherwise leave me be; it wears me no less to heal small hurts than great."

"Oh," Scaurus said in a small voice. He had not known that. There was, he realized, a lot he did not know about the healer-priests' art. Styppes and his kind could work cures that had left Gorgidas in envious despair, but it seemed the Greek also had skills they lacked.

Thinking back to Gaius Philippus' remark of a little while before, the tribune wondered what sort of bargain Styppes was.

That evening Helvis did not appear. Marcus waited inside his tent until the legionary camp slept around him, hoping she would come. At last, knowing she would not, he blew out the lamp and tried to sleep himself. It was not easy. When Helvis and he were first partnered, sharing the sleeping-mat with her had made it hard for him to doze off. Now, alone, he missed her warm presence beside him.

All what you're used to, he thought. He tossed irritably. What he was getting used to was not sleeping.

Videssos' coastal plain was as flat a land as any, but to the tribune the next day's march was all uphill. There was a brief flurry of excitement late in the afternoon when a couple of Namdalener scouts emerged from a clump of woods to take a long look at the imperial army, but neither the Khatrishers' yells as they gave chase nor Gaius Philippus' lurid oaths after Drax' men escaped succeeded in rousing Scaurus from his torpor.

Munching absently on a husk-filled chunk of journeybread, he walked down the *via principalis* as dusk fell. As always, his own tent was midway between the two entrances on the camp's main street, with the surveyors' white flag just in front of it. He was about to lift the canvas tent flap when the sound of a familiar voice made him spin on his heel.

Yelling, "Papa! Papa!" Malric swarmed down the *via principalis* toward him. Because the Roman camp was always built to the same simple formula, even a five-year-old could find his way in it with confidence.

"I missed you, Papa," Malric said as Marcus bent to hug his stepson. "Where were you? Mama said you were in the fighting yesterday. Were you very brave?"

"I missed you, too," Marcus said, adding, "and your mother," as Helvis, carrying both Dosti and her traveling chest, came up to him. Seeing the tribune, Dosti wriggled in her arms until she set the toddler down. He staggered over to Scaurus; his legs grew steadier under him every day. The tribune gathered his son in.

"Papa," Dosti announced importantly.

"So I am." Marcus stood up; Dosti started undoing the leather straps of one of his *caligae,* reached up to bat at his scabbarded sword.

"You might say hello to me as well," Helvis said.

"Hello," he said cautiously, but she tilted her face up to be kissed as if nothing was wrong. A knot came undone in his chest; he had not known how tight it was till it loosened. Risking a smile, he raised the tent flap. Malric darted in, shouting, "Come on, slowcoach!" to Dosti, who followed as best he could. Helvis stooped to enter. Marcus went in after her.

The talk was deliberately ordinary for a long time: bits of gossip Helvis had picked up among the women, the tribune's account of the storming of the castle. At last he asked it straight out: "Why did you come back?"

She looked at him sidelong. "It's not enough I did? Must you always dig down under everything?"

"Habit," he said, waving at the camp all around them. "I have to."

"The plague take your habits," Helvis flared, "aye, and your senseless love for creaking Videssos, too." Marcus waited for the fire to grow hotter, but instead she laughed, more at herself than to him. "Why did I come back? If it was once, it was five thousand times from Malric: 'Where's Papa? When is he coming back? Well, why don't you know?' And Dosti fussed and cried and wouldn't stop." Even in the flickering lamplight, she looked worn.

"Is that all?"

“What do you want me to say? That I missed you? That I wanted to come back because I cared about you?”

“If that’s so, I want very much for you to say it,” he answered quietly.

“What does it matter to you, with your precious Empire to care about?” she said, but her face softened. “It is so. Oh, this is hard. There you were fighting against my people—my kinsmen even, for all I know—and what was I doing? Praying to Phos you’d come through safe. I thought I didn’t care—until you went into danger. A heart’s easy to harden with nothing at stake, but—damn it anyway!” she finished, caught between conflicting feelings.

“Thank you,” he said. He went on, “When I was sixteen I was sure everything was simple. Here I am twenty years later and, by the gods, twenty times more confused.” Helvis smiled and frowned at the same time, not quite pleased by his automatic translation of the Latin oath. Even there, he thought, I have to be careful. Still . . . “We stumble on somehow, don’t we?”

“So far,” she said. “So far.”

There were more of Drax’ men the next day, not scouts but a good fifty hard-looking horsemen who rode, lances couched, not far out of bowshot on the army’s flank. They shouted something at Utprand’s Namdaleni, but distance blurred their voices so no words were clear. “Bold-faced sods, aren’t they?” Gaius Philippus said.

Zigabenos thought so, too. He sent off the Khatrishers to drive the rebel mercenaries away. Drax’ men pulled back to forest cover in good order. Laon Pakhymer did not order his archers into the woods after them, unwilling to sacrifice the mobility that was their chief advantage. After a while his men rode off to catch up to the rest of the imperials. Drax’ troopers emerged and took up their dogging post once more.

When evening came the rebels did not camp near Zigabenos’ army, but trotted purposefully southwest. Watching them go, Gaius Philippus scratched at the scar on his cheek. “We’re for it tomorrow, I expect. That troop’s not on their own; they’re a detachment off a big bunch and act like it.”

He pulled out his sword, tested the edge with his middle finger.

"Have to do, I suppose. I don't like fighting these bloody islanders. They're big as Gauls and twice as smart."

After full darkness Marcus saw a faint orange glow on the south-western horizon. He did not remember any good-sized town just ahead of them, which left only Drax' men. His mouth tightened. If they were so close, it would indeed be battle tomorrow.

A messenger came to the Roman camp with orders from Mertikes Zigabenos: "We'll march in extended line tomorrow, not in column." The Videssian general expected it, too, then. His aide continued: "You foot soldiers will be on the left, with the Khatrishers covering you. My lord will take the center, with Utprand's Namdaleni on the right."

"Thanks, spatharios," the tribune said. "Care for a mug of wine?"

"Kind of you, sir," the Videssian said with a grin, looking years younger as his official duty fell away. He took a pull, screwed up his face in surprise. "Rather dry, isn't it?" His second sip was more cautious.

"As dry as we could find," Marcus answered; almost all Videssian wine was too sugary for the Romans' taste. Making conversation, he asked, "Why are the islanders on the right?" If Zigabenos was wary of them, better to put them in the center, where they could be watched—and checked—from either wing.

But the spatharios had an answer that showed his commander had also been thinking, though not along Scaurus' lines: "The right's their place of honor, sir." The tribune nodded thoughtfully; with proud Utprand, an appeal to honor was never wasted. The Videssian finished his wine and hurried away to pass the word to Laon Pakhymer.

Marcus wished the battle had developed sooner; as it was, Helvis and most of the other legionaries' women were here, instead of in a camp of their own farther from the upcoming fight. When he said as much to Gaius Philippus, the senior centurion answered, "They're likely safer here, sir. The imperials take no pains with their fieldworks."

"That's so," the tribune said, consoled. "Still, we'll leave half a maniple behind when we move out tomorrow. Under Minucius, I think."

"Minucius? He'll feel shamed at being left out of the fighting, sir. He's young." The senior centurion spoke as though the word covered a host of faults.

"It's an important job nonetheless, and he's a sensible lad." Marcus' eyes grew crafty. "When you give him the order, explain to him how he'll be protecting his Erene."

Gaius Philippus whistled in admiration. "The very thing. He dotes on the wench." Was that derision or envy in his voice? Scaurus could not tell.

The morning dawned clear and surprisingly cool, with a brisk sea breeze blowing the humidity away. "A fine day," Marcus heard one of the Romans say as they broke camp.

"A fine day to be hamstrung on, beef-head, if you don't tighten that strap on your greave," Gaius Philippus snarled. The soldier checked it; it was quite tight enough. The senior centurion was already rasping away at someone else.

Khamorth irregulars came galloping, waving their fur caps over their heads and shouting, "Big horses! Lots of big horses!" A ripple of excitement ran through the imperial army. Soon, now.

They topped a slight rise and came down into the almost flat valley of the Sangarios, one of the Arandos' minor tributaries. A wooden bridge spanned the muddy little stream. The rebels' camp was visible on the far side of the river, but their commander had chosen to draw them up in front of the bridge.

"Drax! Drax! The great count Drax!" the Namdaleni shouted as their foes came into sight. The call was deep and steady as the beat of a drum.

"Utprand!" "Videssos!" "Gavras!" The answering battle cries were various but loud.

"I credited this precious Drax with more sense," Gaius Philippus said. "Aye, the land doesn't slope enough to matter, but if we once push them back they'll go into the river, and that'll be the end of 'em."

Marcus remembered something Nephon Khoumnos used to say: "If ifs and buts were candied nuts, then everyone would be fat." If that was an omen, he misliked it; the dour Videssian general was long dead, slain by Avshar's wizardry.

Zigabenos, who had once been Khoumnos' aide, knew better than to exhaust his troops by charging too soon. He kept them well in hand as they advanced. The Namdaleni moved slowly forward to meet them. Drax' men wore sea-green surcoats and had green streamers fluttering from their lances.

Where was Drax' banner? If the right was the islanders' place of honor, Scaurus had expected to see it bearing down on him. But it was nowhere to be found—until the tribune spied it at the opposite end of the Namdalener line. Suspicion flared in him. What was Drax scheming?

Like an armored thunderbolt, Utprand hurled himself at that taunting banner, breaking the steady line the imperial army had maintained. By squads and platoons his men followed, until half a thousand knights bore down on the rebel count.

"Traitor! Robber!" Their war cries rang over the pounding of their horses' hooves.

"Drax! Drax! The great count Drax!" Shouting, too, Drax' horsemen swung lances down and dug spurs into their mounts to meet them. They had another cry as well, and a premonitory shiver went down Scaurus' spine: "Namdalen! Namdalen! Namdalen!"

"Go on! Go on! Back him, you milk-livered, cheese-faced dogturds!" That was Gaius Philippus shouting, profanely praying for some miracle to take his voice across the field and make Soteric's men, and Clozart's, and Turgot's, join Utprand and his loyal retainers in their charge.

A few did, but a trickle, ones, twos, and fives. Most sat their horses, waiting. If Utprand could cast Drax down, perhaps they would advance . . . but Utprand and his followers were alone on the field, and Drax had more than half a thousand knights to throw against them.

Lances shattered. Horses fell, screaming worse than men. Riders flew from saddles to be trampled under iron-shod hooves. The sun sparkled off steel as swords were bared. Utprand's wedge of men, fighting all the more grimly for knowing themselves betrayed, still surged toward their enemy's standard.

Scaurus cheered them on, but not for long, for Drax' right bore down on him, every lance, it seemed, aimed straight at his chest. The Khatrishers were still skirmishing with the onrushing Namdaleni, peppering them with arrows. A knight here, another there, sagged in their saddles as they were hit. But the light horse in front of them could not really stop their charge. One Khatrisher, bolder than his friends, rode in close to slash at an islander with his saber. The Namdalener swerved his horse so it struck his foe's pony shoulder to shoulder. The smaller mount stumbled and went down. An islander speared its rider as if he were a chunk of meat to be impaled on a belt-knife. The sea-green wave rolled over the corpse.

"Stand firm now, you *hastati*! The horses don't want to spear themselves," Gaius Philippus was shouting.

"*Pila* at the ready . . ." Marcus called. He waited, dry-mouthed, as Drax' men neared with frightening speed. "At the ready . . . loose!" He swung his arm down; the buccinators' horns echoed his command.

Hundreds of javelins darted forth as one, followed by another volley and another. Horses and riders went sprawling, killed or wounded; knights behind lost their footing in turn. Some of the horsemen reacted quickly enough to catch the *pila* on their shields—which were shaped, Scaurus thought in one of those strange, clear moments he knew he would remember forever, like the kites Videssian boys flew. It did them less good than they might have hoped. The long, soft-iron shanks of the *pila* bent on impact, making them doubly useless: not only did they foul the shields, but the Namdaleni could not throw them back.

But Drax' men were already fearfully close when the rain of javelins began. Their charge was blunted, slowed. It could not be stopped. A few of their horses drew up rather than running onto the *hastae;* more, spurred on by their riders, crashed through the line of heavy spears. "Drax! Drax! The great count Drax!" Their shout never faltered.

Had it not been for the flexibility of the Romans' maniples, the system that let them fight in small units and shift eight-man squads to meet trouble wherever it occurred, the Namdalener charge would have smashed them to ruin in minutes. Scaurus, Gaius Philippus, Junius Blaesus, Bagratouni—all of them screamed orders, directing legionaries to where they were needed most.

A lancehead, its steel discolored with rust but still deadly, jabbed past the tribune's shoulder. Behind him a Roman grunted, more in surprise than pain. The lance, now dipped in red, ripped free. The legionary's scream drowned in up-bubbling blood.

A hurled stone smashed off the nasal of the lancer's conical helm. He swore in island patois, shook his head groggily. Marcus sprang forward.

Sudden fear on his face, the Namdalener tried to beat his thrust aside with the shaft of his lance. The tool was too clumsy, the man too slow. Scaurus' point punched through his chain gorget and into his neck. The lance slipped from his hand. He would have fallen, but in the press he could not for some minutes.

Another Namdalener, also on horseback, slashed down at the tribune, who caught the blow on his shield. The knight grunted and cut, again and again, his sword striking sparks from the bronze facing of Marcus' *scutum*. He was a clever warrior; each cut came from a different, newly dangerous angle. The Roman's shield arm started to ache.

He pivoted on his left foot, thrusting at the rider's jack-booted leg. With a veteran's instinct, the Namdalener twitched it out of the way, but for a horseman that was not enough. His mount took the stab in the barrel. Its eyes wide with pain it could not understand, it reared and then foundered, pinning the islander beneath it before he could kick free of the stirrups. His cry of pain was cut short as another horse trampled him.

Someone pounded the tribune's shoulder. His head whipped round; it was Senpat Sviodo, who waved a scolding finger under his nose. "That was not sporting," the Vaspurakaner said.

"Too bloody bad," Marcus growled, for all the world like Gaius Philippus.

Senpat's mobile features curdled into a frown. "The Romans are a very *serious* people," he declared, and winked at the tribune.

"To the crows with you," Scaurus said, laughing. And one worry, at least, he thought, had come to nothing at all, for Gagik Bagratouni's band of refugee Vaspurakaners was fighting as fiercely as any of Scaurus' troops. The thick-shouldered *nakharar* himself dragged a Namdalener from the saddle, to be finished by his men. Mesrop Anhoghin outdueled another; the Roman thrusting-stroke he had learned let him use his long arms to best advantage.

"This Drax is no great shakes as a general," Senpat yelled in Marcus' ear. "He should have learned from last year's battle that his knights can't break our line. They pay the price for trying, too." That was so. With their charge stalled, the Namdaleni grew vulnerable not only to the legionaries but also to the Khatrishers, who plied them with arrows and began to stretch wide to turn their flank.

But if Drax' tactical skills left something to be desired, the great count was a clever, insightful strategist. Sudden commotion broke out on the imperials' right wing. Scaurus glanced in that direction, but saw nothing—too many horses and riders in the way. He grimaced in annoyance; in most fights his inches gave him a good view of the field, but not today.

All too soon, he had no need to see; the rising tide of battlecries from the right told him all he had to know: "Namdalen! Namdalen! Namdalen!" The shout swelled and swelled, far beyond the noise Drax' men alone could make. Cries of fury and fear came from the Videssian center; the island mercenaries had turned their coats.

There was a lull in the assault on the legionaries. The commander of Drax' right wing, a snub-nosed Namdalener who had to be older than he looked, held up his shield on his lance. It was not painted white, but Marcus guessed he meant it as a sign of truce. "What do you want?" he called to the officer.

"Join us!" the islander shouted back, his accent nearly as thick as that of Utprand, who was surely dead by now. "Why t'row your lives away for not'ing? Up Namdalen and away wit' old Videssos! The future belongs to us!"

The legionaries answered that for themselves, an overwhelming roar of rejection. "Up Namdalen with a hoe handle!" "It'd be us you turned treacher on next!" That one hit home; if the Romans sometimes got on better with the men of the Duchy than they did with the imperials, it was for the islanders' plain speech and straightforwardness. Utprand, although ruthless as a wolf, had been an utterly honest man, while Drax outdid the Videssians in double-dealing. Gaius Philippus' jeer spoke for many: "Why should we give you what you're not men enough to take?"

A slow flush of anger ran up the Namdalener's face. He lowered the upraised shield, settled his helm's bar nasal more firmly on his short nose. "On your heads be it," he said. The islanders surged forward once more.

Their second charge, though, was not half so fierce as the first had been. That puzzled Scaurus, but after a moment he understood. All Drax' knights needed to do here was to keep the legionaries in play. As long as they could not go to the aid of Zigabenos' Videssians in the center, that was enough.

Laon Pakhymer saw that, too, and with bantam courage flung his Khatrishers at the solid Namdalener ranks. The light horsemen's spirit was equal to anything, but man for man, horse for horse, they were grossly overmatched in close combat. "Gutty little bastards, aren't they?" Gaius Philippus said with nothing but respect in his voice. He watched the doomed attack; there was nothing else he could do.

At last flesh and blood could take no more. The Khatrishers broke, riding wildly in all directions, for the time being wrecked as a fighting force. Pakhymer galloped after them, still shouting and trying to bring them back for one more charge, but they would not heed him.

His flank cover ruined, Marcus drew his line back and to the left, anchoring the end of it to a small stand of fig trees. The Namdaleni did not hinder the maneuver; it drew him further from the center. He knew that and hated it, but he could do Zigabenos no good by being surrounded and destroyed, either.

In any case, the Videssian general was being driven leftward, too, pressed from the front by Drax' men and from the right by the Namdaleni who had been his own. But Zigabenos, as Scaurus knew, was resourceful; though his position could hardly have been worse, he still had a stratagem left to try.

The battlefield din shrieked in Scaurus' ears. When a great roar swallowed it as a whale might gulp a spratling, he thought for a terrible second that he had been struck a mortal blow and was hearing the sound of death. But the noise was real; troopers on both sides clapped hands to their heads and spun about, looking for its source. Then the tip of shadow touched the tribune, and terror with it.

Long as the Amphitheater, thick as the city's Middle Street was wide, the dragon soared over the battle on batwings vast enough to shade a village. It roared again, a sound like the end of the world; red-yellow as molten gold, flame licked from the fanged cavern of its mouth. Its eyes, big as shields, wise as time, black as hell, contemptuously scanned the quarreling worms below.

But there are no dragons, Marcus' mind yammered. In his disbelief he must have spoken aloud, for Gaius Philippus jerked his head upward. "Then what do you call that?"

Men shouted and ducked and tried to hide; horses, plunging and rearing, did their best to bolt. Riders jounced on their bucketing mounts and were thrown by the score. Though the Videssians were no more able to defend than the Namdaleni to attack, the pressure which vised them eased.

The dragon sideslipped in the air, sun glinting on silver scales. The great wings beat, once and then again, like the heavy breathing of a god. The beast stooped on the Namdaleni. Fire shot from its mouth now, making the incendiary the imperials brewed seem no more than embers. The islanders scattered before it, clawing at one another in their effort to escape.

Suddenly, incongruously, Gaius Philippus' sweat-streaked face creased in a grin. "Are you daft, man?" Scaurus yelled, waiting for the beast to turn and burn him, too.

"Not a bit of it," the senior centurion answered. "Where's the wind of its passage?" He was right, the tribune realized; those wings, when they worked, should have stirred a gale, but the air was calm and still, even the early morning breeze gone.

"Illusion!" he cried. "It's magicked up!" Battle magic was a touchy thing; most wizardries melted in the heat of combat. Indeed, because that was so, generals often ignored sorcery in their plans. Zigabenos, holding back until the last moment, made the most of it from sheer surprise.

But what one wizard could accomplish, another could undo. Even as the dragon dove toward the islanders' ranks, it began to fade. Its roar grew distant, its shadow faint, its flame transparent. It would not vanish, but a ghost held no terror for man or beast. Now and again it firmed somewhat as the Videssian magicians tried ever more desperate spells to maintain the seeming, but their Namdalener counterparts vitiated each one in turn.

The men of the Duchy re-formed with a trained speed and discipline Marcus had to admire, though it meant ruin for his side. "Namdalen! Namdalen!" Their shout once more dominated the field. And now they fought with greater ferocity than before, as if to make amends for their momentary panic.

The snub-nosed wing commander bawled an order. His horsemen struck forward—not at the legionaries this time, but at the join between their maniples and the Videssian regiment to the right. The move was full of deadly cunning; coordination between units of the polyglot imperial army was never what it should be. Romans and Videssians each hesitated a few seconds too long, and got no chance to repair their mistake. Voices deep-throated in triumph, the Namdaleni swarmed into the gap they had forced.

"Form square!" Marcus ordered. The buccinators echoed him. He bit his lip in anger and dismay. Too late, too late, the islanders were already round his flank.

The Namdalener officer, though, had a feel for the essential. He swung his knights in against the Videssian center, already hard-pressed from right and front. Surrounded on three sides, the imperials shattered. Zigabenos and a forlorn rear guard fought on, but most of the Videssians had no thought beyond saving themselves. The men of the Duchy pounded after them, cutting them down from behind.

Compared to breaking the Videssians, the legionaries were a secondary objective. They formed their hollow square with only token interference from the islanders. "Blow 'retreat,'" Scaurus ordered the buccinators. The bitter call rang out.

"Back to camp?" Gaius Philippus asked.

"Do you think we can do any good here?"

The senior centurion's eyes measured the battlefield. "No, it's buggered right and proper." As if to underscore his words, a fresh burst of shouting from the right had Zigabenos' name in it. Dead or captured, Marcus thought dully. The Videssian general's standard had fallen some time before, the Empire's sky blue and golden sun trampled in the dust . . . and the Empire with it, all too likely.

IV

VARATESH AND HIS FIVE FOLLOWERS RODE SOUTH LIKE WINDBLOWN leaves, their gray cloaks swirling around them. Their talk was an endless botheration to him, a string of thieveries, rapes, murders, and tortures, all proudly recounted and embellished. He had done worse than any of them, but he did not brag of it. It made him ashamed. Forfeit the company of good men, he thought for the thousandth time, and what you have left is offal—harden yourself to it. He could not.

He had killed his twin brother at seventeen, in a quarrel over a serving girl. No one ever believed Kodoman drew knife on him first, though it was so. Kinslayer his clan named him and punished him accordingly. They did not kill him, for he was the khagan's son, but cast him out, driving him naked from their tents onto the steppe.

In its way that, too, was a death sentence; the spirit went out of ostracized men, so they perished from aloneness as much as from hunger, cold, or wild beasts. But the injustice of it was a flame burning in young Varatesh's breast, a flame to sustain him where a lesser man would have yielded to malignant fate and died. He came back to steal a horse; he had to, he told himself, to survive. The guard was about his size; a swift blow from behind, and he had clothes as well. Of course he only stunned the man; he was sure of that, though the fellow had not moved by the time he rode away.

Bad luck somehow followed him after that. More than once he was on the point of being adopted into a new clan when word of his past caught him up and he was spurned once more. The insult of it rankled still; who were those arrogant chieftains, to presume to judge him on such rumors? One way or another, the insults were avenged. Before long, no khagan in his right mind would have invited Varatesh to join him and his. As his past grew blacker, so did his future; he could not wade to acceptance through blood.

Banned from the clans by no fault of his own—for so he always saw it—Varatesh, ever bold, formed his own. The plains had always known outlaws—scattered skulkers, often starving, distrusting each other and afraid of their betters. Varatesh gave them a standard to rally to, a blank black banner that openly proclaimed them for what they were. At last he was the chief he should have been, with a growing host behind him—and he hated them, almost to a man. Better, he thought sometimes, if Kodoman's dagger had found his heart.

Such thoughts availed him nothing. He reined in to consult the talisman he carried. As always, the crystal sphere was transparent when he first put it in his hands, but at his touch it began to swirl with orange mist. Soon all its depths were suffused with orange—save for one patch, which remained stubbornly clear. He rotated the sphere; however he turned it, the clear area stayed just east of south, as if drawn by some sorcerous lodestone. And it was larger than it had been yesterday.

"We gain," he told his companions. They nodded, smiling like so many wolves.

In fact, Avshar had explained to him, it was not magic that kept the entire crystal from coloring, but the absence of magic. "There is a traveler on the plains who carries a blade proof against my spells," the wizard-prince had said. "We've met before, he and I. If you would, I'd have you take him for me and fetch him here to your tents, where I can pry his secrets from him at leisure."

A cold, greedy hunger was in the white-robed giant's voice, but Varatesh did not hear it. For Avshar he bore admiration and regard not far from love. The sorcerer was outcast, too, driven, he said, far from Videssos in some political convulsion. That alone would have been enough to make a bond between them. But Avshar also used the renegade chieftain's son with exactly the sort of respectful deference Varatesh felt should have been his by right. He rarely received it from his followers, most of whom were ruffians long before they became outlaws. To have the wizard—a mighty one, as he had proved in many more ways than a bit of crystal—freely grant it eased Varatesh's suspicions as nothing else could have. His quality was recognized at last, and by one himself of high estate, even if an outlander.

That had given Varatesh pause, the first few days after Avshar appeared before his tent. The wizard used the steppe tongue like a true Khamorth, not some lisping imperial . . . and no one saw his face. He always wore either a visored helm or mantling so thick only the faintest hint of eyes could be made out. But he was not blind; far from it.

After a very short while, though, doubts somehow disappeared, and both Avshar's curious arrival—*why* had the sentries not reported a traveler?—and personal habits came to be nothing more than matters for idle speculation.

Perhaps he has hideous scars, Varatesh thought compassionately. One day he will see I esteem him for himself, not the fleshly mask he wears.

With a nomad's patience, the plainsman was willing to wait. For now he would help his friend in the task he had been set; it never occurred to him to wonder how Avshar had come to set him tasks. He booted his horse forward.

"No, damn it, I want nothing to do with that miserable piece of pointed iron in my kit," Gorgidas growled at camping time, as he had every day since they left the village. Every day saw him more irritable, too; his face itched and felt rough as a rasp as his beard started growing in. And, to his mortification, it seemed to be mostly white, though his hair was still dark but for a thin dusting of silver at the temples. He wished he had his razor back.

"Listen to the silly man, now!" Viridovix exclaimed to everyone who would listen—the friendly feud between Celt and Greek entertained the whole party. "When you were with the legion, with its thousands of men and all, the lot of 'em could look after you. The now, though, it's but this wee few of us. We have to watch out for our own selves and maybe canna be sparing the time for one puir doit too proud to learn swordplay."

"Oh, go howl. I've managed to come this far in my life without the knack for killing people, and I don't care to pick it up now. I'm too old to learn such tricks anyway." He looked resentfully at the Gaul, who was his own age, near enough, but whose sweeping mustachios were still bright red.

"Too old, is it? Sure and you're a day younger than you'll be tomorrow." Viridovix waited to see if that shot would hit, but the physician merely set his chin. The Celt switched to Latin so only Gorgidas would understand: "Forbye, if you're not too old to start bedding women, now, sure and the sword shouldna come too hard."

The day was warm, but ice leaped up the Greek's spine. "What mean you?" he said sharply.

"Softly, softly," Viridovix said, seeing his alarm. "Naught with harm in it for you. But sith you've tried the one new thing, why not the other?"

Gorgidas sat unmoving, staring past the Gaul. Viridovix left him to himself for most of a minute, then asked with an impudent grin, "Tell me now, how is it by comparison?"

The Greek snorted. "Find out for yourself, you barbarian ape." He had lived under the shadow of the Roman army's law too long to be easy with others knowing he preferred men to women. In the legions, those who did so faced being beaten to death by their fellow soldiers as punishment on discovery.

Even the thought of a *fustuarium* was enough to freeze the smile on his lips. He sat a while, considering; he did not like the idea of being a burden to his companions. Pikridios Goudeles, with more tact than Gorgidas had thought he had, helped solve the dilemma. "Possibly the brave Viridovix," he said, pronouncing the Celt's name with care, though Videssians tended to stumble over it, "would instruct us both. I have no skill at swordplay, either."

Skylitzes had been tossing a handful of dry sheepdung on the fire. At Goudeles' words he looked up, his usually dour features showing amazed delight. The spectacle of the plump bureaucrat wielding a blade promised amusement beyond his wildest dreams. He kept silent, afraid a taunt might make Goudeles change his mind.

Gorgidas unsheathed the *gladius* Gaius Phillippus had given him, hefted it experimentally. It seemed short and stubby compared to the longsword Viridovix bore; the Romans favored blades no more than two feet long, for they relied on the stab rather than the slashing stroke. The leather-wrapped grip fit Gorgidas' hand seductively well; he held a tool perfectly designed for its intended use.

"Heavier than your pens, eh?" Arigh said, stepping toward the fire with the results of his brief hunt: a rabbit, a striped ground squirrel, and a fair-sized tortoise. The Greek nodded, scratching the side of his face for the dozenth time that day. Already his beard was thicker than Arigh's; the Arshaum, unlike the Khamorth, were not a whiskery folk. As if to compensate, they rarely trimmed the few hairs that did appear, but let them grow in a thin tuft at the point of their chins.

Goudeles, of course, had brought no sword. He borrowed a saber from one of Agathias Psoes' troopers, a curved, single-edged blade with a very short back edge, called a shamshir in the Khamorth tongue, a yataghan by Arigh. The Videssian handled it with even more uncertainty than Gorgidas showed; the Greek, at least, had seen combat at first hand.

But after a flourish that almost took off his own ear, Goudeles said grandly to Viridovix, "Impart to us your martial art."

"That I will." As the soldiers gathered round to watch, the Celt set his pupils in the guard position, making sure they carried their left arms well behind them. "Keeping them out o' harm's way and balancing you both, you see. If you've shields you'll stand more face-to-face to get full advantage from 'em, but no use complicating things the now."

He adjusted them once more and stepped back to survey his handiwork. Then, without warning, he tore his own blade free and leaped at his students with a bloodcurdling shriek. They stumbled away, horrified. The watchers guffawed. "There's you first pair of lessons together," Viridovix said, not unkindly. "The one is, never relax around a man with a sword, and t'other, a good loud yell never did you any harm, nor your foe any good."

Even as teacher, the Gaul made a relentless opponent. Gorgidas' arm and shoulder ached from parrying his slashes. So did his ribs; Viridovix had thumped them with the flat of his blade more than once. The contemptuous ease with which he got through infuriated the Greek, as Viridovix had known it would. Where Gorgidas had been all but forced to take sword in hand, he soon worked in grim earnest, panting breaths hissing out between clenched teeth. Once Viridovix had to pirouette neatly to keep from being spitted on his point; the Greek lacked the experience to know how dangerous his thrust was.

"That poxy Roman blade," the Gaul said. He was sweating as freely as his pupil. "You kern, you were watching the legionaries and never let on—you almost let the air out of me there."

Gorgidas began an apology, but Viridovix slapped him on the back and cut it short. "Nay, 'twas well done." He whirled on Goudeles. "Now, sirrah, your turn. And at ye!"

"Oof!" the pen-pusher said as the Celt's blade spanked his side. He lacked any feel for aggression; whatever strokes he made were purely to defend himself. Within that limitation, though, he showed some promise. His movements were economical, and he had a gift for guessing the direction the next blow was coming from. Lankinos Skylitzes showed disappointment.

"It's good you're not trying to go beyond yourself," Viridovix said. "If you learn enough to stay alive a while, sooner or later a mate'll rescue you, the which would do a dead corp no good at all, at all."

But after a while he grew bored with an opponent who would not take the fight to him. His own strokes grew quicker and harder, and when Goudeles, retreating desperately now, threw up his saber in a counter, the Gallic longsword met it squarely. The pen-pusher's blade snapped clean across; the greater part flew spinning into the fire. Taken by surprise, Viridovix barely managed to turn his sword in his hand so he did not cut Goudeles in two. As it was, the Videssian fell with a groan, clutching his left side.

Viridovix knelt by him, concerned. "Begging your pardon, indeed and I am. That one was not meant to land."

"Mmph." Goudeles sat up gingerly. He hawked and spat. Gorgidas saw the spittle was white, not pink-tinged—the bureaucrat had no truly dangerous hurt, then. Goudeles looked at the stub of his blade. "I did not realize I was facing you with a weapon as flawed as my own skill."

"Not flawed!" protested the trooper from whom he'd borrowed it. He was still young enough for his beard to be soft and fuzzy; his name was Prevails, Haravash's son, testifying to his mixed blood. "I paid two goldpieces for that sword; it's fine steel from the capital."

Goudeles shrugged, winced, and tossed him the broken saber. He caught the hilt deftly. "Look!" he insisted, showing everyone that what was left of the blade had the suppleness befitting a costly weapon. Once he had satisfied himself and his comrades of that, his eyes slowly traveled to Viridovix. "Phos, how strong are you?" he whispered, awe in his voice.

"Strong enough to eat the pits with the plums—or you without salt." But despite the gibe, the grin stretched thin across Viridovix' strong-cheekboned face. Gorgidas could guess his thoughts. There were times when his sword and Scaurus', spell-wrapped by the druids of Gaul, were far more than ordinary blades in this world where magic was real as a kick in the belly. Usually it took the presence of sorcery to bring out their power, but not always.

The Celt sat cross-legged by the fire. He drew that strangely potent sword, studied the druids' marks that had been stamped into the metal while it was still hot. They meant nothing to him; the druids guarded their secrets well, even from the Gallic nobles.

For a moment the marks seemed to glow with a golden life of their own, but before Gorgidas was sure he had seen it, Viridovix resheathed his blade. Some chance reflection from the firelight, the Greek thought. He yawned and sighed at the same time, too tired to worry about it long.

He also ached. Swordplay, like horsemanship, called on muscles he rarely used. He knew he would be stiff come morning. *Ten years ago I would have been fine*, he protested to himself. The internal answer came too soon: *ten years ago you weren't forty-one*.

He gnawed at a rabbit leg, washed down some of the tasteless nomad-style wheatcakes with swigs of kavass, and fell asleep the moment his feet reached the end of his bedroll.

Varatesh tested the night breeze with a spit-moistened finger; out of the south, as he had expected. The wind came off the sea in spring and summer, bringing fair weather with it. In fall it would shift, and not even a man born on the plains relished a steppe winter. Every year the shamans begged the wind spirits not to turn, and every year found themselves ignored. Foolishness to waste good prayers thus, the renegade thought.

He had counted on a south wind when he led his little band across the track of the man he sought and his companions. They had ridden on after dusk to catch up with the larger party, using as their guides the stars and Avshar's talisman; in the darkness its orange smoke glowed with a glowworm's pale cold light. Now their quarry's camp lay straight north, the embers of its campfire a red smudge against the horizon.

Luckily there was no moon, or sentries might have seen Varatesh's men approach. But in the faint starglimmer they were so many shadows sliding up, and they moved as quietly as any shades. Varatesh's feet chafed in his boots. He was not used to walking any distance, but he had left the horses behind with one of his men; even muzzled, they were too likely to give themselves away.

"What now?" a nomad whispered. "From the trail the filthy pimps' sons left, they've got twice as many as we do, and then some."

"Much help they'll get from that," Varatesh replied. He checked the wind; it would not do to have it shift now. It was steady. He grunted in satisfaction, reaching inside his leather tunic for the second of Avshar's gifts. The jar was veined alabaster, eggshell-thin, with a wax-sealed silver stopper. Even unopened, it had the feel of magic to it, a magic like the wizard-prince's crystal, subtler and somehow more dangerous than the familiar charms the shamans used. Varatesh's men backed away from their leader, as if wanting no part in what he was about to do.

He cut the sealing wax with a hard thumbnail, stripped it off, and threw it away. Though the jar was still tightly shut, he smelled the faint, sweet odor of narcissus. That was dangerous; he held his breath as a wave of dizziness washed over him, hoping it would pass. It did. Moving quickly now, he yanked the stopper free and tossed the little jar in the direction of the camp a few hundred yards away. He heard it shatter, though the throw was gentle. He did not think the noise would be noticed in the camp, but no matter if it was; any investigator would only meet Avshar's sorcery the sooner.

Varatesh hurried back to his comrades upwind; together they drew back farther, taking no chances—as they had been warned, this was not a magic that chose between friend and foe. "How long do we wait?" someone asked.

"A twelfth part of the night, the wizard said. By then the essence will have dispersed." Varatesh looked west, studying the sky. "When the star that marks the Sheep's left hock sets, we move. Be watchful till then—if they have a sentry posted far enough off to one side, he may not be taken by the spell."

They waited, watching the star creep down the deep-blue bowl of heaven toward the edge of the earth. No outcry came from the camp ahead. Varatesh's spirits rose; all was just as Avshar had foretold.

The white spark of light winked out. The nomads rose from their haunches and walked toward the camp, sabers ready in their hands. "My legs hurt," grumbled one of them, no more comfortable on foot than his leader.

"Shut up," Varatesh snapped, still wary. The outlaw glared at him. He was sorry for his hard words as soon as they were out of his mouth; it hurt him to have to use men so. Back in his own clan, he thought, a simple headshake would have conveyed his meaning. But he rode with his clan no more, and never would again, unless he came one day as conqueror. These oafs with whom he was forced to share his life paid soft manners no mind. Often even curses would not make them listen, and obedience had to be forced with fists or edged steel.

"Look here!" a nomad said, pointing to one side. The huddled shape was a sentry, now curled on his side in unnatural sleep. Varatesh smiled—it was always good to see a magic perform as promised. Not that he doubted Avshar, but a sensible man ran no risks he did not have to. An outlaw's life, even an outlaw chief's life, was risky enough as it was.

The five plainsmen came into the fire's circle of light. Almost as one, they exclaimed at the strange sight of strings of fallen horses, flanks slowly rising and falling in the grip of Avshar's spell. Varatesh laughed nervously. It had not occurred to him that the sorcery would fell animals along with men.

A dozen men lay unconscious by the fire. With the caution of a beast of prey, Varatesh examined their horses' trappings. He frowned. From the look of things, fifteen of the beasts were being ridden. Counting the sentry he had already seen, that left two men unaccounted for. He trotted back into the darkness. If the sentries spaced themselves in a triangle round the fire, a good sensible plan, the missing ones would be easy to find—unless Avshar's magic had somehow missed them, in which case, he thought, there would be arrows coming out of the night.

The missing guardsmen were close to where he had expected them to be. A drop of sweat ran down his forehead nonetheless; the sorcery's success had been a very near thing. From the awkward way one of the men had fallen, he had been walking back toward the campsite when sleep overcame him. Perhaps he thought he was taken ill and, like a good soldier, headed in for a replacement—as luck would have it, the worst thing he could have done. He had headed straight into the spell instead of away from it.

When Varatesh returned, he found one of his men bending over a sleeper, a thin chap with the scraggly beginnings of a pepper-and-salt beard. The chieftain's foot lashed out, kicking the outlaw's saber away before it could slice the fellow's exposed throat.

The nomad yelped. He cradled his injured right hand in the other. "You've gone soft in the head," he growled, resenting the spoiled kill. "Why ruin my sport?" The other three outlaws, who had been looking forward to the same amusement, grouped themselves behind him.

"Denizli, you are a cur, and the rest of you, too!" Varatesh did not bother to hide his disgust. "Slaying the helpless is women's work—it suits you. If you take such delight in it, here!" His hands well away from sword and dagger, he turned his back on them.

They might have jumped him, but at that moment one of the supposedly ensorceled men by the campfire sat up not six feet from Varatesh and demanded in sleepy, accented Videssian, "Will you spalpeens give over your yattering and let a tired fellow sleep?" His hand was on his sword hilt, just as it had been when he dozed off; he faced away from the outlaws and must have assumed from their Khamorth speech that they were members of his own squad of horsemen arguing among themselves. He did not seem alarmed, only mildly annoyed.

The would-be mutineers froze in surprise; they had thought the members of the embassy party as insensate as so many logs. But Varatesh was more clever than his followers, and knew more. If Avshar's quarry owned a blade that defeated the wizard's magics, why should it not also defend him against this one? Reasoning thus, Varatesh had equipped himself with a bludgeon. He pulled it out now, took two steps forward, and struck the complainer, who was no more than half-awake, a smart blow behind the right ear. Without so much as a groan, the man fell flat, once more as unconscious as his comrades.

The Khamorth chieftain whirled, ready to face his men's challenge. Their uncertain stances, the confusion on their faces, told him they were again his. As if nothing had happened, he ordered them, "Come turn this chap over so we can see what we have." They obeyed without hesitation.

To this point, things had gone as Avshar had predicted, but when Varatesh got a good look at the man he had stunned, he suddenly felt almost as befuddled as his companions had when the fellow sat up and spoke.

Avshar's description of his enemy had been painted with the clarity of hate: a big man, blond, clean-shaven, but otherwise of a Videssian cast. The man at Varatesh's feet was big enough, but there the resemblance to the sorcerer's picture ended. He had blunt features and high, knobby cheekbones; true, he shaved his chin and cheeks, but a great fluffy mustache reached almost to his collarbones. And while his hair was light, it was more nearly fire-colored than golden.

The outlaw scratched his beard, considering. He still had one test to make. He drew forth Avshar's crystal and held it close to the unconscious man. Though he waited and waited, no color appeared in its depths; it might have been any worthless piece of glass. The absence of magic was absolute. Reassured, he said, "This is the one we seek. Denizli, go out and fetch Kubad and the horses."

"What for? And why me?" the nomad asked, not wanting to walk any further than he had to.

Varatesh swallowed a sigh, sick to death of being cursed to work through men unable to see past the tips of their beards. With such patience as he had left, he explained, "If we bring the horses here, we won't have to carry this great hulk out to them." He let some iron come into his voice, "And you because I say so."

Denizli realized he would get no backing from his companions, who were all relieved Varatesh had not chosen them. He trotted clumsily away, pausing once or twice to rub at his blistering heels.

Donkey, Varatesh thought. But then, it seemed even Avshar's wisdom had its limits. When he had time, he would have to ponder that.

The man he had clubbed moaned and tried to roll over. Varatesh hit him again, a precisely calculated blow delivered without passion. It would not do to strike too hard; he remembered the sentry in his father's clan. No, no, he told himself for the thousandth time, the fellow had only been knocked cold. Still, he was more careful now.

Hoofbeats in the darkness heralded Kubad's approach. Denizli with him looked happier on horseback. At least he had the wit to remount, Varatesh thought. Kubad looked around the campfire with interest. "Worked, did it?" he remarked economically. "Can we plunder them?"

"No."

"Pity." Of the five Varatesh had with him, Kubad was far the best. He slid down from his horse, walked to the side of his chief, who was still standing over the red-haired man. "This the one the wizard wants?"

"Yes. Get one of the remounts over here; we'll tie him aboard." They slung the unconscious man over the horse's back like a hunting trophy, bound his hands and feet beneath the beast's belly. Varatesh took his sword.

"How long is your charm good for?" Kubad asked. "You don't want to butcher these sheep—" Denizli had been talking, then, "—so likely they'll come after us when they wake. And there's more o' them than there is of us."

"We'll have a day's start, from what I was told. That should be plenty. Smell the air—the night's clear, aye, but rain's coming before long. What trail will they follow?"

In the crimson glow of the campfire, Kubad's smile seemed dipped in blood.

Viridovix awoke to nightmare. The driving pain in his head left him queasy and weak, and when his eyes came open he groaned and squinched them shut again. He was facing directly into the rising sun, whose brilliance sent new needles of agony drilling into his brain. Worse even than that was the work of some malevolent sorcerer, who had reversed sky and horizon and set both of them bobbing like a bowl of calf's-foot jelly. His sensitive stomach heaved. Only when he tried to reach up to shield his face from the sun did he discover his hands were tied.

His moan alerted his takers to his returning awareness. Someone said something in the plains speech. The jouncing stopped. Very carefully, Viridovix opened one eye. The world was steady, but still upside down. He let his head hang loosely. Gray-brown dirt swooped toward him; a sharp stem of grass poked up to within a couple of inches from his forehead. There was a brown, shaggy-haired leg on either side of him. I'm on a horse, he told himself, pleased he could think at all.

After more talk in the Khamorth tongue, one of the nomads came over to him. In his undignified posture, Viridovix could only see the man from the thighs down. That was enough to send alarm shooting through him, for alongside a saber the plainsman bore the Gaul's sword.

Viridovix had learned only a few words of the plains language, none of them polite. He used one now, his voice a ghastly croak. Almost instantly he realized his rashness; his captor could enjoy revenge at leisure. He tried to gather his wits so he could take a blow manfully, if nothing else.

But the nomad only laughed, and there seemed to be no menace under the mirth. "I will cut you loose, yes?" he said in good Videssian, with only a trace of his people's guttural accent. His voice was a surprisingly light tenor, a young man's voice. He went on, "Please do not plan any folly. There are two men with bows covering you. I ask again, shall I cut you down?"

"Aye, an you will." The Celt saw no point in refusing; trussed as he was, he could do nothing, even without the pounding in his head. The Khamorth bent beneath the horse's barrel. His dagger bit through the rawhide thongs that lashed Viridovix' wrist to his ankles.

The Gaul tumbled to the ground, limp as a sack of meal. His nausea abruptly overwhelmed him. As he spewed, the Khamorth held his head so he would not foul himself, then gave him water to clean his mouth. The kindness was in its way more frightening than brutality would have been. To brutality, at least, he would have known how to respond.

After two or three tries he managed to sit. He studied his captor as best he could, though his vision was still blurred and went double on and off. The Khamorth *was* young, likely less than thirty, though the great bushy beard he wore after his people's custom helped obscure his youth. He was a bit taller than most plainsmen and carried himself like one used to leading. His eyes, though, were strange; even when he looked straight at Viridovix, they seemed far away, peering at something only he could see.

Fighting dizziness, the Gaul turned his head to see what allies the nomad had. As promised, two plainsmen had nocked arrows in their short bows. One drew his shaft back a few inches when Viridovix' eyes met his. He had a most unpleasant smile.

"Hold, Denizli!" the chief said in Videssian for the Gaul's benefit, then repeated the command in his own speech. Denizli scowled, but did as he was told.

There were three more Khamorth simply relaxing on their horses. They watched Viridovix as they might a wildcat they had ridden down, a dangerous beast who should get no chance to use his fangs. The lot of them were typical enough plainsmen, if on the hard-bitten side. It was their leader who put trepidation in the Celt's heart, the more so because he did not seem to belong on the steppe. He had more depth than his followers and, with his beard trimmed, would not have been out of place at the imperial court. Finesse, thought Viridovix, that was the word.

In his pain and confusion the Gaul took a bit of time to notice that none of his comrades had been taken. When he did, he burst out, "What ha' ye done wi' my mates, y'blackhearted omadhaun?"

The nomad chieftain frowned a moment; as was often true, Viridovix' brogue thickened in times of stress. But when he understood, the Khamorth laughed and spread his empty hands. "Nothing at all."

Oddly, Viridovix believed him. He was sure any of the other five would have delighted in the killing, but not this man. "What is it you want o' me, then?" the Celt asked, not reassured.

The answer, though, was mild enough. "For now, let me wash your head, so your cuts do not fester." Varatesh poured some kavass onto a scrap of wool, then knelt by Viridovix. The Celt winced when the stinging stuff touched his cut and swollen scalp, but the nomad daubed away as gently as Gorgidas might have done. "I am called Varatesh, by the way," he remarked.

"I'd be lying if I said I was pleased to make your acquaintance," the Gaul told him. Varatesh smiled and nodded, quite kindly—or so it would have seemed had Viridovix not been his prisoner.

The nomad's body screened him from one of the archers. As if his weight were too much for him, Viridovix slumped against Varatesh's shoulder—and then grappled for the longsword at the plainsman's belt.

Only then did he realize how hurt and fuddled he was; Varatesh twisted away and bounced to his feet before the Celt's move was well begun.

The nomad shouted for his bowmen not to fire. He looked down at Viridovix, and there was no kindness on his handsome face now. With chilling deliberation, he kicked the Gaul in the point of the elbow. "Play no games with me," he said, still quiet-voiced.

Viridovix barely heard; sheets of red and black fire were passing in front of his eyes. The pain in his head, anguish a moment before, receded to a dull, all but friendly ache. Varatesh might not slaughter for the sport of it, but that only made his torments worse when they came.

"I doubt whether Avshar cares what shape you are in when he meets you," the Khamorth said. He paused, waiting to see how Viridovix met the name.

"Och, be damned to you and him both," the Gaul said, trying not to show the chill he felt. He blustered, "My comrades'll be catching up with you long before you can bring me to him." He had no idea how true that was; but if Varatesh had let them live, he might as well worry about them.

One of the other nomads laughed. "Hush, Kubad," Varatesh said, then turned back to Viridovix. "They're welcome to try," he went on placidly. "In fact, I wish them luck."

When the Celt could stand, his captors put him on one of their remounts. They took no chances on his escape, tying his feet under the horse and his hands behind him; the plainsman called Kubad guided his mount on a lead. Trying to gain more freedom of any sort, he protested, "At least be letting me have hold of the reins. What if I slip off?" He meant it; he felt anything but well.

Kubad had enough Videssian to answer him. "Then you drag." Viridovix gave up.

As the nomads rode north over the plains, the Gaul began to see that, by comparison, his own party had been lazing along. The steppe ponies trotted on and on, tireless as if driven by some clockwork. Despite the wide detour the plainsmen took round the herds of some clan, they covered nearly as much ground in one day as Viridovix was used to doing in two.

The only stops they made were to answer nature's calls; Viridovix found it hard to relieve himself with an arrow aimed at his midriff. The Khamorth ate in the saddle, gnawing on barklike sun-dried strips of beef and lamb. They did not pause to feed their prisoner, but halfway through the day Varatesh, courteous as if he'd never killed a man, held a flask of kavass to Viridovix' lips. He drank, both from thirst and in an effort to dull the pounding hurt in his head. The fermented milk did not help much.

Dirty-gray clouds like the underbellies of so many sheep came scudding up out of the south as the afternoon wore to a close. Kubad said something in his own language to Varatesh, who bobbed his head as if acknowledging a compliment. The wind grew brisker and began to feel damp.

The Khamorth leader picked a small creek with an overhanging bank as a campsite. "Rain tonight," he told Viridovix, "but we sleep dry here—unless the stream rises. I do not think it will."

"And what if it does?" The Gaul, hurt and also exhausted from staying in the saddle without being able to use his hands, did not really care, but tried to discommode Varatesh in any small way he could.

He failed. "Then we move," the nomad answered, busying himself with the fire. It was tiny and smokeless, not one to advertise their presence. This time the Khamorth shared their travelers' fare with Viridovix, untying him so he could eat, but always watching him so closely he could do nothing more. When he was through Varatesh bound him once more, testing each knot so carefully that the Gaul hated him for his thoroughness.

The plainsmen drew straw for their watches; Viridovix gathered himself to do something—he knew not what—as soon as he saw the chance. But his body betrayed him. Despite the misery in his head, despite the discomfort of having his arms tied behind his back, he yielded to sleep almost at once.

The gentle plashing of rain in the rivulet a few feet away woke him some hours later; Denizli, who had drawn third watch, was on sentry go. Varatesh had chosen his campsite perfectly. The projecting streambank left it snug and dry, just as he had said. Actually, the Celt had not doubted him; even in his cruelty, the outlaw chief was competent.

Viridovix rolled out toward the rain. Denizli growled something threatening in his own tongue and hefted his bow. "Sure and I just want to soak my puir battered noddle," the Celt said, but Denizli only grunted and lifted the bow a couple of inches further.

Swearing at his luck, Viridovix perforce drew back. "Arse-licking eunuch," he said. He knew he was gambling, but beyond grunting again Denizli did not respond. Here, at least, was one nomad who had no Videssian. The Gaul cursed him for several minutes, a profane stew of the imperial tongue, Latin, and Celtic. Feelings slightly eased, he tried to find some tolerable position in which to go back to sleep. The rain, he thought, looked to be lasting a while.

Gorgidas stirred and grumbled as a raindrop splashed against his cheek. Another coldly kissed his ear, a third spattered off his left eyelid. He scrabbled at his bedroll, trying to pull it over his head without really rousing. Before he could, half a dozen more drops landed on his face, leaving him irretrievably awake. "By the dog," he muttered in Greek, an oath of annoyance. The weather had seemed good enough when he fell asleep.

He winced as he sat, for his head gave a savage twinge. He wished for raw cabbage to deal with his hangover, but wondered what he had done to deserve one. Kavass was potent, aye, but the little he'd had at the evening meal should not have left him as crapulent as this.

Others were waking, too, and groaning and cursing in such a way that the Greek guessed they felt no better than he. Only when he began to look around did he notice the campfire had gone out. He frowned. The ground, as yet, was barely damp—why were only ashes left of the good-sized blaze they'd set not long before?

Agathias Psoes had the same thought. "What's wrong with you sheeps' heads?" he shouted to his troopers. "Can't you even keep a bloody fire going?" Their replies were mumbles; the evidence of their failure was only too plain.

"How many Khamorth does it take to start a fire?" Arigh asked rhetorically, and then answered his own question: "Ten—one gathers the brushwood while the other nine try to figure out what to do next."

"Heh, heh." Psoes barked a short fragment of laugh, enough for politeness' sake. Though he was not of Khamorth blood himself, most of his squad was, and he naturally took their part when an outsider taunted them.

Pikridios Goudeles, on the other hand, found the Arshaum's gibe funny, chuckling quietly for nearly a minute. Gorgidas allowed himself a wry smile; Arigh took every chance, it seemed, to twit his people's eastern neighbors on the steppe.

It was then that Gorgidas realized Viridovix' booming laugh had failed to ring out at his friend's joke. Was the accursed Gaul still sleeping? Gorgidas peered through the darkness and the raindrops, which were coming thicker now. He could not see the Celt. "Viridovix?" he called.

There was no answer. He called again, with equal lack of success. "Probably gone off somewhere to drop his trousers," Lankinos Skylitzes guessed.

Gorgidas heard footsteps squelching toward the camp and thought for a moment Skylitzes was right. But it was one of the sentries. "Hallo the camp!" the trooper said. "Are you daft there, to let your fire die? Keep talking, the lot of you, so I can find you."

When the sentry came in, he asked, "Is everything well? I had something odd happen to me." He spoke with elaborate unconcern, trying to mask his worry. "I was out there watching and started to feel faint. I headed in to get a relief, but I reckon I didn't make it—next thing I knew, it was raining on me. Very strange—seems like there's a smith pounding out stirrups in my head, but I drank water because I knew I had to be sober for watch. What hour is it, anyway?"

As it turned out, no one knew. Nor did they argue about it long, for just then one of the horses gave a puzzled-sounding snort and scrambled to its feet, followed within minutes by the rest of the animals. Ignoring their own headaches, Psoes' men and Skylitzes rushed over to them, shouting in mixed Videssian and the Khamorth tongue. For the first time, Gorgidas understood something was truly amiss; horses did not go down of their own accord.

The horsemen clucked and fussed over their beasts, trying to learn why they had fallen. Lankinos Skylitzes walked back toward the dead campfire. "Gorgidas?"

"Here."

"Where? Oh." The soldier almost stumbled over him. "Sorry—bloody dark." Skylitzes' voice softened. "I've heard you are a healer. Would you see to the horses? They seem all right, but—" He spread his hands, a motion the Greek saw only dimly.

Gorgidas understood the request, but it did not please him. "I'm a physician no more," he said shortly. That was too abrupt, he decided, so he went on, "Even if I were, I know nothing of animals. Horseleeching is a different art from doctoring men." And a good deal lower one, he did not add.

Skylitzes caught his annoyance nonetheless. "I meant no offense." Gorgidas dipped his head impatiently, then regretted it as his headache flared. Skylitzes asked, "Has Viridovix turned up?"

"No. Where could he have wandered off to, anyhow? Where did he lay out his sleeping-mat? If he's on it snoring, I'll wring his lazy neck."

"You'd need to wait your turn, I think." Skylitzes squinted as he peered through the rain. He pointed. "Over there, wasn't it?"

"Was it?" Gorgidas took himself to task for not paying closer heed before he slept; if a historian—or a doctor, for that matter—failed to notice details, what good was he? He was proud of his powers of observation, and here, when he needed them, they let him down.

Skirting the ashes of the campfire—and still wondering why they were so cold—the Greek walked in the direction Skylitzes had indicated. Sure enough, there were blankets and a thin traveling mat spread on the ground; they were beginning to get soaked now. Beside them was a knapsack Gorgidas recognized as Viridovix' and the Celt's helmet with its seven-spoked bronze wheel of a crest. Of Viridovix himself there was no sign.

The commotion in the camp made the two remaining sentries come in to see what was toward; both reluctantly admitted falling asleep at their posts. "Trouble yourselves not," Pikridios Goudeles said pompously, "for no harm resulted."

Agathias Psoes growled, as any good underofficer would at the notion of his men dozing on watch. And Gorgidas shouted, "No harm? Where's Viridovix?"

"To that I must confess my ignorance. The man is your comrade, and of your people. Why should he choose to wander off?"

Gorgidas opened his mouth, shut it again; he had no idea. He did know how useless it was to explain that he and the Celt were no more of the same people than Goudeles and a Khamorth.

The rest of the night was dank and miserable. No one went back to sleep, and not just the pattering rain stopped them. The entire party was much more awake than their midnight rousing called for, but unpleasantly so; a good part of the desultory talk centered on their aching heads.

"Been drunk without a hangover before," Arigh remarked, "but I never had the hangover without the drunk." As if to correct the fault, he swigged from the kavass-skin that was almost always near him.

Toward morning the clouds grew tattered for a while, revealing a thin cheese-paring of a moon low in the east. Too thin, too low—"We've lost a day!" Gorgidas exclaimed.

"Phos, you're right," Skylitzes said, making his god's circular sun-sign over his breast. He raised his hands to the damp heavens and muttered a prayer. Nor was he the only one; Psoes and the Videssians in his squad imitated him, while the troopers who still followed Khamorth ways poured kavass out on the ground to propitiate the less abstract powers they worshiped. Even Goudeles, as worldly a man as Videssos grew, prayed with the soldiers.

"Some spirit has touched us. We should sacrifice a horse," Arigh said, and the Khamorth cried out in agreement.

Gorgidas listened to his companions with growing exasperation. While they babbled of gods and spirits, his logical mind saw the answer only too clearly. "We've been magicked asleep so someone could snatch Viridovix," he said, and, a moment later, carrying his train of thought to its conclusion, added, "Avshar!"

"No," Skylitzes replied at once. "Were it Avshar, we should be waking in the next world. There is no mercy in him."

"His minions, then," the Greek insisted. He remembered the potent blade the Gaul carried, but did not mention it; the fewer who knew of it, the less likely word of it would reach the wizard, should Gorgidas prove wrong by some lucky chance.

He did not think he was. It was growing steadily lighter; he walked over to examine Viridovix' bedroll once more. His breath hissed out as he saw the bloodstains on the Celt's blankets. He held them up, displaying them to the rest of the party. "A kidnapping while we were spelled to sleep!" he said.

"And even so, what of that?" Goudeles said. The seal-stamper sounded petulant; he was used to the comforts of Videssos and did not relish sitting unprotected in the rain and mud of the trackless steppe. He went on, "When weighed against the mission with which we were entrusted, what is the fate of one barbarian mercenary? Once our embassy is successfully completed—which boon Phos grant—then, with the augmentation of manpower the addition of the Arshaum will yield us, we may properly search for him. But until such augmentation should come to pass, he remains a secondary consideration."

Gorgidas gasped, not wanting to believe his ears. "But he may be hurt, dying—he surely is hurt," the Greek said, touching the brown stains on the cloth. "You would not leave him in the enemy's hands?"

If Goudeles was embarrassed, he did not show it. "I would not cast myself into them, either, and bring to nothing the purpose for which I was dispatched."

"The pen-pusher is right," Skylitzes said, looking as though the admission left a bad taste in his mouth. "The Empire's safety overrides that of any one man. Your countryman is a doughty fighter, but he is only one. We need hundreds."

Neither of the Videssians knew Viridovix, save on the journey. Gorgidas turned to Arigh, who had roistered with the Celt for two years. "He is your friend!"

Arigh tugged at his straggling chin whiskers, plainly uncomfortable with the Greek's bald appeal. Personal ties counted for more with him than with the imperials, but he was a khagan's son and understood reasons of state. "It grieves me, but no. The farmer-folk speak true, I fear. I betray a trust now whatever I do, but I act for my clan before I act for myself. V'ridrish is no easy prey; he may yet win free."

"Curse you all!" Gorgidas said. "If you care nothing for what happens to your comrade, stand aside for one who does. I'll ride after him myself."

"That is well said," Arigh said quietly. Several of the troopers echoed him. Furious, Gorgidas ignored them all, sweeping possessions into his rucksack.

But Skylitzes came over to put a hand on the Greek's shoulder. Gorgidas cursed again and tried to shake free, but the stocky Videssian officer was stronger than he. "Let loose of me, you god-detested oaf! Why should you care if I seek my friend? I cannot matter to you any more than he does."

"Think like a man, not an angry child," Skylitzes said softly. The rebuke was calculated to touch the Greek, who prided himself on his rationality. Skylitzes waved, an all-encompassing gesture that swept round the horizon. "Go after Viridovix—" Like Goudeles, he said the name carefully. "—if you will, but where will you go?"

"Why—" the Greek began, and then stopped in confusion. He rubbed his bristly chin; a beard, he was finding, could be a useful adjunct to thought. "Where do your reports place Avshar?" he asked at last.

"North and west of where we are now, but that news is weeks old and worth nothing now. You've seen how the plainsmen move, and no law makes the damned wizard-prince stay with any one clan."

"Northwest is good enough."

"Is it? I've seen you, outlander; you lack the skill to follow a trail—not that the rain will leave you one." Skylitzes went on remorselessly, "And if you do somehow catch up to your foes, what then? Are you warrior enough to slay them all singlehanded? Are you warrior enough even to protect yourself if a nomad chooses to make sport of you? Will that sword of yours help, should you buckle it on instead of leaving it in your kit?"

Gorgidas started; sure enough, he had not thought of the *gladius* Gaius Philippus had given him, and had left it tucked away with his scrolls of parchment. For the first time in many years, he wished he were skilled with weapons. It was humiliating that he could not stop some chance-met, unwashed, illiterate barbarian who might enjoy killing him simply to watch him die.

He rummaged through his sack for the sword, but threw it angrily back in when he found it. It could not cut Lankinos Skylitzes' logic. "West, then," he said, hating the necessity that impelled his words. *Ananke,* he thought: life's harshest master.

When Skylitzes offered a sympathetic handclasp, the Greek did not take his hand. Instead he said, “Keep drilling me on my swordplay, will you?” The officer nodded.

Gorgidas’ thoughts were full of irony as he scrambled onto his horse. He had left Videssos for the plains to change from doctor to historian. Change he was finding aplenty, but hardly what he had wanted. Things long excluded from his life were forcing their way in: women, weapons—but precious little history yet. It might have been funny, had he been without greater concerns.

The rain poured down from an indifferent sky.

V

The retreat fared better than Marcus had dared hope. With victory in their hands, the Namdaleni were more eager to chase small bands of fugitives than to tackle a good-sized detachment still under arms. A couple of companies of horsemen made tentative runs at the legionaries, but went off in search of easier prey when they failed to dissolve in panic flight.

"Cowards get what they deserve," Nevrat Sviodo remarked as she passed the body of a Videssian speared in the back. Scorn filled her voice. She had fought side by side with her husband. Her quiver was almost empty, her saber had blood on it, and her forehead was cut and bruised from a thrown stone, luckily only a glancing blow.

"Aye, that's the reward for running higgledy-piggledy," Gaius Philippus agreed. The senior centurion was not downcast in defeat; he had seen it before. "There's ways to lose as well as ways to win. By the Sucro, now, my mates did well even though we lost, and at Turia, too. If the old woman hadn't shown up, we'd have given the boy a good drubbing and sent him back to Rome." He smiled at the memory.

"The old woman? The boy?" Nevrat looked at him in confusion.

"Never mind, lass; it was a long time ago, back where the lot of us came from. These Videssians aren't the only ones with civil wars, and I chose the wrong side in one."

"So you were with Sertorius, then?" Marcus said. He knew the senior centurion had been of Marius' party. After Sulla beat the last of the Marians in Italy, Quintus Sertorius refused to yield Spain to the winners. Winning the Spanish natives to his side, he fought on guerilla-style for eight years, until one of his own subordinates murdered him.

"So I was. What of it?" Gaius Philippus challenged. His loyalty, once given, died hard.

"Not a thing," the tribune said. "He must have been a fine soldier, to face up to Pompey the Great."

"'The Great?'" Gaius Philippus spat in the dusty roadway. "Compared to what? As I said, if Metellus hadn't saved his bacon at Turia, he'd be running yet—if he could. We wounded him there, you know."

"I hadn't realized that. I was still in my teens then."

"Yes, I suppose you would have been. I was a little younger than you are now, I think." He wiped his face with the back of his hand. Most of the hair on his scarred forearm was silver. "Time wins the war, no matter what becomes of the battles."

The sun was still high in the west when the legionaries came into sight of their camp again. There were dead horses and riders outside, and a squad of Namdaleni studying the palisade at a respectful distance. They trotted off when they recognized the newcomers.

Minucius met Scaurus at one of the entrances to the *via principalis.* The young underofficer's salute was as much a gesture of relief as of respect. "Good to see you, sir," he managed.

"And you," Marcus said. He raised his voice so everyone could hear: "Half an hour! Knock down the tents, find your women and tots, and then we travel. Anyone slow can make his excuses to the islanders—we won't be here to listen to them."

"I knew it went wrong," Minucius was saying. "First the plainsmen running, and then the Videssians, with Drax' men on their heels. Did Utprand turn traitor, then?"

"No, but his men did. He's dead."

"So that was the way of it," Minucius growled. His large hands folded into fists. "I thought I knew some of the good-for-naughts who tried coming over the stakes. You saw the welcome we gave 'em—they went off to have a go at something less lively, like the imperials' camp over past the trees." He hesitated; uncertainty seemed out of place on his rugged features. "I hope we did right, sir. There was, ah, some as wanted us to open up and join 'em."

"Some, eh?" the tribune said, seeing through Minucius' clumsy directions. "I'll tend to that; don't you worry about it." He slapped the underofficer on the back. "You did well, Sextus. Go on, get Erene and your children. I want some distance between us and Drax before he decides to make his lads stop plundering and finish us off."

Drax might do that at any time, Marcus thought as Minucius hurried away—perhaps this moment, perhaps not until morning. Had the tribune been leading the Namdaleni, he would have attacked the legionaries at once. But Drax had been a mercenary far longer than Scaurus: with booty in front of his men, he might not dare pull them away. Might, might, might . . . Marcus wished the Namdalener count were less opaque.

The camp bubbled and seethed like limestone splashed with vinegar. Soldiers and their kin shouted each other's names over and over, wandering here and there as they searched for one another. "Lackwits," Gaius Philippus muttered. "If the silly hens'd stay by their men's tents they'd get found easy enough."

"Those whose men are still here to find them," Marcus said, and the senior centurion had to nod. As fights went, this one had not cost the legionaries overmuch; the center of the imperial army had borne the brunt. Still, men were down who would never rise again; too many, too many. How long would it be before there were no Romans left?

In the camp's central forum, Styppes was doing his best to hold off that evil day. Scaurus gave credit where due; the healer-priest's fat face was dead pale from the strain of his labor. He hurried from one moaning, wounded soldier to the next, never pausing long enough to heal a man completely, but giving him a chance at life before going on to another bleeding trooper. He gulped wine in the moments between patients, but, seeing his work, Marcus did not care.

Helvis stood by the tribune's tent. They shared a quick hug, then Scaurus began uprooting tent pegs. Malric gave what he thought was help until Marcus growled at him to get out of the way. His hands automatically went through the motions of folding the tent for travel.

"Even after we've won, you have no use for us?" Helvis asked.

"Look around you," Scaurus suggested. "This is the only 'we' I know; it's far past time you understood that."

Outside the camp a Namdalener yelled something. Marcus could not tell what it was through the din, but the island drawl was unmistakable. "The only 'we'?" Helvis said dangerously. "What would you do if that was Soteric out there?"

Marcus squeezed air from between layers of the collapsed tent, tied the tent cord around it. He thought of his brother-in-law's work of the day. "Right now I believe I'd kill him."

Whatever answer she had started to make froze on her lips. The tribune went on wearily, "There are no chains on you, dear, but if you come with me you'd best see the folk here inside as 'we.' Come or not, as you please. I haven't the time to argue."

He thought for a long moment the brutality of that was more than she would bear. But Dosti squirmed in her arms; she comforted him, at first absently, then with real attention. She looked at him, at Scaurus, while the palm of her left hand lightly touched her belly. "I'll come with you," she said at last.

Marcus only grunted. He was wrestling the folded tent into his pack. As with a snake swallowing a rabbit, the engulfing looked impossible but was accomplished even so. Somehow his little wooden chest fit, too. The chair and table would have to stay behind—no time to load them on a mule. He swung the pack onto his shoulders; Romans were their own best mules.

Helvis wore an odd, wistful look. He impatiently started to turn away, but her words spun him back: "There are times, dear, when you make me think so much of Hemond."

"What? Why?" he asked, startled. She seldom spoke of Malric's father to the tribune, knowing the mention of Hemond made him touchy and remembering how annoyed he grew when she carelessly called him by her dead husband's name.

"By the Wager, it's not for how you act!" Remembering, she smiled, her eyes soft. "When he wanted something of me, he'd laugh and joke and poke me in the ribs, jolly me along." She cocked a rueful eyebrow at him. "Where you set things out like a butcher slapping a hunk of meat on the table, and if I don't like it, to the ice with me."

Marcus felt his ears grow hot. "Where's the likeness, then?"

"You knew Hemond. He'd have his way, come fire or flood—and so will you. And so do you, again." She sighed. "I'm ready."

The legionaries traveled in a hollow square, with their families and the wounded in the center. The Namdaleni dogged their tracks, as Marcus had known they would. Without cavalry of his own, he could do nothing about it. He counted himself lucky only to be watched. From the noise coming out of the captured Videssian camp, Drax was treating most of his men to a good round of plundering.

Videssian stragglers attached themselves to Scaurus' band by ones and twos, some afoot, others on horseback. He let them join; some were still soldiers, and any mounted troops could be useful, as scouts if nothing more.

One of them brought word of Zigabenos' fate: captured by the Namdaleni. One more piece of bad news among the many—Marcus was dismayed but not surprised. It was also something he had expected to hear, whether true or not. He asked the imperial, "How do you know that's so?"

"Well, I ought to. I seen it," the trooper answered; his upcountry accent made Scaurus think of Phostis Apokavkos. He glared at the tribune, as spikily indignant as any Videssian at having his word questioned. "They drug him off his horse; Skotos' hell, if he hadn't been wounded, they never would a-done it. He gave 'em all the fight they wanted and some besides. The plague take all Namdaleni anyways."

"You saw him taken and did nought to stay it?" Zeprin the Red rumbled ominously. The burly Haloga, long an imperial guard, still carried in his heart the shame of not dying with the regiment of his countrymen who vainly defended Mavrikios at Maragha. It was no fault of his own; the Emperor had sent him away to take command of the imperial left wing. He blamed himself regardless. Now, axe in hand, he glowered at the bedraggled Videssian before him. "What sort of soldier do you call yourself?"

The trooper hawked and spat. "A live one," he retorted, "which is a sight better than the other kind." He stared back with deliberate insolence.

Zeprin's always florid complexion darkened to the color of blood. He roared out something in his own tongue that sounded like red-hot iron screaming as it was quenched. Before either Marcus or the Videssian could move, his axe jerked up, then smashed down through the man's helmet, splitting his skull almost to the teeth. He toppled, jerking, dead before the blow was through.

The Haloga tugged his axe free. "Craven carrion," he growled, cleaning the weapon on a clump of purslane. "A man who will not stand by his lord deserves no better."

"We might have learned something more from him," Marcus said, but that was all. If legionaries broke and ran in large numbers, they could be decimated: one in ten chosen at random for execution to requite their cowardice. Before he took service, the tribune had reckoned the punishment hideous in its barbarity; now he thought of it without revulsion. The change shamed him. War fouled everyone it touched.

The Arandos was a fat brown stream, several hundred yards across. Bridges spanned it, but Drax' men held their watchtowers. Perhaps they could be forced, but that would take time, time the legionaries did not have. Had Drax not had so many bands of fugitives to hunt down, he would have overrun them already instead of giving them these three days of grace. The Namdalener was like a dog surrounded by so many bones he did not know which one to take up and gnaw. Scaurus, on the other hand, felt like a hare with the nets closing in.

Hoping against hope, he sent out Videssians to ask the peasants if they knew of a ford, reasoning that they would be more inclined to talk to their countrymen than to aliens like the Romans. He almost shouted when Apokavkos brought back a big-eared codger who came straight to the point: "What's it worth to ye?"

Another twanger, the tribune thought. He answered, "Ten goldpieces—on the other side of the river."

"You on a cross if you're lying," Gaius Philippus added. The local scratched his head at that—the Videssians did not practice crucifixion. But the threat in the senior centurion's voice could not be missed. Still, the farmer nodded agreement.

He led the legionaries east along the Arandos until they were well out of sight of any bridge. Then he slowed, squinting across the river for some landmark he did not name. At last he grunted. "There y'are," he said, pointing.

"Where?" To Scaurus, the stretch of water looked no different from any other part of the Arandos.

"Nail the lying bastard up," Gaius Philippus said, but in Latin. Not understanding him, the farmer pulled the knee-length tunic that was his only garment over his head and, naked, stepped into the river.

He was promptly in up to his outsized ears, and Marcus thought seriously of what to do with him. The peasant, though, seemed unabashed. He turned around, grinning a wet grin. "Spring flood's not as near done as I'd'a liked, but come ahead. It don't get no deeper."

Holding his sword over his head, the tribune followed. His inches were an advantage; the water reached his chin, but no higher. Two and three at a time, the legionaries followed. "No more'n that," their guide warned. "The track ain't what you call wide." He splashed forward, now bearing a few paces left, now a few right, now pausing as if to feel about with his toes.

"The gods help us if the damned islanders come on us," Gaius Philippus said, looking back nervously. He stepped into a deep place and vanished, to emerge a moment later, spluttering and choking. "Ordure," he growled.

Marcus was glad for the Romans' training, which included swimming as an essential part. Even when they stumbled off the narrow ford, they were able to save themselves; luckily the Arandos' current was not strong. Only one man was lost, a Vaspurakaner who sank and drowned before he could be rescued. The mountaineers, alas, were no swimmers; their streams were tiny trickles in summer, torrents spring and fall, and frozen solid when winter came.

When the tribune squelched up onto the south bank of the river, the Videssian peasant greeted him with outstretched palm. Scaurus eyed him meditatively as he fumbled in his wet belt-pouch. "How do I know you'll not sell the secret of the ford to the first Namdaleni who ride by?"

If he expected some guilty start, he was disappointed. With mercenary candor, the fellow answered, "I'd do it, excepting they wouldn't buy. Why would they? They hold the bridges." His regret was perfectly genuine.

"Listen to the man!" Senpat Sviodo exclaimed. He was checking to make sure his pandoura had taken no harm during the crossing. "Is it any wonder these Videssians are ever at strife with themselves?"

"Probably not." Marcus paid his guide, who examined each coin carefully, biting a couple of them to see if they were real soft gold.

"Not bad," the farmer remarked. "I could've broken a tooth on that one of Ortaias' you gave me, but it's only the one." In lieu of anywhere else to carry them, he popped the coins into his mouth; his left cheek sagged under their weight. "Much obliged to you, I'm sure," he said blurrily.

"Likewise," Scaurus answered. Children were squealing and splashing each other as their mothers and the legionaries carried them across the stream. Some of the women got carried, too: the very short ones, and those whom pregnancy had made awkward. Helvis, tall and strong, made the passage on her own. She brought Dosti herself; a trooper carried Malric. Her linen blouse and long, heavy wool skirt clung to her magnificently as she came out of the water.

With regret, the tribune pulled his eyes away and looked down along the riverbank to where several of Gagik Bagratouni's men were sitting glumly, mourning their drowned comrade. The sight made him ask the peasant, "Why not drive a row of stakes into the riverbed so the ford would be safe?"

"And let everyone know where it's at?" The local shook his head in amazement. "Thank ye, nay."

"What do you use it for that's so secret?" Marcus asked, but when he saw the Videssian's hand come out he said hastily, "Never mind. I don't want to know enough to pay for it."

"Thought not." The farmer waited until the last legionaries were done with the ford, then waded back into the Arandos. When he got to the north bank he discovered someone had made off with his tunic. Peering across the river, Marcus waited for an angry outburst. There was none. Mother-naked, the Videssian disappeared into the brush that crowded close to the stream.

"Why should he care?" Senpat said. He bulged his own cheek out comically. "He's still ahead nine goldpieces and change, even without the old rag."

There were Namdaleni on the far side of the Arandos. The legionaries were two days south of the river when they came headlong onto a pair of the islanders, sitting their mounts with the easy arrogance of men who feel themselves lords of all they survey. That arrogance vanished like smoke in the wind when they came out from behind a stand of scrubby oaks and spied Scaurus' column. He saw them exchange horrified glances. Then they were riding madly across a wheat field, spurring their heavy horses like racing steeds as they dashed toward the river.

For a moment Marcus rocked back on his heels, as startled by the encounter as the men of the Duchy. Then he remembered he, too, had horsemen, a good score of Zigabenos' men. "After them!" he shouted.

The Videssians moved hesitantly at first, as if fighting had not occurred to them. The foot soldiers' cheers, though, put fresh heart in them, as did the sight of the Namdaleni in full flight. The islanders were a bare hundred yards ahead of their pursuers when they disappeared over a low rise.

The imperials soon returned, trotting proudly now. They led one horse and held up a pair of fine mail shirts and two conical helms with bar nasals. "Where's the other beast?" someone called.

"We had to shoot it," one of them said.

"Idiots!" "Bunglers!" "A pack of damned incompetents, the lot of you!" The Videssians accepted the good-natured chaffing for the praise it was.

"That's all to the good," Gaius Philippus said. "They feel like men again; we'll get some use out of them."

"You're right," Marcus said. "But how many men does Drax have, anyway? I'd hoped he was just holding the line of the Arandos against whatever the Videssian grandees south of the river could scrape up to throw at him, but he looks to be coming right at them. Whatever you say about him, he doesn't think small, does he?"

"Hmm." The senior centurion considered that. "If he spreads himself too thin, the Yezda will see to him, whether we do nor not."

"That's so," Marcus admitted, disquieted. He had not even seen one of the invading nomads for almost a year and a half; it was easy to forget them in the tangles of the Empire's civil wars. Yet without them, those wars would not have happened, and they roamed the highlands like distant thunderheads.

"Not distant enough," Gaius Philippus said when Scaurus spoke his conceit aloud.

The stand of oaks was bigger than the tribune had guessed. It went on for miles. Part of some noble's estate? he wondered. Half-ripe acorns, dirty green with tan, ribbed tops, nestled between sharp-lobed leaves. He heard a boar grunting somewhere out of sight among the trees; all pigs loved acorns.

The legionaries scuffed through the gray-brown, tattered remnants of last autumn's fallen leaves. The sound was soothing, like surf on a beach.

Discordant footfalls ahead roused Scaurus to alertness once more. A man burst round a corner of the forest path. His chest heaved with his exertion; blood splashed his tunic and the dust of the road from a great cut across his forehead. The terror on his face turned to disbelieving joy as he recognized the Videssian horsemen with the legionaries.

"Phos be praised!" he gasped. His words stumbled over each other in his urgency: "A rescue! Quick, my lord, the outland devils—murder!"

"Namdaleni?" Marcus demanded—was there no end to them? At the fellow's nod, he snapped, "How many?"

The man spread his hands. "A hundred, at least." He hopped up and down, ignoring his wound. "Phos' mercy, hurry!"

"Two maniples," the tribune decided. Gaius Philippus nodded in grim agreement; the men of the Duchy were no bargain. In the same breath, Scaurus went on, "Blaesus, your men; aye, and yours, Gagik!" Bagratouni understood the order, though it was in Latin. He shouted in his own throaty tongue; his Vaspurakaners yelled back, clashing their spears on their shields. The *nakharar's* contingent was oversized for a proper maniple; a hundred Namdaleni would be outnumbered three to one.

Gaius Philippus shook the wounded Videssian, who was wobbling now that he had stopped his dash for life. "Which way, man?" the veteran demanded.

"Left at the first fork, then right at the next," the man said. He daubed at his forehead with his sleeve, staring in disbelief at the bright blood. Then he doubled over and was sick in the road. Gaius Philippus grunted in disgust, but shouted out the directions for all the troopers to hear.

Marcus pulled his sword free. "At a trot!" he said, and added, "The shout is 'Gavras!'" The legionaries pounded after him.

The first fork was only a furlong or so down the forest track, but the second was a long time coming. Feeling the sweat running itchily under his corselet, Scaurus began to wonder if he'd missed it. But the Videssian's gory trail told him he had not. The blood in the roadway was still fresh and unclotted; the man must have run as if the Furies nipped his heels.

The Romans were not as fast, but the pace they set was enough to make their Vaspurakaner comrades, most of them heavy-set, rather short-legged men, struggle to keep up. "There up ahead, past the rotten stump," Gaius Philippus said, pointing; sure enough, the path did split. The senior centurion's voice was easy; he could jog along far longer than this without growing winded.

As the fork neared, Marcus heard shouts and the clash of steel on steel. "Gavras!" he yelled, the legionaries echoing him. There was a startled pause ahead, then the cry came back in Videssian accents, along with roars of anger and dismay from Namdalener throats.

The legionaries charged down the right fork of the path, which opened out into a clearing in the oak woods. A double handful of Videssians, four mounted and the rest on foot, were pushed into a compact, desperate circle by hard-pressing Namdalener horsemen. Men were down on either side; the islanders looked to be gathering themselves for a last charge to sweep their enemies away.

As his maniple deployed into battle line, *pila* ready to cast, even stolid Junius Blaesus burst out laughing. "A hundred?" he said to Scaurus. "Looks to me, sir, like we've brought a mountain to drop on a fly."

If the little clearing held thirty islanders, the tribune would have been surprised. The men of the Duchy gauped as legionaries kept pouring out of the woods. Finally the fellow Marcus took to be their commander because of his fine saddle and horse and the gold inlay on his helm threw back his head and laughed louder than Blaesus had. "Down spears, lads," he called to his knights. "They have us, and no mistake."

The Namdaleni followed his order, warily in the case of those still fronting their intended victims. But the Videssians, as surprised as their foes by their deliverance, were content to lean on their weapons and sob in great breaths of air; they were in no condition to attack.

The mercenary captain rode slowly up to Scaurus. The Romans

around the tribune raised javelins threateningly, but the islander paid them no mind. He held his shield out to Scaurus. "Give me a blow for my honor's sake," he said, and Marcus tapped the metal facing with his sword. "Well struck! I yield me!" He took off his helmet to show he had surrendered. His men followed suit.

Under the helm the Namdalener had a smiling, freckled face and a thick head of light brown hair; like most of his countrymen, he shaved the back of his head. As had been true of the islanders in the motte-and-bailey fort north of the Sangarios, he did not seem disturbed at yielding; these things were part of a professional soldier's life.

His squadron was as casual; one of them said, quite without rancor, to the imperials they had just fought, "We'd have had you if these whoreson Romans hadn't come along." Having served side-by-side with them in the capital, the Namdaleni knew more about the legionaries than did the Videssians they had saved.

Scaurus set his troopers to disarming the islanders, then walked over to salute the Videssian leader. The man's highbred horse and the air of authority he wore like a good cloak made him easy to pick out. He must have been nearly sixty, but a vigorous sixty. His hair and close-trimmed beard were iron gray, and, while his middle was thick, his shoulders did not sag under the weight of armor.

His eye held a twinkle of irony as he returned Marcus' salute. "You do me too much honor. The weaker should bow and scrape, not the stronger. Sittas Zonaras, at your service." He bowed in the saddle. "My rank is spatharios, for all that tells you."

Even as the tribune gave his name, he decided he liked this Zonaras. In the cloud-cuckoo-land of Videssian honorifics, spatharios was the vaguest, but few imperials would poke fun at their own pretensions.

"I've heard of you, young fellow," Zonaras remarked, apparently adding the last phrase to see if Scaurus would squirm. When he got no response, he probed harder. "Baanes Onomagoulos had things to say about you, none of which I'd care to repeat to you face-to-face." One of the noble's retainers shot him an alarmed look.

"Did he?" Marcus said, alert beneath his casual mask. It was not surprising Zonaras knew the late rebel; this was the country from which Onomagoulos came. That he would admit knowing him was something else, an extraordinary gesture of trust when offered to a man who served Baanes' foe.

"Onomagoulos rarely said much good about anyone," the tribune said, and Zonaras nodded, his own face impassive now, as if wondering whether he had made a mistake. His eyes cleared as Marcus went on, "I think being lamed embittered him. He wasn't so sour before Maragha."

"That's so," the Videssian said. As if relieved to back away from a dangerous subject, he glanced toward the men of the Duchy. "What will you do with them? They think they own the country for no better reason than their bandit chief's say-so."

After the Sangarios, Marcus thought gloomily, they had better reason than that. He thought for a few seconds. "Perhaps Drax will exchange them for Mertikes Zigabenos."

The legionaries must have outmarched news of the battle, for Zonaras blinked in amazement, and his men exclaimed in alarm. "Drax holds the guards commander?" Zonaras said. "Grave news. Tell it me."

Scaurus set it forth. Zonaras listened impassively until he spoke of the desertion of the Namdaleni who had marched with the Imperial Army, then cursed in black anger. "Skotos freeze all treachers' privates," he growled, and from that moment on the tribune was sure he had taken no part in Onomagoulos' revolt. When Marcus was done, Zonaras sat silent a long while. At last he asked, "What will you do now?"

"What I can," the tribune answered. "How much that may be, I don't know."

He thought Zonaras might snort in contempt, but the Videssian noble gave a sober nod. "You carry an old man's head on your shoulders, to fight shy of promising Phos' sun when you don't carry it on your belt." Zonaras scratched his knee as he watched Scaurus. "You know, outlander, you shame me," he said slowly. "It is not right for hired troops to be more willing to save Videssos than her own men."

Marcus had thought that since his first weeks in the Empire, but few Videssians agreed. Long used to their power, they took it for granted—or had, until Maragha. The Roman, whose homeland had grown mighty only in the century and a half before his birth, was not so complacent.

Zonaras broke into his thoughts, reaching down to take his hand. "What I and mine can do for you, we will," he pledged, and squeezed with a strength that belied his years. Scaurus returned the clasp, but wondered how much help one backwoods noble was likely to give.

The next day's march was a revelation to the tribune, not least because all of it was over Sittas Zonaras' land. Toward evening the legionaries made camp beside his sprawling villa, which nestled in a narrow valley. The setting sun shone purple off the highlands to the south and east. "We've done well," Zonaras said with no little pride.

"Aye, belike, and an elephant's plump," Gaius Philippus said.

Marcus had known intellectually of the broad estates and peasant villages Videssian grandees controlled. Only now did he start to feel what that control meant. Around the capital, brawling city life replaced the nobles' holdings, and in the westlands' central plateau the soil was too poor to allow a concentration of wealth such as Zonaras enjoyed.

His acres included fine vineyards and gardens; a willow plantation by the stream that ran past him home; meadows where horses and donkeys, cattle, sheep, and goats grazed; forests for timber and animal fodder; poor grapevines climbing up hillside trees; and the oak woods where he had met first the Namdaleni and then Scaurus, which yielded acorns not only to be the wild boar he hunted, but also to his own herd of pigs.

On the march the tribune had seen no fewer than five presses for squeezing out olive oil. There were herders in the fields with the flock; the chief herdsman, a solid, middle-aged man without the least touch of servility, had warily come up to greet Zonaras after the noble assured him at some distance that the long column of legionaries behind him was friendly.

"Glad of it, sir," the man had answered, "else I'd have raised the countryside against 'em." He tore up a scrap of parchment with something written on it; probably the numbers and direction of the intruders, Marcus thought. He was not surprised the herder chief knew his letters. In Rome, too, a man with such a responsible job would have to be able to read and write.

And while the legionaries who heard the fellow's promise to his lord snickered at it, Scaurus suspected it should not be taken lightly. Nor was Gaius Philippus laughing. Unlike most of the Romans, he knew the other side of irregular warfare. "All the folk in all these villages we've passed through seem plenty fond of Zonaras here," he said to the tribune. "It'd be no fun having them bushwhack us and then fade off through the woods or into the hills before we could chase 'em." He spoke Latin, so Zonaras caught his name but no more.

Marcus understood the senior centurion's logic and also suddenly understood why the bureaucrats back in Videssos the city so hated and feared the provincial nobles. It would literally take an army to make Zonaras do anything he did not care to do, and there were scores of nobles like him.

Indeed, even an army might not have sufficed to bring Zonaras back to obedience. He could defend with more than an armed peasantry. As the legionaries discovered when they reached his family seat, the noble kept a band of half a hundred armed retainers. They were not quite professional troops, as they made most of their living by farming, but what they lacked in spit and polish they made up for with unmatched knowledge of the area and the same strong devotion to their lord the chief herdsman had shown.

Once, Scaurus knew, the farmer-soldiers' first loyalty had been to the Empire. But years of harsh taxes made them seek protection from the grandees against the central government's greed. The local nobles, ambitious and powerful, were glad to use them to try to throw off the bureaucrats' yoke once for all. To survive, the pen-pushers in the capital hired mercenaries to hold them in line . . . and so, Marcus thought as the legionaries planted stakes on their rampart, these endless civil wars, first an Onomagoulos rebelling, then a Drax. He grunted. Without Videssos' civil strife, the Yezda would be out beyond the borders of Vaspurakan, not looking down like vultures over Garsavra.

"Well, what of it?" Helvis responded when he remarked on that. "If Videssos used no mercenaries, the two of us would not have met. Or would that thought please you these days?" There were challenge and sadness both in her voice; the question was not rhetorical.

"No, love," he said, touching her hand. "The gods know we're not perfect, but then only they are. Or Phos, if you'd rather," he amended quickly, seeing her mouth tighten. He cursed his clumsy tongue; he had no real belief in the Roman gods, but spoke merely from habit.

Gaius Philippus had also heard the tribune's first comment. "Hrmp," he said. "If the Videssians didn't hire mercenaries, they'd have killed the lot of us as soon as we came into this crazy world."

"There is that," Scaurus admitted. Gaius Philippus nodded, then hurried off to swear at a Vaspurakaner who had been foolish enough to start to relieve himself upstream from the camp. The luckless trooper found himself with a week of latrine duty.

Marcus was left thoughtful. Gaius Philippus rarely broke in when he and Helvis were talking. Was the senior centurion trying in his gruff way to keep things smooth between them? Considering his misogynism, the notion was strange, but the tribune was strapped for any other explanation. He murmured a sentence in archaic, rhythmic Greek. Helvis looked at him strangely.

"'Everything you say, my friend, is to the point,'" he translated. Everything was in Homer somewhere.

Zonaras' wife was a competent, gray-haired woman named Thekla. His widowed sister Erythro lived with them. Several years younger than Sittas, she was flighty and talkative, and had a gift for puncturing the calm front he cherished.

Erythro was childless; her brother and Thekla had had a daughter and three sons. The girl, Ypatia, reminded Marcus a little of Alypia Gavra in her quiet intelligence. She was betrothed to one of the nobles in the hills to the south. The man stood to inherit Zonaras' estates, for his only surviving son, Tarasios, was a pale, consumptive youth. He bore his illness with courage and laughed at the coughing fits that wracked his thin frame, but death's mark was on him. Along with many men of lower rank from the holding, his two brothers had fallen at Maragha, fighting under Onomagoulos.

Despite that, Zonaras had not supported his neighbor's rebellion against Thorisin Gavras. "As Kalokyres says, in civil war the prudent man sits tight." Scaurus smothered a smile when he heard that; the last man he had known who was fond of quoting the Videssian military writer was Ortaias Sphrantzes, a miscast soldier if ever there was one.

Framed in black, portraits of the grandee's dead sons hung in his dining hall. “They’re crude daubs,” Erythro told Marcus in the confidential manner she liked to affect. “I’ll have you know my nephews were handsome lads.”

“All your taste is in your mouth, darling sister,” Sittas Zonaras rumbled. He and Erythro argued constantly, with great enjoyment on both sides. If she spoke well of wine, he would drink ale for the next fortnight to irritate her, while she kept urging him to drown all the cats on the estate—but stroked them when he was not there to see it.

Actually, Scaurus agreed with Erythro here. By the standards of the capital, the paintings were the product of a half-schooled man, no doubt a local. Still, they gave Marcus an idea. A couple of days after the legionaries encamped by Zonaras’ villa, he went to Styppes, saying, “I’d ask a favor of you.”

“Ask,” Styppes grunted, ungracious as usual. At least, thought the tribune, he was sober.

“I’d like you to paint an icon for me.”

“For you?” Styppes’ eyes narrowed within their folds of flesh. “Why should an unbeliever want a holy image?” he asked suspiciously.

“As a gift for my lady Helvis.”

“Who is a heretic.” The healer-priest still sounded surly, but Scaurus had his arguments ready; he had played this game with Videssians before. It took some time and some shouting, but after a while Styppes sullenly admitted that right devotion could lead even heretics toward the true faith—his own. “Which holy man would you have me depict, then?”

The tribune remembered the temple in Videssos Helvis had been visiting when rioting broke out against the Namdaleni in the city. “I don’t know the name of the saint,” he said, as Styppes curled his lip, “but he lived on Namdalen before it was lost to the Empire—Kalavria, it was called, wasn’t it? He has a shrine dedicated to him in the capital, not far from the harbor of Kontoskalion.”

“Ah!” the healer-priest said, surprised Scaurus had a choice in mind. “I know the man you mean: the holy Nestorios. He is portrayed as an old bald man with his beard in two points. So the heretics of the Duchy revere him yet, do they? Very well, you shall have your icon.”

“My thanks.” Marcus paused, then felt he had to add, “A favor for a favor. When I find time, I'll pose for your image of the holy—what did you call him?—Kveldulf, that was it."

"Yes, yes, that's good of you, I'm sure," Styppes said, abstracted. The tribune thought he was already starting to plan the icon, but as he turned to go he heard the priest mutter under his breath, "Phos, I'm thirsty." Not for the first time, he wished jolly, capable Nepos preferred life in the field to his chair in theoretical thaumaturgy at the Videssian Academy.

Over the next few days Scaurus was too busy to give Styppes or the icon much thought. Zonaras' villa and his little private army were well enough to face a rival grandee, but the tribune had few illusions about their ability to withstand Drax' veterans. The legionaries dug like badgers, strengthening the place as best they could, but his worries only deepened. The best, he knew, was none too good; he simply did not have enough men.

He used Zonaras' retainers and his other Videssian horsemen to spy out the Namdaleni. Every day they reported more islanders south of the Arandos, but not the great column of knights the tribune feared. The men of the Duchy began building a motte-and-bailey fort a couple of hours' ride north of Zonaras' oak woods. "Drax is busy somewhere and doesn't want us interfering," Gaius Philippus said.

Marcus spread his hands in bewilderment. Not all of what the Namdalener count did made sense. "No, all it does is work," the senior centurion replied. A good Roman, he valued results more than methods.

The tribune released one of his Namdalener prisoners at the edge of the woods, using him as a messenger to offer Drax the exchange of his fellows for Mertikes Zigabenos. Their freckled captain, who called himself Persic Fishhook from a curved scar on his arm, said confidently, "No problem. We'll be free in a week, is my guess. Thirty of us are worth a Videssian general any day, and then some." While they waited to be swapped, the islanders cheerfully fetched and carried for the legionaries; even as captives, they and the Romans got on well.

When he got back to Zonaras' holding, Marcus was intrigued to find Styppes on his hands and knees in the garden by the villa, turning up lettuce leaves. "What are you after?" he called to the healer-priest, wondering what sort of medicinal herbs grew along with the salad greens.

He blinked when Styppes answered, "I need a good fat snail or two. Ah, here!" The priest put his catch in a small burlap bag.

"Now I understand," the tribune laughed. "Snails and lettuce make a good supper. Will you boil some eggs with them?"

Styppes grunted in exasperation as he got to his feet. He brushed once at the mud on the knees of his blue robe, then let it go. "No, lackwit. I want them to let me finish the image of the holy Nestorios." He made Phos' sun-sign over his heart.

"Snails?" Marcus heard his voice rise in disbelief.

"Come see then, scoffer." Wondering whether Styppes was playing a prank on him, the Roman followed him to his tent. They squatted together on the dirt floor. Styppes lit a tallow candle that filled the tight space with the smell of burning fat. The priest rummaged in his kit, finding at last a large oyster shell. "Good, good," he said to himself. He took one of the snails from his bag, held it over the candle flame. The unfortunate mollusc bubbled and emitted a thick, clear slime. As it dripped, Styppes caught it in the oyster shell. The other snail suffered the same fate. "You see?" the healer-priest said, holding the shell under Scaurus' nose.

"Well, no," the tribune said, more distressed at the snails' torment than he had been in several fights.

"Bah. You will." Styppes poured the slime onto a hand-sized marble slab and added powdered gold. "You will pay me back, and not in new coin," he warned Scaurus. Next came a little whitish powder—"Alum"—and some sticky gum, then he stirred the mix with a brass pestle. "Now we are ready—you will admire it," he said. He took out a pair of badger-fur brushes, one so fine the hairs were fitted into a goosequill, the other larger, with a wooden handle.

Marcus drew in a breath of wonder when he saw the icon for the first time. Styppes' sketches had shown him the priest had a gift, but they were only sketches. The delicate colors and fine line, the holy Nestorios' ascetic yet kindly face, the subtled shadings of his blue robe, his long, thin hands upraised in a gesture of blessing that reminded the tribune of the awesome mosaic image of Phos in the High Temple in the capital . . . "Almost I believe in your god now," he said, and knew no higher praise.

"That is what an image is for, to instruct the ignorant and guide them toward its prototype's virtues," the healer-priest replied. His plump hand deft as a jeweler's, he dipped his tiny feather-brush in the gold pigment on his piece of marble. Though he held the icon close to his face as he worked, his calligraphy was elegant; the gilding, even wet, shone and sparkled in the dim candlelight. "Nestorios the holy," Marcus read. Styppes used the larger brush to surround the saint's head with a gleaming circle of gold. "Thus we portray Phos' sun-disk, to show the holy man's closeness to the good god," he explained, but the tribune had already grasped the halo's meaning.

"May I?" he said, and when Styppes nodded, he took the wooden panel into his own hands. "How soon will it be ready for giving?" he asked eagerly.

Styppes' smile, for once, was not sour. "A day for the gilding to dry, then two coats of varnish to protect the colors underneath." He scratched his shaved head. "Say, four days' time."

"I wish it were sooner," Marcus said. He was still not won over to this Videssian art of symbol and allegory, but there was no denying that in Styppes' talented hands its results were powerfully moving.

The priest reclaimed the icon and set it to one side to dry undisturbed. "Now," he said with an abrupt change of manner, "where did I toss those snails? Your supper idea wasn't half bad, outlander; have you any garlic to go with them?"

Laon Pakhymer appeared at the legionaries' camp like the god from a machine in a Roman play: no one set eyes on him until suddenly he was there. He flipped Scaurus the wave that passed for a salute among his easygoing folk; when the tribune asked how he had managed to ride through not only Zonaras' picket posts but also the Namdaleni, he answered airily, "There's ways," and put a finger by the side of his nose.

Sextus Minucius exclaimed, "I'll bet you used that old geezer's ford."

"Aren't you the clever young fellow?" Pakhymer said with mild irony. "And what if I did?"

"What did he gouge you for?" Gaius Philippus asked.

The Khatrisher gave a resigned shrug. "A dozen goldpieces."

The senior centurion choked on his wine. "Jove's hairy arse! You ought to go back and kill the bugger—he only got ten for the lot of us."

"Maybe so," Pakhymer answered, "but then, you hadn't just come from Kyzikos." He looked uncommonly smug, like a cat that knew where cream came from.

"What difference does it make where you—" Marcus began, and then stopped, awe on his face. Kyzikos housed an imperial mint. No one in this world had ever heard of Midas, but in Kyzikos the Khatrishers could come close to making his dream real. The tribune did not even think of pointing out that they were stealing the Empire's gold; he had learned mercenaries served themselves first. What he did say was, "Drax won't love you for emptying the till."

"Too bad for Drax. You're right, though; he's thrown a good deal at us, trying to drive us out. And so he has, but our pockets are full. I never did see such a payday." His pockmarked face was dirty, his beard wind-matted and snarled, his clothes ragged, but he was blissful nonetheless. Gaius Philippus stared at him with honest envy.

"No wonder the Namdaleni have been so easy on us, with Kyzikos to go after," Minucius said.

"It's like I guessed, sir," Gaius Philippus said to Scaurus. "But Drax is making a mistake, grabbing at the treasure first. Once his enemies are gone, it falls into his lap, but if he takes the gold and leaves us around, we may find some way to get it back."

"He doesn't have it," Pakhymer pointed out. "Still, I take your meaning even so. I have something planned to make old Drax jump and shout."

"What will you do?" Marcus asked with interest. For all his slapdash ways, that Khatrisher was a clever, imaginative soldier.

"Oh, it's done already." Pakhymer seemed pleased at his own shrewdness. "I spread some of Kyzikos' gold around where it would do the most good—it's on its way up to the central plateau. If the damned islanders are busy fighting Yezda, they can't very well fight us."

The tribune gaped. "You bribed the nomads to attack Drax?"

"So we fought them a couple of years ago. What of it?" Pakhymer was defiant and defensive at the same time. "We fought the islanders last year when they served Ortaias, and now again. One war at a time, I say."

"There's a difference," Marcus insisted. "Drax is an enemy, aye, but not wicked, only power-hungry. But the nomads kill for the joy of killing. Think on what we saw on the road to Maragha—and after." He remembered Avshar's gift, hurled into the legionaries' camp after the fight—Mavrikios Gavras' head.

Pakhymer flushed, perhaps recalling that, too, but he answered, "Any man who tries to kill me is wicked in my eyes, and my foe's foe my friend. And have a care the way you say 'nomad,' Scaurus; my people came off the same steppe the Yezda did."

"Your pardon," the tribune said at once, yielding the small point so he could have another go at the large one. "Bear this in mind, then—once you invite the, ah, Yezda down into the lowlands, even if they do hurt Drax, still you set the scene for endless fighting to push them back again."

"Is that bad? Why would the Videssians hire mercenaries, if they had no one to fight?" Pakhymer was looking at him strangely, the same look, he realized, he had seen several times on Helvis.

He sighed. Without meaning to, the Khatrisher had fingered the essential difference between himself and Scaurus. To Laon Pakhymer, the Empire was a paymaster and nothing more; its fate meant nothing to him, save as it affected his own interests. But Marcus found Videssos, despite its flaws, worth preserving for its own sake. It was doing—had done for centuries—what Rome aspired to: letting the folk within its borders build their lives free from fear. The chaos and destruction that would follow a collapse filled him with dread.

How to explain that to Pakhymer, who, for the sake of a temporary triumph, would have two packs of wolves fight over the body of the state he thought he was serving? Marcus sighed again; he saw no way. Here was his quarrel with Helvis, come to frightening life. The Khatrisher would make a desert and call it peace.

His gloom lifted somewhat as the council shifted focus. Pakhymer intended bringing all his countrymen south of the Arandos; that would give the Romans the scouts and raiders they badly needed. If Thorisin could piece together some kind of force to keep Drax at play in the north, perhaps the legionaries would not be outnumbered to the point of uselessness. And if Gaius Philippus could do with these half-trained Videssians what Sertorius had with the Spaniards, they might yet make nuisances of themselves. If, if, if . . .

He was so caught up in his worries that, when the officers' meeting broke up, he walked past Styppes as if the healer was not there. "I like that," the fat priest said. "Do a favor and see the thanks you get for it."

"Huh?" Scaurus brightened. "It's done, then?" he asked, glad to have something to think about beside Namdaleni on the march.

"Aye, so it is. Now you notice me, eh?" Marcus held his peace under the reproach; whatever he said to the healer-priest was generally wrong. Styppes grumbled something into his beard, then said, "Well, come along, come along."

When the tribune had the icon in his hands, his praise was as unstinting as it was sincere. Styppes was ill-tempered and overfond of wine, but his hands held more gifts than healing alone. Unmoved by Scaurus' compliments, he began, "Why I waste my talent for a heathen's heretic tart—" but Scaurus retreated before he was at full spate.

He found Helvis sitting under a peach tree outside the camp, mending a tunic. She looked up as he came toward her. When she saw he was going to sit by her, she jabbed her needle into the shirt, one of Malric's—and put it aside. "Hello," she said coolly; she did not try to hide her anger over the tribune's refusal to take her countrymen's side against Videssos. He was tired of the way policy kept getting between the two of them.

"Hello. I have something for you." The words seemed flat and awkward as soon as they were out of his mouth. With a sudden stab of shame, he realized he had too little practice saying such things, had been taking Helvis too much for granted except when they fought.

"What is it?" Her tone was still neutral; probably, Marcus guessed unhappily, she thinks I have underwear for her to darn.

"Here, see for yourself," he said, embarrassment making his voice gruff as he handed her the icon.

The way her eyes grew wide made him sure his guess had been all too close to the mark. "Is it for me? Truly? Where did you get it?" She did not really want an answer; her surprise was speaking. "Thank you so much!" She hugged him one-armed, not wanting to lay the image down, then made Phos' sun-sign at her breast.

Her joy made Scaurus glad and contrite at the same time. While happy to have pleased her, he knew in his heart he should have thought to do so long ago. He had ill repaid her love and loyalty—for why else would she stay with him despite their many differences? Nor did he think of her as only a bed warmer, a pleasure for his nights; love, he thought with profound unoriginality, is very strange.

"Who is it?" Helvis demanded, breaking his reverie. Then in the same breath she went on, "No, you don't tell me, let me work it out for myself." Her lips moved as she sounded out Styppes' golden letters one by one; in less than three years Marcus, already literate in two other tongues, had gained a grasp of written Videssian far better than hers. "Nes-to-ri-os," she read, and, putting the pieces together, "Nestorios! The island saint! However did you remember him?"

The tribune shrugged, not wanting to admit Styppes had provided the name. He felt no guilt over that; in a faith he did not share, it was enough he had recalled the holy man's existence. "Because I knew you cared for him," he said, and from the touch of her hand he knew he had the answer right.

Sentries escorted a pair of Namdaleni into Scaurus' presence. "They've come under truce-sign, sir," a Roman explained. "Gave themselves up to our pickets at the oak woods, they did." The men of the Duchy favored the tribune with crisp salutes, although one looked distinctly unhappy. And no wonder, Marcus thought; it was the islander he had sent to Drax with his exchange offer.

"Hello, Dardel," he said. "I didn't expect to see you again."

"Nor I you," Dardel answered mournfully.

The other Namdalener saluted again. Scaurus had seen that handsome, snub-nosed face before, too, on the right wing of Drax' army at the Sangarios. Now the officer looked elegant in silk surcoat and gold-inlaid ceremonial helm. "Bailli of Ecrisi, at your service," he said smoothly, his Videssian almost without trace of island accent. "Allow me to explain. As my suzerain the great count and protector Drax must decline your gracious proposal, he deemed it only just to return to you the person of your prisoner."

So Drax had a new title, did he? Well, no matter, thought Marcus; he could call himself whatever he chose. "That is most honorable of him," the tribune said. He bowed to Bailli. Not to be outdone in generosity by Drax, he added, "Of course Dardel will be free to return with you when you leave here."

Bailli and Dardel both bowed, the latter in delight. Scaurus said, "Why does the great count reject my offer? We are not rich here, but if he wants ransom for Zigabenos as well as his men free, we will do what we can."

"You misunderstand the great count and protector's reasons, sir," Bailli said. Marcus suddenly distrusted his smile; it said too plainly he knew something the tribune did not. The Namdalener went on, still smiling, "Chief among them is the fact that, being a loyal lieutenant to my lord Zigabenos, he cannot compel him to accept an exchange he does not wish."

"What?" Marcus blurted, astonished out of suaveness. "What farce is this?"

Bailli reached under his surcoat. His guards growled in warning, but all he produced was a sealed roll of parchment. "This will explain matters better than I could," he said, handing it to Scaurus. The tribune examined the seals. One he knew—the sun in golden wax, the mark of the Empire of Videssos. The other seal was green, its symbol a pair of dice in a wine cup. That would have to be Drax' mark. Scaurus broke the seals and unrolled the parchment.

The great count's man had been eyeing his exotic gear. He said, "I don't know, sir, if you read Videssian. If not, I'd be happy to—"

"I read it," Marcus said curtly, and proceeded to do so. He recognized Drax' style at once; the great count wrote the imperial tongue as ornately as any Videssian official. That was part of what made him such a deadly foe; he aped the Empire's ways too well, including, Scaurus saw as he read on, its gift for underhanded politics.

The document was not long, nor did it need be. In four convoluted sentences it proclaimed Mertikes Zigabenos rightful Avtokrator of the Videssians, named the great count Drax his "respected commander-in-chief and Protector of the Realm," urged all citizens and "soldiery whether Videssian or foreign" to support the newly declared regime, and threatened outlawry and destruction for any who resisted. Drax' signature, in fancy script with a great flourish underneath, completed the proclamation; Zigabenos' was conspicuously absent.

Marcus read it all through again, damning the great count at every word. The man had to be a genius at intrigue, to do so much damage in so little space. By working through a Videssian puppet, he took away the stigma of being an invader and permanently compromised Zigabenos in Thorisin Gavras' eyes. The rightful Emperor could not be sure Zigabenos was not willingly cooperating with Drax. And Zigabenos, no mean machinator himself, would see that for himself—and might really help the great count from fear of what would happen to him if Drax' revolt failed. The tribune's head started to ache. The more he thought, the worse things looked.

He rolled up the parchment to hand it back to Bailli. The two pieces of Drax' seal fit neatly together, edge to edge. In his choice of emblem, at least, Scaurus thought, he was a Namdalener; the men of the Duchy loved to gamble.

Bailli sniggered when he remarked on that. "Look again."

The tribune did, then swore and threw the parchment to the floor, for what were dice in a wine cup but loaded dice?

VI

"Tell me," Varatesh said to Viridovix as he helped his prisoner dismount after another long day of travel, "why did you dye your hair and mustache that hideous shade? And why have you grown the mustache but no beard? By the spirits, you stand out more among plainsmen this way than as you were."

"Will you give over havering anent my looks? It's no beauty y'are your own self." He tried to smooth his long mustachioes, sadly draggled by days of steady rain. With a rawhide strap binding his wrists, he made a clumsy job of it.

"Do not toy with me," Varatesh said, mild-voiced as usual. "I will only ask my question once more." The outlaw chief made no threats, as his riders would have. His cruelty was subtler, letting the Gaul find his own terrors to imagine.

"A pox take you, man. My own face this is on the front o' my head, and nought but." Viridovix glared at the Khamorth, afraid and exasperated at the same time. "What is it I'm supposed to look like, anyway?" he demanded.

"As Avshar set you forth," Varatesh said, and Viridovix felt a chill at the wizard-prince's name. Every day the roughgaited steppe pony he unwillingly rode brought him closer to a meeting he did not want.

"Well, how is that, you kern? I'm not likely to be reading the villain's mind, nor wanting to, either."

Kubad snarled at the insults and fingered his knife in its sheath. What Videssian he understood was mostly vile, just as Viridovix could curse in the plains speech. But Varatesh waved his rider to silence. When he was on the trail of something, such trifles were like false scents to a hunting hound, distractions to be screened out. "As you wish," he said to the Celt. "Your height matches Avshar's picture of you, but he makes your hair out to be dark yellow, not this roan of yours, and calls you clean shaven, though that, I know, means not much. Nor do you look like any imperial I've seen, and he said you might be a Videssian but for fair hair and light eyes."

"Sure and I'd never be that, Varatesh dear," Viridovix said, and then laughed in the Khamorth's face.

"What do you find so funny?" The outlaw chief's tone was dangerous; like most men habitually unsure of themselves, he could not stand being mocked.

"Only that your puir soft-noodled wizard sent you off chasing fish, fur, or virgin's milk. I ken the man you mean, and he's no friend of Avshar, Scaurus isn't, nor a bad wight for all he's a Roman." The alien names meant nothing to Varatesh, who waited with angry impatience. Enjoying himself for the first time since he was taken, the Gaul went on, "If it's the Scaurus you're after, lad, you've a farther ride than the one you took to nab me, for he's still back in the Empire, indeed and he is."

"What?" Varatesh barked. He did not doubt his prisoner's word; the relish Viridovix took in making him look a fool was too obvious. His men were shouting questions at him. With poor grace, he translated what the Celt had said. That his own men lost respect for him was worse than Viridovix' glee; who cared what an enemy thought?

"Avshar won't be pleased," Kubad said, a remark that hung in the air like the smell of lightning.

It was Denizli's turn to half draw his dagger. He smiled evilly. "If this son of a spotted mare's no one Avshar wants, we can have our sport with him here and now." He did pull the knife free, held it under Viridovix' eyes.

"Loose my hands and do that, hero," the Celt growled.

"What does he say?" Denizli said. When Varatesh told him, his smile grew wider. "Tell him I will loose his hands for him—one finger at a time." He stepped toward Viridovix again.

Varatesh nearly let him have his way, but a sudden thought made him cry, "No! Wait!" and knock his rider's blade to one side. Twice now in days he had robbed Denizli of the pleasure of the kill. The renegade sprang at him with an oath, dagger slashing out. But it bit only empty air; Varatesh, who seemed impossible to surprise, had already danced aside.

His own knife leaped into his hand. The other Khamorth—Kubad and his comrades Khuraz, Akes, and Bikni—made no move to interfere. In their brutal world, strength alone gave the right to lead.

Varatesh took a cut arm, but a moment later Denizli was writhing in the mud, shrieking as he clutched his hands to his gashed belly. Varatesh stooped over him and cut his throat, as a merciful man would.

Viridovix caught his eye. "Well fought," he said. "I wish it had been me to do it." He meant the compliment; he took fighting too seriously for idle flattery. Varatesh was fast and supple as a striking snake.

The Khamorth shrugged. "Bury this garbage," he said to the four remaining riders. Obeying with no back answers, they stripped the corpse and started to dig; the sodden ground made the work easy. Varatesh turned back to the Gaul. "Riddle me this: if you are not the man my comrade Avshar seeks, how did his magic lead me to you? How did his sleeping-charm not fell you? And how is it you bear a sword like the one this—what was his name?—Scaurus carries?" His Khamorth accent made it sound like "Skrush."

"Begging your pardon and all, but if I'm not the man himself is after, how should I know the answers to your fool questions?"

Varatesh smiled, but thinly. "Just what Avshar will ask you, I think. I will leave it to him, then." For the first time Viridovix was glad of the rain. It hid the sweat that sprang out on his forehead. That sword—he wished he knew more about the sorceries the druids had laid in it. But the Celtic priests revealed their secrets to no one outside their caste. Initiates spent up to twenty years memorizing their lore, for they would not commit it to writing . . . and now they were a world away, and a lost world, to boot.

"Your honor!" he called as Varatesh started to leave. When the Khamorth paused, he went on, "Now that that pig's bladder of a Denizli is after having no further use for his cloak, could I sleep under it tonight? A dry snooze'd be a rare pleasure after this cursed soppy weather." The nomads' cloaks, of greasy wool, shed the rain like ducks' feathers, while the Gaul, in his cloth, had been constantly sodden. Luckily it was warm; a chill likely would have put a fever in his lungs.

"Well, why not? You do have the look of a drowned pup." Varatesh gave his men the order. There were a couple of startled looks, and Kubad quickly spoke up in protest, but Varatesh's answer seemed to satisfy the nomad. The outlaw leader said to Viridovix, "You'll take Kubad's instead. It has a hole in it, and he'll keep Denizli's for himself."

"That will do me, and I thank you."

The Khamorth untied his hands so he could eat, but, as always, kept him covered while loose and rebound them with a fresh strip of rawhide as soon as he was done. When he asked to go out to answer a call of nature, they also bound his ankles together so he had to take tiny hobbling steps. Again, an archer accompanied him.

He had not gone far when he slipped and fell with a splash into a man-sized puddle. His guard laughed and made no effort to help him up. Suspecting a trap, he watched from a safe distance, bow drawn, as the Celt floundered. At last Viridovix struggled back onto his feet. If he had been wet before, he was drenched now. "Och, for a copper I'd piss on *you,*" he said to the nomad, but in Gaulish. Recognizing the tone if not the words, the Khamorth kept on laughing. Viridovix glowered at him. "Well, you blackguard, you're not so smart as you think y'are," he said, and his guard laughed even more.

Sodden as he was, the sheepskin cloak did nothing to keep him dry. He curled under it nonetheless. Four of the five nomads slept; Varatesh drew first watch. After his stint was done he woke Akes, who sat grumpily in the rain waiting until it was time for him to rouse Kubad. Every so often, as Varatesh had done, he would glance over at Viridovix, but the Celt was no more than an unmoving lump in the darkness.

For all his pretended sleep, Viridovix was frantically if quietly busy under the sheepskin. His thrashings in the puddle had not been accidental; he had thoroughly soaked the rawhide straps that tied him. Wet, the hide had far more stretch in it than it did dry. Ever so slowly and carefully, not daring to risk detection, he moved his wrists back and forth, up and down, until at last—it was halfway through Kubad's watch—he hooked a thumb under the edge of the hide strip and worked it up over his hands. He clenched his fists over and over, trying to get full feeling back.

Kubad had a skin of kavass with him to help while away the time. All the better, Viridovix thought. The top of the cloak hid his smile. He yawned loudly and half sat, making sure he kept his arms behind him.

He looked around as if just locating the sentry he had been anxiously watching all the while.

At the motion Kubad eyed him, but the nomad knew his captive was safely tied. He lifted the skin to his mouth. "How about a nip for me, too, Khamorth darling?" Viridovix called. He kept his voice very low; he hardly wanted to wake Kubad's mates—least of all Varatesh. Varatesh smelled trouble as a bear smelled honey.

But Kubad ambled over and squatted by the Gaul. "You wake thirsty, eh?" he said, holding the skin to Viridovix' lips.

As he drank, Viridovix felt a tiny twinge of guilt at betraying the nomad's friendly act. He stifled it—how friendly had Varatesh's bandits been when they kidnapped him?

"Another?" Kubad asked. The Gaul nodded. The nomad bent closer to present the skin again, and Viridovix lunged forward to take him by the throat. The skin of kavass went flying. By good fortune, it landed on the wool cloak so it did not splash and give the Celt away.

Kubad was an experienced fighter, but he was taken by surprise and made a mistake that proved fatal. Instead of reaching for his dagger, his first, instinctive reaction was to try to break Viridovix' grip on his neck. But the Gaul had desperation's strength, his strangling fingers pressing up under the angle of Kubad's jaw. Too late the nomad remembered the knife. It was his last thought, and his hands would not obey him, falling limp at his sides.

Viridovix let the corpse down into the mud. He took the dagger himself—a curved weapon with a heavy, lozenge-shaped pommel—and cut the strip of hide that bound his ankles. He made himself wait until the aches and tingles of returning circulation were gone before he moved. "You've only the one chance, now, so don't go wasting it from impatience," he muttered.

The rain drumming down masked his noise as he slid toward the nomads; here was revenge for the taking. But he paused as he stooped over the first of them. Kubad had been a fair fight, but he could not bring himself to murder sleeping men. Eighty-nine kinds of a fool Gaius Philippus'd call you, he said to himself as he sheathed the weapon. Reversed, it would do for a club.

Three times he struck—none of them gentle, for he did not intend to have any of the Khamorth wake with a howl. That left Varatesh.

The outlaw chief woke with a blade tickling his throat. Self-possessed as usual, he sent his right hand slithering toward his belt-knife, hoping the motion would be invisible under the thick cloak. "Dinna try it," Viridovix advised. He held a second dagger, sheathed and reversed, in his left hand. "Sure and I'll slit your weasand for you or ever you get it out." Varatesh considered, decided he was right, and seemed to relax. Viridovix was undeceived.

"Not knowing how hard-pated your lads are, I'll make the farewells brief," the Gaul said.

That startled Varatesh as the reversal of fortunes had not. "You're free and did not kill them?"

"Kubad's dead," Viridovix answered matter-of-factly, "but the rest'll have no worse than the fierce sore head you gave me. As will you," he added, and clubbed the outlaw chief. Varatesh slumped.

Thinking the Khamorth might be shamming, Viridovix drew back warily, but his left-handed blow had been strong enough. Working quickly, he tied all four of the unconscious plainsmen. One wasn't, quite, and had to be flattened a second time. He took all their weapons he could find, loaded them onto a packhorse, then buckled on his own sword. It made a pleasant weight at his hip.

Varatesh's eyes opened while the Celt was still tying the horses' lead lines together. He started working at his bonds at once, making no effort to disguise it—had Viridovix intended to kill him, he would have been dead by now. "We'll meet again, outlander," he promised.

"Aye, belike, but not soon, I'm thinking, e'en once you do get loose," Viridovix said, finishing his work with the animals. "You'd look the proper set o' mooncalves, now, chasing after me afoot, and me with your horses and all."

Varatesh paused, looked at him with grudging respect. "I hoped you would not think of that; many southrons would not have." He started to shake his head, then winced and gave it up as a bad job.

"And besides," Viridovix went on, grinning, "you'll have the demons' own time finding a trail in this muck." The Khamorth scowled, remembering how he had said that to Kubad about Viridovix' comrades. Now the shoe was on his foot and it pinched. So would his boots, soon enough, he thought sourly.

The Gaul swung himself into the saddle. "A pox on your skimpy stirrup leathers," he grumbled; with his long legs, his knees were nearly under his chin. He dug a heel into the steppe pony's ribs, cuffed it when it tried to buck. "None o' that, now!" One by one, as their leads went taut, the nomads' three dozen horses followed the beast he rode. The lilting air was whistling came straight from the Gallic forests. And why not? he thought, there's just myself the now, so I can be me—aye, and like it, too, with none to say they don't understand.

He whistled louder.

Gorgidas muttered an obscenity as a raindrop hit him in the eye, blurring his vision for a few seconds. "I thought we were done with this cursed weather," he complained.

"Why wait till now to carp?" Lankinos Skylitzes asked. "We've been out from under the worst of it almost all day. If you'd ridden north instead of west, you'd still be soaking it up like a sponge."

Arigh nodded. "It'll get drier the further west you go. In Shaumkhiil, my people's land, these week-long summer storms don't happen much. Winter, now, is another tale." He shuddered at the thought of it. "Videssos has spoiled me."

"I wonder why that's so," Gorgidas said, curious in spite of himself. "Perhaps your being further from the sea has something to do with it. But no—how could you have wet, snowy winters if that were so?" He thought briefly, then asked. "Or is there some other sea to the north, from which your winter storms could gather moisture?"

"Never heard of one," Arigh said without much interest. "There's the Mylasa Sea between the plains and Yezd, but that's south of my folk, not north, and hardly more than a big lake anyhow."

Surprisingly, Goudeles said to Gorgidas, "Well reasoned, outlander. The Northern Sea does run some distance west of the Haloga lands, how far no man knows, but cold and drear throughout." He gave an elegant grimace of distaste. "It must be the cause of the harsh weather good Arigh mentions."

"How do you know that, Pikridios?" Skylitzes challenged. "Far as I've heard, you never set foot outside Videssos till now."

"A fragment of poetry I came across in the archives," the bureaucrat replied blandly. "Written by a naval officer—a Mourtzouphlos, I think; they're an old family—not long after Stavrakios' time, when the Halogai still minded their manners. Quite an arresting little thing, really; one is quite taken with the strangeness of it, almost as if the author were portraying another world. Rocks and ice and wind and odd, bright-beaked shore birds with some flatulent name he must have borrowed from the local barbarians: 'auks,' I think it was."

"Well, auks to you, too," Skylitzes said, defeated by the pen-pusher's barrage of detail. Goudeles dipped his head in a smug half-bow. Gorgidas thought he heard Skylitzes grind his teeth.

"Your pardon, gents," Agathias Psoes broke in, practical as a Roman, "but that looks to be a good place to camp, there up ahead by the stream." The underofficer pointed; as if at the motion, a small flock of ducks came quacking down from the gray sky. Psoes smiled like a successful conjurer; his men unshipped their bows. Gorgidas' stomach rumbled at the thought of roast duck.

But the first bird that was shot let out a loud squawk, and its flockmates took wing, evading the fusillade of arrows the troopers aimed at them. "Shut up in there," the Greek said as his belly growled again. "It's cheese and wheatcakes after all."

Sword drill came before supper. To his dismay, Gorgidas was starting to look forward to it. There was an animal pleasure in feeling his body begin to learn the right response to an overhand cut, a thrust at his belly, a slash at his calf. The practice was like the Videssian board game that mimicked war, but played with arm and eye and feet as well as mind.

Feet—at last he was working on ground firm enough to make footwork mean something more than just staying upright. "A man-killer soon," Skylitzes said, dancing back from a stab.

"I don't want to be a man killer," the Greek insisted. Skylitzes ignored that and came back to show him how he had given the thrust away. The taciturn Videssian officer was a good teacher; better, Gorgidas thought, than Viridovix would have been. He was more patient and more systematic than the mercurial Celt and remembered his pupils were altogether untrained. Where Viridovix would have thrown up his hands in disgust, Skylitzes was willing to repeat a parry, a lunge, a sidestep thirty times if need be, until it was understood.

When Gorgidas was done, he went down to bathe in the stream, leaving Pikridios Goudeles to Skylitzes' tender mercies. Skylitzes worked the seal-stamper harder than Gorgidas; the Greek was not sure how much of that was because he was a better student than Goudeles and how much because Goudeles and the soldier did not get along. He heard Goudeles yelp as Skylitzes spanked his knuckles—getting some of his own back for that arctic epic.

A green and brown frog no bigger than the last joint of Gorgidas' finger sat in a bush near the edge of the stream. If it had not peeped suddenly, he never would have noticed it. He shook his finger at it. "Hush," he said severely, "before you send all our Khamorth running for their lives." His stomach gurgled again. "And you, too."

They came to a good-sized river the next day; Psoes identified it as the Kouphis. "This is as far west on the Pardrayan steppe as I've come," he said.

"We're halfway to the Shaum, near enough," Arigh said, and Skylitzes nodded. He spoke little of his travels, but if he knew the Arshaum speech along with that of the Khamorth, likely he had gone much farther than the Kouphis.

The river ran north and south. They rode upstream, looking for a ford, and came level with what looked like a heap of building-stones on the far bank. They set Gorgidas scratching his head—what were they doing here in the middle of the flat, empty plain? Two of Psoes' troopers had heard of the stone-pile, but they were little help; they called it "the gods' dung heap."

Skylitzes gave a rare laugh. "Or the Khamorth's," he said quietly, so Psoes' men would not hear. "It's what's left of a Videssian fort, after two hundred-odd years of sacks and no upkeep."

"What?" Gorgidas said. "The Empire ruled here once?"

"No, no," Skylitzes explained. "It was a gift from the Avtokrator to a powerful khagan. But when the khagan died, his sons quarreled, and the nomads went back to living clan by clan."

Pikridios Goudeles stared across the Kouphis at the ruin and burst into laughter himself. "That? That pile of rubble is Khoirosphaktes' Folly?"

"You know of it, too?" Gorgidas asked, forestalling Lankinos Skylitzes; the soldier, it seemed, was not willing to believe Goudeles knew anything.

The bureaucrat rolled his eyes, a gesture that somehow brought with it a whiff of the capital despite the shabby traveling clothes that had quickly replaced his fine robes. "Know of it? My inquisitive friend, in Videssos' accounting schools it is the paradigm of failing to measure cost against results. The goldpieces squandered on shipping artisans and stone from the Empire! And for what? You see it for yourself." He shook his head. "And that says nothing of the elephant."

"Elephant?" the Greek and Skylitzes said together. In Videssos as in Rome they were rare breasts, coming from the little-known lands south of the Sailors' Sea.

"Oh, indeed. One of the khagan's envoys had seen one—at a menagerie, I suppose—and told his master about it. So there was nothing for it but that the barbarian had to have a look at it, too. And the Avtokrator Khoirosphaktes, who, I fear, drank too much to know when to leave well enough alone, shipped it to him. Oh, the gold!" Goudeles looked pained to the bottom of his parsimonious soul.

"Well, out with it, man!" Gorgidas exclaimed. "What did the khagan do with his elephant?"

"Took one look and shipped it back, of course. What would *you* do?"

"Och, beshrew me, sure and I've gone and made a hash of it," Viridovix said, cocking hands on hips in irritation. The inky-black night was at last graying toward another cloudy morning, and the Celt, to his disgust, realized he had been riding east ever since he escaped from Varatesh. The corners of his eyes crinkled. "There's a bit o' good in everything," he told himself, "that there is. The omadhaun'd never think to look for me going this way—he must credit me for better sense."

He gnawed at his mustache as he thought, then swung south, planning to ride in a large circle around Varatesh's camp; he had a healthy respect for the outlaw chief. "I should have put paid to the son of a mangy ferret, for all he spared my mates," he said, speaking aloud again to hear the good Celtic words flow off his tongue. "One fine day he'll cause me more grief, sure as sure."

A horse which had started to graze while he paused jerked its head up with a sharp neigh of protest as its lead rope came taut again. "Dinna say me nay," the Gaul told it, still unhappy with himself. "Too late for your regrets, as for mine."

As the day wore on, the sun finally began to burn its way through the storm clouds. The rain grew fitful, then stopped. "Well, the gods be praised," Viridovix said, and looked about for a rainbow. He did not find one. "Likely that knave of a Varatesh stole it," he muttered, only half joking.

In one small way, the rain and clouds and mist had been a comfort to him, for they closed in his circle of vision and did not make him cope with the plains' vast spaces along with his other miseries. But with the clearing weather, the horizon seemed to draw back veil after veil until, as in his first days on the steppe, he felt like a tiny speck moving through infinity. "If there were but one wee star in all the sky, sure and it'd be no lonelier than I," he said, and bellowed out endless songs to hold aloneness at arm's length.

His banshee shout of glee when he spied a herd of cattle moving far to the south sent his horses' ears pricking up in alarm. After a moment's reflection, though, he squelched it, wondering which was worse, no neighbors or bad ones. "For if I can see them, sure as sure they can see me. Och, wouldn't the little Greek be proud now, to hear me play the logician?"

His reasoning was rewarded, if that was the word, within minutes. A handful of Khamorth peeled away from their cattle and came toward him at a trot. "And what will they do when they find a stranger with these horses and all?" he asked himself; he did not care for the answer he reached. Then he recalled the heavy bows the nomads carried and grew unhappier yet.

He wished for his helm and his cape of scarlet skins to let him cut an impressive figure. His traveling clothes were muddy, wet, and drab to begin with; he surveyed himself with distaste. "Sure and it's a proper cowflop I look," he said mournfully. He cursed Varatesh anew. The outlaw, a scrupulous thief, had stolen only the Gaul and his sword.

At that thought he yelled laughter; his lively spirits could not hold gloom for long. He leaped down from his horse, pulled his ragged tunic over his head, and scrambled out of baggy trousers. He threw them on his pony's back. Naked, blade in hand, he waited for the plainsmen.

"Now they'll have somewhat to think on," he said, still grinning widely. The breeze ran light fingers over his skin. He felt no strangeness, readying himself to fight bare. For as long as the bards recalled, there had been Celts who went naked into battle, wanting no more armor than their fighting rage. He roared out a challenge and strode toward the nomads.

The grin turned sour on his face as he saw the arrows nocked in their double-curved bows, but he was not shot out of hand. The Khamorth gaped at him—what sort of crazy man was this pale, copper-haired giant? They talked back and forth in their own language. One pointed at Viridovix' crotch and said something that was probably rude; they all laughed. Curiosity would not keep this pack at bay long; already the arrows were beginning to bear on him.

He took another long step forward; the plainsmen raised their bows menacingly. "Is it that any o' you lumping buggers is after having the Videssian?" he shouted, his whole stance a defial.

As it happened, none of them spoke the imperial tongue. But their colloquy after the question let him pick out their leader, a lean, hard-faced barbarian whose curly beard tumbled halfway down his chest. "You!" the Celt shouted, and pointed at the Khamorth with his sword.

The nomad gave back a stony glare. "Aye, you, you sheep-futtering spalpeen!" Viridovix said, repeating the insult in his vile Khamorth. As the plainsman slowly reddened, the Gaul gestured, daring him to come out face to face in single combat.

He knew the risk he ran. If the Khamorth was secure in his dominance over his comrades, he would just order them to kill the Celt and then ride on, unruffled. But if not . . . The plainsmen were watching their chief very closely. Silence stretched.

The nomad snarled something; he was angry, not afraid. He reminded Viridovix of a stoat as he slipped off his pony—his motions had a fluid, quick purposefulness that warned the Celt at once he would be no easy meat. The nomad's shamshir slid from its leather sheath, down which writhed polychrome beasts of prey in the contorted Khamorth style. He sidled forward, taking the Gaul's measure as he advanced.

Curved sword met straight one, and at the first pass Viridovix gave back a pace. Quick as a ferret indeed, he thought. He parried a cut at his upper thigh, then threw his arm back to avoid another. Smiling now, enjoying the game, the plainsman bored in to finish him, only to be brought up short by the Celt's straight-armed thrust—not for nothing had Viridovix spent years with the Romans. But his sword, unlike Scaurus', had no sharp stabbing point, and the nomad's shirt of thick sueded leather kept it from his vitals. The Khamorth grunted and stepped back himself.

Each having surprised the other, they fenced warily for a time, both looking for some flaw to use to advantage. Viridovix hissed as the very point of his foe's blade drew a thin line across his chest, then growled in disgust at his own clumsiness when he was pinked again, this time on the left arm. His ancestors, he decided, were great fools—fighting naked, there was just too much to guard. The nomad was unmarked. Viridovix was stronger than the Khamorth and had a longer reach, but in the long run speed would likely count for more.

"Well, then, we maun be keepin' it brief," he said to himself and leaped at the plainsman, raining blows from all directions, trying to overwhelm him by sheer dint of muscle. His opponent danced away, but his boot heel skidded in the trampled mud, and he had to block desperately as Viridovix' blade came slashing down. He turned the stroke, but his own sword went flying, to land point down in the muck.

"Ahh," said the Khamorth from their horses.

With their leader at his mercy, as he thought, Viridovix had no intention of killing him—there was no telling what the plainsmen might do after that. But when he stepped confidently forward to pluck the nomad's knife from his belt in token of victory, the Khamorth chopped at his wrist with the hard edge of his hand, and his own sword dropped from suddenly nerveless fingers.

"No you don't, you blackhearted omadhaun!" the Gaul shouted as his foe grabbed for the dagger. He grappled, wrapping the nomad in a bear hug. The Khamorth butted like a goat, crashing the top of his head up into Viridovix' chin. The Celt saw stars, spat blood from a bitten tongue, but his left hand kept its clamp on his opponent's right wrist. He punched the plainsman in the back of the neck again and again—not sporting, maybe, but effective. At last, with a soft little groan, the Khamorth slumped to the mud.

Sweat glistening all over his body, Viridovix retrieved his sword and faced the mounted nomads. They stared back, as uncertain as he was. "I've not killed him, you know," the Gaul said, gesturing toward their chief, "though he'll wish I had for the next few days." He still got blinding headaches from the clubbing Varatesh had given him.

He squatted beside the plainsman, who was just beginning to revive. The rest of the nomads hefted their bows in warning. "It's no harm I mean him," Viridovix said; they did not understand that any more than they had his previous speech, but relaxed somewhat when they saw him help their comrade sit. The barbarian moaned and held his head in his hands, still half unconscious.

One of the Khamorth tossed his bow to the man beside him, dismounted, and walked up to Viridovix, his empty hands spread in front of him. He pointed to the Celt. "You," he said. Viridovix nodded; that was a word he knew. The nomad pointed to the string of steppe ponies the Gaul was leading. "Where?" he asked. He repeated it several times, with gestures, until Viridovix understood.

"Oh, it's these beauties you'd be knowing about, is it? I stole 'em from Varatesh, indeed and I did," the Celt said, proud of his exploit, not just because it had let him escape, but for its own sake as well. In Gaul as among the nomads, stock raiding was a sport, in fact almost an art.

"Varatesh?" Three of the Khamorth spoke the name at the same time; it was all they had caught of what Viridovix had said. Even their stunned leader jerked his head up, but let it fall with a groan. They hurled excited questions at the Gaul. He waved his hands to show he could not follow.

The dismounted nomad shouted his friends down. "You and Varatesh?" he asked Viridovix with a wide, artificial smile, then repeated the question, this time with a fearsome scowl on his face.

"Aren't you the clever one, now?" the Celt exclaimed. "Me and Varatesh," he said, and screwed up his face into the most terrible grimace he could imagine, slashing the air with his sword for good measure. Only then did he realize the nomads might be friendly to the outlaw. Well, no help for it, and a lie had the same chance of getting him into trouble as the truth.

But he got the answer right. The plainsmen broke into smiles for the first time. The dismounted one offered his hand for Viridovix to clasp. He took it warily, shifting his sword to his own left hand, but the Khamorth's friendliness was genuine. "Yaramna," he said, tapping himself on the chest. He pointed to his companions on their horses: "Nerseh, Zamasp, Valash," then to his chief: "Rambehisht."

"More sneeze-names," Viridovix sighed, and gave his own. Then he had two inspirations, one on the other's heels. He retrieved Rambehisht's saber and gave it back to the plainsman. Rambehisht was hardly up to standing yet, let alone showing thanks, but his comrades murmured appreciatively.

Then the Gaul walked back to his horses, retrieving his trousers and tunic from the back of the one he had been riding. He used his sword to cut some of the animals' leads, and presented each of the plainsmen with half a dozen beasts. The string he kept for himself had been Varatesh's; in such matters he trusted the outlaw chief's judgment.

He could not have picked a better friendship-offering from all the world's wealth. All the Khamorth but Rambehisht crowded round Viridovix, wringing his hand, pounding his back, and shouting in their own language. Even their leader managed a wan smile, though it looked as if moving his face in any way hurt. Viridovix had tried to give him some of the best animals he had, not wanting to make a permanent enemy if he could help it.

With more gestures and the few words the Celt knew, Yaramna indicated they would soon be riding back to his clan-mates' tents. "The very thing I was hoping you'd say," Viridovix replied. Yaramna understood his grin and nod better. The Khamorth made a wry face at his failure to communicate; he finally made Viridovix realize that some men of his clan did speak Videssian. "We do the best we can, is all," the Celt shrugged. He had already made up his mind to learn the plains tongue.

He laughed suddenly. Yaramna and the other Khamorth looked at him, puzzled. "Nay, it's nought to do with you," Viridovix said. He had never thought a day would come when he started to sound like Scaurus.

Varatesh's hands were puffy and swollen still, the marks from the thongs Viridovix had used to bind him carved deep and red and angry on his wrists. If the Gaul had not missed the little knife he always carried in a slit pouch on the side of one boot, he would still be tied. But Khuraz had wriggled over through the mud to get it out and then, working back-to-back with Varatesh, managed to cut his bonds—and his wrists and hands, more than once.

The outlaw clenched painful fists and tried with little success to ignore the hoofbeats of agony in his skull. He did not like to lose at anything, least of all to a man who should have been his helpless prisoner. Nor did he relish the week or more of a hiking he and his comrades had ahead of them unless they could steal horses. And least of all he liked the prospect of explaining to Avshar how the fat partridge had slipped through his nets. Avshar's anger would be bad enough, but to have the wizard-prince think him nothing but a thick-witted barbarian after all . . . he bit his lip in humiliated fury.

When the wave of black anger passed, he found he could think again, despite the pain. He reached inside his tunic for the crystal charm Avshar had given him. Holding it carefully in clumsy fingers, he watched the orange mist suffuse its depths.

"East," he grunted in surprise, peering at the clear patch the orange would not enter. "Why is the worthless dog moving east?" He wondered if the crystal had gone awry, decided it had not. But when captured, the red-haired stranger had been heading west, and in company with an Arshaum. Varatesh tugged at his beard. He distrusted what he did not understand.

"Who gives a sheep turd where he's going?" Bikni asked from the ground. "Good riddance, says I," Akes echoed, also sitting in the wet dirt. Varatesh's three surviving followers were all sick and shaken from Viridovix' bludgeoning. So was their chief, but his will drove him, while they were content to lie like dogs in their own vomit.

"Avshar will care," he answered; battered as they were, his henchmen flinched. "And I care," he added. He had made sure to get the knife back from Khuraz and showed it now.

"It's a long walk back to our mates," Bikni whined. "No horses, no food, no arms—and you know what your bloody toy dagger is worth, Varatesh. Not much."

"So we walk. I will get home if I have to eat all three of you along the way. And," Varatesh said very softly, "I will be even."

When he strode north, the other three Khamorth, moaning and lurching and grumbling, followed, just as a lodestone will draw dead iron in its wake.

Prevails, Haravash's son, came galloping back toward the embassy party from his station at point. "Something up ahead," the young trooper called.

" 'Something,' " Agathias Psoes muttered, rolling his eyes. The underofficer shouted, "Well, what is it?"

At that point they both dropped into the Videssian-Khamorth lingua franca used at Prista, and Gorgidas lost the thread of their conversation. After days with no more than an occasional herd on the horizon, anything would be a relief, simply to break the boredom of travel. Arigh claimed the Shaum river, the great stream that marked the border between the Khamorth and his own Arshaum, was close. The Greek had no idea how he knew. One piece of the endless steppe was identical to the next.

"What are they jabbering about?" Goudeles said impatiently. The bureaucrat from the capital could no more follow the bastard frontier dialect than could Gorgidas.

"Your pardon, sir," Psoes said, returning to the formal imperial speech. "There's a nomad encampment in sight, but it doesn't seem right somehow."

"Where are their flocks?" Skylitzes asked. He turned to Prevails. "This place of many tents, where is?" He was at home in the jargon Videssians and nomads used together.

"You'll see it as soon as you top the next rise," the trooper answered, smiling as he switched styles so Goudeles, Arigh, and Gorgidas could understand.

Skylitzes' habitual frown deepened. "That close? Then where *are* their bloody flocks?" He looked this way and that, as if expecting them to pop out of thin air.

Just as Haravash's son had said, the encampment was visible when the embassy party rode to the top of the gentle swell of land ahead. Recalling the bright tents of the Yezda he had seen too often in Vaspurakan and western Videssos, Gorgidas was looking for a similar gaudy spectacle. He did not find one. The camp seemed somber and quiet—too quiet, the Greek thought. Even at this distance, he should have been able to see cookfires' smokes against the sky and horsemen riding from one tent to the next, if as no more than fly-sized specks.

"A plague?" he wondered aloud, remembering his Thucydides, and Athens wasted at the start of the Peloponnesian War. His scalp prickled. Plagues were beyond any doctor's power to cure—though who knew what wonders a healer-priest could work?

Goudeles, who should have known, said, "The expedient course, to my mind, would be to take a broad detour and avoid the risk." For some obscure reason, it comforted Gorgidas that the Videssian feared disease as much as he.

"No," Lankinos Skylitzes said. Goudeles started a protest, but the officer cut through it: "Plague might have killed the plainsmen's herds, or it might have left them untouched. It would not have made them run away."

"You're right, Empire man," Arigh said. "Plagues only make people run." His slanted eyes mocked Goudeles.

"As you wish, then," the bureaucrat answered, doing his best to show unconcern. "If the fever melts the marrow inside my bones, at least I know I shall be dying in brave company." Still an awkward horseman, he urged his mount into a trot and rode past Arigh toward the encampment. Looking less sly and smug than he had a few seconds before, the Arshaum followed, with the rest of the embassy behind them.

Skylitzes' logic only partly reassured Gorgidas; what if a pestilence had struck some time before, and the nomads' animals wandered off in the interim? But when his comrades exclaimed in alarm as three or four ravens and a great black vulture flapped into the sky on spying the oncoming horsemen, the Greek leaned back in his high-cantled saddle in relief. "When did death-birds become a glad sign?" Psoes asked.

"Now," Gorgidas replied, "for they mean there is no plague. Scavengers either shun corpses that die of pestilence or, eating of them, fall victim to the same disease." Unless, of course, the fearful part of his mind whispered, Thucydides had it wrong.

But as the embassy party came closer, it grew clear no pestilence had brought the camp low—or none save the pestilence of war. Wagons were gutted shells, some tilting drunkenly with one wheel burned away. Tent-frames held only charred remnants of the felts and leathers that had stretched across them. The tatters waved in the wind like a skeleton's fleshless fingers; death had ruled long here.

A few more carrion birds rose as the riders entered the murdered encampment—not many, for the best pickings were mostly gone. The stench of death was fading; more bone than rotted flesh leered sightlessly up at the newcomers, as if resenting life's intrusion into their unmoving world.

The bodies of men and women, children and beasts lay strewn about the tents. Here was a plainsman with the stub of his blade in his hand, the rest a few feet away. Broken, it was not worth looting. An axe had cleaved the man's skull. Close by him was what once had been a woman. Her corpse was naked, legs brutally spread wide. Enough flesh clung to her to let Gorgidas see her throat had been slashed.

With the legions and then in Videssos, the Greek had known more violent death than he liked to remember, but here he saw a thoroughness, a wantonness of destruction for its own sake that had made his flesh crawl. He looked from one of his companions to the next. Goudeles, who knew little of war, was pale and sickened, but he was not alone. Psoes' soldiers, Skylitzes, even Arigh, who seemed to pride himself for hardness—what they saw shocked them all.

No one seemed able to speak first, to break the silent spell of horror. At last Gorgidas said, as much to himself as to the rest, "So this is how they wage war, here on the plains."

"No!" That was Skylitzes, Agathias Psoes, and three of his troopers all together. Another raven cawed indignantly at the near-shout and waddled away, too stuffed to fly. Psoes, quicker-tongued than Skylitzes, went on, "This is not war, outlander. This is madness." To that Gorgidas could only dip his head in agreement.

"Even the Yezda are no worse than this," the Greek said, and then, his agile mind leaping: "And they, too, came off the steppe—"

"But it was in Makuran—Yezd, now—they learned to follow Skotos," Psoes said, and all the Videssians spat in rejection of the dark god. "The plainsfolk are heathen, aye, but fairly clean as heathens go." Gorgidas had heard otherwise in Videssos, but then Psoes was closer to the Khamorth than men who lived in the Empire proper. He wondered whether that intimacy made the underofficer more reliable or less. The Greek tossed his head. History was proving as maddeningly indefinite as medicine.

The brief moment of abstraction was shattered when his sharp eyes spied the symbol hacked into the shattered side of a cedar box. He had seen those paired side-by-side three-slash lightning bolts too often in the ruins of Videssian towns and monasteries to fail to recognize Skotos' mark now. He pointed. Psoes followed his finger, jerked as if stung; he, too, knew what the mark meant. He spat again, sketched Phos' sun-circle on his breast. Skylitzes, Goudeles, and the Videssian troopers followed suit.

Arigh and the Khamorth, though, were puzzled, wondering why their companions chose to excite themselves over a rude carving in the midst of far worse destruction.

"I would not have thought it," Skylitzes and Psoes said in the same breath. Skylitzes dismounted, squatted beside the profaned chest. The pious officer spat yet a third time, this time directly on the mark of Skotos. Pulling flint and steel from his belt, he cracked them together over a little pile of dead grass. The fire did not want to catch; the grass was still a bit damp from the recent rain.

"Varatesh's renegades. It must be," Psoes said over and over while Skylitzes fumed and his fire did not. The underofficer sounded badly shaken, as if searching for any explanation he could find for the butchery all around him. "Varatesh's renegades."

"Ah." Skylitzes had coaxed his blaze to life. He put the cedar box at one corner of it. As the flames fed on the tinder, they began licking the wood as well. Skotos' symbol charred, vanished. "Thus in the end light will cast out darkness forevermore," Skylitzes said. He and all the Videssians made the sun-sign again.

As the embassy party left the raped camp behind, Gorgidas wondered aloud, "Where are the nomads learning of Skotos?"

"A wicked god for wicked men," Goudeles replied sententiously. To the Greek, that sort of answer was worse than useless. Until this horror, the plainsmen had struck him as men like any others—barbarous, yes, but their natures a mix of good and bad. Nor was Skotos native to the steppe; neither the troopers of Khamorth blood nor Arigh had recognized his mark.

Yet in Yezd the incoming nomads took to the evil deity with savage enthusiasm—and, on reflection, that was not right either. Before the nomad conquest, Yezd had been Makuran, an imperial rival to Videssos, but a civilized one. And the Makurani had a religion of their own, following their beloved Four Prophets. Whence the cult of Skotos, then, and where the link between distant Yezd and an encampment still all too close?

Lankinos Skylitzes had no trouble making a connection. "Avshar travels with Varatesh," he said, as to a stupid child.

The explanation satisfied him completely, and Gorgidas flushed, angry he had not seen it himself. But the Yezda, the Greek remembered, were already entering Makuran half a century ago. A chill ran up his spine—what, then, did that make Avshar?

Valash came galloping back toward the horsemen from his station at point. He called something in his own language. The rest of the Khamorth shouted back, glee on their bearded faces. Even dour Rambehisht grudged a smile, though the look he gave Viridovix was unreadable.

"Camp at last, I'll be bound, and about time, too. Now we get down to it," the Gaul said. He had spent four days helping the nomads tend their cattle while Zamasp rode in to fetch herders to replace them. The work was thoroughly dull; cattle were stupid, and the more of them there were together, the stupider the lot of them seemed to get. Even so, he had not been able to enjoy the release mindless tasks sometimes bring, not with his life still held by nomads who were not his friends.

Yaramna rode close to the Celt. The plainsman was on one of the animals Viridovix had given him. "Good horse," he said, slapping its neck affectionately. Viridovix understood the second word from a Khamorth obscenity; the plainsman's action gave him the first.

"Glad you like him, indeed and I am," he answered, and Yaramna was as quick to grasp his meaning, if not the sense of each word.

The Khamorth camp sprawled across the plain, with tents and wagons set down wherever their owners chose. Viridovix guffawed. "Sure and Gaius Philippus'd spit blood, could he see these slovens. Not a proper Roman camp at all, at all. Welladay, free and easy always did suit me better."

And yet, his years with the legionaries made him frown when he saw—and smelled—piles of garbage by each tent, when men pissed wherever they happened to be when they felt the urge, as casually as the grazing horses that wandered through the camp. That was no way to make a proper encampment, either. His own Celts were a cleanly folk, if not so much given to order as the Romans.

The sight of a stranger in the camp, especially one as exotic as the Gaul, made the nomads shout and point. Some shied away, others came crowding in for a closer look. One toddler, bolder than some warriors, ran forward from a cookfire to touch the tip of the stranger's boot as he rode by. Viridovix, who was fond of children, brought his pony to a careful stop. "Boo!" he said. The tot's eyes went very round. He turned and fled. Viridovix laughed again; the child's trousers, otherwise like his elders', had no seat in them. "Foosh! Isn't that a sly way to do things, now!" he exclaimed.

The tot's mother snatched it up and spanked its bare rump, a use for the bottomless pants the Celt had not thought of. "Puir bairn!" he said, listening to its outraged howls.

Valash led his comrades and Viridovix to a round, dome-shaped tent larger and more splendid than any of the rest. A wolfskin on a pole in front of it marked it as the clan-chief's; so did the two sentries eating curded cheese by the entranceway. Beasts and demons in the writhing nomad style were embroidered on the green felt tent; similar scenes were painted on the frame of the wagon that would haul the disassembled tent across the steppe. Rank on rank of baggage carts stood beside it. The chests they carried were shiny with tallow to protect them from the rain.

All that was wealth only a chief enjoyed, the Gaul saw. Most of the tents were smaller and of thinner stuffs, light enough so one man could pitch them and so a horse could bear their fabric and the sticks that made up their framework along with a goodly part of the rest of a nomad family's goods. Where the clan leader had dozens of carts by his tent, most of the tribesmen made do with three or four—or sometimes none. Viridovix revised his estimate; the plains life might be free, but it was far from easy.

One of the sentries licked his horn spoon clean and glanced up at Valash's group. He pointed at Viridovix, asked something in the Khamorth tongue. They went back and forth for a few seconds. The Celt caught the name "Targitaus" repeated several times; he gathered it belonged to the chief. Then the sentry surprised him by saying in accented Videssian, "You wait. Targitaus, I tell him you here."

As the plainsman started to duck inside the tent, Viridovix called after him, "Your honor, is himself after having the Empire's speech?"

"Oh, yes. He go Prista many times—trade. Raid once, but long time gone." The sentry disappeared. Viridovix sighed in relief; at least he would not have to explain himself through an interpreter. Trying to use an interpreter for vigorous speech was like trying to yell underwater—noise came through, but not much sense.

The sentry came out. He spoke to the Khamorth, then to Viridovix: "You go in now. You see Targitaus, you bow, yes?"

"I will that," the Celt promised. He dismounted, as did the plainsmen. The second sentry took charge of their horses while the first one held the tent flap open; it faced west, away from the wind. Sensible, Viridovix thought, but the idea of passing a steppe winter in a tent made the red-gold hairs on his arms stand up as if he were a squirrel puffing out its fur against bad weather.

He dipped his head to pass through the entranceway, which was low even for the stocky Khamorth. When he raised his eyes again he whistled in admiration. The Romans, he discovered, were tyros when it came to tents. This one was big as any four legionary tents, a good dozen paces across. White fabric lined the inside, making it seem larger still by reflecting the light of the fire in the very center and butter-burning lamps all around the edge. Leather bags along the northern side held more of Targitaus' goods; the men of his household had hung their bows and swords above them. Cooking utensils, spindles, and other women's tools went along the southern edge of the tent. Between them, opposite the entrance, was a great bed of fleeces and felt-covered cushions. Not an inch of space was wasted, but the tent did not seem cramped.

That was a small miracle, for it was full of people, men on the northern side, women to the south. There was a low couch—the only bit of real furniture in the tent—between the cookfire and piled-up bedding. Remembering what the sentry had told him, Viridovix bowed to the man reclining on it, surely Targitaus himself.

"So. You take long enough to notice me," the nomad chief said to the Gaul; Valash and the rest of the Khamorth had already made their bows. Targitaus' Videssian was much more fluent than his sentry's but not as good as Varatesh's. He did not seem much angered. The Celt studied the man who would decide his fate. Targitaus was middle-aged and far from handsome—paunchy, scarred, with a big, hooked nose that had been well broken a long time ago and now pointed toward the right corner of his mouth. His full gray beard and the uncut hair under his fur cap gave him something of the look of a gone-to-seed dandelion. But in their nest of wrinkles, his brown eyes were disconcertingly keen. A noble himself in Gaul, Viridovix knew a leader when he saw one.

"You look like an 'Alugh," Targitaus remarked; with his guttural accent it took the Gaul a moment to recognize "Haloga." The Khamorth went on, "Come round the fire so I get a better see at you." Accompanied by Rambehisht, Yaramna, and the others, Viridovix picked his way through the men's side of the tent. Nomads sitting on pillows or round cloths leaned aside to let them pass.

"Big man," Targitaus said when the Celt stood before him. "Why you so big? You wear out any horse you ride."

"Aye, well, so long as it's not the lassies complaining," Viridovix murmured. Targitaus blinked, then chuckled. The Gaul smiled to himself; he had gauged his man aright.

The men on the ground to the right of the chief's couch translated his words and the Celt's so the plainsmen could understand. He was the first smooth-faced Khamorth Viridovix had seen; his cheeks were pink and shiny in the firelight. His voice was between tenor and contralto. He wore a robe that his corpulent frame stretched tight.

Seeing the Celt's glance, Targitaus said, "This Lipoxais. He is *enaree* of clan."

"'Shaman,' you would say in Videssian," Lipoxais added, his command of the imperial speech near perfect. The melting look he gave Viridovix made the Gaul wonder whether the *enaree* was a eunuch, as he had first thought, or simply effeminate.

"Shaman, yes," Targitaus nodded impatiently. "Not to talk of words now." He measured Viridovix up and down, his eyes flicking to the longsword at the Celt's hip. "You tell me your story, hey, then we see what words need saying."

"That I will," Viridovix said, and began at the point of his kidnaping.

The chief stopped him. "No, wait. What you doing Pardraya in first place? You no Empire man, no Khamorth, no Arshaum either—that plain enough, by wind spirits!" His laugh had a wheeze in it.

With a sinking feeling, Viridovix told the truth. As Lipoxais translated, an angry muttering rose from the plainsmen round the fire. "You go to lead Arshaum through Pardraya and you want my thanks and help?" Targitaus growled. He touched his saber, as if to remind himself where it was.

"And why not? I deserve the both of 'em." Targitaus stared; Lipoxais raised a plucked eyebrow. Outface the lot of them, Viridovix told himself; if they see you yielding so much as a digit, it's all up. He stood straighter, looking down his long nose at the Khamorth chief. "The more o' the Arshaum are after fighting in Videssos, the fewer to tangle with you. Is it not so?"

Targitaus scratched his chin. Lipoxais' smooth, high voice finished rendering the Gaul's words into the plains tongue. Viridovix did not dare look around to see how the nomads were taking what he said, but the hostile rumbling died away. "All right. You go on," Targitaus said at last.

The hurdle leaped, Viridovix warmed to his tale and won his listeners to him when they understood he and Varatesh were foes. "The brother-slayer, eh?" Targitaus said, and spat in the dirt in front of his couch. "Few years gone by, he try to join clan. His story even worse than yours—he not just leave things out, he tell lies, too." He looked Viridovix full in the face, and the Celt could not help flushing. "Go on," Targitaus said. "What next?"

Viridovix started to warn the nomads of Avshar, but they did not know the wizard-prince's name and so did not fear him. The gods grant they don't find out, the Gaul thought, and went on to tell of his escape from Varatesh. That brought shouts from the plainsmen as it was interpreted, and a "Not bad," from Targitaus. Viridovix grinned; he suspected the Khamorth was short with praise.

"In the dark and all I rode east instead of west and came on your lads here," the Celt finished. "Belike you'd sooner have the tale o' that from them."

Interrupting each other from time to time, the nomads told their side of the meeting with Viridovix. Early on, Targitaus' jaw fell. "Naked?" he said to the Gaul.

"It's a way my people have betimes."

"Could be painful," was all the chief said. His men went on to describe the fight with Rambehisht. Targitaus snapped a question at the stern-featured nomad. "What do you have to say for yourself, losing to a naked man?" Lipoxais translated.

The Gaul tensed. Rambehisht was fairly important in the clan; if he shouted denunciations now, it might not be pleasant. But he answered his chief with a shrug and a short phrase. "He beat me," Lipoxais rendered tersely. Rambehisht added another, slightly longer, sentence: "My head still hurts—what more can I say?"

"So." After that single syllable, Targitaus was quiet for a long time. At last the Khamorth chief turned to Viridovix. "Well, outlander, you are a fighter if nothing else. You have gall, to meet a man like that."

"Have gall? Indeed and I am one."

"So," the plainsman repeated, scratching his head. "What next?"

"If I were after asking you for an escort to the Arshaum country, you'd have my head for fair, I'll wager," Viridovix said. He did not need the nomads' growls as Lipoxais translated; he had put out the idea to let it be knocked down and make his real proposal the more attractive.

“How’s this, then, your honor? It’s a nasty neighbor you have in this kern of a Varatesh, the which ye can hardly say nay to. Now you’ve a grudge against him, and I’ve one, too, the gods know—” No Videssians were here to shout “Heresy!” at that. “—and like enough some o’ your other clans hereabouts, too. Would it not be a fine thing to put the boot to him once for all, aye, and the mangy curs as run with him?” And Avshar, too, he thought, but did not name him again.

Guttural mumbles round the fire as the listening nomads considered. “Grudge?” Targitaus said softly. “Oh my yes, grudge.” He leaped to his feet, shouted something in the plains speech. “Does it please you, brothers?” Lipoxais gave the words to Viridovix. The roar that came back could only be “Aye!” A meat-eater’s smile on his face, Valash slapped the Gaul on the back.

But Targitaus, as leader, had learned caution. *“Enaree!”* he said, and Lipoxais stood beside him. “Take your omens, say if this will be good or bad for clan.”

Lipoxais bowed his head and put both hands over his face in token of obedience. Then he turned to Viridovix, saying quietly, “Come round here behind me and put your hands on my shoulders.” The *enaree*’s flesh was very warm and almost as soft as a feather cushion.

From inside his robe Lipoxais drew a piece of smooth white bark two fingers wide and about as long as his arm. He cut it into three equal lengths, wrapped it loosely round his hands. Viridovix felt him suddenly go rigid; his head snapped back, as a man’s will in the throes of lockjaw. The Celt could look down at the *enaree*’s face. His mouth was clenched shut, his eyes open and staring, but they did not see Viridovix. Lipoxais’ hands moved as if they had a will of their own, twisting and untwisting the lengths of bark round his fingers.

The mantic fit went on and on. Viridovix had no idea how long it should last, but saw from the worry growing in Targitaus’ eyes that this was not normal. He wondered whether he should shake Lipoxais out of his trance, but hesitated, afraid to interfere with a magic he did not understand.

The *enaree* returned to himself about when Viridovix was making up his mind to shake him whether it ruined the charm or not. Sweat dripped from his face; his robe was wet under the Gaul’s hands. He staggered, righted himself with the air of someone getting his land legs after a long time at sea. This time no longing was on his face when he looked at Viridovix, only awe and a little fear. "There is strong magic around you," he said, "your own and others." He shook his head, as if to clear it.

Targitaus barked something at Lipoxais, who answered at some length before turning back to Celt. "I could see little," he explained, "through so much sorcery, and that little was blurred: fifty eyes, a doorway in the mountains, and two swords. Whether these are signs of good or ill I do not know."

Plainly unhappy at not learning more, Targitaus reflected, his chin in his hand. At last he straightened, stepping forward to clasp Viridovix' hand. "As much chance for good as for bad," he said, "and Varatesh's ears need trimming—down to the neck, I think." He sounded jovial, but the Gaul thought he would not be a good enemy to have.

"So," the Khamorth chieftain went on; he seemed to use the word as a pause to gather his thoughts. "You swear oath with us, yes?"

"Whatever pleases your honor," Viridovix said at once.

"Good." Targitaus switched to the plains tongue. A young man who had his eyes and his prominent nose—the later unkinked—brought a large earthenware bowl and a full skin of kavass. No ordinary nomad brew was this, but dark, strong, and heady, with a rich aroma like ale's. "Karakavass—black kavass," Targitaus said, pouring it into the bowl. "The lords' drink."

But he did not drink of it yet; instead, he pulled a couple of arrows from a quiver and put them point-down in the bowl, then followed them with his shamshir. "Your sword, too," he said to Viridovix. The Celt drew it and put as much of the blade as would fit—a bit more than half—into the bowl. Targitaus nodded, then unsheathed his dagger and took Viridovix' hand. "Do not flinch," he warned, and made a small cut on the Celt's forefinger. Viridovix' blood dripped into the bowl. "Now you me," Targitaus said, giving him the knife. He might have been carved from stone as the Gaul cut him. Their bloods mingled now—a strong magic, Viridovix thought approvingly.

Lipoxais began a chanted prayer; the gutturals of the Khamorth language sounded strange in his high voice. From time to time Targitaus spoke in response. As the *enaree* prayed on, Targitaus said to Viridovix,

"Swear by your powers to act always as a brother to this clan and never to betray it or any man of it."

The Gaul paused only a moment, to think which of his gods would best hear his oath. "By Epona and Teutates I swear it," he said loudly. Horse-goddess and war-god—what better powers to call on with the nomads? As he spoke their names, the druids' marks on his enchanted blade glowed golden. Lipoxais' eyes were closed, but Targitaus saw.

"Magics of your own, yes," he muttered, staring at his new-sworn ally.

When Lipoxais' chant was done, the Khamorth chief took his weapons from the bowl. Viridovix did the same, drying his sword on his shirttail before putting it back in its sheath. Targitaus stooped, carefully lifted the bowl to his lips. He drank, then handed it to the Celt. "We share blood, we share fate," he said, with the air of one translating a proverb. Viridovix drank, too; the karakavass was mouth-filling, smooth on his tongue as fine wine, warm and comforting in his belly.

Once the Gaul's drinking sealed him to them, Targitaus' lieutenants rose from their sitting-cloths and came up to share the bowl. Servants rolled the cloths into tight cylinders so not a crumb of precious food would be spilled.

"You are one with us now," Targitaus said, punctuating the remark with a belch. "More kavass!" he called, and new skins were broached: not the dark, earthy brew in the ceremonial bowl, but strong enough. Viridovix drank deep, passed the skin to Valash next to him. Another came his way a moment later, then another. His ears began to buzz.

Targitaus' wolfskin cap kept wanting to slide down over the chief's left eye. He pushed it back, looked owlishly at Viridovix. "You one with us," he said again, his accent rougher than it had been a few minutes before. "You should be glad; it is the right of a man. Do you see a wench who pleases you?"

"Well, fry me for a sausage!" the Gaul exclaimed. "I never looked." That he had paid no attention to the women in the tent was a measure of his anxiety.

Now he made amends for the lapse. There were times when loneliness stabbed like a knife, remembering the pale Celtic women with hair sun-colored or red to match his own. But he was not one to live in the past for long and took his chances where he found them. He grinned, thinking of Komitta Rhangavve.

It was not that he expected any such high-strung beauties in Targitaus' tent. Like the Vaspurakaners, the Khamorth were heavier-featured than the Videssians. The faces of their men often held great character, but the women tended to have a stern, forbidding aspect to them. Their clothes did not soften their appearance, either; they wore trousers, tunics, and cloaks identical in cut to those of the plainsmen, and of the same furs and leathers. In place of the men's inevitable fur caps, though, they wore conical headdresses of silk, ornamented with bright stones, and topped by crests of iridescent feathers from ducks and pheasants. That helped, but not enough.

Worse still, Viridovix thought as his eye roved, a good many of the women on the southern side of the tent had to be the wives of Targitaus' officers: chunky, far from young, and some of them looking as used to command as the nomad chief. He had had enough of that last from Komitta. They were surveying him, too, with a disconcerting frankness; he was as glad he could not understand their comments.

Then he paused. Not far from Targitaus' couch was a girl whose strong features, as with Nevrat Sviodo, had their own kind of beauty. It was her eyes, the Celt decided—they seemed to smile even when the rest of her face was still. She met his glance as readily as did the older women by her, but without their coarse near-mockery. "That's a likely-looking lass," he said to Targitaus.

The Khamorth's thick eyebrows went up like signal flags. "Glad you think so," he said dryly, "but pick again, a serving-girl, if you please. That is Seirem, my daughter."

"Och, begging your pardon I am," Viridovix said, reddening. He was very much aware of his fragile place here. "How is it I'm to tell the wenches from some laird's lady?"

"By the bughtaq, of course," Targitaus answered. When he saw the Gaul did not know the word, he gestured to show he meant the Khamorth women's headdress. Viridovix nodded, chiding himself for not noticing that detail. Along with jade and polished opals, Videssian goldpieces ornamented Seirem's bughtaq; she was plainly no slavey.

The Celt's gaze settled on a woman of perhaps twenty-five, without

Seirem's lively face, but attractive enough and nicely rounded. Except for a few reddish stones and a very small piece of jade, her headdress was plain. "She'll do me, an it suit you," he said.

"Who?" Targitaus put down the skin of kavass from which he had been slurping. "Oh, Azarmi. Aye, why not? She serves my wife Borane."

Viridovix waved her over to him. One of the richly adorned women, a particularly heavy-set one, said something that set all her companions rolling in helpless mirth. Azarmi shook her head, which only made the old women laugh harder.

The Gaul offered her kavass from the skin Targitaus had laid aside. With no language in common, it was hard to put her at ease. She did not pull away when he touched her, but did not warm to him either.

So it proved later, too, when the bedding was spread round the banked fire. She was compliant and did not seem resentful, but he could not excite her. Piqued and disappointed, he thought hungrily of Seirem asleep a few feet away until he drifted off himself.

"My father has it from his grandfather," Arigh said, "that when the Arshaum first saw the Shaum, they took it for an arm of the sea."

"I believe it," Gorgidas said, looking down at the slate-blue river flowing majestically southwest toward the distant Mylasa Sea. He shaded his eyes; the reflection of the afternoon sun sparkled dazzlingly bright. He tried to guess how wide the river was, and failed—a mile and a half? Two miles? Whatever the answer, the Shaum made the Kouphis, the Arandos, any stream Gorgidas had seen in Gaul or Italy or Greece, into a pygmy by comparison.

He wiped his forehead with the back of his hand, felt grit rasp his skin. Goudeles, still foppish even in plains costume, brushed a bit of dry grass from his sleeve. "As if reaching this stream was not trial enough, however shall we cross it?" he asked no one in particular.

A good question, the Greek thought. The nearest ford would be hundreds of miles north. It would take a demigod to bridge the Shaum, and who on the wood-scarce steppe knew anything of boatbuilding?

Skylitzes bared his teeth in a smile. "How well do you swim, Pikridios?"

"Over that distance? At least as well as you, by Phos."

"The horses are better than either of you," Arigh said. "Come on." He led them down to the bank of the Shaum, dismounted and stripped, then climbed back on his horse. The rest of the embassy party did likewise. Arigh directed, "Ride your lead beast out until he has to swim, then slide off and keep a good grip round his neck. I'll go last; here, Psoes, you lead my string with yours. I'll take just the one animal and make sure nobody else's horses decide to stay on land." He drew his saber, tested the point with his thumb.

Gorgidas hefted the oiled leather sack in which he kept his precious manuscript. Catching the Arshaum's eye, he said, "I'll hold on with one hand—this has to stay dry." The nomad shrugged; if the Greek cared to take chances for the sake of some scratchings, that was his affair.

Surveying Goudeles' pudgy form, Lankinos Skylitzes said, "You'll float better than I do, anyhow, pen-pusher." Goudeles sniffed.

Gorgidas twitched the reins and urged his mount forward. It tried to swerve when it realized he wanted it to go in the river, but he kicked it in the ribs and kept it on a straight course. It swung its head back resentfully. He booted it again. Like a bather testing the water with one toe, it stepped daintily in, then paused once more. *"Ithi!"* the exasperated Greek shouted in his own tongue. "Go on!" As he swung a foot free of the stirrups for another kick, the horse did.

It gave a frightened snort when its hooves no longer touched ground, but then struck out strongly for the far bank. Seen from only a few inches above the water, that seemed impossibly far away. Back on the eastern bank, a trooper's remount balked at entering the Shaum. Arigh prodded it with his sword. It neighed shrilly and bolted in, dragging the two beasts behind it along willy-nilly.

The Shaum's current was not as strong as Gorgidas had expected. It pulled the swimming horses and their masters south somewhat, making the journey across the river longer than it would have been, but did not really hamper their swim. The water was cool and very clear. The Greek could look down to the rocks and river plants on the bottom. About halfway through the crossing he started in alarm—the dun-colored fish rooting about on the bottom was longer from nose to wickedly forked tail than his horse was. "Shark!" he shouted.

"Nay, no sharks in the Shaum," Skylitzes reassured him. "They call it a mourzoulin hereabouts; the Videssian name is sturgeon."

"I don't care what they call it," the Greek said, frightened out of curiosity. "Does it bite?"

"No, it only has a little toothless sucker-mouth for worms and such."

"Salted, the eggs are very fine," Goudeles said with relish. "A rare delicacy."

"The flesh is good smoked," Prevails Haravash's son added. "And from the swim bladder we make—what is the word for letting some light through?"

"Translucent," Goudeles supplied.

"Thank you, sir. Yes, we make translucent windows to fit into tent panels."

"And if it had a song, I suppose you'd use that, too," Gorgidas said darkly. The ugly brute still looked dangerous.

Prevails took the Greek seriously. "On the plains we use everything. There is too little to waste." Gorgidas only grunted, keeping an eye on the sturgeon, or mourzoulin, or whatever it was. It paid him no attention. After a while, he could not see it any more.

By the time the western bank drew near, his arms were exhausted from holding the mouth of his leather bag above water, even though he had taken to switching it from one to the other. That also meant his grip on his horse was not what it should have been. The shore was only about thirty yards away when he and the animal parted company. He thrashed frantically—and felt his feet scrape bottom; the steppe pony was still too short to touch. Now it was his turn to help his horse. Sighing with relief, he did so, and led the beast and his remounts up onto the land of Shaumkhiil. Save that the river was behind him, it seemed no different from Pardraya to the east.

Skylitzes splashed ashore a few feet away from him. He reached into the bag and dug out a stylus. "How do you spell 'mourzoulin'?" he demanded. Looking resigned, Skylitzes told him.

Robes swirling about him, Avshar paced his tent like a caged panther. His great height and long strides made it seem cramped and tiny, built for a race of dwarfs. The sorcerer lashed out with a booted foot. A cushion flew across the tent, rebounded from the tight-stretched felt of the wall, and an image of a black-corseleted warrior hurling a brace of three-spiked thunderbolts thumped to the ground.

The wizard-prince swung round on Varatesh. "Incompetent!" he snarled. "Lackwitted, poxy maggot! You puling, milk-livered pile of festering dung, cutting your filthy heart out would be revenge too small for your botchery!"

They were alone; even in his rage, Avshar knew better than to revile the outlaw chief in front of his men. The wizard's contempt, the lash of his words, burned like fire. Varatesh bowed his head. More than anything else, he wanted the regard of this man, and bore abuse for which he would have killed any other.

But he reckoned himself slave to no one and said, "I was not the only one to make mistakes on this venture. The man you sent me after was not the one I found. He—"

Avshar dealt him a tremendous backhand buffet that stretched him in the dirt of the tent floor. He rose tasting blood, his head ringing. He slid into fighter's crouch. He had loved Kodoman, too, and Kodoman also stuck first . . . "Who are you, to use me so?" he whispered, tears stinging his eyes.

Avshar laughed, a laugh as black as the mail his icon showed. He swept aside the mantlings that always hid his face. "Well, worm," he said, "who am I?"

Varatesh whimpered and fell to his knees.

VII

"Here," Thekla Zonara said, handing a servant a silver candlestick. "This will fit in the load you're packing." When the man held it in confusion, she took it from him and stowed it away. "And this," she added, edging in beside it a gilded silver plate decorated with a hunting scene in low relief.

"We must save these, too," her sister-in-law Erythro cried, running up with an armload of brightly glazed earthenware cups. "They're too lovely to be left for the Namdaleni."

"Merciful Phos!" Sittas Zonaras said. "Why not pack up the pigs' swill troughs while you're about it? That's worthless junk; the islanders are welcome to it. There's little enough time for this move as is. Don't waste it worrying over excess baggage." He shook his head in mock annoyance.

"And don't you waste it bickering with Erythro," his daughter Ypatia told him.

The nobleman sighed and turned to Scaurus. "Women should never be allowed to be sensible, don't you think, outlander?"

Still holding her cups, Erythro faced up to the Roman like a pugnacious sparrow. "Why ask him? What does he know of sensible? He brought the Namdaleni down on us in the first place. Were it not for him, we'd still be snug here instead of trekking into the hills like so many Khamorth following their herds."

"Enough!" Sittas said; now his irritation was real. "Were it not for him, I'd be dead in the woods or captive with all the estate for ransom. Had you forgotten that?"

"Well, yes, I had," Erythro said, not a bit abashed. "This move has me all in a frenzy, and no wonder, too!" She bent and piled the cups on top of the candlestick and plate. Her brother rolled his eyes and looked pointedly at Ypatia, who pretended not to notice.

Though at first Marcus had thought Erythro's comment monumentally unfair, on reflection he was not so sure. Plenty of nobles in the westlands were coming to terms with the Namdaleni and the "Emperor" Mertikes. "You might have been able to do the same, Sittas, were it not for my men being here," the tribune finished. Erythro smirked.

"Don't encourage her," Zonaras said. He went on, "Me, make common cause with bandits and heretics? I'd sooner see this villa burned over my head than bend the knee to Drax and his straw man. Nay, I'm glad to be with you."

The villa might burn regardless, the tribune thought unhappily. For all their entrenching, for all the manpower Pakhymer and his Khatrishers added, if Drax threw the whole weight of his army against the legionaries, they would be crushed. And that full weight was coming; Pakhymer's scouts said the Namdalener column would cross the Arandos tomorrow. So it was retreat again, this time south into the hills.

Leaving the Zonarai still arguing over what was to go and what had to be left behind, Scaurus went outside. Lowing cattle and milling sheep streamed past; the herdsmen needed no urging to get their flocks out of the oncoming army's way. "Come on, keep them moving!" the chief herder was shouting. "No, Stotzas, don't let them drink now. Time enough for that later, when everyone's passed through."

Gaius Philippus, who already had the Romans ready to travel, watched the herder with respect. "He'd make a good officer," he said to the tribune.

Marcus had an inspiration. "Well, why not make him one, then? Who better to lead your irregulars?"

The senior centurion stared. "By the gods, sir, that's a triple six!" The two Romans smiled at each other briefly. In Videssian dice, sixes were the worst throw, not the best—the sort of little thing that left the legionaries permanently alien here. "You there!" Gaius Philippus called.

"You want me?" the herder chief said without turning his head. "Wait a bit." He deftly disentangled two flocks, sent them up separate passes so they would not compete for fodder. That done, he walked over to the Romans, nodded in the same respectful but unservile way he had to Zonaras. "Do something for you?"

"Yes, ah—" Marcus paused, not knowing his name.

"Tarasikodissa Simokattes," he said. Seeing the Romans flinch, he relented. "They call me Ras."

"And a good thing, too," Gaius Philippus muttered, but in Latin.

Scaurus felt much the same, but went on, "When you first saw us, you spoke of raising the countryside." Ras nodded again. "You know weapons, then?"

"Aye, somewhat. Bow, spear, axe. I'm no great shakes with a sword in my hand—not enough practice."

"Like to fight, do you?" Gaius Philippus asked.

"No." The answer was quick and definite.

The senior centurion beamed, the expression sitting oddly on his usually dour face. "You were right, Scaurus. I can use this one." He turned back to Simokattes. "How would you like to make a lot of Namdaleni wish they'd never been born?"

Ras studied him, his face as elaborately guileless as Gaius Philippus'. The two of them, bearded Videssian herdsman and Roman veteran, had a good deal in common, Marcus thought. But the senior centurion's bait was too tasty not to be nibbled. "Tell me more," Simokattes said.

Gaius Philippus smiled.

The senior centurion was less happy two mornings later, when he looked back on Zonaras' villa as the legionaries tramped up into the hills. "We should have torched the place," he said to Marcus. "It'll make Drax a lovely strong point."

"I know," the tribune said, "but if we did burn it, what would the highland nobles think they had to gain by siding with us? If we don't leave what they have unharmed, they'll see us as just another set of barbarians, bad as the Namdaleni."

"Maybe so," Gaius Philippus said, "but they don't have much use for us if they see us as weak, either." Scaurus grunted; there was too much truth in that for comfort. Would antagonizing Zonaras by destroying the villa do more harm than leaving Drax a base? He wished for a surer sense of when tactics had to override strategy.

"It's something you learn by doing it wrong every so often at first," Gaius Philippus said when he complained about that. The veteran added,

"Of course, if your mistake is too big, it kills you, and you don't learn much after that."

"You always relieve my mind," Marcus said dryly. He saw a stir of motion to the north, at the head of the valley that sheltered Zonaras' villa. "We pulled out none too soon—here come the islanders. Think the rear guard will do any good?"

"Under young Tarasios? Not a chance." The senior centurion sounded regretful but certain. He called to a trooper, "You there, Florus—run fetch that herder fellow Ras back here. He ought to see this." The Roman saluted and trotted off.

The hectic flush of fever in his face, Tarasios Zonaras had refused to join the retreat to the hills. "No," he had said in the bubbling whisper that was all he had left of his voice, "here I stand. I have little enough time anyway. Fighting for my land is a faster and better end than I looked for." His kinsfolk had not been able to sway him, and Scaurus had not tried; his Stoic training taught that a man could decide when to let go of life. About a score of his father's troopers had chosen to stand with him.

Ras Simokattes came back with the Roman. "What is it, outlander?"

"Just watch," Gaius Philippus said.

The men of the Duchy, sensible veterans, fanned out into a skirmish line as they entered the valley, taking no chances on an ambush. Their advance quickened as they saw the abandoned legionary camp, and looked up into the hills and spied their opponents' withdrawing column.

They were close to the villa when Tarasios and his followers burst from the cover of a stand of apple trees and charged, sabers gleaming as they spurred their horses forward. In the distance everything was tiny and silent and perfect, a realistic painting that somehow moved. An islander toppled from his saddle, then another. But the Namdaleni, after a panicky moment, fought back. More and more knights rode up, to ring Tarasios' band with steel.

Simokattes' glance flicked to the young Zonaras' kin. His face carved by harsh lines of grief, Sittas watched the unequal fight; now and again his hands twitched on his horse's reins as he pantomimed a blow that should be struck. His wife and daughter wordlessly embraced, while Erythro wept. The herder-chief, his own strong rough hands curling into fists, gave his attention back to the battle below. It was already almost over.

"What do you see?" Gaius Philippus asked him.

"A brave man," Simokattes replied quietly.

"Aye, maybe so, but a stupid one regardless." Simokattes turned in anger, but the senior centurion went on as earnestly as Marcus had ever heard him. "Think on it, Ras, and think well. Soon enough it'll be you leading men against the islanders, and not ones with the skill or arms Tarasios had behind him. What did he do? He broke cover instead of fighting from it, and he attacked a great many men with a few instead of the other way round. Brave? What good was his bravery to him—or to the troopers who followed him?" In the valley, no Videssians were still horsed. "The task is to hurt the enemy, not your own men."

The chief herdsman was silent for some time. At last he said, "You're a hard man, Roman."

"That's as may be, but I've been at this filthy trade thirty-odd years now and I know what's so. This is what you signed on for, you and your talk of raising the countryside. If you haven't the stomach for it, go back to your cows."

Simokattes swung at him, a blow born largely of frustration. With unhurried quickness, Gaius Philippus ducked and stepped forward, at the same time seizing the herder's arm and twisting it behind his back until he gasped with pain. The senior centurion let him go at once, slapped him on the shoulder. "What you think of me is your affair, but listen to me. It'll save your neck one day." Simokattes gave a brusque nod and walked away.

"He'll do," Gaius Philippus said, watching his back.

"Did you have to be so hard on him?" the tribune asked.

"I think so. Amateurs come to this business with all sorts of stupid ideas."

Marcus' own bitter knowledge, gained the past three years, made him add, "Precious little room for gallantry, is there?"

"That for gallantry." The senior centurion spat in the dust. "It wasn't Achilles who took Troy." Scaurus stared; if Gaius Philippus, with hardly a letter to his name, could draw lessons from Homer, he was the prince of poets indeed!

Judging from what Drax had done in the past, the tribune thought he would try to seal off the passes leading south, but not do any serious campaigning in the hills south of the Arandos. But the great count, perhaps seeing final victory just ahead of him, showed more aggressiveness than Scaurus expected of him. Not only did quick motte-and-bailey forts got up in well-placed spots at valley mouths and on hillsides, but Namdalener patrols slashed into the hill country, looting and burning right up to the legionaries' heels.

Marcus did not need Sittas Zonaras' reproachful gaze to tell him he had to stop that quickly, if he could. If the islanders could raid where they chose, what use for the Videssians to back the legionaries against them? He thought for a while, then went to see Laon Pakhymer.

The Khatrisher was firing grapes at a miniature motte-and-bailey made of dirt and sticks. "I wish it were that easy," Scaurus said; Pakhymer's toy catapult was doing a good job of destruction.

"It's simpler when they don't shoot back," Pakhymer agreed, taking careful aim. He touched the trigger; the little catapult bucked. A bit of wood flew from the castle on the bailey. Marcus waited with increasing impatience as the Khatrisher reloaded. At last Pakhymer looked up, a sly smile on his pockmarked face. "Ready to burst yet?"

The tribune had to laugh at his impudence. "Not quite."

"I was afraid you'd say that. You expect my lads to earn what they got at Kyzikos, then? Aye, do you; I can see it in your eyes. What is it this time?"

Marcus told him. He tugged at his unkempt beard as he considered. "Yes, that could happen, if we have a proper guide riding with us."

"I'll see to it Simokattes gets you one."

"All right, you're on. Three days from now, you said?" At Scaurus' nod, the Khatrisher remarked, "The problem, as I see it, will be not biting off too big a chunk."

"Exactly." As usual, the tribune thought, Pakhymer had a keen sense of what was required—and not much inclination to use it. The Khatrisher examined another grape. He shook his head sadly. "Not round enough," he said, and ate it. "Care for one?" He laughed when Marcus pretended not to hear.

Scaurus thought the fat green bush he was crouching behind was wild parsley. Whatever it was, its little pale yellow flowers were pungent enough to make his eyes water. He bit down hard on his upper lip to keep from sneezing. Nothing was happening yet, but if he started he did not think he could stop, and it would be soon now.

Half a dozen Khatrishers entered the valley, spurring their little ponies for all they were worth. Now and again one would turn to fire at the men of the Duchy close behind.

The Namdalener leader was a stocky youngster named Grus. Though young, he had learned caution; he ordered his double squadron to halt and craned his neck to study the canyon walls. But Ras Simokattes and Gaius Philippus had set their trap well. Though Junius Blaesus' maniple lay in wait for the islanders to advance, no telltale glint of sun off steel, no untoward motion gave them away. Grus whooped and waved his men on.

Hand clutching sword, Marcus waited until all the Namdaleni, even the rear guard, had entered the valley. He nodded to the buccinator beside him. The cornet blared, a single long note. With cries of "Gavras!" legionaries leaped from behind shrubs and tree trunks and stands of brush and dashed down the steep-sloping canyon walls at the islanders.

The two knights of the rear guard brutally jerked their horses round and started up the valley again—not cowardice but sense, to bring help to their mates. A *pilum* thudded into the belly of one beast. It crashed to the ground, screaming, and rolled over its rider. The other horseman was nearly at the mouth of the canyon when three legionaries pulled him out of the saddle.

Grus, cursing, tried to pull his men into a circle. But one Roman came rushing down toward them, far ahead of his comrades. It was Titus Pullo; he bellowed, "Come on, Vorenus! We'll see which of us is the better man!" Another legionary bolted out of the pack; Lucius Vorenus was pounding after his rival and swearing at the top of his lungs.

Pullo cast his *pilum* at very long range, but his throw was true; a Namdalener on the fringe of Grus' milling circle took the javelin in his thigh. He screamed and fell from his horse. Pullo darted forward to finish him off and strip his corpse, but a pair of islanders covered their wounded comrade. One of them rammed his own heavy lance clean through the thick wood and leather of the Roman's *scutum*. The iron point caught the buckle of his sword belt and twisted it to one side; when he reached for the *gladius* he grabbed only air. The Namdaleni rained sword strokes on him. He went over on his back to get the most use from his fouled shield.

Then Lucius Vorenus, in a berserk fury Viridovix might have envied, was on the islanders, screaming, "Get off him, you pimps, you dogs, you bleeding vultures! He's a fig-sucker, but even a fig-sucking Roman's worth the lot of you!" He killed the Namdalener who had thrust his spear at Pullo, beating the man's light kite-shaped shield aside with his own heavier one and then stabbing him in the side at the join in his shirt and mail.

The second islander and one of his countrymen, perhaps thinking Pullo dead and out of the fight, turned all their attention to Vorenus, who was hard-pressed to defend himself. But Pullo was far from dead. Having finally managed to draw his sword, he cast aside his worthless *scutum,* scrambled to his feet, and jabbed the *gladius* into a horse's rump. Blood spurting, the beast bucketed away, its rider clinging to its neck and trying in vain to bring it under control.

"Bastard!" Vorenus panted.

"You're the whore's get, not me!" Pullo retorted. They fought back-to-back, raving at each other all the while. By then the rest of the Romans were reaching the Namdaleni, and the pressure on the two of them eased.

Trapped, outnumbered, pelted by javelins, the islanders began surrendering one after the other. But Grus, mortified at falling into the ambush, came rushing at Marcus on foot; his horse was down, hamstrung by a *gladius*. "Yield yourself!" the Roman called.

"To the ice with you!" Grus shouted, almost crying with rage and chagrin. The tribune raised his shield against a whirlwind attack. Grus must have been drawing on the same furious energy that powered Vorenus and Pullo; he struck and struck and struck, as if driven by clockwork. He paid no thought to defense. More than once he left himself open to a killing blow, but Marcus held back. The little battle was already won, and the Namdalener officer might be worth more as prisoner than corpse.

Gaius Philippus bent, found a stone of good hand-filling size. He let fly at close range; the rock clanked off the side of grus' conical helmet. The Namdalener staggered, dropped his guard. Marcus and the senior centurion wrestled him to the ground and disarmed him. "Nice throw," the tribune said.

"I saw you didn't want to kill him."

Ras Simokattes looked in confusion from the two officers to where Pullo and Vorenus were accepting their comrades' praise. "What are you foreigners, anyway?" he asked Scaurus. "Here you two go out of your way to keep from letting the air out of this one—" He nudged Grus with his foot. "—while that pair yonder's a couple of bloodthirsty madmen."

The tribune glanced over to the two rival legionaries. Junius Blaesus was congratulating them now. Marcus frowned; the junior centurion seemed unable to see past the obvious, something the tribune had noticed before. He turned back to Simokattes. "Bide a moment, Ras. You'll see what we are." Then, to the Romans: "Pullo, Vorenus—over here, if you would."

The troopers exchanged apprehensive looks. They broke away at once from their mates, came to attention before Scaurus. "I hope your rivalry is done," he said mildly. "Now each of you has saved the other; that should be plenty to put you at quits." He spoke Videssian, for the chief herdsman's benefit.

"Yes, sir," they said together, and actually sounded as if they meant it.

"To say it was bravely done would be to waste words. I'm glad the both of you came through alive."

"Thank you, sir," Pullo said, smiling; Vorenus relaxed with him.

"No one said at ease, you!" Gaius Philippus rasped. The legionaries stiffened. The apprehension returned to their faces.

"Both of you are fined a week's pay for breaking ranks in the charge," Scaurus went on, no longer mild. "Not only do you endanger yourselves by bringing your feud along to combat, you also gamble with your comrades' safety. Never again—d'you understand me?"

"Aye, sir," they answered, both very low.

"What were you playing at?" Gaius Philippus demanded. "You might as well have been a couple of Gauls over there." That was his worst condemnation for disorderly soldiers; Vorenus flushed, while Pullo shuffled his feet like a small, naughty boy. Both were a far cry from the ferocious warriors of a few minutes before. When Scaurus dismissed them, they went quietly back to their comrades.

"Well, what are we, Ras?" the tribune asked Simokattes.

"A pack of bastards, if you want to know," Grus said from the ground.

"Quiet, you," Gaius Philippus said.

Simokattes had watched in disbelief as the Romans took their dressing-down; he had never known soldiers trained to such obedience. He scratched his head, rubbed at a leathery cheek. "Damned if I could tell you, but I'm glad you're not against me."

"Bah!" said Grus.

Isolated in the southeastern hills, Marcus longed for news of the wider world, but had all but given up hope of having any when an imperial messenger, a dapper, foxy-faced little man, made his way through the Namdaleni and was scooped up by a Khatrisher patrol. "Karbeas Antakinos, I'm called," he said when they brought him to the tribune. His sharp eyes flicked round the legionary camp, missing nothing.

"Good to see you, good to see you," Marcus said, pumping his hand.

"Very good to be here, let me tell you," the courier said. His speech had the quick, staccato rhythm of the capital. "The ride was hellish—damned Gamblers all over the lot." He used the Videssians' insulting nickname for the men of the Duchy, who returned the favor by calling the imperials Cocksures. The Roman swallowed a sigh; he had no patience for the bickering between Phos' sects.

He also remembered Drax' gift for treachery. "Let me have your bona fides," he said to Antakinos.

"Yes indeed." The Videssian rubbed his hands together briskly. "I was to ask you his Imperial Majesty's opinion of hot-tempered women."

Scaurus relaxed; Thorisin had used that recognition signal before. "That they're great fun, but wearing."

"Has a point, does he?" Antakinos chuckled. He had an easy laugh that went well with his resonant tenor. "I remember a girl named Panthia—but that's another story. To business: how do you stand here?"

"It's stalemate, for now. The islanders don't go poking their noses into these hills any more, not after a couple of little lessons we taught them, but I can't get loose, either. There's too many of them down here. Can Gavras draw them off?"

The messenger grimaced. "Not a prayer. He just led two regiments to Opsikion, opposite the Duchy, to fight off a Namdalener landing there."

"Bloody wonderful," Gaius Philippus said. "I suppose we might have known it was coming."

"Aye," Antakinos said. "Phos be praised it's only freebooters and not the Duke. Speaking of which, pirates from the Duchy have shown up off the westlands, too. Three days before I set out, Leimmokheir came into port after chasing four of them away and sinking a fifth. And you can be sure more than those are lurking about."

"By the gods," Scaurus said, dismayed into Latin. He returned to the imperial tongue. "You're telling me, then, that we are as great a force as the Avtokrator has left."

"In essence, yes," the courier agreed unhappily. "In truth, I'll be glad to tell him how strong you are. After the, ah, misfortune at the Sangarios, he feared all of Zigabenos' army had been destroyed or turned traitor with its general." Damn the great count Drax, Marcus thought, while Antakinos finished, "But you do not have the look of defeated men to you."

"I should hope not," Gaius Philippus snorted.

Laon Pakhymer walked up in time to hear the last exchange. "No indeed," he said, eyes twinkling, "for your men fear you worse than Drax. All he can do is kill them." The senior centurion snorted again, but did not seem displeased.

"You traveled through the lands the islanders hold," Marcus said to Antakinos. "How are the folk there taking to their rule?"

"Interesting question." Antakinos eyed him with respect. "Thinking of stirring them up, maybe? His Majesty said you were a tricksy one. Well, here's how it is: out in the countryside they'd take kindly to roasting Gamblers over a slow fire, the peasants 'cause they steal and the nobles because some of their number have been dispossessed to give their estates to men from the Duchy." The messenger pursed his lips. "The towns, I fear, are the other way round. Drax takes tribute from 'em, aye, but less than they paid Videssos—and the townsfolk count on the Namdaleni to protect them from the Yezda."

Laon Pakhymer shook his head very slightly, but Antakinos noticed and raised a curious eyebrow. To Scaurus' relief, the Khatrisher did not explain himself. That ploy still made the tribune's hackles rise.

"Well, what if there's more of the sods coming by than we thought when we laid the ambush?" The speaker was a tall, lanky farmer in rough homespun and a thick leather jerkin. He clutched his boar spear uncertainly.

Gaius Philippus held onto his patience with both hands. These raw Videssian recruits had neither Roman discipline nor the impetuosity of the Spaniards Sertorius had forged into so dangerous a guerilla army. But all the two hundred or so men hunkered down around him were volunteers, either refugees from the lowlands or hillmen who wanted more of soldiering than squabbling with the noble a couple of valleys over.

The senior centurion said to his listeners, "You don't need me to answer a question like that. Who'll tell him?" A score of hands rose, Ras Simokattes' first. Gaius Philippus pretended not to see Zonaras' chief herdsman. "You, there—yes, you with the gray streak in your hair."

The man stood, clasped his hands behind his back and dipped his head, as if to some half-forgotten childhood teacher. "If there's too many, we stay in hiding," he said diffidently. A light hunting bow was at his feet.

"That's the way of it!" Gaius Philippus approved. "And don't be ashamed to do it, either. Unless the odds are all with you, don't get gay with the islanders. They have better gear than you and they know what to do with it, too. Just like me." He grinned a lazy grin.

Watching the lesson, Marcus saw the veteran's would-be marauders sober as they remembered his demonstration of a couple of days before. In full panoply, he had invited any four of his pupils to come at him with the hand-weapons they had. The fight did not last long. Reversing his *pilum*, he knocked the wind out of one assailant, ducked the scythe-stroke of another and broke the spearshaft over his head. Whirling, he let the third Videssian's club whack into his shield, then hit him under the chin with the *scutum*'s metal-faced edge. Even as the man sank, Gaius Philippus was drawing his sword and sidling toward his last foe, who carried a short pike. The fellow was brave enough, rushing forward to jab at the Roman, but Gaius Philippus, graceful as a dancer, stepped inside the thrust and tapped him on the chest with his sword. Two men unconscious, one helpless on the ground, the fourth white-faced and shaking—not bad, for a minute's work.

A good dozen men slipped out of camp that night.

But for the ones who stayed, the senior centurion was proving a better teacher than Scaurus had expected. In fact, he showed a zest for the assignment he did not always bring to his ordinary duties. Like any job, those had become largely routine as the years went by. The new role seemed to take him back to his youth, and he plunged into it with more enthusiasm than the tribune had seen from him since they knew each other.

The veteran was saying, "Make your strike, do as much mischief as you can, and get away fast. Sometimes it doesn't hurt to ditch your weapons." That would have been blasphemous advice to give to full-time soldiers. But to guerillas, it made sense. "Without 'em, who's to know who you are?"

"And when they chase us?" someone asked.

"Scatter, of course. And if you get out of sight for a minute or two, you can stop running. Just bend down in a field and pull weeds like you belonged there. They'll ride past you every time." Gaius Philippus' smile was altogether without the cynical cast it usually bore. "You can have a lot of fun at this business."

Marcus dug a finger into his ear. The senior centurion, as hardened a professional as ever lived, calling soldiering fun? Reliving one's youth was all very well, but from Gaius Philippus that seemed like second childhood.

Ruelm Ranulf's son was pleased with himself as he and his squad of Namdaleni rode south toward the hills where resistance still simmered against his liege lord Drax. Not for a moment did he think of himself as subject to any Emperor Zigabenos. That piece of play-acting was for the Videssians to chew on.

He paused to light a torch. Twilight was almost gone, but he wanted to keep moving. With luck, he could join Bailli by midnight. That was what pleased him; when he'd set out from Kyzikos, he had expected to be on the road another day, but the ford over the Arandos that gaffer had shown him saved hours skirting the bank looking for a bridge and then doubling back. He touched his wallet. It had been well worth the goldpiece, and the old man looked as though he hadn't seen many lately.

A moth flew in tight circles round his torch. The night was warm and very still; he could hear the faint whirr of its wings. A bat swooped out of the blackness, snatched the bug, and was gone almost before he was sure he'd seen it.

"Damned flittermouse," he said, making the sun-sign on his breast to ward off the evil omen. His men did the same. The Namdaleni called bats "Skotos' chickens," for without the dark god's help, how could they see to fly so unerringly by night?

As the hills came nearer, stands of brush and shadowy clumps of trees grew more common than they had been north of the Arandos. That rich low plain was the most intensively farmed and most productive land Ruelm had ever seen. By the austere standards of the duchy, even this was plenty fine enough.

A lapwing piped in the undergrowth to the side of the roads. "Peewit!" it said, following the call with a long whistle. Ruelm was mildly surprised to hear a day bird so long after dusk. Then the first arrow whispered out of the night, and the knight behind him swore in startlement and pain as it stuck in his calf.

For a second Ruelm sat frozen—no enemies were supposed to be here. The Romans and the Videssian and Khatrisher ragtag and bobtail clinging to their skirts had been driven well up into the hills.

Another arrow hissed past his face, so close a rough feather of the fletching tickled his cheek. Suddenly he was soldier again. He threw the torch as far as he could—whoever these night-runners were, no sense lighting a target for them. He was drawing his sword as they broke cover and rushed.

He slashed out blindly, still half dazzled by the torchlight, felt the blade bite. Behind him, the trooper who was first wounded yelled as he was dragged from the saddle; his cry cut off abruptly. Others replaced it—backcountry Videssian voices shouting in mixed triumph and, he would have taken oath, fear.

The darkness gave the savage little fight a nightmare quality. Whirling his horse round to go to the aid of his men, Ruelm saw his foes as shifting black shadows, impossible to count, almost impossible to strike.

"Drax!" he shouted, and tasted sour fear in his mouth when only two men answered.

A hand pulled at his thigh. He kicked at his assailant; though his boot met only air, the man skipped back. He roweled his horse's flank with his spurs. The gelding reared, whinnying. Well-trained as a warhorse, it lashed out with iron-shod hooves. A man's skull shattered like a smashed melon; a bit of brain, warm, wet, and sticky, splashed on Ruelm's forehead, just below his helmet.

Then, with a great scream, the gelding foundered. As he kicked free of the stirrups, Ruelm heard a Videssian cry, "Hamstrung, by Phos!" Boots and bare feet scuffed in the dirt of the roadway as more came running up like so many jackals.

The islander lit rolling and started to scramble to his feet, but a club smashed against the chain-mail neckguard that hung from his helm. Stunned, he fell to his knees and then to his belly. His sword was torn away; greedy hands ripped at the fastenings of his hauberk. He groaned and tried to reach for his dagger. "'Ware!" someone shouted. "He's not done yet!"

A harsh chuckle. "We'll fix that!" Still dazed, he felt rough fingers grope under his chin, jerk his head back. "Jist like a sheep," the Videssian said. The knife stung, but not for long.

Accompanied by Sittas Zonaras and Gaius Philippus, Scaurus walked toward the truce-site Bailli of Ecrisi had suggested. "Here, Minucius," the tribune said, pausing, "this is close enough for you and your squad." The young underofficer saluted; they were a good bowshot away from where Bailli and a pair of his lieutenants were waiting. A double handful of dismounted Namdaleni lounged on the ground a similar distance north of their leaders.

"Hello, islander," Scaurus called as he came up. "What do we need to talk about?"

But Bailli was not the suave, self-assured officer who had delivered Drax' proclamation a few weeks before. "You scum," he snarled, his neck corded with fury. "For two coppers I'd stake you out for the crows. I thought you a man of honor." He spat at the Roman's feet.

"If I'm not, why risk a parley with me? We're enemies, true, but there's no need to hate each other."

"Go howl, you and your pretty talk," Bailli said. "We took you and yours for honest mercenaries, men who'd do their best for him who pays them, aye, but not stoop to such foulness as you're wading in. Murders in the night, tavern stabbings, maimed horses, thefts to drive a man mad—"

"Why blame us?" Marcus asked. "First off, you know we Romans don't war like that—as I say, you must, or you'd not be here talking with me. And second, even if we did, we couldn't, for it's you who pinned us back in these hills."

"Seems someone in the flatlands isn't fond of you," Gaius Philippus said, as casually as if remarking on the weather.

Bailli was near the bursting point. "All right! All right! Loose your stupid peasants, if that's how you care to play this game. We'll root them out if we have to chip down every tree and burn every cottage from here back to the city. And then we'll come back to deal with you, and you'll wish for what we gave your cowardly skulkers."

Gaius Philippus said nothing, but an eyebrow twitched. To Bailli it could have meant anything; to Marcus, it showed he was not worried by the threat.

"Will there be anything more, Bailli?" the tribune asked.

"Just this," the Namdalener officer said heavily. "At the Sangarios you fought your men as well as you could and as cleanly, too. Then afterwards in the talks over your exchange scheme, you were gracious even when they did not turn out as you wanted. So why this?"

The honest perplexity in his voice deserved a straight answer. Marcus thought for a moment, then said, "'Doing me best,' as you call it, is all very well, but it's not my job. My job is to hold things together, and one way or another I intend to do it."

He treasured the look of unreserved approval Gaius Philippus gave him, but knew he had made no sense to Bailli. Roman stubbornness was a trait without counterpart in this world; neither sly Videssians, happy-go-lucky Khatrishers, nor proud upstart Namdaleni fully appreciated it.

Yet Bailli was no fool. Just as Scaurus had quoted him, now he threw the tribune's words back in his face. "'One way or another,' is it? How much thanks do you think you'll win from the Empire's nobles, outlanders, if you teach the assassin's trade to peasants with manure between their toes?" He looked Zonaras in the eye. "And you, sirrah. When you go out to collect your rents, will you feel safe riding past any bush big enough for a man to hide behind?"

"Safer than when your bravoes set on me," the Videssian retorted, but he tugged thoughtfully at his beard all the same.

"You remind me of the man in the story, who threw himself on the fire because he was chilly. On your head be it—and it probably will." Bailli turned back to Scaurus. "We buried that northbound rider of yours—Antakinos, wasn't it?"

If he knew the name, he was not bluffing. Marcus wondered how many couriers had been taken before they ever reached him. "Did you?" he said. "Well, *vale*—farewell!"

Bailli grunted, plainly hoping for some larger reaction. He nodded to his lieutenants, who had been glowering at the tribune and his comrades with even less liking than their leader showed. "Come on; we've given him his warning, and more than he deserves." With almost legionary precision, the Namdaleni turned on their heels and tramped back to their waiting knights.

As Scaurus, Gaius Philippus, and Zonaras moved toward Minucius' guard squad, the senior centurion had all he could do to keep from smirking. "That one'll be the best recruiter we ever had. There's nothing like seeing your farm torn to bits and your neighbors killed to give you the idea of which side you should be on."

"Aye, likely so," Marcus said, but abstractedly. Bailli's jab over the consequences of encouraging a guerilla among the Videssian peasantry troubled him more than he had shown the islander. When he gave Gaius Philippus a free hand, he had not thought past the immediate goal of making Drax' life miserable. He was doing that, no doubt; Bailli's spleen was a good measure of it. But the Namdalener, blast him, was right—the marauders who took up arms against the men of the Duchy would not magically unlearn their use once the war was done. How long before they realized a disliked landowner or imperial tax-agent bled as red as an islander?

Zonaras might have been reading his thoughts. He clapped the tribune on the back, saying, "I don't expect to be bushwhacked tomorrow, Scaurus, no, nor next year either."

"I'm glad," Marcus answered. He consoled himself by thinking that in Videssos, as in Rome, the great landowners were too powerful. Their grip needed loosening. The Empire had been stronger when it relied on its freeholding peasantry than now, with the provincial nobles at odds with the pen-pushers in the capital, and with the state's defenses in the hands of unreliable mercenaries like the Namdaleni—or the Romans.

But that evening Pakhymer laughed at him when he retorted what Bailli had said. "And you were the one who got huffy at me for doing what needed doing with the Yezda."

"There's a difference," Marcus insisted.

"In a pig's arse," the Khatrisher said cheerfully; the tribune had known he would not see it. "You load your side of the Balance as heavily as you can, then hope for the best." Orthodox Videssian thought held that Phos would one day vanquish his wicked rival Skotos. Pakhymer's folk, whose very nation sprang from the chaos of barbarian invasion, were not so optimistic. In their view the fight between good and evil was evenly matched, thus the metaphor of the balance. To the imperials, even to the Namdaleni, it was foul heresy. Independent as always, the Khatrishers clung to it regardless.

Marcus was glad he was indifferent to theology.

Gaius Philippus had come to respect Pakhymer's opinions; the pockmarked little cavalry commander had a habit of being right. Picking a bit of raisin out from between his teeth, he said to Scaurus, "You're the one who keeps track of these cursed imperial politics, sir. Will they see us as ogres for using their clients to fight the islanders?"

"Only the ones who are ogres themselves, is my guess. They're the ones who have something to fear." Marcus eyed the veteran curiously; such worries were unlike him. "Why should it trouble you?"

"No reason, really," the senior centurion said, but his sheepish smile rang false. Marcus waited. Gaius Philippus stumbled on, "After all, what with the Yezda and Zemarkhos' fanatics between here and Aptos, likely no trouble from this would ever reach there."

"Aptos?" The Romans had wintered there after Maragha, but it was more than a year since they left the small town, and Scaurus had hardly thought of it since.

Gaius Philippus seemed to regret opening his mouth in the first place. The tribune thought he was going to clam up, but he plunged ahead: "The local noble's widow there—what was her name? Nerse Phorkaina, that was it—is a fine lady. What with raising up her son, and the Yezda, and Zemarkhos' holy war against everything, I'd rather she didn't think we'd given her a new headache. That would be a poor return for good guesting."

"So it would," Marcus agreed solemnly. What was her name, indeed, he thought. He was sure Gaius Philippus remembered everything there was to remember about Phorkos' widow, down to what stones she favored in her rings. But the senior centurion was so used to despising women that Scaurus doubted he would ever admit feeling otherwise, even to himself.

The short-hafted axe bit into the black mulberry's trunk again and again. Chips flew. Bryennios the woodcutter grunted in satisfaction as the tree began to totter. Long years of use had polished the axe handle smooth as a maiden's skin beneath his callused palms. He walked round to the other side of the mulberry, deepened his undercut with a few strokes, then went back to the main cut. He grunted again. Sure enough, he'd be able to drop the tree in the space where the old alder had stood until the storm three winters past. That would make chopping it into timber so much easier.

The breeze shifted, bringing with it the sharp odor of wood smoke. Bryennios made another wordless noise, this one anything but pleasant—it was not Tralles the charcoal-burner at work. Houses in his hamlet were going up in flames. He could hear women wailing in the distance, and Namdaleni shouting to each other.

As if thinking of the men of the Duchy had conjured them up, three came riding toward him down the forest track. "You, there!" one shouted; his lazy island accent swallowed the last *r.* Bryennios sneered, but to himself. The Namdaleni were all armored and carried their long lances at the ready. The woodcutter swung his axe again. The mulberry groaned. A few more strokes and it would fall.

"Belay that!" the islander shouted. The seaman's word meant nothing to Bryennios, who had seen no water greater than a pond, but the sense was plain. He lowered the axe.

Pretending not to, he eyed the Namdaleni as they approached. Two might have been Videssians for looks had they not shaved; the third was fair-haired, with eyes of a startling green. All of them were big, strapping men, overtopping him by half a head or more, but his shoulders were wider than theirs, his arms thick with muscle from his trade.

"What do you want of me?" he asked. "I have work to do—more work, thanks to the lot of you." He did not bother hiding his bitterness.

The older of the two dark Namdaleni, their spokesman, wiped at his forehead with the sleeve of his green surcoat. Soot and rusty sweat came away in a short clean streak. The rest of his face was filthy. "You want to be spared such visits, eh?" he said.

Bryennios looked at him as at any idiot. "Who would not?"

"A point." The islander smiled thinly. "Well, we aren't pleased to have a supply wagon torched and two guards knocked over the head. Have any ideas about whose clever scheme that was? We'd pay well to learn his name."

The woodcutter shrugged, spread his hands. The Namdalener snarled in disgust, mockingly imitated his gesture. "You see how it is, then. If we can't find out who these rebels are, we have to teach everyone the price of sheltering them." Bryennios shrugged again.

"You mi' as well talk to the clot's axe," the blond islander said. "It'd tell you more." His emerald stare stabbed at Bryennios; the down-pointing bar nasal on his helmet gave him the aspect of a brooding falcon. At last he jerked hard on his horse's reins, wheeling the beast around. His comrades followed.

Bryennios attacked the mulberry again. After a few savage swings it fell just where he had known it would. He stepped forward to lop off the bigger branches. He muttered a short prayer of thanks that the men of the Duchy had not taken the blond knight's sour advice and examined his axe. The dark red crusted stain at the top of the handle did not come from sap.

"Why are they pulling out? I haven't a clue," the Khatrisher scout said to Scaurus, as cheeky as any of his people. "You want whys, see a magician. Whats I'm pretty good at, and I tell you the Namdaleni are breaking camp."

The tribune fumbled in his pouch, tossed the horseman a goldpiece. "Whatever the reason, good news deserves a reward." The Khatrisher made it disappear before Marcus thumped his forehead at his folly. "After Kyzikos, you should be paying me."

"It won't go to waste, even so." The Khatrisher grinned smugly.

The tribune rode back to his vantage point with him. No great horseman, Scaurus blessed the stirrups that gave him a fighting chance to stay on the large, unreliable beast between his thighs.

A glance from the hilltop crag told him the scout was right. Bailli's Namdaleni had used the legionary camp by Zonaras' villa as their own main base. Now it lay deserted; Marcus reached the observation post in time to see the last of the Namdalener column ride north out of the valley. Even at some distance, he could see how tightly bunched they were—a hostile countryside was the best argument against straggling.

Watching the retreat as he was, he took a while to notice that a garrison still held Zonaras' strong-walled home. So it proved over the next few days all along the line the islanders had set up to contain the legionaries. Their striking force was gone, but they still stood strongly on the defensive.

When the riders who did sneak past the Namdalener forts reported that the main body of islanders was hurrying northwest toward Garsavra, Laon Pakhymer looked so pleased with himself that Marcus wanted to throttle him. "You see, even the Yezda can be useful," the Khatrisher general said. "One man's trouble is the next fellow's chance."

"Hmmp," Scaurus said. He still hoped the men of the Duchy would smash the Yezda, though he had to admit he would not be brokenhearted to see them weakened in the smashing. He did not mean to sit idly by while they battled. If a couple of the islanders' motte-and-baileys fell, the way would open for the legionaries to go down into the coastal plain once more. The hills made a good refuge, but nothing would be decided here—and the lush lowlands were much better able to feed any army. He was sick of barley and lentils, and even those were running low.

Naturally, Zonaras wanted his villa to be the first strong point freed, but the tribune had to tell him no—its approaches were too open, and the building itself too strong. The elderly noble shook his head ruefully. "There's praise I could do without."

Marcus chose several more likely targets to attack. For himself he picked a fort that was new Namdalener construction, a few miles west of Zonaras' holding. The valley it sat in was a guerilla center; strife between them and the islander garrison had made many of the local peasants flee, and the men of the Duchy were working their fields. Looking out from between the branches of an almond grove, the tribune thought they were doing a good job of it, too.

There was no signal. When he judged the moment ripe, Pakhymer sent a few dozen horsemen riding hell-for-leather into the valley. They trampled through the rich green fields, slashing the growing grain with their sabers to leave as wide a track of destruction as they could. Some carried smoking torches, which they hurled here and there. Others darted toward the small flock of sheep grazing just outside the motte and started driving them into the hills.

From a quarter mile away, Marcus could hear the roars of outrage in the fort, could see men running about on the wall and shooting a few useless arrows at the pillagers outside. Then a wooden gangboard thudded down over the deep moat. Knights stormed over it, their horses' hooves echoing thunderously. Peering through the leaves, the tribune counted them as they came. Thirty-eight, thirty-nine . . . his spies' best guess was that the castle held fifty or so.

While panicked sheep ran every which way, the Khatrishers regrouped to meet the threat, using their ponies' quickness and agility for all they were worth. They peppered their heavily armored foes with arrows; Scaurus saw an islander clap his hands to his face and slide back over his horse's tail. Two of Pakhymer's men rushed toward a Namdalener who had gotten separated from his mates, one to either side. Watching from concealment, the tribune bit his lip. What would it take to convince the Khatrishers they could not stand up against islanders in close combat? Covering his left side with his shield, the Namdalener chopped the man on his right from the saddle, then used a clever backhanded stroke to send the other reeling away with a gashed forearm. The rest of the islanders shouted to applaud the feat of arms.

As if their morale was broken, the raiding party sped toward the hills, the men of the Duchy pounding after them. Now the Khatrishers' light horses were not putting out quite their best speed; they seemed unable to pull away from the islanders' ponderous chargers. Yelling and brandishing their lances, the Namdaleni held hotly to the pursuit.

Scaurus watched the gap between islanders and fortress increase. He turned to the maniple which had spent an uncomfortable night with him under the almonds. "All right, lads, at the trot!" he shouted. They burst from concealment and rushed toward the castle, carrying hurdles and bundles of brush to fill the moat.

They were almost halfway there before any of the Namdaleni spied them approaching from the side; the riders were intent on the chase, while the handful still inside the fortress had no eyes for anything but their comrades. Then one of the men on the earthwork wall let out a horrified bellow. The tribune was close enough to see mouths drop open in dismay. Islanders darted toward the gangboard, to drag it up before the legionaries reached it. Scaurus bared his teeth in a grin; he had not counted on that much luck.

The thick oak planks were heavy, and the passage of horses and mail-clad knights had driven the wooden bridge deep into the soft earth of the rampart. Marcus heard the islanders grunting and swearing with effort, but the outer edge of the gangboard had hardly moved when his *caligae* thudded onto it.

He dashed forward, doing his best not to think of the moat that yawned below. An islander, his nails broken and hands black with dirt, gave up the futile effort to shift the bridge and stepped out onto it, drawing his sword as he did. Marcus' own Gallic longsword was already in his hand. "Horatius, is it?" he panted. But unlike the span the legendary Roman hero had held against the Etruscans, this one was wide enough for three or four men to fight abreast. Before more Namdaleni could join the first quick-thinking one, Scaurus assailed him from the front, Minucius from the left, and another Roman from the right. He defended himself bravely, but three against one was a fight that could only last seconds. The soldier toppled, bleeding at throat, groin, and thigh. Cheering, the legionaries trampled over his corpse and swarmed into the castle's bailey. A couple of Namdaleni tried to fight; most threw down their arms in despair.

By then the knights chasing the Khatrishers realized the snare they had fallen into. They spun their horses and came galloping back toward the fort, spurring desperately. But the Khatrishers turned round, too, and became pursuers rather than pursued. The islanders, with more at stake than the raiders, ignored their arrows as best they could, though one charger after another rode on riderless.

"Come on, put your backs into it!" Scaurus shouted. With many more hands than the Namdaleni had used, the legionaries strained at the gangboard. They yelled as it pulled free of the clinging earth and went tumbling into the moat. It was well made; the tribune did not hear timbers crack as it hit.

Outside the castle, the islanders milled round in confusion, shut out of their own fortress and at a loss what to do next. The Khatrishers' archery suggested that lingering was not the wisest course. Looking glumly back over their shoulders, they trotted north, presumably to join their main force. Pakhymer waved to Marcus, who returned it; the assault had gone better than he had dared hope.

He spent the night in the captured fort, waiting for reports from his officers. A rider attached to Gagik Bagratouni's force came in just after sunset, to announce a success as complete and easy as the tribune's. Junius Blaesus took his target, too, but at the cost of some hard fighting. "What went wrong?" Marcus asked.

"Started his charge too damned soon," the Khatrisher scout answered, not shy about criticizing someone else's officer. "The Namdaleni managed to reverse themselves and hit him before he made it to the castle. He's brave enough, though—ducked a lance and speared one right off his horse, he did." The Katrisher tugged his ear, trying to remember something. "Ah, that's it—your friend Apokavkos lost the little finger on his right hand."

"Pity," Scaurus said. "How is he taking it?"

"Him? He's angry at himself—told me to tell you he cut instead of thrusting, and the last time he'll make that mistake, thank you very much."

That left only Gaius Philippus unaccounted for. Marcus was not much worried; the senior centurion's target was farthest from his own. But early next morning a rider came in to report flat failure. He was vague about what had happened; Scaurus did not hear the full story until he saw Gaius Philippus back at the Roman camp a few days later. He had pulled the legionaries out of the captured forts, leaving Videssians behind instead, a mixture of nobles' retainers and irregulars—troops plenty good for garrison duty.

"One of those things," the senior centurion shrugged. "The Khatrishers went whooping into the fields fine as you please, but the whoresons inside had a couple of stone-throwers in their castle, which we didn't know about till they opened up. Good aimers, too. They squashed two horses and took the head off a rider neat as you please. That discouraged the rest considerably, and what was supposed to be a fake skedaddle turned real mighty fast." He spooned up some mutton stew. "Can't say I blame 'em much. We sat under some peaches till it was dark again, then left. Some of my men have taken a flux from eating green ones, the twits."

Despite the veteran's misfortune, Scaurus knew he had gained a solid success. His mouth watered at the prospect of getting down into the plain; a full summer in the hills would leave them picked bare and his troops starving. True, all Drax' forces together could crush the legionaries, but Drax had problems of his own.

Senpat Sviodo made as if to throw his pandoura away in disgust after producing a chord even Scaurus' insensitive ear recognized as spectacularly unmusical. "I wish we were back in the highlands," he said. "It's too muggy down here; there's no way to keep gut strings in tune with all this humidity. Ah, my sweet," he crooned, holding the pandoura as he might

Nevrat, "you deserve strings of finest silver. And," he added, laughing, "if I lavished money on you thus, perhaps you'd not betray me, fickle hussy."

With an enthusiast's zeal, he went on to explain the advantages and disadvantages of different kinds of stringing. Marcus fought to hide boredom; not even Senpat's easy charm could make him find music interesting, and the day's march had left him worn.

He was glad of the excuse to break away when Lucius Vorenus came up. "What now?" he asked. "What's Pullo done that you don't care for?"

"Eh?" Vorenus blinked. "Oh, nothing, sir. That valley scuffle's made fast friends of us. In fact, we're on sentry go together, over at the east gate. And just rode up, sir, is a Yezda who'd have speech with you."

"A what?" It was Scaurus' turn to gape. Senpat's Latin was enough to catch the name of his people's foes; he struck a jangling discord that had nothing to do with whether his strings were in tune. The tribune felt his mouth tighten. "What would a Yezda have to say to me?"

"I wouldn't know, sir. He's out there with a white rag tied to his bow; he doesn't carry a spear, or have a helmet to put on it, for that matter. Dirty-looking beggar," Vorenus added virtuously.

Marcus exchanged glances with Senpat. The Vaspurakaner's face showed an odd mixture of puzzlement and hostility; Scaurus felt much the same. "Bring him in," he said at last. Vorenus saluted and trotted off.

Despite the legionary's unflattering description, Marcus expected a more impressive figure than the Yezda cut—some high officer, perhaps, with Makurani blood in his veins along with the infusion from the steppe—tall, thin, handsome, with delicate hands and mournful liquid eyes, like the captain who had defended Khliat against Mavrikios Gavras. But only a scruffy nomad on a pony followed Vorenus, looking for all the world like any of the Khamorth in imperial service. Not a soldier gave him a second look. Yet his presence here, not far from Kyzikos, was a knife at Videssos' throat.

The Yezda, for his part, seemed no more happy to be in his enemies' camp than Marcus was to have him there. He turned his head nervously this way and that, as if looking for escape routes. "You Scaurus, leader of this peoples?" he asked, his Videssian labored but understandable.

"Aye," the tribune said stonily. "What would you?"

"I Sevabarak, cousin to Yavlak, who is leaders of clans of Menteshe.

He send me to you to ask how much money you gots. You need plenties, I think."

"And why is that, pray?" Marcus asked, still not caring to have anything to do with Yezda.

Sevabarak was not offended; indeed, he seemed amused. "Because we—how you say?—whale stuffings out of oh-so-tough knightboys last week. Damn sight more than pissworthy Empire can do," he said. Then, ticking off names on his fingers, he went on, "We gots Drax, we gots Bailli, we gots what's-his-name Videssian thinks he's Empire—"

"Emperor," Scaurus corrected mechanically. Beside him, Senpat Sviodo's eyes were round and staring. So, for that matter, were his own.

Sevabarak waved the interruption aside. "Whatever. We gots. We gots Turgot, we gots Soteric, we gots Clozart—no, I take back, him dead, two days gone. Anyway, we gots shitpot full Namdalenis. You wants, you buy back, plenty monies. Otherwise," and his eyes grew cruel and eager, "we see how long we stretch them lives out. Some last weeks, I bet."

But Marcus paid no attention to the threat. Here was a broken rebellion handed to him on a golden plate—and if the legionaries moved quickly, they still might keep the Yezda off the coastal plain. And thinking of gold . . . "Pakhymer!" he shouted. This might cost more than the legionaries had, and he was ready to swallow all the Khatrisher's "I-told-you-so's" to get it.

VIII

THE GREAT WAIN CREAKED, MOVING ACROSS THE GENTLY ROLLING steppe on wheels tall as a man. Gorgidas sat cross-legged on the polychrome rug of goats' hair, paring away at his stylus' point with the edge of his sword; not what Gaius Philippus had hoped he'd use the weapon for, he thought, chuckling. He tested the point on the ball of his thumb. It would do. He opened a three-leafed tablet, frowned when he saw how poorly he'd smoothed the wax after transcribing his last set of jottings onto parchment.

He tugged on his left ear as he thought. His stylus hurried across the tablet, tiny wax curls spiraling up from it. "In sweep of territory, neither Videssos nor Yezd compares favorably with the nomads to the north. Indeed, should those nomads somehow unite under a single leader, no nation could stand against them. They do not, however, govern themselves with great wisdom or make the best use of the vast resources available to them."

He studied what he had written—not bad, something of a Thucydidean flavor to it. His script was small and very neat. As if that mattered, he said to himself with a snort. In all this world, only he read Greek. No, not quite: Scaurus could stumble through it after a fashion. But Scaurus was in Videssos, which seemed unimaginably far away from this wandering train of Arshaum wagons.

Beside him, Goudeles was making notes of his own for an oration he intended to give to Arigh's father Arghun, the khagan of the Gray Horse clan, when at last they reached the chieftain. It would not be long now, a couple of days at most. Lankinos Skylitzes, well padded with fat cushions, was sound asleep, ignoring the occasional jounce of a wheel bumping over a rock. He snored.

Gorgidas set the stylus moving again. "It is not surprising, then, that the Arshaum should have succeeded in driving the Khamorth to the eastern portion of the steppe, which extends further west than any man's knowledge of it; the former folk has adapted itself more completely to the nomadic way of life than the latter. The very tents of the Arshaum, 'yurts,' in their dialect, are set upon large wheeled carts. Thus no time is wasted pitching or breaking camp. They followed their flocks forever, like dolphins in a school of tunny."

The comparison pleased him. He translated it into Videssian for Goudeles. The pen-pusher rolled his eyes. " 'Sharks' might he better," he said, and followed that with a muttered, "Barbarians!"

Gorgidas chose to think that remark was meant to apply to the Arshaum and not to him. He resumed his scribbling: "Because the plainsfolk do not act as a single nation, both Videssos and Yezd try to win them over clan by clan. By attracting such prominent khagans as Arghun to their side, they hope to influence less important leaders to join the faction that looks to be a winner." He put his stylus down, asked Goudeles, "What do you suppose this Bogoraz is up to?"

Skylitzes opened one eye. "No good for us, I'm sure," he said, and went back to sleep.

"I fear he's right," Goudeles said, sighing. The Yezda ambassador had also come to woo Arghun. Until their khagan chose one side or the other, the Arshaum were carefully keeping Bogoraz and his retainers separate from the Videssian party.

Inspiration failing him, Gorgidas stowed tablet and stylus and stuck his head out the flap of the yurt. Agathias Psoes, riding beside the felt tent on wheels, nodded a greeting; he kept his squad on alert, not relying on the nomads to keep Bogoraz and his handful of retainers from mischief.

The Greek turned to the young plainsman guiding the yurt's team of horses. "May your herds increase," he said in polite greeting, using up a good deal of what he had learned of the sibilant Arshaum tongue.

"May your animals be fat," the nomad replied. Like most of his people, he was short and lean, with a wiry strength to him. He was flat-faced, swarthy, and almost without a beard; a fold of skin at the corner of each eye gave them a slanted look. When he smiled, his teeth were very white.

Suede fringes and brightly dyed tassels of wool ornamented his sheepskin trousers and leather coat. He wore a curved sword and dagger and a quiver on his back; his bow was beside him on the wooden seat. He smelled strongly of the stale butter he used to oil his straight, coarse black hair.

It was later than Gorgidas had thought. The sun was sliding down the sky toward a low range of hills that barely serrated the western horizon. They were the first blemishes on the skyline he had seen for weeks. Beyond them was only more steppe.

Two riders came out of the west, one straight for the Videssian embassy's yurt, the other peeling off toward that of Bogoraz. Yezd's banner, a leaping panther on a field of brownish red, fluttered above it. It was a nice touch; Gorgidas wished the Empire had been as forethoughtful.

The messenger said something in his own language to the Greek, who tossed his head to show he did not understand. The nomad shrugged, tried again in bad Khamorth; only a few Ashaum knew Videssian. Gorgidas ducked inside the tent and shook Skylitzes awake; the officer spoke the local tongue fluently.

Grumbling, Skylitzes went out and talked with the messenger for a few minutes. "We're to meet the clan's shamans tonight," he reported to his companions. "They'll purge us of any evil spirits before we're taken to the khagan." Though he had experience with the customs of the steppe peoples, his unsmiling features were more dour than usual. "Pagans," he said under his breath, and made the sign of Phos' sun on his breast. Goudeles, by contrast, did not seem unduly perturbed at the prospect of going through a foreign ritual.

Outside, the messenger was still talking with the yurt driver, who clucked to his horses. The ungreased axles screeched as the wagon swung southward. Gorgidas looked a question at Skylitzes, who said, "He's taking us to where the shamans are."

An hour or so later the yurt rumbled down into a broad valley. Looking out, the Greek saw that Bogoraz's wain was a couple of hundred yards behind. Twoscore Arshaum horsemen rode between the yurts, making sure Psoes' troopers did not mix it with the Yezda soldiers who guarded Bogoraz. The rest of the wagons with which both parties had been traveling had gone on ahead to Arghun.

A lone tent on wheels stood in the valley, its horses grazing around it. A man got down from it, torch in hand; Gorgidas was too far away to see more than that his costume was strange. Then the yurt-driver said something to the Greek. "Come inside," Skylitzes said. "He says it ruins the magic if we see the sacred fires lit." Gorgidas obeyed with poor grace; how could he learn if he was not allowed to observe?

The yurt drove up close enough for him to hear the crackle of flames; he heard Bogoraz' rolling into place beside it. The driver called out to someone. The reply came back in a reedy tenor, an old man's voice. "We can go out now," Skylitzes said. He turned to stare at Goudeles. "Phos' name, are you still working on that rubbish you spew?"

"Just finding the proper antithesis to balance this clause here," the bureaucrat replied, unruffled. He ostentatiously jotted another note, watching Skylitzes fume. "This will have to suffice," he said at last. "So much is wasted in translation, in any case. Well, come along, Lankinos—it's not I who's keeping them waiting now." And sure enough, the pen-pusher was out the tent flap first.

Bogoraz was alighting from his yurt as well, but Gorgidas hardly noticed him; his attention was riveted on the shamans of the Arshaum. There were three of them, two straight and vigorous, the third stooped with age—he must have answered the Videssian party's driver. They were dressed in ankle-length robes of suede, covered with so many long shaggy fringes sewn on that they seemed more beasts than men. All three wore snarling devil-masks of wood and leather painted in hideous greens, purples, and yellows, adding to their inhuman aspect. Silhouetted against the fires they had set, they capered about, calling out to each other now and then. Their voices echoed, hollow, inside their masks.

Gorgidas watched the display with interest, Skylitzes with active suspicion. But Pikridios Goudeles bowed to the eldest shaman with the same deep respect he might have shown Balsamon, the patriarch of Videssos. The old Arshaum bowed creakily in return and said something.

"Well done, Pikridios," Skylitzes said grudgingly. "The geezer said he didn't know whether to take us or the Yezda first, but your good manners made up his mind for him."

Goudeles bowed again, as deeply as his plump form would allow. The pen-pusher was self-indulgent and bombastic, Gorgidas thought, but he was a diplomat, too.

So, in his way, was Bogoraz. He saw at once he would not be able to change the shaman's decision and so did not try, folding his arms over his chest as if the entire matter was beneath his notice.

Again, Gorgidas watched him out of the corner of his eye. The shamans were busy at their fire, chanting incantations and throwing fragrant frankincense into the flames. The old man rang a bronze bell while his two assistants kept chanting. "Driving away demons," Skylitzes reported.

Then the elder drew out a small packet from beneath his long coat, tossed its contents over the fire. The flames flared up in pure white heat, dazzling Gorgidas' sight and making sweat start on his brow. A blot of darkness against the glare, the shaman approached the Videssian party and spoke. "What?" Skylitzes barked in Videssian. Collecting himself, he spoke in the Arshaum tongue. The shaman repeated himself, gesturing as if to say, "It's all quite simple, you know."

"Well?" Goudeles demanded.

"If I understand him, and I'm afraid I do," Skylitzes said, "he wants us to prove we mean Arghun no harm by walking through the bonfire there. If our intentions are good, he says, nothing will happen. If not—" the officer hesitated, finished, "the fire does what fire does."

"Suddenly being first is an honor I would willingly forego," Goudeles said. Skylitzes, unshakable in the face of physical danger, seemed close to panic at the idea of trusting his safety to a heathen wizard's spell. Gorgidas, who did his best to disbelieve in anything he could not see or feel, wondered why he was not similarly afraid himself. He realized he had been watching the old shaman as closely as if he were a patient; the man glowed with a confidence as bright as the blaze he had called up.

"It will be all right, I think," he said, and was rewarded with matched unhappy looks from Goudeles and Skylitzes, the first time they had agreed with each other in days. Then the old Arashaum grasped at last that the Videssian group had doubts. Waving to reassure them, he took half a dozen backward strides—and was engulfed by flames. They did not burn him. He danced a few clumsy steps in the heart of the fire, while Goudeles' party—and Bogoraz, off to one side—stared at him. When he emerged, not a fringe on his fantastic costume was singed. He waved again, now in invitation.

Goudeles had his own peculiar form of courage. Visibly pulling himself together, he said to no one in particular, "I did not fall off the edge of the map to work an injury on a nomad." He walked briskly up to the edge of the flames. The old shaman patted him on the back, then took his hand and escorted him into the bonfire. The blaze leaped up around them.

Lankinos Skylitzes was biting his lip when Goudeles' voice, full of relief and jubilation, rose above the crackle of the fire. "Quite whole, thank you, and no worse than medium rare," he called. Skylitzes set his jaw and stepped forward. Unnervingly, the old shaman appeared from out of the flames. The officer made Phos' sun-sign over his heart once more, then reached to take the shaman's outstretched hand.

"Here," Skylitzes called a few moments later, laconic as usual. Then the shaman was beckoning to Gorgidas. For all his confidence, the Greek felt a qualm as he came up to the bonfire. He narrowed his eyes to slits against the glare and wondered how long it would be before Goudeles' feeble joke turned true.

The old Arshaum's hand, though, was cool in his, gently urging him into the flames. And as soon as he stepped into the fire, the sensation of heat vanished; it might have been any summer's evening. He was not even sweating. He opened his eyes. The white light surrounded him, but no longer blinded. He looked down at the coals over which he walked and saw they were undisturbed by his passage. Beside him the shaman hummed tunelessly.

Darkness ahead, total after the brilliance that had bathed him. A sudden blast of heat at his back told him he was past the spell. He stumbled away from the fire. Goudeles caught and steadied him. As he regained his vision, he saw Skylitzes gazing back at the blaze like a man entranced. "All light," the officer murmured, awe-struck. "Phos' heaven must be thus."

Goudeles was more practical. "If it has anything to do with Phos, it'll fry that rascal of a Bogoraz to a crackling and do the Empire a great service."

Gorgidas had nursed that same hope, but a few minutes later the shaman came through the fire with the Yezda envoy in hand. At last the Greek had to pay him attention. If he had hoped Wulghash, the khagan of Yezd, would send out some half-barbarous chieflet, he saw at once he was to be disappointed.

Bogoraz was plainly of the old stock of Makuran, the state that had treated with Videssos as an equal for centuries until the Yezda swarmed down from the steppe to conquer it. In his late middle years, he stood tall and spare. He turned for a moment to look at the old shaman; outlined against the flames, a strong hooked nose gave him the brooding profile of a hawk.

His sight clearing, Wulghash's ambassador noticed the Arshaum party and came up to them with a mocking half bow. "An interesting experience, that," he remarked; he spoke the imperial tongue with old-fashioned phrasing but only the faintest hint of his native accent. "Who would have thought these barbarians had such mages among them?"

His eyes were hooded, again like a hawk's; Gorgidas could make out nothing in their black depths. The rest of his face had a lean power in it that was in good accord with his build. His chin was strong and jutting, his cheekbones sharply carved. A thick graying beard, tightly curled like his hair, covered his jaw and cheeks; he let his mustaches grow long enough to hide most of his upper lip. It was a good mouth to keep concealed, wide, with full lips that could easily wear either harshness or sensuality.

The Yezda's presence roused Skylitzes from his golden dream. He touched the hilt of his sword, growling, "I should take care of what the fire bungled."

Bogoraz met him glare for glare, unafraid. The envoy of Yezd carried no weapons; he toyed with the bright brass—or were they gold?—buttons on his coat of brown wool, cut longer behind than before. Under the coat he wore a caftan of some light fabric, striped vertically in muted colors. "Why do you think me less pure of heart than yourself?" he asked, gesturing in sardonic amusement. Gorgidas was struck by his hands, which were slim and elegant, with long tapering fingers—a surgeon's hands, the Greek thought.

"Because you bloody well are," Skylitzes said, ignoring subtleties.

"Softly, my friend." Goudeles laid a hand on the officer's arm. "The truth must be that this is a wizard himself, though shy of admitting it, with spells to defeat the flames." Though he still spoke to Skylitzes, he watched Bogoraz for any telltale response to his probe.

But Bogoraz would not rise for it. "What need have I of magic?" he asked, his smile showing no more of his thoughts than a shaman's mask might. "Truly I wish this Arghun no harm—so long as he does what he should." The mask slipped a trifle, to show the predator behind it.

Viridovix sipped from the skin of kavass. Beside him Targitaus, who had passed it to him, belched loudly and patted his belly. "That is a well-made tipple," he said, "smooth and strong at the same time, like the hindquarters of a mule."

"A mule, you say?" Viridovix needed Lipoxais' translations less each day; he was beginning to understand the Khamorth tongue fairly well, though he still answered in Videssian when he could. "Sure and it tastes like a mule's hind end. I miss my wine."

Some of the plainsmen chuckled, others frowned to hear their traditional drink maligned. "What did he say?" asked Targitus' wife Borane; like most of the women, she had no Videssian. The nomad chieftain explained. Borane rolled her eyes, then winked at the Celt. She was a heavy-featured woman, losing her looks and figure to middle age; as if to turn aside the advancing years, she affected a kittenishness that went poorly with her girth.

Her daughter Seirem showed her one-time beauty like a mirror reflecting an image twenty years gone. "If our blood-cousin does not care for kavass," Seirem said to Targitaus, "maybe he would enjoy the felt tent."

"What was that last?" Viridovix asked Lipoxais; he had caught the words, but not the meaning behind them.

" 'The felt tent,' " the *enaree* translated obligingly. He took the phrase too much for granted to think it needed explaining.

"By my prize bull's pizzle," Targitaus said, "he doesn't know the felt tent!" He turned to his servants. "Kelemerish! Tarim! Fetch the hangings, the cauldron, and the seeds."

The servants rummaged with alacrity in the leather sacks on the northern side of the tent. Tarim, the younger of the two, brought Targitaus a two-eared round cauldron of bronze, full almost to the top with large flat stones. Targitaus sat it in the cookfire to heat. Kelermish gave his chieftain a fist-sized leather bag with a drawstring top. He opened it and poured a nondescript lot of greenish-brown stems, seeds, and crushed leaves into the palm of his hand.

Seeing Viridovix' bewilderment, he said. "It's hemp, of course."

"Will your honor be making rope, then?" The Gaul wished Gorgidas were with him, to wring sense from this fiddle-faddle. Targitaus only snorted. Tarim and Kelermish were closing in the space round the fire with felt blankets hung from the ceiling of the pavilion, making a tent within a tent.

The Khamorth chief looked into the cauldron; the stones were beginning to glow red. He grunted in satisfaction, fished the bronze pot out of the fire by one ear with a long-shanked fork. As he carefully set it in front of Viridovix, his household crowded closer to the Gaul. "You shall have the fine seat tonight."

"Shall I now? And what'll I do with all these rocks? A hot stone's all very well wrapped in flannel for a cold winter's bed, but not for much else I can see. Sure and I can't eat the kettleful of 'em for you."

Had Targitaus been a Videssian, he would have responded to Viridovix' raillery with some elaborate persiflage of his own. As it was, he dumped the handful of leafy rubbish he was holding onto the red-hot stones. A thick cloud of smoke puffed out. It did not smell like the burning grass Viridovix had expected. The odor was thicker, sweeter, almost spicy; of themselves, the Gaul's nostrils twitched.

"What are you waiting for?" Targitaus said. "Don't waste the fine seat; bend down and take a deep breath."

Lured by that intriguing scent, Viridovix leaned over the cauldron until he was close enough to feel the heat radiating up into his face. He sucked in a great lungful of smoke—and then choked and coughed desperately as he tried to blow it out. His chest and windpipe felt as if he had swallowed olive coals. Tears ran down his cheeks. "Och, my puir scorched thrapple," he wheezed, voice a ragged ghost of his usual smooth baritone.

The plainsmen found his splutters funny, which only made things worse. "It's one way to blow the smoke around," Targitaus chuckled, inhaling a less concentrated draft and holding it in his lungs until the Gaul wondered that he did not burst. Other nomads were doing the same and smiling beatifically.

"He's new to it, father. I think you did that on purpose," Seirem accused. "Let him have another chance."

The chieftain's bushy eyebrows and bent nose made it impossible for him to look innocent, whether he was or not. He threw more seeds and leaves on the hot stones; a fresh cloud of fumes rose from them. He waved an invitation to Viridovix.

This time the Celt breathed more cautiously. He could not help making a wry face; however inviting the stuff smelled, it tasted like charred weeds. He coughed again but, gritting his teeth, held most of the smoke down. When he finally let it out, he saw his breath come forth, as he might on a cold winter morning.

That was interesting. He thought about it for a few seconds. They seemed to stretch endlessly. That was interesting, too. He looked at Targitaus through the murky air, which got murkier as the chieftain kept adding dried hemp to the cauldron. "Whisht! A rare potent smoke y'have there."

Targitaus was holding his breath again and did not answer. Viridovix was not put out. He inhaled deeply himself, felt the fumes' soft heaviness behind his eyes.

The sensation was very different from too much wine. The Gaul made a rowdy drunk, always ready for a song or a fight. Now he simply felt insulated from the world in a pleasant sort of way. He knew he could get up and do anything at need, but did not see the need. Even thinking was getting to be more trouble than it was worth.

He gave it up, leaning back on his elbows and watching the nomads around him. Some were sprawled out, limp as he was. Others stalked, low-voiced. Lipoxais was playing a lively song on a white bone flute. The notes seemed to glitter in the air and pull Viridovix after them.

His eyes found Seirem's. A slow smile spread over his face; here was an exercise he would not be too lazy to enjoy. But this was no village of serfs, worse luck, and Seirem no peasant wench to be rumpled at a whim. "Och, the waste of it," he said in his own tongue.

Borane did not miss the lickerish look the Gaul sent her daughter.

She said something to Seirem, too fast for Viridovix to follow. They both laughed uproariously; the nomads were an earthy folk. Seirem hid her face in her hands, peeped at the Celt through interlaced fingers, a coyness that was pure affectation. His grin was wider.

"What was she after telling you?" he asked.

The two women were laughing again. Borane made a hand gesture that showed she did not mind. Still giggling, Seirem answered him: "Something Azarmi said about you—that you were as tall as you were tall."

In a strange language, with his wits fuzzy with fumes, it took Viridovix a little while to work that through. When he did, he chuckled himself. "Did she now?" he said, and sat a bit straighter, the better to display one sort of height, at least.

Hoofbeats thundered in the night outside the tent; Targitaus' sentries exchanged shouts with the riders, then one of them peered through the entranceway and called for his master. Simply making himself sit had been no small feat for Viridovix, but Targitaus, swallowing an oath, stood at once and pushed his way through the crowd of nomads and out past the felt hangings round the fire. Some cool, fresh air got in as he left; the Celt gulped it gratefully.

He heard a man yelling something at the Khamorth chieftain. There was a moment of silence before Targitaus bellowed furiously. He stormed back into the tent. "Up, you lazy sons of lizards! We've had a herd hit!"

The plainsmen scrambled to their feet, shouting curses and questions. The hangings came down with magical speed; the Khamorth clambered for their bows and swords, their corselets of boiled leather. A few clapped on iron caps, but most kept their usual fur headgear.

Broad face dark with anger, Targitaus glared at Viridovix for his slowness. "Come on, outlander—I want you with us. This stinks of Varatesh's work."

"Well, well," Goudeles said in surprised admiration. "Who would have thought the barbarians had such a sense of style?"

The comment was made *sotto voce* as the Videssian embassy approached the Gray Horse clan's ceremonial yurt, where Arghun awaited them. Gorgidas had to agree with the pen-pusher. The Arshaum ceremony was not much less impressive than the one with which the Videssian *hypasteos* Rhadenos Vourtzes had tried to overawe the Romans at Imbros when they were first swept into the Empire.

Here, instead of parasol bearers as a sign of rank, a stalwart nomad stood spear in hand in front of the khagan's yurt. Others, not part of the ritual but real guards, flanked it on either side with drawn bows. Just below the standard-bearer's glittering spearhead dangled three horsetails, symbols of the clan. The warrior was so still he might have been cast in bronze.

So, too, was the single horse that drew the ceremonial yurt. Though only a steppe pony, its coat, which was gray, had been curried till it shone, and its shaggy mane and tail combed and tied with ribbons of orange and gold. It was splendidly caparisoned, with cheekpieces of carved wood and golden harness-ornaments in the shape of griffins' heads. To impress the eye further, it bore a magnificent orange felt saddlecloth, held in place by straps of gilded leather at chest, belly, and tail. On the sides of the cloth, applique-work griffins attacked goats, which were shown cowering away from the fierce mythical beasts.

The yurt itself was silent and closed atop its two-wheeled cart. Unlike all the others Gorgidas had seen, it was the only half-round, with a black wool curtain screening its flattened front. Three more horsetails hung on a slim standard above it.

The standard-bearer could move after all; he spun on his heel and called out to that blank forbidding curtain. Gorgidas caught the phrase "embassy from Videssos"; he had heard it often enough since crossing the Shaum.

There was a moment in which he wondered whether anyone was behind the curtain, but then it was pulled aside, the pause plainly a dramatic effect. Black felt lined the interior of the yurt, to make the figure of Arghun himself, seated on a high-backed chair covered with shining gold leaf, all the more imposing.

Arghun was a more weatherbeaten version of his son Arigh, who stood at the right hand of the throne and smiled in greeting as the Videssians came up. The khagan's hair and straggling chin whiskers were iron-gray rather than black and his face carried deeper lines than his son's, but it was easy to see what the years would do to Arigh. Arghun wore the same furs and fringed hides as the rest of his people, of fine cut but not extraordinarily so. The only sign of his rank Gorgidas could see on his person was the gray horsetail of his clan that he wore at his belt.

To the khagan's left stood a tall, lithe young man of perhaps eighteen, who bore a family resemblance to him and Arigh both, but was far handsomer than either. He was very much aware of it, too; his eye was disdainful as he surveyed the approaching diplomats. With high cheekbones, clear golden skin, and nostrils that arched like gullwings from his slim nose, his presence struck Gorgidas like a blow. Nor did his raiment detract from it: he wore a golden belt, tunic and trousers almost as elaborately fringed as a shaman's, and fine leather shoes embroidered with silver thread.

Goudeles, as head of the mission, stepped forward and went to one knee before the khagan; not the full proskynesis the Avtokrator of the Videssians would receive, but only a step away from it. He bowed low to Arigh and the unknown prince at Arghun's left. Skylitzes, who would serve as translator, followed suit.

"Your majesty Arghun, mighty khagan, your highness prince Arigh—" the titles rolled smoothly off Goudeles' tongue. Then he hesitated in urbane embarrassment. "Your highness prince, ah—"

Arigh spoke across the throne. The young man favored Goudeles with a smile, half-charming, half-scornful. He answered with a single short sentence; his voice was tenor, sweet and self-assured. "His name is Dizabul; he is Arghun's son," Skylitzes interpreted.

"*Younger* son," Arigh emended pointedly, eyeing Dizabul with scant liking. With the sublime arrogance perfect beauty can give, his brother pretended he did not exist.

Ignoring the byplay—or seeming to; the pen-pusher missed very little—Goudeles presented the members of his embassy to Arghun and his sons. Gorgidas surprised himself with the depth of the bow he gave Dizabul; to look at, truly the most striking youth he had seen in years, if rather petulant.

While the khagan greeted the ambassadors, the rest of the clan of the Gray Horse watched from their yurts, which had been drawn discreetly away from their ruler's. More heads appeared at tent flaps and wicker-barred windows when Skylitzes rendered Goudeles' next words into the Arshaum tongue: "His Imperial Majesty Thorisin Gavras has sent the khagan gifts."

Several of Agathias Psoes' troopers stepped forward to present the Emperor's gifts; the underofficer had impressed the solemnity of the occasion on them with a profane bluntness that reminded Gorgidas of Gaius Philippus. Now they played their roles perfectly, advancing one by one to set their presents in front of Arghun's yurt, then withdrawing once more.

"His Imperial Majesty offers gold in token of our future friendship." A small but heavy sack of leather clinked musically as a soldier laid it on the thick, low grass.

Arigh spoke to his father. Skylitzes' mouth twitched in an almost-smile as he translated, "All old coins; I saw to it myself." Arigh was canny enough to insist on best value; the turmoil in Videssos' recent decades had forced the Empire to cheapen its goldpieces with lesser metals. Arghun's smile said he knew that, too. Dizabul looked elaborately bored.

Goudeles was thrown off stride for a moment, but recovered smoothly. "Silver for the khagan!" Prevalis Haravash's son brought up a larger sack to set beside the first. The jingle was higher-pitched than that of gold, but still sweet.

"Jewels for the khagan's treasury, or for his ladies: rubies, topazes, opals like fire, pearls like moonlight!" When the next trooper set his gift down, Goudeles opened the sack and displayed a glowing pearl in the palm of his hand. Gorgidas gave him high marks for shrewdness; living so far from the sea, Arghun might never have seen a pearl. The khagan leaned forward to examine it, nodded, sat back once more.

"Fine vestments for your majesty." Some of the robes were cloth-of-gold, others of samite or snowy linen, heavily brocaded, bejeweled, and shot through with gold and silver thread. Here at last was stuff to rouse Dizabul's interest, but his father seemed indifferent in the finery.

"Last, as a mark of honor, the Avtokrator presents you with boots striped in the imperial scarlet." Only the Videssian Emperor wore footgear all of scarlet; for him to share the color even in this way was a signal act of deference. Duke Tomond of Namdalen did not presume to wear red boots.

Speaking through Arigh, Arghun said, "These are fine gifts. Are there words to go with them?"

"Will a cock crow? Will a crow caw?" Skylitzes murmured in Videssian as Goudeles visibly gathered himself for a flight of rhetoric. Arigh snickered but, being pro-Videssian, did not explain the ridicule to his father.

Goudeles himself could only glower at his comrade out of the corner of his eye. He began the opening address he had been toying with for days: "O valiant Arghun, our great Emperor—" He had a bureaucrat's revenge on Skylitzes there, loading that "great" with so much stress as to make the word a travesty. "—using me as his messenger, indicates that fortune should always be auspicious for you, as you take pleasure in treating with the Empire of Videssos, and also as you show kindness to us its legates. May you always conquer your enemies and despoil your foes. May there be no malice between us, as far as is possible; such exists only to cleave asunder the establishment of friendship."

"Slow down, curse you," Skylitzes whispered frantically. "If I don't know what you're talking about, how do you expect them to?"

"They don't need to, really," Goudeles answered under cover of a dramatic gesture. "I'm saying what has to be said at a time like this, that's all." He bowed once more to Arghun, and finished, "The people of the clan of the Gray Horse and however many subjects they may have are dear to us; may you not hold our affairs otherwise." He stepped back a pace to show the oration was done.

"Very pretty," Arigh said; his years in Videssos let him appreciate Goudeles' performance more readily than his father or brother could. "I—" The khagan interrupted him. He nodded, abashed; in Arghun's presence he was no hotspur, but an obedient son. He said, "My father would like to reply through me. No offense to you, Lankinos, you speak very well, but—"

"Of course," Skylitzes said quickly.

"We are honored to hear the khagan's remarks," Goudeles added.

Gorgidas braced himself for another high-flown speech. Instead, Arghun fell silent after two sentences. His son translated: "My thanks for the presents. As for your embassy, I will decide what to do when I have also heard the man from Yezd."

Goudeles frankly gaped. "That's all?" he squeaked, surprised out of elaborate syntax. He looked as if he had been stabbed, then slowly led the Videssian party to one side. " 'My thanks for the presents,' " he muttered. "Bah!" He swore with unbureaucratic imagination.

"You spoke well, but the nomads' style is different from yours," Gorgidas told him. "They admire Videssian rhetoric, though—remember Olbiop? And Arghun strikes me as a prudent leader. Would you expect him to say yes or no without listening to both sides?"

Slightly consoled, Goudeles shook his head. "I wish he would," Skylitzes said. But Bogoraz of Yezd was already coming up to the khagan's yurt. Skylitzes' stare was as intense as if they were meeting on the battlefield.

The Yezda envoy, like Goudeles, went to one knee before Arghun; the dignity of his salute was marred when the black felt skullcap he wore fell to the ground as he dipped his head. But he quickly regained the advantage when he spoke to the khagan in the Arshaum tongue.

"A plague!" Gorgidas and Goudeles said together. The Greek went on, "That can't help influencing Arghun, whether he realizes it or not."

"Hush!" said Skylitzes, and after listening for a moment, "Less than you'd think. The scoundrel has a mushy Khamorth accent, good for making any Arshaum look down his flat nose."

"What's he saying?" Goudeles asked; he had no more of Arghun's language than did Gorgidas.

"Same garbage you were putting out, Pikridios. No, wait, here's something new. He says Wulghash—Skotos freeze him!—knows what a great warrior Arghun is, and sends him presents fit for a warrior."

At Bogoraz's imperious wave, one of his guardsmen laid a scabbard of enamel-decorated polished bronze before the khagan. With a placating glance at the Arshaum bowmen, the ambassador drew the curved sword to display it to Arghun. It was a rich and perfect product of the swordsmith's art, from hilt wrapped in gold wire to gleaming blade. After a ceremonial flourish, Bogoraz sheathed it again and presented it to the khagan.

Arghun drew it himself to test the balance, smiled with genuine pleasure, and buckled it to his belt. Smiling, too, Bogoraz gave similar blades to his sons; they differed only in that their hilts were wrapped with silver rather than gold. Dizabul fairly licked his lips as he took his weapon from the Yezda; even Arigh unhesitatingly wore his.

For the moment all but forgotten, the Videssian party watched their reaction in dismay. Skylitzes ground his teeth. "We should have thought of that."

"Aye," Goudeles agreed mournfully. "These plains barbarians are fierce folk; they take more kindly to edged metal than robes of state, where our own people, I think, would esteem them equally."

Trying as he usually did to find general rules from the examples life offered him, Gorgidas said, "It's wrong to judge others by one's own standards. We Greeks burn our dead, while the Indians—" He stopped, reddening, as the others turned to stare; India—Greece, too!—meant nothing here.

Bogoraz's parade of costly weaponry continued: daggers with hunting scenes picked out on their blades with gold leaf; double-curved bows reinforced with horn, buffed and waxed till they sparkled; arrows of fragrant cedar fletched with iridescent peacock plumes, in quivers of snakeskin; spiked helmets ornamented with jewels.

Dizabul chose to wear every item the Yezda gave him; by the time Bogoraz was done, he looked like a walking armory. Caressing the hilt of the new sword, he turned and spoke to his father. His voice carried; plainly he meant it to. Bogoraz gave the Videssian embassy a satisfied smirk.

Skylitzes, on the other hand, worked his jaws harder than ever. He grated, "The pup is all for throwing us out now, or filling us full of holes with his new toys. He's calling us 'the worthless hucksters Arigh brought.' "

Arghun's elder son bristled at that and began a hot response. The khagan snarled at him and Dizabul both. Dizabul started to say something more, but subsided when Arghun half rose from his throne.

Collecting himself, Arghun turned back to Bogoraz, who had affected to notice nothing. But some of the Yezda's top-loftiness fell away when Arghun dismissed him as abruptly as he had Goudeles. "The gifts are splendid, he says," Skylitzes reported, "but any alliance needs more thought." The Videssian officer seemed almost unbelieving.

"He *is* a clever leader," Gorgidas said.

"Indeed he is; he milks both sides impartially," Goudeles said. He sounded as relieved as Skylitzes. "Well, good for him. The game's still even."

Viridovix dismounted without grace, but with a great groan of relief. Three hard days in the saddle had left him sore and stiff to the point of anguish. As he had before, he marveled at the endurance of the plainsmen; once mounted, they seemed made into—what was the Greek word for beings half man, half horse? Unable to remember, he mumbled a curse.

The air did not lend itself to such musings; it was thick with the sickly-sweet stench of death. And Targitaus was watching, grim-faced, as the Gaul paced about trying to stomp blood back into his calves and feet. "Another ride like that and I'll be as bowlegged as you Khamorth laddies." Not knowing the word for "bowlegged," he illustrated with gestures.

He failed to amuse the nomad chieftain, who said, "Save your jokes for the women. Nothing to laugh at here." Viridovix flushed. Targitaus did not notice; he had already turned back to the carnage spread before him.

It must have been worse a week before, when his herders found it, still fresh. Yet even after the scavengers had feasted, what was left was quite bad enough. Half a hundred cattle had been lured away from the herd, and then—what? "Slaughtered" was too gentle a word for the massacre here.

The ground was still dark from the blood that had soaked into it when the cows' throats were cut. The killing alone would have been enough to make this no ordinary raid. Cattle were for herding and for stealing, not liquidation. The steppe was too harsh to let a tradition of wanton killing grow; even in war, winners simply took herds and flocks from their defeated foes—herds and flocks were war's object, not its target.

But not here, not now. These beasts sprawled in death were more pitiful than warriors fallen on a battlefield; beasts have no choice in their fate and no chance to avert it. And that fate had been cruel, viciously so.

Great cuts had been made in the carcasses, and filth smeared into them to spoil the meat. The hides were not only gashed, but also rubbed with some potent caustic that made them worthless, too. Targitaus' clan could have salvaged nothing from the animals even if they had been discovered the hour after they died.

The chief's son Batbaian paced from one mutilated cow to the next, shaking his head and tugging at his beard as he tried without success to understand what he saw. He turned helplessly to his father. "They must be mad, as dogs are, to do this!" he burst out.

The clan leader said sadly, "I wish you were right, boy. This is Varatesh's way of trying to make me afraid and make me sorry for sheltering the outlander here." He bobbed his head, so like Batbaian's, at Viridovix.

To the Gaul, though, the savagery he saw here called up another memory, of a body outside the walls of Videssos the city, when the legionaries were helping Thorisin Gavras lay siege to the Sphrantzai within. Along with other torments, poor Doukitzes' outraged corpse had borne a name sliced into its forehead: Rhavas. As soon came clear, that needed but a rearrangement of letters to reveal the killer.

"It's Avshar's sport I make this," he said. "I've tried to tell you of him till the now and made no headway at it—the which I canna blame you for, as you'd not seen the way of him. But hark, an you will." In the Khamorth speech as best he could, in Videssian when it failed him, he spoke of Doukitzes and much else: of the wizard-prince's duel with Scaurus when the Romans first came to Videssos the city; of Maragha and afterward, and Mavrikios Gavras' head flung into the legionary camp; of the Grand Courtroom in the capital, and Avshar's sorcery for making the worst of his rogues invulnerable to steel.

The obscenity and cruelty of that last tale shook the plainsmen. "He made his magic with a woman, you say?" Targitaus demanded, as if he thought his ears were tricking him.

"Aye, and with her unborn wean ripped from her," the Celt replied. The plainsman shuddered. Where the slaughter of his beasts left him coldly furious, here was malice worse than he had dreamed possible.

With youth's temerity, Batbaian cried, "Let's be rid of him, then—

burn his tent over his head and all who follow him, too!" Looking at their cattle, with Viridovix' words still hanging over them, the Khamorth shouted, "Aye!"

And, "Aye," said Targitaus as well, but softly. Where his clansmen had only caught the horror in the Gaul's tale, he also saw what it revealed of Avshar's power. "Aye," he said again, and added, "if we can."

He looked at Viridovix, not happily. "I see it is time to gather the clans against Varatesh and this Avshar of yours."

"Past time," Viridovix said at once, and Batbaian gave a vigorous nod. Despite Targitaus' ringing promises of war on the outlaw chief, weeks had dragged by without much happening.

The chief looked uncomfortable. "You come from Videssos, outlander, where the khag—er, the Emperor, tells his men, 'Do this,' and they do it or lose their heads. It is not like that on the plains. If I go to Ariapith of the Oglos River clan, or Anakhar of the Spotted Cats, or Krobyz of the Leaping Goats and tell them we should clean out Varatesh together, the first thing they will say is, 'Who leads?' What do I answer? Me? They will say I try to set my Wolfskins up as Royal Clan, and have nothing to do with me."

"Royal Clan?" the Celt echoed.

"Sometimes a clan will get the better of all the ones around it and rule the steppe for a while, even for a man's life, until they get free and pull it down." Ambition glowed in Targitaus' eyes. "Every khagan dreams of founding a Royal Clan and has nightmares his neighbor will do it first. So each watches the next, and no one gets too strong."

"So that's the way of it, eh?" Suddenly Viridovix found himself on familiar ground. In Gaul before the Romans came, the tribes were constantly jockeying for position, squabbling and intriguing for all they were worth. The Aedui had held pride of place until the Sequani allied with the Ubii from over the Rhine and usurped their dominant position. In the process, though, they had made Ariovistus the German the most powerful man in Gaul. . . .

The Celt's eyes sparked green; he whooped with glee and clapped his hands together. "How's this?" he said to Targitaus, who had swung round in surprise, half drawing his sword. "Suppose you're after telling old Crowbait o' the Spotted Hamsters, or whatever his fool name is, that

Varatesh is aiming to make his piratical spalpeens Royal Clan, the which is nothing less than true. Sure and he'd piss himself or ever he let that happen, now wouldn't he?"

He could all but hear the wheels spinning inside the nomad chief's head. Targitaus looked at Batbaian, who was staring at Viridovix with awe on his face; the young are easily impressed on hearing things they have not thought of for themselves. "Hmm," said Targitaus, and the Gaul knew he had won.

Batbaian exclaimed, "Guide your herds right in this, father, and it'd be you who'd be Royal Clan khagan!"

"Me? Nonsense, boy," Targitaus said gruffly, but Viridovix saw the thought had struck him before his son voiced it. He chuckled to himself.

Dizabul stabbed the last strip of broiled rabbit from the boiled-leather bowl he held in his lap, chewed noisily with the good manners of the steppe. He leaned forward; the cook lifted more sizzling meat from the griddle with a pair of wooden tongs, refilled his bowl. He sat back with a smile of thanks. Turning to his left, he murmured something to Bogoraz and flourished the elegant dagger the Yezda envoy had given him. That dazzling smile flashed again.

Slurping kavass from a golden goblet, Gorgidas covertly admired the young man, whose beauty stirred a pleasant pain in him. In the nomad way, Arghun had provided women for the Videssian embassy, but though Gorgidas was finding he could perform with them for necessity's sake, they did not satisfy him. After each coupling he felt as a sailor might who turned at sea to a shipmate to relieve his lusts although caring nothing for love of men ashore.

With a stab of pain and loss, he remembered Quintus Glabrio's slim, quiet, intent face, remembered the mixed amusement and distaste with which the junior centurion had spoken of his time with a Videssian girl. "Damaris deserved something different from me, I suppose," he'd said once, adding with a wry laugh, "*She* certainly thought so after a while." That liaison had broken up in spectacular style, along with much crockery.

Thinking of Glabrio helped put Dizabul in perspective. The Roman had been a man, a partner, while the Arshaum princeling showed every sign of being no more than a much-coddled younger son, with spiteful temper to match. Moreover, Gorgidas had learned, he had a son and two daughters of his own by slaves and serving girls.

The Greek drank again. Still, no denying he was lovely.

In his musings over Dizabul, Gorgidas had given scant attention to the great banquet tent. That did it less than justice; it was as important to the Arshaum as the Imperial Palace was to Videssos and had proportional splendor lavished on it. The yurt was the largest he had seen on the plains, easily forty feet across and drawn by a team of twenty-two horses.

Outside, its thick, felt panels had been chalked white to make it stand out against the drab steppe. Now the Greek noticed the silk hangings that lined the stick framework within, work as splendid as any the Empire could boast. The shimmering fabric was dyed saffron and green; the embroidered horses galloping across it were executed with the barbaric vigor that characterized nomad art.

Arghun, his sons, and the rival embassies sat round the cookfire on rugs of thick, soft wool. The clan's elders made a couple of larger circles around them. The Arshaum sat cross-legged, with either boot hiked onto the opposite thigh. Their guests sprawled every which way—unless practiced from birth, the nomad posture was fiendishly uncomfortable.

At his father's right, Arigh twisted himself into the position for a while, then gave it up with a rueful headshake and a loud creak from his knees. "You've been in Videssos too long," Skylitzes told him.

The look Dizabul gave his brother said he would have liked it better had Arigh stayed there longer still.

"Until we got here, I didn't know you had a brother," Goudeles said to Arigh; Gorgidas was not the only one who'd seen that poisonous stare.

"I'd almost forgotten him myself," Arigh said, dismissing Dizabul with a wave of his hand. "He was just a brat underfoot when I left for the Empire seven or eight years ago—hasn't changed much, looks like." He spoke Videssian so his brother would not understand, but Gorgidas frowned when Bogoraz whispered behind his hand to Dizabul. A flush climbed the young man's high cheekbones, and the scowl he sent Arigh's way made his earlier glower seem loving by comparison.

Servants scurried back and forth, filling goblets from silver pitchers of kavass and fetching food for the Arshaum not within arm's length of the cook. Along with the rabbit Dizabul enjoyed, there was an enormous roasted bird. "Eh? It's a crane," Arigh said in reply to Gorgidas' question. "Good, too—haven't eaten one in years." With that nomad way he had no trouble; his strong white teeth ripped meat away from a legbone. The Greek controlled his enthusiasm. The bird was tasty, but tough as leather.

The mutton and tripes were better, as were the cheeses, both hard and soft; some of the last had sweet berries stirred through them. As well as the kavass, there was fresh milk from cows, goats, and horses, none of which tempted Gorgidas. He would have paid a pretty price for real wine or a handful of salted olives.

When he remarked on that, Arigh shook his head with a grimace of disgust. "Wine is a good thing, but in all the time I was in Videssos I never got used to olives. They taste funny, and the imperials put them in everything. And the oil stinks." Arshaum lamps burned butter, which to the Greek's nose had its own pervasive, greasily unpleasant smell.

Conversation in the banquet tent was halting, and not only because of the language barrier. Arigh had warned the Videssian embassy that Arshaum custom did not allow serious business to be discussed at feasts. It let Gorgidas enjoy his food more, but left him bored with the few snatches of talk he could follow.

Bogoraz, who had a gift for rousing trouble without seeming to mean to, skated close to the edge of what custom permitted. Without ever mentioning his reasons for coming onto the steppe, he bragged of Yezd's might and the glory of his overlord the khagan Wulghash. Skylitzes kept translating his boasts and grew angrier by the minute. Satisfaction and sardonic amusement in his eyes, Bogoraz stayed on his course, never saying anything against Videssos in so many words, but hurting its cause with every urbane sentence.

After a while, Skylitzes' knuckles grew white on the stem of his goblet. The clan councilors were beginning to chuckle among themselves at the fury he had to hold in. "I'll tell that sleazy liar something!" he growled.

"No!" Arigh and Goudeles said together. The pen-pusher went on, "Don't you see, he'll have you in the wrong if you answer him."

"Is this better, to be nibbled to death with his sly words?"

Surprised at his own daring, Gorgidas said, "I know a story that might put him in his place."

Skylitzes, Goudeles, and Arigh all stared at the Greek. To the Videssians he was almost as much a barbarian as the Arshaum, not to be taken seriously; Arigh tolerated him largely because he was Viridovix' friend. "You won't break custom?" he warned.

Gorgidas tossed his head. "No, it's just a story." Goudeles and Skylitzes looked at each other, shrugged, and nodded, at a loss for any better idea.

Bogoraz, whose Videssian was certainly better than the Greek's, had listened to this exchange with amiable disdain, seeing that Gorgidas' companions did not put much faith in him. His heavy-lidded eyes screened his contempt as Gorgidas dipped his head to Arghun and, with Arigh translating, said, "Khagan, this man from Yezd is a fine speaker, no doubt of it. His words remind me of a tale of my own people."

Beyond what was required for politeness, the Arshaum chieftain had not paid Gorgidas much attention either. Now he looked at him with fresh interest; in a folk that did not read, a tale-teller was someone to be respected. "Let us hear it," he said, and the elders fell quiet to listen.

Pleased Arghun had swallowed the hook, Gorgidas plunged in: "A long time ago, in a country called Egypt, there was a great king named Sesostris." He saw men's lips moving, fixing the strange names in their memories. "Now this Sesostris was a mighty warrior and conqueror, just as our friend Bogoraz says his master Wulghash is." The smile slipped on the Yezda's face; the sarcasm he relished was not so enjoyable coming back at him.

"Sesostris conquered many countries, and took their princes and kings as his slaves to show how powerful he was. He even put them in harness and made them pull his, er, yurt." As the Greek had heard the story, it was a chariot; he made the quick switch to suit his audience.

"One day he noticed that one of the princes kept looking back over his shoulder at the yurt's wheels. He asked the fellow what he was doing.

"And the prince answered, 'I'm just watching how the wheels go round and round, and how what was once at the bottom is now on top, and what used to be high is brought low.' Then he turned round again and put his shoulder into his work.

"But Sesostris understood him, and they say that, for all his pride, he stopped using princes to haul his yurt."

The strange sounding mutter of conversation in a foreign tongue picked up again as the Arshaum considered the tale, talked about it among themselves. One or two of them sent amused glances toward Bogoraz, thinking back to his boasts. As befit his station, Arghun held his face expressionless. He said a few words to his elder son, who turned to Gorgidas. "He thanks you for an, ah, enjoyable story."

"I understood him." Repeating his half bow to the khagan, the Greek tried to say that in the Arshaum speech. Arghun did smile, then, and corrected his grammar.

Bogoraz, too, wore a diplomat's mask, set so hard it might have been carved from granite. He aimed his hooded eyes at Gorgidas like a snake charming a bird. The Greek was not one to be put in fear by such ploys, but knew he had made an enemy.

IX

Garsavra, once reached, made all the factional strife Marcus had seen in Videssos seem as nothing. On the march west the legionaries had captured and sent back to the capital upwards of a thousand Namdaleni, fleeing their defeat at the hands of the Yezda in the small, disordered bands any beaten army breaks into. A hundred or so still held the motte-and-bailey outside Garsavra, defying Roman and Yezda alike. The tribune did not try to force them out; they were more useful against the nomads nosing down from the plateau than dangerous to his own men.

There were already Yezda in Garsavra when the legionaries got there. The town was not under their control; before Scaurus' troops arrived, it was under no one's control—which meant no one kept them out, either. Attacking them hardly seemed politic while haggling with their chief, so the tribune pretended not to notice them.

The nomads caused little trouble, going through the town like tourists and marveling at the huge buildings. Compared to Videssos the city or Rome, it was a sleepy provincial capital, but to men who lived their lives in tents it was strange and exotic beyond belief. The Yezda traded in the marketplace for civilization's luxuries and fripperies. Marcus saw one of them proudly wearing a white-glazed chamberpot on his head in place of the ubiquitous nomad fur cap. He would have told the nomad what he had, but the fellow's comrades were so admiring he did not have the heart. Quite a few local Videssians saw it, too; it gave the Yezda a new nickname, which might make trouble later.

That was the least of the tribune's problems with the locals. Faced as they were with the threat of attack from the central highlands, he had expected them to join together in receiving the legionaries favorably. Moreover, he needed them to do so. Even with Pakhymer's contribution, he was still eight thousand gold pieces short of the twenty thousand Yavlak demanded for his important captives. He had dispatched messages to the capital, but had no confidence they would bring the quick results he needed. With Thorisin Gavras fighting in the east, no one in Videssos had the driving will to hurry the imperial bureaucracy along. Scaurus knew that bureaucracy too well; he planned to raise the money he needed from the people of Garsavra and repay them when the pen-pushers finally got around to shipping gold west.

Expecting any large number of Videssians to agree about anything, however, as he should have remembered, was so much wishful thinking. True, many Garsavrans favored Thorisin—or said so, loudly, while the Emperor's troops held their city. But almost as many still held to the lost cause of Baanes Onomagoulos; the rebellious noble Drax had crushed before revolting in his turn had held huge estates not far south of Garsavra. Dead, especially dead at foreign hands, no one remembered his faults. The arrogant, liverish, treacherous little man was magically transformed into a martyr.

By contrast, a third party was sorry to see the Namdaleni beaten and imperial rule restored. Antakinos had warned Marcus the islanders were popular in the cities they had taken, and his warning was true. Drax had a smaller state to run than the Empire and so did not tax his towns as heavily as the imperials had. From novelty if nothing else, that was enough to gain him a good-sized following.

As subject people will, some of the Garsavrans had gone over to their conquerors' ways, even to the extent of worshiping at the temple Drax had converted to the Namdalener rite for his own men to use. The idea infuriated Styppes, who got into a shouting match with a Namdalener priest he happened to run into in the city marketplace.

Scaurus, who had been dickering with a tremor over the price of a new belt, looked up in alarm at the bellow of, "Seducer! Greaser of the skid to Skotos' ice!" Face crimson with rage, fists clenched in righteous wrath, the healer-priest shouldered his way toward the man of the Duchy, who held a fat mallard under each arm.

"By the Wager, conceited Cocksure, yours is the path to hell, not mine!" the islander yelled back, facing up to him. His priestly robe was a grayer shade of blue than Styppes'; he did not shave his head, as Videssian priests did. But his faith in his own righteousness was as strong as any imperial's.

"Excuse me," Marcus whispered to the leather seller. At a trot, as if heading into battle, he hurried toward the two priests, who were swearing at each other like a couple of cattle drovers. If he could get Styppes away before argument turned to riot . . . Too late. A crowd was already gathering. But they were crying, "Debate! Debate! Come hear the debate!" This was a diversion they had enjoyed before, with local clerics against the Namdaleni. Now they came running to hear what the new priest had to offer.

Styppes glared about as if not believing his ears. Scaurus was equally surprised, but much happier. They might get away without bloodshed after all. The tribune winced as Styppes clapped a dramatic hand to his forehead and declared, "Misbelief is to be rooted out, not discussed."

"Heh! I'll talk to *you*," the Namdalener said. He was about forty, with tough, square, dogged features that seemed better suited to an infantry underofficer than a priest. Almost as heavy as Styppes, he bore his weight better, more like an athlete gone to seed than a simple glutton. He gave an ironic bow. "Gerungus of Tupper, at your service."

Styppes coughed and fumed, but the crowd, to Marcus' relief, kept shouting for a debate. With poor grace, the healer-priest told Gerungus his name. "As you are the heretic, I shall begin," the Videssian said, "and leave you to defend your false doctrines as best you can."

Gerungus muttered something unpleasant under his breath, but shrugged massive shoulders and said, "One of us has to." His Videssian was only slightly accented.

"Then I shall commence by asking how you islanders come to pervert Phos' creed by appending to it the clause 'on this we stake our very souls.' What authority have you for this addition? What synod sanctioned it, and when? As handed down from our learned and holy forefathers, the creed was perfect, as it stood, and should receive no valueless codicils." Marcus raised his eyebrows. Here in his area of expertise, Styppes showed more eloquence than the tribune had thought in him. Cries of approval rang from the crowd.

But every Videssian priest who disputed with Gerungus challenged him so. His answer was prompt: "Your ancient scholars lived in a fool's paradise, when the Empire ruled all the way to the Haloga country and Skotos' evil seemed far away. But you Videssians were sinners, and Skotos gained the chance to show his power. That is how the barbarians came to wrest Khatrish and Thatagush from you, aye, and Kubrat that was. For Skotos inspired the wild Khamorth from the steppe and corrupted you so you could not resist. And it grew plain Skotos' power is all too real, all too strong. Who knows whether Phos will prevail in the end? It could turn out otherwise."

Now Styppes was white, not red. "A Balancer!" he exclaimed, and the crowd growled menacingly. To the imperials, Khatrish's belief in the evenness of the struggle between good and evil was a worse heresy than the one the Namdaleni professed.

"Not so, if you give me leave to finish," Gerungus returned steadily. "Neither you nor I will be here to see the last battle between Phos and Skotos. How can we know the outcome? But we must act as if we were sure good will triumph, or face the eternal ice. I take the gamble proudly—'on this I stake my very soul.'" He stared round, defying the crowd. Marcus looked, too, and saw the Videssians unwontedly quiet. Gerungus' oratory was not as florid as Styppes', but effective all the same.

The tribune saw Nevrat Sviodo standing behind Gerungus, her thick black hair curling down over her shoulders. She smiled when their eyes met. She made a slight motion of her hand to indicate the intent crowd, then pointed toward Scaurus and nodded, as if including the two of them but no one else. He nodded back, understanding perfectly. As a Vaspurakaner, she had her own version of Phos' faith, while the Roman stood outside it altogether. Neither could grow heated over this debate.

Styppes was blowing and puffing like a beached whale, gathering his wits for the next sally. "Very pretty," he grunted, "but Phos does not throw dice with Skotos over the universe—the twin ones of 'the suns' for peace and order against the double six of 'the demons' for famine and strife. That would put chaos at Phos' heart, which cannot be.

"No, my friend," the healer-priest went on, "it is not so simple; there is more knowledge in Phos' plan than that. Nor does Skotos have need of dice to work his ends, with such as you to lead men toward falsehood from the truth. The dark god's demons record each sin of yours in their ledgers, aye, and the day and hour it was committed, and the witnesses to it. Only true repentance and genuine belief in Phos' true faith can rub out such an entry. Each blasphemy you utter sets you one step closer to the ice!"

Styppes' passion was unmistakable, though Scaurus thought his logic poor. As the healer-priest and his Namdalener counterpart argued on, the tribune's attention wandered. It stuck him that, with a few words changed, Styppes' account of the demons in hell and their sin ledgers could have been a description of the imperial tax agents' account books. He did not think the resemblance coincidental and wondered whether the Videssians had noticed it for themselves.

A wisp of stale, stinking smoke made the tribune cough as he trod up the steps of the Garsavran provincial governor's hall, a red brick building with columns of white marble flanking the entrance way. Heavily armed squads of legionaries stood prominently in the marketplace and prowled the town's main streets, making sure riot would not break out afresh. Had the one just quelled erupted a few days earlier, he would have blamed it on tension from the theological debate. As it was, he suspected the rich merchants and local nobles waiting for him inside, the men who would have to pay to help buy Drax and his comrades from the Yezda. If they could drive the Romans out of Garsavra, their purses would be safe—and too many of them were pro-Namdalener to begin with.

He was glad of his own officers at his back. They all wore their most imposing gear, with crested helms, short capes of rank, and mail shirts burnished bright, the better to overawe the Garsavrans. A buccinator followed, carrying his horn as he might a sword.

Scaurus ran memorized phrases from his address over and over in his mind. Styppes, grumbling as usual, had helped him work on it. His own Videssian was fine for casual conversation, but in formal settings the imperials demanded formal oratory, which was nearly a different language from the ordinary speech. The Gavrai now and then got away with bluntness, but that was partly because everyone assumed they had the high style at their disposal. The tribune's unadorned words would merely mark him as a barbarian, and today he needed to seem a representative of the imperial government, not some extortionate brigand.

Styppes still thought the speech too plain, but it was as ornate as the Roman could stand.

He turned to Gaius Philippus, who had listened to him rehearse. "What would Cicero think?"

"That fat windbag? Who cares? Caesar's worth five of him on the rostrum; he says what he means—and with all due respect, I think Caesar'd puke right down the front of his toga."

"Can't say I'd blame him. I feel like Ortaias Sphrantzes."

"Oh, it's not as bad as *that,* sir!" Gaius Philippus said hastily. They both laughed. Ortaias never used one word when ten would do—especially if eight of them were obscure.

Marcus motioned the buccinator forward; he preceded the legionary party into the governor's audience chamber. The tribune got his first glimpse of the locals, a score or so of men who sat talking amiably with each other and fanning themselves against the late summer's humid heat.

The sharp note of the trumpet cut through their chatter. Some of them jumped; all craned their necks toward the doorway through which Scaurus was coming. He looked neither right nor left as he took his seat in the governor's high chair and rested his arms on the exquisite rosewood table in front of it. A lot of fundaments had been in that seat lately, he thought: a legitimate governor or two, Onomagoulos, Drax, Zigabenos perhaps, and now himself—and better him than Yavlak.

His officers stood behind him: Gaius Philippus, Junius Blaesus, and Sextus Minucius frozen to attention; Sittas Zonaras lending a Videssian touch to the party; Gagik Bagratouni a powerful physical presence in Vaspurakaner armor; and Laon Pakhymer half-amused, looking as if he were playing at charades.

He rose, looking over his audience. They stared back, some as impressed as he had hoped, others bored—most of those had the sleek look of merchants—two or three openly hostile. Not a bad mix, really, no worse than he had faced in the town senate of Mediolanum—how long ago it seemed!

He took a deep breath. For a frightening moment he thought his address had fled, but it came back to him when he began to speak: "Gentlemen, you were chosen by me today for this council; pay heed now to my words. You know how the Namdalener wickedly subdued the cities of the west; he collected tribute from you, ravaged your villages and towns in his illegal rebellion, and treated men's bodies evilly, subjecting them to unbearable exaction of their few resources. Therefore it is amazing to me, gentlemen of Garsavra, how easily you are deceived by those who have outwitted you and seek your help at the cost of your blood. They are the very ones who have done you the greatest harm, for what sort of benefit did you gain from this rebellion, other than murders and mutilations and the amputation of limbs?"

He almost laughed at the pop-eyed expression on the face of the fat man in the second row, who was in the wine trade. Likely the fellow had never heard an outlander say anything more complex than, "Gimme another mug."

Relishing his speech for the first time, the tribune continued: "Now those who would help the Namdalener have stirred you to anger and strife, yet contrived to keep their own property undamaged." Let them be suspicious of each other, Marcus thought. "At the same time, however, they still claim protection of the Empire and seek to cast the blame for their actions on the innocent. Is it expedient for you, gentlemen, to allow those who fawn on the rebel to wring advantage from you thus?

"For by Phos' assent," Marcus continued, with a phrase Styppes had suggested, and one Scaurus would not have thought of otherwise, "you see that the Namdalener is a prisoner. Now that we are delivered from his wickedness, we must ensure that he does not escape, like smoke from the oven. And he who captured him now asks his price."

Seeing he was getting to the meat of the matter, his listeners leaned forward in anticipation. "If the Emperor were not campaigning far away, or if the barbarian holding the Namdalener allowed a delay, I would hurry to Videssos to collect that price. As you see, however, this is impossible, nor do I myself have the necessary money. Therefore it will be necessary for each of you to contribute according to his ability, lest the Yezda decide to ravage your land while awaiting his payment. I declare to you that this is the situation as it exists and pledge that, as much as you pay, it shall be restored to you by the Emperor."

He sat down, waiting for their response; they looked as pleased with the prospect of parting with their gold as he had expected. The fat wine merchant spoke for them all when he said, "Pay us back? Aye, no doubt, just as the shearer gives the sheep back their wool."

Privately, Marcus would have admitted he had a point; like any state, Videssos was happier to gather money than to spend it. What he said, though, was, "I have some influence at the capital, and I do not let the folk who help me be forgotten." They understood that; the patron-client relationship was less formal in Videssos than in Rome, but no less real. But hereabouts they were the powerful men, unused to depending on anyone else, let alone a foreign mercenary.

Zonaras spoke up. "This one has a strange habit; when he says he'll do something, he does it." He told how the legionaries had held the Namdaleni out of the hills and organized the irregulars to carry the war to them in the lowlands. "And all that," he said, "seemed a lot less likely than collecting from the treasury."

"Nothing is less likely than collecting from the treasury," the fat man insisted, drawing a short laugh. But he and his companions had listened attentively; because Zonaras was a Videssian, they were more inclined to believe him than the tribune.

One of the local nobles, a lean, nearly bald man whose back was bent with age, struggled to his feet, leaning on a stick. He stabbed a gnarled finger at Scaurus. "It was you, then, taught our farmers to be brigands, was it?" he shrilled. With his jutting nose and thin ruff of white hair, he looked like an old, angry vulture. "Two of my wells fouled, stock run off or killed, my steward kidnapped and branded. You brought this down on me?" He stood straighter in his outrage, brandishing the stick like a sword.

But from the back of the chamber someone called, "Oh, stifle it, Skepides. If you'd shown your tenants any fairness the past fifty years, you'd have nothing to moan about."

"Eh? What was that?" Not catching the jibe, Skepides turned back to Scaurus. "I tell you this, sir, I'd sooner deal with the Namdaleni than a seditionary like yourself, Skotos take me if I wouldn't. And I'll have no more to do with this scheme of yours." Slowly and painfully he made his way to the aisle. He hobbled out. Two or three of the Videssians followed him.

"Try to talk them round," Marcus urged. "The more who share the cost, the less it falls on each of you."

"And what will you do if none of us goes along?" another merchant asked. "Take our gold by force?"

The tribune had waited for that question. "By no means," he said promptly. "In fact, if in your wisdom you choose not to help me, I intend to do nothing at all."

His audience broke into confused babble, all but ignoring him. "He won't compel us?" "Ha! What trick is this?" "To the ice with him! Let him buy his barbarians with his own money!" That last sentiment, or variations of it, had wide support. It was the plump winedealer who had the wit to ask the Roman, "What do you mean, you'd do nothing at all?"

"Why, just that." Marcus was innocence itself. "I would simply take my troops back to the imperial city, as my job would be done here, or so it seems to me."

That produced worse commotion among the Videssians than his first announcement had. "Then who'd save us from the Yezda?" someone yelled.

"Why should I care about that?"

"By Phos," the man blustered, "you've used enough wind showing what a fine imperial you are." Behind Scaurus, Gaius Philippus chuckled quietly. "Now when it comes down to protecting imperial citizens, you'd rather run away." Merchants and nobles shouted agreement—all but the wine seller, who was looking at the tribune with the grudging respect one sharper sometimes gives another.

"If you are citizens, act like it," Marcus growled, slamming his fist down on the table. "Your precious Empire has kept you fat and safe and prosperous for more years than any of you can reckon, and I doubt you have any complaint over that. But when trouble comes and it needs your help, what do you do? Bawl like so many calves looking for their mothers. By your Phos, gentlemen, if you aren't willing to give aid, why should you get it? I tell you this—if I am one single goldpiece short ten days from now, I *will* pull out, and you can make your own bargain with Yavlak. And a very good day to you all."

His officers trailing, he strode out of the audience chamber, leaving dead silence behind.

"Me, I would you thrash for so talking," Gagik Bagratouni remarked as they came out into the late afternoon sun. "But as you say, these fat so very long. They pay, I think."

"I wouldn't have had to browbeat you into it," Marcus said. "Vaspurakan is frontier country, and borderers know what has to be done." He sighed. "If I admire the Empire for keeping its people secure, I suppose I shouldn't blame them for being selfish as well. They've never had not to be."

He caught motion out of the corner of his eye, swung round on Gaius Philippus. "And what in the name of the gods are you up to?"

The senior centurion gave a guilty start and jerked his hands away from his dagger. The thin keen blade stayed where he had wedged it—between the drums of one of the columns by the entranceway of the governor's hall. "I've wanted to do that for years," he said defensively. "How many times have you heard toffs going on and on about columns so perfectly made you couldn't get a knife blade between the drums? I always thought it was so much rubbish, and here I've proved it." He retrieved the dagger.

Marcus rolled his eyes. "It's a good thing Viridovix isn't here to see you, or you'd never hear the last of it. Columns, now!" He smiled to himself all the way back to the legionary camp.

The next morning a very respectful Garsavran delegation appeared to announce they were having difficulty in allotting payments proportional to wealth. The stall was so blatant Marcus almost laughed in their faces. "Come along, my friends," he said, and returned to the governor's residence. After a winter's struggle with the intricacies of the whole Empire's tax structure at Videssos the city, the local receipts were child's play. An hour and a half later he emerged from the records office and handed the nervously waiting Garsavrans a list of amounts due, down to the fraction of a goldpiece. Defeat in their eyes, they took it and slipped away.

He had all the payments within two days.

With the constant strain and motion of campaigning, he knew he had not given Helvis much time or attention the past couple of months. Sometimes he thought that pleased her just as well. If they were not together much, they could not quarrel, and she still bitterly resented his loyalty to the Empire. And as her pregnancy progressed, her desire for him faded. The same thing had happened when she was carrying Dosti; he bore it as best he could.

Once they set down a long-term camp outside Garsavra, however, they could not keep ignoring each other—and Soteric's captivity gave Helvis a new and urgent worry. The evening after Scaurus sent a heavily armed party to buy the Namdalener prisoners from Yavlak, she asked him, "What do you plan to do with them once you have them?"

She held her voice tight-reined, but he could hear the fear that rode it. Still, she urged no action on him, having learned that the easiest way to turn him against an idea was to push for it too strongly. In the lamplight her deep blue eyes were enormous as she waited for his reply.

"Nothing at once, past holding them and sending word to Thorisin. That choice is for him to make, not me."

He braced for an explosion, but was startled when her eyes swam with tears, and she scrambled clumsily to her feet to embrace him, saying brokenly, "Thank you, oh, thank you!"

"Here, what's this about?" he said, taking her shoulders and holding her at arm's length so he could see her face. "Did you think I'd kill them out of hand?"

"How was I to know? After what you said in camp after the battle where—" She could not put a pleasant face on that, so she drew back quickly. "After the battle, I feared you might."

Her gaze went to the image of the holy Nestorios atop her little traveling shrine. "Thank you," she whispered to the saint, "for saving Soteric."

Marcus stroked her hair. "I said that in the heat of rage. That does not excuse it; I'm not proud of it. But I haven't the stomach for butchery. I thought you knew me better."

"I thought I did, too." She moved close to him, smiled when her belly touched him at the same time as her breasts. But her face grew sober again as she looked up and tried to read his. "Still, even after so long I think sometimes I don't know you at all."

His arms tightened around her. He often felt the same toward her and realized their recent isolation had done nothing to help that. Even so, he did not tell her what was in his mind—that Thorisin Gavras, Avtokrator of the Videssians, was not apt to view captured rebel chiefs kindly. The holy Nestorios notwithstanding, Soteric was a long way from saved.

The note was in Latin, and ambiguous to boot: "We have your packages. Coming in three days." Marcus read it twice before he noticed the Roman "d" was replaced by its Videssian equivalent. Little by little the Empire wore away at them all.

On the morning of the third day a Khatrisher messenger told the tribune the company he had sent out was within a couple of hours of Garsavra. "Very good," he breathed, full of relief. So Yavlak had kept his bargain after all—one hurdle overleaped.

To intimidate the islanders still holed up in their fortress outside the town, Marcus paraded almost his entire army past the castle, leaving behind only enough men to hold the legionary camp against a sally. The men of the Duchy watched him from their walls of heaped-up earth. They would be getting hungry in there soon, he thought; time enough to deal with them then.

Even so short a distance west of Garsavra, the land began to slope sharply upwards toward the central plateau. The Arandos, slow and placid in the lowlands, bumped down over cataracts to reach them. The great boulders were almost lost in seething white foam. Its greatest tributary, the Eriza, flowed down from the north to meet it; Garsavra sat at their junction.

Scaurus' guide clung to the southern bank of the Arandos, which surprised him not at all. On the plateau the rivers were the only sure source of water in summer.

He saw dust ahead, low, widespread cloud that meant men on foot—the light cavalry of the Yezda would have kicked it up in high, straight columns. He exchanged grins with the Khatrisher scout, who gave the thumbs-up gesture Pakhymer's hand had picked up from the Romans.

Then Marcus spied the marching square of legionaries, flanked by a thin cordon of Khatrisher archers to hold off any raiders that might appear—and to round up any Namdalener who somehow broke out of that hollow square.

Junius Blaesus saluted the tribune with the air of a man glad to lay down a heavy burden. "Here they are, sir, all the ones Yavlak had alive: three hundred and—let me see—seventeen. I set out with, ah, twenty-one who died on the march—they were badly wounded to start with, and I couldn't see much the Yezda had done for 'em. I didn't want to leave them behind, though," he finished anxiously.

"You did right," Marcus assured him, and watched his broad peasant face glow with pleasure. Earnest though Blaesus was, responsibility frightened him.

The tribune turned from the junior centurions to the Namdaleni in his charge. The islanders were a far cry from the proud, confident troops who had set out to wrest Videssos' westlands from the Empire. Patchy beards straggled up their gaunt cheeks. Most walked with a forward list, as if drawing themselves up straight took more vigor than they had. Almost every man limped, some from wounds, the rest because the Yezda had stolen their boots and left them only cloths with which to wrap their feet. They wore tattered rags of surcoats and trousers; like the boots, their mail shirts were the nomads' spoils. Their eyes were hollow and uncaring as they plodded along.

So this was victory, Scaurus thought. He felt like a captain of one of Crassus' fire brigades back at Rome, turning a profit from the misfortune of others by buying burning property on the cheap.

Here and there a face, an attitude stood out from the general run of prisoners. Mertikes Zigabenos' luxuriant black whiskers made him easy to pick out in the throng of new, scraggly beards. So did his expression of absolute despair, painful to see even among so much misery. He would not lift his head when Marcus called his name. Beside him walked Drax, whose short beard was startlingly red. The great count's left arm in a filthy sling. He was not ashamed to meet Scaurus' eye, but his own steady gaze was as unfathomable as ever.

Not all the Namdaleni had forgotten they were men. The veteran Fayard, who had been a member of Hemond's squadron when Marcus arrived at Videssos the city, marched where the troopers around him shambled. He threw the tribune a sharp salute, followed it with a shrug, as if to say he had thought they would meet again, but not like this. Somehow he had kept himself fit, making the best of whatever came his way.

Soteric, too, was straight as a plumb bob. That stubborn erectness was what first made Marcus know him; beard and haggardness added years to his looks, so he seemed older than the tribune when in fact he was not thirty. A half-healed, puckered scar seamed his forehead. He glared at his brother-in-law like a trapped wolf. With little sympathy in him, he expected none.

"Traitor!" Soteric shouted, and the tribune did not doubt he meant it. A strange word, he thought, after the fight at the Sangarios. But Helvis' brother was so full of the righteousness of his cause that he was blind to any other. Some of that was in Helvis, too. Not as much, Marcus thought thankfully.

He turned to Styppes, saying, "Do what you can for their hurts." Not all of those, he saw, had come in battle; some islanders carried the mark of the lash or worse.

The healer-priest had scant relish for his task. "You ask too much of me," he said, sounding for once very much like Gorgidas. "Many I will not cure, for they have had long to fester. And these are heretics and enemies as well."

"They fought for the Empire once," Marcus pointed out, "and many will again, with your help." Styppes scowled at him. Scaurus started to argue further, but found he was talking to the priest's back. Styppes was pushing past Blaesus' men to reach the wounded Namdaleni.

Gaius Philippus was trying not to smile. "What is it with that one? Does he always have to growl a while before he goes to work?"

"You're a fine one to talk. The gods help any legionary in your way after something goes wrong," Scaurus said. The veteran did grin then, acknowledging the hit.

It was drawing toward evening when the legionaries and their captives reached Garsavra. Scaurus led them past the Namdalener-held fortress once more, an implied threat that the men of the Duchy in his hands might become hostages for the castle's surrender. The ploy worked less well than he had hoped. The haler prisoners raised a cheer to see the motte-and-bailey still holding out, a cheer the knights on its rampart echoed.

Soteric gave Marcus a look filled with ironic triumph.

Nettled, the tribune paraded his army and the captured Namdaleni down Garsavra's chief street to the town marketplace as a spectacle for the people. That was not quite a success, either. The Garsavrans were less fond of such shows than their jaded cousins in the capital. The verge of the roadway was embarrassingly empty as the legionaries tramped between the baths and the local prelate's residence, a domed building of yellow stucco every bit as large and important as the governor's hall. The clatter of hobnailed *caligae* on cobblestones all but drowned the spatters of applause the few spectators did dole out. Most of the townsfolk ignored the parade, preferring to go about their business.

But that did not mean the Garsavrans paid no attention to the arrival of the Namdalener prisoners. The town began to heave like a man after a stiff dose of hellebore, and street fights broke out fresh. One faction wanted to lynch the islanders out of hand. To his dismay, Scaurus found this group including not only those who hated the Namdaleni, but also some who had collaborated with them while they held Garsavra and now wanted to make sure details of their collusion never came forth.

"They'd be as glad to work for Yavlak," he said, disgusted.

"Aye, well, it's for us to see they never have the chance," Gaius Philippus answered calmly, too cynical to be much upset by another proof of man's capacity for meanness.

But for every man ready to roast the islanders over a slow fire, another wanted to free them and start the rebellion all over again. Marcus began to wish he had settled down to besiege the men of the Duchy in their motte-and-bailey, however wasteful of troops and time that was. He was sure they slipped into town from time to time; with Garsavra wall-less, it was impossible to keep them out. And their presence was a constant reminder to the Garsavrans of their brief rule. Every third housefront, it seemed, had "Drax the Protector" scrawled on it in charcoal or whitewash.

The tribune did his best to get his captives fit for travel east, thinking that once the bulk of them were out of Garsavra the turmoil would die down. He also wanted to show the townsfolk that the islanders themselves had to recognize the Empire's superiority. The ceremony he worked out borrowed from both Roman and Videssian practices.

In the center of the marketplace he drove two *pila* butt-first into the ground, then lashed a third across them, a little below head height; he set a portrait of Thorisin Gavras atop the crosspiece. Then he gathered the Namdalener prisoners—all save Drax, his leading officers, and the luckless Martikes Zigabenos—in front of his creation in groups of ten. Legionaries with bared swords and Khatrisher archers stood between them and the watching Garsavrans.

"As you bend your necks to pass under this yoke," Scaurus said to the prisoners—and to the crowd, "so do you yield yourselves up to the rightful Avtokrator of the Videssians, Thorisin Gavras."

Group by group, the islanders subjugated themselves, stooping beneath the Roman spear and the image of the Videssian Emperor. As they emerged on the far side, Styppes swore each group to a frightful oath calling down curses on themselves, their families, and their clans if ever they warred against the Empire, or even sat silent while others spoke of such war. And group by group the Namdaleni swore, "On this we stake our very souls." The healer-priest glowered at the form their oath took, but Marcus was well pleased. The men of the Duchy were more likely to obey an oath that followed their own usage than one imposed on them by the imperials.

The ritual of surrender went perfectly through about two-thirds of the Namdaleni. Then Styppes, in the middle of swearing yet another group to loyalty, swayed and collapsed. As he had been gulping from a large wineskin all through the ceremony, Marcus was more annoyed than concerned. There was a brief delay as a couple of Romans dragged him to one side and another pair hurried off to fetch the prelate of Garsavra, a white-bearded, affable man named Lavros.

Marcus rescued the written-out oath from where it had fallen by Styppes. Lavros quickly read it to himself, then nodded and started to administer it from the beginning to the waiting Namdaleni, who had been laughing and joking among themselves. Fayard, who happened to be in the group being sworn, called out, "Here now, your honor, we've done that bit already!"

"I doubt you'll suffer any lasting harm from doing it again," Lavros said, unruffled, and kept right on with the whole oath. The men of the Duchy made their pledge, and the ceremony went on.

Thirty Khatrishers accompanied the Namdalener prisoners Scaurus sent back to Videssos the city. They were as much to protect the islanders from Ras Simokattes' irregulars as to keep them from escaping; Namdaleni who traveled through the countryside unarmed or in small parties took their lives in their hands.

Every so often the tribune worried about Bailli's angry outburst at the edge of the southeastern hills. The men of the Duchy were beaten, but the guerillas showed no sign of shutting up shop. One problem at a time, Scaurus told himself, echoing Laon Pakhymer.

Bailli and his fellow officers were a problem in themselves. Marcus had not sent them east with the common soldiers, not caring to risk their getting away on the journey—they were too dangerous to run loose. He kept them shut up in the governor's residence, waiting for an order from Thorisin on their fate. That solution was not ideal either, for as soon as the Garsavrans realized they were there the town broke out in new turmoil—or rather the same old one.

They had quarrels within their ranks as well; Mertikes Zigabenos sent Scaurus a request to be quartered apart from the Namdaleni who had made an unwilling Emperor of him. The tribune complied—he was much more sympathetic to Zigabenos' plight than that of, say, Drax or Soteric. The only Namdalener marshal who roused his pity was Turgot of Sotevag, who was nearly out of his mind with worry over his mistress Mavia. Scaurus remembered her from the capital, a startlingly blonde girl less than half Turgot's age. With the rest of the islanders' women, she had stayed in Garsavra when they rode west against the Yezda and, Marcus thought, likely fled when news came of their defeat. That, he had seen after Maragha, was part of a mercenary's life, too. But Turgot would not hear it, swearing she had promised to wait for him.

After a week of this, Drax' patience wore thin. "And what's a promise worth?" he snapped. When he heard of it, Marcus thought the remark showed more of the great count's nature than he usually let through his self-possessed facade.

Imprisonment was not a usual Roman penalty, its place being taken by corporal punishment, fines, or sentence of exile. Inexperienced jailers, the legionaries paid for learning the trade. One morning a shaking guardsman woke Scaurus to report Mertikes Zigabenos' cell empty.

"A pox!" the tribune said, leaping off his sleeping-mat. Helvis murmured drowsily as he threw a mantle over his shoulders, then leaped up in alarm when he shouted for the buccinators to sound the alarm. By the time Dosti's first frightened wail rang out, Marcus was already out in the *via principalis* setting up search teams.

Going through Garsavra house by house, he was gloomily aware, was a task that had been beaten before he began. And yet when the legionaries quickly found their fugitive, the news was no great delight. Zigabenos was on his knees at the altar of Garsavra's main temple to Phos, which was set behind the city prelate's home. Clinging to the holy table with hands pale-knuckled from the force of his grip, the reluctant Avtrokrator cried, "Sanctuary!" over and over, as loud as he could.

The tribune found a Roman squad standing uncertainly outside the temple doorway. A body of locals was gathering, too, plainly not willing to see Zigabenos dragged from the shrine by force. Nor did the legionaries seem eager to go in after him. Some of them had taken to Phos themselves since coming to the Empire, and temples were refuge-places in the Roman world as well.

Rubbing sleep from his eyes, Lavros the prelate arrived at the same time Marcus did. He placed himself in the entrance to block the tribune's path. Making Phos' sun-sign on his breast, he said loudly, "You shall not take this man away against his will. He has claimed sanctuary with the good god." The swelling crowd shouted in support, pressing forward despite the Romans' armor, swords, and spears.

"May I go in alone and speak with him, at least?" Scaurus asked.

His mild reply took Lavros by surprise. The senior priest considered, running the palm of his hand across his shaven skull. "Will you put aside your weapons?" he asked.

Marcus hesitated; he did not like the idea of parting with his potent Gallic blade. At last he said, "I will," and stripped off sword and dagger. He handed them to his squad leader, a solid trooper named Aulus Florus. "Take care of these," he said. Florus nodded.

As Lavros stood aside to let the tribune pass, he whispered, "And what's all this in aid of?" Marcus shrugged; he heard the ghost of a laugh behind him as he stepped into the temple.

It was laid out like all of Phos' shrines, with the altar in the middle under the dome, and seats radiating out in the four cardinal directions. The mosaic in the dome was a poor copy of the one that graced the High Temple in the capital. This Phos was stern in judgment, but not the awesome, spiritually potent figure that made any man unsure of his own worthiness.

A prickle of unease ran through the Roman as he came down the aisle. If Zigabenos had somehow armed himself . . . but the Videssian guards officer tightened his grasp on the altar still further and kept up his cry of, "Sanctuary! In Phos' name, I claim sanctuary!"

"There's but the one of me, Mertikes," Marcus said. He spread his hands to show they were empty. "Can we talk?"

In the flickering candlelight Zigabenos' eyes were haunted. "Shall I say aye, then, when you haul me off to the headsmen? Why should I ease your conscience for you?" A veteran of imperial politics, he knew the usual fate of failed rebels.

Marcus only waited, saying nothing. A painful sigh escaped Zigabenos. His shoulders sagged as the tribune's silence let him realize how hopeless his position was. "Damn you, outlander," he said at last, voice old and beaten. "What use to this farce, after all? Thirst or hunger will drive me out soon enough. Here; you have me, for what joy it brings you." He let go the altar; Scaurus saw sweat beaded on the polished wood where his hands had been.

Seeing the clever Zigabenos succumbing thus to fate wrenched at the tribune. He blurted, "But you must have had some plan when you fled here!"

"So I did," the Videssian said. His smile was bitter. "I would have yielded up my hair and turned monk. Even an emperor thinks three times before he sends the knives after a man sworn to Phos. But I was too quick—the shrine was dark and empty when I got here, with no priest to give my vow to. Wretched slugabeds! And now it's you here instead. I always thought you a good soldier, Scaurus; I could wish I was wrong."

Marcus hardly heard the compliment; he was shouting for Lavros. The prelate hurried toward him, concern overriding his usual good nature. "I hope you'll not try to cozen me into believing this suppliant has changed his mind—"

"But I have, reverend sir," Zigabenos began.

"No indeed," Scaurus said. "Let it be just as he wishes. Fetch all the people in and let them see the man who was forced to play the role of Avtokrator now make amends for what he was compelled to do, by assuming the garments of your monks."

Lavros and Mertikes Zigabenos both stared at him, the one in delight, the other in blank amazement. The priest bowed deeply to Scaurus and bustled up the aisle, calling to the crowd outside. "You'll let me?" Zigabenos whispered, still unbelieving.

"Why not? What better way to get you out of the political life for good?"

"Thorisin won't thank you for it."

"Then let him look to himself. If he put Ortaias Sphrantzes in a blue robe after getting nothing but ill from him, he shouldn't grudge you your life. You served him well until your luck tossed sixes at you." Marcus felt an absurd pleasure at remembering the losing Videssian throw and being able to bring it out naturally.

"I threw my own 'demons,' trusting the Namdaleni too far."

"So did Thorisin," the tribune pointed out, and Zigabenos really smiled for the first time since Scaurus had reclaimed him from the Yezda.

They had little more chance for talk; the temple was filling fast with chattering Garsavrans. Scaurus took a seat in the first row of benches, leaving Zigabenos alone by the altar. In his shabby cloak, he was a poor match for its silver-plated magnificence.

Lavros had disappeared for a few minutes. He returned bearing a large pair of scissors and a razor with a glittering edge. A second priest followed him, a swarthy, stocky man who carried an unadorned blue robe and bore a copy of Phos' sacred writings, bound in rich red leather, under his arm. The townsfolk grew quiet as they strode toward the holy table in the center of the shrine.

Zigabenos lowered his head toward Lavros. The scissors snipped, shearing away his thick black hair. Once there was only stubble on his pate, Lavros wielded the razor. Zigabenos' scalp gleamed pale, and seemed all the whiter when compared to his sun-weathered face.

The short, swarthy priest held out the leather-bound volume to the officer, saying formally, "Behold the law under which you shall live if you choose. If in your heart you feel you can observe it, enter the monastic life; if not, speak now."

Head still bent, Zigabenos murmured, "I will observe it." The priest asked him twice more; his voice gained strength with each affirmation. After the last repetition, the priest bowed in turn to Zigabenos, handed his book to Lavros, and invested the new monk with his monastic garb. Again following ritual, he said, "As the garment of Phos' blue covers your naked body, so may his righteousness enfold your heart and preserve it from all evil."

"So may it be," Zigabenos whispered; the Garsavrans echoed his words.

Lavros prayed silently for a few moments, then said, "Brother Mertikes, would it please you to lead this gathering in Phos' creed?"

"May I?" said Zigabenos—no, Mertikes, Scaurus thought, for Videssian monks yielded up their surnames. His voice was truly grateful; the tribune had yet to meet a Videssian who took his faith lightly. Mertikes was a strange sight, standing by the rich altar in his severely plain robe, a little trickle of blood on the side of his newly shaved head where the razor had cut too close. But even Scaurus the unbeliever was oddly moved as he led the worshipers in the splendid archaic language of their creed, "We bless thee, Phos, Lord with the great and good mind, by thy grace our protector, watchful beforehand that the great test of life may be decided in our favor."

"Amen," the Garsavrans finished, and Marcus found himself repeating it with them. Lavros said, "This service is completed." The crowd began to stream away. Mertikes came up to squeeze Scaurus' hand with his own strong clasp. Then Lavros said gently, "Come with me, brother, and I will take you to the monastery and introduce you to your fellow servants of Phos." Head up now, not looking back, the new monk followed him.

That crisis solved itself neatly, but was only peripheral to the greater problem of the captive Namdalener lords. A week after Zigabenos became Brother Mertikes, a mob tried to storm the provincial governor's hall and free Drax and his comrades. The legionaries had to use steel to drive the rioters back, leaving a score of them dead and many more wounded. They lost two of their own as well, and after that the Romans could only walk Garsavra's streets by squads. Three nights later the townsmen tried again. This time Marcus was ready for them. Khatrisher archers on the roof of the hall broke the mob's charge before it was well begun, and none of the tribune's men was hurt.

He knew, though, that he did not have the troops to hold down sedition forever, not and watch Yavlak, too. And so he met with the Namdaleni in their confinement. Soteric gave a sardonic bow. "You honor us, brother-in-law. I've seen my sister a few times, but you never deigned visit before."

And Bailli sneered. "Still sweating, are you? I hope they wring all the water from your carcass." Drax' lieutenant was far from forgetting the peasant irregulars.

The great count himself sat quiet, along with Turgot. Marcus guessed that Turgot did not care what he was about to say; Drax' silence was likelier from policy.

The tribune nodded to Bailli. "Yes, I'm still sweating. I don't fancy going through another night like the couple just past and I don't intend to, either. And so, gentlemen—" He looked from one islander to the next. "—something will have to be done about you. Easiest would be to strike off your heads and put them on pikes in the marketplace."

"Whoreson," Soteric said.

Drax leaned forward, alert now. "You'd not say that if it was your plan."

"I'll do it if I have to," Marcus answered, but he admired the great count's quickness all the same. "Truly, I'd sooner not—it's Thorisin's place to judge what you deserve. But I won't chance the townsfolk freeing you. You're too dangerous to the Empire for that." Drax bowed slightly, as if acknowledging praise.

"What do you leave us with, then?" Soteric demanded scornfully.

"Your bare lives, if you want them. Do you?" The tribune waited. As the Namdaleni saw he meant the question, they slowly nodded, Turgot last of all. "Very well, then . . ."

"You're getting good at these spectacles," Gaius Philippus said out of the corner of his mouth. "The locals'll think twice before they get gay." A hollow square of legionaries in full battle dress stood at attention in the center of the Garsavran marketplace, *pila* grounded, staring stolidly out at the hostile Videssians around them. A raw northerly breeze whipped their cloaks back from their shoulders.

"I'm glad the weather's holding off," Marcus said. When the wind came from the north, rain and then snow were bound to follow. The tribune was happy to be next to the small fire in the center of the Romans' square—until a blown spark stung his calf behind his greave. He cursed and rubbed.

The buccinators' horns brayed; heads turned toward the maniple tramping into the marketplace, its swords drawn and menacing. Taller than their Roman captors, Drax and Bailli, Soteric and Turgot were easy to recognize in the center of the column.

Marcus glanced toward Ansfrit, the captain of the Namdalener castle, to whom he had granted a safe-conduct to his drama. Ansfrit looked as though he wanted to try a rescue on the spot, but the fearsome aspect of Scaurus' troopers was enough to intimidate the Garsavrans.

The maniple merged with the hollow square. Legionaries frogmarched their prisoners up to the tribune, two to each islander. In front of them strode Zeprin the Red. The enormous Haloga cut an awesome figure in the gleaming gilded cuirass of Imperial Guards—freshly regilded for the occasion, in fact. He saluted Scaurus Roman-style, shooting right fist out and up. "Behold the traitors!" he cried, bass thundering through the open market.

Barefoot, shivering in the wind in thin gray linen tunics, fists clenched tight with tension, the men of the Duchy awaited judgment. The silence stretched. Then the crowd of Garsavrans around the square of the legionaries parted as if fearing disease, to let a single figure through. Like Spartan hoplites of the world Scaurus had known, Videssian executioners wore red to make the stains of their calling less evident. Only the man's black buskins were not the color of blood.

There were Yezda in the crowd; the tribune saw them staring admiringly at the tall, angular, masked shape of the executioner. Here was pomp and ceremony to suit them, he thought with distaste.

No help for that—he was bound to go on with what he had devised. "Hear me, people of Garsavra," he said; Styppes had been glad to help with *this* speech. "As traitors and rebels against his Imperial Majesty Thorisin Gavras, Avtokrator of the Videssians, these wretches deserve no less than death. Only my mercy spares them that." But as his listeners began to brighten, he went on inexorably, "Yet as a mark of the outrage they have worked on the Empire, and as fit warning to any others who might be mad enough to contemplate revolt, let the sight of their eyes be extinguished and let them know Skotos' darkness forevermore!" By Videssian reckoning, that constituted mercy, for it avoided capital punishment.

But a moan rose from the crowd, overtopped by Ansfrit's bellow of anguish. The Garsavrans started to surge forward, but Roman *pila* snapped out in bristling hedgehog array to hold them off.

Inside the hollow square, the four Namdaleni jerked as if stung. "Blinded?" Drax howled. "I'd sooner die!" The islanders wrenched against their captors' grip and, with panic strength, managed to tear free for an instant. But for all their struggles, the legionaries wrestled them to the ground and held them there, pulling away the hands with which they vainly tried to shield their eyes.

Tunelessly humming a hymn to Phos, the executioner put the tip of a thin pointed iron in the fire. He lifted it every so often to gauge its color; his thick gloves of crimson leather protected him from the heat. Finally he grunted in satisfaction and turned to Scaurus. "Which of 'em first?"

"As you wish."

"You, then." Bailli happened to be closest to the executioner, who went on, not unkindly, "Try to hold as steady as you can; 'twill be easier for you so."

"Easier," Bailli mocked through clenched teeth; sweat poured down his face. Then the iron came down, once, twice. Tight-jawed no longer, the snub-nosed Namdalener screamed and screamed. The scent of charring meat filled the air.

Pausing between victims to reheat his iron, the executioner moved on to Turgot and Drax, and then at last to Soteric. Helvis' brother's cries were all curses aimed Marcus' way. He stood unmoved over the fallen

Namdaleni and answered only, "You brought this upon yourselves." The burned-meat smell was very strong now, as if someone had forgotten a roasting joint of pork.

The legionaries helped their groaning, sobbing prisoners sit, pulling thick black veils over their eyes to hide the hot iron's work. "Show them to the people," Scaurus commanded. "Let them see what they earn by defying their rightful sovereign." The troopers who formed the hollow square opened lanes to let the crowd look on the Namdaleni.

"Now take them away," the tribune said. No one raised a hand to stop the islanders from being guided back to their captivity in the governor's hall. They stumbled against each other as they staggered between their Roman guards.

"Ansfrit," Marcus called. The Namdalener captain approached, fear and rage struggling on his pale face. Scaurus gave him no time to compose himself: "Surrender your castle to me within the day, or when we take it—and you know we can—everyone of your men will suffer the same fate as these turncoats. Yield now, and I guarantee their safety."

"I thought you above these Videssian butcheries, but it seems the dog apes his master."

"That's as may be," the tribune shrugged, implacable. "Will you yield, or shall I have this fellow—" He jerked his head toward the red-clad executioner. "—keep his irons hot?" Under his shiny leather mask, the man's mouth shaped a smile at Ansfrit.

The Namdalener flinched, recovered, glared helplessly at Scaurus. "Aye, damn you, aye," he choked out, and spun on his heel, almost running back toward the motte-and-bailey. Behind his retreating back, Gaius Philippus nodded knowingly. Marcus smiled himself. Another pair of troubles solved, he thought.

The druids' marks on his blade flared into golden life, scenting wizardry, but it was scabbarded, and he did not see.

Far to the north, Avshar laid aside the black-armored image of Skotos he used to focus his scrying powers. A greater seer than any *enaree,* he cast forth his vision to overleap steppe and sea, as a man might cast a fishing line into a stream. The power in Scaurus' sword was his guide; if it warded the hated outlander from his spells, it also proclaimed the Roman's whereabouts and let Avshar spy. Though he could not see the tribune himself, all around him was clear enough.

The wizard-prince leaned back against a horsehair-filled cushion of felt. Even for him, scrying at such a distance was no easy feat. "A lovely jest, mine enemy," he whispered, though no one was there to hear him. "Oh yes, a lovely jest. Yet perhaps I shall find a better one."

News somehow travels faster than men. When Scaurus got back to the legionary camp, Helvis met him with a shriek. "Animal! Worse than animal—foul, wretched, atrocious brute!" Her face was dead white, save for a spot of color high on each cheek.

Legionaries and their women pretended not to hear—a privilege of rank, Marcus thought. They would have gathered round to listen to any common trooper scrapping with his leman.

He took Helvis by the elbow, tried to steer her back toward their tent. "Don't flare at me," he warned. "I left them alive, and more than they deserved, too."

She whirled away from him. "Alive? What sort of life is it, to sit in a corner of the marketplace with a chipped cup in your lap, begging for coppers? My brother—"

She dissolved in tears. The tribune managed to guide her into the tent, away from the camp's watching eyes. Malric, he guessed, was out playing; Dosti, napping in his crib, woke and started to cry when his mother came in sobbing. Marcus tried to comfort her, saying, "There's no need for that, darling. Here, I've brought a present for you."

Helvis stared at him, wild-eyed. "So I'm your slut now, to be bought with trinkets?"

He felt himself reddening and damned his clumsy words; the Videssian oratory was turgid, but at least it could be rehearsed. This, now—"See for yourself," he said brusquely, and tossed her a small leather pouch.

She caught it automatically, tugged the drawstring open. "This is a gift?" she stuttered, confusion routing fury for a moment. "Chunks of half-burned fat?"

"I hoped you might think so," Scaurus said, "since each of your precious islanders—aye, your honey-mouthed brother, too—clapped them over his eyes as my troopers fought 'em in the dirt."

Her mouth moved without sound, something the tribune had heard of but never seen. At last she whispered, "They're not blind?"

"Not a bit of it," Marcus said smugly, "though Turgot flinched and got an eyebrow seared off, the poor mournful twit. A pretty joke, don't you think?" he went on, unaware he all but echoed his deadliest foe. "All the riots and plots in town have collapsed like a popped bladder, and Ansfrit's panicked into giving up lest he earn what Drax got."

But Helvis was not listening to him any more. "They're not bl—" she started to scream, and then bit the palm of his hand as he clapped it over her mouth.

"You don't know that," he said, stern again. "You've never heard that. Apart from the legionaries who wrestled them down and a few others close enough to see what happened, the only one who knows is that butcher in his suit of blood, and he's well paid to keep quiet. D'you understand me?" he asked, cautiously taking his hand away.

"Yes," she said in so small a voice they both laughed. "I'd pretend anything, anything, to keep Soteric safe. Oh, hush, you," she added to Dosti, plucking him out of the crib. "Everything is all right."

"All right?" Dosti said doubtfully, and followed it with a hiccup. Marcus scratched his head; every time he looked at his son, it seemed, Dosti had something newly learned to show him.

"All right," Helvis said.

X

THE SIEGE TOWER RUMBLED ACROSS THE BOARD. "GUARD YOUR EMperor, now!" Viridovix said, scooping up a captured foot soldier—no telling when he might be useful, coming back into play on the Gaul's side.

Seirem twisted her mouth in annoyance, blocked the threat with a silverpiece. He pulled the siege tower back out of danger. She advanced her other silverpiece a square, reaching the seventh rank of the nine-by-nine board. With a smile, she turned the flat piece over to reveal the new, jeweled character on its reverse. "Promote to gold," she said.

"Dinna remind me," he said mournfully; as a more powerful goldpiece, the counter attacked his prelate and a horseman at the same time. The prelate was worth more to him; he moved it. Seirem took the horseman. It was like the Videssians, Viridovix thought, to have money fight for them in their board game—and to grow more valuable deep in enemy territory.

He wondered how long the board and men had wandered with the nomads, an unplayed curiosity. No doubt some plainsman had brought the set back with him from Prista, taken by the rich grain of the oaken game board, by the inset lines of mother-of-pearl that separated square from square, and by the ivory pieces and the characters on them, made from emeralds and turquoise and garnets. In Videssos the Gaul had learned the game on a stiff leather board, with counters crudely hacked from pine. He admired it tremendously, most of all because luck played no part in it.

In the Empire he had only been a fair player; here he was teaching the game, and still ahead of his pupils. Seirem, though, was catching on fast. "Too fast by half," he muttered in his own Celtic speech; she had turned the captured horseman against him, with wicked effect.

It took a sharp struggle before he finally subdued her, trapping her emperor in a corner with his siege tower, prelate, and a goldpiece. She frowned, more thoughtfully than in anger. "Yes, I see," she said. "It was a mistake to weaken the protection around him to throw that attack at you. You held me off, and there I was in the open with no help around to save me." Her fingers reset the board. "Shall we try again? You take first move this time; my defense needs work."

"Och, lass, for the wee bit you've played, you make a brave show of it." He advanced the foot soldier covering a silverpiece's file, opening the long diagonal for his prelate. Seirem frowned again as she considered a reply.

Watching her concentrate, he thought how different she was from Komitta Rhangavve. Once he had managed to steal a whole day with Thorisin Gavras' volcanic mistress; the gameboard was a pleasant diversion between rounds. Or it should have been, but the Celt had never learned the courtier's art of graceful losing. One game Komitta beat him fairly; the next he managed to win. She'd screeched curses and hurled the board, pieces and all, against a wall. He never did find one of the spearmen.

Here was Seirem, by contrast, paying the price of trouncings to learn the game, her fine dark eyes full of thought while she waited for his next move. She also had a sweet, low voice and was equally skilled with the pipes and the light women's bow. Yet Komitta, with her passion for rank, would have called her barbarian, or worse. "Honh!" the Celt snorted, again in his own language. "The bigger fool her, the vicious trull!"

"Will you be all night?" Seirem asked pointedly.

"Begging your pardon, lass; my wits were wandering." He moved a foot soldier and promptly regretted it. He tugged at his mustaches. "Sure and that was a rude thing to do!"

From the fireside where she was gossiping with a couple of other women, Borane glanced over at the game-players. She recognized the tone Viridovix used toward her daughter, perhaps better than he did; after so many casual amours, he was not ready to admit to himself that he might feel something more for Seirem. But for those with ears to hear, his voice gave him away.

Targitaus stamped into the tent, face like thunder. He, too, was bright enough to see how Seirem had become the outlander's favorite partner at the gameboard. But when he growled, "Put your toys away!" and followed that with an oath that made Borane's friends giggle, the Gaul was not panic-stricken; he had seen this fury before.

"Who's said us nay the now?" he asked.

"Krobyz, the wind spirits blow sleet up his arse! May his ewes be barren and his cows' udders dry. What did you call his clan, V'rid'rish, the Hamsters? You were right, for he has the soul of a hamster turd in him." He spat into the fire in absolute disgust.

"What excuse did he offer?" Seirem asked, trying to pierce her father's anger.

"Eh? Not even a tiny one, the shameless son of a snake and a goat." Targitaus was not appeased. "Just a no, and from what Rambehisht says, he counts himself lucky not to come back with a hole in him for his troubles."

Viridovix grimaced as he helped Seirem put the pieces away, hardly noticing that their hands brushed more than once. "That's not good at all. Every one o' these spalpeens should be seeing the need to put the fornicating bandits down, and too many dinna for me to think the lot of 'em fools. A pox on Varatesh, anyhow; the omadhaun's too clever by half. Belike he's got his hooks into some o' the nay-sayers."

"You have it, I think," Targitaus said heavily. "The rider I sent to Anakhar said the whole clan was shaking in their boots to move against the outlaws. I doubt we'll see help from them, any more than from Krobyz. We have better luck with the clans east of the Oglos, where fear of the whoreson doesn't reach. That Oitoshyr, of the White Foxes, fell all over himself promising help."

"Easy enough to promise," the Gaul said. "What he does'll count for more. He's far enough away to say, 'Och, the pity of it. We didna hear o' the shindy till too late,' and have no one to make him out a liar."

Targitaus scaled his wolfskin cap across the tent, grunted in somber satisfaction when it landed on the leather sack nearest the pile of bedding. "A point. Should I thank you for it?"

Lipoxais the *enaree,* who had been quietly grinding herbs with a brass mortar and pestle, spoke up now. "Think of the animal's tail as well as its head." A Videssian would have said, "Look at the other side of the coin," Viridovix mused. The *enaree* went on, "Oitoshyr runs less risk of you dominating him if you win than your neighbors do, because he is far away. That should make him more likely to join us."

"Do you say that as a seer?" Targitaus asked eagerly.

"No, only as one who's seen a good deal," Lipoxais answered, smiling at the distinction with as much pleasure as an imperial might have taken over such wordplay.

"Still not bad," Viridovix said. He had gained a great deal of respect for the *enaree*'s shrewdness in the weeks since he came to Targitaus' clan. He was still not sure whether Lipoxais was a whole man—unlike most of the Khamorth, he kept his modesty, even in the cramped conditions of nomadic life. Whole or not, nothing was lacking from his wits.

A pessimist by nature, Targitaus had no trouble finding new worries. "For all the allies we may bring in, what good will they do us, V'rid'rish, if your Avshar is as strong as you say? Will he not help Varatesh's renegades ride over us no matter what we do?"

The Celt chewed at his lower lip; he lived with that fear, too. But he answered, "It's a tricksy thing, battle magic, indeed and it is. Even himself may have it turn and bite him." Lipoxais nodded vigorously, his chins hobbling. Sorcery frayed all too often in the heat of combat.

A fresh thought struck Viridovix. "Sure and it was a braw scheme, for all the Romans thought of it," he exclaimed, and then remembered: "Nay, they said 'twas first used against 'em." He reddened when he realized that, of course, his listeners had no idea what he was talking about. Targitaus was standing with folded arms, impatiently drumming his fingers on his elbows.

The Gaul explained how the legionaries had frightened a band of Yezda out of a valley one night by tying fagots to the horns of a herd of cattle, then lighting the sticks and stampeding the crazed beasts at the nomads. He did not make light of his own role either, for he had ridden at the head of the herd and sworded down one Yezda who did not panic. "But the rest o' the kerns were running for their lives, shrieking like so many banshees," he finished happily. "They must have thought it was a flock o' demons after 'em—and likely so would Varatesh's rogues."

All of the Khamorth, though, even Seirem, even Borane's gossip partners, looked at him in horror. When Targitaus made as if to draw his sword, Viridovix saw how badly he had blundered, but did not know why. Lipoxais reminded his chief, "He is not of us by blood and does not know our ways."

Muscle by muscle, the khagan relaxed. "That is so," he said at last, and then to Viridovix, "You fit well with us; I forget how foreign you are in truth." Viridovix bowed at the implied compliment, but Targitaus was speaking to him now as to a child. "Here on the plains, we do not let fire run wild." The nomad's wave encompassed the vast, featureless sea of grass all around. "Once started, how would it ever stop again?"

Coming as he did from damp, verdant Gaul, Viridovix had not thought of that. He hung his head, muttering, "Begging your pardon, I'm sorry." But he had the quick wits to see that the ploy might still be used, or something like it. "How would this be, now?" he said, and gave them his new idea.

Targitaus ran his hand through his beard as he thought. "I've heard worse," he said—highest praise.

Seirem nodded in brisk satisfaction, as if she had expected no less.

His sons flanking him, councilors grouped around him, Arghun found the key question and asked it directly of the rival embassies: "Why should my people take service with one of you instead of the other?"

Perhaps Goudeles had expected some polite conversation before getting down to business, for he did not have his answer instantly ready. When he hesitated, Bogoraz of Yezd seized the chance to speak first. Forehead furrowed in annoyance, Goudeles—and Gorgidas with him—listened to Skylitzes' whispered translation: "Because Videssos is a cow too tired and old to stay on its legs. When a beast in your own herds—may they increase—cannot keep up, do you rope another to it to help it along for its last few days? No, you slaughter it at once, while it still has flesh on its bones. We invite you to help with the butchering and share the meat."

Against his will, Gorgidas found himself respecting Bogoraz' talents. His argument was nicely couched in terms familiar to the Arshaum and doubly effective because of it.

Yet Goudeles, though robbed of the initiative, thought quickly on his feet. "Having seen his own Makuran collapse at the first shout, Bogoraz may perhaps be forgiven for his delusion that such decay has befallen us as well. He ministers to his new masters well."

Arigh interpreted for his father and the elders. "Your pun didn't translate," Skylitzes muttered when the plainsman's version was through.

"Never mind. I meant it for Bogoraz," the bureaucrat answered. The shot went home, too; the Yezda envoy gave him a fierce glower. Goudeles was not bad at finding weaknesses himself, Gorgidas thought. Serving overlords only a generation off the steppe had to be humiliating for Bogoraz, who was as much a man of culture as the Videssian.

"I give Wulghash all my loyalty," the ambassador said, rather loudly, as if to convince himself. He must have succeeded, for he returned to the attack: "Yezd is now a young, strong land, filled with the vigor fresh blood brings. Its time is come, while Videssos falls into shadows."

Proud in the full power of his strength, Dizabul threw back his head. As Bogoraz doubtless intended, he identified Yezd's situation with his own. But Gorgidas wondered if the envoy had not outsmarted himself. There were few young men among Arghun's councilors.

One of the oldest of them, a man with a scant few snowy locks combed across his skull, slowly rose and tottered toward Bogoraz. The diplomat frowned, then yelped in outrage as the Arshaum reached out and plucked a hair from his beard. Holding it at arm's length, he peered at it with rheumy eyes. "Fresh blood?" he said, slow and clear enough so even Gorgidas and Goudeles could understand. "This is as white as mine." He threw it on the rug.

"Sit down, Onogon," Arghun said, but as much in amusement as reproof. Onogon obeyed, as deliberately as he had risen. Several of the elders were chuckling among themselves; Bogoraz barely hid his fury. Abuse would have been easier for him to bear than mockery.

Gorgidas, for his part, started when he heard the old man speak. The devil-mask had distorted the chief shaman's voice, but the Greek still knew it when he heard it again—a powerful ally to have, if ally he was. Gorgidas reached forward to tap Goudeles on the shoulder, but the pen-pusher was speaking again.

"Our presence here gives the lie to the Yezda's foolish effrontery," he said. "As it always has, Videssos stands."

Bogoraz bared his teeth in a shark's smile. "Khagan, the senile Empire has no bigger liar than this man, and he proves it out of his own mouth. I will show you the state Videssos is in. This Goudeles, when he offered you his desperate tribute, paid you in old coin, not so?"

"Oh, oh," Skylitzes said under his breath as Arghun nodded.

"See, then, what the Empire mints these days and tell me if it stands as it always has." And Bogoraz reached into his wallet, drew forth a coin, and cast it at the khagan's feet.

Even from several paces way, Gorgidas could see what it was—a "goldpiece" of Ortaias Sphrantzes, small, thin, poorly shaped, and so adulterated with copper that it was more nearly red than honest yellow.

Bogoraz retrieved the coin. "I would not cheapen myself by offering you so shabby a gift," he said to Arghun.

The dramatic flourish hurt as badly as the damning money itself. It grew very quiet in the banquet tent, which now served another function; all the Arshaum watched Goudeles to see what response he had.

He stood a long time silent, thinking. Finally he said, "That was the coin of a usurper, a rebel who has been put down; it is not a fair standard to judge by." All true, though he did not tell the Arshaum he had followed Ortaias until Thorisin Gavras took Videssos. Just as if he had served Gavras all his life, he went on, warming to his theme, "Now we have an Emperor who is strong-willed and to be feared, well able to do that which is necessary in administering the state, both in war and in the collection of public revenues."

"Sophistry," Bogoraz fleered in Videssian. The Arshaum tongue lacked the concept, so he was blunter: "Lies! And your precious Emperor had best be skilled at war, for it is not merely Yezd he fights; his paid soldiers from Namdalen have revolted against him, and in the east he wars with the Duchy itself. His forces are divided, spread among many fronts; since we are fighting no one but Videssos, it is plain victory will soon be ours."

Gorgidas, Skylitzes, and Goudeles exchanged glances of consternation. Isolated on the plains for months, they knew nothing of events in the Empire; it was only too likely Bogoraz had fresher news than theirs. The very set of his body, the enjoyment he took from his revelation, argued for its belief.

The Greek had to admire Goudeles then. Rocked as he was by Bogoraz' announcement, the seal-stamper laughed and bowed toward the Yezda envoy as if he had brought good news. "What nonsense is this?" Bogoraz said suspiciously.

"None at all, sir, none at all." Goudeles bowed again. "May all be well for you, in fact, for though born a man of Yezd, you have testified to the courage of Videssos and not hidden the truth out of fear."

"You have gone mad."

"No, indeed. For unless the Videssian power was distracted, as you said, and was extending its army against various foes, do you think the Yezda could stand against it in battle? Were we facing Yezd alone, even its name would be destroyed along with its army."

It was a brave try, but Bogoraz cut through words with a reminder of real events. "We fared better than that at Maragha. And now we and Namdalen grind Videssos to power between us." He made a twisting motion with his hands, as though wringing a fowl's neck.

The Arshaum murmured back and forth; Goudeles, at last with the look of a beast at bay, had no ready answer. Beside him Skylitzes was as grim. In desperation, Gorgidas spoke to Arghun: "Surely Yezd is a more dangerous friend for you than Videssos. The Empire is far away, but Yezd shares a border with your people."

If he expected the same success the tale of Sesostris had brought him, he did not gain it. When his words were interpreted, the khagan laughed at him. "We Arshaum do not fear the Yezda. Why should we? We whipped them off the steppe into Yezd; they would not dare come back."

That reply hardly pleased Bogoraz more than the Greek; he might have mixed feelings toward his overlords, but he did not care to hear them scorned.

And Skylitzes seized on Arghun's words as a drowning man would grab a line. "Translate for me, Arigh," he said tensely. "I must not be misunderstood." Arigh nodded; he had watched Bogoraz take control of the debate with as much anxiety as the Videssians. If their cause went down to defeat, his as their sponsor suffered, too—and Dizabul's grew brighter, for backing the right side.

"Tell your father and the clan enders, then, that Gorgidas here is right, and Yezd menaces your people even now."

Understanding the officer's Videssian, Bogoraz shouted angry protest. "More twaddle from these talksmiths! If words were soldiers, they would rule the world."

"More than words, Yezda! Tell the khagan, tell his elders why Yezd is making cats'-paws of the Khamorth outlaws by the Shaum, if not to use them against the Arshaum. Then who would be between whom?" With wicked precision, Skylitzes imitated Bogoraz's neck-twisting gesture. The Videssian officer might lack Goudeles' flair for high-flown oratory, but with a soldiers' instinct he knew where a stroke would hurt.

The clan leaders' eyes swung back to Bogoraz, sudden hard suspicion in them. "Utterly absurd, your majesty," he said to Arghun. "Another load of fantastic trumpery, no better than this suet-bag's here." The broad sleeve of his coat flapped as he pointed at Goudeles. He sounded as sure of himself as he had when wounding the Videssians with word of Drax' revolt.

But Skylitzes still had his opening and pounded through it, "How is it that Varatesh and his bandits struck west over the Shaum this past winter, the first time in years even outlaws dared act so?"

The Gray Horse clan was far enough from Shaumkiil's eastern marches that Arghun had not heard of the raid. He snapped a question at the elders. Onogon answered him. Triumph spread over Skylitzes' saturnine face. "He knows about it! Learned from another shaman, he says."

Bogoraz remained unshaken. "Well, what if these renegades, or whatever they are, came cattle-stealing where they don't belong? They have nothing to do with Yezd."

"No?" Gorgidas had never heard so much sarcasm packed into a single syllable. "Then how is it," Skylitzes asked, "that Avshar rides with these renegades? If Avshar is not second in Yezd after Wulghash, it's only because he may be first."

Now the Yezda envoy stared in dismay and disbelief. "I know nothing of this," he said weakly.

"It's true, though." That was not Skylitzes, but Arigh. "This is what I spoke of, father, when I rode ahead of the embassy." Skylitzes interpreted for Gorgidas and Goudeles as Arigh told the elders of Viridovix' kidnapping on the Pardrayan steppe, and of the part Avshar's magic had played in it.

"You see he did not scruple to attack an embassy," Goudeles put in, "contrary to the law of all nations, who recognize envoys' persons as sacrosanct."

"What have you to say?" Arghun asked Bogoraz. As usual, the khagan kept his face impassive, but his voice was stern.

"That I know nothing about it," the Yezda ambassador repeated, this time with more conviction. "This Avshar has not been seen in the court at Mashiz for two years and more, since he took up the army that won glory for Wulghash at Maragha." An eyebrow quirked, a courtier's grimace. "There are those who would say Wulghash has not missed him. Whatever he may or may not have done after he last left Mashiz should not be held to Yezd's account, only to his own."

"Khagan!" That was Skylitzes, shouting in protest; Goudeles clapped a dramatic hand to his forehead. The officer cried out, "If your men go to tend a herd five days away from your yurt, they still ride under your orders."

Several of the councilors behind Arghun nodded in agreement. "Well said!" came Onogon's thin voice. But others, unable to take seriously a threat from the despised Khamorth, still seemed to think Bogoraz' arguments carried more weight, nor did Dizabul pull away from the man whose cause he backed. The deadlock held.

The khagan gestured to both embassies in dismissal. "It is time for us to talk among ourselves on what we've heard," he said. His own eyebrow lifted in mild irony. "There is a bit to think about." Bogoraz and the Videssian party ignored each other as they left the banquet tent; the driver whistled his horses to a brief halt so they could alight.

Once back in their own yurt, Goudeles threw himself down on the rug with a great sigh of relief. "Scratch one robe," he said. "I've sweated clean through it." A serving girl, understanding tone if not words, offered him a skin of kavass. "Phos' blessings on you, my sweet," he exclaimed, and half emptied it in one great draught.

"Save some," Skylitzes ordered. After he had drunk, he slapped the bureaucrat on the back. Ignoring Goudeles' yelp, he said, "Pikridios, I never thought I'd see the day when you disowned the Sphrantzai and spoke up for Thorisin—aye, and sounded like you meant it."

"Professional pride compelled," the bureaucrat said. "Should I let a mere Makuraner get the better of me, how could I show my face in the chancery again? And as for your precious Gavras, my hardheaded friend, if he had given me my just deserts, I would still be comfortably ensconced there."

"If he had given you your just deserts," Skylitzes retorted, "you'd be short a head, for your embassy to him during the civil war."

"Such details are best forgotten," Goudeles said with an airy wave. The pen-pusher went on, "The shock of my sensibilities here on the barren steppe is punishment enough, I assure you. So far from being the safe center of the cosmos, Videssos seems an island in a barbarous sea, quite small, lonely, and surrounded by deadly foes."

Now Skylitzes was staring at him. "Well, Phos be praised! You really have learned something."

"If the two of you can hold off singing each other's praises for a bit," Gorgidas said pointedly, "you might send that skin this way."

"Sorry." Skylitzes passed it to him. As the Greek drained it, the Videssian officer said, "We might find you a line or two while we're singing. You gave me the idea to warn the Arshaum of Avshar's games."

"Aye, aye, aye." After the tension in the banquet tent, the kavass was hitting Goudeles hard; his round cheeks were red, and his eyes a little glassy. He nodded as if his head were on springs, bobble, bobble, bobble. "And that parable about what's-his-name, your king with the funny name. That took Bogoraz' high-necked pretensions down a peg, yes it did." He giggled.

"Glad to help," Gorgidas said, warming to their praise. He remembered something he had caught in the arguments before the khagan and spoke it before he could lose it again: "Did you notice how Bogoraz slighted Avshar? Are there splits among the Yezda?"

"Never a court without 'em," Goudeles declared loudly.

"Even if there are, what use can we make of it here?" Skylitzes asked, and the Greek had to admit he did not know.

"Not to worry about that, my dears," Goudeles said. His elegant syntax was going fast, but his wits still worked. "Now we got—*have*—an idea of where the clan elders stand, we throw gold around. Works pretty good, most times." He giggled again. "Wonderful stuff, gold."

"It would be even more so if Bogoraz didn't have it, too," Gorgidas said. Goudeles snapped his fingers to show what he thought of that.

The pony's muscles flexed between Viridovix' thighs as the beast trotted over the plain. The Celt held the reins in his left hand; the right was on the hilt of his sword. He tried to look in every direction at once. Riding to war, even in a scouting party such as this, was new to him; he was used to fighting on foot.

The steppe's broad, flat reaches also oppressed him. He turned to Batbaian beside him. "What's the good of being a general, now, with the whole country looking all the same and not a place to lay an ambush in the lot of it?"

"A gully, a swell of land to hide behind—you use what you have. There's plenty, when you know where to look." The khagan's son eyed him with amusement. "A good thing you aren't leading us. You'd get yourself killed and break my sister's heart."

"Sure and that'd be a black shame, now wouldn't it?" Viridovix whistled a few bars of a Videssian love song. His soldier's alertness softened as he thought of Seirem. After so many women, finding love in place of simple rutting was an unexpected delight. As is often true of those whose luck comes late, he had fallen twice as hard, as if to make up for squandered years. "Och, she's a pearl, a flower, a duckling—"

Batbaian, who could remember his sister as a squalling tot, made a rude noise. Viridovix ignored him. "At least you have nothing to fear for her sake," the young Khamorth said. "With so many clans sending men to fight Varatesh, the camp has never been so large."

"Many, yes, but not enough." That was Rambehisht, who led the patrol. As sparing of words as usual, the harsh-featured plainsman pierced to the heart of the matter. Targitaus' army grew day by day, but many clans chose not to take sides, and some few ranged themselves with Varatesh, whether from fear of Targitaus or a different kind of fear of the outlaw chief and Avshar.

The scouting party's point rider came galloping back toward his mates, swinging his cap in the air and shouting, "Horsemen!" Viridovix' blade rasped free of its scabbard; the plainsmen he rode with unslung their bows and set arrows to sinew bowstrings. On this stretch of steppe other horsemen could only be Varatesh's.

A few minutes after the outrider appeared, the patrol spied dust on the northwestern horizon. Rambehisht narrowed his eyes, taking the cloud's measure. "Fifteen," he said. "Twenty at the outside, depending on remounts." The numbers were close to even, then.

The opposing commander must have been making a similar calculation from what he saw, for suddenly, before his men came into view, he swung them round sharply and retreated as fast as he could go. Batbaian let out a yowl of glee and punched Viridovix in the shoulder. "It works!" he shouted.

"And why not, lad?" the Celt said grandly, swelling with pride as he accepted congratulations from the plainsmen. Even Rambehisht unbent far enough to give him a frosty smile. That truly pleased Viridovix, to have the man he had beaten come to respect him.

Behind them, the six or eight cattle that accompanied the patrol took advantage of the halt to snatch a few mouthfuls of grass. Each of the beasts had a large chunk of brush tied behind it and threw as much dust into the air as a couple of dozen men. "The polluted kerns'll be after thinking it's whole armies chasin' 'em," Viridovix chuckled.

"Yes, and tell their captains as much," Rambehisht said. He was a thoughtful enough warrior to see the use of confusing his foes.

"And we must have a double handful of patrols out," Batbaian said. "They'll be running from so many shadows they won't know when we really move on them." He gazed at Viridovix with something close to hero worship.

Feeling pleased with themselves, the scouts camped by a small stream. To celebrate outfoxing the enemy, Rambehisht slit the throat of one of the cattle. "Tonight we have a good feed of meat," he said.

Viridovix scratched his head. "I'm as fond o' beef as any man here, but how will you cook him? There's no wood for a fire, nor a pot to seethe him in, either."

"He'll cook himself," the plainsman answered.

"Och, aye, indeed and he will," Viridovix scoffed, sure he was the butt of a joke. "And belike come morning the corp of him'll grow feathers and fly off tweeting wi' the burdies."

After Rambehisht opened the cow's belly, a couple of nomads dug out the entrails and tossed them into the stream. It turned to silvery turmoil as fish of all sizes swarmed to the unexpected feast. A couple of large, brown-shelled turtles splashed off rocks to steal their share. Another was staring straight at Viridovix. It blinked deliberately, once, twice.

Rambehisht proved as good as his word. Arms gory to the elbows, he stripped hunks of flesh from the beast's bones and made a good-sized heap of the latter. To the Celt's surprise, he proceeded to light them; with the marrow inside and the fat still clinging to them, they burned well. The resourceful Khamorth then threw enough meat to feed the patrol into a bag made of the cow's raw hide, dipped up water from the stream and added it to the meat, and hung the makeshift cauldron over the fire with a javelin. Before long boiled beef's mouth-watering scent filled the air, mixing with the harsher smell of the burning bones.

Most of the nomads stuck strips of raw meat under their saddles, to rough-cure as they rode along. There the Celt declined to imitate them. "I'd sooner have salt on mine, or mustard, thanking you all the same. Horse sweat doesna ha' the same savor."

What Rambehisht had cooked, though, was delicious. "My hat's off to you," Viridovix said, and so it was—with the coming of night he had laid aside the bronze-studded leather cap he wore. He belched magnificently. As any plainsman would, Rambehisht took it for a compliment and dipped his head in reply.

Patting his belly, the Gaul rose and ambled over to the creek, well upstream from the offal in it—a precaution the Romans had taught him. The water was cool and sweet. He dried his mustaches on his sleeve and saw that same fat turtle still sitting on its boulder. He flapped his arms, screeched, "Yaaah!" Horrified, the little animal flapped its legs insanely, trying to swim before it was in the water. After a moment it collected the few wits it had and dove into the stream.

"Och, what a terror I am," Viridovix laughed. He remembered Arigh's joke with the frogs at Prista, looked in vain for the turtle. "Puir beastie! If you were but a puddock, now, you could take revenge on the lot of us wi' a single peep."

Varatesh listened in consternation as the scout babbled, "It's a horde, I tell you. From the dust, there must be hundreds of 'em coming this way.

You'd best believe we didn't stick around for a closer look, or I wouldn't be here to warn you."

The outlaw chief bit his lip, wondering how Targitaus had conjured up such an army. Seven patrols, now, had sighted big forces moving on his camp. Even discounting their reports by half, as any sensible leader did, his enemies were showing more vigor than they ever had before. If they kept pushing forward, they would drive him back toward the Shaum—or over it. He weighed the risks, wondering whether Targitaus could be as dangerous as the Arshaum. A raid was one thing, a fine piece of bravado, but to try to establish himself in Shaumkhiil . . .

White robes swirling around him, heavy boots clumping in the dirt, Avshar emerged from his tent and strode toward the outlaw chief. Varatesh could not help flinching; the scout, who knew far less than he, cringed away from the wizard-prince. "What lies is this coward grizzling out?" Avshar demanded, cruelly disdainful.

Varatesh glanced up at the veiled face, not sorry he could not meet those masked eyes. He repeated the rider's news, adding out of his own concern, "Where are they getting the men?"

Avshar rubbed mailed hands together, a tigerish gesture of thought. He swung round on the scout. "Whose patrol are you with?"

"Savak's." The renegade kept his answer as short as he could.

"Savak's, eh? Then you *are* a coward." As the scout began to protest, Avshar's booted foot lashed out and caught him in the belly. He spun away and fell, retching, to the ground. In showy contempt, the wizard-prince turned his back on him. The rider would have tried to kill any outlaw, even Varatesh himself. From Avsahr he crept away.

The sorcerer turned back to Varatesh, deigning to explain. "Your escaped swordsman rides with the 'army' Savak's putrid carrion fled from, which makes it easier for me to track them with my scrying. Shall I tell you how they grow their soldiers?"

"Yes." Varatesh's hands had balled into fists at Avshar's viciousness and scorn. At mention of Viridovix they tightened further. He was not glad to be reminded of how the Celt had bested him. Nothing had gone right since that red-whiskered rogue appeared on the plains.

When the wizard-prince was done, Varatesh stood rigid with fury at the trick. The gall of it all but choked him. "Cattle?" he whispered.

"Brush?" Realization burst in him. "All their bands must be so!" His voice rose to a roar, summoning the camp. "Ho, you wolves—!"

"Here's that lad back again," Viridovix said. His comrades sat their horses calmly as the point rider came toward them. After days of frightening off Varatesh's patrols without fighting, they looked forward to doing it again.

When Rambehisht saw the cloud of dust behind the scout, though, his sneer became a worried frown. "Lots of them, this time," he said, and unshipped his bow. The rest of the Khamorth did the same.

"Is it a brawl, now?" the Gaul asked eagerly.

Rambehisht spared him one sentence: "They aren't here to trade tunics with us." Then the plainsman was shouting, "Spread out, there! Quick, while there's time! Oktamas, fall back with the remounts. And kick those cattle in the arse, somebody; they're no good to us anymore."

Horsemen grew visible through the dust, trotting forward at a good clip. Rambehisht's "spread out" order confused Viridovix for a moment. Used to infantry fights, his natural inclination would have been to gather his forces for a charge. Then the first arrow whizzed past his head, and he understood. A headlong rush would have been pincushioned in seconds.

Nomads were darting every which way, or so it seemed, snapping off shots at what looked like impossible ranges. Yet men screamed when they were hit, and horses, limbs suddenly unstrung, went crashing to the steppe. It was deadly and confusing, and the Gaul, an indifferent rider with a weapon whose reach was only arm's length, was of little use to himself or his comrades.

His ignorance of the plains' fluid way of fighting almost got him killed or captured in the first moments of the skirmish. Varatesh's men outnumbered Rambehisht's patrol, which promptly gave ground before them. For Viridovix, retreat and defeat were as one word. He held his ground, roaring defiance at the outlaws, until Batbaian shouted, "Fall back, fool! Do you want to see Seirem again?"

That brought the Celt to his senses as nothing else could have. It was nearly too late. Already one of the outlaws was past him and twisting in the saddle to fire. Viridovix slammed his heels into his horse's flanks. It sprang forward, and the arrow flew behind him.

"Try that again, you black-hearted omadhaun!" Viridovix yelled, spurring straight at the nomad. Without time to nock another shaft, the plainsman danced his mount aside. The Gaul thundered by. He rode hard, bent low over his horse's neck. An arrow point scraped the bronze at the very crown of his protective cap, sending a shiver through him. He could feel his back muscles tightening against a blow.

But quivers were emptying, and shamshirs came out of scabbards as the fight moved to closer quarters. Even then engagements were hit-and-run as horses carried riders past each other; a slash, a chop, and then wheel round for the next pass. Suddenly Viridovix, with his long, straight sword, owned the advantage.

Then he heard an enemy horseman cry his name. His head whipped round—he knew that voice. Varatesh drove his horse forward, shouting, "No tricks between us now and no truce either!"

"Sure and Avshar's pup has slipped his leash!" the Celt retorted. Varatesh's swarthily handsome features twisted with rage. He struck, savage as a hunting hawk. Viridovix turned the blow, but it jolted his arm to the shoulder. His own answering slash was slow and wide.

Varatesh spun his horse faster than Viridovix could. The Gaul was quickly finding he did not care for mounted fighting. Afoot, he had no doubt he could cut Varatesh to pieces, for all the outlaw chief's speed and ferocity. But a horse was as much a weapon as a sword, and one at which the plainsman was a master.

With a deft flick of the reins, the renegade drove his mount to Viridovix' shield side, cutting across his body at the Celt. A Khamorth might have died from the unexpected stroke. Viridovix, though, was used to handling a far heavier shield than the boiled-leather target he bore and got it in front of the slash. But his roundhouse reply was a poor thing which just missed cutting off his own horse's ear.

Though Varatesh's blow had failed, the Gaul realized he could not let the outlaw keep the initiative—he was too dangerous by half for that. "Get round there, fly-bait!" he roared, jerking his horse's head brutally to the left. The beast neighed in protest, but turned.

This time Viridovix was as quick as his foe. Varatesh's eyes went wide with surprise as the Celt bore down on him. His shamshir came up fast enough to save his head, but Viridovix' stroke smashed it from his fingers. The renegade gasped an oath, wondering if his hand was broken. He drew his dagger and threw it at the Celt, but the cast was wild—he had no feeling above his wrist.

In plainsman style, Varatesh was not ashamed to flee then. "Come back, you spineless coistril!" Viridovix cried. He started to gallop after him, then glanced round, looking for comrades to join him in the chase. "Well, where are they all gone to?" Most of Rambehisht's men were a quarter-mile south and still retreating in the face of the outlaws' superior numbers.

The Gaul paused, of two minds. There was Varatesh ahead, disarmed and temptingly close. If Viridovix had the faster horse, he could overhaul him and strike him down, but he would surely cut himself off from his mates in the doing. Then his choice was made for him, for two of the outlaw chief's men were riding to his rescue, one with a bow.

The little battle had only increased Viridovix' respect for the potent nomad weapon. He wheeled his horse away from the threat. The Khamorth fired twice in quick succession, his last two arrows. One of the shafts darted over the Celt's shoulder. Of the other he saw nothing. Short, he thought, and turned back to shake his fist at the bowman.

An arrow was sticking in the high cantle of his saddle. He blinked; the archer was tiny in the distance. "Fetch the executioner!" he exclaimed. He tugged the shaft out, wondering how long it had been there. "Did you fly all this way, or were you riding?" The arrow gave no answers. He threw it to the ground.

It took another hour of skirmishing to shake free of Varatesh's followers. At last they gave up. Their horses were not as fresh as those of Rambehisht's patrol, and Varatesh was too canny to let his men be caught on tired animals. Having accomplished his main purpose—turning his enemies' advance—he drew back.

"The grandest sport of all!" Viridovix shouted to his comrades as they reformed. The Gaul was still exhilarated from the fighting. It was not the hand-to-hand he was used to, but all the more exciting for its strangeness. Not until he brushed a sweaty arm over his cheek did he discover he was cut, whether from a sword or an unnoticed arrow-graze he never knew.

Several Khamorth were wounded, but even a plainsman with an arrow through his thigh grinned through clenched teeth at the Gaul's words. Like him, the nomads enjoyed war for its own sake. They had every reason to be proud, Viridovix thought. Badly outnumbered, they had only lost one man—the corpse was slung over a remount—and given Varatesh's hard-bitten bandits all they wanted.

Even gloomy Rambehisht seemed satisfied as the patrol made camp under lowering skies. "They paid for everything today," he said, gnawing on the flattened chunk of meat he had carried under his saddle.

"Yes, and dearly!" Batbaian said. He was tending to an arrow wound in his horse's hock. His voice cracked with excitement; combat was still new to him, and he swelled with pride on facing it successfully.

Viridovix smiled at his enthusiasm. "A pity the spalpeens twigged to the kine," he said.

"Any trick is only good till the other fellow figures it out." Rambehisht shrugged. "We got farther than we would have without 'em, pushed the outlaws back and our own camp forward." He looked up at the gathering clouds. "Rain soon anyway, and then no dust to raise."

The death of Onogon the shaman delayed whatever choice of allies the Arshaum were going to make. The clanswomen bewailed his passing, while the men mourned in silence, gashing their cheeks with knives to mark their grief.

"As for me, I'd just as soon cut my throat," Pikridios Goudeles remarked, knowing Onogon's loss hurt the cause of Videssos.

Arigh visited the imperial embassy's yurt the next day, his self-inflicted wounds beginning to scab. He glumly sipped kavass, shaking his head in disbelief. "He's really gone," the Arshaum said, half to himself. "Somewhere down inside me, I didn't think he could ever die. All my life he's been just the same—he must've been born old. He looked as if a breeze would blow him over, but he was the wisest, kindest man I ever knew." Perhaps it was his years in Videssos, perhaps his deep grief, but, nomad custom notwithstanding, Arigh was close to tears.

"There will be no mourning in Bogoraz's tent," Goudeles said, still thinking of the Empire's interest.

"That's so," Arigh said indifferently. His private sorrow dimmed such concerns.

More sensitive to the plainsman's mood than was Goudeles, Skylitzes said, "I hope his passing was easy."

"Oh, yes. I was there—we were arguing over you folk, as a matter of fact." Arigh gave Goudeles a tired, mocking smile. "He finished a skin, stepped outside to piddle. When he got back, he said his legs were heavy. Dizabul, curse him, laughed—said it was no wonder, the way he guzzled. Well, to be fair, Onogon took a chuckle from that.

"But he kept getting worse. The heaviness crept up his thighs, and he could not feel his feet, not even with a hard pinch. He lay down on his back, and after a bit his belly grew cold and numb, too. He covered up his face then, knowing he was going, I suppose. A few minutes later he gave a sort of a jerk, and when we uncovered him his eyes were set. He showed no pain—that old heart just finally stopped, is all."

"A pity," Skylitzes said, shaking his head—as much tribute as the pious officer could render to a heathen shaman.

Gorgidas had all he could do to keep from crying out. Suddenly the historian's cloaking he had assumed sloughed away, to reveal the physician beneath. To a doctor, Onogon's death screamed of poisoning, and he could name the very drug—hemlock. Arigh's account described its effects perfectly; especially in the old, it would seem a natural death to those who did not know them.

When the plainsman finally left, the Greek told his comrades what he guessed. Skylitzes grunted. "I can see it," he said judiciously.

"Oh, indeed, Bogoraz has it in him to kill," Goudeles said. "No doubt of that. But what good does knowing do us? If we put it about, who would believe us? We would but seem to be slanderers and do ourselves no good. Unless, of course," he added hopefully to Gorgidas, "you have a supply of this drug with which to demonstrate? On an animal, perhaps."

"Now there's a fine idea, Pikridios," Skylitzes said. "He shows the stuff off, and they think we blew out the old bastard's light. Just what we need."

"I have none in any case," Gorgidas said. "When I became a physician I swore an oath to have nothing to do with deadly drugs, and was never tempted to break it." He sat unhappily, head in his hands. It ached in him that Goudeles should be right. He hated poisons, the more so because physicians had such feeble countermeasures. Most so-called antidotes, he knew, came from old wives' tales and were good for nothing.

The women Arghun had bestowed on the embassy knew no Videssian, but Gorgidas', a tiny, exquisite creature named Hoelun, had no trouble understanding his dismay. She gently touched his slumped shoulder, ready to knead away his trouble. He shrugged her away. When she withdrew, silent and obedient as always, he felt ashamed, but only for a moment. Revenges on Bogoraz kept spinning through his mind; Onogon deserved better than to be murdered for the sake of a war hundreds of miles away.

He laughed without humor at one particularly bloodthirsty vengeance. Viridovix, he thought, would be proud of him—a fine irony there.

The shaman's funeral occupied the next several days. He was buried rather than burned, common custom on the fire-wary steppe. A sleeping-mat was set in the center of a great square pit, and Onogon's body, dressed in his wildly fringed shaman's garb, laid on it. A roof of woven brush set atop poles formed a chamber over the corpse; the Arshaum buried gold cups with it, while Tolui, the shaman who had succeeded Onogon as the clan's chief seer, sacrificed a horse over the grave. The blood spurted halfway across the brush roof below.

"A good omen," Arigh said as the horse was tipped into the pit. "He will ride far in the world to come." Almost all the clan elders were at the graveside, watching servants begin spading earth into the tomb. Gorgidas watched them in turn, trying to gauge what they were thinking. It was next to impossible; mourning overlay their features, and in any case they were as impenetrable a group of men as he had seen.

The Greek's own short temper rose to watch Bogoraz make his way among them, exuding clouds of sincere-sounding sorrow—like a squid shooting out ink, he thought. Dizabul was at the Yezda's side; Arshaum heads turned to hear him laugh at some remark Bogoraz made.

Wulghash's legate and Goudeles played out their game of bribe and counterbribe, promise and bigger promise. "Insatiable," the Videssian groaned. "Three times now, I think, I've paid this Guyuk to say aye, and if Bogoraz has been at him four for a no, then all the gold's for nothing."

"Terrible, when you can't trust a man to stay bought," Gorgidas murmured, drawing a crude gesture from Goudeles and a rare smile from Skylitzes.

Whether they finally concluded there was nothing left to milk or they came to a genuine decision, the Gray Horse Arshaum sent riders out to the neighboring clans, inviting them to send envoys to a feast at which the choice would be announced. "Clever of Arghun," said Skylitzes, who had a better feel for Arshaum usages than his comrades. "He can make clear which side he favors at the start of things, and by their custom the other won't be able to complain."

The envoys came quicker than Gorgidas had expected; he still found it hard to grasp how much ground the nomads could cover when they needed to. Two of them promptly reached for their blades when they saw each other and had to be pulled apart. Arghun ordered them kept under watch, just as he had the rival embassies from the powers to the south.

Even the banquet yurt was too small to hold all the feasters. After carefully clearing a stretch of earth, the Arshaum dug three firepits: a small central one for Arghun, his sons, and the ambassadors, with larger ones on either side for the khagan's councilors and the envoys from other clans. The nomads unrolled rugs around each fire, initiating the layout of a tent as closely as they could.

"One way or the other, it will be over soon now, and there's some relief," Goudeles said, trying to get the creases out of a brocaded robe that had been folded in a saddlebag for several weeks. He was not having much luck.

"Unless they choose against us, and offer us up to Skotos to seal their foul bargain," Skylitzes said. He patted his sword. "I'll not go alone."

Changing into his own meager finery, Gorgidas reflected on the inconsistencies that could dwell in a man. Skylitzes got on well with the Arshaum, liked them better than he did Goudeles, some ways. But in anything touching religion, he kept all the aggressive intolerance that characterized Videssians. The pen-pusher was far more broad-minded there, though to him the plainsmen were so many savages.

"Well, let's be off," Goudeles said with forced lightness. The suave calm he cultivated was frayed.

Gorgidas felt himself the center of all eyes as the Videssian party walked toward the feast. Agathias Psoes and his men anxiously watched the embassy, while the Arshaum themselves seemed as curious as its members about whether they would be friends or foes.

The evening was cool, with a smell of rain in the air. As well, the Greek thought, that the Arshaum had made their choice at last; another week or so and the fall storms would begin in earnest—and good luck to an outdoor feast then!

The leaping flames in the fire pits gave an inviting promise of warmth. Goudeles might have been reading Gorgidas' mind, for he said, "Tonight I almost would not mind tramping through the coals." He pulled his robe more tightly about him. After months in tunic and trousers, Videssian ceremonial costume was drafty.

The Greek scowled when he saw Bogoraz climb down from his yurt. Wulghash's emissary, urbane as always, waved and hailed his rivals. "Wait for me, if you would. We shall learn our fate together." A smile was on his full lips as he came up. It did not reach his eyes, but that meant nothing. It never did.

The Yezda diplomat's small talk, though, was its usual polished self. "See what an eminent audience we shall perform before tonight," he said, and the sneer in his voice was delicate enough to make Goudeles lift an envious eyebrow.

Most of the Arshaum were already in their places; some had begun to eat, and the skins of kavass were traveling among them. They grew quiet as they spied the two embassies approaching out of the twilight. With a nod to his sons to follow him, Arghun rose to meet them.

Gorgidas looked from one face to the next, trying to find his answer before the khagan gave it. Arghun was unreadable and seemed faintly amused, as if savoring the suspense he was creating. Nor was anything to be gleaned from Arigh, who stood impassive, yielding the moment to his father. But when the Greek saw Dizabul's ill-concealed pout, he began to hope.

Arghun stepped forward, embraced Goudeles, Skylitzes, and Gorgidas in turn. "My good friends," he said. He greeted the Yezda envoy with a nod, civil but small. "Bogoraz." He paused for a moment to make sure he was understood, then said, "Come. The food is waiting."

Behind the Videssian embassy, Psoes whooped with joy. "All you can drink tonight, lads!" he shouted, and then it was his men's turn to cheer. Bogoraz' guards, wherever they were, were silent.

The Yezda envoy managed a courteous bob of the head for Goudeles. "I would have won, without so clever an opponent," he said. Beaming, the Videssian bowed in return. He would have had equally insincere compliments for his rival had their places been reversed, and they both knew it.

When Dizabul started to say something, Bogoraz hushed him. "I know you did all you could for our cause, gracious prince. Now let us enjoy the fare your father offers. This custom your people have of not speaking of important matters at meals is wise, I think." Taking the arm of Arghun's younger son, he sat by the fire and fell to with good appetite.

Sitting in turn, Gorgidas gave him a slit-eyed look. He was still only catching about one word in three of the Arshaum speech, but tone was something else. Bogoraz did not sound like a defeated man.

"Aye, no doubt he has front," Skylitzes allowed, dipping a strip of roast mutton into dark-yellow mustard. The Videssian officer's eyes went wide when he tasted it. "Kavass," he wheezed, and gulped to put out the fire.

Warned just in time, the Greek offered his own similarly anointed hunk of meat to Arigh, who said, "Thanks," and devoured it. "Too hot for you, eh?" he chuckled. "Well, I never got used to that vile Videssian fish sauce, either." Gorgidas, who was fond of liquamen, nodded, taking his point.

The kavass was flowing fast; their decision made, the Arshaum saw no reason to hold back. Gorgidas did not feel like waking up to a pounding head come morning. In Greek style, he was used to watering his wine when he wanted to stay close to sober. The serving girl looked at him as if he was mad, but fetched him a pitcher and a mixing cup anyway. The fermented mares' milk was not improved for being diluted to half strength.

"A useful trick, that," said Goudeles, who did not miss much. "You give the look of drinking twice as much as you really do." His eyes sparkled with triumph. "Tonight, though, I don't care how much I put down."

On Arghun's left, Bogoraz was eating and drinking with a fine show of unconcern. Dizabul matched him draught for draught and, being young, soon grew drunk. "Things would have been different if *I* had been khagan," he said loudly.

"You're not, nor likely to be," Arigh snarled.

"Quiet, both of you," Arghun said, scandalized. "Have you no respect for custom?" His sons obeyed, glaring at each other, Arigh suspicious of Dizabul for threatening his position, Dizabul hating Arigh—whose existence he had almost forgotten—for returning and destroying his. Strife fit for a tragedian, Gorgidas thought—Euripides, perhaps, for there was no easy right and wrong here.

Despite Arghun's warning to his sons, the feast bent Arshaum propriety to the breaking point. It was, after all, the occasion for announcing an alliance, and one by one the envoys from the neighboring clans found their way over to the central firepit to meet the Videssian ambassadors. Some spoke to Bogoraz as well, but most seemed ready to follow Arghun's lead; the Gray Horse clan held the widest pastures and was thus the most influential on the plains of Shaumkhiil.

The succession of tipsy barbarians soon bored Gorgidas, who did not envy his companions for having to be cordial toward each of them in turn. Sometimes being unimportant had advantages.

The only nomad who briefly managed to rouse the Greek's interest was the envoy of the Black Sheep clan, the most powerful next to Arghun's. His name was Irnek; tall and, for an Arshaum, heavily bearded, he carried himself with an air of sardonic intelligence. Gorgidas feared he might favor Bogoraz simply from ill will between his clan and that of the Gray Horse, but Irnek, after a long, cool, measuring stare, ignored the Yezda diplomat.

That slight and others like it seemed to reach Bogoraz at last. Where before he had kept his wits about him at all times, tonight he drank himself clumsy. After almost emptying a skin of kavass with one long draught, he dropped it and had to fumble about before he was able to pick it up and pass it on to Arghun. "My apologies," he said.

"No need for them." The khagan drained it, smacked his lips thoughtfully. "Tangy." He called for another.

Gorgidas was gnawing meat from a partridge wing when Arghun

uncoiled from his cross-legged seat and stomped in annoyance. "My cursed foot's fallen asleep."

Arigh laughed at him. "If I'd said that, you'd say I was still soft from Videssos."

"Maybe so." But the khagan stamped again. "A plague! It's both of them now." He tried to stand and had trouble.

"What's wrong?" Gorgidas asked, not following the Arsham speech.

"Oh, nothing." Arigh was still chuckling. "His feet are asleep." Arghun rubbed the back of one calf, his face puzzled.

Gorgidas' eye swept to Bogoraz, who had opened his coat and was wiping his forehead as he talked with Dizabul. Suspicion exploded in the Greek. If he was wrong he would have much to answer for, but if not—he seized the dish of mustard in front of Arigh, poured in water till it made a thin, pasty soup, and pressed the bowl into the Arshaum prince's hands.

"Quick!" he cried. "Give this to your father to drink, for his life!"

Arigh stared. "What?"

"Poison, you fool!" In his urgency, politeness was beyond Gorgidas; it was all he could do to speak Videssian instead of Greek. "Bogoraz has poisoned him, just as he did Onogon!"

The Yezda ambassador leaped to his feet, fists clenched, face red and running with sweat. He bellowed, "You lie, you vile, pox-ridden—" and then stopped, utter horror on his features. The expression lasted but a moment, and haunted Gorgidas the rest of his life.

Then everyone was crying out, for Bogoraz burst into blinding white flame, brighter by far than the bonfire by him. His scream cut off almost before it began. He seemed to burn from the inside out, a blaze more furious with every passing second. And yet, as he kicked and writhed and tried to run from the fate he had called down on himself, his flaming body gave off no heat, nor was there any stench of burning. Onogon's magic and the protective oath he had extracted from Bogoraz had not been enough to save himself, but they served his khagan still.

"Oath-breaker!" cried Tolui, the new shaman, from among the clan elders. "See the oath-breaker pay his price!"

Mouth working in terror, Dizabul scrambled away from the charring ruins of what had been his friend.

Arghun stood transfixed, gaping at the appalling spectacle. Gorgidas had no time for it. He seized the mustard from Arigh once more, thrust it on the khagan. "Drink!" he shouted, by a miracle remembering the Arshaum word. Automatically, Arghun obeyed. He suddenly bent double as the emetic took hold, spewed up kavass and food.

Under the sour smell of vomit was another, sharper, odor, the telltale scent of hemlock. Gorgidas barely noted it; Bogoraz' hideous end had banished any doubts he might have had.

After vomiting, Arghun went to his knees and stayed there. He touched his thighs as if he had no feeling in them. Gorgidas' lips tightened. If the poison reached the khagan's heart he would die, no matter that he had thrown most of it up. "Keep him sitting!" the Greek barked at Arigh, who jumped to support his father with arm and shoulder.

The physician shouted for Tolui, who came at the run, a short, middle-aged nomad with a surprisingly deep voice. Through Arigh, Gorgidas demanded, "Have you any potions to strengthen a man's heart?"

He almost cried out for joy when the shaman answered, "Yes, a tea made from foxgloves."

"The very thing! Brew some quick and fetch it!"

Tolui darted away. Gorgidas thrust a hand under Arghun's tunic; the skin at the khagan's groin was starting to grow cool. The Greek swore under his breath. Arghun, bemused a moment before, was turning angry; hemlock left the victim's mind clear to the end.

Dizabul hesitantly approached his father, knelt to take his hand. Against every Arshaum custom, there were tears in his eyes. "I was wrong, father. Forgive me, I beg," he said. Arigh snarled something short and angry at his brother, but Gorgidas could guess how much that admission had cost the proud young prince.

Before Arghun could reply, a handful of concubines rushed toward him, shrieking. He shouted them away with something close to his healthy vigor, grumbling to Arigh, "The last thing I need is a pack of women wailing around me."

"Will he pull through?" Goudeles asked Gorgidas. He was suddenly full of respect; they were in the Greek's province now, not his.

The physician was feeling for Arghun's pulse and did not answer. His fingers read a disquieting story; the khagan's heartbeat was strong, but slow and getting slower. "Tolui! Hurry, you son of a mangy goat!" the Greek shouted. To get more speed, he would have called the shaman worse, had he known how.

Tolui came trotting up, holding a steaming two-eared cup in both hands. "Give that to me!" Gorgidas exclaimed, snatching it away from him. The shaman did not protest. A healer himself, he knew another when he saw one.

"Bitter," Arghun said when the Greek pressed the cup to his lips, but he drank it down. He sighed as the warm brew filled his stomach. Gorgidas seized his wrist again. The foxglove tea was as potent in this world as in his own; the khagan's heartbeat steadied, then began to pick up.

"Feel how far the coldness has spread," Gorgidas ordered Tolui.

The shaman obeyed without question. "Here," he said, pointing. It was still below Arghun's navel—an advance, but a tiny one.

"If he dies," Arigh said, voice chill with menace, "it will not be a horse sacrificed over his tomb, Dizabul; it will be you. But for you, this cursed Bogoraz would have been run out long since." Sunk in misery, Dizabul only shook his head.

Arghun cuffed at his elder son. "I don't plan on dying for a while yet, boy." He turned to Gorgidas. "How am I doing?" The physician palpated his belly. The hemlock had moved no further. He told the khagan so.

"I can feel that for myself," Arghun said. "You seem to know this filthy poison—what does it mean? Will I get my legs back?" The khagan's eyebrows shot up. "By the wind spirits! Will I get my prick back? I don't use it as much as I used to, but I'd miss it."

The Greek could only toss his head in ignorance. Men who puked up hemlock were not common enough for him to risk predictions. As yet he was far from sure Arghun would survive; he had not thought past that.

Lankinos Skylitzes held a wool coat, a long light robe, and a black felt skullcap in front of him. "What is this, a rummage sale?" Gorgidas snapped. "Don't bother me with such trash."

"Sorry," the Videssian officer said, and sounded as if he meant it; like Goudeles, he was taking a new look at the physician. "I thought you might be interested. It's all that's left of Bogoraz."

"Oh."

Gorgidas felt Arghun's pulse again. The khagan's heart was still beating steadily. "Get me more of that foxglove tea, if you would," the Greek said to Tolui. Arigh smiled as he translated. He knew Gorgidas well enough to realize his return to courtesy was a good sign. The physician added, "And bring back some blankets, too; we should keep the poisoned parts as warm as we can."

Gorgidas stayed by Arghun through the night. Not until after midnight was he sure he had won. Then at last the chill of the hemlock began, ever so slowly, to retreat. As the sky grew light in the east, the khagan had feeling halfway down his thighs, though his legs would not yet answer him.

"Sleep," Arghun told the Greek. "I don't think you can do much more for me now—and if you prod me one more time I may wring your neck." The twinkle in his eye gave the lie to his threatening words.

The physician yawned until his jaw cracked; his eyes felt full of grit. He started to protest, but realized Arghun was right. His judgment would start slipping if he stayed awake much longer. "You rout me out if anything goes wrong," he warned Tolui. The shaman nodded solemnly.

Waking Skylitzes and Goudeles, who had dozed off by the fire, Gorgidas headed back with them toward the Videssian embassy's yurt. "I'm very glad indeed old Arghun chose us over the Yezda," the pen-pusher said.

"I should hope so," Skylitzes said. "What of it?"

Goudeles looked round carefully to make sure no one who understood Videssian was in earshot. "I was just thinking that if he had not, I might have been foolish enough to essay something drastic to change his mind." The plump bureaucrat patted his paunch. "Somehow I don't think I would have burned so neatly as Bogoraz. Too much fat to fry, you might say. Rrrr!" He shuddered at the very notion.

XI

"A MESSENGER?" SCAURUS REPEATED. PHOSTIS APOKAVKOS NODDED. The tribune muttered to himself in annoyance, then burst out, "I don't want to see any bloody messenger; they only come with bad news. If he's not from Phos himself, I tell you, I'll eat him without salt. If some tin-pot noble wants to complain that my men have lifted a couple of sheep, let him do it himself."

Apokavkos grinned self-consciously at the near-sacrilege. "Next best thing to Phos, sir," he said in careful Latin; though he clung to the Empire's religion, he acted as Roman as he could, having got a better shake from the legionaries than his own folk ever gave him. He rubbed his long, shaven chin, continuing, "From the Emperor, he is."

"From Thorisin?" Marcus perked up. "I'd almost given up on getting word from him. Go on, fetch the fellow." Apokavkos saluted and hurried out of what had been the provincial governor's suite of offices. Raindrops skittered down the windowpane behind the tribune.

The messenger squelched in a few minutes later. Despite his wide-brimmed leather traveling hat, his hair and beard were soaked; there was mud halfway up his knee-high boots. He smelled of wet horse.

"This is a bad storm, for so early in the season," Marcus remarked sympathetically. "Care for some hot wine?" At the man's grateful nod, the Roman used a taper to light the olive oil in the small brazier that sat at a corner of his desk. He set a copper ewer of wine atop the yellow flame, wrapped his hand in a protective scrap of cloth when he was ready to pick it up and pour.

The imperial messenger held his cup to his face, savoring the fragrant steam. He drank it off at a gulp, to put something warm in his stomach. "Have another," Marcus said, sipping his own. "This one you'll be able to enjoy."

"I do thank you. If you'll let me have that rag—ah, thanks again." The Videssian poured, drank again, this time more slowly. "Ah, yes, much better now. I only wish my poor horse could do the same."

Scaurus waited until the courier set this cup down empty, then said, "You have something for me?"

"So I do." The man handed him a tube of oiled silk, closed at either end with a wooden plug and sealed with the imperial sunburst. "Waterproof, you see?"

"Yes." Marcus broke the seal and unrolled the parchment inside it. He set it on the polished marble desktop with his cup at one end and the corner of an abacus at the other to keep it from spiraling up again.

The script was plain and forceful; Scaurus recognized the Emperor's writing at once. The note had Gavras' straightforward phrasing, too, with none of Drax' rhetorical flourishes added. "Thorisin Gavras, Avtokrator, to his captain Marcus Aemilius Scaurus: I greet you. Thanks to some pen-pusher's idiocy, your latest letter did not get out of the city till I came here, so I have it only now. I say well-done to you; you have served me better than I could have hoped. I have sent some of your islander prisoners to enjoy the winter in garrison duty on the Astris and will exchange the rest for my own men whom the brigands captured. That will take time, as I drove them off the mainland at Opsikion with much loss, though I fear pirate raids still continue all along our coasts. As soon as possible, I will send the Garsavrans gold to repay what you took from them—I trust you have receipts." The tribune smiled at the sly reference to his brief bureaucratic career. He read on: "Bring Drax and the remaining rebel leaders here at once, with as small a detachment as may be counted on to prevent their escape—do not weaken Garsavra's garrison more than you must. Head the detachment yourself, that I may reward you as you deserve; your lieutenant has enough wit to hold his own in your absence. Done at Videssos the city, nineteen days after the autumn equinox."

Marcus thought rapidly, then looked up at the messenger. "Six days, eh? You made good time, riding through such slop."

"Thank you, sir. Is there any reply?"

"Not much point to one. You'll only beat me to the capital by a few days. Tell his Majesty I'm carrying out his orders—that should be enough."

"I'll do it. Can I trouble you for some dry clothes?"

"Aye, it should be easy enough duty," Gaius Philippus said. "The Yezda won't be doing much in this weather, not unless they teach their little ponies to swim." Sardonic amusement lit his face. "And come to that, you'll have a jolly little tramp through the bog, won't you?"

"Don't remind me," Marcus said. He longed for a good Roman road, wide, raised on an embankment to keep it free of mud and snow, solidly paved with flat square stones set in concrete. Each fall and spring, with the rains, Videssos' dirt tracks turned into bottomless quagmires. That they were easier on horses' hooves than paving stones did not, to the tribune's way of thinking, make up for their being useless several months out of the year.

"Will two dozen men be enough?" the senior centurion asked.

"To keep four from getting loose? They'd better be. And with women and children and what-have-you, the party will look plenty big to discourage bandits—not that the bandits won't be chin-deep in slime themselves. Besides, I have my orders, and there's no doubt Thorisin's right—you'll have more need of troops here than I will. I'm sorry I'm stealing Blaesus from you."

"Don't be. Most of your men are from his maniple, and he knows them. And while he's gone," Gaius Philippus continued with his usual practicality, "I get the chance to bump Minucius up a grade for a while. He'll do well."

"You're right. He has the makings of a centurion in him, that one." Scaurus grinned at the veteran. "You're bumping up a grade yourself."

"Aye, so I am, aren't I? I hadn't thought of that, but I'll remember when the time comes to deal out the pay, I promise."

"Go howl," the tribune laughed.

The rain pelted down, whipped into almost horizontal sheets by a fierce north wind. Thus, while the Namdalener prisoners' departure from

Garsavra made a little procession, few townsfolk watched it. Senpat and Nevrat Sviodo rode ahead of the main body of legionaries as scouts. In the midst of the Romans came the four islanders, at Scaurus' command still wearing their veiling. Baggage-mules and donkeys for the soldiers' families followed, while Junius Blaesus led the five-man rear guard.

The legionaries were plodding past the graveyard just outside Garsavra when the tribune looked back through the storm and saw a lone figure riding after them. "Who is it?" he yelled back to Blaesus. The howling wind swept away the junior centurion's answer. Uselessly wiping at his face, Marcus filled his lungs to shout again.

Before he could, Styppes came splashing up to him, astride a scrawny, unhappy-looking donkey that made heavy going of his bulk. The rain had soaked the healer-priest's blue robe almost black. Looking down at Scaurus afoot, he announced, "I shall accompany you back to the city. I have been away from my monastery too long, and there are perfectly capable healers at Garsavra to tend to your soldiers there."

As it often did, his peremptory tone grated on the tribune. "Please yourself," he said shortly, but in truth he was not sorry to have Styppes' company this once—not with Helvis carefully riding sidesaddle a hundred feet behind and due in less than three months. He had tried to persuade her to stay at Garsavra, but when she refused he yielded. After all, he thought, she was not likely to see her brother again.

Styppes' donkey stepped into a particularly deep patch of mire—what had been a rut in the road in drier times—and almost stumbled. The healer-priest pulled sharply on the reins. The beast recovered, but gave him a reproachful look.

Scaurus' sympathies lay with the donkey. Marching during the rainy season was an exercise suited to Sisyphos, save that the tribune's burden, instead of rolling down a hillside in the underworld to be hauled up anew, only grew heavier. Every step was hard work. The mud clung to his *caligae* and made a soft sucking sound of protest every time he pulled his leg free. In some stretches, he could not lift his legs at all, but had to slog forward pushing a mucky wake ahead of himself. He began to envy his prisoners, burdened by neither armor nor packs.

As eagerly as he looked forward to camping at the end of the day, the halt proved hardly better. Camp was a slapdash affair; he did not have the men to dig in with, and the weather foredoomed that anyhow. It was impossible to start a fire in the open. The Romans and their companions made miserable meals half-heated over braziers or olive-oil lamps, in their tents.

"Are you all right?" the tribune asked Helvis as he clashed flint and steel over tinder that was not as dry as it should have been. *Click, click!* The metal and gray-yellow stone seemed to laugh at him.

Helvis toweled at her hair. "Stiff, tired, drowned—otherwise not bad," she said, smiling wryly. While on donkeyback she had worn a thick, belted, woolen cloak, now cast aside, but her yellow linen shift had got wet enough to mold itself to her belly and swelling breasts. She toweled again, harder. "I must look like that monster your people have, the one whose head is all over snakes."

"The Medusa?" Marcus said, still clicking away. "No, not really. When I look at you, only one part of me turns to stone." She snorted. He paid no attention, bending over the little pile of tinder to blow gently on the orange spark that had caught at last. As it burst into flame, he sighed in relief. "There, that's done; now we can close the tent flap."

Helvis did, while the tribune lit lamps. When he started to ask, "Is the baby—" she cut him off firmly.

"The baby," she declared, "is better than I am, I'm sure. And why not? He's out of the cold and damp. He gave me such a kick when I got down from that mangy hard-backed beast that I thought he was this one." She nodded at Malric, who was rolling a giggling Dosti over and over on the sleeping mat. Bored from having ridden all day, he had energy to spare. Helvis gave a little shriek. "Not into the mud!" She sprang forward, too late.

Later, after both boys had finally fallen asleep, she took Marcus' hand, guided it to her belly. Her skin was warm and smooth as velvet, taut from pregnancy. The tribune smiled to feel the irregular thumps and surges as the baby moved within her. "You're right," he said. "He's lively."

She stayed quiet so long he wondered if she'd heard him. When she finally spoke, he heard unshed tears in her voice. "If it is a boy," she said, "shall we call him Soteric?"

He was silent himself after that, then touched her cheek. "If you like," he said, as gently as he could.

"I remember marching from Videssos to Garsavra in a week's time," Marcus said to Senpat Sviodo. "Why is it so much farther from Garsavra back to Videssos?"

"Ah, but the land knows you and loves you now, my friend," Senpat answered, cheery despite his bedraggled state. The brightly dyed streamers that hung from his three-pointed Vaspurakaner hat were running in the rain, putting splotches of contrasting colors on the back of his cloak; his precious pandoura was safe inside a leather bag behind him. Grinning, he went on, "After all, did it not love you, why would it embrace you so? It fairly cries out for you to stay with it forever."

"You can laugh, up there on your horse," Scaurus growled, but Senpat's foolishness pleased him, even so.

As for the rich black loam of the Empire's coastal lowlands, he was ready to consign it to the Namdaleni, the Yezda, or Skotos' demons for that matter. The soil grew progressively more fertile and quaggier, too, as the sea drew closer. Traveling across it when it was wet was like trying to wade through cold, overcooked porridge. The tribune's party was almost alone on the road. He had no trouble understanding that—only mad men or desperate ones would go journeying in the fall rains.

"And in which of those classes do you fit?" Senpat asked when he said that aloud.

"You're here with me—judge for yourself," Marcus came back. Something else occurred to him. "I begin to see why the symbol of Videssian royalty is the umbrella."

Early the next morning Styppes' donkey fell again, throwing him into the ooze. He came up spluttering and cursing in most unpriestly fashion, face, beard, and robe plastered with mud. The donkey did not rise; it had broken a foreleg. It brayed piteously when Bailli, who knew more of horseleeching than any of the Romans, touched the shattered bone. "I doubt you'll trust me with a knife, so cut its throat yourself," he said to Marcus. Turning to Styppes, he went on, "As for you, fatty, you'll use your own hooves from here on out."

"Skotos' ice is waiting for you, insolent heretic," Styppes said, trying to wipe the muck from his face but only spreading it about. From the glare he gave Bailli, it was plain he did not like the idea of marching for several days.

The donkey squealed again, a sound that tore at Scaurus' nerves. He said, "Why not heal it, Styppes?"

The Videssian priest purpled under his coat of mud. He shouted, "The ice take you, too, ignorant heathen! My talent lies in serving men, not brute beasts. Do you want me to prostitute myself? I have no idea how the worthless creature is made inside and no interest in learning, either."

"I was but looking to help," the tribune began, but Styppes, insulted and petulant, was in full spate and trampled the interruption. He railed at Marcus for every remembered slight since the day they met, dredging up things the Roman had long forgotten.

The entire party came to a halt to listen to his tirade, or try not to. A couple of legionaries knelt in the mud to tighten the ankle-straps on their *caligae;* Helvis, as she often did, urged her donkey forward so she could talk to her brother and the other islanders. The Romans paid no attention to her, understanding why she had come with them. Turgot reached out to touch Dosti's fair hair. He shook his head in pain as he remembered his lost Mavia.

Scaurus bent and put the donkey out of its pain. It kicked once or twice and was still. Styppes railed on.

"Be quiet, you bloated, bilious fool," Drax said at last. "Are you a four-year-old bawling over your broken toy?" He did not raise his voice, but the flash of cold contempt in his eyes brought Styppes up short, mouth opening and closing like a fresh-caught fish.

Drax bowed slightly to Marcus. "Shall we get on with it?" he said, as courteously as if they were on their way to a feast or celebration. The tribune nodded, admiring his style. He called out an order. The company lurched forward.

"By the gods, sir, there were times I thought we'd never make it," Junius Blaesus said to Scaurus as the dirty gray of the afternoon's rainy sky darkened toward night, "but it's getting close now, isn't it?"

"So it is," the tribune said, brushing back a loose lock of hair that crawled like a wet worm down his cheek. "A day and a half, maybe, to the Cattle-Crossing. In decent weather it'd be half a day."

A six-man mounted party splashed west past them, kicking up muck and earning curses from the legionaries. Here among the suburbs of the capital, there was a good deal of local traffic. It made the roads worse, something Marcus had not thought possible. He had his prisoners resume their black veils full-time; in the less crowded country further west he had only made them clap on the veiling once or twice a day when someone approached. This was safely imperial territory and the charade was probably unneeded, but where Drax was concerned he took few chances.

More splashing from up ahead, and another rider loomed out of the rain—Nevrat. Her head turned as she searched for Scaurus in the gloom. She smiled when she saw him, teeth flashing against her dark skin. "I've found us a campsite," she said, "a farm with a good stone horse barn to keep our, ah, guests warm and safe. I looked it over. It has little slit windows—" She held her hands a palm's breadth apart to show him. "—and a door that bars from the outside."

"Perfect," Marcus exclaimed. "The great count won't break out of that." He had made Junius Blaesus virtually ring the prisoners' tent with sentries each night. Behind stone and wood, though, they'd be safe enough. A single sentry each watch should do, giving his troopers a much-needed rest.

The farmer on whose land the barn stood was a toplofty little man whose prosperity was made plain enough by the very fact that he owned several horses. He tried to bluster when the tribune asked to use the barn, naming two or three minor court officials who, he declared, "will not be pleased to hear of my being mistreated in this way!"

Annoyed, Marcus dug out Thorisin Gavras' letter and wordlessly handed it to the man, who went red and then white as he saw the imperial signature. "Anything you desire, of course," he said rapidly, and shouted for his farmhands. "Vardas! Ioustos! Come quick, you lazy wretches, and drive the horses into the field!"

The two men emerged from a little cottage set to one side of the main farmhouse, one of them still chewing at a mouthful of supper. Having won his point, the tribune could afford to be gracious. He waved them back. “Let the beasts be. The men inside will have no fire, and the animals’ heat will help keep them warm.”

Vardas and Iuostos looked toward their master, whose name Scaurus did not know. “As he pleases,” the farmer said; they went back to their interrupted meal. Now ingratiating, the short tubby man said to the Roman, “You will honor me by joining me for supper?”

“Thank you, no.” An hour of nervous chatter from this fellow, arrogant and servile by turns, was not to Marcus’ taste. He gave an excuse that let the man save face. “I have to see to setting up camp.”

“Ah.” The farmer nodded wisely, as if understanding what a great labor that was. He bobbed a stiff bow, turned, and fled back into his house. Marcus laughed silently at his retreating back.

The legionaries, whose tents were going up nicely without any supervision, greeted his orders with barely muffled cheers. They did whoop out loud when Blaesus volunteered to take a turn at the barn door himself. Grinning with pleasure at their response, the junior centurion said, “Why not? It’s easier than sleeping, almost.”

“You’d better not sleep, Junius,” the tribune said, driving a tent peg into the muddy ground—at last, something the rain made easier. His tone was bantering, and Blaesus still smiled, but not as widely as he had. The *fustuarium* waited for sentries who dozed at their posts.

Once the tent was up, Scaurus dried himself as best he could. Malric and Dosti fell deeply asleep as soon as their dinner was done. “What did you do, beg a potion from Styppes?” the tribune whispered to Helvis as she covered the two boys. “They’ve been hellions since we set out.”

“Not far wrong,” she said, rising. She tossed him a half-empty wineskin. “I gave them each a good nip while you were busy.”

“Did you? Whatever for?”

She gave him a slow sidelong look. “For us,” she said, her voice thick and sweet as the unwatered wine in the skin.

He scarcely had time to set it down before she stepped smiling into his arms. He kissed her in glad surprise; her desire turned fickle when she was carrying a child.

Her fingers toying with him, she undid his sword belt, pulled down his metal-studded military kilt. “Such complications,” she murmured. Scaurus kissed her eyes and then her ear, having already tugged her simple shift over her head. He blew out the lamps. Together, they slipped to the sleeping mat.

After a while she turned her back on him; he slid into her from behind. The posture, made for slow, lazy love, was easy on them both, her for her pregnancy and him for his weariness after days of pushing through mud. She sighed and wriggled closer.

When he was spent, he rolled lazily onto his back, whistling up into the darkness. Malric stirred, muttering something. "Hush, dear," Helvis said softly. Marcus was not sure which of them she was talking to until she groped for the wineskin, found it, and gave her son a long swallow. He smacked his lips, then turned over and went back to sleep.

"There," Helvis said to the tribune. "Tonight, no interruptions." She pressed herself against him, her hand busy once more.

"Easy there," he said. "I'm fine."

"I think you're fine," she said, mischief in her voice, and did not stop.

"I'm not sure anything will happen." But as he spoke, he felt himself rising to her touch. His arms tightened around her.

"You are the noisiest man," she grumbled, kindly, a bit later, pushing him away from her; his gasps had wakened Dosti. Every pore content, he did not answer. She quieted the baby the same way she had Malric, then returned to the tribune's side.

After a while, she touched him again. He looked at her, bemused, but there was not enough light to read her expression. "You're asking too much, you know," he said sleepily.

She laughed at him. "Times I've said that to you, you sulked for days. See how it feels to be mouse instead of cat, sir? But I want you, and I'll have you."

He stroked her hair, damp now with sweat as well as rain. So was his own. "There is a difference, though. If I can't, I can't."

"There are ways," she said, and used one. It took a while, but he discovered she was right. Amazement gave way to delight. Drowned in her flesh, he sank into as profound a sleep as he had ever known.

Helvis waited for what seemed an endless time, listening to Scaurus' slow, steady breathing and the beat of the rain on the tent. He did not stir when she moved away from him and got to her feet; her mouth twisted in vexation as his seed dribbled down her thigh. She was glad he had not been able to see her face.

She dressed quickly, pinning her heavy cloak closed over her shift. She found the wineskin with her fingers and slipped it into a deep pocket. Then she felt the ground until she came upon his sword belt.

The broad-bladed dagger slid free of its sheath with a tiny scrape of metal against metal. It was heavier in her hand than she had expected. She looked down at the sleeping tribune, hardly more than a deeper shadow in the darkness. Her grip tightened on the hilt. . . . She bit her lip till she tasted blood, shook her head violently. She could not. The knife went with the wineskin.

Malric whimpered as she picked him up, but did not wake. Dosti made no complaint at all, snoring and breathing wine fumes into her face. She held both of them under her outspread cloak so the raindrops would not wake them when she went outside, and thanked Phos that Marcus had pitched his tent just to one side of the horse barn. She did not think she could carry Malric far.

She wished she were not pregnant. It made her slow-moving and clumsy, and what would be necessary would be all the more dangerous.

The chilly rain beat against her face as she shouldered the tent flap open and stepped out into the night. She did not look back at Marcus, but around to take her bearings. There was the barn, with the sentry in front of it. She wondered who he was.

Most of the legionaries' tents were behind her; she could see lamplight under a couple of flaps. Snatches of pandoura music came sweet through the storm, Senpat Sviodo whiling away the time. Closer by she heard Titus Pullo laugh at a joke Vorenus told. Relief seeped through her; it would have been impossibly difficult with either of them on guard. They were too alert by half. All these Romans, she knew too well, were fine soldiers, but the ex-rivals surpassed the rest.

She wondered how long the watchman had been on duty. Was his turn just starting or almost done? She could not gauge the time, not with moon and stars swaddled in clouds. Gamble, then—her lips thinned in a humorless smile as she realized the Videssians' scornful nickname for her people, like most caricatures, fit somewhat.

And Marcus did not believe at all.

She squashed carefully through the mud, as if toward the latrines dug behind the horsebarn. If anyone was there, she could still withdraw in safety—and leave her brother and the other Namdaleni to the judgment of the Avtokrator of the Videssians. It did not bear thinking of.

No one squatted over the noisome slit trenches. She breathed a prayer of thanks to Phos for his protection; confidence soared in her. As soon as the barn's wall screened her from the view of the Roman sentry, she stepped under the shelter of its broad, overhanging eaves. She dug her face into the hollow of her shoulder, wiping the rain from her eyes. Then she stooped and set her sleeping children in the small dry space by the gray stone wall.

"Back soon, my dears," she breathed, though the wine in them meant they did not hear. The sight of Dosti tore at her. She felt whore and deceiver both, to have used his father so. But blood, faith, and folk were ties older and stronger than two and a half years of what was sometimes love with Scaurus.

She straightened, found the tribune's knife, and held it concealed in the flowing sleeve of her cloak. Her heart pounded, her breath came short and fast, not in the passion she had counterfeited but from fear. Recognizing it helped steady her. She turned the corner of the barn and came up to the man on guard.

She was sure she would have no chance of sneaking up on him—she had never seen a Roman sentry woolgathering on watch. So she came openly, splashing and complaining in a loud voice about the dreadful weather.

"Who—?" the Roman said, tensing as he peered through the rain and dark. "Oh, it's you." He relaxed, gave a rueful chuckle. "Aye, it's hideous, isn't it? And to think I was chuckleheaded enough to volunteer to stand out in it. Here, come under the eaves; it's a little drier, though not much, not with this cursed north wind."

"Thank you, Blaesus."

"What can I do for you, my lady?" the junior centurion asked, an open, friendly man with no suspicion in him. He knew Helvis was a Namdalener, in the same way he knew Senpat Sviodo was a Vaspurakaner or Styppes a Videssian. It meant little to him—as well find danger in Scaurus himself as in his woman.

"I have some sweetmeats here Marcus thought you might like," she said, stepping closer. Her hands, Blaesus saw, were sensibly hidden against the cold and wet in her mantle's broad sleeves. He felt his face flush with gladness. Truly the tribune was an officer in ten thousand, to think of sharing tidbits with a sentry.

The knife was in the Roman's neck before he saw it glitter. He tried to scream, but blood gushed into his mouth, tasting of iron and salt. He knew a moment's chagrin—he should have been more careful. Scaurus had spoken to him about that before.

The thought was dizzy, distant as he fought in vain to breathe through the fire and flood in his throat. His knees gave way. He fell face-down in the muck.

A legionary stuck his head into Marcus' tent and shouted, "Sir!"

"Hmm? Wuzzat?" The tribune rolled over, grunted at the contact between the cold sleeping mat and his backside.

The trooper—it was Lucius Vorenus, he realized—blasted sleep from him. "Blaesus is murdered, sir, and the islanders fled!"

"What? Ordure!" Scaurus sprang to his feet, groping for clothes. Suddenly wakened with such news, it took him a few seconds to notice that Dosti and Malric had not begun to howl, that Helvis was not beside him. At the jakes, he thought.

But his sword belt hefted wrongly when he seized it. His fingers found the empty sheath. "Murdered?" he barked tensely at Vorenus. "How?"

The legionary's voice was grim. "Stabbed through the throat like a pig, sir."

"No," Scaurus whispered, half prayer, half moan, finding a horrid pattern in the night's events. Bare-chested and barefoot, he burst past Vorenus and ran for the horse barn. The trooper splashed after him, making heavier going through the mud in his mail shirt and *caligae*. "Is Helvis back of the barn with the children?" Marcus flung over his shoulder.

"At the latrines? I don't think so, sir. Why?" Vorenus said, puzzled and panting.

"Because they're not in my tent either," the tribune grated, tasting the cup of desperation and betrayal, "and my dagger is missing."

Vorenus' jaw shut with an audible click.

Still looking surprised, Blaesus' corpse leaned against the wall of the barn, by the opened door. Vorenus said, "When I came to relieve him, I thought he'd been taken ill until I shifted him and spied—that." A second mouth gaped in the junior centurion's neck. The trooper went on, "The door was shut when I got here, I suppose so anyone looking from camp would see nought amiss. But there's not a Namdalener in there now, or a horse either."

"There wouldn't be," Scaurus agreed. "Do Nevrat and Senpat still have theirs?"

"I don't know, sir. I came to you first, and their tent's some way from yours."

"Go find out; if they do, we'll need them. Rouse the camp, send out searchers—" Not that they'll find anyone, he jeered to himself, not with them afoot and the islanders mounted and with the gods knew how long a start. But maybe by some miracle Helvis was nearby after all, wondering what the commotion was about. He winced at the unlikelihood. As Vorenus started to dash away, the tribune added, "And fetch me Styppes."

Vorenus saluted and was gone. Marcus looked down at Blaesus' body, saw both his scabbards gaping wide as his throat. A *gladius* and a couple of daggers for the Namdaleni, then, he thought—not much. His mind, numbed by disbelief, chewed doggedly on trivia to keep from working at the empty tent a hundred feet away. The real pain would come soon enough.

Vorenus' yells tumbled the legionaries from their tents in alarm. Scaurus heard him switch from sonorous Latin to Videssian. Nevrat Sviodo's clear contralto pierced the rain: "Yes, we have them." The islanders had not risked entering the camp; Marcus doubted he would have himself.

A black shadow stumped toward the horse barn—Styppes, from its angry forward lean and its width. As he drew near, the tribune heard him muttering to himself. The healer-priest grunted in surprise when he saw Scaurus half-naked by the doorway. "If you called me to cure your chest fever," he said with heavy sarcasm, "I cannot until you catch it. But you will."

Reminded of the rain and cold, Marcus began to shiver; he had not noticed them. As baldly as he could, he told Styppes what had happened. Save for what had passed inside his tent, he held back nothing, knowing it would have been useless. He finished, "You know something of magic—can you learn where they fled? We may catch them yet. They cannot travel quickly, not with a pregnant woman."

"That heretic slut—" Styppes growled. He got no further; Scaurus knocked him down.

The priest slowly got to his feet, dripping and filthy. Marcus expected him to storm off in fury. Instead he groveled, saying, "Your pardon, master!" The tribune blinked, but he had not seen the murder in his own eyes. Styppes went on, "I know a spell of searching, but whether it will work I cannot say—that skill is not mine. Would you set a silversmith at an anvil and have him beat out swords?"

"Try it."

"I will need something belonging to one of the fugitives."

"I'll bring it to your tent," the tribune told him. "Wait for me there." He went back to his own at a gluey trot. Something belonging to one of the fugitives would be easy to get there.

Mounted and armed, Senpat and Nevrat Sviodo loomed over him. "What do you want of us?" Senpat asked, his voice carefully neutral. Surely the whole camp knew by now, and waited to see what Marcus would do.

"Take half a dozen men with you, ride back to the last big farm, and commandeer however many horses they have," he said. "We're going after them, and when I dogged Ortaias Sphrantzes after Maragha I learned it's no use chasing riders on foot."

The young Vaspurakaner nodded and started to ride away, shouting for Romans to join him. Nevrat leaned down from her saddle, close enough for Scaurus to read the compassion on her face. "I'm sorry," she said quietly. "The fault is partly mine. Had I not found this place, you would have gone on as you had been doing, and none of this would have happened."

He shook his head. "As well blame the pompous little man who built the barn. I set the guard as I did, and I—" He could not go on.

Nevrat understood, as she often seemed to. She said, "Do not blame her too much. She did not act out of wickedness, or, I think, from hatred of you."

"I know," the tribune said bleakly. "That makes it harder to bear, not easier." He shook free of the comforting hand Nevrat held out. She stared after him for a long moment, then rode to join her husband.

Back at his tent, Marcus threw his tribune's cape over his wet shoulders. Helvis' traveling chest was where she had left it, off to one side of the sleeping mat. He flipped up the latch and fumbled in the chest. Near the top, under an embroidered tunic, he came across a small, flat square of wood—the icon he had given her a few months before. His eyes squeezed shut in pain; he pounded a fist down onto his thigh. As if to give himself a further twist of the knife, he picked up the image and carried it to Styppes.

"A good choice," the healer priest said, taking it from him. "Phos' holiness aids any spell cast in a good cause, and the holy Nestorios, as you know, has a special affinity for the Namdaleni."

"Just get on with it." Scaurus' voice was harsh.

"Remember, I have not tried this in many years," Styppes warned. The ritual seemed not much different from one Nepos had used to seek a lost tax-document for the tribune at the capital. After prostrating himself before the icon, Styppes held it over his head in his right hand. He began chanting in the same ancient dialect of Videssian Phos' liturgy used. His left hand made swift passes over a cup of wine, in which floated a long sliver of pale wood. One end of the sliver had been dipped in blue paint that matched his priestly robes.

His chant ended not with a strong word of command, as Nepos' had, but imploringly; his hand opened in supplication over the cup. "Bless the Lord of the great and good mind!" Styppes breathed, for the chip of wood was swinging like a nail drawn toward a lodestone. "Southeast," the healer-priest said, studying the blue-tipped end.

"Toward the coast, then," Marcus said, almost to himself. Then, to Styppes once more, "You'll ride with us, priest, and cast your spell every couple of hours, to keep us on the trail."

Styppes looked daggers at him, but did not dare say no.

The pursuit party rode out near dawn, mounted on a strange assortment of animals: a couple of real saddle horses beside Senpat's and Nevrat's; half a dozen packhorses, two of which were really too old for this kind of work; and three brawny, great-hoofed plow horses. "A miserable lot," Senpat said to Marcus, "but I had to scour four farms round to get 'em. Most folk use oxen or donkeys."

"The islanders aren't on racers either," the tribune answered. The turmoil in the Roman camp had roused the farmer whose beasts were gone, and Scaurus' ears were still ringing from his howls of outrage. Mixed with the curses, though, was a good deal of description; even with the inevitable exaggeration of his horses' quality, Marcus doubted they would tempt the Videssian cavalry much.

The rain died away into fitful showers and finally stopped, though the stiff north wind kept whipping bank after bank of ugly gray-black clouds across the sky. Styppes, who had brought a goodly supply of wine with which to work his magic, nipped at it every so often to stay warm. It did nothing for his horsemanship; he swayed atop his plow horse like a ship on a stormy sea.

Marcus, taller and heavier than his men, also rode one of the ponderous work animals. Feeling its great muscles surge under him, he reflected that he was at last beginning to react like a Videssian. Styppes' spell of finding was but another tool to grasp, like a chisel or a saw, not something to make a man gasp in lumpish terror. And for traveling quickly, a horse was better than shank's mare.

Other thoughts bubbled just below the surface of his mind. He fought the anguish with his stoic training, reminding himself over and over that nothing befell a man which nature had not already made him fit to bear, that there was no point to being the puppet of any passion, that no soul should forfeit self-control of its own accord. The number of times he had to repeat the maxims marked how little they helped.

Whenever the legionaries rode past a herdsman or orchard keeper, the tribune asked if he had seen the fugitives. "Aye, ridin' hard, they was, soon after dawn," a shepherd said at mid-morning. "They done some-thin'?" His weather-narrowed eyes flashed interest from under a wool cap pulled low on his forehead.

"I'm not out for the exercise," Scaurus retorted. Even as the herder gave a wry chuckle, he was booting his horse forward.

"We're gaining," Senpat Sviodo said. Marcus nodded.

"What will you do with Helvis when we catch them?" Nevrat asked him.

He tightened his jaws until his teeth ached, but did not answer.

A little later Styppes repeated his spell. The chip of wood moved at once, to point more nearly east than south. "There is the way," the healer-priest said, sounding pleased with himself for having made the magic work twice in a row. He took a healthy swig from the wineskin as reward for his success.

As the coast grew near, the ground firmed under the horses' hooves, with sand supplanting the lowlands' thick, black, clinging soil. Terns soared overhead, screeching as they rode with wild breeze. The horses trotted past scrubby beach plums loaded with purple fruit, trampled spiky saltwort and marram grass under their feet.

The sea, gray and threatening as the sky, leaped frothing up the beach; Scaurus licked his lips and tasted salt. No tracks marred the coarse yellow sand. "Which way now?" he called to Styppes, raising his voice above the booming of the surf.

"We will see, won't we?" Styppes said, blinking owlishly. Marcus' heart sank as he watched the priest's lurching dismount. The wineskin flapped at his side like a crone's empty dug. He managed to pour the last few drops into his cup, but a fuddled smile appeared on his face as he tried to remember his magic. He held the icon of the holy Nestorios over his head and gabbled something in the archaic Videssian dialect, but even the tribune heard how he staggered through, fluffing half a dozen times. His passes, too, were slow and fumbling. The sliver of wood in the wine cup remained a mere sliver.

"You worthless sot," Scaurus said, too on edge to hold his temper. Muttering something that might have been apology, Styppes tried again, but only succeeded in upsetting the cup. The thirsty sand drank up the wine. The tribune cursed him with the weary rage of hopelessness.

Titus Pullo gestured southward. "Smoke that way, sir, I think!" Marcus followed his pointing finger. Sure enough, a windblown column was rising into the sky.

"We should have spied that sooner," Senpat Sviodo said angrily. "A pox on these clouds; they're hardly lighter than the smoke themselves."

"Come on," Marcus said, swinging himself back into the saddle. He thumped his heels against the plow horse's ribs. With a snort of complaint, it broke into a jarring canter. The tribune turned his head at a shout; Styppes was still struggling to climb aboard his horse. "Leave him!" Scaurus said curtly. Sand flying, the pursuit party rode south.

They rounded a headland and saw the bonfire blazing on the beach less than a mile away. Marcus' pulse leaped. There were horses round that fire, and others walking free not far away, grazing on whatever shore plants they could find. Senpat whooped. "Gallop!" he shouted, and spurred his horse forward. The others followed.

Jouncing up and down, his eyes tearing from the wind of his passage, Scaurus had all he could do to hold his seat. The legionary Florus could not, and went rolling in the sand while his horse thundered away. Vorenus jeered as he rode by the helpless trooper, then almost joined him when his packhorse stumbled.

Because the Romans had to give all their attention to their horsemanship, Nevrat Sviodo was first to spot the warship lying offshore. Its broad, square sail was tightly furled in the stiff breeze; small triangular topsail and foresail held it steady in the water. Its sides and decking were painted sea green, to make it as near invisible as could be.

The color reminded Marcus of Drax' tokens. He knew with sudden sick certainty that this was no imperial craft, but one of the Namdalener corsairs hunting in Videssian waters.

A moment after Nevrat cried out, the tribune spied the longboat rowing out to meet its parent vessel. He saw the wind catch a woman's hair and blow it in black waves round her face. A smaller shape sat to either side of her. She was looking toward the beach and pointed back at the oncoming legionaries. She called out something at the same time; though he could not hear the words, Scaurus knew that sweet contralto. The rowers picked up their stroke.

The boat was hardly two hundred yards from shore. Fitting an arrow to his bow, Senpat Sviodo rode out till his horse was belly-deep in the sea. He drew the shaft to his ear, let fly. Marcus muttered a prayer, and did not know himself whether or not he asked for Senpat's aim to be true.

He saw the arrow splash a few feet to one side of the longboat. The rowers pulled like men possessed. Senpat nocked another shaft, then swore vilely as his bowstring snapped when he drew it back. Nevrat rushed forward to hand him her bow, but it was a lighter one that did not quite have the other's range. Senpat fired; the arrow fell far short of its mark. He shot again, to prove to himself the first had been no fluke, then shook his head and gave Nevrat back her bow. Knowing they were safe, the oarsmen eased up.

Scaurus' cheeks were wet. He thought the rain had started again, then realized he was weeping. Mortified, he tried to stop and could not. He stared at the sand at his feet, his eyes stinging.

Once the longboat and its occupants were recovered, the islanders unreefed their mainsail. It seized the breeze like a live thing. When the tribune raised his head again, there was a white wake under the ship's bow. The steersmen at the stern leaned hard against their twin steering oars. The corsair heeled sharply away from land, driving east with the wind at its beam. No one on deck looked back.

Afterward, Marcus remembered little of the next two days; perhaps mercifully, grief, loss, and betrayal left them blurred. He must have returned the horses, both stolen and appropriated, for he was afoot when he entered the capital's chief suburb on the western shore of the Cattle-Crossing, the town the Videssians simply called "Across."

What stuck in his mind most, oddly, should have been least likely to remain. Senpat and Nevrat, trying to free him from his black desperation, bought a huge amphora of wine and, carrying it together, hauled it up the stairs to the cubicle he had rented over a perfumer's shop. "Here," Senpat said, producing a mug. "Drink." His brisk tenor permitted no argument.

Scaurus drank. Normally moderate, this night he welcomed oblivion. He poured the wine down at a pace that would have left Styppes gasping. Though they did not match him cup for cup, his Vaspurakaner friends soon sat slack-jointed on the floor of the bare little room, arms round each other's shoulders and foolish smiles on their faces. Yet he could not reach the stupor he sought; his mind still burned with terrible clarity.

The wine did loose deep-seated memories he had thought buried forever. As the returning rain pattered on the slates of the roof and slid through shutter slats to form a puddle by his bed, he paced up and down declaiming great stretches of the *Medea* of Euripides, a play he had learned when studying Greek and hardly thought of since.

When he first read the *Medea,* his sympathies were with the heroine of the play, as its author intended. Now, though, he had committed Jason's hubris—maybe the worst a man can fall into, taking a woman lightly—and found himself in Jason's role. He found, too, as was often the case in Euripides' work, that misery was meted out equally to both sides.

Senpat and Nevrat listened to the Greek verses in mixed admiration and bewilderment. "That is poetry, truly," Senpat said, responding to sound and meter with a musician's ear, "but in what tongue? Not the one you Romans use among yourselves, I'm sure." While he and his wife knew only a little Latin, they could recognize it when they heard it.

The tribune did not answer; instead he took another long pull at the wine, still trying to blot out the reflections that would not cease. The cup shook in his hand. He spilled sticky purple wine on his leg, but never noticed. Even Medea, he thought, had not seduced Jason before she worked her murders and fled in her dragon-drawn chariot.

"Was any man ever worse used by woman?" he cried.

He expected no answer to that shout of despair, but Nevrat stirred in her husband's arms. "As for man by woman, I could not say," she said, looking up at him, "but turn it round, if you will, and look at Alypia Gavra."

Marcus stopped, staring, in mid-stride. He hurled the half-empty wine cup against a wall, abruptly ashamed of his self-pity. The ordeal Mavrikios Gavras' daughter had endured outshone his as the sun did the moon. After Ortaias Sphrantzes' cowardice cost her father his life at Maragha, Ortaias—whom flight had saved—claimed the throne when he made his way back to the capital; the Sphrantzai, the bureaucratic family supreme, had produced Emperors before. And to cement his claim, Alypia, whose house opposed everything his stood for, had been forced into marriage with him.

But Ortaias Sphrantzes, a foolish, trivial young man with more bombast than sense, was only a pawn in the hands of his uncle Vardanes. And Vardanes, whose malignance was neither mediocre nor trivial, had coveted Alypia for years. Dispossessing his feckless nephew of her, he kept her as slave to his lusts throughout Ortaias' brief, unhappy reign. When the Sphrantzai fell, Scaurus had seen her thus and seen her spirit unbroken despite the submission forced from her body.

Turning his back on the spattered wall, he knelt clumsily beside Nevrat Sviodo and touched her hand in gratitude. When he tried to speak his thanks, his throat clogged and he wept instead, but it was a clean weeping, with the beginning of healing in it. Then at last the wine reached him; he did not hear Nevrat and her husband when they rose and tiptoed from the room.

It was cold in the Hall of the Nineteen Couches, and the tribune felt very much alone as he made his report to Thorisin Gavras. The Sviodos had crossed with him to the capital, and Styppes—for whatever his company was worth—but Marcus had sent his Romans back to Gaius Philippus at Garsavra. Without the Namdaleni to guard, there was no point keeping them; Gaius Philippus could use them, and in Garsavra they did not risk the Avtokrator's wrath.

He told the truth, as much of it, at least, as had happened outside his tent. Thorisin was silent when he finished, studying him stony-faced over steepled fingers. When I first met him, Marcus thought, he would have worn his feelings on his sleeve. But he was learning the emperor's art of never revealing too much; his eyes were perfectly opaque.

Then the imperial façade cracked across and showed the man behind it. "Damn you, Scaurus," he said heavily, the words ripped from him one by one, "why must I always love you and hate you at the same bloody time?"

The officers who sat in council with him stirred. The Roman did not know many of them well, nor they him. They were most of them younger men, come to prominence under the Emperor's eye this past campaigning season while the tribune was far away in the westlands; so many of the marshals who had served with Scaurus under Mavrikios Gavras were dead or in disgrace as rebels—or both.

"Your Highness, you cannot credit this tale, can you?" protested one of the new men, a cavalry officer named Provhos Mourtzouphlos. The disbelief on his handsome, whiskery face—like several other soldiers round the council table, he imitated Thorisin's carelessness about hair and beard—was manifest. Heads bobbed in agreement with him.

"I can," the Emperor replied. He kept on examining Scaurus, as if wondering whether the tribune had left something out. "I haven't said I do, yet."

"Well, you ought to," Taron Leimmokheir told him abruptly. His, at least, was a familiar face and voice; as always, the drungarios of the fleet's raspy bass, used to roaring out commands at sea, sounded too big for any enclosed space, even one the size of the Hall of the Nineteen Couches. Smiling at Marcus, he went on, "Anyone with the courage to come back to you after such misfortunes deserves honor, not blame. And what if the fornicating Gamblers got away in the end? There's no New Namdalen over the Cattle-Crossing, and for that you have only the outlander here to thank."

Mourtzouphlos sent an aristocrat's sneer toward the gray-bearded admiral, who had risen from the ranks by dint of courage, strength, and—rare among Videssians—unswerving, outspoken honesty. The cavalryman said, "No wonder Leimmokheir speaks up for the foreigner. He owes him enough."

"So I do, and proud to own it, by Phos," the drungarios said.

The Emperor, though, frowned, remembering how Leimmokheir had sworn loyalty to Ortaias before he knew Thorisin had survived Maragha—and how, with his stubborn loyalty, he refused to go back on that oath. He also remembered the assassination attempt he had blamed on the admiral, and the months Leimmokheir had spent in prison until Scaurus proved him guiltless—and touched off Baanes Onomagoulos' revolt by showing him to be the man behind the plot.

Thorisin passed a weary hand in front of his eyes, then scratched his left temple. The dark brown hair there was thinner than it had been when Marcus and the legionaries came to Videssos, and more streaked with gray as well. At last he said, "I think I do believe you, Roman. Not for what Taron here says, though there's truth in that, too. But I know you have the wit to make a better lie than the yarn you spun, so it's most likely true. Aye, most likely," he repeated, half to himself. Then, straightening abruptly on his gilded chair, he finished, "Stay in the city a while; you needn't hurry back to Garsavra. That lieutenant of yours is plenty able to hold the town when winter slows everyone to a crawl, Yezda and us alike."

"As you wish, of course, sir," Marcus said, saluting. The Emperor was right; if anything, Gaius Philippus was a better tactician than Scaurus. But the order was strange enough to make the tribune ask, "What would you have me do here?"

The question seemed to catch Thorisin Gavras by surprise. He scratched his head again, thinking. After a few seconds he answered, "For one thing, I want a full report in writing from you, covering what you've told me today in more detail. The Namdaleni are demons to fight; anything I can learn from what you did to them will be useful. And, oh yes," he went on, struck by a happy afterthought, "you can ride herd on the plague-taken pen-pushers as you did last winter."

Marcus bowed, but he was somber as he took his seat. Although Thorisin professed believing him, he did not expect he would be trusted to command again any time soon.

The Emperor had already dismissed him from his mind. He looked round the hall. "Now for the next piece of good news," he said. He unrolled a square sheet of parchment, elaborately sealed and written in a large, gorgeous hand. Gavras held it as if it gave off a bad smell. "This little missive is from our dear friend Zemarkhos," he announced sardonically, and began to read aloud.

Stripped of the fanatic priest's turgid phrasing, the proclamation declared Amorion and the westlands surrounding that city the rightful principality of Phos on earth and hurled venomous anathemas at Thorisin and Balsamon the patriarch of Videssos. "By which the madman means we've no taste for massacring Vaspurakaners," the emperor growled. He tore the parchment in half, threw it behind him. "What do we do about such tripe?"

The council threw out a few suggestions, but they were all half-hearted, suicidal, or both. The plain truth was that, since a wide stretch of territory held by the Yezda—whom Zemarkhos hated almost as much as he did heretics within his own faith—separated Amorion from imperial troops, Thorisin could not do much but fume.

He glared at his advisors for being as unable to get around that as he was himself. "No more brilliant schemes, the lot of you?" he asked at last. Silence answered. He shook his head in disgust. "No? Go on, then. This council is dismissed."

Servants swung back the Hall of the Nineteen Couches' mirror-bright bronze doors. Videssos' officers trooped out. Marcus wrapped himself in his cape to ward off the icy breeze. At least, he thought, the bureaucrats kept their offices warm.

Videssian troops occupied two of the four barracks halls the legionaries had used in the palace complex; a company of Halogai, newly come from their cold northern home, was quartered in the third. The last stood empty, but Scaurus had no desire to rattle around in it like a pebble inside a huge Yezda drum. Instead, he took up residence in an empty second-floor room of the bureaucrats' wing of the compound that held the Grand Courtroom. The seal-stampers greeted him with wary politeness, recalling his meddling in business they considered theirs alone.

He worked in a desultory way on the report the Emperor had requested, but it seemed stale and flat even as he wrote it. He could not attach any importance to it; in trying to numb himself to the shock of Helvis' leaving him as she had, he pulled away from the rest of the world as well. He moved in a gray haze that had nothing to do with the weather.

He did his best to disregard the knock on his door—which he kept closed most of the time—but it went on and on. Sighing, he rose from a low chair by the window and lifted the latch.

Waiting outside, beringed hands on hips, was a plump, smooth-cheeked man of uncertain age, clad in a robe of saffron silk shot through with green embroidery—one of the eunuchs who served the Videssian Emperors as chamberlains. "Took you long enough," he sniffed, giving Marcus the smallest bow protocol allowed. He went on, "You are bidden to attend his Imperial Majesty this evening in his private chambers at the beginning of the second hour of the night." The Videssians, like the Romans, divided day and night into twelve hours each, beginning respectively at dawn and sunset.

Marcus started; Thorisin had ignored him in the week since the officers' council. He asked the chamberlain, "Does he expect my account of the western campaign? I'm afraid it's not quite done." Only he knew how much an understatement that was.

The eunuch's shrug set his puddingy jowls shaking. "I know nothing of such things, only that an attendant will come to lead you thither at the hour I named. And I hope," he added, putting Scaurus in his place, "you will be prompter in greeting him than you were for me." He turned his back on the tribune and waddled away.

The attendant proved to be another eunuch, somewhat less splendidly robed than his predecessor. He started shivering as soon as he stepped from the well-heated wing of the Grand Courtroom into the keen night breeze. Scaurus knew a moment of sympathy. He himself wore trousers, as most Videssians did when not performing some ceremonial function. He did not miss his Roman toga; the Empire's winters demanded warmth.

The cherry trees surrounding the imperial family's personal quarters sent bare branches reaching skeletal fingers into the sky—no fragrant blooms at this season of the year. A squad of Halogai stood guard at the doorway, their two-handed axes at the ready. In fur robes of otter and white bear and fox and snow leopard over gilded cuirasses, the big blond men seemed perfectly at ease. And why not, the tribune thought—they were used to worse weather than this. They eyed him curiously; he looked as much like one of them as like an imperial. They discussed him in their own guttural language as the chamberlain led him by; he caught the word "Namdalen" spoken in a questioning tone.

The entrance hall still showed scars from the fighting this past spring, when Baanes Onomagoulos had slipped a murder-squad into the city to try to do away with Thorisin. The legionaries, opportunely returning from a practice march, had foiled that. Scaurus glanced at a portrait of the great conquering Emperor Laskaris, now seven and a half centuries dead. As always, the tribune thought Laskaris looked more like a veteran underofficer than Avtokrator of the Videssians, but now a bloodstain marred the lower left quadrant of his image, and sword strokes had chipped at the hunting scenes of the floor mosaics over which the tribune walked.

The chamberlain paused. "Wait here. I will announce you."

"Of course." As the eunuch bustled down the passage, Marcus leaned against a wall and studied the alabaster ceiling panels. They were dark now, of course, but the translucent stones were cut so thin that during the day they lit the hall with a pale, shifting, pearly light.

The imperial servitor vanished round a corner, but he did not go far. Scaurus heard his own name spoken, heard Thorisin's impatient reply: "Well, fetch him." The eunuch reappeared, beckoned Marcus on.

The Emperor was leaning forward in his chair, as if willing the Roman into the room. On a couch beside him sat his niece; Marcus' heart gave a painful thump to see her. As was often true, especially since her torment at the hands of Vardanes Sphrantzes, Alypia's face wore an abstracted expression, but warmth came into her fine green eyes as Marcus entered.

Remembering his etiquette, the tribune bowed first to Thorisin, then to the princess. "Your Majesty. Your Highness." The eunuch frowned when he did not prostrate himself, but Thorisin, like Mavrikios before him, had always tolerated that bit of republican Roman stubbornness.

Now, though, his finger darted forward. "Seize him!" Two Halogai sprang out from behind the chamber's double doors to lock Scaurus' arms back of him in an unbreakable grip. Struggle would have been useless; the burly warriors overtopped even the tribune's inches by half a head. Like some of the sentries outside, they wore their hair in thick braids that hung down to the small of their backs, but there was nothing effeminate about them. Their hands were big as shovels, hard as horn.

Surprise and alarm drove discretion from the tribune. "This is no way to get a proskynesis," he blurted.

A smile flickered on Alypia's face, but Thorisin's remained hard. "Be silent," he said, and then turned to the other occupant of the room. "Nepos, is that hell-brew of yours ready yet?"

First seeing Alypia and then being collared by the Haloga giants, Marcus had hardly noticed the tubby little priest, who was busily grinding gray, green, and yellow powders together. "Very nearly, your Majesty," Nepos replied. He beamed at the Roman. "Hello, outlander. It's good to see you again."

"Is it?" Scaurus said. He did not like the sound of "hell-brew." Nepos was mage as well as priest, and a master at his craft, master to the point of teaching theoretical thaumaturgy at the Videssian Academy. The tribune wondered if he was so expendable as to be only an experimental animal. He had no relish for life since Helvis had forsaken him, but there were ends and ends. Nepos, cheerfully oblivious, poured his mixed powders into a golden goblet of wine, stirred it with a short glass rod.

"Can't use wood or brass for this, you know," he said, perhaps to Thorisin, perhaps to Marcus, perhaps only because he was used to lecturing. "They'd not be the better afterward." The Roman gulped despite himself.

The Emperor fixed him with the same searching glance he had brought to bear in the Hall of the Nineteen Couches. "After you let the islanders loose, outlander, my first thought was to put you on the shelf and leave you there till the dust covered you up. You've always been too thick with the Namdaleni for me to really trust you." The irony of that almost jerked laughter from Scaurus, but Thorisin was going on, not altogether happily, "Still and all, there are those who think you truly are loyal, and so we'll find out tonight." Alypia Gavra would not meet the tribune's eye.

Nepos raised the goblet by its graceful stem. "Do you remember Avshar's puppet," he asked Marcus, "the Khamorth who attacked you with the spell-wound knife after you bested Avshar at swords?" The tribune nodded. "Well, this is the same drug that wrung the truth from him."

"And he died when you were done questioning him, too," Scaurus said harshly.

The priest gestured in abhorrence. "That was Avshar's sorcery, not mine."

"Give it to me, then," the tribune said. "Let's be done with it."

At Thorisin's nod, the Haloga who pinioned Scaurus' right arm let go. The Avtokrator warned, "Spilling it will do you no good. There'll just be another batch, and a funnel down your throat."

But when the goblet was in his hand, Marcus asked Nepos, "Is there only just enough, or a bit more?"

"A bit more, perhaps. Why?"

The tribune sloshed a few drops of wine onto the floor. "Here's to that fine fellow Thorisin, then," he said. The Videssians frowned, not understanding; he heard one of the Halogai behind him grunt in confusion. It was the toast of Theramenes the Athenian to Kritias when forced to take poison in the time of the Thirty Tyrants after the Peloponnesian War.

He swallowed the wine at a single draught. Beneath the sweetness he could taste Nepos' drugs, tart on his tongue, but also numbing. He waited, wondering if he would start to gibber, or thrash about on the floor like a poisoned dog.

"Well?" Thorisin Gavras growled at Nepos.

"The effects vary from case to case, from person to person," the priest replied. "Some take longer to respond than others." Scaurus heard him as if from very far away; the whole of his mind was suffused with a golden glow. Of all the things he had expected, this godlike feeling was the last. It was like an orgasm that went on and on, but with all the pleasure gone and only transcendence left.

Someone—it was the Emperor, but that did not matter to him—was asking him something. He heard himself answering. Why not? Whatever the question was, it could only be trivial next to the immanence in which he drifted. He heard Thorisin swear; that was not important either. "What drivel is he mouthing?" the Avtokrator said. "I can't follow a word of it."

Alypia Gavra said quietly, "It's his birth-speech."

"Well, he should use ours, then."

Marcus obeyed, untroubled; one language was as good as another. The questions came faster: why had he let Mertikes Zigabenos take refuge in a monastery? "I thought that if you could do as much for Ortaias Sphrantzes, who deserved worse, then I could for Mertikes, who deserved better."

A grunt from Thorisin. "Is he truly under, priest?"

Nepos peeled back one of Scaurus' eyelids, waved a hand an inch in front of his face. The tribune neither flinched nor blinked. "Truly, your Majesty."

Gavras laughed ruefully. "Well, I suppose I had that coming. Still, Zigabenos hadn't a tenth the political muscle the Sphrantzai carry, and only fear of that saved Ortaias' scrawny neck." Alypia made a sound in the back of her throat that might have meant anything or nothing.

Why had the tribune only pretended to blind the Namdalener marshals at Garsavra?

"I wanted to do nothing that could not be undone later. You might have had some use for them that I did not know." Thorisin grunted again, this time in satisfaction, but Marcus went on, "And Soteric was Helvis' brother, and I was sure she would leave me if I harmed him. I did not want her to leave me."

The Roman, who had not bothered to close his eye after Nepos pulled it open, saw but did not notice the look of triumphant suspicion Gavras shot his niece. "Now we come down to it," the Emperor said. "So you did not want the doxy gone, eh?"

"No."

"Tell me, then, how it happened she escaped, and the whole nest of snakes with her. Tell me *everything* about that: what she did, what you think she did, what you did, what you thought while you were doing it. Damn you, Scaurus, I'll know your soul for once."

Drugged as he was, the tribune stood silent a long time. The grief Thorisin was probing could touch the tranquility of a god. "Answer me!" the Emperor shouted, and Scaurus, his will overborne by the other's, began again. While one part of him listened and bled, the rest told exactly how Helvis had worn him down into drowsiness. The worst of it was knowing he would remember everything after Nepos' potion no longer held him.

As he droned on, Nepos reddened in embarrassment. The Haloga guardsmen muttered back and forth in their own tongue. And Alypia Gavra turned on her uncle, saying angrily, "In Phos' name, stop this! Or why not flay the skin from him while you're about it?"

At the word "stop," Marcus obediently did. But Thorisin's voice was cold as he told Alypia, "This was your idea, to have the truth from him. Now have the stomach to sit and hear it, or else get out."

"I would not stay to see anyone stripped naked against his will." Her face was pale as she whispered, "I know the taste of that too well." She stepped past Marcus and was gone.

"Bah!" Thorisin seemed to notice Scaurus was not talking. "Go on, you!" he roared. The tribune told him of the pursuit; of the beacon fire that had drawn the Namdalener corsair; of Helvis, her sons, and the rest of the islanders escaping the beach in the raiders' longboat. "And what did you do then?" the Emperor asked, but quietly; Marcus' account of that desperate, futile chase had left him without his hectoring tone.

"I cried."

Thorisin winced. "To the ice with me if I blame you for it," he said to himself. "Alypia had the right of it after all; I've raped an honest man." Very gently then, to Scaurus, "And what then, and why?"

The tribune shrugged; the Halogai were still at his back, but no longer restrained him. "Then I came to the city here, to you. There was nothing else for me to do. How could I flee to a monastery, when I do not follow your god? And if Drax was wrong to turn rebel, so would I have been. Besides, I would have lost."

Thorisin gave him a very odd look. "I wonder. I do wonder."

XII

Seirem pressed her lips against Viridovix'; he hugged her to him. "You're *too* tall," she said. "My neck gets stiff when I kiss you."

"Make yourself used to it, girleen, for you'll be doing a lot of it after we're back from the squashing o' that flea of a Varatesh," the Gaul answered. A measure of his fancy for her was that he passed up the obvious bawdy comeback to her words. Between them there was no need for such artificial warmers; they were pleased enough with each other as they were.

She hugged him. "You be after comin' back, hear?" she said, mimicking his brogue so perfectly they both laughed.

"Mount up, you lazy groundling!" came Targitaus' gruff bellow. "You think we have time to waste on your mooning about?" But the khagan was fighting a smile, and next to him Batbaian grinned openly.

"Och, the corbies take you," Viridovix said, but after a last squeeze he let Seirem go and swung up into the saddle. As it often did, his steppe pony snorted a complaint; he was heavier than most Khamorth.

Targitaus looked over to Lipoxais. "You promised ten days of decent weather," he said, half-threateningly. It was no small matter. The first autumn rains had already fallen, and war among the nomads depended on clear skies. Wet bowstrings made a mockery of their chief fighting skill.

The *enaree* shrugged, flesh bobbling inside his yellow wool robe. "I saw what I saw."

"I wish you'd seen who would win," Targitaus grumbled, but not in real complaint. The passion that surrounded battle clouded foretelling. "We'll have to find out, then," the chieftain said. He raised his voice to a shout. "We ride!" Batbaian raised the wolf standard of the clan, and the

Khamorth clucked their horses into motion. Scouts trotted ahead, with flank guards out to either side.

"You, too, wretched beast," Viridovix said, snapping the reins and digging his boots into the pony's sides. He turned to wave a last good-bye to Seirem and was almost pitched off the horses's back when it shied at a blowing scrap of cloth. He clutched its mane, feeling a fool.

Perhaps over the last few years he had grown more used to Roman discipline than he suspected, for the army Targitaus led seemed a very disorderly thing. Indeed, he could be said to lead it only because more plainsmen rode round his standard than any other. But no one could make the other clan-chiefs follow his orders if they did not care to. They fought Varatesh for their own reasons, not his.

A dozen separate bands of nomads, then, rode north and west against the outlaws. They ranged in size from the double handful in white fox caps who followed Oitoshyr to the several hundred with Anakhar of the Spotted Cats, a contingent second in size only to Targitaus'. Anakhar's wavering had abruptly stopped when he discovered that Krobyz, his hated neighbor on the steppe, favored Varatesh. "If that goat's arse is for him, there's reason enough to smack him down," he had declared, and joined Targitaus forthwith.

Beyond finding Varatesh and then fighting him, they had no plan of action. When Viridovix suggested working one out, Targitaus and the rest of the clan leaders looked at him as if he had fallen from the moon. The Celt had to laugh when he thought of it. "As if I'd have listened to a Roman spouting such balderdash," he said to himself. Even so, he worried a little.

"One thing," Batbaian said, "the rains have laid the dust to rest."

"They have that, and not sorry I am for it," Viridovix agreed. Going to fight without choking on the grit his comrades kicked up was a pleasure he had not known since Gaul. Clouds covered the sun every few minutes, sending shadows racing over the plains. The day was cool, the air crisp and clean. Sometimes, tramping across Videssos' dry plateau, he'd thought the whole country made of dust.

After a moment, he said, "But outen the dust, how are the scouts to be spotting the kerns we're after?" Batbaian blinked; he had not thought of that. Viridovix worked up a fair-sized anger—was nothing without its drawbacks?

Targitaus stretched his mouth in what was not quite a smile. "For one thing, they have the same problem with us. For another, scouts who don't pay attention to what's ahead of them end up dead, and that keeps 'em lively."

"Well, you have the right of it there," the Gaul allowed.

The nomad army seemed larger than it was, thanks to the string of remounts behind each plainsman. The rumble of hooves on damp ground reminded Viridovix of the constant murmur of the sea. "But it doesna make me want to gi' back my breakfast," he said happily.

He thought of Arigh's jibe about horsesickness and was glad there was nothing to it. Though he still could not stomach the half-raw beef the Khamorth used for iron rations, he munched on wheatcakes and curded cheese, washed them down with kavass. He wished for something sweet, wine or fruit or berries. When Rambehisht passed him a chunk of honeycomb and the heady tang of wild clover filled his mouth, he was content with the world. "A braw lass, a good scrap to go to, and e'en a bit o' honey when you need it most," he said to no one in particular. "Who could want for more?"

After the Khamorth camped that night they went from fire to fire, trading news, telling tales, and gambling with a bizarre assortment of money, some of it so worn Viridovix could not tell whether it had been minted in Videssos or Yezd. There were also square silver coins stamped with dragons or axes, whose like he had not seen. "Halugh," a nomad explained. The Gaul won several goldpieces and one of the Haloga coins, which he pocketed for luck.

The next day's travel was much like the one before. The steppe seemed endless, and the plainsmen with whom Viridovix rode the only men on it. But when the evening fires went up, there was a faint answering glow against the northern horizon. Men checked harness and gear; here a nomad tightened a girth, there another filed arrow-points to razor sharpness, while two more practiced sword-strokes on horseback, making ready for what would come tomorrow.

Viridovix woke before dawn, shivering from the cold. In Gaul the trees would have been gorgeous with autumn's colors; the only change the steppe grass showed was from green to grayish yellow. "Sure and it's bleak enough, for all its size," he mumbled around a mouthful of cheese.

The Khamorth teased the handful of older men left behind to guard the remounts. The latter gave back good as they got: "When you're done beating the bastards, drive 'em this way. We'll show you what we can do!"

Clan by clan, the plainsmen mounted. As they rode north they shook themselves out into a rough battle line. Targitaus' band held the right wing. Eyeing the gaps between clans and the ragged front, Viridovix consoled himself by thinking that Varatesh's bandits would keep no better ranks.

Moving dots against the steely sky, the outlaws appeared. A murmur ran down the line; men nocked arrows and freed swords in scabbards. Varatesh's men drew closer with a speed that Viridovix, still used to foot campaigns, found dismaying. He waved his sword, howling out a wild Celtic war cry that startled his comrades; what it did to the foe was harder to tell.

Skirmishers traded arrows in the shrinking no-man's-land between the armies. A pair of nomads dueled with sabers. When the outlaw slid from his saddle, a cheer rang out from his foes.

It clogged in Viridovix' throat when he spied in the center of the enemy line a white-robed figure riding a black horse half again the size of the steppe ponies around it. "Well, you didna think himself'd stay away," he muttered. "Och, would he had, though." The Gaul thought his side outnumbered the bandits, but who knew how many men Avshar was worth?

No time for thought after that—the two main bodies were shooting at each other now. The arrows flew, bitter as the sleet that could be only days away. Useless in the long-range fight, the Celt watched over the edge of his small, light shield. The deadly rhythm had a fascination to it: right hand over left shoulder to pull a shaft from the quiver, nock, draw, a quick glance for a target, shoot, and over the shoulder again. The plainsmen methodically emptied their quivers. Now and again the measured cadence would break down: a curse, a grunt, or a scream as a man was hit, or a wild scramble to leap free of a foundering horse before it crushed its rider.

Varatesh watched in astonishment as Avshar wielded his great black bow. It was built to the same double-curved pattern as any nomad bow, but not even the burliest outlaw could bend it. Yet the wizard-prince used it as Varatesh might a child's weapon, killing with his wickedly barbed shafts at ranges the outlaw chief would not have believed a man could reach. His skill was chillingly matter-of-fact. He gave no cry of triumph when another shot struck home, nor even a satisfied nod, but was already choosing his next victim.

An arrow whined past Varatesh's cheek. He ducked behind his horse's neck—futile, of course, if the shaft had been truly aimed. He fired back, saw a rider topple. He wondered if it was the man who had shot at him. "No," Avshar said, reading his thought. The wizard-prince's voice held scornful mirth. "Why should you care, though? He would have been glad enough to kill you." That was true, but even truth from Avshar left a sour taste.

The wizard's eye traveled the enemy line for new targets. He wheeled his horse leftward, steadying it with his knees. He drew the black bow back to his ear, but as he shot Varatesh reached out and knocked his wrist aside. The arrow flew harmlessly into the air.

The wizard-prince seemed to grow taller in the saddle, glaring down at Varatesh like an angry god. "What are you playing at, fool?" he rasped, a whisper more menacing than any other man's roar of rage.

The outlaw chief quailed as Avshar's wrath fell on him, but his own anger sustained him. "The red-haired one is mine," he said. "You may not have him."

"You speak to me of 'may not,' grub? Remember who I am."

That memory would stay with Varatesh forever. But he summoned all that was left of his own pride and flung it back at Avshar: "And you, sorcerer, remember who I am." Afterwards, he thought it the bravest thing he had ever done.

The wizard-prince measured him with that terrible unseen stare. "So," he said at last, "another tool turns and bites me, does it? Well, for all that your mother was a cur, you make a better one than that scrannel Vardanes, who thought only of his prick in the end." He spread his hands in ironic generosity. "Take the red-haired one, then, if you can. I make you a present of him."

"He is not yours to give," Varatesh said, but only to himself.

As fighters on both sides began running out of arrows, the battle lines drew closer. Shamshirs flashed in the autumn sun; a nomad near Viridovix gaped at the spouting blood where two fingers of his left hand had been sheared away. "Tie 'em up!" Targitaus shouted. The rider came out of his stupor. Cursing furiously, he wrapped a strip of wool over the wound and tied it tight with a leather thong.

An outlaw rode straight for the Gaul; Viridovix booted his horse on to meet him. Straight sword rang off curved one. With the lighter weapon, the Khamorth slashed again before Viridovix had recovered. He leaned away from the stroke, turned the next one with his shield. His own cut laid the nomad's leg open. The rider cursed and dropped his guard. Viridovix brought his blade round in a backhand swipe. It crunched into the renegade's cheek. Blood spattered; the Khamorth's fur cap flew from his head. Dead or unconscious, he fell from the saddle, to be trampled by his own horse.

Rambehisht had cannily saved his arrows till the fighting came to close quarters. At point-blank range his bow, reinforced with horn, could drive a shaft right through a man, or pin him to his horse. Then his own animal toppled, shot just below the eye. Lithe as a cat, he kicked free of the stirrups before it fell, and faced an oncoming bandit sword in hand.

Mounted man against one afoot, though, was a contest with an ending likely grim. Viridovix, who was not far away, howled out a wild Gallic war cry. It froze the outlaw for the moment the Celt needed to draw close. Rambehisht ran forward, too. Suddenly it was two against one; the horseman tried to flee, but in the press he could not. Seizing his left calf, Rambehisht pitched him off his beast. Viridovix leaned down to finish him off. Rambehisht leaped onto the steppe pony before it got away. He drew, fired, and hit a nomad riding up behind the Gaul.

Viridovix jerked his head round at the bandit's cry of pain. "Thank you, Khamorth darling. That one I hadna seen."

"Debts are for paying," the dour plainsman answered. Viridovix frowned, wondering if Rambehisht intended to pay back his beating one day as well.

No time to fret over might-be's. Three brigands spotted Viridovix at once. By luck, one of Targitaus' men took the closest out of the fight with a well-cast javelin. The other two bored in on the Gaul. He let out another ululating shriek, but it did not daunt them. Thinking fast, he spurred toward one, then clapped his bronze-studded leather cap from his head and hurled it in the other's face. He wheeled his horse with a skill he hardly knew he had, smashed his sword down on the head of the distracted renegade's beast. The luckless horse dropped, stone dead. Viridovix never knew what happened to its rider. He was already whirling back to face the other bandit, but the outlaw fled before him.

He laughed gigantically. "Back to your mother, you skulking omadhaun! Think twice or ever you play a man's game again!" Blood flew from his sword as he brandished it overhead. This was what the battlefield was for, he thought—bending the foe to your mastery, whether by steel or force of will alone. Intoxicating as strong kavass, the power tingled in his veins.

He brushed his long hair back from his eyes, looked round to see how the bigger fight was going. It was hard to be sure. These cavalry battles took up an ungodly lot of room and ebbed and flowed like quicksilver. Worse, he had trouble telling his own side from the outlaws at any distance.

There was, he saw, a battle within a battle in the center of the field, with Anakhar's Spotted Cats in a wild melee with Krobyz' Leaping Goats. Most of Varatesh's nonoutlaw allies seemed to be bunched there, from the standards waving over them. They might fight along with his blank black banner, but were not eager to join too closely with the renegades who followed it.

As a result, Anakhar's men were outnumbered and hard-pressed. Targitaus waved to his son to ride to their rescue. Batbaian led a company leftward. Unlike Viridovix, he knew friend from foe at a glance. His horsemen plugged what had been a growing gap, making the enemy give ground. Heartened, the Spotted Cats fought with fresh vigor.

Targitaus took the rest of his men on a flanking move round the outlaws' left. Avshar met them head-on, leading half a hundred of Varatesh's hardest brigands, scarred rogues who knew every trick of fighting, fair and foul. They were steeped in evil but far from cowards, giving no quarter and asking none.

On his huge stallion, Avshar stood out from the Khamorth around him like a war galley among rowboats. His fearsome bow was slung over his shoulder; he swung a long straight sword with deadly effect. "Another oaf!" he cried as one of Targitaus' riders drove at him. The blade hissed as it cleaved air and bit into the plainsman's neck. "That for your stupidity, then, and Skotos eat your soul forever!"

Viridovix raised his voice to carry through the battle clamor: "Avshar!" The wizard-prince's head came up, like a dog taking a scent. "Here, you kern!" the Celt yelled. "You wanted Scaurus, but I'll stand for him the now!"

"And fall, as well!" Avshar spurred past one of his own men. "Out of my way, ravens' meat!" He brought his sword up in mock salute as he neared the Gaul. "You will make Varatesh angry, gifting me with your life so."

Viridovix barely beat the wizard's first stroke aside, turning the flat of the blade with his shield—the edge would have torn through it. The heavy horse Avshar rode let him carry the full panoply he always wore beneath his robes—his shield was a kite-shaped one, faced with metal, on the Namdalener pattern. The gear made the Gaul's boiled leather seem flimsy as linen.

You'll not beat this one on strength, the Gaul thought as he turned his horse for the next pass, nor on fear either. That left wit. He remembered the lesson he had learned in his fight with Varatesh: a horse was as important as a sword. It was doubly true of Avshar's huge charger, which reared to dash the brains from a dismounted nomad with its iron-shod hooves.

The wizard-prince brought it down and sent it charging at Viridovix, who dug spurs into his own mount. When they met, his slash was aimed not at Avshar in his mail, but at the stallion. He had intended to deliver the same crushing blow he had used against the outlaw's mount, but misjudged the speed the charger could deliver. Instead of crashing down between the beast's eyes, the sword tore a great flap of skin from the side of its neck.

That served nearly as well as the stroke he had intended, for the wounded animal screamed in shock and pain and bucked frantically, almost throwing Avshar. Bellowing in rage, the wizard-prince had to clutch its mane to keep from going over its tail. And even though he held his seat, the wounded animal would not answer the reins; it ran off at full gallop, carrying him out of the fight.

"Come back, ye blackguard!" Viridovix howled gleefully. "It's only just begun that I have."

Avshar spun in his saddle, shouting a curse. For a moment the battlefield swayed and darkened before the Gaul's eyes. Then the druids' marks on his blade flashed golden as they turned aside the spell. His vision cleared. He squeezed the sword hilt gratefully, as if it were a comrade's hand.

The battle hung, undecided, for some endless time, with no lull long enough to let the fighters do much more than sob in a few quick breaths or swig at skins of water or kavass. The sun had passed west of south before Viridovix fully realized he was moving forward more often than back.

"Press 'em, press 'em!" Targitaus shouted. "They're going to break."

But as his horsemen gathered themselves for the charge that would finish the outlaws, yells of alarm came from the center and left, the most dreaded cry on the steppe: "Fire!" Clouds of thick black smoke leaped into the air, obscuring the renegades. Targitaus' face purpled with rage. "Filthy cowards! Better to die like men than cover a retreat that way."

Then Viridovix heard Avshar's gloating laughter and knew all his hopes were undone, for the flames spread faster than any natural fire, and at the direction of a malignant will. Horses shrieked and men screamed as the advancing walls of fire swept over them. But they were merely caught by accident in the web of the wizard-prince's design. He used his blaze to net his foes as a hunter would drive hares into his meshes, trapping them in small pockets between fiery sheets that raced between and behind horses faster than any beast could hope to run.

As the main body of their enemies was caught, Varatesh's brigands took fresh heart, while the clans that rode with them saw Avshar's prowess with mingled awe and terror. They drove against the untrapped remnants of Targitaus' army with redoubled force. Now all the weight of numbers was on their side. There was no checking them. The retreat that followed was close to rout.

Viridovix tried to stem it singlehanded, slashing his way through the enemy ranks toward Avshar. The wizard-prince was afoot, having dismounted from his wounded charger the better to direct his sorcery. The Gaul's desperation burned bright as the wizard's flames; few outlaws dared stand against him.

Varatesh and a band of outlaws rode to Avshar's rescue, but the wizard needed no protection. He gave Viridovix a quick glance, gestured, sent a tongue of flame licking his way through the grass. The Celt spurred toward it regardless, confident his sword would carry him past the magic. The druids' marks on the blade glowed as he thundered toward the fire.

But his mount knew nothing of sorcery and shied at the flames ahead, its eyes rolling with panic. For all his roweling, it would go no further. He cried out to Epona, but the Celtic horse-goddess held no power in this world. Avshar's image wavered through the flames, tauntingly out of reach.

"All right, then, I'll go my ain self," the Celt growled, fighting to steady the beast enough to let him climb down. But Varatesh chose that moment to loose a hoarded arrow at him. It missed, but sank deep into his horse's rump. The beast squealed and leaped into the air, almost throwing him. It bolted away, out of control. That was, perhaps, as well for Viridovix; goaded by pain, the steppe pony outran the bandits pursuing it. Avshar's vengeful laughter burned in the Gaul's ears.

When he finally made his horse obey him, he could only join the fragments of Targitaus' shattered army in their retreat. The renegades and their allies let them go. They were hovering like carrion flies round Avshar's prisoning walls of fire, which burned on, fierce as ever, long after the grass that should have been their only fuel was gone.

Black as despair, smoke filled all the autumn sky.

Krobyz bowed low in the saddle as Varatesh rode by. Exhausted as he was, the outlaw chief flushed with pleasure at the acknowledgement of his prowess from a legitimate khagan. This, he told himself, was what he had been reaching toward for so many years. At last he had earned the place which belonged to him by right, and that despite the foes he did not deserve. His lip curled—they had seen his might today.

The crackling flames ahead reminded him the triumph had not been entirely his. As if to reinforce that reminder, Avshar came up beside him. But the wizard-prince only waved toward the warriors trapped in his blazing cells. "What is your pleasure with them?"

Varatesh was ready to be magnanimous in victory. "Let them surrender, if they will."

Shrugging, Avshar called to the plainsmen in the nearest fiery box. "Yield yourselves to Varatesh, grand khagan of the Royal Clan of Pardraya!" The unexpected title made the outlaw chieftain blink. Why, so I am, he thought proudly.

The box held Oitoshyr and his three or four surviving clansmen, their white fox caps dark with dust and soot. Oitoshyr was wounded, but not ready to quit. "Bugger Varatesh, the grand pimp of the plains," he shouted, "aye, and you, too, you hulking turd!"

The wizard-prince looked a question to Varatesh. Furious at the rebuff, he spat in the dirt. Avshar took that as answer and gestured with his left hand. One wall of flame holding the White Foxes turned transparent, then died. Varatesh waved a hundred bandits in. Grinning, they set about the butchery they had been waiting for. Oitoshyr took a long time to die.

After that, surrenders came one on the other. Varatesh was staggered by the victory he had won. No bard sang of, no *enaree* remembered, a battle with so many prisoners taken. There must have been a thousand in all; as each flame pocket opened, his men swarmed over them like locusts, taking weapons, armor, and horses as spoils of war. He wondered how long he could feed them.

"Why should you?" Avshar said. "Give them back to their own worthless clans."

"And have them take up arms against me again the next day? I did not think you such a trusting soul."

The sorcerer laughed, deep in his throat. "Well said! But if you could get them off your hands, and at the same time prove your supremacy to every petty chief on the steppe?" He paused, waiting for Varatesh's response.

"Go on," the plainsman urged, intrigued.

Avshar laughed again and did.

"I thank you, but no," Gorgidas told Arghun for what must have been the twentieth time. "When the imperial embassy goes back to Videssos, I intend to go with it. I am a man made for cities, just as you belong here on the plain. I could no more be happy following the flocks than you could in the Empire."

"We will speak of this again," the khagan said, as he did each time Gorgidas declined to stay with the Arshaum. Arghun leaned back against a pile of cushions in the Videssian embassy's yurt and stretched a blanket of rabbit fur over his legs. Feeling had returned to them, but not full use. The khagan needed two sticks to walk and still could not sit a horse.

His gratitude for his life, though, knew no bounds. He had showered the Greek with presents: a knee-length coat of marten's fur so soft it almost did not register to the fingers; a string of fine horses; a falcon with blood-colored eyes—no hawker, Gorgidas had been able to decline that in good conscience; a splendid bow and twenty arrows in a quiver covered in gold leaf, which he discreetly passed on to Skylitzes, who could use it; and, perhaps at Tolui's urging, a supply of all the herbs the nomads reckoned medicinal, each in a little bone jar with a stopper carved from horn.

"You are starting to speak our language well," Arghun went on.

"My thanks," Gorgidas said, rather insincerely. Like most Greeks, he thought his own supple, subtle tongue the one proper speech for a civilized man. Learning Latin had been a concession to serving in the Roman army, Videssian a necessity in this new world. In a generous moment, he might have admitted each had a few virtues. But the Arshaum speech was fit only for barbarians. As he had written, "It is a tongue with more words for the state of a cow's hoof than for that of a man's soul. No more need be said."

Thunder rumbled in the distance; Arghun curled his fingers in a protective sign. Rain pounded against the yurt's tight-stretched felt. In a normal year, the plainsmen would have been moving toward their winter pastures. This fall, though, the flocks went south with boys and graybeards, while warriors gathered to avenge the attack on the Gray Horse khagan.

A pony splashed up to the yurt, which slowed to let the rider swing himself up onto it. Dripping, Arigh slithered through the tent flap. He sketched a salute to his father. "The standard is ready," he reported.

Goudeles cocked a sly eyebrow at Gorgidas. "Here's something for your history, now; you can style this the War of Bogoraz' Coat."

The Greek rubbed his chin; he hardly noticed the feel of his whiskers any more. "You know, I like that," he said. He rummaged in his kit for tablet and stylus, then scribbled a note in the wax. To unite the Arshaum clans, they had chosen to fight, not behind any tribal banner, but under the symbol of their reason for going to war.

The exchange had been in Videssian, but Arghun, catching the Yezda's name, asked to have it translated. When Arigh rendered it into the plains speech, his father let out a short, grim laugh. "Ha! If any more of him was left, that would go up on a lance instead of his coat."

"And rightly so," Lankinos Skylitzes said. He hesitated, then went on carefully, "You are building a potent army here, khagan."

"Yes," Arghun said, pride in his voice. "Are you not glad to have friends so strong?"

The imperial officer looked uncomfortable. "Er, of course. Yet traveling to Prista in such force might alarm the Pardrayan Khamorth—"

"As if that mattered," Arigh snorted. He drew a finger across his throat and made a ghastly gurgling noise. "This to them if they dare turn on us. I hope they try."

Skylitzes nodded, but he was a dogged man and plowed on with his chain of thought. "And should such an army reach Prista, it would be hard to find shipping enough to transport it easily to Videssos."

Angry and baffled, Arigh said, "What's chewing on you, Lankinos? You come all this way for men and now you have them and don't want them."

But Arghun was eyeing Skylitzes with new respect. "Ride lightly on him there, son."

"Why should I?" Arigh looked resentfully at the Videssian.

"Because he knows his business." Seeing his son still mutinous, Arghun began to explain: "He came to us for soldiers for his own khagan."

"Well, of course," Arigh broke in. "What of it?"

"This army here is *mine,* as he sees. He has the right to wonder how I will use it, and if it might be more dangerous to him than the enemies he already has."

"Ahh," said Arigh, taking the point. Goudeles seemed chagrined at missing it himself, while Gorgidas dipped his head, admiring Skylitzes' subtlety.

The officer saluted Arghun, plainly relieved he was not annoyed. "If I may ask straight out, then, how will you use it?"

"I will hurt Yezd as much as I can," Arghun said flatly. "Arigh is right, I think; the Khamorth will stand aside for us when they see we mean them no harm—or, if not, the worse for them. But the easiest way to Mashiz is through Pardraya, and that is the way I aim to take." He bowed to the envoys from Videssos. "You will ride with us, of course."

"An honor," Skylitzes said.

Goudeles, on the other hand, looked like a man who had just been stabbed. Even more than Gorgidas, he longed for a return to the city and now saw it snatched away from him at the whim of this barbarian chief. "An honor," he choked out at last.

"Back to sword practice, Pikridios," Skylitzes chuckled, understanding him perfectly. The pen-pusher did not quite stifle a groan.

"This yurt will have to go, too," Arigh said, grinning as he rubbed salt in Goudeles' wounds. "Just a good string of horses, maybe a light shelter tent to keep the snow off at night."

"Snow?" Goudeles said faintly.

"Speak my tongue, please," Arghun grumbled; his son had dropped into Videssian to talk to the imperials. When he had caught up with the conversation, the khagan nodded in sympathy with Goudeles. "Yes, I know the snow is a nuisance. It will slow us up badly. But if we leave as soon as the clans have gathered, we should be nearing Yezd come spring."

"That's not precisely what I was worrying about," the bureaucrat said. He buried his face in his hands.

The nomads rode through steppe winters every year, following their herds. Knowing it could be done did not make the prospect appetizing. Gorgidas said the first thing that came to his mind. "Arigh, I'll need a fur cap like yours, one with—" He gestured, unsure of the word. "—ear flaps, by choice."

The plainsman understood him. "You'll have it," he promised. "That's a good job of thinking ahead, too; I knew a man who froze his ears in a blizzard and broke one clean off without ever knowing it till they thawed."

"How delightful," Goudeles muttered, almost inaudibly.

Gorgidas remembered something else. "Avshar is still loose in Pardraya."

That sobered his Videssian colleagues, and even Arigh, but Arghun said, as others had before, "A wizard. We have wizards of our own."

"Keep them moving, curse it!" Valash shouted. Viridovix nodded; he stood tall in the saddle, flapped his arms, and howled Gallic oaths. The flock of sheep picked up its pace by some meaningless fraction. Snug in their thick coats of greasy wool, they were more comfortable in the cold fall rain than the men who herded them.

The storms had come back two days ago, as Lipoxais foresaw, and made the nomads' retreat that much worse. There were not enough men to drive the herds as fast as they could go, either. That Targitaus had put a lubber like Viridovix to work was a measure of his desperation. Women were riding drover, too, and boys hardly old enough to have their feet reach the stirrups.

The Celt bullied a knot of sheep back into the main flock. He was glad Targitaus had any duty for him at all. It would have been easy to pile blame for the disaster on the foreigner—the more so as Batbaian had not returned with his father. Dead or captured, no one knew.

But Targitaus said only, "Not your fault, you fought well." If he did not want to see much of Viridovix after the fight, the Gaul found that easy to understand and kept his distance as best he could. It meant he could not spend much time with Seirem, but that would have been so anyhow. Targitaus drove his family no less than the rest of the clan; his daughter's hands were chafed and blistered from riding with the animals.

"*Get* along there, you gangling fuzz-covered idiot pile o' vulture puke!" Viridovix roared at a ewe that kept trying to go off on its own.

The black-faced beast bleated indignantly, as if it knew what he was calling it.

Valash darted away from the Celt to keep more sheep in line. The young Khamorth's face was drawn with fatigue as he rode back. "This job is too big for two," he said. He shook his head; rainwater flew from his beard.

"Aye, well, maybe not much longer to it, I'm thinking," Viridovix said. "Sure and that son of a serpent Varatesh couldna be finding us the now, not with the rain and all to cover our trail." There had been no serious pursuit after the battle, none of the harrying the Celt had dreaded. For what it was worth, Targitaus had brought off his retreat masterfully.

Valash looked hopeful at the Gaul's words, but as they left his mouth Viridovix cursed himself for a fool. Avshar could track him by his sword as easily as a man following a torch through the night. For a moment he thought of throwing it into the muck to break the trail. But before his hand touched the sword hilt he jerked it away and spat in defiance. "If the whoreson wants it, let him earn it."

Darkness came swiftly these fall nights, thick clouds drinking up the light almost before the sun they hid was set. The Khamorth traveled as long as they could see the way ahead, then ran up their tents, largely by feel. The camp was cheerless—so many men missing or dead, others wounded, and all, men and women alike, exhausted.

Wrapped in a thick wool blanket, Viridovix huddled close to the cookfire in Targitaus' tent. The khagan's greeting was a grunt. He ate in gloomy silence, new lines of grief scored into his cheeks.

The Gaul made a cold supper of cheese and smoked mutton sausage, declined the blackberries candied in honey that Seirem offered him. "Another time, lass, when I'm more gladsome than now. The sweet of 'em'd be wasted on me, I'm thinking."

Lipoxaïs the *enaree* ate greedily; the thick juice ran sticky down his chin. "How can you pig it so?" Viridovix asked him. "Does it not fair gag you, wi' your folk in sic straits?"

"I take the pleasures I can," Lipoxais said shortly, his high voice expressionless, his jowly, beardless face a mask. Viridovix took a large bite of sausage and looked away, his own cheeks reddening. He had his answer about the *enaree*'s nature and found he did not want it.

"I wasna after the shaming of you," he muttered.

The *enaree* surprised him by laying a pudgy hand on his arm. "I suspect I should be honored," he said, a hint of a twinkle in his fathomless dark eyes. "How many times have you apologized for a clumsy tongue?"

"Not often enough, likely." Viridovix thought about it. "And I wonder whyever not? There's no harm to me and maybe some good to the spalpeen I'm after slanging."

Lipoxais glanced over to Seirem. "You're civilizing him."

"Honh!" Viridovix said, offended. "Am I a Roman, now? Who wants to be civilized?" After a while he realized the *enaree* had borrowed the Videssian word; it did not exist in the Khamorth speech. "Shows what he knows," the Gaul said to himself, and felt better.

"All right, I made a mistake!" Dizabul said, slamming his fist against the floor of the yurt. It hurt; he stared at it as if it had turned on him, too. He went on, "Is that any reason for everyone to treat me like a bald sheep? Is it?"

Yes, Gorgidas thought, but he did not say so. Dizabul was at an age where yesterday receded into the mist and tomorrow was impossibly far away. It seemed monstrously unfair to him still to be held accountable for his choices after their results became clear. But the elders remembered, and treated him as they would anyone who backed the wrong side. It stung; he was used to acclaim, not snubs.

He was, in fact, desperate enough to talk with the Greek, whom he had ignored before. Gorgidas did not suffer fools gladly, but Dizabul sometimes got off the subject of his own mistreatment and would answer questions about the history and customs of his clan. He was not stupid, only spoiled, and knew a surprising amount of lore. And his beauty helped the Greek tolerate his arrogance.

He was, indeed, so striking a creature that Gorgidas found himself tempted to play up to him with exaggerated sympathy. That made him angry at himself, and in reaction so short with Dizabul that the boy finally glared at him and shouted, "You're as bad as the rest of them!" He stomped off into the rain, leaving Gorgidas to reflect on the uses of self-control.

The Greek and Goudeles went into serious training for war. The pen-pusher never made even an ordinary swordsman, but Gorgidas surprised the Arshaum with his work with the *gladius*—at least on foot. "For the nomads," he recorded, "accustomed as they are to cutting at their foes from horseback, employ a like style when not mounted and are thus confounded facing an opponent who uses the point rather than the edge."

He hung a merciful veil of silence over his own efforts with the saber and the slashing stroke.

Even so, his progress satisfied Skylitzes. "No one would mistake you for a real soldier, true, but you've learned enough so you won't be butchered like a sheep. . . ." The officer rounded on Goudeles, who was rubbing a knee he had twisted trying to spin away from the plainsman with whom he had been practicing. Skylitzes rolled his eyes. "Unlike this one, who might as well tattoo 'rack of mutton' on his forehead and have done."

"Hrmmp," the bureaucrat said, still sitting in the mud. "I daresay I do better on the field than one of these barbarians would in the chancery. And what do you want from me? I never claimed a warrior's skills."

"Neither did the Hellene," Skylitzes retorted, startling Gorgidas, who had not realized the Videssian knew what his people called themselves.

The officer's praise did not altogether please him. He loathed war with the deep and sincere loathing of one who had seen too much of it too closely. At the same time, he was driven to do whatever he tried as well as he could. Having decided he needed the rudiments of the soldier's trade, he set about acquiring them as conscientiously as he had his medical lore, if not with the same burning interest.

He blinked, suddenly understanding how Gaius Philippus could see soldiering as just another trade, like carpentry or leatherworking. He would never like that perspective, but it was no longer alien to him.

He had to laugh at himself. Who would have thought insight could come from learning butchery? He remembered what Socrates had told the Athenians: "For a human being, an unexamined life is not worth living." And Socrates had fought in the phalanx when his *polis* needed him.

He must have murmured the Greek aloud, for Goudeles asked, "What's that?"

He translated it into Videssian. "Not bad," the pen-pusher said. "He was a secret agent, this Socrates?" Gorgidas threw his hands in the air.

When they got back to the yurt, Gorgidas carefully scraped the dirt from his horsehide boots before going in. Goudeles and Skylitzes followed suit, having learned he was much easier to live with if they went along. As a result, the yurt was undoubtedly cleaner than it had been when it housed plainsmen.

Goudeles cocked an eyebrow at the Greek. "What will you do when we move east, and it'll be a tent over bare mud?"

"The best I can," Gorgidas snapped. He did not think he had to apologize for his fastidiousness. He had long since noticed that wounds healed better when kept clean and sick patients recovered faster in clean surroundings. He had taken that as a general rule and applied it all through his way of living, reasoning that what aided against ill health might also help prevent it.

"Don't mock him over this one, Pikridios," Skylitzes said. He stretched full length on the rug with a grunt of pleasure. "Nothing wrong with coming back to something that's dry and isn't brown."

"Oh, no doubt, no doubt," Goudeles allowed. "But I'll never forget Tolui's face when our friend here called him a filthy ball of horse droppings for tracking mud on the carpet." Gorgidas had the grace to look shamefaced, the more so as the shaman had come to talk about the medicinal plants Arghun had given him.

"Well, still and all, I think the yurt's a more comfortable place now that he's taken charge of it than it was when our wenches were still here," Skylitzes said.

"Have it any way you like." The bureaucrat was working at his knee again and rolling up his sheepskin trousers for a look at it. It was already turning purple. Even so, he managed a leer. "You must admit, they had an advantage he lacks."

"First time I've heard it called that," Skylitzes snorted.

Gorgidas laughed, too, and not very self-consciously. With no other choice available, he had been more successful with women than he would have imagined possible. Hoelun had helped that immensely; her desire to please was so obvious it would have been difficult—to say nothing of churlish—not to respond in kind. He found himself missing her now she was gone. But he missed acting according to his own nature more.

"Are you a crazy man, to come riding into our camp this way?" Targitaus demanded, glowering at the outlaw. "Put that fool white shield away—why should I care about your truce sign?" His hand twitched eagerly toward his sword.

Varatesh's rider matched the chieftain stare for disdainful stare. He was about forty, with a proud, hard face that might have been handsome but for his eyes, which were set too close together and, with their slitted lids, showed only cruelty. His horse and gear were of the finest, probably loot from the recent battle. He did not offer his name, but answered with a jeer, "Go ahead, kill me, and see what happens to your precious clansmen and their friends then."

The spirit seemed to go out of Targitaus. His shoulders sagged; Viridovix, watching, would have sworn his cheeks slumped, too. "Say on," he said, and his voice suddenly quavered like an old man's.

"Thought you'd see sense," the outlaw said. He was enjoying his mission; he rubbed his hands together as he got down to business. "Now that we've seen a new Royal Clan come to be, it's time the rest of the steppe recognized what's what—starting with you and yours."

As nothing else could have, that stung Targitaus back to life. His face purpled with fury. He roared, "You bastard, you cheese-faced crock of goat piss, you frog!" It was the deadliest Khamorth insult, and the outlaw's lips skinned back from his teeth in anger. Targitaus paid no attention, storming on, "You go tell Varatesh he can lick my arse, for I'll not lick his!" The clansmen around him shouted their approval.

The tumult gave Varatesh's man the time he needed to recover his temper; the renegade chief had not chosen foolishly. As the yells died down to mutters, the outlaw spread his hands in conciliation and spoke as mildly as he could. "Who spoke of licking arses? You know Varatesh is stronger than you. He could crush you as a boy squeezes a newt in his fist." Viridovix scowled at the heartless comparison, which let him see into the outlaw's soul, soft words or no. "But he does not. Why should he? One way or another, you will be his subjects. Why not willingly?"

"And put the Wolf under your bandits' black flag? Never."

"All right, then," the outlaw said, with the air of a man beaten down by hard bargaining. "He will even make you a present."

Targitaus spat in contempt. "What gift would I take from him?"

"He will give you back all the prisoners he holds and ask no ransom for them."

"You toy with me," Targitaus said. But he saw the terrible, haunted hope on the faces of his people, and when he repeated, "Toy," doubt was in his voice.

"By my sword, I do not," Varatesh's man said. The nomads fell silent and looked at each other, for among their warrior folk the worst renegade would think three times before he broke that oath.

Unable to check himself, Targitiaus burst out, "Is Batbaian among them?"

"Aye, and luckier than most. By my sword I swear it."

Dismay filled Viridovix as he heard Targitaus heeding the bandit. He cried, "Sure and your honor canna take the omadhaun's lies for truth, can you now? What's the word of a Varatesh worth, or an Avshar?" A few heads bobbed in agreement, but not many.

With his son in Varatesh's hands and a straw to grasp, the nomad chief answered, "V'rid'rish, I followed your path once, and see what it gained me." The Gaul's jaw fell at the reversal, and at the unfairness of it, but Targitaus went on with worse: "So where do you find the brass to urge a course on me now?"

"But—"

Targitaus overrode him with a slashing gesture. "Be grateful your neck is not the price asked for, for I would trade you for Batbaian and my clansmen." The Celt bowed his head; he had no reply to that.

Having decided to treat with his foes, Targitaus dickered with all his skill and wrung the most from his wretched bargaining position. He argued concession after concession from Varatesh's man, making the renegade agree that, as he took the risk of halting his clan, none of Varatesh's men should be allowed to approach the camp with the column of prisoners.

"You understand the captives will be unarmed and afoot," the outlaw warned.

"Aye, aye," the chieftain said impatiently. "Had we won, we'd have plundered you." Once his mind was made up, he moved ahead at full speed. He exchanged oaths with the outlaw, calling on the spirits to avenge any transgressions in the terms agreed upon.

Viridovix watched morosely from the edge of the crowd of Khamorth. Few of them would speak to him; for the first time in weeks he felt himself once more an alien among them. Seirem's smile said she had not forgotten him, but he wondered how long he would enjoy it now that her father had turned against him. In a way, the couple of sentences Rambehisht ostentatiously gave him cheered him more. "Maybe it's not me that's crazy after all," he said to himself, tugging at his mustache.

The agreement went forward regardless. "Ride hard," Targitaus told Varatesh's man. "Truce or no truce, we will not stay here long."

The renegade nodded. He kicked his shaggy dun pony into a trot, lifted his shield of truce on his lance so none of Targitaus' patrolling pickets would attack him on his return to his master. A stray breeze brought back his laughter as he rode out of camp.

"Ah, we can set them free after all," Avshar said. "How noble for us." He sipped kavass with a hollow reed that went through a slit in his visored helm. Somehow he still managed the proper nomad slurp.

Varatesh had been drinking hard for days. He wished he had never given the orders that went with the prisoner release. Far too late for regrets or turning back now, he thought. "Yes, let them go," he said. The thing was done, and he had to live with it. His hand shook as he lifted the skin to his mouth; he gulped without tasting what he drank.

"They're coming!" the rider called as he rode into camp. The Khamorth cheered; everyone was milling about among the tents, the men armed, the women in holiday best, wearing their finest bughtaqs and long flounced festival shirts of wool dyed in horizontal bands of bright color. The day cooperated with their celebration. It was cold but clear, the last storm having blown itself out the night before.

Tension and fear mingled with the joy. Wives, daughters, brothers of missing men, all hoped their loved ones were prisoners and knew some of those hopes would be broken.

“The bastards tied them together, it looks like,” Targitaus’ scout was reporting. “They’re in lines of twenty or so, one bunch next to the other.”

There was an angry rumble from the nomads, but Targitaus quelled it. “So long as they’re coming,” he said. “Ropes come off, aye, and other bonds as well.” His clansmen growled eagerly at that, like the wolves that were their token.

From beside Viridovix, Seirem called, “How do they look?” Her hand held the Gaul’s tight enough to hurt. He knew how much she wanted to ask for word of Batbaian, and admired her for holding back to keep the scout from being deluged in similar questions. He squeezed back; she accepted the pressure gratefully.

“I didn’t ride close, I fear,” the plainsman said “As soon as I saw them, I turned round and came here to bring word.” Seirem bit her lip, but nodded in understanding.

“Let’s go out to meet them!” someone shouted. The Khamorth started to surge forward, but Targitaus checked them, saying, “The agreement was to receive them here, and we shall. For now we are weak; we cannot afford to break any part of it. Yet . . .” he added, and the nomads nodded, anticipating the day.

Waiting stretched. Then a great cry went up as the first heads appeared over a low swell of ground a few hundred yards from the camp. Heedless of the khagan now, his people pelted toward them. He trotted with them, not trying to hold them back any longer. Still hand in hand, Viridovix and Seirem were somewhere near the center of the crowd. He could have been at the front, but slowed to match her shorter strides.

More and more freed captives stumbled into view, roped together as the scout had said. Viridovix whistled in surprise as he saw their numbers. “Dinna tell me the blackguard’s after keeping his promise,” he muttered. Seirem looked up at him curiously; he realized he had spoken Gaulish. “Never you mind, love,” he said in the plains speech. “Seems your father had the right of it, and glad I am for it.”

“So am I,” she said, and then, with a little gasp, “Look, it’s Batbaian, there at the front of a line!” They were still too far away for Viridovix to recognize him, but Seirem had no doubts. She called her brother’s name and waved frantically. Batbaian’s head jerked up. He spotted Viridovix, if not his sister, and wagged his head to show he had heard; with his hands tied behind him, he could not wave back.

As they hurried closer, Seirem suddenly flinched, as if struck. "His eye—" she faltered. Her own filled with pain; there was only an inflamed empty socket under Batbaian's left brow, the lid flapping uselessly over it.

"Och, lass, it happens, it happens," Viridovix said gently. "The gods be praised he has the other, and home again to heal, too." Seirem's hand was cold in his, but she managed a nod. She had seen enough of war's aftermath to know how grim it could be.

The returning captives only added more proof of that as they shambled forward. Many limped from half-healed wounds; more than one had only a single hand to be roped behind his back.

Seirem was recognizing more plainsmen now. "There's Ellak, heading up another column. The spirits be kind to him; he's lost an eye, too. And Bumin over there—you can always tell him because he's so bowlegged—oh, no, so has he. And so has Zabergan, and that tall man from the Spotted Cats, and Nerseh there—" She looked up at Viridovix, fear on her face. It congealed in him, too, like a lump of ice under his heart. He recalled what sort of gifts Avshar gave.

The rush from the camp reached the prisoners, and welcoming shouts turned to cries of horror. Women screamed and wailed and fainted, and men with them. Others reeled away to spew up their guts on the muddy ground. One man drew his saber, cut his brother from a file of captives, then cut him down. Before anyone could stop him, he drew the blade across his own throat and fell, spouting blood.

For what Seirem had seen at the columns' heads was such mercy as Avshar and Varatesh had shown. The file leaders had been left with an eye apiece, to guide their lines over the steppe. Every man behind them was blinded totally; their ruined eyes dripped pus or thick yellow serum in place of the tears they would never shed again. It took time for the atrocity to sink in: a thousand men, with half a hundred eyes among them.

Lipoxais, his usually pink face dead pale, went from column to column, pressing soothing herbs on the most cruelly mutilated nomads and, perhaps as important, offering a kindly voice in their darkness. But the hopeless magnitude of the task exhausted the *enaree*'s medicines and overwhelmed his spirit. He went to his knees in the mud, weeping with the deep, racking spasms of a man not used to tears. "Fifty eyes! I foretold it and knew not what I saw!" he cried bitterly. "I foretold it!"

The short hairs on the back of Viridovix' neck prickled up as he remembered the *enaree*'s mantic trance. What else had Lipoxais seen? A mountain doorway and a pair of swords. The Gaul shivered. He spat to avert the omens, wanting no part of the rest of Lipoxais' prophecies.

Targitaus was staring about like a man who knew he was awake but found himself trapped in nightmare all the same. "My son!" he groaned. "My clan! My—" He groaned again, surprise and pain together, and clutched at his head—or tried to, for his left arm would not answer his will. He swayed like an old tree in a storm, then toppled, face down.

Seirem shrieked and rushed to his side, Viridovix close behind. Borane was already there, gently wiping mud from Targitaus' cheeks and beard with the sleeve of her festive blouse. And Lipoxais, torn from his private grief, came at the run.

"Cut me loose, curse it!" Batbaian shouted. Someone slashed through the rope that held him to his fellow captives. Deprived of their one sighted comrade, they froze in place, afraid to move. Batbaian, his hands still tied behind him, pushed through the crowd and clumsily knelt beside his father.

The right side of Targitaus' face was still screwed up in anguish, the left slack and loose as if made from half-melted wax. One pupil was tiny, while the other filled its iris. The chieftain's breath rattled in his throat. While his family, the rest of the Khamorth, and Viridovix watched and listened helplessly, it came slower and slower till it stopped. Lipoxais closed his staring eyes. With a moan, Borane clutched at Targitaus, trying to squeeze life into him once more and trying in vain.

XIII

Although Marcus passed the ordeal of the drug, the Emperor did not summon him again. Thorisin lacked the front of a Vardanes Sphrantzes, to savor dealing with a man he had shamed. The tribune was as pleased to be left alone. Eventually he finished his report and sent it to the Avtokrator by messenger. A scrawled acknowledgment returned the same way.

Gaius Philippus kept Garsavra under control. Yavlak's Yezda tried raiding farms near the town not long after Scaurus reached the capital. The report the senior centurion sent him was a model of terseness: "They came. We smashed 'em."

The tribune was glad to hear of the victory, but less so than he would have imagined possible a few weeks before. The constant murmurous shuffle of parchment insulated the bureaucrats' wing of the Grand Courtroom from such struggles. And knowing the Romans had done well without him only made Marcus feel more useless.

He stayed at his desk or in his room most of the time, narrowing his world as much as he could. There were few people in Videssos he wanted to see. Once, rounding a corner, he found one of Alypia's servants knocking at his door. He ducked back out of sight. The servant left, grumbling. Scaurus shrank from facing the princess after revealing himself to her under Nepos' elixir, all his private griefs private no more.

Without Senpat and Nevrat Sviodo, he would have been altogether reclusive. And the first time they came calling, he did not intend to answer. "I know you're there, Scaurus," Senpat called through the door. "Let's see if I can pound longer than you can stand." Aided by his wife, he beat out such a tattoo that the tribune, his ears ringing, had to give in.

"Took you long enough," Nevrat said. "I thought we'd have to stand here and drip all night." The finery the two Vaspurakaners were wearing was rather the worse for rain.

"Sorry," Marcus mumbled untruthfully. "Come in; dry off."

"No, you come out with us," Senpat said. "I think I've found a tavern with wine dry enough to suit you. Or if not, drink enough and you won't care."

"I soak up enough wine by myself, thanks, dry or sweet," Marcus said, still trying to decline. Along with the patter of raindrops against his window, the grape eased him toward such rest as he got.

But Nevrat took his arm. "Drinking by yourself is not the same," she declared. "Now come along." Left with only the choice of breaking away by force, the tribune came.

The tavern was not far from the palace compound. Scaurus gulped down a cup of wine, grimaced, and glowered at Senpat Sviodo. "Only a Vaspurakaner would call this syrup dry," he accused. The "princes" favored even sweeter, thicker vintages than the Videssians drank. "How is it different from any other wine hereabouts?"

"As far as I can tell, it isn't," Senpat said breezily. While Scaurus stared, he went on, "But the lure of it pried you out of your nest, not so?"

"I think your wife laying hold of me had more to do with it."

"You dare imply she has charms I lack?" Senpat mimed being cut to the quick.

"Oh, hush," Nevrat told him. She turned to Marcus. "What's the use of having friends, if they don't help in time of trouble?"

"I thank you," the tribune said. He reached out to touch her hand, let go of it reluctantly—any small kindness could move him these days. Her smile was warm.

"Another thing friends are good for is noticing when friends' mugs are empty," Senpat said. He waved to the tap-man.

Scaurus found Nevrat was right. When he holed up in his cubicle with a bottle, all he got was stuporous and sad. With Senpat and Nevrat, though, wine let him receive the sympathy he would have rejected sober. He even tried to join in when one of the men at the bar started a round of drinking songs, and laughed at the face Senpat made to warn him his ear and voice were no truer than usual.

"We must do this again," he heard himself saying while he stood, a little unsteadily, outside his doorway.

"So long as you promise not to sing," Senpat said.

"Harumph." With drunken expansiveness, Marcus embraced both Vaspurakaners. "You are good friends indeed."

"Then as good friends should, we will let you rest," Nevrat said. The tribune sadly watched them go. They, too, were swaying as they made their way down the corridor toward the stairs. Senpat's arm slid round his wife's waist. Marcus bit his lip and hurried into his room.

That small sting at the end did not badly mar the evening. Scaurus' sleep was deep and restful, not the sodden oblivion that was the most he dared hope for since Helvis left him. The headache he woke with seemed a small price to pay. When he went up to the office where he worked, he nodded to the bureaucrats he was overseeing, the first friendly gesture he had given them.

He found the pen-pushers easier to supervise than they had been the year before. None had Pikridios Goudeles' talent for number-shuffling, and they all knew Marcus had managed a draw with their wily chief. They did not have the nerve to try sneaking much past him.

Going through page after page, scroll after scroll of tax accounts without finding a silver bit out of place was encouraging in a way, but also dull. The tribune worked away with mechanical competence; he was not after excitement.

Seeing Scaurus in a mood rather less dour than he had shown before, one of the bureaucrats came up to his desk. "What is it, Iatzoulinos?" the tribune asked, looking up from his counting board. Even without his eyes to guide them, his fingers flicked through an addition with blurring speed; long practice with the beads had made him adept as any clerk.

"This has the possibility of providing you with some amusement, sir," Iatzoulinos said, holding out a scroll. The pen-pusher was a lean, sallow man of indeterminate age. He spoke the jargon of the chancery even on matters that had nothing to do with finance; he probably used it when he made love, Marcus thought scornfully.

He wondered what so bloodless a man would find funny. "Show me."

"With pleasure, sir." Iatzoulinos unrolled the strip of parchment. "You will note first that all required seals have been affixed; to all initial appearances, it is a proper document. Yet note the inexpert hand in which it is written and the childishly simple syntax. Finally, it purports to be a demand on the capital for funds from a provincial town—" Iatzoulinos actually laughed out loud; he saw the joke there as too obvious to need spelling out.

Scaurus studied the document. Suddenly he, too, began to laugh. Iatzoulinos looked gratified, then grew nervous as the tribune did not stop. At last the pen-pusher said, "I pray your pardon, sir, but you appear to have discovered more risibility here than I had anticipated. Do you care to impart to me the source of your mirth?"

Marcus still could not speak. Instead, he pointed to the signature at the bottom of the parchment.

Iatzoulinos' eyes followed his finger. The color slowly faded from his narrow cheeks. "That is your name there," he said in a tiny voice. He glanced fearfully at Scaurus' sword—he was not used to overtly deadly weapons in the chancery, which dealt with the subtler snares of pen and ink.

"So it is." The tribune finally had control of himself. He continued, "If you check the file, you'll also find an imperial rescript endorsing my request here. The citizens of Garsavra did the Empire a great service in contributing their own funds to obtain the Namdalener prisoners from Yavlak. Simple justice required repayment."

"Of course, of course. I shall bend every effort toward the facilitation of the reimbursement process." In his dismay, Iatzoulinos was practically babbling. "Illustrious sir, you will, I hope, grasp that I intended no offense in any remarks that may perhaps have appeared at first hearing somewhat slighting."

"Don't worry about it." Scaurus got up and patted the unfortunate bureaucrat on the shoulder. There was no way to explain he actually felt grateful to Iatzoulinos; not even with Senpat and Nevrat had he laughed so hard.

"I shall draft the memorandum authorizing the dispatch of funds posthaste," Iatzoulinos said, glad of an excuse to edge away from the Roman.

"Yes, do," Marcus called after him. "Gaius Philippus, who heads the Garsavra garrison these days, lacks my forbearance." Iatzoulinos' sidling withdrawal turned into a trot.

Shaking his head, the tribune sat again. Even the relief his laughter brought was mixed with misery. He would rather have been at Garsavra himself, with his countrymen, than lonely and under a cloud at the capital. And thinking of how he had acquired the men of the Duchy only reminded him how he lost them afterward.

A few days later, the chamber was rocking with merriment when he came in the door. He caught snatches of the bad jokes the pen-pushers were throwing back and forth: ". . . knows which side his bread is buttered on, all right." "Buttered-Bun would be a better name for him." "No, you fool, for her—"

Silence fell as the bureaucrats saw him. After Iatzoulinos' disaster, they did not include him in their glee. He walked past clerks who avoided his eyes, listened to their conversation abruptly turn to business.

Stung, he sat down, opened a ledger, and began adding a long column of figures. This once, he wished he needed conscious thought to work the abacus. It would have taken his mind away from the hurt he felt.

"Play some more tunes, Vaspurakaner!" someone called through shouted applause. A score of throats took up the cry, until the tavern rang with it.

Senpat Sviodo let his pandoura rest in his lap for a moment, flexed his hands to loosen them. He sent a comic look of dismay toward the corner table where Marcus and Nevrat were sitting.

Nevrat called something to him in their own language. He nodded ruefully and rolled his eyes. "I'm sorry," she said to Scaurus, dropping back into Videssian. "I told him he could have been here drinking with us if he'd left the lute at home."

"He enjoys playing," the tribune said.

Nevrat raised an eyebrow. "Oh, indeed, and I enjoy sugarplums, but I'd burst if I tried eating a bushel basket full."

"All right." Marcus yielded the point. Senpat had only intended playing a song or two, more for his own amusement than anyone else's. But he found a wildly enthusiastic audience, not least among them the taverner, who had all but dragged him to his current seat atop the bar. His Vaspurakaner cap lay beside him, upside down. He had been singing a couple of hours now, with the crowd around him too thick and too keen to let him go.

They cheered all over again at the first chords of a familiar tune and roared out the chorus: "The wine gets drunk, but you get drunker!"

"He should spin that one out as long as he can," Marcus said. "Maybe they'll all pass out and give him a chance to get away."

The taverner might have been thinking along with him. Two barmaids labored to keep the mugs of the throng round Senpat filled; two more, carrying large jugs of wine on their hips, went from table to table.

Nevrat held out her cup for a refill. Scaurus declined; his was still half full. Nevrat noticed. "You're stinting tonight."

"You should understand that, you and your sugarplums."

She smiled. "Fair enough." Then she grew serious, studying him like a theologian pondering a difficult text. She held her voice neutral as she remarked, "You have been drinking deep lately, haven't you?"

"Too deep, maybe."

Her face cleared. "I thought as much myself, but I doubted it was my place to say so. Although," she added quickly, anxious that he take no offense, "no one could blame you, considering—"

"Aye, considering," he finished for her. "Still and all, you can only look at the world from the inside of a bottle so long. After that, you just see the bottle."

Remembering why he drank, he looked downcast enough for Nevrat's dark brows to come together in concern. She reached out to touch his hand. "Is it still so bad?"

"I'm sorry." He needed a deliberate effort to come back to himself. "I didn't think it showed so much."

"Oh, someone who passed you in the street might not notice," she said, "but we've known each other some years now, you and I."

"So we have." Thinking about it, he realized he knew Nevrat and Senpat about as well as he did any non-Romans, knew Nevrat better than any woman in this world save Helvis—thinking of her made him grimace again, though he did not know it—and Alypia Gavra. And no imperial ceremonial hedged in Nevrat.

Before he quite realized it had, his hand tightened on hers. It was strange to feel a woman's hand callused from the sword hilt, like his own; reins and the bow had also hardened Nevrat's palm and fingers. She looked at him in surprise, but did not draw away.

Just then, Senpat finished his song. He scrambled down from the bar in spite of fresh shouts for more, saying, "No, no! Enough, my friends, enough!" The sound of his voice, unaccompanied by pandoura, made Marcus jerk back as if Nevrat's hand had burst into flame.

"Well, well, how do we fare here?" Senpat said after he finally fought his way through the crush to the corner table. "What have you two been plotting while they held me hostage? Up to no good, I don't doubt."

The tribune was glad he still had wine in his cup. He drained it, which let him avoid answering.

After a tiny pause, Nevrat said, "No reason for you to doubt it." She used the same noncommittal tone she had with Scaurus a few minutes before.

He winced. It must have been his conscience nipping at him, for Senpat noticed nothing amiss. He hefted his cap, which jingled with the copper and silver his audience had tossed in. "You see?" he said. "I should have been a minstrel after all."

Nevrat's snort told what she thought of that. "Put the money in your belt-pouch," she said. "You'll need your hat—the rain's started again."

"When does it ever stop, these days?" Senpat upended the cap; a couple of coins rolled off the table onto the floor. "Let be," he said when Nevrat started to pick them up. "Something to make the sweepers happy." He stowed his pandoura in a soft leather sack, then glanced at Marcus. "It'll be dryer than you are, without a hat."

"Dryer than any of us." The reply sounded lame in the tribune's ears, but it served well enough. Sometimes a laconic way had its advantages.

"Sometimes I think you take better care of your toy than you do of me," Nevrat said, bantering much as she usually did.

"Why not?" Senpat came back. "You can take care of yourself."

"I'm glad you think so."

Nevrat's answer was tart enough that Marcus half turned toward her, wondering if she might have meant it for him as well. Senpat only chuckled, saying, "Truly a viper's tongue tonight." He thrashed about, as if bitten by a snake. Nevrat mimed throwing a plate at him, but she was laughing, too. Marcus' lips twitched; Senpat was incorrigible.

He slung his pandoura over his shoulder, jammed his Vaspurakaner cap down as far as it would go on his head. He made for the door, Nevrat close behind him. Scaurus followed more slowly. He thought for a moment of staying until the rain let up, but that might take days. Besides, as he had said to Nevrat, after a while drinking grew to be for its own sake alone. He knew himself too well to pretend to be blind to that.

A Videssian tried to pull Nevrat into his arms. She swung away, plucked the wine cup from his hand, and, smiling sweetly, poured it over his head. "Never mind," she said to Senpat, who had spun round, his hand darting to his knife. "I *can* take care of myself."

"So I see." He stayed wary, wondering if anyone would take it further. Marcus shouldered through the crowd to help at need.

The imperial was coughing and swearing, but the fellow next to him growled, "Stifle it, you fool. You had that coming, for fooling about with someone else's woman." The drenched man looked round for support and found none. With his music, Senpat was everyone's hero tonight, even if he and his wife were outlanders.

Marcus gasped at the cold rain and briefly regretted deciding to leave. He turned up the collar of his coat to give the back of his head what protection he could, and looked down at the puddles growing between the cobblestones. That did not do much to keep the raindrops off his face.

Senpat and Nevrat splashed along beside him. Their heads were down, too. Scaurus' eyes kept returning to Nevrat. He swore at himself under his breath and reflected that the man in the tavern who had upbraided the other Videssian might as well have been talking to him instead.

On the other hand, Nevrat had not upended a cup of wine on him, either. He dimly realized the state he was in, when so small a thing could be a reason for optimism.

The rain turned to sleet. A dripping courier brought a message to the tribune at his office in the Grand Courtroom. "Fancier digs than you had at Garsavra," he said, handing Scaurus the parchment.

"Hmm? Oh, yes." Marcus had not noticed it was the same man who had delivered Thorisin's dispatch ordering him to the capital.

He broke the seal, felt mixed loneliness and pleasure at seeing angular Latin letters rather than the snaky Videssian script. As always, Gaius Philippus' note was to the point; he found writing too hard to waste words. The scrawled message said, "The locals are paid off, them as didn't die of shock. Now where's *our* back wages?"

The tribune scribbled a reminder to himself. When he looked up, the courier was still there. "Yes?"

The fellow shifted his feet; water squelched. "Last time I saw you, you fed me hot wine," he said pointedly.

"I'm sorry." Marcus reddened. He took care of the rider, apologizing again for his discourtesy. It was not even that he resented the man for starting him on his disastrous journey; he had simply been thoughtless. In a way, that was worse.

Mollified at last, the courier gave him a salute before going off to deliver the rest of his dispatches. Scaurus, his conscience somewhat assuaged, decided not to let another chance to show good manners pass by.

"I've just had word you sent the Garsavrans the money the fisc owed them," he said to Iatzoulinos. "I want to thank you for attending to it promptly."

"Once you pointed out the urgency, I did my best to implement your request," the bureaucrat said. What else was I going to do, with you looking over my shoulder? his eyes added silently, faint contempt in them. Marcus pursed his lips, annoyed that civility could be taken as a sign of weakness.

His voice hardened. "I trust you will also be punctual in seeing that the pay for the garrison at Garsavra—the garrison of my countrymen—does not fall into arrears."

"Accounts for military expenditures are maintained in an entirely different ledger," Iatzoulinos warned. "The policies of the present government have occasioned so many transfers of funds that I have difficulty being certain if this request can be expedited so readily as the last."

The tribune's tours in the chancery, especially this latest one, had made him understand how, to the pen-pushers who spent all their time here, ledgers became more real than the men whose deeds and needs they recorded. Gaius Philippus would have another opinion about that, he thought.

He said, "Garsavra is important in holding the Yezda at bay. The Emperor would not care to hear of disaffection among the troops there. And, as I told you, I am one of them, and I know them. Their current commander is not a man to make an enemy of."

"I will exert every effort," Iatzoulinos said sulkily.

"A fine idea. If you work as hard to pay the Romans as you did for the people of Garsavra, I'm sure their wages will reach them very soon."

Marcus gave the bureaucrat a friendly nod and returned to his desk. Iatzoulinos actually permitted a smile to touch his thin face for a moment, which let the tribune hope the warning had sunk home without stinging too much.

In spite of his gloom, he suddenly smiled himself. Iatzoulinos might think him a nuisance, but the pen-pusher would run shrieking from a meeting with Gaius Philippus.

"Three pieces of silver?" The leatherworker's stare was scornful. "This is a fine belt, outlander. See the tooling? See the fine tanning? See how strong it is?" He tugged at it.

"It doesn't come apart in your hands," Scaurus observed dryly. "If it did, someone would have lynched you long since, and you would not be standing here trying to cheat me. Still, perhaps if I offered you four, you might be so ashamed at your ill-gotten gains that you would keep quiet and leave off letting the whole plaza of Palamas know what a thief you are."

"I, a thief? Here you try to rob me without even drawing sword. Why, after the price I had to pay for the cowhide, after the hard labor I lavished on it, I would be stealing from my own children to let it go for seven."

They eventually settled on six silver coins, a quarter of a goldpiece. Marcus was vaguely displeased; had his heart been in the haggle, likely he could have got the belt for five. He shrugged. He could not really make himself care. These days, there was not much he did care about.

At least he had the belt. The one he was wearing was old and frayed.

He unbuckled it, slid off his sword and dagger, and leaned them against his leg. Holding up his trousers with one hand, he began threading the new belt through the loops.

He was fumbling for the one behind his back when a cheery voice said, "Aye, that's the hard one; I remember from the days when I wore breeches."

"Nepos!" The tribune started, then had to make a quick grab to keep from losing his trousers—and his dignity. He whirled to face the priest, and his weapons fell clattering to the flagstones. His face scarlet, he stooped to retrieve them, and almost lost his pants again.

"Here, let me help you." Nepos lifted Scaurus' knife and sword out of the slush on the pavement. He waited until the tribune had the belt on, then handed them back to him.

"Thank you," Marcus said stiffly. He did not want to have anything to do with Nepos, not after he had drugged him and then listened with Thorisin and Alypia as he bared his soul.

If Nepos sensed that, he did not show it. "Good to see you," he said. "You've been as hard to catch as a cockroach lately. Do you just scuttle along the edges of the walls, or have you actually figured out a way to disappear into the wainscoting?"

"I haven't had much use for people," Marcus said lamely.

"Well, considering what you've been through, one could hardly blame you." Seeing the Roman's face freeze, Nepos realized the blunder he had made. "Oh, my dear fellow, your pardon, I pray you."

"You will excuse me, I hope." Voice as expressionless as his features, Scaurus turned to go.

"Wait! In Phos' name, I beg you."

Reluctantly, Marcus stopped. Nepos was not the sort of priest who kept his god's name on his lips every moment of the day. When he called on Phos, he had important reason, or so he thought.

"What do you want with me?" The tribune could not contain his bitterness. "Haven't you seen enough to glut you already?"

"My friend—if I may still call you such . . ." Nepos waited for some sign from Scaurus, but the tribune might have been carved from stone. Sighing, the priest went on, "Let me tell you how deeply I regret how that entire affair turned out . . . as does the Emperor himself, I might add."

"Why? It didn't hurt *him* any."

Nepos frowned at the harsh way Marcus spoke of Thorisin, but continued earnestly, "But it did, in reducing you. His Majesty had the right to ensure you were involved in no sedition against him, but when it came to probing in such, uh, intimate detail into your private affairs . . ." Nepos hesitated again, casting about for some way to go on without doing more damage. Finding none, he finished, "He should have stopped his questions sooner."

"He didn't," Marcus said flatly.

"No, and as I told you, he is sorry for it. But he is also stubborn—think back to the case of Taron Leimmokheir if you doubt that. And so he is slow in admitting any error, even to himself. Nevertheless, please note he has you in the same important post you held last year."

"It's not as important as the command at Garsavra," the tribune said, still unwilling to believe.

"No, but fill it well, raise no further suspicions, and I daresay you will have your old rank back again come summer, when campaigning season is here again."

"Easier for you to say than for Thorisin to do."

Nepos sighed again. "You are a stubborn man, Scaurus—in gloom as in other things, I see. I leave you with a last bit of advice, then: judge by the event, not before it."

Marcus blinked. Nepos' admonition might have come from the lips of a Stoic philosopher. The priest bent his plump frame into a half-bow and departed. The wan winter sun gleamed off his naked pate.

Scaurus frowned, watching him go. Nepos might think him somber, but the priest was lighthearted himself, which probably made him double any good things Thorisin had said and halve the bad. If the Emperor really wanted him back in meaningful service, he could have restored him by now. No, the tribune thought, he was still out of favor with Thorisin—and that, as Nepos had recommended, was judging by the event.

He shook his head. The motion made him catch sight of another familiar face. Like Scaurus, Provhos Mourtzouphlos was taller than most imperials and so stood out from the crowd that filled the plaza of Palamas.

The handsome aristocrat was also frowning. He was—Marcus stiffened, his long-dormant soldier's alertness suddenly waking—he was watching Nepos. The priest's robe and shaven pate were easy to spot as he walked through the square.

Then Mourtzouphlos' gaze swung back to the tribune. Marcus caught his eye, nodded deliberately. Mourtzouphlos grimaced, turned, and began haggling with a man who carried a brazier and a wicker basket full of shrimp.

Interesting, Scaurus thought, most interesting indeed. He started toward the palace complex. After half a minute or so, he turned back, as if he had forgotten something. Mourtzouphlos might be holding a roasted shrimp by the tail, but he was also definitely keeping an eye on the tribune. In fact, he had come a few paces after him. Seeing that Scaurus realized what he was about, he stopped in confusion and chagrin.

At first the Roman was furious, certain Thorisin Gavras had set Mourtzouphlos on him. So much for Nepos' optimism, he thought. But then he decided the Emperor had no need to put such an inept spy on his trail. If he wanted someone to watch Scaurus secretly, the tribune would never know it.

What, then? The only thing he could think of was that Mourtzouphlos was suspicious of his influence with Thorisin, and that seeing him talking to Nepos—who certainly did have the Emperor's ear—had alarmed the aristocrat. But Mourtzouphlos was in Thorisin's good graces himself. If he thought Scaurus was a rival, perhaps it was so.

Gardeners raked the last withered autumn leaves from the broad lawns that surrounded the buildings of the palace quarter. They nodded respectfully as the tribune walked past. He returned their salutes automatically. They meant nothing; the gardeners were too low in the hierachy to risk offending even someone out of favor. Mourtzouphlos' jealousy, though, was the first good news Marcus had had in some weeks.

He spun on his heel. A bowshot behind him, Provhos Mourtzouphlos abruptly found a bare-branched tree fascinating. He did not acknowledge or seem to notice the cheerful wave Scaurus sent him.

A grin felt strange on the tribune's face, but good.

Marcus' pleased mood lasted through the afternoon. He lured an answering smile out of Iatzoulinos, no small accomplishment. The bureaucrat even unbent far enough to tell him a joke. He was astonished; he had not realized Iatzoulinos knew any. He did not tell it well, but the effort deserved notice.

Dinner also seemed uncommonly enjoyable. The roast lamb really was lamb, not gamy mutton; the peas and pearl onions were cooked just right; enough snow had fallen for the taverner to offer ice and sweet syrup for dessert. And so, when Scaurus went back to his chamber a little past sunset, he felt it was the best day he'd had since coming to Videssos the city.

Darkness came quickly in late fall; the tribune was not ready to sleep. He lit several lamps, rummaged about till he found Gorgidas' history, and began to read. He wondered how the Greek and Viridovix were faring on the steppe. With a guilty start, he knew he had hardly thought about them since—his mind searched for a painless way to say it—since things went wrong.

He was trying to unravel an elaborate passage when the knock on the door came. For a moment, he did not notice it. Then it was only an unwelcome distraction, and he did his best to ignore it. He found Greek hard enough giving it his full attention.

"Must you always pretend you're not in? I can see the light under the door."

He sprang to his feet, rolled the book up as fast as he could. "Sorry, Nevrat, I didn't expect you and Senpat tonight." He hurried to the door and pulled it open. "Come in."

"I thank you." Nevrat stepped past him. "Always good to visit you; the pen-pushers heat their digs well." She undid the heavy wool scarf she was wearing in place of the bright silk one she preferred, let her fleecy coat fall open.

Marcus hardly noticed her making herself comfortable; he was still eyeing the empty corridor outside his room. "Where's Senpat?" he blurted.

"Singing—and drinking, I imagine—at the wine shop we've all been visiting. I chose not to go along."

"Ah," Scaurus said, more a polite noise than anything else. He hesitated, then asked, "Does he know you're here?"

"No."

The word seemed to hang in the air between them. Marcus started to shut the door, paused again. "Would you rather I left it open?"

"It's all right; close it." Nevrat sounded amused. She looked round the tribune's rather bare quarters. Her eye fell on the book he had so hastily set down. She opened it, frowned at the alien script—the Greek alphabet looked nothing like Videssian or her native Vaspurakaner. Helvis had reacted the same way, Marcus recalled; he bit his lip at the unbidden memory.

To cover the stab of hurt, he waved Nevrat to the room's only chair. "Wine?" he asked. At her nod, he pulled a bottle and cup from the top drawer of the pine chest next to his bed. He poured for her, then sat on the bed, leaning back against the wall.

She raised any eyebrow. "Aren't you having any? You said you'd gone moderate, not teetotal."

"Perish the thought!" he exclaimed. "But, you see, I have just the one cup."

Her laughter filled the little room. She drank, then sat forward to pass him the cup. "We must share, then."

His fingers brushed hers as he took it. "Thank you. I hadn't planned to do much entertaining here."

"So I see," she said. "Certainly it's not the lair a practiced seducer would have."

"As is only fitting, because I'm not." He filled the cup again, offered it to her.

She took it but did not drink at once, instead holding it and contemplating it with an expression so ironic that Scaurus found himself flushing. "I didn't mean it like that," he protested.

"I know you didn't." Nevrat raised the cup to her lips to prove it. She passed it to him, went on, "Marcus, I have cared for you as long as we've known each other."

"And I for you, very much," he nodded. "Aside from everything else, without you these past weeks would have been . . . well, even worse than they are. I owe you so much for that."

She waved that aside. "Don't speak foolishly. Senpat and I are happy to do whatever we can for you."

He frowned; she had not mentioned her husband since she sat down. But as they talked on, Senpat's name did not come up again, and the tribune found his hopes rising. He remembered the joke he had heard from Iatzoulinos. Judging by Nevrat's laughter, he told it better than the seal-stamper had.

"Oh, a fine story," she said. " 'What in Skotos' name was that?' " Repeating the punch line set her chuckling again. Her black eyes glowed; her grin was wide and happy. She was, Scaurus thought, one of those uncommon women whose features grew more beautiful with animation.

A lamp went out. The tribune got up. He took out a little bottle of oil, filled the lamp, and relit the wick with one of the others. He had to pass close by Nevrat to get back to his seat on the bed. As he did, he reached out to stroke her dark, curly hair. It was coarser under his fingers than he had imagined.

She rose, too, and turned to face him. He stepped forward to embrace her.

"Marcus," she said.

Had she spoken his name another way, he would have gone on to take her in his arms. As it was, she might have held up Medusa's head, to turn him to stone in his tracks. He searched her face, found regret and compassion there, but not eagerness to match his own.

"It's no good, is it?" he asked dully, already sure of the answer.

"No," she said. "I'm sorry, but it's not." She started to put a hand on his shoulder, then arrested the gesture. That was worse than her words.

"I should have known." He had to look away from her to continue. "But you were always so caring, so sympathetic, that I hoped—I thought—I let myself think . . ."

"Something more might be there," she finished for him.

He nodded, still avoiding her eyes.

"I saw that," she said. "I did not know what to do, but finally I decided we had to speak of it. Truly I do not want any man but Senpat."

"The two of you are very lucky," Marcus said. "I've thought so many times." Holding his voice steady was rather like fighting after taking a wound.

"I know we are," she said quietly. "And so I came tonight to say what I had to say—and instead we ended up chatting like the friends we've always been. That silly story of yours about the rich man who wanted to be an actor—" Thinking of it, she smiled again, but only for a moment. "I suppose I just thought I could let things go on as they had. But then—"

"Then I had to make a mess of it," he said bitterly.

"No!" For the first time, Nevrat sounded angry. "I don't blame you for it. How could I? After what happened to you, of course you hope to find again the happiness you once knew. But—I am as I am, and I cannot be the one to give it to you. I'm sorry, Marcus, and sorrier that now I've hurt you, too, when that is the last thing I ever wanted."

"It doesn't matter," Scaurus said. "I brought it on myself."

"It matters very much," Nevrat insisted. "Can we go on now as friends?" She must have sensed his thoughts, for she said quickly, "Think now, before you say no. How do we—either of us—explain to Senpat what went wrong?"

The tribune found himself promising to keep the friendship going. To his surprise, he also found himself meaning it. Not being an outgoing sort, he had too few friendships to throw any casually away. And whatever he wished was there with Nevrat, they did genuinely like and care for each other.

"Good," she said crisply. "Then we need not break our next meeting-day—three days from now, wasn't it?"

"Yes."

"I'll see you then. Truly, I will be glad to. Always believe that." Nevrat smiled—a little more cautiously than she would have before, Marcus judged, but not much—and stepped out into the hallway, closing the door behind her.

Her footsteps faded. Scaurus put the wine away. It was probably for the best, he told himself. Senpat was a good man as well as a close friend. He had no business trying to put cuckold's horns on him. Down deep, he knew that perfectly well.

He kicked the side of the cheap pine chest as hard as he could. It split. Pain shot up from his toe. He heard the jug of wine break. Swearing at fate, his damaged foot, and the wine, he used a rag to mop up the mess. By luck, the jar was almost empty, so only one tunic was ruined.

He gave a sour laugh as he blew out the lamps and crawled into bed.

He should have known better than to think he was having a good day. Since Helvis left, there were no good days for him.

He was still limping as he climbed the stairs to his office two days later. His right big toe was twice its proper size and had turned purple and yellow. The day before, one of the pen-pushers had asked what happened.

"I gave the wardrobe in my room a kick." He'd shrugged, leaving the bureaucrat to assume it was an accident. Sometimes literal truth made the best lie.

Seeing him abstracted, a middling-important scribe tried to sneak some fancy bookkeeping past him. He spotted it, picked up the offending ledger, and dropped it with a crash on the luckless seal-stamper's desk.

"You piker," he said contemptuously to the appalled bureaucrat. "Last winter, Pikridios Goudeles used that same trick to get himself an emerald ring with a stone big enough to choke on, and here you are, trying to steal a miserable two and a half goldpieces. You ought to be ashamed."

"What—what will you do with me, illustrious sir?" the pen-pusher quavered.

"For two and a half pieces of gold? If you need it so badly, keep it. But the next time I find even a copper out of place in your books, you'll see how you like the prison under the government offices on Middle Street. That goes for all of you, too," Marcus added for the benefit of the rest of the bureaucrats, who had been listening and watching intently without seeming to.

"Thank you, oh, thank you, merciful and gracious sir," the would-be embezzler said over and over. Marcus nodded curtly and started back to his own desk.

He remembered something as he passed Iatzoulinos. "Have you arranged to send the Romans at Garsavra their pay?" he asked.

"I would, ah, have to check my records to be certain of that," Iatzoulinos answered warily. No, Scaurus translated without effort.

He sighed. "Iatzoulinos, I've been patient with you. If you make

Gaius Philippus angry, I don't think he will be. I know this man; you don't. Take it as a warning from one who means you well."

"I shall, of course, attend to it at once," Iatzoulinos said.

"See that you do." The tribune folded his arms and waited. When Iatzoulinos realized he was not going to leave, the pen-pusher set aside the project he had been working on and picked up the ledger that dealt with military expenditures in the westlands. He inked a pen and, with poor grace, began drafting a payment authorization. Satisfied for the moment, Marcus moved on.

He jumped as a hailstone rattled off the window. His sore foot made him regret it. Winter would be here in earnest soon, he thought; the storm that blew in yesterday had already covered the lawns of the palace complex with a snowy blanket. The tribune hoped the weather would stay bad awhile. Despite his promises to Nevrat, he was not ready to face her and Senpat together quite so soon as tomorrow. Maybe the snow would force them to put things off.

His office and his room were both pleasantly warm. He was glad the bureaucrats heated their wing of the Grand Courtrooms so lavishly. Then he thought of his friends on the steppe and was even gladder.

XIV

THE WIND HOWLED AND MOANED LIKE A DEEP-VOICED HOUND GONE mad, driving snow into Batbaian's face and frosting Viridovix' ruddy mustaches. A thick, short beard hid his cheeks and chin; he had not shaved in weeks and did not know when he would have the chance again. He swore when a gust sneaked under his heavy fur greatcoat and chilled his back. The coat did not fit him very well. It had been made for one of Varatesh's riders, but the fellow had no use for it now.

The Gaul gave a gusty sigh. His breath puffed out white. He sighed again, remembering the felt tent and how breathing smoke had bemused him. His face hardened. Targitaus' tent was smoke now, and the tents of all his clan, and the clansmen with them.

Timing pitilessly exact, Varatesh had given the Wolves three days to thrash with caring for nearly a thousand blinded men who could do nothing to help themselves—and with the torment their coming brought. Then he struck, and shattered the clan.

Viridovix and Batbaian were herding an outlying flock of sheep when the blow fell, or they would have perished with the rest. As it was, when evening came they rode into camp and found massacre waiting for them. In his way, Varatesh was a gifted leader, to instill order into his cutthroats: they had descended on their foes, killed, raped, looted, and gone, probably all in two hours' time.

Gaul and nomad rode together through silence so thick it echoed; even the yapping little dogs that had run scavenging from tent to tent were slain. For Viridovix, shock piled on shock left an eerie calm; Batbaian's face was twisted in agony too deep for words. Every so often one of them would nod to the other when he came across the body of someone he cared for. There was dour Rambehisht, with three dead outlaws around him and an arrow in his back. If he had planned vengeance on

Viridovix, he would never have it now. And Lipoxais, yellow *enaree*'s robe soaked with blood. And Azarmi the serving wench, her skirt on the ground beside her. She still wore a blood-soaked blouse; the outlaws had not bothered tearing it off before their sport, only stabbed through it when they were done.

Filled with the same dreadful surmise, Batbaian and Viridovix leaped from their horses and ran for what had been Targitaus' tent. It leaned drunkenly to one side, half its framework broken. And inside their worst fears were realized. Borane's dead fist clutched a dagger. The blade was stained—she had fought before she died. But she was fat and getting old; Varatesh's men had merely slaughtered her. By all the signs, Seirem had not been so lucky.

Viridovix cursed himself for memory; the anguish flared in him, red and agonizing as when he had first seen Seirem's corpse. He wished for the thousandth time that he had never known his few short weeks of love, or that he had died with the one who gave it to him.

"And what's a wish worth?" he said to himself. "Damn all anyway." A bitter tear ran down his cheek.

Batbaian turned at the sound of his voice. "That does no good," he said stonily. "It will only freeze to your skin." The dead khagan's son was no more the near-boy he had been till summer; he seemed to have aged ten years in as many weeks. His face was thinner, with lines of suffering carved into his forehead and at the corners of his mouth.

He had been the one who suggested firing the camp. "It will warn off any other herders who might still be alive," he had said, "and might lure Varatesh's riders back." A cold, hungry light kindled in his eye then, and he patted his bow-case. He and Viridovix found an ambush point; it would not do to give their lives away without as rich a revenge as they could take.

But the renegades had not returned, no doubt thinking the smoke came from an overturned lamp or smoldering torch that had set the encampment ablaze. When it was clear they would not, Batbaian took the patch from his ruined eye and threw it to the ground. "When I kill them, let them know what I am," he said.

His score stood at four now, one ahead of the Gaul's.

They lived as outlaws, one of the many reversals since the war against

Varatesh went so disastrously awry. Now the bandit chief and his brigands lorded it over the steppe and hunted its one-time leaders like vermin. But as Varatesh himself had shown, running them to earth was no easy task. A goat here, a sentry there, two horses stolen somewhere else—the blowing winter snow covered tracks. It was the hardest life Viridovix had ever known, but it could be lived.

Hands clumsy inside thick gloves, they fought their tent into place as evening fell. Despite the windbreak of snow they piled in front of it, the raw north wind still found its way through the felt. They huddled in blankets next to the bonfire, roasting chunks of mutton over it. No problem keeping meat fresh in winter, Viridovix thought—the trick was thawing it again.

He rubbed grease from his chin and licked his fingers clean. Let the Romans try to live in this cold with their journeybread and porridges, he thought. Red meat was all that kept up a man's strength here.

Instead of wiping it away, Batbaian smeared the mutton fat over his cheeks, nose, and forehead. "Helps against frostbite," he said. He spoke seldom, these days, and always to the point.

"Next time, lad," Viridovix nodded. He drew his sword, examined it for rust. In the cold and constant wet it spread all too easily. He scoured away a tiny fleck of red, rust or dried blood. "Wouldna hurt to rub the blade wi' fat, either."

A wolf howled in the distance, a bay chill as the night. One of the horses snorted nervously.

"North again come morning?" Viridovix said.

"Oh yes." Batbaian's lips opened in a humorless smile. "Where better than down their throats? Richer pickings, too—more flocks. More men." His one eye gleamed in the sputtering firelight. The other socket was a ghastly shadow.

The Gaul nodded again, but through a smothering sense of futility. Not even killing could bring back what he had lost. "Is it any use at all, at all?" he cried. "We skulk about pretending it's some good we're about, slaying the spalpeens by ones and twos, but I swear by gods it's nobbut a sop to our prides. It no more hurts 'em than the grain a pair o' wee mice steal'll make the farmers starve."

"So what will you do? Fold up and die?" A nomad's harsh contempt rode Batbaian's voice for the comparison and for the despair as well. "We're not the only men in Pardraya who'd tie Varatesh in a rope of his own guts."

"Are we not, though? Too near it, I'm thinking. Them as'd try it did, and see what we got for it. And as for the rest, there's no more will in 'em than your sheep; they'll follow whoever leads 'em. Precious few have the ballocks to go after a winner."

"Leave if you like, then. I'll go on alone," Batbaian said. "At least I'll die as a man, doing as I should. And I say again, even without you I won't be alone forever. Pardraya is a wide land."

"Not wide enough," Viridovix came back, stung by the plainsman's dismissal and wanting to wound him in return. Then he hesitated. "Not wide enough," he repeated softly. His eyes went wide. "Tell me at once, Khamorth dear, would you ride away from Varatesh the now—och, and from Avshar, too—for a greater vengeance later, and mayhap one you might live through in the bargain?"

Batbaian's glare seized him, as if to drag his meaning out by force of will. "What does dying soon or late mean to me? But make me believe in a greater vengeance, and I will follow you off the edge of Pardraya."

"Good, for you'll need to," the Celt replied.

"A pox!" Gorgidas said, clutching too late at the top of his head. The freezing wind tore his otter-fur cap free and sent it spinning over the snowy ground. He ran cursing after it, his naked ears tingling in the cold.

The nearby Arshaum laughed and shouted bad advice. "Kill it!" "Shoot it!" "Quick, it's getting away! Stab it with that thrusting-sword of yours!"

Recapturing the flyaway headgear, the Greek whacked it against his trousers to get the snow off—and to work off his own annoyance. Then he jammed it back in place, and swore again as a last, freezing clump came loose and horrified the back of his neck.

Skylitzes' mouth was twitching; Goudeles did not try to hide a grin. "Now you see why all plainsmen, east or west of the Shaum, swear by wind spirits," he said.

He meant it as a joke, but it brought Gorgidas up short. "Why, so they do," he said. "I hadn't noticed that." He reached for the tablet on his belt—it hung at his right hip, where most men would carry a dagger. He scrawled a note, writing quickly but carefully. When he set stylus to wax in this weather, great chunks wanted to come away from the wood.

"That's nothing," Arigh said when he complained. "One winter a long time ago, a man went out riding without remounts and his horse broke a leg. He tried to yell for help, but it was so cold no one heard him till his shout thawed out next spring. That was a few months too late to do him any good, I fear."

Arigh told the story with so perfect a dead-pan air that Gorgidas wrote it down, though he added pointedly, "I have heard this, but I do not believe it." If that sort of disclaimer was enough to let Herodotos sneak a good yarn into his history when he found one, it should be good enough for him, too.

Arghun hobbled out of his tent, leaning on Dizabul. Arigh sent his brother a glance that was still full of mistrust. The khagan's elder son shouted for quiet, a shout the officers of the Gray Horse clan took up. The riders gathered round their chief. The rest of the Arshaum, attracted by the motion, also drew near, so that Arghun soon commanded the whole army's attention.

An attendant led the khagan's horse through the crowd. "See if you two can work with each other for once," Arghun said to his sons. Dizabul scowled; Arigh nodded, though his lips pursed. Together they helped their father into the saddle.

Arghun's hands curled lovingly on the reins he had not held for so long. But his legs were still all but useless. Arigh had to place his booted feet in the stirrups and then lash them there so they would not slip out. Even so, pride glowed on the khagan's face. A great cheer rang from the nomads to see him mounted once more; to them a man who could not ride was only half alive.

"Fetch the standard," Arghun said to the attendant, who hurried back with the spear that carried Bogoraz' long coat. Arghun held it high over his head so even the most distant rider could see it. "To Mashiz!" he cried.

The Arshaum host was silent for a moment, then echoed the cry, brandishing their swords, bows, and javelins. "Ma-shiz! Ma-shiz!

Ma-shiz!" The noise dinned in Gorgidas' ears. Still roaring the war call, the plainsmen dashed to their horses, leaving a great trampled place in the snow to show where they had stood.

Almost as at home on horseback as an Arshaum, Skylitzes was grinning as he mounted. "I can hardly care whether this comes off or not," he called to Goudeles. "Either way we make Wulghash sweat to hold against us."

"No one could sweat in this weather," the pen-pusher said firmly, scrambling onto his own beast. "And it had best work, or my mistress will be most disappointed."

"Your mistress? What of your wife?"

"She inherits."

"Ah." Skylitzes started to say something more, but a fresh round of cheers from the nomads drowned him out. Still carrying the standard, Arghun rode east, his back straight in the high-cantled saddle, only the firm set of his mouth showing the strain he felt. As usual, his two sons flanked him; perhaps, thought Gorgidas, each was afraid to let the other have their father to himself for long. Singly and by bands, the Arshaum streamed after them.

Goudeles wanted to show the Videssian presence by riding in the van beside the khagan, but Skylitzes vetoed that. "Why wear out our horses breaking trail?" he asked with a veteran's experience. "You wait a bit, and he'll drop back to us." He soon proved right; for all Arghun's will, he could not set the pace for long.

The khagan threw questions at Skylitzes about the land east of the Shaum and especially about the mountains of Erzerum, which stretched between the Mylasa Sea and the Videssian Sea and separated Yezd from the Pardrayan steppe. The discussion on the ways and means of mountain warfare quickly bored Gorgidas. Despite Arghun's disappointed look, the Greek went searching for Tolui to talk about plant lore, something nearer his own heart.

"One of the ground roots you gave me smells like—" Gorgidas stopped, annoyed, not knowing the name in the Arshaum speech. "Orange, about so long, fatter than my thumb."

"Carrot," the shaman supplied.

"Yes, thanks. All my people do with it is eat it. What do you use it for?"

"We mix it with nightshade and wild rue in honey. It cures—" Tolui used another word Gorgidas did not know. The shaman grinned and made an unmistakable gesture.

"I understand: hemorrhoids." In a folk as much in the saddle as the Arshaum, the Greek could see how piles would be a common problem. He asked, "Is it given by mouth, or put directly where, ah, it will do the most good?"

"By mouth. For the other, we make an ointment of goose or partridge fat, egg white, fennel, and oil of wild roses, then smear it on. It soothes well."

Gorgidas dipped his head in agreement. "It should. You might also try mixing honey with that, I think. Honey is good for relieving inflammations generally."

That sort of conversation pleased the Greek much more than arguments over the best way to sniff out an ambush in a pass. After a while he guiltily remembered that he had come to the plains as historian, not physician. He asked Tolui, "Why do your people and the Khamorth differ so much from each other in your looks and in the build of your bodies?"

Tolui frowned. "Why should we be the same as the Hairies?" His voice carried as much disdain as a Greek's would, talking about barbarians.

"I'm looking to learn, not to offend you," Gorgidas said hastily. "To a foreigner like me, you and they seem to live on similar land under much the same kind of weather. So I wondered why the two folk are not the same as well." They should have been, if the doctrine Hippokrates put forward in *Airs, Waters, Places* was correct, as the Greek had always believed.

Tolui, though, operated with an entirely different set of assumptions. Mollified by Gorgidas' explanation, he said, "I will tell you. We Arshaum were the first race of men. The only reason there are Khamorth is that one of our men, many lives ago, was without a woman too long and futtered a goat. The Khamorth were the get of that union; that is why they are so disgustingly shaggy."

"I see." Gorgidas suddenly regretted his whiskers. He wrote Tolui's fable down; it was an interesting bit of lore, if nothing else. And Hippokrates was not doing so well here; he wrote that steppe nomads were stocky or plump, hairless, and of a ruddy complexion. The Khamorth met only the first criterion, the Arshaum the second, and neither people the third.

The Greek rubbed his earlobe between thumb and forefinger. "Tell me more about this goat."

Viridovix peered down into the valley of the Shaum through swirling snow. "Well, where's the other side o' the fool stream, now?" he said indignantly, as if Batbaian had hidden it on purpose.

"Oh, it's there," the Khamorth said. "All we have to do is get to it—and then persuade the devils across the river not to kill us on sight." He spoke with morbid anticipation; Viridovix' notion of begging help from the Arshaum had horrified him, fey though he was. Next to them, Avshar was a new terror; tales of the Arshaum frightened naughty children into behaving.

The Gaul pretended not to notice his gloom. "One thing at a time. Once we're after crossing the river, then we think on the folk as live there." He did not give Batbaian a chance to argue, but clucked to his horse and trotted toward the Shaum. Shaking his head, Batbaian followed.

Had Viridovix been a more experienced horseman, he would have known better than to set a fast pace downhill through snowdrifts that hid the ground below. His pony whinnied in terror as a forefoot came down in some unseen hole. It stumbled and fell, throwing the Gaul. He was lucky; he had the wind knocked out of him as he hit the ground, but the thick blanket of snow cushioned him from worse damage.

But he had heard the horse's legbone snap. As he was struggling to his feet, Batbaian dismounted and put the animal out of its pain. Blood steamed in the snow. Batbaian turned to the Gaul. "Help me butcher it," he said. "We'll take as much as we can carry." Viridovix pulled out his dagger. He did not care for the thick, gluey taste of horse, but it was better than an empty belly.

When the gory task was done, Batbaian said only, "We'll take turns on the beast that's left. It'll make a path for the man on foot." He did not waste time railing at the Gaul; Viridovix knew what his carelessness had cost them. They would be at walking pace from here on, and their one remaining animal, the Celt thought, would have to carry their gear all the time.

Once they reached the riverbank, though, Viridovix wondered if they would go any farther at all. The Shaum did not flow swiftly; it iced over in winter. But it was so wide that a stretch of a couple of hundred yards still ran free in the center of the stream, with pieces of ice crashing against each other in the current as they bobbed their way south.

The Gaul shivered, looking out toward the frigid black water. "I wouldna try to swim it," he said to Batbaian. "Three strokes and you'd be another icicle."

"Look there, though," the plainsman said, pointing downstream. A broad cake of drift ice had run against the farther edge of the ice, and a couple of smaller ones against it. Water splashed over them, but they made a bridge of sorts.

"We'd not get the pony across that," Viridovix protested.

"No, but then we wouldn't anyhow. He'd crash through where a man can crawl on his belly and spread his weight on the ice. Are you still set on this mad scheme of yours?"

"I am that."

"Well, then." Batbaian slid down from the saddle, went up to touch his horse's nose. Before Viridovix knew what he was doing, he slit the beast's throat. It gave a reproachful, dreadfully human cough as its legs buckled and it went down.

"Are you witstruck?" the Gaul cried.

"No. Think through it," Batbaian said, sounding like a Roman. "If he can't cross with us, he's more use dead than alive. Don't stand there gaping—give me a hand getting the hide off." His knife was already busy; Viridovix helped mechanically, wondering if the nomad really had lost his wits.

Batbaian had not. After another rough job of worrying chunks from the horse's flank and hock, he used the hides as a sack to hold the meat, their knocked-down tent, and his pack. "Give me yours, too," he told the

Celt, who undid it from his back. Batbaian lashed the hide closed, hefted it. "Weighs less than a man," he said, satisfied. He added another length of rope. "You see? We'll haul it behind us, far enough away so it won't put extra strain on the ice."

"And aren't you the cleverest little chappie, now?" Viridovix said admiringly. In his Gallic forests he might have done as good a job of improvising, but here on the plains it took the Khamorth to see what to do with what they had.

Batbaian shrugged the praise away; it meant nothing to him. He dragged the hide downstream along the bank until he was even with the ice jam in the Shaum. Viridovix followed. At the very edge of the river the Khamorth handed him the rope. "You take this. I'll go first and scrape the snow away so we can tell how the ice is."

"And why not me for that?" the Gaul said, wanting to do something, at least, of importance.

But Batbaian replied, "Because I'm lighter," which was unanswerable. He stepped onto the ice. It held his weight, but he walked slowly and very carefully, planting each foot before he raised the other. "Wouldn't do to slip," he said with forced lightness.

"You're right there," Viridovix said. He moved as cautiously as the Khamorth.

From behind them came an excited baying and yapping, then snarls as a band of wolves fell on the Gaul's dead horse. He looked back, but they were lost in the blowing snow. He heard bones crunch. "Might you step it up a bit, Batbaian dear?"

"No." The plainsman did not turn his head. "Going through the ice is the bigger risk. They won't be after us, not with two horses to keep them happy."

"Sure and I hope you're right. If I'm eaten I'll not forgive it." The Celt made sure his blade was loose in its scabbard. The idea of facing wolves on the treacherous ice chilled him worse than the biting north wind.

He scowled when one of the beasts, driven away from the first carcass, found the second one. More came running to gorge themselves; the noise of their feasting seemed almost at his elbow. Now he could see them, back by the riverbank. He cursed and half drew his blade when one of them trotted onto the frozen river, but its feet flew out from under it, and it sprawled on its belly. With a startled yip, it fled back to land. "Ha! You like it no better here than I," Viridovix said.

"Shut up," said Batbaian. "This is getting tricky." They were almost to midstream. The Khamorth picked his way with even greater care now, for there were patches where the Shaum's water showed dark through the ice. He skirted them as long as he could, staying with the ice that was thick enough still to be white. At last, he sighed, defeated. "No help for it now," he said, and went down on his belly to wriggle forward.

Viridovix' thick coat kept the worst of the cold from him, but his knees burned to the ice's kiss. Memory floated into him, of sliding on a frozen pond in Gaul one winter when he was very small, of the squeals of glee from the other children and the sight of bare-branched trees all around. No trees here, not for miles. He squirmed faster to catch up with Batbaian.

They were side by side when they came to the edge of the ice pack. Seen close up, the tumbled slabs of ice ahead were far less promising as a way across than they had looked from the bank. Batbaian waved the Celt to a halt while he considered. "As fast as we can," he decided. "I don't know how long this first one will hold us."

"But what if we break it free?"

The Khamorth shrugged. "Then we have a raft. Maybe we can steer it to the far side."

"Honh!" Viridovix said, but Batbaian was already gathering himself for the rush. He scrambled from the pack onto the chunk of ice ahead. It groaned under his weight. With a final, frantic slither, he rolled onto the next slab.

As soon as the plainsman was off the first piece of ice, Viridovix clambered onto it, the horsehide sack bumping after him. It rocked alarmingly. The sudden, queasy motion reminded the Gaul of a pitching boat. "None o' that now," he said to himself, wrestling with his weak stomach. Freezing water soaked his trousers. He yelped and tried to move faster.

The thin ice crackled beneath him; a network of cracks appeared, spreading fast. "Hurry!" Batbaian yelled. With a last desperate lunge, the Celt tumbled onto the next block, hauled their gear after him. Widening lines of inky-black water showed as the last chunk of ice shifted and started to break up.

Batbaian gave a sarcastic dip of his head. "I hope you didn't forget anything back there."

"Only my anvil." Viridovix managed a winded grin; the Khamorth bared his teeth in what might have been a smile. He inched ahead. This chunk of ice was thicker than the last one, but more precariously placed. It teetered and swayed as the two men crawled across it. Batbaian grunted in relief as he swarmed onto the last frozen cake. He helped pull Viridovix up after him. "My thanks," the Gaul said. "One of my hands is fair frozen."

"If the tinder isn't soaked, we'll have a fire as soon as we get to the other side," Batbaian promised. For the first time he sounded as if he thought they would make it.

There was one dreadful moment when Viridovix thrust his left arm through the ice into the frigid Shaum up to the elbow. He waited for the pack to split and drop him into the river, but it held; the weak spot proved no bigger than a man's head. He wriggled his arm out of his sleeve and pressed it against his body to try to put some tiny warmth back in it.

Then Batbaian was shouting ahead of him—there was sand and dirt under the snow, not ice. Viridovix lurched onto the land and lay gasping like a fish cast up by the stream. The Khamorth fought the horsehide sack; it had frozen nearly hard. He used the lead pommel of his dagger to hammer tent pegs an inch or two into the iron-hard ground. Viridovix gave what one-handed help he could in spreading the felt fabric of the tent over its framework of sticks. They scrambled into it together, groaning with relief to be out of the ceaseless, piercing wind.

Clumsy in his thick mittens but careful all the same, Batbaian opened the bone box that held bark and dry leaves. He looked inside. "Ah," he said. He rummaged in his kit for flint and steel. He pushed the snow to one side, found a few flat stones so he would not have to set the tinder on damp ground. After several tries he got a small fire going. He scraped fat from the inside of the roughly butchered horsehide, cut more strips from the hunks of horsemeat. The fat ran as it melted and stank foully, but it burned. "What I wouldn't give for a few handfuls of dry horsedung," Batbaian said.

Viridovix huddled close to the fire. He held his left arm over it, trying to chafe back feeling. "Hack off a couple of gobbets there and set 'em up to roast," he said through chattering teeth. "E'en horsemeat'll be good in my belly. And if you're keen to be dreaming of turds, why go ahead, and may you ha' joy of 'em. As of me, I'll think on mulled wine, and thank you just the same."

On the eastern bank of the Shaum, a wolf lifted its head in suspicion. A low growl rumbled deep in its throat; the hair stood up on its shoulders and ridged along its back. The oncoming rider did not falter. The growl turned to whine. The wolf slunk out of the horseman's path; the pack scattered before him as he trotted down to the very edge of the frozen stream.

He dismounted. His white robes, swirling in the wind, might almost have been blowing snow themselves. Hands on hips, he stared across the river. Even he could not see the tent on the far shore, but he knew it was there. This once his great size and the weight of mail on his shoulders worked against him; for one of his bulk, there was no crossing the Shaum. He felt of the ice in his mind and knew it would not hold him.

He cursed, first in the guttural Khamorth speech, then in archaic Videssian, slow and full of hate. "Winter, then, shall my work complete," he said in the same language. "Skotos will aid his servant thus, I trow." He swung himself back into the saddle, wheeled his horse, and rode east.

The wolves were a long time returning.

Tied together so they would not lose each other in the storm, Batbaian and Viridovix slogged west. Shaumkhiil was as featureless as the Pardrayan plain, but there was no danger of wandering in circles. As long as they kept the wind blowing against their right sides, they knew they could not be far wrong.

They had yet to see an Arshaum, which left Viridovix angry and frustrated and Batbaian, as far as the Gaul could tell, secretly relieved; down deep he still seemed to believe they were ten feet tall and armed with fangs.

Maybe the Arshaum ate sheep at a gulp and spat out the bones, but eat sheep they did. The Gaul and Khamorth came on a dozen or so that must have strayed from their main herd. Viridovix ate mutton until he missed the horsemeat he had had to make himself choke down. Batbaian, a skillful jackleg tailor, sewed scraped sheepskins together into cloaks the two wanderers wore over their greatcoats.

They needed the extra layer of warmth; the weather was the worst Batbaian had seen. To Viridovix it was appalling beyond belief: snow, ice, ravening wind, endless days without glimpse of sun or stars through thick black clouds. The storms on the Videssian plateau had been bitter, but they were storms, each with beginning and end. This went on and on, as if summer left the world for good.

"It's dogging us, I'm thinking," Viridovix shouted through the screaming gale.

"What's that?" Batbaian yelled back. He was only a yard in front of the Celt, but the wind flung words away.

"I say the blizzard's after dogging us, to pounce when it's worn us down." Viridovix had meant it as a figure of speech, but suddenly wondered if it were not truth. Batbaian turned round and mouthed a name. The Gaul could not hear it, but he knew what it was. His shudder, for once, had nothing to do with cold. He thought again about throwing away his sword, this time more seriously than he had before.

The storm blew harder, as though it acknowledged Avshar as its parent. The wind hurled stinging snow into Viridovix' eyes. He shielded them with his hands as best he could, stumbling ahead all but blind. The icy blast fought his every forward step; it was like trying to walk through ocean waves.

A savage gust stopped him and Batbaian in their tracks. "The tent!" the plainsman shouted. "This will kill us if we stay in it!" Viridovix cursed as he tried to drive the pegs; the ground had frozen so hard it did not want to take them. Somehow he and Batbaian forced the felt over its framework. Like animals darting into a nest, they scrambled for shelter.

The raging wind seemed to scream louder once they were out of it. Viridovix rubbed at his legs, stamped his feet; his boots were thick and lined with several layers of felt, but his toes turned to ice each day regardless. "Sure and I understand the now why you were mooning over horseapples back there," he said. "A sheepshit fire's better than none."

"This is the last of it, worse luck," Batbaian said. Fat caught more easily, but once alight the uncured dung burned longer and, to the Celt's surprise, cleaner than the drippings the Khamorth always caught from his meat. Viridovix had hesitated almost a day over eating anything cooked on a dung fire, but hunger broke down his qualms.

He sighed in relief as the fire began to give off a little warmth. The snow and ice clinging to his mustaches started melting; he wiped his face on his cloak. The wool was rank and greasy, but he did not mind. "Mutton again," he grumbled.

"We're almost to the end of that, too," Batbaian said. "You'll like it better than empty, I'd bet."

"Truth that." Viridovix skewered a hunk on his dagger, held it over the flames. His belly rumbled at the smell. "Sure and my insides think so."

A poorly planted tent peg tore out of its hole. The wind smacked it against the side of the tent like a flung stone. Batbaian's head came up in alarm. "We've got to set that again," he exclaimed, "before—" The second peg came loose as he was scrambling to his feet. The gale roared in under the bottom of the tent, lifted the felt free of its framework. Viridovix clutched it for a moment. Then, with what sounded like mocking laughter, the storm ripped it from his hands and sent it flapping away over the steppe.

"After it!" Batbaian screamed. "We won't last a day without it!" He flung the last words over his shoulder as he vanished into the blowing snow.

Viridovix plunged after him. He had not gone twenty paces when he knew he was in trouble. Ahead, Batbaian might have been snatched from the face of the earth. The fire was lost behind him. He cried the Khamorth's name again and again, howled out Gallic war cries. If there was any answer, the wind blew it away.

Still shouting, he ran with the wind at his back for a while. In the blizzard, Batbaian could have been almost at his elbow, and would not have known it. He stopped, irresolute. If Batbaian had caught the runaway tent fabric, what would he do with it? Stay and wait for Viridovix or try to bring it back to what was left of the frame? "Och, a murrain take it," the Celt muttered. "Whichever way I guess'll turn out wrong."

He dug in his pouch and found the square Haloga coin he had won. He tossed it in the air, caught it with both hands. When he uncovered it, a dragon leered at him. "To the tent, then." He turned to face the bitter wind. It stung like fire against his face; he was glad of his new beard, and wished it were heavier.

He tried to follow his own footprints back, but the storm was already blowing snow over them. They grew fainter as he watched. He thought he was getting close when they finally gave out altogether. He fought panic. There had to be some way—the wind! If it had held steady, he could use it to steer his way back.

It must have shifted. After a while he knew he had gone too far. He cast about blindly then, hoping luck would serve where wit had failed. It did not. He stood shivering, pounding his hands together and wondering what to do next. No food, no fire, no shelter—he could feel the heat draining from his body and knew Batbaian had been right; the storm could kill quickly.

"If only the cursed snow'd stop so a body could use the eyes of him," he said, shaking his head like a baffled bear. It seemed ready to snow forever, though, thick gusts of white powder blowing by almost horizontally.

Realizing he had to shield himself from the ravening gale, he knelt and began pushing up a heap of snow as a windbreak. The storm swept it away about as fast as he piled it up, but at last he had a waist-high wall that blocked the worst of the wind. He crouched behind it, knowing his makeshift would do no good if the storm did not blow itself out soon.

The numbness came insidiously; he hardly noticed when he could no longer feel his nose, his feet, his forearms. In a way it was a relief, for they did not hurt any more. His mind grew numb, too, slipping into a frigid lassitude in which he knew he was dying but lacked the will to care. He had always thought he would fight death to the end, but the irresistible cold stripped his defenses one by one and left him nothing to strike back at. He did not notice closing his eyes; what was there to see, in any case?

He slept.

"Bloody ghastly," Goudeles shouted over the shrieking wind.

"What are you complaining about, Pikridios?" Skylitzes said beside him. "With your blubber you're likely warmer than any of us." The officer rode hunched over the right side of his pony's neck to gain a little protection from the blizzard.

The brute power of the plains winter chilled Gorgidas' heart as much as it did his body. A child of the sunny Mediterranean, he was ill-equipped to face miles of snow and ice; they daunted him worse than sudden death on the battlefield. No wonder the Videssians gave Skotos a frozen lair, he thought.

He turned to Arghun, asking, "Is it always so fierce?"

The khagan's face, like his own, was smeared so thick with grease that it glistened even in this murky light. "I have seen storms as bad as this, a few," he answered, "but never one that lasted so long. And it grows worse as we ride east, which is strange. Usually the fouler weather stays to the west." A gust kicked snow into his face. He coughed and bundled his robe of long-haired goatskin tighter around him. Since his poisoning he felt the cold more than his followers, and the Greek could only guess the hardship he was enduring. No complaint passed his lips, though, nor a suggestion that the Arshaum army slow its advance.

A pair of scouts came riding back through the nomads toward the khagan, one a few yards ahead of the other. The leader bobbed his head in salute, spoke with faint distaste: "We found a Hairy, sir, freezing in the snow, and some other foreigner with him."

Arghun's brows shot up. "A Khamorth? On our side of the river?"

"Outlaw?" Skylitzes rapped.

"That or a madman, or maybe both. No horse, and he's lost an eye sometime not long ago—not pretty. Just an idiot Khamorth, rolled in felt."

"Oh, a pox on him," the second scout burst out as he came abreast of his companion. He was younger than the other man, with lively, humorous eyes. "Tell them about the fire-demon."

The first picket made a rude noise. "You and your fire-demons. If he is one, this storm's put him out for good. Even money he's frozen dead by now—he didn't look to be far from it, and I shouldn't wonder, either, lying in the snow in only his coat."

"Well, I still say he's no natural breed of man," the younger Arshaum insisted. "Or will you tell me you've seen his like before, with hair and whiskers and great long mustache the color of polished bronze?"

Gorgidas, Skylitzes, and Goudeles shouted together. The scout started; Arghun's horse shied at the outcry. "Our this friend is," Gorgidas said to the khagan, losing grammar in his excitement.

Skylitzes nodded. "That could only be one man."

Gorgidas swung round on the scouts. "You left him there to freeze, you idiots?"

"And up your arse, too," the leader of the two retorted. "What do we want with foreigners on Arshaum land?" That included the Greek, his glare said.

But Arghun roared, "Hold your tongue, you! These foreigners here are our allies, and this one saved my life. If their friend dies in the snow, you'll wish you had, too." The khagan's temper was usually mild; the plainsmen quailed at his outburst.

"Take me to him," Gorgidas said. The outriders obeyed without a word. "Gallop, damn you!" the Greek shouted. The three spurred their horses forward, snow flying. Goudeles and Skylitzes in their wake, they pounded through and then past the Arshaum army.

Gorgidas wondered how the nomads knew just where to ride in this howling white wilderness. Steering by the wind, no doubt, and by landmarks they recognized but which meant nothing to his untrained eyes. His own eyes stung and watered from the headlong pace, and his nose, despite the coating of fat that covered it, felt like an icicle in the center of his face. These flat-featured nomads were better suited than he to life in a steppe winter.

"There," the younger scout said, pointing ahead through the swirling snow. The Greek spied the ponies first, then the dismounted Arshaum beside them—no, he saw as he drew near, one of the squatting figures had to be a Khamorth, from its heavy beard. He dismissed the man from Pardraya from his thoughts. If the fellow was well enough to move around like that, he was not going to freeze in the next few minutes.

"Out of my way!" Gorgidas shouted, leaping down from his horse. The three Arshaum huddled round the shape in the snow jumped to their feet, reaching for swords. The scouts who had fetched the Greek were shouting, too, explaining to their comrades who he was.

He paid them no attention, bending down over Viridovix' prone form. When he pulled him over onto his back, he thought the Celt was dead. His flesh was pale and cold; his head rolled limply on his neck. He did not seem to be breathing.

The Greek cradled Viridovix' face in his hands. Just so had he held Quintus Glabrio when an arrow killed his lover, helpless for all his skill. And now another one dear to him—true, in a different and lesser way—he could not save. Futile rage and frustration tore at him; would he never be of any use?

Then he jumped—was that a pulse in the Gaul's throat? It came again, so slow and faint he hardly dared believe he felt it.

Afterwards, he never remembered thinking what to do next. His dogged rationality had been Nepos' despair when the priest-mage tried to teach him the Videssian healing art. "Never mind how or why," Nepos had shouted once. "Know that you must—and you will." But for the Greek that was worse than no explanation, and he never did succeed.

His lover's wound could have been the trigger to free him from the grip of reasoned thought and let the healing gift burst forth, but Glabrio had died before he hit the ground. Not even the Videssian art could raise the dead. And so Gorgidas had turned his back on it in his anguish over the failure—for good, he thought.

Now, though, desperation lifted him outside himself, stripped away everything but the need to save his friend. Seeing him suddenly stiffen above Viridovix, Goudeles pushed aside an Arshaum who was about to take him by the shoulder. The nomad spun round in anger. "Shaman," the bureaucrat said, pointing to the Greek. "Let him be." The Arshaum's slanted eyes went wide. He nodded and stepped back.

Gorgidas, staring down at the Celt's white face, never noticed the byplay. He felt his will gather into a single hard point, like the sun's rays focused by a burning glass. This was where he had always fallen short, trying to force that focused will outward. But it leaped forward before he consciously tried to project it.

A conduit, a channel—he sensed Viridovix' failing body as if it were his own; sensed the ravages of cold and exposure that froze fingers and cheeks, reached deep into entrails; sensed the chilled blood in its thick, sluggish motion through the Gaul's veins.

In that first dizzying rush of perception the Greek was almost swept away, almost lost himself in the Celt's distress. But his stubborn reason would not let him be submerged; he *knew* who he truly was, no matter what sense impressions his mind was receiving. And the conduit ran both ways—in the same instant he felt Viridovix flood in on him, he was also reaching out to reverse, repair, revive.

Quicken the heart; send warmth surging into belly, streaming into arms and legs. Strengthen lungs, and speed them, too—they had barely been sipping the frigid air. More delicate work: feel the damage of frost in fingers, toes, cheeks, ears, eyelids—melt it gently, gradually, let the new flow of blood work with his power. The poor makeshift words for what he did came later. In the crisis they meant nothing. The healing went on at a level far below words.

The Celt stirred under his hands like a restless sleeper, muttered some drowsy protest in his own musical speech. His eyes, green as the Gallic forests, came open, and there was intelligence in them. Then Gorgidas truly realized what he had accomplished. Joy leaped in him, joy and as crushing a weariness as he had ever known: the price of the healer's art.

Viridovix had not thought he would wake again, surely not with this new hot tide of strength flowing through him. As he stretched and—oh, miracle!—felt all his limbs answer him, he thought for a moment he had passed to the afterworld; he could not imagine feeling so well in this one. The hands gently touching his face, then, might belong to some immortal maid, to make him glad through eternity.

But when he looked up, the face he saw was a man's, thin, tense, etched with lines of triumph and harsh fatigue. "Foosh!" he said. "No lassy you, more's the pity."

Gorgidas rolled his eyes and laughed. "No need to ask whether you're healed. By the dog, do you think of nothing else, you satyr?"

Viridovix' sudden flinch of pain made the Greek wonder if he was in fact healed, but all the Gaul said, very quietly, was, "Aye, betimes I do." Viridovix struggled to sit. The blood roared in his ears, but he fought his dizziness down. "Batbaian!" he exclaimed. "Is he after being found?"

Hearing his name, Batbaian hurried over to the Celt, still swaddled in the thick felt fabric of the tent. He seemed glad for any excuse to sidle away from the Arshaum, who were eyeing him like a pack of wolves sizing up a stray hound. Skylitzes and Goudeles crouched by Viridovix, too; the Videssian officer steadied him with a strong right arm, while the bureaucrat pressed Gorgidas' hand in congratulation.

"Are you all right, now?" Viridovix said to Batbaian, dropping into the Khamorth speech. Gorgidas followed it with difficulty; he had not used that language in months.

"I'm well enough, thanks to this," the nomad answered, shaking snow from the felt. He looked in wonder at Viridovix. "But how is it you're here to ask me? You shouldn't be, not after being out in the blizzard with no cover."

"Truth that." There was wonder on Viridovix's face, too, but aimed at Gorgidas. "He healed me, must be." Almost accusingly, he said to the physician, "I didna think you could."

"Neither did I." Now that it was done, the Greek longed for nothing so much as the warm inside of a tent, a deep draught of kavass, and his bedroll to take him through the long winter night—and most of the next day, if he could get away with it.

But Viridovix was saying, "If it's a druid of leechcraft you are now, Gorgidas dear, have a look at Batbaian and the eye of him, and see if there's somewhat to be done for the puir lad."

The Greek sighed, a long, frosty exhalation; no doubt Viridovix was right. "I'll do what I can." He leaned toward the young Khamorth, who drew back in suspicion, still full of mistrust for anyone who had anything to do with the Arshaum. "Hold still," Gorgidas said in Videssian. Though he hardly spoke the imperial tongue, Batbaian understood it enough to obey.

Gorgidas sucked in his breath sharply when he took a good look at the nomad's ruined socket. Not having paid any real attention to Batbaian, he had assumed the Khamorth's eye lost to sword or arrow in some steppe skirmish. But the scar he saw was wrong for that: too large, too round, too neat, with the look of cautery to it. His gently probing fingers confirmed the impression. "How did you come by this?" he asked.

Voice cold as the north wind, Batbaian told him. He did not have the Videssian for all of it, but Viridovix and Skylitzes helped interpret, and his final, plunging gesture was graphic enough. Skylitzes, hardened soldier though he was, turned his head and was sick in the snow. He bent down and scooped up more to clean his mouth.

"Aye, that was the way of it," Viridovix said grimly. "A sweet fellow, Avshar." With a grunt of effort, the Celt fought his way to his feet. He stood swaying but triumphant. "And a deal to pay him back for, that there is." His face grew bleak once more, his eyes far away. "That there is," he repeated softly. He touched his sword, drawing strength from the thought of revenge.

Then he seemed to come back to himself, and asked Gorgidas, "Is anything to be done for the eye, now?"

The Greek had to toss his head in his people's no. He knew he could heal again; like a boy's first spending of his seed, the one success promised more. But that knowledge was useless here. "Time has given the wound such healing as it will have. Had I seen it when it was fresh, the best I could have done would have been to bring it to the state it is in now. The art works with what it finds; it cannot give back what is lost."

Viridovix' nod was unhappy, Batbaian's only impatient—he wore the mutilation as a reminder to himself of what he owed.

Goudeles sneezed. The sound reminded Gorgidas that the blizzard had not gone away simply because he had found Viridovix. The Gaul could freeze all over again—and so could the rest of them. The physician ran back to his horse, pulled a blanket from his saddlebag, and wrapped Viridovix in it.

The Celt accepted it absently; being alive, being warm enough to feel the snow stinging his cheeks, was enough to savor. He hardly heard Gorgidas when the Greek asked him if he could ride, but the physician's impatient growl got through. "I can that," he said, and managed the ghost of a chuckle. "Dinna fash yoursel'."

He mounted behind Gorgidas, Batbaian back of Skylitzes. The physician's pony snorted resentfully at having to carry two; Gorgidas got it moving with the rest regardless. "Your riding's better than it was," Viridovix said.

"Yes, I know. I have many useless talents these days," the Greek said, tapping the *gladius* that swung at his left hip. He paused, and added wonderingly, "And a real one, it seems."

The ride west to the Arshaum army was short; the nomads had been pushing forward at their own steady pace while Gorgidas labored over the Gaul. Outriders yelled challenges. The scout leader answered with loud praise for Gorgidas' healing talents. The physician's mouth quirked in a wry smile. Now that he had done something worth talking about, the picket was glad enough to claim a share of it.

Viridovix did not know the Arshaum language, beyond a few obscenities Arigh had taught him. But his eyes grew wide as he took in the size of the approaching force. "The lot of you've not been wasting your time, have you now?" he said to Gorgidas. The Greek tossed his head.

Then there was a shout: "V'rid'rish!" Arigh rode up at a near-gallop, clumps of snow flying under his horse's hooves. His grin as white as the landscape around them, he pounded the Gaul's back. "I wanted to kill someone when I found the scouts who came across you were gone again before I knew about it."

"Blame me for that," Gorgidas said. Like Arigh, he spoke Videssian so Viridovix could understand.

"Blame, is it?" the Celt snorted. "Pay him no mind, Arigh darling. A little later and there'd only be the frozen corp of me here, the which'd be no good for saying hello."

"You're without a horse, I see," Arigh said—the nomads' first priority. "Take a couple from my string."

"Obliged," Viridovix said. "Might you also be having one for Batbaian my friend?"

Arigh's grin disappeared as his glance slid to the Khamorth. His lip curled; for the first time, he reminded Gorgidas of Dizabul. "Your taste in friends has gone down," he said.

"Has it now?" Viridovix said. "Well, belike you have the right of it; I keep picking khagans' sons." He locked eyes with the Arshaum prince.

With his swarthy skin and the thick layer of grease on his face, it was impossible to see whether Arigh flushed, but after a few moments he walked his horse over to Batbaian. He had learned a little of the Khamorth speech traveling across Pardraya to Prista and the Empire; now he used it to ask, "A horse—you need?"

Batbaian had stiffened as the Arshaum came up to him; he jerked in surprise to hear his own language. Then he nodded with a dignity beyond his years. "I thank you," he said. He fumbled at his belt, undid the dagger there—fine metalwork, with a leaping stag in high relief on the bronze sheath—and offered it to Arigh. "A gift for a gift."

The smile returned to Arigh's face; he accepted the knife, clapped Batbaian on the shoulder. The watching Arshaum murmured in approval. Few of them, probably, had understood Arigh when he made his gift to Batbaian, but his return gesture needed no words. "The Hairy acts as a man should," Gorgidas heard one nomad say, and his companion's reply: "Why not? He's seen a fight or two, looks like—that scar's not pretty."

Arigh said, "Skylitzes, Gorgidas, bring 'em along to my father. We can all hear what they have to say then." He rode off toward the gray horsetail standard.

Viridovix bowed to Arghun as best he could riding double. The khagan was frailer than he had expected and sat his horse with difficulty; the Gaul wondered if he had been ill. He was soft-spoken, without the blustery temper Targitaus had used to browbeat his clansmen, but the Arshaum hurried to obey when he said something. Now he studied Batbaian cautiously, Viridovix with lively curiosity. He said something in the sibilant Arshaum tongue.

"He didn't believe Arigh when he told him of your looks," Gorgidas translated, "but he sees he was telling the truth after all."

"Honh!" Viridovix said. In Latin he went on, "And I never set eyes on such a lot of slant-eyed flat-noses in all my days either, but no need to tell him that, I'm thinking. Give him top o' the day instead."

Gorgidas did. Arghun nodded at the courtesy, then said, "I'd be curious to know how the two of you happened to come here." It was phrased as a request, but was plainly a command; Gorgidas put it into Videssian for Viridovix and Skylitzes into the Khamorth language for Batbaian.

"Up to me to start, it is," Viridovix said, and began to tell of what had befallen him since Varatesh snatched him from the camp. The outlaw's name raised a growl from a few of the Arshaum by Arghun, the ones whose clans wandered closest to the Shaum. They remembered his raid over the winter the year before, and its savagery. The Gaul was soon talking faster than Gorgidas could easily interpret; Arigh helped him when he faltered.

Another horseman pushed his way through the crowd gathering round the newcomers. What a dandified sprout, Viridovix thought; he wore furs and leather as if they were silk and cloth-of-gold, and even in the wind and snow he somehow kept his pony perfectly groomed, its mane braided with bright red ribbons.

"Father, I—" Dizabul began.

Arghun cut him off. "Whatever it is, it'll have to keep, boy. These foreigners bear important news."

The young prince's handsome face clouded as he looked Viridovix' way, the more so because of Arigh beside him. But when he spied Batbaian his jaw dropped. "Am I less than a Hairy, now?" he began angrily.

But Arghun silenced him again, this time with a gesture of dismissal. "Go on, redbeard," he said.

"Not bad, not bad," he said, laughing, when the Gaul told of the trick with the cattle he had suggested to drive Varatesh's men back. By then Viridovix and Batbaian were speaking alternately as they described the events that had led up to the attack on the outlaws and their allies.

The khagan snapped sharp questions about the battle itself. Hearing it in detail reminded Gorgidas all too much of the catastrophe at Maragha. Avshar's battle magic, whatever might be true of others', did not fail in the heat of combat. If the soldiers he led could fight on anywhere near even terms, that sorcery would be enough to spell victory for them.

And the aftermath of victory—the Arshaum prided themselves on their hardness, but more than one cried out in loathing and horror as Batbaian, his voice dispassionate as if it had all happened to some stranger, spoke of endless red-hot irons. They flinched again when Viridovix told of the winners' cruel toying with their enemies' hopes, and of Targitaus' seizure when the dreadful truth came clear. Apoplexy, thought Gorgidas, sickened but unsurprised.

After that, the story of the sack of the camp seemed almost anticlimax, though Viridovix felt the thin scabs tear open and the pain flow out like blood when he thought of Seirem. "So there it stands," Batbaian finished. "Varatesh, the spirits dung on him, has Pardraya, and Avshar him, or so it looked to me when I was in their hands. Next to them," and Batbaian looked Arghun full in the face, beyond fear now, "even you Arshaum are a good choice. So we came to beg your help, if you care to give." The Khamorth glanced at the warriors all around, said dryly, "You may not need me to persuade you to move east."

Arghun stroked his wispy beard. He turned to Gorgidas. "This is the Avshar you have spoken of, the one from Yezd?"

"Aye," said the Greek, echoed by words or nods from his friends and comrades.

The khagan said, "I had not intended to leave much of Yezd on its wheels in any case. Your wizard will be one more yurt to knock down." Arghun folded his arms with the serene confidence of a man who has not known defeat. The Arshaum who heard his declaration cheered; they, too, were sure only victory was possible when facing Khamorth and other weaklings.

Their guests, who had seen the wizard-prince's handiwork, were less sanguine, but saw little point in saying so. "As well explain music to a deaf man," Goudeles muttered. "One way or another, they'll find out."

"Or another," Gorgidas agreed gloomily. Having warned Arghun over and over of the deadly might he would face, the physician was coming to understand the nature of the curse Apollo had laid on Kassandra.

Winter's short day and the raging storm combined to force the Arshaum to an early halt. "Will you share my tent?" Gorgidas asked Viridovix as they dismounted. "I want to examine you—I can hardly believe you're alive." As nothing else could, curiosity held wariness at bay.

"I am that, thanks to you," the Celt said. He poked Gorgidas in the ribs. "I'll come wi' you, though its nobbut the carcass o' me you're hankering after."

"Bah!" From anyone but Scaurus or Viridovix, the crack would have frightened the Greek; and the tribune, he thought, would never have made it—too mannerly by half. As it was, he was obscurely pleased. He looked Viridovix up and down. "You flatter yourself."

"Do I now?" Chuckling, the Gaul helped him set up his tent. "This is better than the one I had, but mind you drive the pegs down firm."

The physician was adept with flint and steel and he soon had a dung fire going. After he and the Gaul had eaten, he seized Viridovix' wrist; the pulse was firm and steady, that of a healthy man. When the fire had warmed the cramped space inside the tent, he had his friend strip off coat and tunic and listened to his lungs. The air whistled smoothly in and out, with none of the damp, soggy sound that would have warned of chest fever. Finally, he examined the Celt's hands and feet, cheeks, nose, and ears for traces of frostbite. He tossed his head. "You're disgustingly well."

"The which is only your fault, so dinna come carping to me over it."

"Scoffer. Truly, though, had you not been a strong, healthy man, you would have been dead long before I got to you." Pride and delighted awe lit the Greek's face as the notion that he had really healed took hold.

Viridovix dressed again with some haste; it was not so warm as all that. He gulped kavass. After months on the steppe, he hardly noticed the faintly sour taste—and it, too, was warmth of a sort. He said to Gorgidas, "You're after hearing what's befallen me—tell me now how the lot o' you fared once I was raped away." The Greek obeyed, talking much of the night away as the wind howled outside. Listening, Viridovix thought the past months had been good ones for Gorgidas. His wit was still biting, but he spoke with a confidence and a sense of his own worth the Gaul had not seen in him since his lover's death—and perhaps not before.

Once the story was done, the physician seemed to change the subject. "Do you remember the argument we had a couple of years ago, not long after we came to Videssos?"

"Och, which one was that?" Viridovix said, grinning and yawning. "There've been so many, and rare sport they are, too."

"Hmm. Well, maybe so. The one I'm thinking of had to do with war and what it was good for."

The reminiscent smile disappeared from Viridovix' face. "So that's the one you mean, is it?" he said heavily, sighing through his thick mustaches. "I'm afeared you had the right of it after all. A cold cruel thing it is, warring, and glory only a word a reeking corp'll never hear again."

Gorgidas stared at the Celt, thunderstruck as if a second head had appeared on his shoulders. This, from the barbarian who exulted in combat for its own sweet sake? "Odd you should say so, when—" the physician began, and then stopped, looking at his friend more closely. He had examined the Gaul's body; now he looked at the man, really saw for the first time the grief that sat behind his eyes and showed at the corners of his mouth and in the deepening lines of his forehead. "You lost more than a battle when you rode with the Khamorth," he blurted.

"Too canny, y'are," Viridovix said, and sighed again. "Aye, there was a lass, Batbaian's sister she was. She's dead now, though not soon enough." After a while he went on, very low, "And part o' me with her. And what was the sense in that, or the use?" he asked the Greek. "None I could see when I found her, puir broken thing, nor the now either. Blood for blood's sake, the which is why I own I was wrong and you right."

Gorgidas thought of Quintus Glabrio, face blank in death. The memory burned in him still, and from his own pain he knew the Gaul's. They sat silent for a time, words no good to them. Then the Greek said, "No little irony here."

"And what might that be?"

"Only that when I brought up that argument I intended to yield it to you."

"Go on with you." Viridovix was as startled as the physician had been before. "You, the chap who wouldna carry a sword, come to relish soldiering? Next you'll be after taking heads and nailing 'em to your gate like a proper Celt."

"Thank you, no. But—" Gorgidas slapped the *gladius* on his hip, which Viridovix had not noticed. "—I wear a blade these days, and I begin to know what to do with it. And perhaps I begin to understand your 'glory.' For is it not true," he said, falling naturally into disputational style even though he was not speaking Greek, "that the idea of winning acclaim from one's fellow will make a man more likely to resist the onslaught of the wicked?"

"Honh!" The Gaul shook his head; having once changed his mind, he held to his new view with a convert's zeal. "An omadhaun'll go after glory no less than an honest man, so where's the use of it there?"

Gorgidas leaned forward with pleasure, sleep forgotten, loving the argument for its own sake. "That's true, but the renown of a good man lives forever, while an evildoer's fame is buried in disgrace. Four hundred years ago Herodotos said of the sycophant at Delphi who carved the

Spartans' name on a golden bowl they did not offer, 'I know his name, but I will not record it.' And no one knows it now."

"He did that?" the Gaul said admiringly. "Now there's a revenge for you. But listen—"

They wrangled through the night, pounding fists onto knees and shouting at each other, quite without rancor: "Thick-skulled woods-runner!" "Hairsplitting knave of a Greek!" Fire and smelly tallow lamps guttered low, leaving them in near darkness. At last the thin murky light of winter dawn began to creep under the tent flap.

Gorgidas knuckled his eyes, suddenly feeling exhaustion catch up with him again. No help for it, not with another day in the saddle ahead. The left side of his mouth quirked up in a wry grin. "Here we sit, not knowing which of us is right and which wrong, but we go on even so."

"Aye, well, what else can we do?" Viridovix rose, stretched, jammed on his fur hat and stuck his head outside. "Come on, laddie, they're stirring out there." The swirl of cold air helped wake Gorgidas. Shivering, he belted his coat shut and followed the Gaul out into the snow.

XV

Marcus was working in his cubicle late one afternoon when he found he needed to go up to the records room to compare a protested assessment to the one levied the year before. He scratched his head; the place was empty. Where were the clerks hunched over registers, their ink-smudged fingers flicking beads on reckoning boards?

Only a single grizzled watchman paced the corridors, and he was making his rounds as fast as he could. When Scaurus hailed him, he looked at the tribune as at any madman. "Go on with you, sir. Who's for work on Midwinter's Day? The lot of 'em left hours ago, they did."

"Midwinter's Day?" Marcus echoed vaguely. He counted on his fingers. "Why, so it is." The watchman was gaping now, exposing a few blackened stumps of teeth. Not even foreigners forgot the chief festival of the Videssian year, the celebration to call the sun back from the winter solstice.

Chilly air bit at Scaurus' nose as he left the pen-pushers' warm den. That had been true last year, too, when he'd been dragged from his desk by Viridovix and Helvis. . . . He kicked at the snow, remembering.

Hardly anyone walked the broad ways of the palace complex; the servants, soldiers, and bureaucrats who made up the Empire's heart reveled with the rest of the city. The plaza of Palamas, just east of the palaces, was a sea of humanity. Venders cried their wares: ale, hot spiced wine, roast goat in cheese sauce, shellfish, squid fried in olive oil and dusted with breadcrumbs, perfumes, jewelry of all grades from cheap brass trash to massy gold encrusted with gems big as a man's eye, minor magic charms, images of Phos and his holy men. Strolling musicians wandered through the crowds, singing or playing pipes, lutes, horns straight or recurved, even a Vaspurakaner pandoura or two, all in the hope of enjoyably separating the frolickers from their coins.

Marcus, who had no ear for music in his best moods, gave them a wide berth. They reminded him of Helvis, who delighted in music, and of his recent fiasco with Nevrat Sviodo. Nevrat went out of her way to be friendly whenever she, Senpat, and the tribune went out, but her manner had a slight constraint that had not been there before. It was, he knew, no one's fault but his own. He growled a curse, wishing he could be free of his memories.

Monks' sober blue robes stood out from the gaudy finery most Videssians wore. Some joined the celebration around them; Scaurus would have bet a good many goldpieces that Styppes was already oblivious to the world. Others led little groups of laymen in prayer or hymns of praise to Phos, forming islets of dignity and deep faith in the jollier, more frivolous throng.

Some, though, abominated all fleshly pleasures, and in their narrow fanaticism devoted themselves only to destroying everything of which they disapproved: Zemarkhos had his spiritual brothers in the city. One such, a dour man whose robe flapped ragged round his scrawny shanks, came panting by the tribune, chasing fine singing youths in masks. Seeing he would never catch them, he shook his fist, shouting, "Your japes profane Phos' holy days! Give your souls to contemplation, not this reckless gaiety! It is a defilement, you witless fools, and Skotos' everlasting ice awaits you!" The young men were long gone. "Bah!" the monk said softly, and looked round for other evil to root out.

Marcus feared the monastic would turn on him; his shaven cheeks and light eyes and hair marked him as an outlander, and so a likely heretic or outright unbeliever. But there was better game close by. A ring of people watched a little dog, its fur dyed green, prance back and forth on its hind legs to the tap of its master's hand-drum. He had trained it to take money from their fingers and scamper back to him with the coins.

"Isn't t'at marvelous?" boomed one of the spectators, a tall Haloga mercenary whose chilly homeland offered no such diversions. His companion, a darkly beautiful whore, smiled up at him, nodding. Her velvet gown, shot through with maroon brocade, clung to her like a second skin. His arm was tight round her waist; now and again his massive hand would slide up to tease the bottom of her breast.

He let her go for a moment, went to one knee; his blond braid, tied with a cord the color of blood, almost brushed the cobbles. "Here, pup!" he called. The dog minced over to take a coin, dropped to all fours to scurry off to the man with the drum. "Gold!" he exclaimed, and bowed low to the Haloga. "A thousand thanks, my master!" The crowd cheered.

But when the mercenary rose, the Videssian monk was stabbing a long bony forefinger into his face. "Filthy, obscene revelry!" he cried. "You poor benighted heathen, you should be at prayer thanking Phos for his mercy in restoring the light for yet another year, not defiling yourself with this lewd creature here!" His glare swung to the courtesan, who returned it; her eyes had glowed at the soldier's lavishness.

The Haloga blinked in surprise at the onslaught. Perhaps he had been briefed about the dangers of inciting Videssian clerics, for his answer was mild enough: "Take your hand away, sir, if you please."

The monk did. He must have thought he had hit the mercenary's conscience, for he softened his harsh commanding tones and tried to speak persuasively. "For all that you are a foreigner, sir, you have the look of a gentleman, so think on what I say. Is your carnal pleasure worth the risk of your soul?"

"Go stifle yourself, you skin-headed vulture!" the tart shrilled. "You leave him alone!" She clutched the mercenary's arm possessively.

"Be silent, trull," the monk said. He kept looking her up and down, as if against his will. Videssian monks were celibate, but he could not tear his gaze away from her invitingly displayed flesh. His words were for the Haloga, but his eyes stayed riveted on the woman. "I grant she's a lovely thing, yet desire is but Skotos' honied bait to trap the unwary."

Marcus grimaced at the sally, though it was not meant for him.

The monk was fairly howling now: "Look at the fine round arse of her, and her narrow waist, oh, and a bosom to make any man weak, in truth—" Scaurus found him almost pitiful to hear, thinking he was condemning the sensual delights he had forsworn, but instead lingering lovingly over them all. "Sparkling eyes and full red lips; sweet as aged wine they must be." He fairly twitched with lust.

The Haloga threw back his head and laughed, a great bass roar loud enough to turn heads over half the plaza. "Bugger me with a pine cone, priest, if you don't need her worse than I do. Here." He tossed a goldpiece at the feet of the monk, who stared at it, popeyed. "Go on," the mercenary told him, "have a good frike on me. I'll find another wench, have no fear; this burgh crawls with queans."

Monk and whore screamed at him together, then at each other. The Haloga turned his broad back on both of them and tramped away. The crowd whooped behind him, loose enough this one day of the year to enjoy a cleric's comeuppance, even at the hands of a heathen.

Nor could Scaurus help smiling; no sea of sorrows was big enough for a man to drown in it altogether. As with Styppes' bilious temper and fondness for the grape, this monk's sad slaverings reminded him that under those blue robes dwelt human beings, perhaps not too different from himself. That was worth remembering. Most times, Videssos' monks roused only dread in him, for fanaticism in the cause of faith was not something a Roman was well equipped to understand.

Thinking of Styppes and his thirst, the tribune bought a cup of wine. It sat warm in his belly. When a man ran through the plaza shouting the praises of the mime troupes performing at the Amphitheater, he drifted south along with a good many others.

The Amphitheater's great oval bowl marked off the southern boundary of the plaza of Palamas. Scaurus paid his two-copper fee and passed through one of the tunnel-vaulted passageways and into the arena. Ushers herded him up ramps and stairways to the very top of the bowl; the mimes had been playing all day, and the Amphitheater was packed.

Seen from so far away, the obelisk, chryselephantine statues, and other memorials of past imperial triumphs that decked the Amphitheater's central spine was almost more impressive than they had been when the tribune stood among them. The tip of the tall granite spike was at the level of his eyes, even here. Not far away from its base bloomed the twelve bright silk parasols that marked the Avtokrator of the Videssians as the same number of lictors with their rods and axes distinguished a Roman consul.

The tribune could not make out Thorisin's features. Somehow that heartened him. He drank more wine, rough cheap stuff that snarled on his palate. Catching his grunt of distaste, the man to his right on the long stone bench said, "A rare vintage—day before yesterday, I think." He was a skinny, bright-eyed little fellow with the feral look of a cutpurse to him.

Marcus smacked his lips. "No, you're wrong. I'm sure it's last week's." The joke was feeble, but he had not made many lately.

His benchmate's reply was lost in the crowd's flurry of applause as a new set of players came out onto the track where, most days, race horses galloped. One of the actors pantomimed stepping in something distasteful and earned a guffaw.

In the Empire's small towns the citizens put on their own skits instead of having professionals entertain them, but all through Videssos the playlets had the same principle behind them. They were fast-paced, topical, and irreverent—on Midwinter's Day, anyone was fair game.

This troupe's first sketch, for instance, featured three chief characters, one of whom, by his robes of state, was obviously the Emperor. The rest of the actors kept getting in his way on various pretexts until at last he stumbled on the other two chief players, a brown-haired woman and a big man wearing a golden wig and Haloga-style furs, thrashing together under a blanket. And oh, the crockery that flew when she—he, actually; the mime troupes were all-male—was discovered! The mock-Emperor had to flee, crossing his arms in front of his face to save it from the barrage of pots and dishes the actor playing his mistress kept pulling from beneath the covers. He only subdued her with the aid of the rest of the players, who had changed into the gilded corselets of Imperial Guards. The pseudo-Haloga tried to hide under that blanket, but a boot in his upraised rump dealt with him.

And that, Marcus thought, doubtless explained why Komitta Rhangavve was not sitting by Thorisin—one lover too many at last, or one too blatant. He suddenly understood the sniggering remarks the bureaucrats had been making, things he had paid no attention to in his gloom.

He turned to his benchmate. "I've been out of the city. When did this happen?"

"A couple months ago, I guess. When the headman got back from that Opsikion place. There's a song about it, goes like this—oh, wait, they're starting up again."

The next skit bored the tribune, but the Videssians around him roared with laughter. It was a satire of some theological debate that had entertained the city this past summer. Only gradually did Scaurus realize that the leading player, a man wearing a huge gray false beard that hung down over the pillow he had stuffed under his threadbare blue robe to fatten himself, was supposed to be Balsamon, ecumenical patriarch of the Empire of Videssos. The real Balsamon was sitting on the Amphitheater's spine not far from the Emperor. He was clad quite properly in the patriarchal regalia: precious blue silk and pearl-encrusted cloth-of-gold, vestments as magnificent in their own way as Thorisin Gavras'. But Marcus—and evidently the whole city—knew he turned comfortably shabby whenever he got the chance.

Thorisin had sat unmoving as he was burlesqued, tolerating Midwinter Day license without enjoying it. Balsamon chortled along with the rest of the Amphitheater when his turn came. He held his big belly in his hands and shook when the actor lampooning him cracked a priestly opponent over the head with an ivory figurine, then ignored the thrashing victim to make sure the statuette was undamaged.

Balsamon shouted something to the mock-patriarch, who cupped a hand at his ear to hear through the noise of the crowd. Whatever it was, Balsamon repeated it. The actor nodded, bowed low in his direction—and walloped the fellow again.

"He's a pisser, that one," Scaurus' raffish neighbor said admiringly as the Amphitheater exploded with glee. Balsamon, as was his way, flowered in the applause. He was much loved in the city, and for good reason.

The mimes darted under the Amphitheater for a change of costume. The first one to re-emerge stepped forth in the furs and leathers of a nomad, with a silver circlet on his head to show he was of some rank. He prowled about fiercely, brandishing a saber and ignoring the hisses and catcalls that showered down on him. Those turned to cheers when another actor came out wearing imperial raiment. But he took no notice of the nomad, turning his back on him and staring off into the distance.

More fur-clad actors emerged, three of them pushing a covered cart over to their chief. He scowled and gnashed his teeth at it, whacking it with the flat of his blade.

There was a flourish of trumpets. Out from the runway strutted a tall man in outlandish military getup, followed by four or five more wearing less splendid versions of the same costume. Marcus frowned, wondering who these apparitions were supposed to be. Their shields were taller than they were. . . . The tribune leaned forward in his seat, feeling his face grow hot.

The pseudo-legionaries far below marched very smartly, or would have, if they had been able to move more than three paces without suddenly changing direction. After a while their leader literally stumbled over one of the mock-nomads, which produced a good deal of startlement and alarm on both sides.

The Yezda chieftain pointed to his cart, then to the figure of the Emperor, who was still aloof from it all. After some comic misunderstanding, the Roman leader paid him a gigantic bag of coins and took possession of the cart. Pantomiming falls in the mud, he and his men wrestled it over to within a few feet of the Emperor.

Marcus' heart sank anew as he watched the mock-legionaries curl up for sleep around the cart. As soon as they were motionless, the four men inside, dressed Namdalener-style in trousers and short jackets, tore the cover off, scrambled out, and danced a derisive jig on their backs. Then, kicking up their heels, they fled for the runway and disappeared.

Still with his back turned, the actor in imperial robes gave a great shrug, as if to ask what could be expected from such hopeless dubs as the ones he had to work with.

The tribune looked at Thorisin. He was laughing now. So much for Nepos' warm words, Marcus thought.

"There's more coming," the little man next to him said as the Roman rose from his seat.

"I'm for the jakes," Scaurus mumbled, sliding crabwise toward the stairs past the row of drawn-up knees. But he did not stop at the latrines. Pausing only to drain another cup of new green wine, he hurried out of the Amphitheater. The crowd's snickers burned in his ears. They would have laughed louder yet, he thought, had the mime troupe known the whole story.

It was nearly dusk; men were lighting torches round the Amphitheater. They crackled in the wind. A cheese-paring of moon sank over the palaces. Marcus started back to his room in the Grand Courtroom, but changed his mind while he was still in the plaza of Palamas. Tonight he needed more of the grape, and every tavern in the city would be open to oblige him.

Turning his back on the palace complex, Scaurus walked through the forum and east along Middle Street. The thoroughfare was nearly as crowded as the plaza. He kept one hand on his belt-pouch; there were more thieves in Videssos than the one he had been sitting by.

The granite pile that housed more government offices, the archives, and a prison took up most of a long block. As the tribune passed the massive building, he heard his name called. His head spun. Alypia Gavra waved his way as she came down the broad black marble steps toward him.

He stood frozen in the street a moment, while revelers surged round him. "Your Highness," he managed at last. Even in his own ears his voice was a startled croak.

She looked about to see if anyone in the crowd had heard him, but no one was paying any attention. "Plain Alypia will do nicely tonight, thank you," she said quietly. She was not dressed as a princess, but in a long, high-necked dress of dark green wool with rabbit fur at the sleeves and collar. If anything, she was more plainly gowned than the women around her, for she wore no jewelry at all, while most of them glittered with gold, silver, and precious stones.

"As you wish, of course," Scaurus said woodenly.

She frowned up at him; the top of her head came barely to his chin. "This ought to be a night for rejoicing," she said. A long, loud thunder of mirth came from the Amphitheater. "Maybe you should go and enjoy the farcers."

He gave a bitter laugh. "I've seen enough of the mimes already, thanks." He had not intended to say anything more, but at her questioning look found himself explaining.

Her eyes widened in sympathy. "They can be cruel," she nodded. Marcus had not seen any of the skits the year before; he suddenly wondered what might have been in them. Alypia went on, "But it's not as if the islanders' escape was all your fault."

"Was it not?" the tribune said, as much to himself as to her. Wanting to get away from that set of memories, he remarked, "To judge by your clothes, you hardly seem ready for a celebration yourself."

"No, I suppose not," she admitted with a brief smile. "I hadn't planned on one. I sent my servants off to keep the holiday early this afternoon and then came here to paw through the archives. That, I thought, would be an all-day job."

It was Scaurus' turn to nod; as an accounts auditor, he had made use of old records himself a few times. The Videssians were marvelous for keeping records, but storing the ones no longer immediately useful was something else again. Even the clerks who kept them often had no idea of what they held. "This was for your history?"

"Yes," she said, seeming pleased he remembered. "I was looking for the general Onesimos Kourkouas' report on an early brush with the Yezda in Vaspurakan, thirty-six, no, thirty-seven years ago. By some accident, it was in the second room I searched. Then again, it was only half as long as I'd thought. So here it is only twilight, and I find myself at loose ends." She studied him. "What do you intend to do the rest of the night? Can it be shared?"

"Your Highness—no, Alypia," Marcus corrected himself before she could, "all I had planned was getting thoroughly sozzled. If you don't get in the way of that, you're welcome to come along; otherwise, I'll see you another day."

He had expected his candor to drive her off, but she said briskly, "A capital idea. Where were you going to go?"

He raised an eyebrow. "I hadn't thought that far ahead. Shall we wander?"

"Why not?" They set out together down Middle Street, away from the palace complex. Around them, the city kept celebrating. Fires blazed at every street corner, and men and women jumped over them for luck. Some, laughing, wore clothes that did not match their gender; Scaurus was almost knocked down by a chubby bearded fellow prancing in skirts. "Careful, there," he growled, in anything but holiday spirit.

Alypia, who understood his pain from her own ordeal, deliberately kept the talk impersonal, not risking a closer touch. Without noticing her tact, the tribune was glad of it. He asked, "How did your Kourkouas find the Yezda?"

"He was horrified by them, by their archery and savagery both. The Vaspurakaners, at first, thought them a race of demons. Some among us thought they were a sending to punish Vaspurakan for its stubborn heresy—until, of course, they invaded Videssos, too."

"That wouldn't do much for that interpretation," the tribune agreed. He spoke with care, not quite sure how vehemently devout Alypia was. From what he had seen, though, he thought her piety more of Balsamon's genial sort than the narrow creed of a Styppes or Zemarkhos. He went on, "I might have reckoned them devils, too, from what they did in the Maragha campaign. And yet Yavlak and his Yezda near Garsavra were vicious cutthroats, aye, but not past human ken. They were happy enough to sell their islander captives back to me instead of torturing them all to death for Skotos' sake."

But thinking of that reminded Scaurus of what had come afterward. He changed the subject in some haste. "Tell me," he said, waving at the square they were entering, "why is this place called the forum of the Ox? I never did know, for all the time I've been here." It was perhaps a third the size of the plaza of Palamas, with none of the latter's imposing buildings.

"There's not much to it, I'm afraid. In ancient times, when Videssos was hardly more than a village, this was the town cattle market."

"Is that all?" he blurted.

"Every bit." Alypia looked at him in amusement. "Are you very disappointed? I could make up a pretty fable, if you like, with plots and wizards and tons of buried gold, but it would only be a fable. Sometimes what's so is a very plain thing."

"I have what I asked for, thanks." He hesitated. "Not even one wizard?"

"Not even one," she said firmly. They crossed the square, which was as full of people as the forum of Palamas. The revelers here were a more motley group than the richer citizens further west. The songs were gamier, the laughter shriller. There was a good sprinkling of town toughs, swaggering in tights and baggy-sleeved tunics; in a new fashion, some had taken to shaving the backs of their heads, Namdalener-style.

Past the forum of the Ox was the coppersmiths' district. The shops on Middle Street were closed now, hiding the ewers and bowls, plates and bells behind stout wooden shutters. The hammer's clang and the patient scratch of burin on metal were silent. Alypia said, "You have an odd way of getting drenched, Marcus. Or did you plan to hike all the way to the wall?"

The tribune flushed, partly in embarrassment and partly in pleasure that the princess still used his praenomen. She had learned enough of

Roman customs to know it was reserved for warm friends, yet kept it after his debacle. He remembered the proverb: prosperity makes friends, adversity tries them.

"As you wish," he said once more, but this time in agreement, not resignation.

Save for the establishments along Middle Street, Scaurus hardly knew the coppersmiths' quarter. When he ventured off the thoroughfare, he found himself in a strange, half-foreign world. The metalworkers' trade was dominated by folk whose ancestors had come from Makuran, and they still clung to some of their western customs. Fewer luck-fires burned here than in the rest of the city; more than once Marcus saw four parallel vertical lines charcoaled on a whitewashed wall or chalked on a dark one.

Following his eye, Alypia said, "The mark of the Four Prophets of Makuran. Some follow them even now, though they dare not worship openly for fear of the monks."

Ironic, Scaurus thought, that the Makuraners faced persecution in Videssos from the worshipers of Phos, and in Makuran itself—Yezd, now—from the followers of Skotos. He asked idly, "What do you think of them?"

Alypia's reply was prompt. "Their faith is not mine, but they are not wicked because of that."

"Fair enough," he said, happy he had judged her rightly. Balsamon had said much the same thing to the Roman when he was newly came to Videssos. Most of their countrymen, smug in righteousness, would have called such tolerance blasphemy.

Alypia on his arm, he wandered the quarter's mazelike side streets for some little time, rejecting one dive because it was full of hooligans who leered out at the two of them, another because it reeked of rancid oil, and a third for its signboard, which prominently displayed the four vertical bars. He had no more desire to meet Makuraner religious enthusiasts than their Videssian counterparts.

The inn he finally chose was a neat two-story building whose sign carried no hidden meanings, religious or political, being merely a bright daub showing a jolly fat man in front of a table loaded with food and drink. The smells that came from inside were some of them unfamiliar but all mouth-watering.

The ground floor of the inn was packed tight with tables, and almost all of those packed with people. Scaurus looked round in disappointment until he spotted a small empty table set against the wall near the open kitchen. "Perfect!" he said, and shouldered his way to it through the crush, Alypia close behind. In summer the blast of heat from braziers and cookfires would have been intolerable, but on Midwinter's Day it was welcome.

Three waiters scurried from tables to kitchen and back again, but the holiday crowd made service slow. The tribune had a chance to look the patrons over: ordinary Videssians for the most part, neither rich nor poor. A few affected Makuraner style, the men, their hair and beards curled into tight ringlets, wearing coats longer behind than in front and their ladies in linen caftans brightly dyed in geometric patterns, with hairnets of silver mesh on their heads. All the talk sounded friendly and cheerful, as if the place's sign had been painted from one of the patrons.

Eventually a server came up. "Hello, stranger, my lady," he said, bowing to Alypia as though he recognized her as a princess. "Phos bless you on the day. What will it be?"

"Wine, for now," Marcus said; Alypia nodded. The man hurried away. Scaurus thought he had Makuraner blood; he was a touch swarthier than most Videssians, with pitch black hair and large, dark, luminous eyes.

The wine arrived with reasonable speed; the waiter poured for them. He said, "My name is Safav." That confirmed the tribune's guess. "If you want more or decide to eat, yell for me." Just then someone did. Safav dodged off toward him.

As Videssians usually did before wine or meat, Alypia Gavra raised her hands and murmured Phos' creed, then spat in the rushes on the floor in rejection of Skotos. Scaurus simply drank. Although she did not seem put out by the omission, Alypia's smile was a bit rueful. "I'm so used to thinking of you as one of us that it sometimes jolts me to remember you have your own customs," she said.

"It does me, too, sometimes," Marcus said. But the traces of his birth-speech gave his Videssian a sonorous flavor it did not have in her mouth and, as usual, he found the wine sticky-sweet on his tongue. "But never for long."

Syrupy the wine might have been, but also potent; it did as much to warm him as the fires at his back. He looked across the table at Alypia. She masked her thoughts well—not from policy, like her uncle, but from pensiveness. He remembered the quiet attraction that had grown between them and wondered whether she chose to do so, too, or as quietly to forget. Behind the cool façade it might have been either.

Was she even fair? he asked himself. Certainly her body lacked Helvis' rich curves—he frowned and cut that thought short. Her face was not as long as Thorisin's or her father's, nor as sharply sculpted; she left her cheeks pale and did nothing to play up her fine green eyes. But there was no mistaking the keen wit and spirit behind them. Conventionally beautiful or not, she was herself, something harder to attain.

A waiter—not their own, but an older man—bustled out of the kitchens past his elbow, cutting into his reverie. "Your pardon, sir," the man said, lifting a square bronze tray higher to make sure it missed the tribune. Agile as a lizard, he slid between tables toward three couples in Makuraner costume. He set enamel bowls before them, ladled soup from a copper tureen. Then, with a flourish, he took the lid from a pan, dug in with a wooden spoon, and plopped light-brown steaming chunks into the soup bowls.

The soup hissed and crackled as though hot metal was being quenched. Scaurus jumped. So, he saw, did Alypia and several of the more Videssian-looking people in the inn. Those before whom it was set, though, ate with gusto. A mystery to be explored! "Safav!"

The waiter handed a patron a plate of broiled prawns and hurried over to the tribune. Marcus asked, "What's the secret of the soup there? Hot pitch, maybe?"

"Sir?" Safav said, confused. Then his face cleared. "Oh, the sizzling rice soup? Would you care for some?"

Marcus hesitated, but at Alypia's nod he said, "Why not?" He was more suspicious than he sounded. All but unknown to the Romans, rice was not common in Videssos either. Despite sputters, the tribune foresaw something on the order of barley mush, not what he wanted for holiday fare.

But when Safav reappeared, the soup bowls he gave Scaurus and Alypia were full of a delicate golden broth rich with peas, mushrooms, and big hunks of shrimp and lobster. "In Makuran, now, this would be lamb or goat, but seafood works well enough," Safav said. Scaurus, waiting for the sizzle, was hardly listening.

With the same flourish the other waiter had shown, Safav whipped the lid from the thick iron pan on his tray and dropped a steaming spoonful into each bowl. They crackled heartily for a few seconds, then sank. "Reminds me of burning ships," the tribune muttered. He prodded the crisp chunk of rice with his spoon, still dubious.

"How is it done?" Alypia asked.

"First boil the rice, then fry it in very hot oil until the moment it starts to scorch. It has to be hot to sizzle, which is why this," Safav said, tapping at the heavy pan. He laid a finger by the side of his nose. "You never heard that from me, my lady, else my cousin the cook comes after me with a big knife. Most people I would not tell; they ask just for talk's sake. But I could see you really want to know." Someone shouted the waiter's name; he bobbed his head shyly and left them.

The tribune gave a tentative taste. The soup was splendid, the crisp rice in it nutlike and flavorful. "What do I know?" he said, and emptied the bowl.

Tuna followed, broiled with oregano and basil; wine; greens with garlic and mint; wine; simmered squid stuffed with lentils and currants; wine; lamb stew with celery, leeks, and dates—another Makuraner dish; wine; squash and beans fried in olive oil; wine; quinces and cinnamon; wine.

Alypia had hold of the conversation without seeming to, deftly steering it to divert him but lay no demands upon him. For all her tact and skill, that game could go on only so long. As the grape mounted to Marcus' head, his responses grew steadily shorter. "Have you done what you set out to do, then?" Alypia said, her tone slyly bantering.

But the tribune was not fuddled, as she supposed. Rather the wine had left his thoughts clear and simple, stripping veils of pretense from him. Too well he remembered standing in front of her like an automaton, nakedly spewing forth his inmost, most secret self under the influence of Nepos' cordial. He stabbed at a chunk of lamb with needless violence.

Sensitive to his swing in mood, Alypia put her goblet down; she had drunk much less than he. She could be direct as well as artful and asked it straight: "What's amiss?"

"What are you doing here with me?" Marcus exclaimed. He stopped in dismay, mouth hanging foolishly open.

"I could ask the same of you," Alypia replied with some heat. But her annoyance was not for his candor, for she went on, "When you sheered off from my servant—oh yes, he saw you—I thought you were angry at me, as you have a right to be. Yet here you sit, peaceably enough. Explain yourself, if you would."

"Angry at you? No, never. I owe you a debt I cannot hope to repay, for finding a way to make your uncle believe me loyal. But—" The tribune fell silent. Alypia waited him out. At last he had to continue. "How could I have anything to do with you, when I blight everything I put my hand to?"

The furious stare she gave him said she was of the Gavras clan after all. "I did not think you would belittle yourself. Who saved my headstrong uncle from Onomagoulos' assassins? Who warned him of Drax, though he would not listen? And who beat Drax in the end? Unless I'm much mistaken, the finger points at you."

"And who let all his prisoners get free, for being, for being—" He had to take a long swallow of wine before he could get it out. "—for being too blind to see his woman was using him as a carter uses a mule? That finger points at me, too, from my own hand."

"There's no denying your Helvis had a hard knot to untie, but I thought better of her." Alypia kept her voice judicious, but her nostrils flared in indignation as she spoke Helvis' name. "But to do as she did, taking advantage of your love for a weapon against you—" She made a gesture of repugnance. "I wish I had not heard that. No wonder you blame me for urging Thorisin to try Nepos' potion."

"Blame you?" Scaurus said, echoing her again. "I just told you I did not; you were doing what you could to help me—and in fact you did. How can there be blame for that? But," he paused to gather his thoughts, "it's hard to meet you, to know what to say, to know how to act, after baring myself before you."

The touch of her fingers was gentle on his. She slowly dipped her head; her eyes were lowered to the tabletop as she reminded him, "Marcus, you have also seen me naked." Her voice was hardly more than a whisper.

The tribune remembered her, calm with Vardanes Sphrantzes' dagger against her throat, her slim body revealed by the transparent silks that were the only garments the elder Sphrantzes allowed her after taking her as plaything from Ortaias. His hand closed tightly around hers. "That was no fault of yours; the crime was Vardanes'."

"Well, did Drax and his comrades escape by your will, then?" Alypia demanded, looking up at him. "We both know the answer to that." She did not seek a reply. Her eyes were far away; she was remembering, too. "Strange," she mused, "that I should thank Avshar in his wickedness for delivering me from my tormentor."

"He gave short measure, as he always does," Marcus said. "Vardanes earned worse than the quick end he got."

She shuddered, still looking backward, but then tried to smile. "Let it lay. I'm sorry I spoke of it." Her hand stayed in his; he touched the writer's callus on her middle finger. He was afraid to say anything. He wondered if he was seeing only what he wished to see, as he had with Nevrat.

When Safav came by, he smiled to himself. Marcus hardly noticed the waiter as he set the spiced quinces on the table and slipped away. In spite of his tension, memory held him again, of Alypia in his embrace, of her lips warm on his—for a few seconds, until she took fright and pulled away. Had that only been this past spring?

"So much between," she murmured, seeming to read his thoughts as she did so often. She was silent again for some time, then drew in a long breath, as if in decision. She said, "As well nothing came of that, don't you think? I was unready to, to . . ." It was her turn to come to an awkward halt. Marcus nodded to show he understood; her eyes thanked him. She went on, "And in any case you had commitments you could not have—should not have—set aside."

"Should I not?" he said bitterly.

By luck, she paid him no attention; she was arguing with herself as much as talking to him. Her face set with resolve a warrior might have envied, she pushed ahead, a sentence at a time. "But your reasons for hesitating are gone now, aren't they? And as for me . . ." Her voice trailed away once more. At last she said, very low, "Marcus, would you see me naked again?"

"Oh, with all my heart," he said, but a moment later felt he had to add, "if you think you can."

"Truly I don't know," she answered. She blinked back tears. "But were you not one to say such a thing as that, I'm sure I could not try." In spite of her determination, her hand trembled in his. He looked at her questioningly. Her nod was short and fierce.

Almost before the tribune could wave for him, Safav appeared. He bent to whisper to Scaurus, "There is a room upstairs, should you want it."

"Damn me," the Roman said, "my head must be transparent as glass tonight." He fumbled in his belt-pouch, pressed coins into Safav's hand.

The waiter stared. "My lord," he stammered, "this is far too much—"

"Take it," Marcus said; a goldpiece more or less seemed a small thing here and now. Safav bowed almost double.

"The second door on the right from the stairs," he said. "A lamp is lit inside; there's charcoal in the brazier, and fresh straw in the mattress, and clean fleeces, too—we made ready for the day."

"Good." Marcus stood with Alypia. She came round the table to him; that his arm went round her shoulder struck him as the most natural thing in the world. Safav bowed again, only to be jerked upright as someone shouted his name. He shrugged comically and scurried away.

One of the men in Makuraner costume gave a sodden cheer as Scaurus and Alypia climbed the stairs. Feeling her flinch, the tribune glared at the tosspot, who was cheerily oblivious to him. But her chin rose in defiance, and she managed a small smile. He lifted his thumb; she knew enough of Roman ways to read his approval. He wanted to hug her on the spot but held back, judging it would only further ruffle her.

The chamber was small, but large enough. Marcus barred the door by the thin light of the promised lamp, which sat on a stool by the bed. He quickly set the brazier going; the room was shuttered against the chill outside, but an icy draft crept in regardless.

Alypia stood motionless in the center of the room while he did what was needed. When he took a step toward her, she started in such trepidation that he froze in his tracks. “Nothing will happen unless you want it to,” he promised. With Roman practicality, he went on, “Warm your hands; it’s cold as a frog in here.” He moved aside to let her at the brazier. She stooped over it, taking him at his word.

Without turning, after a while she said, “Blow out the lamp.” Scaurus did. The flame sprang up for an instant, then was no more. The dim-glowing charcoal in the brazier turned the whitewashed walls the color of blood.

He waited. She came to him slowly, almost defiantly, as if her body were a restive horse she controlled by main force. When he put his hands on her shoulders, she did not pull away, but lifted her face to him. It was a strange kiss; while her lips and tongue were alive against his, she stood so rigid he did not dare sweep her into a full embrace.

She drew back, studying him in the near-darkness. “How does a soldier make so gentle a man?” she said.

He did not think of himself so, but had learned she meant such questions seriously. With a shrug, he answered, “You know soldiering is not the trade I started with. And,” he added softly, “I am not at war with you.”

“No, never,” she murmured. Then he did draw her close, and she came more readily into his arms. He stroked the back of her neck, brushed her hair aside to touch her ear. She shivered, but more from fear, he thought, than sensuality. She retreated a couple of steps, eyeing the bedding by the wall. “Please, you go first,” she said to Scaurus, turning her back again. “I’ll come to you in a minute.”

As Safav had promised, the straw beneath the muslin ticking was fresh and sweet-smelling, the wooly fleeces thick and warm. Marcus lay facing the wall. Someone had scrawled a couple of words on it in charcoal, too smeared now to read in the faint red light.

From behind him, Alypia said, “And patient, too,” with something close to her usual detached irony. There was a bit of silence, followed by a small, annoyed snort as a bone fastener on her dress refused to obey her fingers. The tribune heard the soft rustle of cloth sliding over skin. The mattress shifted as she let herself down onto it.

As his mouth found hers, she whispered, "I hope you will not be too disappointed in me."

Some time later he stared into her eyes; in the near-dark they were as unreadable as the scribble on the wall. "'Disappointed'?" he said, still dazed with delight. "You must be daft."

To his surprise, she twisted angrily in his arms. "You are kind, dear Marcus, but you need not pretend with me. I know my clumsiness for what it is."

"By the gods!" he said, startled into Latin for a moment. In Videssian he protested, "If that was clumsiness, I doubt I'd live through talent." He laid her hand over his heart, still racing in his chest.

She looked past his shoulder. Her voice was absolutely toneless. "*He* said there was no hope for me in such matters, but he would undertake to train me even so." She did not, perhaps could not, force the name out, but Scaurus knew whom she meant. Of themselves, his hands folded into fists.

She did not seem to notice; he might as well not have been there. "I fought him, oh, how I fought him, until one day he let me see he took pleasure from my struggles. After that," she said bleakly, "he trained me—aye, like a dog or a horse. Small mercies when I learned something enough to suit him. When I failed . . ." She shivered into silence.

"It's over," he said, and tasted the emptiness of words. Then he cursed foully in every tongue he knew. That did no good either.

After a while, Alypia went on, "Whenever he finished with me, he would curl his lip in disgust, as if someone had offered him a plate of bad fish. To the end, he despised me as couch-partner. Once I dared to ask him why he came back over and over and over, if I did not satisfy him." Marcus waited helplessly as she paused, remembering. "That was the only time I saw him smile, in all the months he kept me. He smiled and said, 'Because I can.'"

The tribune wished he had not wasted his curses before. He gathered her to him, hugged her close. "Listen to me," he said. "Vardanes, Skotos take him, savored your suffering."

"The very word," she said from against the side of his neck. "He was a connoisseur in all things, torment among them."

"Then why believe what he told you of yourself as a woman?" he demanded. "One more lie, to bring you affliction." He ran his fingers down the curved column of her spine, a long slow caress; kissed her with soft brush of lips. "For it was a lie, you know."

"I pleased you?" she whispered, doubting still. "Really?"

"If snow is 'cool,' or the ocean 'moist,' then yes, you 'pleased' me."

She gave a strangled hiccup of laughter, then burst into tears, clinging to him tightly. She wept against his shoulder for a long time. He simply held her, letting her cry herself out as he had with Senpat and Nevrat.

Finally she was spent and lay quiet in his arms. He tilted her face up to his. He had intended a gentle kiss, of understanding and sympathy rather than passion. But she responded with an intensity not far from desperation. A proverb he had heard somewhere, from the Namdaleni perhaps, briefly ran through his mind: "Tear-filled eyes make sweet lips." Then thought was lost, for Alypia clung to him once more, with a new kind of urgency.

They both gasped when it began again, gentleness forgotten. His lips bruised hers and were bruised in turn; her nails scored his back. She tore her mouth free, said half-sobbing into his ear, "What wonder, to want!" When she cried out in amazed joy, he followed an instant later.

After that, it was some time before either of them cared to move. At last Alypia said, "You're squashing me, I'm afraid."

"Sorry." Marcus shifted his weight; sweat-slick skin slid. They both laughed. "Who would have thought anyone could sweat in this hailstone of a room?"

"Who would have thought . . ." She let her voice trail away. She set her hand on his side, but did not speak.

"What, love?"

Alypia smiled, but answered, "Nothing." That was so patently untrue it hung in the air between them. She amended it at once. "Or nothing I know how to say, at any rate." He mimed scratching his head; she made a face at him. "Witling!"

She was serious, though, as he soon saw. "All I knew of man and woman was cruel sport. But Marcus, you have met with better than that. When you and—" She stopped, gestured in self-mockery. "The romances say one should never seek comparisons."

The romances, Marcus thought, knew what they were talking about. He realized he had scarcely thought of Helvis since fleeing the Amphitheater. Now he could no longer avoid it. Alypia stirred beside him; he saw his silence was frightening her. He said slowly, "The only comparison that matters is that you are here and want to be, while she—is in Namdalen by now, I suppose."

She sighed and snuggled against him. Her whisper sounded like, "Thank you."

But once reminded, he kept slipping back to the stepson he had come to care for, to his own son, to the child Helvis was carrying—or would it be born now? probably—and to the way that had been taken from him. "One thing more, after all," he said harshly. "You would never use your body as a weapon against me."

Her hand clenched on his upper arm, hard enough to hurt. She willed it open. "No," she said. "Never that."

She sat up. The brazier's faint red light softened her features, blurring her resemblance to her father, but she had her own measure of Mavrikios Gavras' directness. "Where do we go from here?" she asked Marcus. "If it pleases you that this should be the affair of an evening, to be forgotten come light, I will understand. That surely is safest."

The tribune shook his head violently, almost as frightened as she had been before. He had seen his life uprooted, all he relied on snatched away, and the prospect of abandoning this gladness filled him with worse dread than the familiar terrors of the battlefield. He and Alypia had cared for each other since not long after the Romans came to Videssos; this was no sudden seduction, to be enjoyed and then thrown aside.

She waved his stumbling explanation aside as soon as she had its drift, bent to kiss him. "I would not force myself on you, either, but I would have grieved to see what might have been, cut short." She abruptly turned practical again. "It won't be easy. You know I am hemmed in by ceremony and servants; chances to slip away will come too seldom. And you must run no risks for my sake. My uncle, did he know, would come after you not with a horsewhip, but the headsman's axe."

"By his lights, it would be hard to blame him," Scaurus said soberly. A mercenary captain—especially one with as alarming a record as the Roman's—the paramour of a childless Emperor's niece? Thorisin could not afford to ignore such a thing, not in Videssos where only intrigue rivaled theology as the national passion.

The tribune thought of the executioner's hot irons, back at Garsavra. He might come to beg for the axe, after a while.

That was the thought of a moment, though. He laughed and stroked Alypia's smooth shoulder.

"What is it, my astonishing, desirable beloved?" she asked, half-embarrassed by the endearments but proud of them as well.

"I was just remembering that a year ago this time, near enough, I was reaming Viridovix up one side and down the other for carrying on with Komitta Rhangavve and here I am playing the same mad game."

"Viridovix?" She frowned in brief puzzlement. "Oh yes, the big copper-haired wild man in your service—a 'Kelt' he called himself, did he not?" Not for the first time, Marcus was impressed by her memory for detail, sharpened, no doubt, by her historical research. He wondered what the Gaul would say about being in Roman service. Something memorable, he was sure.

Alypia suddenly giggled as she made a connection. "So *that's* why he disappeared off onto the plains with Goudeles and the Arshaum—Arigh." She found the name.

"Aye. He and Komitta quarreled, and she went crying rape to Thorisin. He didn't care to wait to find out whether she'd be believed."

Alypia's nostrils flared in an unmistakable sniff. "Komitta would quarrel with Phos as he came to bear her soul to heaven. And as for the other, your friend was hardly the first to know her favors—or the last. I think in the end my uncle was glad she grew flagrant enough to give him the excuse to be rid of her." She giggled again. "Truly, without it I don't think he'd have had the nerve."

Having seen some of Komitta Rhangavve's rages, Scaurus could well believe that. "What happened to her after she was caught with the Haloga?" he asked, recalling the first skit he'd watched in the Amphitheater.

"Thorisin packed her off to a convent outside the city—and a tidy sum he had to pay the reverend mother to take her, too; her reputation was there ahead of her. The northman—Valthjos his name was, called Buttered-Bread after their fashion of giving nicknames—had to sail for home. He was supposed to be in disgrace, but he carried a gold-inlaid axe and a jewel-set scabbard I know he didn't have when he got to Videssos."

The rough justice in that sounded like Thorisin, and the story explained more of the pen-pushers' jokes, but Marcus was grimly certain he would not escape so lightly if discovered with Alypia. She was no mistress of whom the Emperor had tired; until Thorisin bred himself an heir, she was the channel through which the Gavras line would descend.

Thinking along with him, Alypia said, "We must make sure you're not found out." She rose from the bed and walked over to the dress which lay carelessly crumpled on the floor. Her nipples stood up with cold; that icy draft was defeating the brazier. Scaurus admired her economical movements as she dressed, then he threw the sheepskins to one side and started to retrieve his own clothes.

"Wait," she said. "Best I go back alone." When he frowned, she said, "Think it out. I'll simply say I fell asleep over my scrolls. Everyone will believe that and pity me for it. Whereas if I returned with you at whatever hour this is, eyebrows would fly up no matter how innocent we were."

He put out his hands palm up, defeated. "You're right. You generally are."

"Hmm. I'm not quite sure I like that." She quickly ran a comb through her hair. "Anyway, no great hardship for you here. The bed is comfortable."

"Not half so much, without you in it."

"A courtier born," she said, but her eyes were warm. She dimpled. "What would your Viridovix say if he found out you'd been bundling with an Emperor's daughter?"

"Him? He'd congratulate me."

"Good for him, then." Alypia hugged the tribune, kissed him hard and quick. "Sleep warm and think of me." They walked to the door together. He unbarred it. Her hand on the latch, she looked up and said softly, "This is but a beginning, I promise you."

"I know that." He opened his mouth, shut it, and shook his head. "There doesn't seem to be anything else to say." She nodded and slipped out the door. He closed it after her.

SWORDS OF THE LEGION

For Alison, Rachel, and Laura again

WHAT HAS GONE BEFORE:

Three cohorts of a Roman legion, led by military tribune Marcus Aemilius Scaurus and senior centurion Gaius Philippus, were ambushed by Gauls. The Gallic leader Viridovix challenged Marcus to single combat. Both bore druids' swords. When the blades crossed, a dome of light surrounded Viridovix and the Romans. Suddenly they were in the world of the Empire of Videssos, a land where the priests of Phos could work real magic. There they were hired as mercenaries by the Empire.

In Videssos the city, capital of the Empire, Marcus was presented to the soldier-Emperor Mavrikios Gavras and his brother Thorisin. Later, at a banquet, he met Mavrikios' daughter Alypia and the sorcerer Avshar. Avshar forced a duel, but when the druids' sword neutralized Avshar's spells, Marcus won. Avshar sought revenge by magic. It failed, and Avshar fled to his homeland Yezd, western enemy of Videssos. Videssos declared war on Yezd.

Troops flooded into the capital, and tension arose between the mercenaries from the island Duchy of Namedalen and the native Videssians over a small matter of religion. Each regarded the other as heretical. The Videssian patriarch Balsamon preached tolerance, but fanatic monks soon started a riot. Marcus led the Romans to quell that. As the riot was ending, Marcus saved the Namdalener woman Helvis. Soon she and her young son joined him in the Roman barracks.

Finally Videssos' army moved west against Yezd, accompanied by women and children. Marcus was pleased that Helvis had become pregnant, but shocked to learn that the left wing was commanded by young and inexperienced Ortaias Sphrantzes, son of the prime minister, Vardanes Sphrantzes.

Three Vaspurakaners joined later—Senpat Sviodo and his wife

Nevrat to act as guides, and the general Gagik Bagratouni. When the fanatic priest Zemarkhos cursed him, Bagratouni threw the priest and his dog into a sack and beat them. Marcus finally intervened.

At last the two armies met. The battle seemed a draw, until a spell from the sorcerer Avshar panicked Ortaias, who fled. As the left wing collapsed, the Emperor was killed and the army routed.

The Romans retreated eastward in order, rescuing the teacher-priest Nepos and being joined by Laon Pakhymer and his mounted Katrishers as cavalry support. They wintered in a friendly town, learning that Ortaias had declared himself Emperor and forced Alypia to marry him.

Thorisin Gavras had wintered in a nearby town with twenty-five hundred troops. In the spring, the legion joined him to march on Videssos the city. The gates were barred, but a group inside the city opened them. As the defenders fled, Avshar, disguised as Ortaias' commander Rhavas, tried foul magic, but was foiled by the swords of Viridovix and Marcus. Avshar retreated, then suddenly vanished.

Thorisin was crowned Emperor. He annulled Alypia's marriage and banished Ortaias to serve as a humble monk. But he was handicapped by lack of funds. He sent Marcus to supervise the accounting "pen-pushing" bureaucrats, and Marcus discovered that many rich landowners did not pay their taxes. The worst offender was a general, Onomagoulos, a former friend of Mavrikios Gavras. Learning this, Thorisin sent Namdaleni under count Drax to deal with Onomagoulos.

He also sent a group north to seek help from the Arshaum. The Greek physician Gorgidas, disgusted at being unable to learn healing magic, joined, as did Viridovix, fleeing a wrathful lover.

Drax overcame and killed Onomagoulos, then declared the western region Namdalener territory under him. Thorisin sent Marcus and the legion to defeat him.

In the north, Viridovix was kidnapped by outlaws working for Avshar. He escaped to a nomad village, which was soon destroyed by the outlaws. Viridovix and young Batbaian fled into a raging blizzard. Meantime, Gorgidas and the others reached the Arshaum leader Arghun. Gorgidas managed to save Arghun when the Yezda envoy tried to poison him, and Arghun mustered an army to help Videssos by striking Yezd.

On the march, they found the almost-frozen Viridovix. Gorgidas saved him, using the healing magic which he had given up on before.

Meantime, Marcus moved against count Drax and his Namdaleni. After a difficult campaign, he defeated them and took the leaders as prisoners. Among them was Soteric, brother of Helvis. She used wine and her body to put Marcus into a sound sleep, then stole out to free the prisoners and go with them, taking Marcus' children. With mixed sadness and shame, Marcus returned to report to Thorisin.

His brief account was not enough for the Emperor. With Alypia watching, Thorisin ordered Nepos to prepare a drug to make Marcus talk freely and truthfully, then inquired all details, even the personal ones. At the end, Thorisin admitted, "I have raped an innocent man."

Marcus returned to his job supervising the pen-pushers, but tried like a hermit to shut the world away. Alypia, however, sympathized deeply with him. Greeting him at a festival, she got him to take her to dinner. And dinner led to other things. . . .

I

"I'd like to have a better look at that one, if I could," Marcus Aemilius Scaurus said, pointing to a necklace.

"Which?" asked the jeweler, a fat, bald little man with a curly black beard. The Roman pointed again. A grin flashed across the craftsman's face; he bobbed a quick bow. "You have good taste, my master—that is a piece fit for a princess."

The military tribune grinned, too, at the unintended truth in the jeweler's sales talk. I intend it for one, he thought. That he did not say; what he did came out in a growl: "With a price to match, no doubt." Best to start beating the fellow down before he named a figure, for Scaurus intended to have the necklace.

The jeweler, who had played this game many times, assumed a look of injured innocence. "Who spoke of money? Here," he said, pressing the chain into Marcus' hands, "take it over to the window; see if it is not as fine as I say. Once you are satisfied of that, we can speak further, if you like."

The shop had its shutters flung wide. The sun shone bravely, though every so often the northerly breeze would send a patch of cloud in front of it, dimming for a moment the hundreds of gilded spheres that topped Phos' temples, large and small, all through Videssos the city. It was still winter, but spring was in the air. Gulls scrawked high overhead; they lived in the Videssian Empire's capital the year around. Closer by, the tribune heard a chiffchaff, an early arrival, whistle from a rooftop.

He hefted the necklace. The thick, intricately worked chain had the massy, sensuous feel of pure gold. He held it close to his face; months of work with tax receipts in the imperial chancery were making him a trifle nearsighted. The nine square-cut emeralds were perfectly matched in size and color, a deep, luminous green. They would play up Alypia

Gavra's eyes, he thought, smiling again. Between them were eight oval beads of mother-of-pearl. In the shifting light their elusive color shimmered and danced, as if seen underwater.

"I've seen worse," Marcus said grudgingly as he walked back to the jeweler behind his counter, and the bargaining began in earnest. Both of them were sweating by the time they agreed on a price.

"Whew!" said the artisan, dabbing at his forehead with a linen rag and eyeing the tribune with new respect. "From your fairness and accent I took you for a Haloga, and Phos the lord of the great and good mind knows how free the northerners are with their gold. But you, sir, you haggle like a city man."

"I'll take that for a compliment," Scaurus said. Videssians often mistook the tribune for one of the big, towheaded north-men who served the Empire as mercenaries. Most of his Romans were short, olive-skinned, and dark of hair and eye, like the folk into whose land they had been swept three and a half years before, but he sprang from the north Italian town of Mediolanum. Some long-forgotten Celtic strain gave him extra inches and yellow hair, though his features were aquiline rather than Gallic sharp or blunt like a German's—or, in this world, a Haloga's.

The jeweler was wrapping the necklace in wool batting to protect the stones. Marcus counted out goldpieces to pay him. The artisan, taking no chances, counted them again, nodded, and opened a stout iron strongbox. He dropped them in, saying, "And I owe you a sixth. Would you like it in gold or silver?"

"Silver, I think." Videssian sixth-goldpieces were shoddy things, stamped from the same dies as the one-third coins but only half as thick. They were fairly scarce, and for good reason. In a purse they bent and even broke, and they were more likely to be of short weight or debased metal than more common money.

Marcus put the four silver coins in his belt-pouch and tucked the necklace away inside his tunic. He would have to cross the plaza of Palamas to get back to his room in the palace complex, and light-fingered men flocked to the great square no less than honest merchants. The jeweler tipped him a wink, understanding perfectly. "You're a careful one. You wouldn't want to lose your pretty so soon after you get it."

"No indeed."

The jeweler bowed, and held the bow until Scaurus left his shop. He waved as the tribune walked past the window. Well pleased, the Roman returned the salute.

He walked west along Middle Street toward the plaza of Palamas. Videssians bustled all around him, paying him no mind. Most of the men wore thick, plainly cut tunics and baggy woolen trousers like his own. Despite the chilly weather, a few favored the long brocaded robes that were more often used as ceremonial garb than street wear. Town toughs swaggered along in their own costume: tunics with great billowing sleeves pulled tight at the wrists and clinging hose dyed in as many bright colors as they could get. Some of them shaved the backs of their heads. The Namdaleni—sometimes mercenaries, sometimes deadly foes for Videssos—had that style, too, but with them it served a purpose: to let their heads fit their helmets more snugly. For Videssos' ruffians it was simply a fad.

The tribune jumped when one of the roughnecks shouted his name and came up to him, hand outstretched. Then he recognized the fellow, more by his bad teeth than anything else. "Hello, Arsaber," he said, clasping hands. The bravo had been one of the men who threw open the gates to the city when Thorisin Gavras took the imperial throne from the usurper Ortaias Sphrantzes, and had fought bravely enough on the Romans' side.

"Good to see you, Ronam," Arsaber boomed, and Marcus gritted his teeth—that idiot usher's mispronunciation at a long-ago banquet looked to be immortal. Cheerfully oblivious, the Videssian went on, "Meet my woman, Zenonis, and these three lads are my sons: Tzetzes, Stotzas, and Boethios. Love, boys, this is the famous Scaurus, the one who beat the Namdaleni and the bureaucrats both." He winked at the tribune. "My bet is, the pen-pushers're tougher."

"Some ways," Marcus admitted. He nodded to Zenonis, a small, happy-looking woman of about thirty in flowered silk headscarf, rabbit-fur jacket, and long wool skirt; gravely shook hands with Tzetzes, who was about six. The other two boys were too young to pay much attention to him—Stotzas was two or so, while Zenonis carried Boethios, a tiny babe swaddled in a blanket.

Arsaber stood by, beaming, as the tribune made small talk with his family. The ruffian would have been the very picture of domesticity but for his outlandish clothes and the stout bludgeon that hung on his belt. After a while he said, "Come on, dear, we'll be late to cousin Dryos'. Roast quails," he explained to Scaurus, pumping his hand again.

The tribune caught himself looking down at his fingers; it was a good idea to count them after shaking hands with Arsaber. He surreptitiously patted his chest to make sure the smiling rogue had not managed to filch away his necklace.

The chance meeting saddened him; it took a while to figure out why. Then he realized that Arsaber's family reminded him achingly of the one he had built up until Helvis found her native Namdalener ties more important than the ones that bound her to him and deserted him, helping her brother Soteric and several other important prisoners escape in the process. The child they had been expecting would only be a little younger than Boethios—but Helvis was in Namdalen now, and Scaurus did not know if it was boy or girl.

In vanished Italy, in a youth he would never see again, he had trained in the Stoic school of philosophy, had been taught to stay untroubled in the face of sickness, death, slander, and intrigue. The sentiment was noble, but, he feared, past his attainment after her betrayal of their love.

The thought of Italy brought to mind the remaining Romans, the survivors of everything this world could throw at them. In many ways he missed them more even than Helvis and his children. They alone shared with him a language, indeed an entire past that was alien to Videssos and all its neighbors. He knew they had spent an easy winter at their garrison duty in the western town of Garsavra; that much Gaius Philippus' three or four brief notes had made clear. But the senior centurion, though a soldier without peer, was only sketchily literate, and his scrawled words did not call up the feeling of being with the legionaries that Scaurus needed in his semi-exile in the capital.

Boots squelching through dirty, half-melted snow, he walked past the block-long red granite pile of a building that housed the imperial archives, various government ministries, and the city prison. His somber mood lifted; he smiled and reached inside his tunic to touch the necklace once more. For all he knew, Alypia Gavra might be going through the archives now, looking for material to add to her history. So she had been doing on Midwinter's Day a few months past, when she happened to encounter the tribune as she left the government offices.

That night a friendship had become much more. Their meetings since, though, were far fewer than Marcus would have wanted. As Thorisin's niece, Alypia was hemmed round with the elaborate ceremonial of an ancient empire, the more so since the Emperor had no legitimate heir.

The Roman tried not to think of the danger he courted along with her. If discovered, he could expect scant mercy. Thorisin sat none too secure on his throne. The Emperor would only see him as an ambitious mercenary captain seeking to improve his own position through an affair with the princess. Scaurus had done great service for him, but he had also flouted Thorisin's will more than once—and, worse perhaps, proved right in doing so.

The plaza of Palamas drove such worries from his head. If Videssos the city was a microcosm of the polyglot Empire of Videssos, then its great square made a miniature of a miniature. Goods from every corner of the world appeared there, and merchants from every corner of the world to sell them. A few nomadic Khamorth crossed the Videssian Sea from the imperial outpost at Prista to hawk the products of the Pardrayan steppe—tallow, honey, wax—at the capital. A couple of huge Halogai, their hair in yellow braids, had set up a booth for the furs and amber of their northern home. Despite the war with Yezd, caravans still reached Videssos from the west with silks and spices, slaves and sugar. A Namadalener trader spat at the feet of a bored-looking Videssian who had offered him a poor price for his cargo of ale; another was displaying a table of knives. A Khatrisher, a lithe little man who looked like a Khamorth but acted like an imperial, dickered with a factor over what he could get for the load of timber he had brought to the city.

And along with the foreigners were the Videssians themselves: proud, clever, vivid, loud, quick to take offense, and as quick to give it. Minstrels strolled through the surging crowds, singing and accompanying themselves on drums, lutes, or pandouras, which had a more plangent, mournful tone. Marcus, who had no ear for music, ignored them as best he could. Some of the locals were not so kind. "Why don't you drown that poor cat and have done?" somebody shouted, whereupon the maligned musician broke his lute over the critic's head. The people around them pulled them apart.

Shaven-headed priests and monks of Phos moved here and there in their blue robes, some exhorting the faithful to pray to the good god, others, on some mission from temple or monastery, haggling with as much vigor and skill as any secular. Scribes stood behind little portable podiums, each with stylus or quill poised to write for folk who had money but no letters. A juggler cursed a skinny carpenter who had bumped him and made him drop a plate. "And to Skotos' ice with *you,*" the other returned. "If you were any good, you would have caught it." Courtesans of every description and price strutted and pranced, wearing bright, hard smiles. Touts sidled up to strangers, praising this horse or sneering at that.

Venders, some in stalls, others wanderers themselves, cried their wares: squid, tunny, eels, prawns—as a port, the city ate great quantities of seafood. There was bread from wheat, rye, barley; ripe cheeses; porridge; oranges and lemons from the westlands; olives and olive oil; garlic and onions; fermented fish sauce. Wine was offered, most of it too sweet for Scaurus' taste, though that did not stop him from drinking it. Spoons, goblets, plates of iron, brass, wood, or solid silver were offered; drugs and potions allegedly medicinal, others allegedly aphrodisiacal; perfumes; icons, amulets, and books of spells. The tribune was cautious even toward small-time wizards here in Videssos, where magic was realer than it had been in Rome. Boots, sandals, tooled-leather belts; hats of straw, leather, linen, cloth-of-gold; and scores more whose yells Marcus could not catch because they drowned each other out.

A shout like the roar of a god came from the Amphitheater, the huge oval of limestone and marble that formed the plaza of Palamas' southern border. A seller of dried figs grinned at Scaurus. "A long shot came in," he said knowingly.

"I'd bet you're right." The tribune bought a handful of fruit. He was popping them into his mouth one at a time when he nearly ran into an imperial cavalry officer, Provhos Mourtzouphlos.

Mourtzouphlos lifted an eyebrow; scorn spread across his handsome, aristocratic features. "Enjoying yourself, outlander?" he asked ironically. He brushed long hair back from his forehead and scratched his thickly bearded chin.

"Yes, thanks," Marcus answered with as much aplomb as he could muster, but he felt himself flushing under the Videssian's sardonic eye. Even though he had ten years on the brash young horseman, who was probably not yet thirty, Mourtzouphlos was native-born, which more than canceled the advantage of age. And acting like a barbarian bumpkin in front of him did not help either. Mourtzouphlos was one of the many imperials with a fine contempt for foreigners under any circumstances; that the Roman was a successful captain only made him doubly suspicious to the other.

"Thorisin tells me we'll be moving against the Yezda in the Arandos valley after the roads west dry," the Videssian said, carefully scoring a couple of more points against Scaurus. His casual use of the Emperor's given name bespoke the renown he had won in the campaign with Gavras against Namdalener invaders around Opsikion in the east, while the tribune toiled unseen in the westlands against the great count Drax and more Namdaleni. And his news was from some council to which the Roman, in disfavor for letting Drax get away in the escape Helvis had devised, had not been invited.

But Marcus had a comeback ready. "I'm sure we'll do well against them," he said. "After all, my legionaries have held the plug of the Arandos at Garsavra the winter long."

Mourtzouphlos scowled, not caring to be reminded of that. "Well, yes," he grudged. "A good day to you, I'm sure." With a flick of his cloak, he turned on his heel and was gone.

The tribune smiled at his stiff retreating back. There's one for you, you arrogant dandy, he thought. Mourtzouphlos' imitation of the Emperor's shaggy beard and unkempt hair annoyed Scaurus every time he saw him. Thorisin's carelessness about such things was part of a genuine dislike for formality, elegance, or ceremony of any sort. With the cavalryman it was pure pose, to curry favor with his master. That cape he had flourished was thick maroon samite trimmed in ermine, while he wore a belt of gold links and spurred jackboots whose leather was soft and supple enough for gloves.

When Marcus came on a vender with a tray of smoked sardines, he bought several of those and ate them, too, hoping Mourtzouphlos was watching.

Rather apprehensively, the tribune broke the sky-blue wax seal on the little roll of parchment. The note inside was in a thin, spidery hand that he knew at once, though he had not seen it for a couple of years: "I should be honored if you would attend me at my residence tomorrow afternoon." With that seal and that script, the signature was hardly necessary: "Balsamon, ecumenical Patriarch of the Videssians."

"What does *he* want?" Scaurus muttered. He came up with no good answer. True, he did not follow Phos, which would have been enough to set off almost any ecclesiastic in the Empire. Balsamon, though, was not typical of the breed. A scholar before he was made into a prelate, he brought quite un-Videssian tolerance to the patriarchal office.

All of which, Marcus thought, leaves me no closer to what he wants with me. The tribune did not flatter himself that the invitation was for the pleasure of his company; the patriarch, he was uneasily aware, was a good deal more clever than he.

His Stoic training did let him stop worrying about what he could not help; soon enough he would find out. He tucked Balsamon's summons into his beltpouch.

The patriarchal residence was by Phos' High Temple in the northern part of the city, not far from the Neorhesian harbor. It was a fairly modest old stucco building with a domed roof of red tiles. No one would have looked at it twice anywhere in the city; alongside the High Temple's opulence it was doubly invisible.

The pine trees set in front of it were twisted with age, but green despite the season. Scaurus always thought of the antiquity of Videssos itself when he saw them. The rest of the shrubbery and the hedgerows to either side had not yet come into leaf and were still brown and bare.

The tribune knocked on the stout oak door. He heard footsteps inside; a tall, solidly made priest swung the door wide. "Yes? How may I serve you?" he asked, eyeing Marcus' manifestly foreign figure with curiosity.

The Roman gave his name and handed the cleric Balsamon's summons, watched him all but stiffen to attention as he read it. "This way, please," the fellow said, new respect in his voice. He made a smart about-turn and led the tribune down a hallway filled with ivory figurines, icons to Phos, and other antiquities.

From his walk, his crisp manner, and the scar that furrowed his shaved pate, Marcus would have given long odds that the other had been a soldier before he became a priest. Likely he served as Thorisin Gavras' watchdog over Balsamon as well as servant. Any Emperor with an ounce of sense kept an eye on his patriarch; politics and religion mixed inextricably in Videssos.

The priest tapped at the open door. "What is it, Saborios?" came Balsamon's reedy voice, an old man's tenor.

"The outlander is here to see you, your Sanctity, at your command," Saborios said, as if reporting to a superior officer.

"Is he? Well, I'm delighted. We'll be talking a while, you know, so why don't you run along and sharpen your spears?" Along with having his guess confirmed, the tribune saw that Balsamon had not changed much—he had baited his last companion the same way.

But instead of scowling, as Gennadios would have done, Saborios just said, "They're every one of them gleaming, your Sanctity. Maybe I'll hone a dagger instead." He nodded to Scaurus. "Go on in." As the Roman did, the priest shut the door behind him.

"Can't get a rise out of that man," Balsamon grumbled, but he was chuckling, too. "Sit anywhere," he told the tribune, waving expansively; the order was easier given than obeyed. Scrolls, codices, and writing tablets lined every wall of his study and were stacked in untidy piles on the battered couch the patriarch was using, on several tables, and on both the elderly chairs in the room.

Trying not to disturb the order they were in—if there was any—Marcus moved a stack of books from one of the chairs to the stone floor and sat down. The chair gave an alarming groan under his weight, but held.

"Wine?" Balsamon asked.

"Please."

With a grunt of effort, Balsamon rose from the low couch, uncorked the bottle, and rummaged through the chaos around him for a couple of cups. Seen from behind, the fat old gray-beard in his shabby blue robe—

a good deal less splendid than Saborios', to say nothing of less clean—looked more like a retired cook than a prelate.

But when he turned round to hand Scaurus his wine—the cup was chipped—there was no mistaking the force of character stamped on his engagingly ugly features. When one looked at his eyes, the pug nose and wide, plump cheeks were forgotten. Wisdom dwelt in this man, try though he sometimes did to disguise it with a quirk of bushy, still-black brows.

Under his eyes, though, were dark pouches of puffy flesh; his skin was pale, with a faint sheen of sweat on his high forehead. "Are you well?" Marcus said in some alarm.

"You're still young, to ask that question," the patriarch said. "When a man reaches my age, either he is well or he is dead." But his droll smile could not hide the relief with which he sank back onto the couch.

He raised his hands above his head, quickly spoke his faith's creed: "We bless thee, Phos, Lord with the right and good mind, by thy grace our protector, watchful beforehand that the great test of life may be decided in our favor." Then he spat on the floor in rejection of the good god's foe Skotos. The Videssian formula over food or drink completed, he drained his cup. "Drink;" he urged the Roman.

He cocked an eyebrow when Marcus failed to go through the ritual. "Heathen," he said. In most priests' mouths, it would have been a word to start a pogrom; from Balsamon it was simply a label, and perhaps a way to get a sly dig in at the tribune.

Of its kind, the wine was good, though as usual Scaurus longed for something less cloying. He beat Balsamon to his feet and poured a second cup for both of them. The patriarch nodded and tossed it down; settling cautiously back into his seat, Marcus worked at his more slowly.

Balsamon was studying him hard enough to make him fidget. Age might have left the patriarch's eyes red-tracked with veins, but they were none the less piercing for that. He was one of the few people who gave the tribune the uncomfortable feeling that they could read his thoughts. "How can I help your Sanctity?" he asked, attempting briskness.

"I'm not *your* Sanctity, as we both know," the patriarch retorted, but again no fanatic's zeal was in his voice. When he spoke again, it was with what sounded like real admiration. "You don't say a lot, do you? We Videssians talk too bloody much."

"What would you have me say?"

"'What would you have me say?'" Balsamon mimicked. His laugh set his soft paunch quivering. "You sit there like a natural-born innocent, and anyone who hadn't seen you in action would take you for just another blond barbarian to be fooled like a Haloga. Yet somehow you prosper. This silence must be a useful tool."

Without a word, Marcus spread his hands and shrugged. Balsamon laughed harder; he had a good laugh, one that invited everyone who heard it to share the joke. The tribune found himself smiling in response to it. But when he said, "Truly, I don't call this past winter prospering," his smile slipped.

"Some ways, no," the patriarch said. "We're none of us perfect, nor lucky all the time either. But some ways . . ." He paused, scratching his chin. His voice was musing as he went on. "What do you suppose she sees in you, anyway?"

It was a good thing Marcus' cup was on the arm of his chair; had it been in his hand, he would have dropped it. "She?" he echoed, hoping he only sounded foolish and not frightened.

"Alypia Gavra, of course. Why did you think I sent for you?" Balsamon said matter-of-factly. Then he saw Scaurus' face, and concern replaced the amusement on his own. "I didn't mean to make you go so white. Finish your wine, get some wind back in your sails. She asked me to ask you here."

Mechanically, the tribune drank. Too much was happening too fast, alarm and relief jangling together like discordant lute strings. "I think you'd best tell me more," he said. Another fear was in there, too; had she had enough of him, and tried to pick an impersonal way to let him know?

He straightened in his chair. No—were it that, Alypia had the decency, and the courage, to tell him to his face. His memories were whispering to him; that was all. Having been abandoned by one woman he had trusted and loved, it was hard to be sure of another.

The twinkle was back in Balsamon's eyes, a good sign. He said blandly, "She said you might be interested to learn that she had scheduled an afternoon appointment with me three days from now, to pick my brains for what I recall of Ioannakis III, the poor fool who was Avtokrator for a couple of unhappy years before Strobilos Sphrantzes."

"And so?" Alypia had been working on her history long before the Romans came to Videssos.

"Why, only that if she happened to go someplace else when she was supposed to be here, in my senility and decrepitude I don't think I'd know the difference, and I'd babble on about Ioannakis all the same."

The tribune's jaw fell; amazed gladness shouted in him. Balsamon watched, all innocence. "I must say this senility and decrepitude of yours are moderately hard to see," Marcus said.

Did one of the patriarch's eyelids dip? "Oh, they come and go. For instance, I suspect I shan't remember much of this little talk of ours tomorrow. Sad, is it not?"

"A pity," Scaurus agreed gravely.

Then Balsamon was serious once more, passing an age-spotted hand in front of his face. "You had better deserve her and the risk she runs for your sake." He looked the Roman up and down. "You just may. I hope you do, for your sake as well as hers. She always was a good judge of such things, but with what she suffered she cannot afford to be wrong."

Marcus nodded, biting his lip. After Alypia's father—Thorisin's older brother Mavrikios—was killed at Maragha, young Ortaias Sphrantzes had claimed the throne and gone through the forms of marriage with her to help cement his place. But Ortaias' uncle Vardanes was the true power in that brief, unhappy reign and took her from his nephew as a plaything. The tribune's hands tightened into fists whenever he thought of those months. He said, "That once, I wished I were a Yezda, to give Vardanes the requital he deserved."

Balsamon's mobile features grew grave as he studied Scaurus. "You'll do, I think." He stayed somber. "You hazard yourself in this, too," he said. The tribune began a shrug, but Balsamon's eyes held him still. "If you persist, greater danger will spring from it than any you have ever known, and only Phos can guess if you will win free in the end."

The patriarch's gaze seemed to pierce the tribune; his voice went slow and deep. Marcus felt the hair prickle on his arms and at the nape of his neck. Videssian priests had strange abilities, many of them—healing and all sorts of magery. The Roman had never thought Balsamon more than an uncommonly wise and clever man, but suddenly he was not so sure. His words sounded like foretelling, not mere warning.

"What else do you see?" Marcus demanded harshly.

The patriarch jerked as if stung. The uncanny concentration faded from his face. "Eh? Nothing," he said in his normal voice, and Scaurus cursed his own abruptness.

After that, the talk turned to inconsequential things. Marcus found himself forgetting to be annoyed that he had not learned more. Balsamon was an endlessly absorbing talker, whether dissecting another priest's foibles, discoursing on his collection of ivory figurines from Makuran—"Another reason to hate the Yezda. Not only are they robbers and murderous Skotos-lovers, but they've cut off trade since they began infesting the place." And he swelled up in what looked like righteous wrath—or laughing at himself.

He picked at a bit of dried eggyolk on the threadbare sleeve of his robe, commenting, "You see, there is a point to my untidiness after all. Had I been wearing that—" He pointed to a surplice of cloth-of-gold and blue silk, ornamented with rows of gleaming seed pearls. "—when I was at breakfast the other day, I might have been liable to excommunication for soiling it."

"Another reason for Zemarkhos," Scaurus said. The fanatic priest, holding Amorion in the westlands in defiance of Yezda and Empire alike, had hurled anathemas at Balsamon and Thorisin both for refusing to acclaim his pogrom against the Vaspurakaners driven into his territory by Yezda raiders—their crime was not worshiping Phos the same way the Videssians did.

"Don't twit me over that one," Balsamon said, wincing. "The man is a wolf in priest's clothing, and a rabid wolf at that. I tried to persuade the local synod that chose him to reconsider, but they would not. 'Unwarranted interference from the capital,' they called it. He reminds me of the tailor's cat that fell into a vat of blue dye. The mice thought he'd become a monk and given up eating meat."

Marcus chuckled, but the patriarch's stubby fingers drummed on his knee; his mouth twisted in frustration. "I wonder how many he's burned since power fell into his lap—and what more I could have done to stop him." He sighed, shaking his head.

In an odd way, his gloom reassured the tribune. After his own failures, it did not hurt to be reminded that even as keen a man as Balsamon could sometimes come up short.

Saborios, certainly as efficient as a soldier if he was not one, had the door open for Scaurus even as he reached for the latch.

Alypia Gavra sat up in the narrow bed and poked Marcus in the ribs. He yelped. She touched the heavy gold of the necklace. "You are a madman for this," she said. "It's so beautiful I'll want to wear it, and how can I? Where will I say it came from? Why won't anyone have seen it before?"

"A pox on practicality," Scaurus said.

She laughed at him. "Coming from you, that's the next thing to blasphemy."

"Hrmmp." The Roman leaned back lazily. "I thought it would look good on you and I was right—the more so," he smiled, "when it's all you're wearing."

He watched a slow flush of pleasure rise from her breasts to her face. It showed plainly; she was fairer of skin than most Videssian women. He sometimes wondered if her dead mother had a touch of Haloga blood. Her features were not as sharply sculpted as those of her father or uncle, and her eyes were a clear green, rare among the imperials.

Mischief danced in them. "Beast," she said, and tried to poke him again. He jerked away. Once he had made the mistake of grabbing her instead and seen her go rigid in unreasoning panic; after Vardanes, she could not stand being restrained in any way.

The sudden motion nearly tumbled both of them out of bed. "There, you see," the tribune said. "That poking is a habit of mine you never should have picked up. Look what it brings on."

"I like doing things as you do," she said seriously. That brought him up short, as such remarks of hers always did. Helvis had tried to push him toward her own ways, which only made him more stubborn in clinging to his. It was strange, hearing from a woman that those were worth something.

He gave a sober nod, one suited to acknowledging something a legionary might have said, then grunted in annoyance, feeling very much a fool. He sat up himself and kissed her thoroughly. "That's better," she said.

Chickens clucked and scratched below the second-story window, whose shutters were flung wide to let in the mild air. Marcus could see the ponderous bulk of Phos' High Temple pushing into the sky not far away. He and Alypia had managed one meeting at this inn during the winter, so had it become a natural trysting place when she was supposed to be visiting Balsamon.

The innkeeper, a stout, middle-aged man named Aetios, shouted at a stableboy for forgetting to curry a mule. The fellow's eyes had sparked with recognition when Scaurus and the princess asked for a room, but the tribune was sure it was only because he had seen them before, not that he knew Alypia by sight. And in any case, with him, silver was better than wine for washing unpleasant memories away. His lumpish face came alive at the sweet sound of coins jingling in his palm.

Alypia made as if to get up, saying, "I really should go see Balsamon, if only for a little while. That way neither he nor I can be caught in a lie."

"If you must," Marcus said grumpily. With the ceremony that surrounded her as niece and closest kin of the Avtokrator, she could steal away but rarely, and the chance she took in doing so hung like a storm cloud over their meetings. He savored every moment with her, never sure it would not be the last.

As if reading his thoughts, she clung to him, crying, "What will we do? Thorisin is bound to find out, and then—" She came to a ragged stop, not wanting to think about "and then." In his short-tempered way, Thorisin Gavras was a decent man, but quick to lash out at anything he saw as a threat to his throne. After the strife he had already faced in his two and a half years on it, the tribune found it hard to blame him.

Or he would have, had the Emperor's suspicions affected anyone but him. "I wish," he said with illogical resentment, "your uncle would marry and get himself an heir. Then he'd have less reason to worry about you."

Alypia shook her head violently. "Oh, aye, I'd be safe then—safe to be married off to one of his cronies. He dares not now, for fear whoever had me would use me against him. Let his own line be set, though, and I become an asset to bind someone to him."

She stared at nothing; her nails bit his shoulder. Through clenched teeth she said, as much to herself as to him, "I will die before I lie again with a man not of my choosing."

Scaurus did not doubt she meant exactly that. He ran a slow hand up the smooth column of her back, trying to gentle her. "If only I were a Videssian," he said. That a princess of the blood could be given to an outland mercenary captain, even one more perfectly trusted than himself, was past thinking of in haughty Videssos.

"Wishes, wishes, wishes!" Alypia said. "What good are they? All we can truly count on is our danger growing worse the longer we go on, and only Phos knows when we will be free of it."

The tribune stared; in Videssos he was never sure where coincidence stopped and the uncanny began. "Balsamon told me something much like that," he said slowly, and at Alypia's inquiring glance recounted the strange moment when the patriarch had seemed to prophesy.

When he was done, he was startled to see her pale and shaken. She did not want to explain herself, but sat silent beside him. But he pressed her, and at last she said, "I have known him thus before. He gazed at you as if to read your soul, and there was none of his usual sport in his words." It was statement, not question.

"You have it," Scaurus acknowledged. "When did you see him so?"

"Only once, though I know the fit has taken him more often than that. 'Phos' gift,' he calls it, but I think curse would be a better name. He has spoken of it to me a few times; that he trusts me to share such a burden is the finest compliment I've ever had. You guessed well, dear Marcus," she said, touching his hand: "He sometimes has the prescient gift. But all he ever learns with it is of destruction and despair."

The Roman whistled tunelessly between his teeth. "It is a curse." He shook his head. "And how much more bitter for a joyful man like him. To see only the coming trouble, and to have to stay steady in the teeth of it . . . He's braver than I could be."

Alypia's face reflected the same distress the tribune felt.

"When was it you saw him?" he asked her again.

"He was visiting my father, just before he set out for Maragha. They were arguing and trading insults—you remember how the two of them used to carry on, neither meaning a word of what he said. Finally they ran out of darts to throw, and Balsamon got up to leave. You could see it coming over him, like the weight of the world. He stood there for a few seconds; my father and I started to ease him back down to a chair, thinking he'd been taken ill. But he shrugged us away and turned to my father and said one word in that—certain—voice."

"I know what you mean," Scaurus said. "What was it?"

"'Good-bye.'" Alypia was a good mimic; the doom she packed into the word froze the Roman for a moment. She shivered herself at the memory. "No use pretending it was just an ordinary leave-taking, though my father and Balsamon did their best. Neither believed it; I've never seen Balsamon so flat in a sermon as he was at the High Temple the next day."

"I remember that!" Marcus said. "I was there, along with the rest of the officers. It troubled me at the time; I thought we deserved a better farewell than we got. I guess we were lucky to have any."

"Was that luck, as it turned out?" she asked, her voice low. She did not wait for a reply, but rushed on, "And now he sees peril to you. I'll leave you, I swear it, before I let you come to harm because of me." But instead of leaving, she clung to him with something close to desperation.

"Nothing the old man said made me think separating would matter," said Scaurus. "Whatever happens will happen as it should." The Stoic maxim did nothing to ease her; his lips on hers were a better cure. They sank back together onto the bed. The bedding sighed as their weight pressed the straw flat.

Some time later she reached up to touch his cheek and smiled, as she often did, at the faint rasp of newly shaved whiskers under her fingers. "You are a stubborn man," she said fondly; in a land of beards, the tribune still held to the smooth-faced Roman style. She took his head between her palms. "Oh, how could I think to leave you? But how can I stay?"

"I love you," he said, hugging her until she gave a startled gasp. It was true but, he knew too well, not an answer.

"I know, and I you. How much safer it would be for both of us if we did not." She glanced out the window, exclaimed in dismay when she saw how long the shadows had grown. "Let me up, dearest. Now I really must go."

Marcus rolled away; she scrambled to her feet. He admired her slim body for a last few seconds as she raised her arms over her head to slide on the long dress of deep gold wool; geometrically decorated insets of silk accented her narrow waist and the swell of her hips. "It suits you well," he said.

"Quite the courtier today, aren't you?" She smiled, slipping on sandals. She patted at her hair, which she wore short and straight. With a woman's practicality, she said, "It's lucky I don't fancy those piled-up heads of curls that are all the rage these days. They couldn't be repaired so easily."

She wrapped an orange linen shawl embroidered with flowers and butterflies around her shoulders and started for the door. "The necklace," Marcus said reluctantly. He was out of bed himself, fastening his tunic closed.

Her hand flew to her throat, but then she let it drop once more. "Balsamon can see it before I tuck it into my bag. After all, what other chance will I have to show it, and to show how thoughtful—to say nothing of daft—you were to give it to me?"

He felt himself glow with her praise; he had not heard much—nor, to be fair, given much—as he and Helvis quarreled toward their disastrous parting. Alypia gasped at the kiss he gave her. "Well!" she said, eyes glowing. "A bit more of that, sirrah, and Balsamon will get no look at my bauble today."

The tribune stepped back. "Too dangerous," he said with what tatters of Roman hardheadedness he had left. Alypia nodded and turned to go. As she did, something rattled inside her purse. Marcus laughed. "I know that noise, I'll wager: stylus and waxed tablet. Who was it the patriarch said, Ioannakis II?"

"The third; the second is three hundred years dead." She spoke with perfect seriousness; the history she was composing occupied a good deal of her time. When Scaurus caught her eye, she said, "There are pleasures and pleasures, you know."

"No need to apologize to me," he said quickly, and meant it. Were it not for her active wit and sense of detail, the two of them could not have met even half so often as they did, and likely would have been discovered long since.

"Apologize? I wasn't." Her voice turned frosty on the instant; she would not stand being taken lightly over her work.

"All right," he said mildly, and saw her relax. He went on, "You might want to compare notes with my friend Gorgidas when the embassy to the Arshaum comes back from the steppe." With a sudden stab of loneliness, he wondered how the Greek physician was faring; despite his acerbic front, he was what Homer called "a friend to mankind."

Many Videssians would have raised an eyebrow at the idea of learning anything from outlanders, but Alypia said eagerly, "Yes, you've told me how the folk in the world you came from write history, too. How valuable it will be for me to have such a different view of the art—we've been copying each other for too long, I fear."

She looked out the window again, grimaced in annoyance. "And now for a third time I'll try and go. No, say not one word more; I really must be gone." She stepped into his arms, kissed him firmly but quickly, and slipped out the door.

Marcus stayed behind for a few minutes; they chanced being seen together as little as they could. Meeting more than once at the same place was a risk in itself, but the inn's convenience to the patriarchal residence weighed against the danger—and Aetios, once paid, asked no questions.

To spin out the time, the tribune went downstairs to the taproom and ordered a jack of ale; sometimes he preferred it to the sweet Videssian wine. Aetios handed him the tall tarred-leather mug with a knowing smirk, then grunted when the Roman stared back stonily, refusing to rise to the bait. Muttering to himself, the innkeeper went off to serve someone else.

The taproom, almost empty when Scaurus had come to the inn early in the afternoon, was filling as day drew to a close. The crowd was mostly workingmen: painters smeared with paint; bakers with flour; carpenters; tailors; a barber, his mustaches and the end of his beard waxed to points; bootmakers; an effeminate-looking fellow who was probably a bathhouse attendant. Many of them seemed regulars and called greetings to each other as they saw faces they knew. A barmaid squeaked indignantly when the barber pinched her behind. One of the painters, who was guzzling down wine, started a song, and half the tavern joined him. Even Marcus knew the chorus: "The wine gets drunk, but you get drunker."

He finished his ale and picked his way out through the growing crowd. He heard someone say to a tablemate, "What's the dirty foreigner doing here, anyway?" but his size—to say nothing of the yard-long Gallic sword that swung on his hip—let him pass unchallenged.

He bore the blade wherever he went. He might have laughed at the power of the druids when he was serving with Caesar's army, but their enchantments, wrapped in his sword and Viridovix', had swept the legionaries from Gaul to Videssos. And in Videssos, with sorcery a fact of life, the two enchanted weapons showed still greater power. Not only were they unnaturally strong in the attack, cleaving mail and plate, but the druids' marks stamped into the blades turned aside harmful magic.

The great golden globes on spires above the High Temple glowed ruddily in the light of the setting sun. After a brief glance their way, Marcus turned his back and walked south toward Middle Street. His progress was slow; traffic clogged Videssos' twisting lanes: people afoot; women on donkeys or in litters; men riding mules and horses; and carts and wagons, some drawn by as many as half a dozen beasts, full of vegetables, fruits, and grain to keep the ever-hungry city fed. Animals brayed; teamsters clapped hands to belt-knives as they wrangled over a narrow right-of-way; ungreased axles screeched.

"Well, go ahead, walk right past me. I'll pretend I don't know you either," said an indignant voice at the tribune's elbow.

He spun around. "Oh, hello, Taso. I'm sorry; I really didn't see you."

"A likely story, with this mat of fuzz on my chin." The ambassador from Khatrish sniffed. A small, birdlike man, Taso Vones would have looked perfectly Videssian except that, instead of trimming his beard as did all imperials save priests, he let it tumble in bushy splendor halfway down his chest. He loathed the style, but his sovereign the khagan insisted on it as a reminder that the Khatrisher ruling class ultimately sprang from Khamorth stock. That they had been intermarrying with their once-Videssian subjects for something close to eight hundred years now was not allowed to interfere with the warrior tradition.

Vones cocked his head to one side, reminding Scaurus more than ever of a sparrow: bright, perky, unendingly curious. "You haven't been out and about much, have you? Thorisin finally let you off the string, eh?" he guessed shrewdly.

"You might say so," the Roman answered, casting about for a story that would cover him. Whatever it was going to be, he knew he would have to work it into the conversation naturally; just throwing it out would make the envoy take it for a lie and, being gleefully cynical about such things, call him on it at once.

But Vones did not seem much interested in Marcus' answer; he was full of news of his own. "Had we not met this way, I'd have come to see you in the next day or two."

"Always a pleasure."

"Always a nuisance, you mean," the Khatrisher chuckled. Marcus' denials were, on the whole, sincere; Taso's breezy frankness was a refreshing relief from the Videssian style, which raised innuendo to a high art. Even Vones, though, hesitated before going on. "I've news from Metepont, if you care to hear it."

Scaurus stiffened. "Do you?" he said in as neutral a tone as he could manage. Metepont lay on the west coast of the island Duchy of Namdalen; more to the point, it was Helvis' town. Sighing, the tribune said, "You'd best give it to me. I'd sooner have it from you than most other people I could think of."

"For which praise I thank you." Vones looked faintly embarrassed, an expression the Roman had not seen on him before. At last he said, "You have a daughter there. My news must be weeks old by now, but from all I know, mother and child were both doing well. She named it Emilia. That's not a Namdalener name; does it come from your people?"

"Hmm? Yes, it's one of ours," Marcus said absently. No reason to expect the Khatrisher to remember his gentile name, not when he'd only heard it a couple of times years ago. He wondered whether Helvis was twisting the knife further, or thought of it as some sort of apology. He shook his head. A child he would never see . . . "How did you learn about it?"

"As you might expect—from the great count Drax. He's hiring mercenaries again, to replace the regiment you broke up for him last year. He had a message of his own for you, too—said he'd like to have you on his side for a change, and he'd make it worth your while to switch."

With studied deliberation, Scaurus spat into the dirt between two flagstones. "He's a fool to want me. Any man who'd turn his coat once'll turn it twice."

Vones laughed at his grimness. "He also said he knew you'd tell him to go to the ice, so get your chin off your chest."

Marcus stayed somber. He could think of a way for Drax to have a chance of prying him away from Videssos: send Thorisin the same message he'd given Taso, and let the Emperor's suspicion do the rest. He wondered if that would occur to the Namdalener. It might; Drax had the mind of a snake. While many islanders aped Videssian ways, the great count could match the imperials at their own intrigues.

Scaurus shook his head again, slowly, like a man bedeviled by bees. The past, it was clear, was not done stinging him yet.

"Hello, look who's coming up behind you," Taso Vones said, snapping his reverie. "Everyone's favorite Videssian officer." The tribune turned to see who had earned that sardonic compliment. He gave a grunt of laughter when he spotted Provhos Mourtzouphlos halfway down the block, almost hidden behind a cart piled high with apples.

The cavalryman looked for a moment as though he would spurn their company, but came up when Taso waved to him. The little Khatrisher bowed from the waist, a paradigm of politeness. "Good evening to you, your excellency. Out slumming, I see." Instead of his usual coxcomb's clothes, Mourtzouphlos was in an ill-fitting homespun tunic, with baggy, mud-colored trousers tucked into torn boots.

He had lost none of his arrogance, though. Looking down his long nose at Vones, he said, "If you must know, easterner, I was hoping a show of poverty would help beat a knave down on the price of a filly." That showed more wit than Marcus would have expected from him.

"And what of you two?" the Videssian went on. "Hatching plots?" He did not bother hiding his disdain.

"Foiling them, if I can," Scaurus said. He gave Mourtzouphlos Taso's news of Drax, adding, "Since you see so much of the Avtokrator these days, best you pass the warning on."

The sarcasm rolled off Mourtzouphlos without sticking, though Taso Vones suffered a sudden coughing fit and had to be slapped on the back. Watching the cavalryman trying to be gracious in his thanks was satisfaction enough for Marcus, though he recovered too quickly to suit the Roman. He had hoped for several minutes of awkwardness, but got only a few sentences' worth.

"Will there be anything more?" Mourtzouphlos asked, for all the world as if Scaurus and Vones had approached him rather than the other way round. When they were silent, he jerked his head in a single short nod. "A pleasant evening to you both, then." He started down the street as though they did not exist.

He actually jumped when Vones called after him, "Did you buy that filly, my lord?"

"Eh?" Mourtzouphlos blinked, collected himself, and said with a scowl, "No; I found some ne'er-do-well's been riding her hard. She's of no value jaded so." He chuckled unpleasantly. "An interesting experience, all the same." And he was off again, swaggering in his shabby boots.

"Self-satisfied bastard," Marcus said as soon as he was out of earshot.

"Isn't he, though?" Taso did a wicked imitation of the officer's nasty laugh. "Like most of that sort, he's satisfied with very little." He plucked at Scaurus' sleeve. "Come with me, why don't you, if you have some gold in your pouch? Come anyway; I'll stake you. I'm for a dice game at a Namdalener tin-merchant's house—you know how the islanders love to gamble. And old Frednis sets a rare table, too. Just wait till you taste the smoked oysters—ah! And the asparagus and crabmeat . . ." He ran his tongue over his lips, like a cat that scents cream.

The Roman patted guiltily at his midriff; these long dull weeks hunched over a desk were putting weight on him. Well, he told himself, you don't *have* to eat much. "Why not?" he said.

Stumbling in the darkness, Scaurus climbed the stone stairs to his small chamber in the bureaucrat's wing of the Grand Court. The hallways, full of the bustle of imperial business during the day, echoed to the slap of his boots. He could still hear Taso Vones singing, faint in the distance, as the Khatrisher lurched off toward his quarters in the Hall of the Ambassadors.

He had not lied, the tribune thought muzzily. Frednis the Namdalener did not stint his guests, not with food nor drink. And the dice were hot; new gold clinked in Scaurus' belt pouch. At any Roman game he would have been skinned, but to the Videssians a double one was a good throw, not a loser: "Phos' suns," they called it.

Pale shafts of moonlight from narrow outer windows guided him down the corridor. He carefully counted doorways as he passed them; the chambers to either side of his own were mere storerooms.

Then his hand was on his sword hilt, for a line of light from a lamp, yellow as butter, slipped out from beneath the bottom of his door. He slid the blade free as quietly as he could. Whoever was inside—sneak thief? spy? assassin?—would regret it. His first thought was of Avshar and wizardry, but the druids' marks on his blade did not glow as they did when magic was near. Only a man, then.

He seized the latch and threw the door wide as he sprang into the room. "Who the—?" he started to roar, and then half choked as his shout was swallowed in a gurgle of amazement.

Gaius Philippus stood in a wary fencer's crouch beside the tribune's bed, *gladius* at guard position; the senior centurion had not lived to grow gray by taking chances. When he saw it was Scaurus coming through the doorway, he swung the shortsword up in salute. "Took you long enough," he remarked. "Must be past midnight."

"What are you *doing* here?" Marcus said, stepping forward to clasp his hand. Not until he felt the other's callused palm against his own did he wholly believe Frednis' wine had not left him seeing things.

"Cooling my heels, till now," the stocky veteran replied, grinning at the tribune's confusion. That was literally true; he was barefoot, his unlaced *caligae* kicked into a corner, one with its hobnailed sole flipped over. He had made himself comfortable during his wait in other ways as well, if the empty jug of wine not far away was any indication.

"And beyond that?" Marcus was smiling, too, mainly at the pleasure of feeling sonorous Latin roll off his tongue; he had not used his birthspeech all winter long. And Gaius Philippus was a Roman's Roman: brave, practical, without much imagination, but stubborn enough to bull ahead on any course he set himself.

His presence was a marker of that last trait, for he explained: "Your bloody damn fool pen-pushers here, sir, haven't sent our lads a single goldpiece the last two months. If they don't see some money pretty fornicating quick they'll start plundering the countryside round Garsavra, and then it's Hades out to lunch for discipline, as well you know. That we can't have."

Scaurus nodded; the legionaries took more delicate handling as mercenaries for Videssos than they had with the full weight of Roman military tradition on them. It was what remained of that tradition that made them as effective as they were in the Empire, where most infantry was no better than rabble. But with their pay in arrears they were tinder waiting for a spark.

The tribune asked, "Why didn't you write me?"

"For one thing, these cursed dirt roads the Videssians insist on using for the sake of their precious horses were arse-deep in mud till a couple of weeks ago, and what were the odds of a letter getting through? For another, I'm not sure I could write that much. It doesn't come easy to me, you know.

"Besides—" Gaius Philippus set his jaw as he came to the meat of things. "—you want something done right, do it yourself. I want you to find me the seal-stamper who bungled this business so I can tell him where to head in. If the damned imperials are going to hire troops to do their fighting for 'em, they'd best treat 'em right. And one of 'em's going to remember it from now on."

Scaurus already knew who the guilty bureaucrat was; the picture of the senior centurion chewing him out in his best parade-ground bellow was irresistible delightful. "I'll do it," he said. "I want to watch: it'll be like throwing a hiveful of wasps on a desk and then whacking it with a stick."

"Aye, won't it just?" Gaius Philippus said with no less anticipation. He gave a satisfied nod. Not for the first time, Marcus thought his features belonged on a sestertius or denarius—his neat, short cap of iron-gray hair; scarred, jutting chin; angular cheekbones; and proud aquiline nose made him ideal for the starkly realistic portraiture of a Roman coin.

The veteran waved round the bare little room, which held no furniture save Scaurus' mattress, a chair that doubled as lampstand, and a much-battered pine wardrobe with a Videssian obscenity carved into one side.

"I thought you lived softer than this," he said. "If this is all Thorisin's giving you, you'd do better coming back to us. When will you, anyway?"

Marcus spread his hands helplessly. "It's not that simple. I'm not in good odor here, after letting Drax go."

"Oh. That," Gaius Philippus said with distaste. Of course he knew the story; the legionaries Scaurus had sent back after the great count escaped would have brought it with them. The senior centurion hesitated, then went on in what was meant for sympathy, "A plague take the scheming bitch." Anger and rough contempt filled his voice; beyond his body's pleasure, he had scant use for women.

Caught between gratitude and the irrational urge to spring to Helvis' defense, the tribune said nothing. After an awkward few seconds Gaius Philippus changed the subject. "The lads miss you, sir, and asked me to give you their best."

"Did they?" Marcus said, touched. "That's good of them." A thought struck him. "Who's in charge there, with you in the city?"

"Well, with you not there after Junius Blaesus, uh, died—" Gaius Philippus got through that as quickly as he could; Helvis had knifed the junior centurion. "—I bumped Sextus Minucius up to his spot." Seeing Marcus raise an eyebrow, he said, "I know he's young for it, but he's shaping well. He's a worker, that one, and nobody's fool. He's tough enough to flatten anyone who talks back, too."

"All right. You know best, I'm sure." With more than thirty years in the legions, the senior centurion made a better judge of soldiers than Scaurus himself, and the tribune was wise enough to realize it. He did ask, though, "How do the outlanders take to him?" Since coming to Videssos, the legionaries had had a good many local recruits to help fill out their ranks; in his Romanness, Gaius Philippus might not even have seen their acceptance of Minucius as a problem.

But his answer showed he had. "Gagik gets on with him fine." Bagratouni headed a two-hundred-man contingent of Vaspurakaners, organized as an oversize maniple; driven from their homeland by the Yezda and then caught in Zemarkhos' pogrom, they fought with a dour, savage valor under their canny *nakharar*. Gaius Philippus' next sentence further reassured Scaurus: "Minucius isn't too proud to ask Bagratouni what he thinks, either."

"That's fine," the tribune said. "I'm glad I had the sense to do the same, with you." He had learned the warrior's trade now, but when he joined Caesar in Gaul, he had been a raw political appointee, very much dependent on his senior centurion. Gaius Philippus grunted at the praise. Marcus asked, "How's Zeprin the Red faring?"

The veteran grunted again, but with a different intonation. "He still just wants to be a common trooper, worse luck."

Marcus shook his head. "Too bad. There's a good man wasting himself." The burly Haloga had been a marshal in Mavrikios Gavras' Imperial Guards, but after he survived Maragha when the Emperor and the rest of the guards regiment were slain he blamed himself and turned his back on officer's rank. Soldiering was all he knew, but he refused to endanger anyone but himself by his actions.

"And Pakhymer?" Scaurus asked.

This time it was a snort from Gaius Philippus. "Pakhymer is—Pakhymer." The two Romans grinned at each other. Laon Pakhymer's brigade of light cavalry from Khatrish was not strictly a part of their command, but the two forces had served side by side since the Maragha campaign. Pakhymer's easy going, catch-as-catch-can style had driven the methodical senior centurion quietly mad all that time. However he did it, though, he generally got results.

"What else do I need to tell you?" Gaius Philippus said to himself, absently scratching at one of the puckered scars on his right forearm; his left, protected by his *scutum*, was almost unmarked. He brightened. "Oh, yes—a pair of new underofficers: Pullo and Vorenus."

"Both at once, eh?" Marcus asked slyly.

"Aye, both at once," Gaius Philippus said, not rising to the tribune's teasing. "You think I had the ballocks to promote one and not the other?" The two legionaries had fought for years over which made the better soldier, a feud that ended only when they saved each other's lives in a skirmish with Drax' Namdaleni.

"No quarrel, no quarrel," Scaurus said in some haste. He sighed; the wine he had drunk at Frednis' was making him low. "Seems you've done a splendid job, Gaius. I don't know why anyone would miss me; you've managed everything just as I would have."

"Don't say that, sir!" Gaius Philippus cried, real alarm in his voice.

"Begging your pardon, but I wouldn't have your bloody job on a bet. Oh, I can handle this end of it: who to promote, who to slap down, which march route to pick, how to dress my line. But the rest of it, especially in this mercenary's game—picking your way through the factions as Thorisin and the pen-pushers square off against each other, knowing when to keep your mouth shut, keeping some shriveled old turd of an officer happy so he doesn't bugger you the minute you turn your back . . . Thank the gods the road from the city to Garsavra's been all over mud what with winter and all, so the damned Videssians weren't able to pull me eight ways at once." He threw up his hands. "Take it back, please. We need you for it!"

It was probably the longest speech Marcus had ever heard him make. Moved, he reached out and clasped the senior centurion's hand. "Thanks, old friend," he said softly.

"For what? The truth?" Gaius Philippus said, outwardly as scornful as ever of any show of emotion. But his hard features could not quite hide his pleasure, and he shuffled his feet awkwardly. He fetched up against the empty jug of wine, which rolled away, bumping on the slightly uneven floor. The veteran followed it with his eyes. "You know," he said, "that wasn't nearly enough. We should have more."

Marcus swallowed a groan. He was already expecting a thick head, but he could not turn the senior centurion down. Gamely he said, "Why not?" for the second time that evening. Come morning, he knew, he would have his answer, but he went out even so.

II

THE ARSHAUM CAMP WOKE WITH THE SUN. SWORDS FLASHED IN THE morning light outside one of the beehive-shaped felt tents; steel rang sweetly against steel. One of the fencers whooped and gave a great roundhouse slash. The other, a smaller man, ducked under it and stepped smartly forward. He stopped his thrust bare inches from his opponent's chest.

"To the afterworld with you, you kern," Viridovix panted, stumbling back and throwing his arms wide in surrender. The Gaul wiped the sweat from his face with a freckled forearm and brushed long coppery hair out of his eyes. "Sure and you must ha' been practicing on the sly."

Gorgidas studied him narrowly. "Are you sure you did not give me that opening?" Physician by training, historian by avocation, the Greek was no skilled swordsman. He had seen too much of war in his medical service with the Roman legions for it to draw him as it did Viridovix. But, having been forced to see he needed a warrior's skills to survive on the steppe, he set about acquiring them with the same dogged persistence he gave to medical lore.

The big Celt grinned at him, green eyes crinkling with mirth. "And what if I did? You were after having the wit to take it, which was the point. Not bad, for a man so old and all," he added, to see Gorgidas fume. Save for the beard the Greek had lately grown, which was streaked all through with white, he might have been any age from twenty-five to sixty; his lean body was full of a surprising spare strength, while his face did not carry much loose flesh to sag with the years.

"You don't have to be so bloody proud. You're no younger than I am," Gorgidas snapped. Viridovix' grin got wider. He preened, stroking the luxuriant red mustaches that hung almost to his shoulders. They were still unsilvered. He had scraped off the beard he grew earlier in the winter, but no gray had lurked there either.

"Boast over what you may," the Greek said sourly, "but both of us wake up to piss oftener of nights than we did a few years ago, when we were on the lazy side of forty. Deny it if you can."

"Och, a hit and no mistake," Viridovix said. "And here's another for you!" He sprang at Gorgidas. The physician got his *gladius* up in time to turn the Gaul's blow, but it sent the shortsword—a gift from Gaius Philippus, and one he had never thought he'd use—spinning from his hand.

"Still not bad," the Celt said, picking it up for him. "I'd meant to spank your ribs with the flat o' my blade that time."

"Bah! I should have held on." Gorgidas opened and closed his fist several times, working flexibility into his numbed fingers. "You have a heavy arm there, you hulking savage." He was too honest not to give praise where it was due, though his sharp tongue diluted it in the giving.

"Well, may you be staked out for the corbies, scoffer of a Greekling." Viridovix swelled with mock indignation. Between themselves they spoke a bastard mix of Latin and Videssian. Each was the only representative of his people in this new world and each felt the pain of his own language slowly dying in him for want of anyone with whom to speak it. Gorgidas kept Greek alive by composing his history in that tongue. But only druids wrote the Celtic speech, so Viridovix was denied even that relief.

Around them the camp was coming to life. Some nomads were tending to their small, shaggy horses while others knocked down tents and rolled the fabric up around the sticks that formed their frameworks. Still more crouched round fires as they breakfasted; the morning was chilly. They mixed water with dry curds and spooned up the thick, soupy, tasteless mix; gnawed at slabs of salted and dried beef, mutton, goat, or venison; or speared horsegut-cased sausages on sticks and roasted them over the flames. Many of them did not have as much as they wanted; supplies were running low.

Mounted sentries trotted in from the perimeter, rubbing at eyes red and tired from their sleepless duty. Others rode out to take their place. The Arshaum grumbled at the tight watch their khagan Arghun kept.

What if they were on the plains of Pardraya, east of the river Shaum, instead of in their own steppelands to the west? Their ancestors had smashed the Khamorth over the river to Pardraya half a century before; few believed the rival nomad folk would dare contest their passage.

For all that, though, the Arshaum were men who enjoyed fighting for its own sake, and Gorgidas and Viridovix were not alone in weapons play. Plainsmen thrust light lances and flung javelins both afoot and mounted. They fired arrows at wadded balls of cloth tossed into the air and at shields propped upright on the ground. Their double-curved bows, reinforced with sinew, sent barbed shafts smashing through the small, round targets—shafts that could pierce a corselet of boiled leather or chain mail afterwards.

A bowstring snapped just as an archer let fly, sending his arrow spinning crazily through the air. "Heads up!" the Arshaum yelled, and all around him nomads dove for cover.

"Why does he go shouting that, the which would do a man no good at all?" Viridovix said. "Riddle it out for me, Gorgidas dear."

"He must have meant it especially for you, you unruly Celt," the physician replied with relish, "knowing you always do the opposite of whatever you're told."

"Honh! See if I'm fool enough to be asking for another explanation from you any time soon."

Not far away, a plainsman thudded into the dirt, flung over his wrestling partner's shoulder; the Arshaum were highly skilled at unarmed combat. Their swordplay was less expert. Several pairs slashed away at each other with the medium-length curved blades they favored. The yataghans, heavy at the point, were all very well for quick cuts from horseback, but did not lend themselves to scientific fencing.

"Had enough?" Gorgidas asked, sheathing his sword.

"Aye, for the now."

They wandered over to watch one of the dueling pairs, perhaps the unlikeliest match in the camp. Arghun's son Arigh was going at it furiously with Batbaian, the son of Targitaus, their blades a silvery glitter as they met each other stroke for stroke.

They were both khagans' sons, but there their resemblance ended. For looks, Arigh was a typical enough Arshaum: slender, lithe, and swarthy, with a wide, high-cheekboned face, short, almost flat nose, and slanted eyes. Only a few black hairs grew on his upper lip and straggled down from the point of his chin. But Batbaian was a Khamorth, with his people's broad-shouldered frame, thick curly beard half hiding his heavy features, and a strong, fleshy beak in the center of his face. He would have been handsome but for the red ruin of a socket where his left eye had been.

The eye he still had was the "mercy" of Avshar and Varatesh the bandit chief. They had taken a thousand prisoners when they crushed the army Targitaus raised against them, and then given those prisoners back to Batbaian's father . . . all but fifty of them with both eyes burned away, the rest left with one to guide their comrades home. Seeing them so ravaged, Targitaus died of a stroke on the spot. Varatesh fell on his devastated clan three days later. As far as Viridovix knew, Batbaian was the only clansman left alive—save himself, whom Targitaus had adopted into the Wolves after he escaped Varatesh and his henchmen. The bandits missed them only because they were attending an outlying herd; they rode in at day's end to find massacre laid out before them.

The Gaul's features, usually merry, grew grim and tight as he fell into memory's grip. Batbaian had had a sister—but Seirem was dead now, and perhaps that was as well, with what she met before she died. Part of Viridovix' heart was dead with her; a tomcat by nature, he had come late to love and lost it too early.

The past winter he and Batbaian had lived the outlaw's life, revenge their only goal. At last he thought to cross west into Shaumkhiil and seek aid from the Arshaum against Varatesh and Avshar, his puppet-master. Batbaian's hate burned away his fear of the western nomads; where the Arshaum despised the Khamorth, the latter had almost a superstitious dread for the folk who had harried them east over the steppe.

Having traveled with the Arshaum force for weeks, though, Batbaian saw that they were men, too, not the near-demons he had thought. And he had earned their respect as well, for the hardships he had borne and for his skill with his hands. His burly build let him shoot farther than most of them, and if he was now giving ground to Arigh, his foe was fast and deceptive as a striking snake.

"The wind-spirits take it!" he cursed in his own guttural tongue, falling back again. In a mixture of bad Videssian—which Arigh understood, having served his father as envoy to the Empire—and worse Arshaum, he went on, "With only eye one, not able to tell how away far you are."

Arigh's grin was predatory, his teeth very white. "My friend, Varatesh's men would not heed your whining, and I will not either."

He pressed his attack, his slashes coming from every direction at once. Then he was staring at his empty hand; his sword lay on the ground at his feet. Batbaian leaped forward and planted a boot on it. He tapped Arigh on the chest with his blade. The watchers whooped at the sudden reversal.

"Why you dirty son of a flop-eared goat," Arigh said without much rancor. "You suckered me into that, didn't you?"

Batbaian only grunted. The summer before he had been hardly more than a boy, full of a boy's chatter and bubbling enthusiasm for everything around him. These days he was a man, and a driven one. He spoke seldom, and his smile, which was rarer, never reached past his lips.

"Puir lad," Viridovix murmured to Gorgidas. "A pity you canna unfreeze the spirit of him, as you did wi' this carcass o' mine."

"I know no gift for that, save it come from within a man's own soul," the physician answered. Then he spread his hands and admitted, "For that matter, when I found you I thought I would have to watch you die, too."

"A good thing you didn't. My ghost'd bewail you for it."

"Hmm. No doubt, if it takes after you in the flesh." But the Greek could not stay flippant long, not where the healing he had worked on Viridovix was concerned.

Ever since he was swept into Videssos with the legionaries, he had studied its healing art, an art that relied not so much on herbs and scalpels as on mustering and unleashing the power of the mind to beat back disease and injury—call it magic, for lack of a better word. He had seen Phos' healer-priests work cures on men he had given up for doomed, and chased after their skill like a hunter trailing some elusive beast.

But the stubborn rationality on which he prided himself would not let him truly accept that curing by mind alone was possible; it ran too much against all his training, all his deepest beliefs. And so for years he tried and, not genuinely believing he could succeed, never did. Only the lash of desperation at finding Viridovix freezing in a fierce steppe blizzard made him transcend his doubts and channel the healing energies through himself and into the Gaul.

He had healed again afterwards, closing and cleansing the bites an Arshaum took from a wolf that would not die with three arrows in its chest. Knowing he could heal made the second time easy. The nomad's gratitude was wine-sweet, and the Greek accepted as a badge of honor the tearing weariness that always followed healing.

"Why for we standing round?" Batbaian demanded. "We should riding be." Without waiting for an answer, he turned away from Arigh and went off to his string of horses to pick a mount for the day's ride.

Behind him, Arigh shook his head. "That one would ride through fire for his revenge."

The Arshaum around him nodded, sympathizing with Batbaian's blood feud. But Viridovix started in alarm, whipping his head round to make sure the Khamorth had not heard the remark. "Dinna say that to him, ever," he warned. " 'Twas Avshar's fires trapped him in the shindy, and all the rest, too." The Gaul shuddered as he remembered those tall, arrow-straight lines of flame darting like serpents over the steppe at the evil wizard's will.

There was compassion under the unfeeling veneer Arigh cultivated, though he often did not let it out. Even when he did, it was usually with a self-deprecating, "All that time in Videssos has left me soft." But now he bit his lip, admitting, "I'd forgotten."

A last delay held up the army's departure a few minutes more. All the tents were down and stowed on horseback save the one shared by Lankinos Skylitzes and Pikridios Goudeles, Thorisin's envoys to Arghun. Skylitzes was long since out and about; the tall imperial officer looked with dour amusement at the sign of his tentmate's sleepiness.

He stuck his head inside the tent and roared, "Up, slugabed! Is this a holy day, for you to spend it all between the sheets?"

Goudeles emerged in short order, but mightily rumpled, tunic on back-to-front, and belt out of half its loops. Rubbing sleep from his eyes, the pen-pusher winced at the ironic cheer that greeted his appearance. "Oh, very well, here I am," he said testily. He glowered at Skylitzes; the two of them were as cat and dog. "Mightn't you have picked a less drastic way to rouse me?"

"No," Skylitzes said. He was that rarity, a short-spoken Videssian.

Still grumbling, Goudeles began to knock down the tent, but made such a slow, clumsy job of it that Skylitzes, with an exasperated grunt, finally pitched in to help. "You bungler," he said, almost kindly, as he tied the roll of tent fabric and sticks onto a packsaddle.

"Bungler? I?" Goudeles drew himself up to his full height, which was not imposing. "No need to mock me merely because I was not cut out for life in the field." He caught Gorgidas' eye. "These soldiers have a narrow view of life's priorities, do they not?"

"No doubt," the Greek answered. As he was already mounted, he sounded a trifle smug. Goudeles looked hurt, one of his more artful expressions. In truth, the bureaucrat was a carpet knight, infinitely more at home in the elaborate double-dealing of Videssos the city than here on the vast empty steppe. But his gift for intrigue made him a sly, subtle diplomat, and he had done well in helping persuade Arghun to favor the Empire over Yezd.

He spent a few seconds trying to restore the point to his beard, but gave it up as a bad job. "Hopeless," he said sadly. He climbed onto his own horse and patted his belly, still ample after close to a year on the plains. "Am I too late to break my fast?"

Skylitzes rolled his eyes, but Viridovix handed Goudeles a chunk of meat. The pen-pusher eyed it skeptically. "What, ah, delicacy have we here?"

"Sure and it's half a roast marmot," the Celt told him, grinning. "Begging your honor's pardon and all, but I was after eating the last of my sausage today."

Goudeles turned a pale green. "Somehow I find my appetite is less hearty than it was, though my thanks, of course, for your generosity." He gave the ground squirrel back to Viridovix.

"Ride, then," Skylitzes snapped. As Goudeles clucked to his horse, though, the officer admitted to Gorgidas, "I'm low myself; we should stop for a hunt soon."

The Greek dipped his head in his people's gesture of agreement. "So am I." He shuddered slightly. "We could go on the nomad way for a while, living off our horses' blood." He did not intend to be taken seriously. The idea revolted him.

Not so Skylitzes; all he said was, "That's for emergencies only. It runs the animals down too badly." He had traveled the steppes before and was at home with the customs of the plainsmen, speaking both the Arshaum and Khamorth tongues fluently.

The Arshaum moved steadily over the Pardrayan plain, their course a bit east of south. Alternately walking and trotting, their ponies ate up the miles. The rough-coated little beasts were not much for looks, but there was iron endurance in them. Gorgidas blessed the wet ground and thick grass cover of approaching spring; later in the year the army would have kicked up great choking clouds of dust.

When afternoon came, the sun sparkled off the waters of the inland Mylasa Sea on the western horizon. Other than that, the steppe was all but featureless, an endless, gently rolling sea of grass that stretched from the borders of Videssos further west than any man knew. As a landscape, Gorgidas found it dull. He had grown up with the endless variety of terrain Greece offers: seacoast, mountains, carved valleys kissed by the Mediterranean sun or dark under forest, and flatlands narrow enough to walk across in half a day.

To Viridovix the limitless vistas of the steppe were not so much boring as actively oppressive. His Gallic woods cut down the sweep of vision, left a man always close to something he could reach out and touch. The plains made him feel tiny and insignificant, an insect crawling across a tray. He fought his unreasoning fear as best he could, riding near the center of the army to use the nomads around him as a shield against the vastness beyond.

Each day he looked south in the hope of seeing the mountains of Erzerum—the peaks that separated Pardraya from Yezd—shoulder their way up over the edge of the world. So far he had been disappointed. "One morning they'll be peeping up, though, and none too soon for me," he said to Batbaian. "It does a body good, knowing there's an end to all this flat."

"Why?" Batbaian demanded, as used to open space as Viridovix was to his narrow forest tracks. His companions also shook their heads at the Celt's strange ways. As he usually did, Batbaian rode with the ten-man guard squad that had accompanied the Videssian embassy out from Prista. Except for Viridovix and Skylitzes, the troopers were the only ones with the army who spoke his tongue, and most of them had Khamorth blood.

The squad leader, Agathias Psoes, was a Videssian, but years at the edge of Pardraya had left him as at home in the language of its people as in the imperial tongue. "Country doesn't matter one way or the other," he said with an old soldier's cynicism. "It's the bastards who live on it that cause the trouble."

Viridovix burst out laughing. "Here and I thought I was rid o' Gaius Philippus for good and all, and up springs his shadow." Psoes, who knew next to nothing of the Romans, blinked in incomprehension.

"What are the lot of you grunting about there?" an Arshaum asked. Viridovix turned his head to see Arghun the khagan and his younger son Dizabul coming up alongside the guardsmen. The men from Shaumkhiil spoke a smooth, sibilant tongue; the harsh gutturals of the Khamorth speech grated on their ears.

With Arghun, though, the teasing was good-natured. He led the Gray Horse clan, the largest contingent of the Arshaum army, more by guile and persuasion than by the bluff bluster Viridovix had used as a chief among the Lexovii back in Gaul.

The Celt translated as well as he could; he was beginning to understand the Arshaum language fairly well, but speaking it was harder. "And what do you think of that, red whiskers?" Arghun asked. Viridovix' exotic coloring fascinated him, as did the Celt's luxuriant mustaches. The khagan grew only a few gray hairs on his upper lip and frankly envied the other's splendid ornament.

"Me? I puts it the other way round. People is people anywheres, but the—how you be saying?—scenery, it change a lot."

"Something to that," Arghun nodded, an instinctively shrewd politician for all his barbaric trappings.

"How can you tell, father?" Dizabul said, his regular features twisting into a sneer. "He talks so poorly it's next to impossible to make out what he says." With a supercilious smile, he turned to Viridovix, "That should be 'I would put,' outlander, and 'people are people,' and 'scenery changes.' "

"I thank your honor," the Gaul said—not at all what he was thinking. Dizabul struck him as Arghun's mistake; the lad had grown up having his every whim indulged, with predictable results. He also loathed his brother and everyone connected with him, which added venom to the tone he took with Viridovix. "Spoiled as a salmon a week out of water," the Gaul muttered in his own speech.

Arghun shook his head at Dizabul in mild reproof. "I'd sooner hear good sense wearing words of old sheepskin than numskullery or wickedness decked out in sable."

"Listen to him and welcome, then," Dizabul snarled, bristling at even the suggestion of criticism. "I shan't waste my time." He flicked his horse's reins and ostentatiously trotted away.

Gorgidas, who was deep in conversation with Tolui the shaman, glanced up as Dizabul rode past. His eyes followed the comely youth as another man's might a likely wench. He was only too aware of the young princeling's petulance and vile temper, but the sheer physical magnetism he exerted almost made them forgettable. He realized he had missed Tolui's last couple of sentences. "I'm sorry. What were you saying?"

"When spring is far enough for the frogs to come out," Tolui repeated, "there is a potion I intend to try on Arghun's lameness. It should be only days now."

"Ah?" said the Greek, interested again as soon as medicine was mentioned. His own knowledge had been enough to save the khagan's life from a draft of hemlock Bogoraz of Yezd had given him when Arghun decided for Videssos, but the paralyzing drug left Arghun's legs permanently weakened. Gorgidas had not been able to work the Videssian styly of healing then, and it did no good against long-established infirmities.

"I need nine frogs," the shaman explained. "Their heads are pithed, and the yellow fluid that comes out is mixed with melted goat fat in a pot. The pot is sealed and left in the sun for a day and in a fire overnight. Then the oil that is left is dabbed on the afflicted joints with a feather. Most times it works well."

"I'd not heard of that one before," Gorgidas admitted, intrigued and a little nauseated. He thought of something else. "Lucky for you Arghun is no Khamorth, or you'd never get near him with that medicine."

Tolui barked laughter. "True. Just another proof the Hairies—" He used his people's contemptuous nickname for the heavily bearded natives of Pardraya. "—hardly rate being called men at all."

"Tomorrow we will hunt," Arghun declared, sitting by the campfire and spooning up the last of his miserable meal of curds and water. A few of his men still hoarded a bit of sausage or smoked meat, while others had knocked over hares or other small game while they traveled; but most were reduced to the same iron rations he carried, or to blood.

"About time. This Pardraya is a paltry place," said Irnek, a tall nomad who led the Arshaum of the Black Sheep clan, next most numerous after the Gray Horses of Arghun and sometimes rivals to them. Puzzlement dwelt in the Arshaum's eyes; he was a clever man, confused by what he was finding. He went on, "It should not be so. This land draws more rain than our Shaumkhiil and ought to support rich flocks. Not from what we've seen, though; I begin to forget the very look of a cow or sheep."

Angry growls of agreement rose from the plainsmen who heard him. They had counted on raiding the herds of the Khamorth as they traversed Pardraya on their way to Yezd, but since they crossed the Shaum those herds were nowhere to be found. They took the occasional stray cow, goat, fat-tailed sheep, but came across none of the great flocks that were as vital to the nomads as a farmer's crops to him.

For that matter, they had seen few Khamorth, not even scouts dogging their trail. The Arshaum took that as but another sign of cowardice, and joked about it. "What do the Hairies do when they see us coming?" to which the answer was, "Who knows? We never get the chance to find out."

The men who traveled with them worried more. Viridovix knew from bitter experience that Avshar could track him by his blade. No magic would bite on it, but that very blankness made it detectable to the wizard-prince. "Sure and it's no happen-so we've not had greetings from the spalpeen. Belike he's brewing somewhat against us."

"A greater concern," Pikridios Goudeles said, "is why no great number of Khamorth have gone over to us. Living under Avshar can scarcely be pleasant."

"A good point," said Gorgidas, who had wondered the same thing.

"Two reasons," Batbaian answered in his labored Videssian. "One, he rules through Varatesh, who is outlaw, yes, but from family of a khagan. He makes a good dog." The plainsman's eye narrowed in contempt.

"That one's more than Avshar's hound," Viridovix disagreed. The time he had spent in Varatesh's clutches made him thoroughly respect the outlaw chieftain's talents.

"I say what I say," Batbaian declared flatly. He stared at the Gaul, challenging him to argue further. Viridovix shrugged and waved for him to go on. "All right. Other reason is that most Khamorth worse afraid of Arshaum than of wizard. I was, so much I did not think of them till you say they might be help in revenge. May be lots of rebels hate Avshar but fear us here, too."

"Something to that," Skylitzes said. "He's also had the winter to deal with uprisings. A lesson or two from him would make anyone thoughtful."

"Thoughtful, forsooth!" Goudeles said. "Are you in a contest of understatement with me, Lankinos? Shall we go on to style this hateful winter just past 'cool,' Phos' High Temple 'large,' and Erzerum 'hilly'?"

Skylitzes' mouth twitched in the grimace he used for a smile. "Fair enough. We could call you 'gassy,' while we were about it."

The bureaucrat spluttered while his comrades laughed. Gorgidas made them serious once more when he asked, "If Avshar does assail us, how are we going to be able to resist him?"

"Fight him, crush him, kill him," Batbaian growled. "Stake him out on plains for vultures to eat. Why else did V'rid'rish bring me here to join you?"

"Crush him, aye, but how?" the Greek persisted. "Many have tried, but none succeeded yet."

Batbaian glared at him as he would have at anyone who questioned the certainty of vengeance. Skylitzes said, "These Arshaum are better warriors than the Khamorth, Gorgidas—and both sides think that's true, which helps make it so."

"What of it?" Gorgidas said. "Avshar need not have the finest soldiers to win. Look at Maragha, look at the battle on the steppe here last fall against Batbaian's father. In both of them it was his magic that made his victory for him, not the quality of his troops."

A gloomy silence fell. There was no denying the physician was right; he usually was. At last Viridovix said, "Very good, your generalship, sir, you've gone and named the problem for us. Are you after having somewhat in mind for solving it, or is it you want the rest of us grumpy as your ain self?"

"To the crows with you," Gorgidas said, nettled at the teasing. "What do I know of ordering battles and such? You were the great war-chieftain back there in Gaul—what would *you* do?"

Viridovix suddenly grew bleak. "Whatever the unriddling may be, I dinna ken it. For fighting the whoreson straight up, I was, and see how well that worked."

Cursing his clumsy tongue, Gorgidas started an apology, but Viridovix waved it away. "It was a question fairly put. The now, the best I know to do is find my bedroll and hope some good fairy'll whisper me my answer whilst I sleep."

"Fair enough." The Greek's eyes were getting sandy, too.

When morning came Viridovix was still without his solution. "Och, it's no luck the puir fairies ha'. They must wear out the wings of 'em or ever they get to this wretched world, the which is so far away and all," he said sadly.

His disappointment was quickly forgotten, though, in amazement over the Arshaum hunt. "Not ones to do things by halves, are they now?" he said to Gorgidas.

"Hardly." The entire Videssian embassy party made up a small part of one wing of the Arshaum army which, led by Arghun, spread out in a long east–west line across the steppe. The other half of the force, under Irnek's command, rode south. Sometime near noon they would also spread out, and then move north as Arghun's followers came down to meet them, the two lines trapping all the game between them.

The Khamorth did not stage such elaborate hunts; Batbaian was astonished to watch the Arshaum deployment. "This might as well war be," he said to Arigh.

"Why not?" the other returned. "What harder foe than hunger? Or do you enjoy the feel of your belly cozying up to your backbone?" It took a good deal to make the grim young Khamorth smile, but his lips parted for a moment.

When Arghun saw his line in position and judged Irnek had taken the rest of the nomads far enough south to shut in a good bag of game, he raised the army's standard high above his head. Fluttering on the end of a lance was Bogoraz's long wool caftan, all that was left of the treacherous ambassador. Like the Videssian party, he had sworn an oath to Arghun's shamans that he meant the khagan no harm and walked through their magic fire as surety for it. When he broke his pledge, the fire claimed him.

With the lifting of the standard, the line rolled forward. The Arshaum who had them pounded on drums, tooted pipes and bone whistles, winded horns. The rest yelled at the top of their lungs to scare beasts from cover.

Trotting along with the rest, Viridovix threw back his head and let out the unearthly wailing shriek of a Gallic war cry. "I don't know about the bloody animals," Gorgidas said with a shudder, "but you certainly frighten me."

"And what good is that, when you're nobbut skin and bones? Och, look, there goes a hare!" An Arshaum shot the little creature at the top of its leap. Backed by his potent bow, the arrow knocked it sideways. It kicked a couple of times and lay still. The plainsman leaned down from his saddle, grabbed it by the ears, and tossed it into a sack.

Viridovix howled again. "Something worthwhile for me to do, then; it's no dab hand at the bow I make, not next to these lads."

"Nor I," the Greek replied. He flapped his arms, bawled out snatches of Homer and Aiskhylos. Whether or not it was his antics that flushed it, another rabbit broke cover in front of him. Instead of running away, the panicked little beast darted straight past his horse. He cut at it with his sword, far too late. The nomad next to him shook his head derisively, mimed drawing a bow. He spread his hands in rueful agreement and apology.

Something went "Honk! Ho-onkk!" a couple of hundred feet down the line. Gorgidas saw a shape running through the grass, a couple of plainsmen in hot pursuit. Then it suddenly bounded into the air, flying strongly on short, stubby wings. The sun shone, metallic, off bronze tail feathers and head of iridescent red and green. "Pheasant!" Viridovix whooped. A storm of arrows brought the bird down. The Gaul fairly drooled. "Age him right, braise him with mushrooms, wild thyme, and a bit o' wormwood to cut the grease—"

"Remember where you are," Gorgidas said. "You'll be lucky if he gets cooked." Crestfallen, Viridovix gave a regretful nod.

A nomad shouted and his horse screamed in terror as a furiously spitting wildcat sprang at them. It clawed the horse's flank, sank its teeth into the Arshaum's calf, and was gone before anyone could do anything about it. The cursing plainsman bound up his leg and rode on, ignoring his comrades' jeers. Gorgidas reminded himself to look at the wound when the hunt was gone. Untended animal bites were almost sure to fester.

More arrows leaped into the sky as the hunters splashed through a small, chilly stream and sent geese and ducks up in desperate flight. Viridovix greedily snatched up a fat goose that had tumbled to earth with an arrow through its neck. "I'll not let anyone botch this," he said, as if challenging the world. "All dark meat it is, and all toothsome, too. O' course," he went on with a pointed glance Gorgidas' way, "I might enjoy the sharing of it, at least with them as dinna mock me."

"I'm plainly doomed to starve, then," the Greek said. Viridovix made a rude noise.

Goudeles said, "If it's praises you seek, outlander, I'll gladly compose a panegyric for you in exchange for a leg of that succulent fowl." He struck a pose—not an easy thing to do on horseback for such an indifferent rider—declaiming, "Behold the Phos-fostered foreigner, magnificent man of deeds of dought—"

"Oh, stifle it, Pikridios," Skylitzes said. "You're still fatter than the damned bird is, and slipperier than goose grease ever was." Not a bit offended, the bureaucrat went right on, the course best calculated to annoy Skylitzes.

"I wish we could bag more of these birds," Gorgidas said. "Too many are getting away."

"We will," Arigh promised, "but there aren't enough to be worthwhile this time." He pointed. "See? Tolui is ready when we come on a big flock."

The shaman was not wearing his usual garb, which differed not at all from that of the rest of the plainsmen: fur cap with ear flaps, tunic of sueded leather, heavy sheepskin jacket—some wore wolf, fox, or otter—leather trousers, and soft-soled boots. Instead, he had donned the fantastic regalia of his calling. Long fringes, some knotted to trap spirits and others dyed bright colors, hung from every inch of his robe and streamed behind him as he rode. A lurid, leering mask of hide stretched over a wooden framework hid his face. Only the sword that swung at his belt said he was human, not some demon's spawn.

Skylitzes followed Arigh's pointing finger, too. The Videssian officer made Phos' sun-sign against evil, muttering a prayer as he did so. Gorgidas caught part of it: ". . . and keep me safe from heathen wizardry." Unafraid of worldly dangers, Skylitzes had all his faith's pious suspicion of other beliefs.

Gorgidas gave a wry laugh; he was in no position to sneer at the soldier. He mistrusted magic, too, of every sort, for it flew straight against the logical set of mind with which he had faced the world since he was a beardless youth. That he worked it himself made him no more easy with it.

He must have been thinking aloud, for Viridovix turned his head and said, "Sure and this is a new world, or had your honor never noticed, being so busy scribbling about it and all? Me, now, I take things as they come, the which is more restful nor worrying anent the wherefore of 'em."

"If you're pleased to be a cabbage, then be one," the Greek snapped. "As for me, I'd sooner try to understand."

"A cabbage, is it? Och, well, at the least you credit me for a head, which is kindlier than you've sometimes been, I'm thinking." Viridovix grinned impishly; just as Goudeles' bombast made Skylitzes growl, his own blithe unconcern irritated Gorgidas more than any angry comeback.

A herd of onagers galloped away from the oncoming riders. The small-eared wild asses could almost have been miniature horses, but for their sparsely haired tails and short, stiff, brushy manes. Three wolves coursed beside them, not hunters now but hunted, fleeing before the Arshaum as from a fire on the steppe.

However hardened they had grown to the saddle, neither Viridovix nor Gorgidas could endure with the Arshaum, who rode as soon as they could walk. The long, hard ride chafed the physician's thighs raw and left the Celt's fundament sore as if he had been kicked. They both groaned as their horses jounced over a low rise and pounded toward another stream.

The drumming thunder of hoofbeats sent a cloud of waterfowl flapping skyward—ducks, geese, and orange-billed swans, whose great wings made a thunder of their own. Birds fell as the nomads started shooting at long range, but again it seemed almost all would evade the arrows.

Gorgidas saw Tolui's devil-masked face turn toward Arghun. The khagan made a short, chopping motion with his right hand. The shaman began to chant; both arms moved in quick passes. He guided his horse with the pressure of his knees alone. A rider in the Greek's world would have been hard-pressed to stay in the saddle thus, but stirrups made it easy for the Arshaum.

Black clouds boiled up over the stream as soon as his spell began, come from nowhere out of a clear sky. A squall of rain, a veritable curtain of water, pelted the escaping birds. It had been only seconds since they took flight, now the sudden deluge smashed them back to earth. Gorgidas heard squawks of terror through the sorcerous storm's hiss.

As quickly as it had blown up, the rain stopped. Water birds lay all along the banks of the stream, some with broken wings, others half drowned, still others simply too stunned to fly. Raising a cheer for Tolui, the plainsmen swooped down on them. They clubbed and shot and slashed, grabbing up bird after bird.

"Roast duck!" Goudeles cried with glee as he bagged a green-winged teal. He thumbed his nose at Viridovix. "You'll not hear that panegyric now!"

"No, nor miss it either," the Gaul retorted. Skylitzes gave a single sharp snort of laughter.

They splashed through the muck Tolui's storm had made. With a glance at the westering sun, Arghun picked up the pace. "We will need daylight for the final killing," he called. His riders passed the word along.

Then Gorgidas heard cheers from the far left end of the line, where scouts stretched out ahead of the main band of hunters. A few minutes later they sounded from the right as well—Irnek's half of the army was in sight. Moving with the smooth precision experience brings, the horsemen on the flanks galloped forward from both parties to enclose the space between and finally trap all the animals in it.

That space grew smaller and smaller as the two lines approached. The beasts within were pressed ever more tightly: wolves, foxes, wildcats, rabbits bouncing underfoot, deer, wild asses, sheep, a few cows, goats. The nomads relentlessly plied them with arrows, pulling one quiverload after another from their saddlebags. The din, with the yelps and screeches and brays of wounded animals mixed with the frightened howls and lowing of those not yet hit and with the hunters' cries, was indescribable.

Driven, hunted, and jammed together as they were, the terrified creatures' reactions were nothing like they would have been in more normal circumstances. They ran this way and that in confused waves, seeking an escape they could not find. And some were desperate enough to surge out against the yelling, waving riders who ringed them all around.

A stag sprang between Gorgidas and Viridovix and was gone, bounding over the plain in great frightened leaps. Arigh whirled in the saddle to fire after it, but missed. Then he and everyone around him cursed in fury as a hundred panicked onagers made a shambles of the hunting line. Other animals of every sort swarmed through the gap.

Agathias Psoes' horse was bowled over when a fleeing wild ass ran headlong into it. The Videssian underofficer sprang free as his mount crashed to the ground, then leaped for his life to dodge another onager. Only the knowledge he had earned with years on the steppe saved him. He frantically laid about him, yelling as loud as he could to make the stampeding beasts take him for an obstacle to be avoided and not a mere man ripe for the trampling. It worked, they streamed past him on either side. When an Arshaum rode close, he clambered up behind the nomad.

Guiding his pony with a skill he had not thought he owned, Gorgidas managed to evade the onagers. He was congratulating himself when Batbaian shouted a warning. The Greek turned his head to find a wolf, a huge shaggy pack leader, bounding his way. It sprang straight for him, jaws agape.

His months of weapon drill proved their worth; before he had time to think, he was thrusting at the snarling beast's face. But his horse could not endure the wolf's onset. It bucked in terror, ruining his stroke. Instead of stabbing through the wolf's palate and into its brain, his *gladius* scored a bloody line down its muzzle, just missing a blazing yellow eye.

The wolf bayed horribly and leaped again. An arrow whistled past Gorgidas' cheek, so close he felt the wind of its passage. It sank between the wolf's ribs. The beast twisted in midair, snapping at the protruding shaft. Bloody foam started from its mouth and nostrils. Two more arrows pierced it as it writhed on the ground; it jerked and died.

"Good shot!" Gorgidas called, looking round to see who had loosed the first arrow. Dizabul waved back at him; he too was busy fighting to keep his mount under control. The Greek tried to read the expression on the prince's too-handsome face, and failed. Then Dizabul caught sight of a gray fox darting away and spurred after it, reaching behind him for another arrow to fit to his bow.

"Well, what about it?" Goudeles asked the physician a few minutes later, when the breakout was contained. The bureaucrat somehow managed to look jaunty even though his face was gray-brown with dust and tracked by streams of sweat. He gave Gorgidas a conspiratorial wink.

"What about what?" the Greek said, his mind back on the hunt.

"You don't play the innocent well," Goudeles told him; he had the Videssian gift for spotting duplicity whether it was there or not. But when he said, "Tell me you weren't wondering whether that shaft was meant for the wolf or you," Gorgidas had to toss his head in a Hellenic no. Dizabul had no reason to love him. He had backed Bogoraz until Gorgidas foiled the Yezda's try at poisoning his father; his pride suffered for finding himself so drastically in the wrong. Then, too, he might well have become khagan if the poisoning had succeeded. . . .

"You're not wrong," Gorgidas admitted. The pen-pusher wet his finger and drew a tally-mark in the air, pleased at his own cleverness.

As the light began to fail, the nomads opened their lines and let the trapped beasts they had not slain escape. They dismounted, drove off the gathering carrion birds, and set about butchering their kills. "Faugh!" said Viridovix, wrinkling his nose. The slaughterhouse stench oppressed Gorgidas, too, but it was hardly worse than battlefields he had known.

The Arshaum set fires blazing in long straight trenches and began to smoke as much of the meat as they could. Arghun hobbled from one to the next with Irnek, supervising the job. "A pity our women and yurts aren't here," Gorgidas heard him say.

"Aye, it is," the younger plainsman agreed. "So many hides, so much bone and sinew wasted because we haven't time to deal with them as we should." Steppe life was harsh; not making the greatest possible use of everything they came across went against the nomads' grain.

While the sweaty work went on, the hunters carved off choice gobbets and roasted them for their day's meal. "Not a bit peckish, are they now?" Viridovix said, between bites of the plump goose he'd taken.

"You do pretty well yourself," Gorgidas replied, gnawing on a leg from the same bird; the Celt had a good-sized pile of bones in front of him. But he was right; the nomads out-ate him without effort. Used to privation, they made the most of plenty when they had it. Seeing them somehow gulp down huge chunks of half-cooked meat reminded the Greek of a time when, as a boy, he had watched a small snake engulfing a large mouse.

Batbaian ate by himself, his back to the fires. As Gorgidas' emptiness faded and he began to be able to think of other things than food, he got up to invite the Khamorth over to talk. When Viridovix saw where he was going, he reached out and held the physician back. "Let the lad be," he said quietly.

Irritated, Gorgidas growled, "What's your trouble? He'll be happier here than brooding all alone."

"That's not so at all, I'm thinking. Unless I miss my guess, the blazes are after reminding him o' the ones Avshar used to snare him. That they do me, and I wasna caught by 'em. If he has somewhat to say, he'll be by, and never you fret over that."

The Greek sat down again. "You may be right. You said something of the same thing to Arigh a few days ago, didn't you?" He eyed Viridovix curiously. "I wouldn't have expected you to be so careful of another's feelings."

Viridovix toyed with his mustaches, as if wondering whether his manhood was questioned. He finally said, "Hurting a body without call is Avshar's sport, and after a bit o' him, why, I've fair lost the stomach for it."

"You're growing up at last," Gorgidas said, to which the Celt only snorted in derision. The physician thought of something else. "If Avshar somehow does not know how large an army has crossed into Pardraya, these fires will give us away."

"He knows," Viridovix said with gloomy certainty. "He knows."

Coincidence or not, two days later a Khamorth rode into the Arshaum camp under sign of truce, a white-painted shield hung from a lance. As he was brought before Arghun and his councilors, he looked about with an odd blend of arrogance laid over fear. He would flinch when the Arshaum scowled at him, then suddenly straighten and glower back, seeming to remember the might he himself represented.

Certainly his bow before the khagan was perfunctory enough to fetch black looks from the plainsmen. He ignored them, asking in his own language, "Does anyone here speak this tongue and yours both?"

"I do." Skylitzes took a long step forward.

The Khamorth blinked at finding an imperial at Arghun's side, but recovered well. He was perhaps forty-five, not handsome but shrewd-looking, with eyes that darted every which way. Half of one of his ears was missing. By steppe standards, he wore finery; his cap was sable, his wolfskin jacket trimmed with the same fur, his fringed trousers of softest buckskin. A red stone glittered in the heavy gold ring on his right forefinger; his horse's trappings were ornamented with polished jet.

"Well, farmer," he said, putting Skylitzes in his place with the nomad's easy contempt for folk who lived a settled life, "tell the Arshaum I am Rodak son of Papak, and I come to him from Varatesh, grand khagan of the Royal Clan and master of all the clans of Pardraya."

The Videssian officer frowned at the insult, but began to translate. Batbaian broke in, shouting, "You filthy bandit, you drop dung through your mouth when you call Varatesh a khagan, or his renegades a clan!" He would have sprung for Rodak, but a couple of Arshaum grabbed him by the shoulders and held him back.

Rodak had presence; he looked down his prominent nose at Batbaian, as if noticing him for the first time. Turning back to Arghun, he said, "So you have one of the outlaws along, do you? Well, I will make nothing of it; he's been marked as he deserves."

"Outlaw, is it?" Batbaian said, twisting in the grip of the Arshaum.

"What did your clan, your *real* clan, outlaw *you* for, Rodak? Was is man-slaying, or stealing from your friends, or just buggering a goat?"

"What I was is of no account," Rodak said coolly; Skylitzes translated both sides of the exchange. "What I am now counts."

"Yes, and what are you?" Batbaian cried. "A puffed-up piece of sheep turd, making the air stink for your betters. Without Avshar's black wizardry, you'd still be the starving brigand you ought to be, you vulture, you snake-hearted lizard-gutted cur, you green, hopping, slimy frog!"

That was the deadliest affront one Khamorth could throw at another; the men of Pardraya loathed and feared frogs. Rodak's hand flashed toward his saber. Then he froze with it still untouched, for two dozen arrows were aimed at him. Moving very slowly and carefully, he drew his hand away.

"Better," Arghun said dryly. "We have experience with treacherous envoys; they do not go well with weapons."

"Or with insults," Rodak returned. His lips were pale, but from anger this time, Gorgidas thought, not fear.

"Insult?" Batbaian said. "How could I make you out fouler than you are?"

"That is enough," Arghun said. "I will settle what he is." Batbaian held his tongue; Arghun framed his orders mildly, but expected them to be obeyed. The khagan returned to Rodak. "What does your Varatesh want with us?"

"He warns you to turn round at once and go back to your own side of the river Shaum, or face the anger of all the clans of Pardraya."

"Unless your khagan makes a quarrel with me, I have none with him," Arghun said. At that, Batbaian cried out again. "Be silent," Arghun told him, then turned to Rodak once more. "My quarrel is with Yezd—this is but the shortest road to Mashiz. Tell that to Varatesh very plainly, yes, and to your Avshar as well. So long as I am not attacked, I will not look for trouble with you Khamorth. If I am . . ." He let the sentence trail away.

Rodak licked his lips. The wars with the Arshaum were burned into the memory of his people. "Avshar comes from Yezd, they say, and is adopted into the Royal Clan; indeed, he stands next to Varatesh there."

"What is that to me?" Arghun's voice was bland. Batbaian suddenly smiled, not a pleasant sight; Viridovix was reminded of a wolf scenting blood. Arghun continued, "You have my answer. I will not turn back, but I make war on Yezd, not on you, unless you would have it so. Take that word to your master."

Skylitzes hesitated before he rendered the khagan's last sentence into the Khamorth speech. "How would you have me translate that?"

"Exactly as I said it," Argun said.

"Very well." The word the Videssian used for "master" meant "owner of a dog."

Rodak glowered at him and Arghun from under heavy brows. "When my chief—" He came down hard on the proper term. "—hears of this, we will see how funny he finds your little joke. Think on one-eye here; before long you may be envying his fate."

He wheeled his horse and rode away. Behind him, Arigh yipped like a puppy. A chorus of laughing Arshaum took up the call, yapping and baying Rodak out of camp. He roweled his horse savagely as he galloped northeast. Batbaian walked over to Arigh and slapped him on the back in wordless gratitude. Chuckling nomads kept barking at each other until it was full dark.

But back at the tent he shared with Viridovix, Gorgidas was less cheerful. He scrawled down what had happened at Rodak's embassy, noting, "The Khamorth are caught between two dreads, the ancient fear of their western neighbors and the new terror raised by Avshar. As the one is but the memory of a fright and the other all too immediate, the force of the latter, I think, shall prevail among them."

As he sometimes did, Viridovix asked the Greek what he'd written. "You're after thinking the shindy's coming, then?"

"Very much so. Why should Avshar let Yezd be ravaged if he can block the attack with these plainsmen, who are but tools in his hand? And I have no doubt he will be able to move them against us."

"Nobbut a tomnoddy'd say you're wrong," Viridovix nodded. He drew his sword, checked the blade carefully for rust, and honed away a couple of tiny nicks in the edge—as tame a reaction to the prospect of a fight as Gorgidas had seen from him. Since Seirem had perished in the massacre of Targitaus' camp, the big Gaul saw war's horror as well as its excitement and glory.

When he was satisfied with the state of the blade, he sheathed it again and stared moodily into the fire. At last he said, "We should thrash them, I'm thinking."

"Then sound as if you believed it, not like a funeral dirge!" Gorgidas exclaimed in some alarm. The mercurial Celt seemed sunk in despair.

"You ha' me, for in my heart I dinna," he said. "Indeed and we're the better fighters, but what's the use in that? Yourself said it a few days ago: it's Avshar's witchering wins his battles for him, not his soldiers."

Gorgidas pursed his lips, as at a bad taste. All Avshar's troops needed to do was hold fast, draw their foes in until they were fully engaged, and the wizard-prince's magic would find a weakness or make one. To hold fast . . . his head jerked up. *"Autò ékhō!"* he shouted. "I have it!"

Viridovix jumped, grumbling crossly, "Talk a language a man can understand, not your fool Greek."

"Sorry." Words poured from the physician, a torrent of them. He forgot himself again once or twice and had to backtrack so the Gaul could follow him. As Viridovix listened, his eyes went wide.

"Aren't you the trickiest one, now," he breathed. He let out a great war whoop, then fell back on his wolfskin sleeping blanket, choking with laughter. "Puddocks!" he got out between wheezes. "Puddocks!" He dissolved all over again.

Gorgidas paid no attention to him. He was already sticking his head out the tent flap. "Tolui!" he yelled.

III

"That's the one," Marcus said, pointing, "his name's Iatzoulinos."

"Third from the back on the left, is it?" Gaius Philippus growled. The tribune nodded, then regretted it. There was a dull, pounding ache in his head, from too much wine and not enough sleep. The senior centurion strode forward, saying, "His name doesn't matter a fart to me and it'll be so much dog dung to him, too, when I'm through with him."

He stamped down the narrow aisleway between the rows of desks. His high-crested helm nearly brushed the ceiling; his scarlet cloak of rank billowed about his shoulders; his shirt of mail clanked at every step. Scaurus leaned against the doorpost, watching bureaucrats look up in horror from their tax rolls, memoranda, and counting boards at the warlike apparition loosed in their midst.

Intently bent over his book of accounts, Iatzoulinos did not notice the Roman's approach even when Gaius Philippus loomed over his desk like a thundercloud. The secretary kept transferring numbers from one column to another, checking each entry twice. Though hardly past thirty, he had an older man's pallor and fussy precision.

Gaius Philippus scowled at him for a few seconds, but he remained oblivious. The senior centurion rasped his *gladius* free. Marcus sprang toward him—he had not brought him here to see murder done.

But Gaius Philippus brought the flat of the blade crashing down on Iatzoulinos' desk. The bureaucrat's ink pot leaped into the air and overturned; beads flew from his counting board.

He leaped himself, staring about wildly like a man waking to a nightmare. With a cry of dismay, he snatched his ledger away from the spreading puddle of ink. "What is the meaning of this madness?" he exclaimed, voice cracking in alarm.

"You shut your sniveling gob, you worthless sack of moldy tripes."

Gaius Philippus' bass roar, trained to be heard through battlefield din, was fearsome in an enclosed space. "And sit down!" he added, slamming the pen-pusher back into his chair when he tried to scuttle away. "You're bloody well going to listen to me."

He spat into the ink spot. Iatzoulinos shriveled under his glare. No shame there, Marcus thought. That glower was made for turning hard-bitten legionaries to mush. "So you're the fornicating cabbagehead's been screwing over my men, eh?" the senior centurion barked, curling his lip in contempt.

Iatzoulinos actually blushed; the red was easy to see on his thin, sallow features. "It may possibly be the case that, due to some, ah unfortunate, ah, oversight, disbursement has experienced, ah, a few purely temporary delays—"

"Cut the garbage," Gaius Philippus ordered. Likely he had not understood half the pen-pusher's jargon. He noticed he was still holding his sword and sheathed it so he could poke a grimy-nailed finger in Iatzoulinos' face. The bureaucrat's eyes crossed as he regarded it fearfully.

"Now you listen and you listen good, understand me?" the veteran said. Iatzoulinos nodded, still watching the finger as though he did not dare look at the man behind it. Gaius Philippus went on, "It was you god-despised seal-stampers first took to hiring mercenaries because you decided you couldn't trust your own troops anymore, 'cause they liked their local nobles better than you. Right?" He shook the secretary. "Right?"

"I, ah, believe something of that sort may have been the case, though this policy was, ah, implemented prior to the commencement of my tenure here."

"Mars' prick, you talk that way all the time!" The Roman clapped his hand to his forehead. He took a few seconds to pick up his chain of thought. "For my money, you were thinking with your heads up your backsides when you came up with that one, but forget that for now. Listen, you mud-brained bastard son of an illegitimate bepoxed she-goat, if you have to have troops that fight for money, what in the name of a bald-arsed bureaucrat do you think they'll do if there's no bloody money?" His voice rose another couple of notches, something Scaurus would not have guessed possible. "If they weren't kind and gentle like me, they'd tear your fornicating head off and piss in the hole, that's what! You'd probably remember better that way anyhow."

Iatzoulinos looked about ready to faint. Deciding things had gone far enough, Marcus called, "Since you are kind and gentle, Gaius, what will you do instead?"

"Eh? Oh. Hrrm." The centurion was thrown off stride for a second, but recovered brilliantly. Shoving his face within a couple of inches of the pen-pusher's, he hissed, "I give you four days to round up every gold-piece we're owed—and in old coin, too, none of this debased trash from Ortaias' mint—or I start saving up piss. Understand me?"

It took three tries, but Iatzoulinos got a "Yes" out.

"Good." Gaius Philippus glared round the room. "Well, why aren't the rest of you lazy sods working?" he snarled, and tramped out.

"A very good day to you all, gentlemen," Marcus said to the stunned bureaucrats, and followed him. He had an afterthought and stuck his head back in. "Don't you wish you were dealing with the nobles again?"

Alypia Gavra laughed when the tribune told her the story. "And did he get the pay for your soldiers?" she asked.

"Every bit of it. It went off to Garsavra by courier, let me see, ten days ago. He's staying in the city until the receipt comes back from Minucius. If it's not here pretty soon, or if it's even a copper short, I would not care to be wearing Iatzoulinos' sandals."

"Rocking the bureaucrats every so often is not a bad thing," Alypia said seriously. "They're needed to keep the Empire running on an even keel, but they are trained in the city and they serve here and begin to think that everything comes down to entries in a ledger. Bumping up against reality has to be healthy for them."

Marcus chuckled. "I think Gaius Philippus was rather realer than Iatzoulinos cared for."

"From what I've seen of him, I'd say you're right." Alypia got out of bed. It was only a few steps to the jug of wine on the table against the far wall. She poured for both of them. The wine was the best this inn offered, but none too good. Compared even to Aetios' tavern, the place was dingy and cramped. The din of hammers on copperware of every sort came unceasingly through the narrow window.

When the tribune put down his cup—yellow-brown unglazed clay, ugly but functional—he caught Alypia watching him curiously. He arched his eyebrows. She hesitated, then asked, "Have you told him about us?"

"No," Scaurus said at once. "The fewer who know, the better."

She nodded. "That's so. Yet surely, if half what you and my uncle have said of him is true, he would never violate your trust. And I know the two of you are close; it shows in the way you work together." She looked the question at him.

"You're right, he'd never betray us," the tribune said. "But telling him would not make me easier and would just make him nervous. He'd see only the risk, and never understand that for you it was worth taking."

"Never say you were not born a courtier, dear Marcus," she murmured, her eyes glowing. He hugged her close; her skin was like warm satin against his.

"Gangway there!" The rough shout came through the window, accompanied by the clatter of iron-shod hooves on paving-stones. With Alypia in his arms, the tribune did not pay the noise much attention, but it registered. The coppersmiths' district was a poor quarter of the city, with horses few and far between.

A few minutes later the inn's whole second floor shook as several men in heavy boots pounded up the wooden stairs. Marcus frowned. "What nonsense is this?" he muttered, more annoyed than alarmed. Better safe, he decided. He climbed to his feet, slid his sword free of its sheath, and wrapped his tunic round his arm for a makeshift shield.

The door came crashing in. Alypia screamed. Scaurus started to spring forward, then froze in his tracks. Four armored archers were in the hallway, bows drawn and aimed at his belly. Half a dozen spearmen crowded after them. And Provhos Mourtzouphlos, a wide smile of invitation on his face, said, "Take another step, outlander, why don't you?"

Wits numb in disaster, the tribune lowered his blade. "No?" Mourtzouphlos said, seeing he would not charge. "Too bad." His voice cracked like a whip. "Then back off!"

The Roman obeyed. "Jove," he said. "Jove, Jove, Jove." It was neither prayer nor curse, simply the first noise he happened to make.

The Videssian bowmen followed. Three kept arrows trained on him while the fourth turned his weapon toward Alypia, who was sitting rigidly upright in bed, the coverlet drawn to her chin to hide her nakedness. Her eyes were wide and staring, like those of a trapped animal.

"No need to aim at her," Marcus said softly. The archer, a young man with a hooked nose and liquid brown eyes that told of Vaspurakaner blood, nodded and lowered his bow.

"You be silent," Mortzouphlos said from the doorway. He suddenly seemed to notice the tribune was still holding his sword. "Drop it!" he ordered, then snapped at the last bowman, "Gather that up, Artavasdos, if you have nothing better to do."

Mourtzouphlos looked Scaurus' unclad frame up and down. "Damned foreign foolishness, scraping your face every day," he said, stroking his own whiskers. His grin grew most unpleasant. "When Thorisin's done with you, you'll likely be able to keep your cheeks smooth without needing to shave." His voice went falsetto; he grabbed at his crotch in an unmistakable gesture.

Marcus' blood ran cold; of themselves, his hands made a protective cup. One of the troopers behind Mourtzouphlos laughed. Alypia came out of her terrified paralysis. "No!" she cried in horror. "Blame me, not him!"

"No one asked your advice, slut," Mourtzouphlos said coldly. "A fine one you make to talk, whoring with the Sphrantzai and then spreading yourself for this barbarian."

Alypia went white. "Shut your foul mouth, Mourtzouphlos," Scaurus said. "You'll pay for that, I promise."

"What are your promises worth?" The Videssian cavalry officer stepped up and slapped him in the face.

Ears ringing, Marcus shook his head to clear it. "Do what you like with me, but have a care how you treat her Majesty the Princess. You'll get no thanks from Thorisin for tormenting her."

"Will I not?" Mourtzouphlos retorted, but with a touch of doubt; his men, reminded of Alypia's title, looked at each other for a moment. Mourtzouphlos pulled himself together. "As for doing what I'd like with you—there's no time for that now, worse luck. Get your trousers on,

Roman," he barked. Scaurus had to swallow a startled laugh; if he began, he did not think he would be able to stop.

Mourtzouphlos rounded on Alypia. "And you, my lady," he said, speaking the honorific like a curse. "Come on, out of there. D'you think I'll leave you to wait for your next customer?" His men leered in anticipation.

"Damn you, Provhos," Scaurus said. Alypia stayed motionless beneath the blanket, dread on her face. After her treatment at the hands of Vardanes Sphrantzes, Marcus knew the humiliation Mourtzouphlos was piling on her might break her forever. When the cavalryman reached out to tear the cover away, he shouted, "Wait!"

"And why should I?"

"Because she is still the Emperor's niece and last living relative. No matter what he may do to me, do you think he'll thank you for making his scandal worse?" That was a keen shot; the Roman could see calculation start behind Mourtzouphlos' eyes. He pressed his tiny advantage: "Give her leave to dress in peace; where will she go?"

Mourtzouphlos rubbed his chin as he thought. At last he jerked a thumb at Scaurus. "Take him out into the hall." As the archers obeyed, he said to Alypia, "I'm warning you, be quick."

"Thank you," she said, to him and Marcus both.

"Bah!" Mourtzouphlos slammed the door. He growled at his troopers, "Well, what are you standing around for? Tie this whoreson up." One of the spearmen jerked the tribune's hands behind him, while a second lashed his wrists together with rawhide thongs.

Before the last knot was tied, Alypia emerged from the cubicle, still tugging at the sleeves of her dark-gold linen dress. She wore her usual dispassionate air like a shield against enemies, but Marcus saw how her hand trembled when she shut the door behind her. Her voice, though, was steady if toneless as she said to Mourtzouphlos, "Do what you must."

"Move, then," he said brusquely. Scaurus stumbled on the stairs; he would have fallen had the archer carrying his sword not grabbed his shoulder. The drinkers in the taproom below stared as the soldiers led their prisoners out. In high spirits once more, Mourtzouphlos tossed a couple of silverpieces to the innkeeper. "This for the custom I may have scared off." The taverner, a lean-faced bald fellow who looked to have no use for on-duty troopers in his place, made the coins disappear.

Two more spearmen were outside keeping an eye on the squad's horses. "Mount up," Mourtzouphlos said. He bowed mockingly to Scaurus. "Here's a gelding for you to ride, instead of your filly. Think on that, outlander."

"You knew!" Marcus blurted in dismay.

"So I did," Mourtzouphlos said smugly. "Saborios has sharp ears, and making sure he was right was worth the time I spent in those cheap, scratchy clothes."

"Saborios!" Scaurus and Alypia said together, exchanging an appalled glance. The princess burst out, "Phos, what will my uncle do to Balsamon?"

"Not a damned thing," Mourtzouphlos answered in disgust. "It would cost him riots, more's the pity." He turned that nasty grin on the tribune again. "The same doesn't apply to you, of course. I only wish I could rout every other greedy mercenary from Videssos so easily. Now ride!"

One of the cavalryman's soldiers had to help Scaurus into the saddle; no horseman, he could not mount without his hands. His mind was whirling as Mourtzouphlos tied a lead to his horse's reins. In principle, ironically, he agreed with the imperial—Videssos would have done better with all native troops.

But Alypia said, "So you would free the Empire of mercenaries, would you, Mourtzouphlos? Tell me, then, you've never made peasants on your estates into personal retainers. Tell me you've never held back tax monies from the fisc." Her voice dripped scorn. Cat-graceful, she swung herself up onto the horse by Scaurus'.

The aristocrat flushed, but he came back, "Why should I give the cursed pen-pushers the gold to spend on more hired troops?" With the provincial nobles converting the Empire's freeholders to private armies and the bureaucrats taxing them into serfdom, no wonder Videssos was short of soldiers. Its manpower pool had been drying up for more than a hundred years.

"Ride!" Mourtzouphlos repeated. He dug spurs into his mount's flank. It bounded forward, and so, perforce, did Marcus' animal. He almost went over its tail; only a quick clutch with his knees saved him. He did not think Mourtzouphlos would mind if he got trampled.

"Make way, in the Emperor's name!" the Videssian officer shouted again and again, trying to hurry through the city's crowded streets. Some of the traffic did move aside to let his troopers pass, but as many riders and folk afoot stopped and turned to gape at him. He would have made better progress keeping quiet, but he crowed out his victory like a rooster.

Marcus endured the journey, distracted from the full mortification of it by his struggle to hold his seat. That so occupied him that he had little chance to turn his head Alypia's way. She rode steadily on, eyes set straight ahead, as if neither the crowd nor her guards had any meaning to her. Once, though, her glance met Scaurus', and she sent him a quick, frightened smile. His horse missed a step, jouncing him in the saddle before he could return it.

After the hurly-burly and close-pressing swarm of humanity in the plaza of Palamas, the palace compound's wide uncrowded lanes were a relief to the tribune, or would have been had not Mourtzouphlos stepped up his squadron's pace to nearly a gallop. A fat eunuch carrying a silver tray scurried onto the edge of the grass as the horsemen thundered by. His head whipped round, and he dropped his platter with a clang when he recognized their prisoners.

They pounded through a grove of cherry trees just beginning to come into fragrant pink blossom and pulled to a halt before a single-story building of stucco trimmed with gleaming marble that was the imperial family's private quarters. Sentries sprang to attention on seeing Mourtzouphlos—or was it for Alypia Gavra? Another eunuch, a steward in a robe of dark red silk embroidered with golden birds, appeared in the entranceway. Mourtzouphlos called, "His Majesty expects us."

"Bide a moment." The chamberlain vanished inside. Mourtzouphlos and his men dismounted, as did Alypia and Scaurus; the tribune managed to slide off his horse without stumbling. Some of the sentries knew him and exclaimed in surprise to see him bound. But before he could answer, the steward returned and beckoned Mourtzouphlos and his unwilling companions forward. "Bring two or three of your guards," he said, indicating the cavalrymen, "but leave the rest here. His Imperial Majesty does not feel they will be required."

Marcus paid no attention to the splendid antiquities he was hurried past, relics of a millenium and a half of Videssian history. The guards frogmarched him along; they did not quite dare mete out the same treatment to Alypia, who walked beside him free of restraint. Prisoner she might be, but, as the tribune had reminded them, she was also the Emperor's niece.

The eunuch chamberlain ducked into a doorway. He started to speak, but Thorisin Gavras irritably broke in, "I know who they are, you bloody twit! Go on, get out of here." Blankfaced, the steward withdrew. Mourtzouphlos led Scaurus and Alypia in to the Avtokrator of the Videssians.

Gavras spun round at their entrance. The motion was lithe, but the Emperor's shoulder sagged just a little, and his eyes were trimmed with red. He looks tired, was Marcus' first thought, followed a moment later by, he looks more like Mavrikios than ever. The burden Avtokrators carried aged them quickly.

But Thorisin remained more impetuous than his older brother had been. "Oh, send your lads back outside, Provhos," he said impatiently. "If we can't handle a girl and a tied man, Phos have pity on us." He slapped the hilt of his saber, an unadorned, much-used weapon in a plain leather sheath.

That seemed to give him an idea. "Artavasdos!" he called after the guards—any Emperor who wanted a long rule knew as many of his men's names as he could. The soldier stood in the doorway. "Is that this wretch's sword you have there?" He jerked a thumb at the Roman. When Artavasdos nodded, he went on, "Well, why don't you fetch it over to Nepos, the sorcerer-priest at the Academy? He's been panting for a long look at it since he found out about it." Artavasdos nodded again, saluted, and disappeared.

Marcus winced as the sword was taken away and felt more naked than he had when Mourtzouphlos and his men surprised him. That druid-enchanted blade, with its twin that Viridovix carried, had swept the Romans from Gaul to Videssos and in the Empire it had proved potent in its own right. He never willingly let himself be separated from it; now his will mattered nothing.

He was dismayed enough to miss Thorisin's words to him. Mourtzouphlos sharply prodded him in the ribs. A frown on his long face, the Emperor repeated, "Still no proskynesis, eh, even for your head's sake? You're a stiff-necked bastard, Roman, and no mistake, but not stiff enough for the axe to bounce off."

"What good would a prostration do?" the tribune said. "You won't spare me on account of it." The proskynesis had not even occurred to him; the custom of republican Rome was to bend the knee to no man.

"Too proud, are you?" Thorisin said. "But not too proud, I see, to sneak out and sleep with my brother's daughter."

"Well said!" Mourtzouphlos exclaimed. Scaurus felt his cheeks go hot; he had no answer for the Emperor.

Alypia said, "It was not as you think, uncle. If anything, I sought him out rather than he me."

"A harlot whoring with a lumpish heathen," Mourtzouphlos fleered. "That makes neither you nor him better, strumpet."

"Provhos," the Emperor said sharply, "I will handle this with no help from you." The cavalryman opened his mouth and closed it again with a snap. Thorisin Gavras' anger was nothing to risk.

"And I love him," Alypia said.

"And I her," Marcus echoed.

Mourtzouphlos seemed about to explode. Thorisin shouted, "What in Skotos' name difference does that make?" He turned to his niece. "I thought you had better sense than to drag the name of our clan through the bathhouses."

"Me?" she said, her voice wild and dangerous. "Me? What of your oh-so-sweet doxy Komitta Rhangavve, who straddled anything that wasn't dead like a bitch in heat, and had you lampooned for it last Midwinter's Day in the Amphitheater in front of half the city?"

Thorisin stopped in his tracks, as if clubbed. He went red, then white. Provhos Mourtzouphlos looked as though he wished he were somewhere else; listening to a family feud in the imperial family could prove unhealthy.

Even more loudly, Alypia went on, "And if you're so concerned to keep us from reproaches, dear uncle, why didn't you put your precious mistress aside when you became Avtokrator, and marry and get yourself an heir?"

In her fury and gallantry she reminded Marcus of an outmatched fencer throwing everything into a last desperate attack, win or die. Thorisin flinched, but growled, "This is not about me, but about you and how what you've done touches me." His voice went up to a roar: "Bizoulinos! Domentziolos! Konon!" The chamberlain who had conducted Mourtzouphlos' party to the Emperor hurried in, along with two other eunuchs. Gavras ordered them, "Take Alypia to her quarters here. See she stays there till I command otherwise; your lives are answer for it."

"That's right!" she cried. "If you have no answer, hide the question away so you need not think about it anymore." The stewards led her away. She cast a last backward look at Scaurus but, not wanting to make his position more hopeless than it already was, said nothing.

"Whew!" said the Emperor, wiping his forehead. "You must be a sorcerer yourself, Roman; I've never seen her so fierce." He laughed humorlessly. "She has the Gavras temper, under all that calm she usually puts on." His stare grew sharp again. "Now—what do we do with you?"

"I am loyal to your Majesty," Marcus said.

"Ha!" That was Mourtzouphlos, but he subsided like a scolded small boy when Thorisin turned his eye on him; all their long past had trained the Videssians to quail before the imperial office's power.

Gavras turned back to the tribune. "Loyal, are you? You have a bloody odd way of showing it, then." He stroked his chin; year by year, his beard was going grayer. "If you were a Videssian, you'd be deadly dangerous to me. You're a good soldier and halfway decent bureaucrat; you might be able to line up both factions behind you. Bad enough as is—tell me to my face you're not an ambitious man."

It was the very word he had known the Emperor would tax him with. "Is that a sin?" he said.

"In a mercenary captain it's a sin past forgiving. Ask Drax."

Scaurus backtracked. "It has nothing to do with my feelings about Alypia. You must know her well enough to know she would recognize advances that came from self-interest for what they were."

"What does an assotted wench know?" Mourtzouphlos sneered, but

Thorisin paused for a moment. If his officer did not, he respected Alypia's clear thinking.

"If I had been a traitor," Marcus pressed on, "would I have stayed with you in the civil war against Ortaias and Vardanes? Would I have warned you against Drax when you sent him out to fight Baanes Onomagoulos? Would I have fought against him last year when he tried to set up his new Namdalen in the westlands?"

"Consorting with an imperial princess without the leave of the Avtokrator is treason for a Videssian, let alone an outlander," Thorisin said flatly, and the tribune's heart sank. "And if you were as pure of heart as you claim, why would you have met with the Namdaleni and plotted abandoning me when it seemed I could not take Videssos from the Sphrantzai? What does your tattling against Drax prove? Any officer will score off his rival if he can. If you despised and suspected him so, why did you let him get away to scheme new mischiefs against me?"

"You know how that happened," Scaurus said, but weakly; it was plain Thorisin would hear no defense. The irony galled the tribune, for he genuinely favored Thorisin's reign. In the troubled times Videssos faced, he could see no chance for a better ruler. And the Empire itself he heartily admired. Despite its flaws, it had given generations union, peace, and, on the whole, good government—ideals republican Rome professed, but failed to live up to.

"What I know," Gavras said, "is that I cannot trust you. That suffices." The tribune heard the finality in his voice. After three civil wars and foreign invasions from west and east, the Emperor would not take chances that touched his safety. With reversed positions, Scaurus likely would have felt the same.

"His head—or any other part you care to take—would be an ornament on the Milestone," Mourtzouphlos suggested. The red granite column in the plaza of Palamas was the point from which all distances were measured in the Empire, and also served to display the remains of miscreants.

"No doubt," Thorisin said. "But I fear his damned regiment would rise if I execute him, and they're dangerous men holding an important position. This needs more thought. He'll be safe enough for the time being locked in gaol, don't you think?"

Mourtzouphlos still seemed disappointed, but managed a nod. "As you say, your Majesty."

"Scaurus and the princess? I can't believe it," Senpat Sviodo said, gesturing theatrically to show his astonishment.

His sweeping wave almost upset his wife's cup of wine. Nevrat Sviodo rescued it with a quick grab. "Tell us more, cousin," she urged. She brushed her thick, black, curly hair back from her face.

"Not much to tell," Artavasdos replied. His eyes flicked this way and that. The three Vaspurakaners were sitting at a corner table in an uncrowded tavern and speaking their own language, but he still looked nervous. Nevrat did not blame him. His news was too inflammatory to be easy with.

"Well, how did you get to be one of the ones who took them?" Senpat asked. He played with the pointed end of his beard, close-trimmed in the imperial fashion to accent his swarthy good looks.

"About the way you'd expect," Artavasdos said. "Mourtzouphlos came to the barracks and ordered my squad out—he said he had a job for us. With his rank, no one argued. He didn't tell us who we were after until we were almost at the inn where they were."

"The princess, though." Senpat was still shaking his head.

"Mourtzouphlos said they'd been at it for a couple of months he was sure of, and maybe longer than that. The way they acted when we broke in on them makes me believe it. They seemed more worried about each other than themselves, if you know what I mean."

"That sounds like Marcus," Nevrat said.

"I knew you and your husband were friends of his, cousin, so I thought you'd better know." Artavasdos hesitated. "Being friends with him might not be a good idea right now. Maybe you should get out of the city for a while."

"So bad as that, Artavasdos?" Nevrat said, alarmed.

The soldier considered. "Well, maybe not. Thorisin is too shrewd to massacre people who know people who've fallen foul of him, I think."

"I hope so," Nevrat said, "or with his temper there'd not be many folk for him to rule." She was not really worried about herself or Senpat;

she thought her cousin had gauged the Emperor's common sense well. But that would not help Scaurus. He was guilty in fact, not by association.

"I can't believe it," Senpat said again.

Nevrat had trouble, too, but for reasons different from her husband's. Senpat did not know that Marcus, in his desperation after Helvis left him, had made a tentative approach to her this past fall. She saw no reason ever to mention it; the tribune had understood she meant the no she gave him.

But now this! She wondered how long the attraction had grown between Scaurus and Alypia Gavra. And, despite wanting no one but Senpat herself, she felt a tiny touch of pique that Marcus should have found someone else so soon after she turned him down.

"What are you laughing at, dear?" Senpat asked her.

She felt herself flushing. She was glad she was as dark as her husband; in the dim tavern, no one could tell. "Me," she said, and did not explain.

The barred door at the far end of the corridor opened with the groan of a rusty hinge. Two guards pushed a creaking handcart through. Another flanked them on either side, with arrows nocked in their bows. All four men looked bored.

"Up, you lags!" one of the archers called unnecessarily. The prisoners were already crowding to the front of their cells; feeding time marked the high point of their day.

Marcus hurried forward with the rest, his belly growling in anticipation. Out of reach on the wall above his head, a torch sputtered and almost went out. He coughed on noxious smoke. Torches gave the prison such light as it had; it was underground, a basement level of the sprawling imperial offices on Middle Street.

A hidden ventilation system carried off enough smoke to keep the air breathable, but only just. Along with the torches, the gaol reeked of moldering straw, unwashed humanity, and full chamber pots. When Mourtzouphlos' troopers had thrown Scaurus into one of the little cells, the stench all but drove him mad. Now, after what he thought was four or five days, he took it for granted.

The cart squeaked down the long, narrow passageway, stopping in front of the cells on either side. One of the guards pushing it handed an earthen jug of water to the prisoner on the left, while the other gave the prisoner on the right a small loaf and a bowl of thin stew. Then they traded sides and pushed the handcart down another few feet.

The tribune passed yesterday's empty jug and bowl back to the guard and took his rations in exchange. The water tasted stale; the bread, of barley and oats, was full of husks and of grit from the millstone. The bits of fish in the stew might have been fresh once, but not any time recently. He spooned it up with a bit of crust, then licked the bowl. There was never enough to satisfy. He paid little attention to his belly's constant grumbling. He was not a good enough Stoic to keep a tight rein on his emotions, but mere bodily discomfort did not matter to him.

After the guards had finished their rounds, there was nothing to do but talk. Marcus did not contribute much; he had got howls of derision when he answered, "Treason," to the fellow who asked him why he had been jailed. The ordinary criminals who made up most of the prison population sneered at "politicals," as they called his kind. Besides, he had nothing new to teach them.

A thief was holding forth on ways to beat locks. "If you have plenty of time, you can work sand down into the bolt hole a few grains at a time until the pin comes up high enough for you to lift it out. It's quiet, but slow. Or, if the lock is in a dark place, you can make a net of fine mesh and attach it to a bit of thread, then push it down into the bolt hole. When the pin gets dropped in, all you have to do is lift and you're home free.

"For quick work, though, a pincer's the thing. Cut a groove in one half and leave the other flat, so you can get a good grip on the pin—it's a cylinder, you see, dropped down into its hole so that half of it's in the doorjamb and ther other half in the bar. Look at the cells across from you, you dips. It's the very same setup they use here, but they're canny enough to keep the locks too far away for us to reach. By Skotos, I'd be out of here in a minute if that weren't so."

Scaurus believed him; he had the matter-of-fact confidence of a man who knew his trade. When he was through, a pompous voice a long way down the corridor began explaining how to color glass paste to counterfeit fine gems. "Ha!" someone else called. "If you're so good, what're you doing here?" His only answer was injured silence.

After that the talk turned to women, the other subject on which the prisoners would go on all through the day. The tribune had a story that would have astonished them—and no intention of telling it.

He slept two or three more times, waking up after each one with new bites. Lice and fleas had a paradise in the filthy straw bedding; he lost count of how many roaches he killed as they skittered across the brick floor. Some of the convicts ate them. He was not hungry enough for that.

His belly told him it was not long before feeding time when a squad of Videssian regular troops came clattering down into the gaol. Their leader showed his pass to the guard captain, who walked along the row of cells until he came to the one that held the tribune. "This him?"

"Let me look," the soldier said. "Aye, that's the fellow."

"He's yours then." The guard produced a key, drew up the bolt, and slid out the bar that held Scaurus' door closed. "Come on, you," he snapped at the Roman.

Marcus stumbled out, then pulled himself to attention as he faced the squad leader. As well go down with the eagle high, his legionary training said, as yield it and go down regardless. "Where are you taking me?" he asked crisply.

"To the Emperor," the Videssian replied. If Scaurus' bearing impressed him, he did a good job of hiding it. He made a sour face. "No—to the bathhouse first. You stink." His men grabbed the tribune by the elbows and hustled him away.

In fresh clothes, even ones that did not fit him well, with his still-damp hair slicked back from his eyes, Marcus felt a new man. The soldiers had finally had to drag him out of the warm pool at the bathhouse. He had soaped twice and scraped himself with a strigil till his skin turned red. He still wore the red-gold beginnings of a beard; razors were hard to come by in Videssos. The whiskers itched and made him look scruffy, constantly reminding him of his time in prison.

He felt a small flicker of relief when his captors took him, not to the Grand Courtroom, but to the Emperor's residence. Whatever lay ahead did not include one of the formal public condemnations the Videssians staged with such pomp and ceremony.

He knew he could not expect to see Alypia with her uncle, but her absence forcibly brought his predicament back to him. Thorisin Gavras wore full imperial regalia, a bad sign; he only donned the red boots, the gem-encrusted purple robe, and the domed crown to emphasize the power of his office. But for the guards, the only soul with Scaurus and the Emperor in the little audience chamber was one of the imperial stewards—Konon, it was—with a scribe's waxed tablet and stylus.

Gavras inspected the Roman. "Are you ready to hear my judgment?" he asked sternly.

"Have I a choice?"

The scribbling steward looked shocked; the Emperor gave a grunt of laughter. "No," he said, and turned forbidding again. "Know that you are convicted of treachery against the imperial house."

Marcus stood mute, hoping the ice he felt in his belly did not show on his face. His sentence rolled down on him like an avalanche: "As traitor, you are dismissed from your post as *epoptes* in the imperial chancery." Though that office had been a plum for Scaurus, whose hopes ran beyond the army life, losing it did not cast him into despair.

But Thorisin was continuing: "Having forfeited our trust, you are also stripped of your command over your Romans and shall be prevented from any intercourse with them, the better to prevent future acts of sedition or rebellion. Your lieutenant Gaius Philippus assumes your rank and its perquisites, effective at once."

Permanent exile from all that was left of his own people, his own world . . . the tribune hung his head; his nails bit into his palms. Low-voiced, he said, "He's a fine soldier. Have you told him of this yet?"

"I shall, but we are not finished here, you and I," the Emperor said. "There is only one standard penalty for treason, as well you know. In addition to such trivia as loss of ranks and titles, you also stand liable to the headman's axe."

After the prospect of exile, the axe seemed a small terror; at least it was quickly done. Marcus blurted, "If you plan on killing me, why did you bother with the rest of that rigmarole?"

Gavras did not answer him directly. Instead he said, "That will do,

Konon." The fat beardless chamberlain bowed and left. Then the Emperor turned back to the Roman, a sour smile on his face. "You would be flattered to know there are people who would sooner I did not execute the sentence—to say nothing of you."

"Are there?" Scaurus echoed.

"Oh, indeed, and a bloody noisy flock they are, too. Alypia, of course, though if you were as innocent as she makes you out, you'd still be a virgin and not in your mess at all. She almost makes me believe it—but not quite.

"And there's Leimmokheir the drungarios of the fleet, a fine, upstanding sort if ever there was one." Gavras cocked an eyebrow at the admiral's unflinching rectitude. "But then, he owes you one. If it weren't for your stubbornness he'd still be jailed, or short a head himself for treason. So how much is his advice worth?"

"You are the only judge of that," Marcus said, but he was warmed to learn Leimmokheir had not forgotten him.

"Those, and a couple more like them, are pleas I can understand." Thorisin looked him up and down. "But how in Phos' name did Iatzoulinos come to send me a good word for you?"

"Did he?" the tribune said, amazed. Then he squelched a laugh; one taste of Gaius Philippus had probably made the pen-pusher hope Scaurus would live forever.

"Aye, he did." Gavras' mouth twisted. "Mistake me not, outlander. There's no doubt of your guilt. But I admit I am forced to wonder just a hair at your motives, and so I will give you a hairsbreadth chance to redeem yourself."

Marcus started to lean forward, but the clutch of the guards brought him up short. "What would you, then?"

"This: put an end to Zemarkhos' rebellion in Amorion. His lying anathemas raise trouble for me all through the Empire, from narrow-minded priests and over-religious laymen alike. Bring that off, and I'd say you'd earned yourself a pardon. More, in fact—if you can do it, I'll make you a noble, and not one with small estates, either. That I pledge to you. I will take oath on it at the High Temple to any priest you name save Balsamon—nay, even to him—if you doubt me."

"No need. I agree," Marcus said at once. Thorisin was short-tempered and suspicious, but the tribune knew he kept his promises. His mind began to buzz with schemes: straight-out conquest, bribery . . . "What force will I have at my disposal?"

"I can spare you a good cavalry horse," the Emperor said. Scaurus started to smile, then checked himself; Thorisin's face was hard, his eyes deadly serious. "Aye, I mean it, Roman. Win your own salvation, if you can. You get no help from me."

One man, against the zealots with whom the fanatic priest had even held the Yezda at bay since Maragha? "It salves your conscience, does it, to send me off to suicide instead of killing me yourself?" The tribune nodded bitterly, no longer caring what he said.

"You are a proved traitor, and mine to do with as I wish," Gavras reminded him. He folded his arms across his chest. "Call it what you will, Scaurus. I need not argue with you."

"As you say. Give me back my sword, then. If I'm to 'win my own salvation,' " Marcus made that a taunt, "let me do it with what is mine."

Thorisin considered. "That is a fair request." He found a scrap of parchment, inked a reed pen, wrote furiously. "Here, Spektas," he said, handing the note to one of Scaurus' guards, "take this to Nepos. When he gives you the blade, bring it back here. The Roman can carry it to his ship."

"Ship?" the tribune said as Spektas hurried away.

"Yes, ship. Did you expect me to send you by road, and maybe find you going off to your Romans and stirring up who knows how much mischief? Thank you, no. Moreover," and the Emperor unbent very slightly, "sea travel's faster than land. If you put in at Nakoleia on the coast north of Amorion, you'll only have a short run inland through Yezda-held territory. And you should get into town in time for the *panegyris*—the trade-fair—dedicated to the holy Moikheios. It draws merchants and customers from far and wide, and should be your best chance to slip in without being spotted."

Scaurus grudged him a nod. Whether Gavras saw it so or not, that was help of a sort. "One more thing," he said to the Emperor.

"What now?" Thorisin growled. "You are in no position to bargain, sirrah."

With the freedom perfect weakness brings, Marcus retorted, "Why not? The worst you can do is take my head, and you can do that anyhow."

The Emperor blinked, then grinned crookedly. "True enough. Say on."

"If I bring Zemarkhos down, you will make a noble of me?"

"I said so once. What of it?"

Scaurus took a deep breath, more than half expecting to die in the next minute. "Should I somehow come back from Amorion, I think I will have shown my loyalty well enough to suit even you. Give me a noble's privilege, then. If I come back, give me leave to court your niece openly, as any noble might hope to do."

"Why, you insolent son of a whore! You dare ask me that, hied here for treason?" Gavras seemed to grow taller in his regalia. One of the guardsmen cursed. Marcus felt the grip on him tighten, heard a sword slide out of its scabbard. He nodded, though he felt fresh sweat prickle at his armpits.

"To the ice with you!" the Emperor exclaimed, and Scaurus thought it was the end. But Thorisin was glaring at him with reluctant respect. "Skotos chill you, I owe Alypia half a hundred goldpieces. She told me you would say that. I didn't think there could be so much brass in any man."

"Well?" Marcus said, but his knees sagged with relief. Had the answer been no, it would have been over already.

"If you return, I will not kill you out of hand for it," the Emperor ground out, word by word. He turned to the guards' squad leader, gestured imperiously. "Take him away!"

"My sword is not here yet," Marcus reminded him.

"Are you trying to find out how close to the edge you can walk, Roman?" Gavras slammed his fist down on the tabletop. "I begin to see why your folk has no kings—who would want the job?" To the guards again: "Let him have whatever gear he wants, but get him out of my sight—wait for his cursed sword outside." And finally to Scaurus once more, it being the Emperor's prerogative to have the last word: "Shall I wish you success, or not?"

The *Seafoam* was a naval auxiliary, an oared cargo-carrier about seventy feet long, with sharp bows and a full stern. She had ten oarports on either side of her hull, as well as a single broad, square-rigged sail, brailed up now that she was in harbor.

Staggering a little under the weight of the heavy kit he carried, Marcus paused at the top of the gangplank. The squad of imperial guards watched him from the dock.

"Permission to come aboard?" he called, recognizing an officer by the knee-length tunic he wore and the shortsword on his hip. Most of his sailors were naked or nearly so, with perhaps a loincloth or leather belt on which to sling a knife.

"Keep at it," the man told his crew, who were stowing pointed wine jars and rounder ones full of pickled fish, along with bales of raw wool and woolen cloth, in the hold. Then he gave his attention to the tribune. "You're our special passenger, eh? Aye, drop down and join us. Give him a hand with his pack, there, Ousiakos!"

The sailor helped ease it to the deck. Rather awkwardly, Scaurus came after it; a true Roman, he was not used to ships. The officer walked up to shake his hand. "I'm Stylianos Zautzes, master of this wallowing tub." The Videssian was in his early forties, whipcord lean, with a grizzled beard, thick bushy eyebrows that met about his nose, and a skin turned to dark leather by years in the sun. When he shed his black, low-crowned cap to scratch his head, the tribune saw he was nearly bald.

Taron Leimmokheir jumped down beside Marcus. The men on deck stiffened to attention, giving him the Videssian salute with right fists over their hearts. "As you were," he said in his raspy bass. The drungarios of the fleet turned to Zautzes. "You take care of this one, Styl," he told the *Seafoam*'s captain, putting an arm round the tribune. "He's a good fellow, for all he's fallen foul of his Majesty. That's not hard to do, as I should know." He flicked his head back to get his mane of silver hair out of his eyes; he had left it long after Thorisin released him from prison.

Zautzes saluted again. "I would anyway, for my own pride's sake. But wasn't he to have a horse? It's not shown up."

"Landsmen!" Leimmokheir said contemptuously. On board ship, things had to be on time and right the first time; there was no room for sloppiness. "I should be able to waste so much time. As is, I can't even stay; I'm off to finish fitting out a squadron for coast patrol. Phos with you, outlander." He squeezed Scaurus' shoulder, pounded Zautzes on the back, and then took a tall step up onto the gangplank and hurried away.

The loading of the *Seafoam* went on. Marcus watched bales of hay tossed into the hold as fodder for his horse. Of the horse itself there was no sign. He shouted a question to the Videssian guardsmen still standing about on the pier. Their leader spread his hands and shrugged.

Zautzes said, "Sorry, Scaurus, but if the beast doesn't turn up by mid-afternoon we'll have to sail without it. I have dispatches to carry that won't keep. Maybe you'll be able to find some sort of animal in Nakoleia."

"Maybe," the tribune said dubiously. The minutes dragged on. He kept one eye on the pier, the other on the sailors to see how close they were to finishing loading.

Two of them dropped a wine jar. Zautzes swore as they swabbed the sticky stuff from the deck and threw the jar's fragments over the rail into the sea. One cut his foot on a shard and limped over to bandage it. Zautzes rolled his eyes in disgust. "You belong behind a plow, Ailouros." The luckless seaman's crewmates promptly took to calling him "Farmer."

Watching the mishap, Marcus forgot about the pier. He jumped at a shout from the gangplank: "Ahoy, or whatever it is you sailor bastards say! Can I get on your bloody boat?"

The tribune whirled. "Gaius! What are you doing here?"

"You know this lubber?" Zautzes demanded, bristling at hearing his beloved *Seafoam* called a boat. When Marcus had explained, the Videssian captain grudgingly called to Gaius Philippus, "Aye, board if you will."

The senior centurion did, grunting as he landed on the deck. He stumbled when he hit, being in full armor—transverse-crested helm, mail shirt, metal-studded leather kilt, and greaves, all polished till they gleamed—with a heavy pack slung on his back. Marcus caught his elbow and steadied him. "Thanks."

"It's nothing." The tribune studied him curiously. "Are you here to see me off? You're overdressed, I'd say."

"To Hades with seeing you off." Gaius Philippus hawked phlegm, but under Zautzes' warning eye spat over the rail. "I'm with you."

"What?" Scenting betrayal from the Emperor, Scaurus reached for his sword hilt. "Thorisin promised you'd take my place once I was gone."

"Oh, he offered it to me. I told him to put it where a catamite would enjoy it." Zautzes' jaw fell; no one spoke thus to the Avtokrator of the

Videssians. Gaius Philippus flicked a glance his way and dropped into Latin. "You can nail me on a cross, sir," he said to the tribune, "before I take a post from the man who robbed you of yours."

"He had his reasons," Scaurus said, also in Latin, and clumsily told the senior centurion what they were. He finished, "So if you want to change your mind, Gavras will likely give you the command no matter what you said to him. He thinks well of you; he's told me so, many times."

Hearing of the tribune's involvement with Alypia for the first time, Gaius Philippus reacted as Marcus had been sure he would. "You must've been balmy, playing with fire like that." He gave his own verdict: "Women bring more trouble than they're worth. I've said it before, and more than once, too."

Not having a good answer, Marcus kept quiet.

"But treason?" the senior centurion went on. "Not a chance. What would you want to throw over Gavras for? Whoever came next'd only be worse."

"So I thought, exactly."

"Of course—you're no thickhead. And I'll not go back, either. I'd sooner be your man than his suspicious Majesty's." He chuckled. "I've finally turned true mercenary, haven't I, when commander counts for more than country?"

"I'm glad," Marcus said simply, adding, "Not that you have much to look forward to, coming with me."

"Zemarkhos, you mean? But there's two of us now, and that doubles our chances, or maybe better. Aye," the veteran said to Scaurus' unspoken question, "Gavras told me where he was sending you." He scratched his head. "Far as I can see, you're lucky. With his temper up, I'm surprised he didn't just kill you and have done."

"Truth to tell, so was I, though I wasn't about to tell him that," Marcus said. "But while I was gathering my gear I thought it over. If Zemarkhos nails me, Thorisin's no worse off than if he'd shortened me himself. If I deal with him in Amorion, well, Thorisin's still stuck with me, but he's rid of his madman priest, who's more dangerous to him than I'd ever be, whether he admits it or not. And if we somehow do each other in, why then Gavras has two hares in the same net."

Gaius Philippus pursed his lips. "Hangs together," he admitted. "It's a good piece of Videssian double-dealing, right enough. They're slicker than Greeks, I swear. Three setups, and he wins them all" He cocked an eyebrow at the tribune. "Only trouble is, in two of 'em you—or rather, *we*—don't."

If the prevailing winds held, Nakoleia was about a week's sail from Videssos. As long as they did, Zautzes let his crew rest easy at the oars and traveled under sailpower alone. The blue-dyed sheet would flutter and flap as the breeze shifted. Scaurus' horse, which had finally arrived, was tethered to the stempost. It twitched its ears nervously at the strange noises behind it for the first few hours out of port, then decided they were harmless and ignored them.

Knowing he would never master the big roan gelding by equestrian skill alone, the tribune did his best to get it used to him and, if he could, well-disposed, too. He curried its glossy coat, stroked its muzzle, and fed it dried apricots and apples begged from the *Seafoam*'s cook. The beast, which had an admirably even disposition, accepted his attentions with an air of deserving no less.

Scaurus proved a good sailor and easily adapted to shipboard routine, stripping down to light tunic and sword belt in the mild spring air. Gaius Philippus had a sound enough stomach, but stayed in trousers and kept on wearing his nail-soled *caligae*. "Give me something with some bite to it," he said, eyeing the tribune's bare feet with disapproval.

"Whatever suits you," Marcus answered mildly. "I thought it best to follow the sailors' lead. They know more about this business than I do."

"If they were all that smart, they'd stay on land." Gaius Philippus drew his *gladius*, tested the edge with his thumb. "Care for some work?" he asked. "No doubt you could use it, after a winter of seal-stamping."

"You're right there," the tribune said. He started to unsheath his own sword, stopped in surprise. A long sheet of parchment was wrapped several times round the blade, held in place with a dab of gum.

"What do you have there?" Gaius Philippus said, seeing him pause.

"I don't know, yet." Scaurus freed his sword from its brass scabbard. He worked the parchment loose, slid it down over the point, and scraped the gum off his blade with his thumbnail.

He unrolled the note. "What does it say? Who sent it?" Gaius Philippus demanded as he came up to peer at the curlicues of Videssian script. Unlike the tribune, he had never learned to read or write the Empire's language, having enough trouble with Latin.

"It's from Nepos," Marcus said. He did not read it aloud, but went through it quickly so he could give Gaius Philippus the gist in Latin.

"Phos prosper you, outlander," the tubby priest and mage had written. "I am glad to have had at last the opportunity to examine this remarkable weapon of yours and only regret the circumstances which made my examination possible. This brief scrawl will summarize what I have learned; the iron-clad ruffian who will return your blade to you is clumping about outside my door even as I write."

Marcus had to smile; he could see Nepos scribbling frantically while Spektas glowered in at him from the corridor. He was sure the guardsman had not managed to hurry Nepos very much.

The tribune read on: "The spells with which your sword is wrapped are of a potency I confess I have not seen. I attribute this to the extremely weak and uncertain nature of magic in your native world, upon which you and your comrades have often remarked. Only charms of extravagant force, it is my guess, would function there at all. Here, however, it is easier to unleash enchantments. As a result, those on your blade, made for harsher circumstances, become wonderfully powerful indeed.

"They are, in fact, so strong I have had great difficulty in evaluating their nature. Testing-spells are subtle things, and the crude strength of your sword's enchantments is too much for them, just as one would not measure the ocean with a spoon. But forgive me; you want what I *do* know.

"Two separate spells, then, are laid on your blade. The first wards the sword and its bearer from opposing magics. This you have seen for yourself, of course, many times. I will only say that it far surpasses in force any such spells I have previously encontered. I wish I could determine how it was cast.

"Because of the warding spell's power, the other cantrip had to be investigated by indirect means, and I fear my results with it are not altogether satisfactory. It is in any case a more subtle enchantment. As far as I can tell, it is a charm somehow intended to protect not merely the individual who carries the sword, but his entire people as well. No Videssian sorcerer could begin to create such a spell, but I hazard that you were brought to Videssos through its agency.

"If I had your red-haired friend's blade to test along with yours, I might have more definite information to offer you—or I might be utterly destroyed. The enchantments are of that magnitude.

"My apologies for not being able to tell you more. I do not think you came here by chance alone, but that is a feeling for which I can offer no proof. I may say, however, that a certain historian with whom we are both acquainted shares my belief. We both wish you success in your trials; the Lord of the great and good mind willing, we shall see you again. Nepos."

The tribune did not translate that last paragraph for Gaius Philippus, but felt a warm glow as he read it. Though Alypia had not had any chance to communicate with him directly, she was clever enough to realize his sword would probably come back to him and somehow got a message where it would do the most good.

He wadded up the parchment and tossed it into the sea.

Gaius Philippus asked a typical, bluntly pragmatic question: "What good does it do you to know how your sword's magicked? You're no wizard, to spell with it."

"Too true. I wish I could, and singe Zemarkhos' beard for him."

"Well, you can't," Gaius Philippus said, "and if you don't pay attention to using it as it should be used, you won't live to face him anyway. So watch yourself!" He lunged at the tribune's chest. Marcus sprang backward as he parried the veteran's next thrust. Seamen crowded around to watch them fence.

IV

The standard flying from the upthrust lance was black as soot, an outlaws' standard once, but now one to make all Pardraya tremble. More than bandits rode in Varatesh's fighting tail now; even the most birth-proud khagans acknowledged him as head of the newly risen Royal Clan and sent their contingents to war at his side. Worse would befall them if they said him nay, and they knew it.

Scowling, Varatesh dug spurs into his pony's flanks. The shaggy little horse squealed and sprang ahead. The great black stallion at its side paced it without effort. Varatesh's frown grew deeper as his glance flicked to the white-robed rider atop the huge horse. Head of the Royal Clan—Royal Khagan—master of the steppe! So everyone proclaimed him, Avshar loud among them, but he and the wizard-prince knew the lie for what it was.

Puppet! The word rang inside his head, sour as milk gone bad. Without Avshar, he would still be a chieflet of renegades, a skulker, a raider—a flea, biting and hopping away before a hand came down to crush him. There were times he wished it were so. He was a killer many times over before Avshar found him, but he had not had any idea of what evil was.

He knew now. These days he never slept without seeing irons heating in the fires, without smelling burned flesh, without hearing men shriek as their eyes were seared away. And he had consented to it, had wielded an iron himself—his skin crept when he thought of it. But through that horror he had become Royal Khagan, had made his name one with fear.

Avshar chuckled beside him, a sound that reminded him of ice crackling on a winter stream. The wizard-prince's mantlings streamed out behind him as his horse trotted southwest. He swaddled himself from head to foot.

"We shall shatter them," the sorcerer said, and chuckled again at the prospect. He spoke the Khamorth tongue with no trace of accent, though not a plainsman. As for what he was—alone on all the steppe, Varatesh had seen beneath his robes, and wished he had not.

"Shatter them," Avshar repeated. "They will rue the insult they gave to Rodak and thus to you as well, my lord." The wizard's terrible voice held no sardonic overtone as he granted Varatesh the title, but the nomad was undeceived. Avshar went on, "Your brave warriors—and a sorcery I have devised for the occasion—shall break the fable of Arshaum invincibility once for all."

Varatesh shivered at the cruel greediness in the wizard-prince's manner, but could find no fault with what he said. The Arshaum were traversing Pardraya without his let—was he a lamb or a kid, for them to ignore as they pleased? "Do the omens promise success?" he asked.

Avshar turned his dreadful unseen stare on the plainsman. Varatesh flinched under it. With a freezing laugh, the wizard-prince replied, "What care I for omens? I am no *enaree,* Varatesh, no puling, effeminate tribesman peering timidly into the future. The future shall be as I make it."

"Do the omens promise success?" Gorgidas asked Tolui. A longtime skeptic, he had scant belief in foretelling, but in this world he was coming to doubt his doubts.

"We will know soon," the shaman said, his voice echoing and unearthly behind the madman's smile of his devil-mask. He reached out for a thin wand of willow-wood; the welter of fringes on the arm of his robe dragged through the dust.

The Arshaum leaders leaned forward in their circle round him. He drew a dagger from his belt and sliced the wand in half lengthwise. "Give me your hand," he said to Arghun. The khagan obeyed without question, and did not draw back when the shaman cut his forefinger. Tolui smeared Arghun's blood on one half of the split willow wand, saying, "This will stand for our army." He stabbed the other half into the soil of Pardraya, so that it came up black with mud. "This serves for the Khamorth."

"I would have my blood you given," Batbaian said.

Even amusement sounded eerie through the mask's unmoving lips.

"The Khamorth who are our enemies, I should have said," Tolui explained. Batbaian flushed. Tolui went on: "Enough now. Let us see what knowledge the spirits will grant, if they see fit to answer me."

The shaman picked up a drum with an oval head; its sides were as heavily fringed as his robe. He rose, tapping the drum softly. Its tone was deep and hollow, a fitting accompaniment to the wordless, crooning chant he began. He danced round the two wands, his steps at first slow and mincing, then higher, faster, more abandoned as he darted now this way, now that, paying no heed to the officers and princes who scattered before him.

A hoarse voice cried out in a nameless tongue ten feet above his head. Another answered, high and girlish. Gorgidas jumped; Lankinos Skylitzes, pale round the mouth, drew Phos' sun-circle on his breast. Gorgidas thought of ventriloquism, but then both voices shouted at once—no trickster could have worked that.

Tolui was dancing furiously. "Show me!" he cried. Drumbeats boomed like thunder. "Show me!" He shouted again and again. The second voice shouted with him, pleading, demanding. The first voice answered, but roughly, in rejection.

"Show me! Show me!" Now a whole chorus of voices joined the shaman's. "Show me!" Then came an angry bellow that all but deafened Gorgidas, and sudden silence after.

"Ah!" said Irnek, and at the same time, Viridovix: "Will you look at that, now!"

The two wands, one red with Arghun's blood, the other dark and dirty, were stirring on the ground like live things. They rose slowly into the air until they reached waist height. All the Arshaum watched them tensely. Viridovix gaped in awe.

Like a striking snake, the muddy wand darted at the one that symbolized Arghun and his men. That one attacked in turn; they both hovered as if uncertain. Then they slowly sank together, still making small lunges at each other. The bloodstained one came to rest atop the other. The Arshaum shouted in triumph, then abruptly checked themselves as it rolled off.

They cried out again, this time in confusion and dismay, as the blood suddenly vanished from the red-smeared wand, which split into three pieces. Their eyes were wide and staring; Gorgidas guessed this was no ordinary divination. Then the wand representing the Khamorth broke into a dozen fragments. Several of those burst into flame; after perhaps half a minute, the largest disappeared.

Tolui pitched forward in a faint.

Gorgidas dashed to his side, catching him before he hit the ground. He pulled the mask from the shaman's head and gently slapped his cheeks. Tolui moaned and stirred. Arigh stooped beside the two of them. He thrust a skin of kavass into Tolui's mouth. The shaman choked as the fermented mare's milk went down his throat, spraying it over Gorgidas and Arigh. His eyes came open. "More," he wheezed. This time he kept it down.

"Well?" Irnek said. "You gave us a foretelling the likes of which we've never seen, but what does it mean?"

Tolui passed a hand over his face, wiped sweat away. He was pale beneath his swarthiness. He tried to sit, and did at the second try. "You must interpret it for yourself," he said, shaken to the core. "Beyond what you saw, I offer no meanings. More magic than mine, and stronger, is being brewed; it clouds my vision and all but struck me sightless. I feel like a ferret who set out after mice and didn't notice a bear till he stumbled over its foot."

"Avshar!" Gorgidas said it first, but he was only half the name ahead of Viridovix and Batbaian.

"I do not know. I do not think the magician sensed me; if he had, you would be propping up a corpse. It was like no wizardry I have touched before, like black, icy fog, cold and dank and full of death." Tolui shuddered. He wiped his face again, as if to rub off the memory of that touch.

Then Skylitzes cried out a name. "Skotos!" he exclaimed, and made the sun-sign again. Goudeles, not normally one to call on his god at every turn, joined him. Gorgidas frowned. He did not follow the Videssian faith, but there was no denying that Tolui's description bore an uncanny resemblance to the attributes the imperials gave Phos' evil opponent.

"What if it is?" said Arghun, to whom Skotos and Phos were mere names. "What business does a spirit you Videssians worship have on the steppe? Let him look out for himself here. This is not his home."

"We do not worship Skotos," Skylitzes said stiffly, and began explaining the idea of a universal deity.

Gorgidas cut him off. "Avshar is no god, nor spirit, either," he said. "When Scaurus fought him in Videssos, he cut him and made him bleed. And beat him, too, in the end."

"That's so," Arigh said. "I was there—that was when I met you, remember, V'rid'rish? Two big men, both good with their swords."

"I didna stay for the shindy, bad cess for me," the Gaul said. "I went off wi' a wench instead, and not one to waste such a braw fight over, either, the clumsy quean." The memory still rankled.

Irnek scratched his head. "I do not like going ahead blind."

"Finding meaning in foretellings that have to do with battles is always chancy," Tolui said, "though it is worth trying. Men's passions cloud even the spirits' vision, and dark spells surround this struggle and veil it more thickly in shadows. Soon we will not need to wonder. We will know."

Arghun's far-flung scouts picked up the approaching army while it was still more than a day's ride northeast of the Arshaum. Against most foes they would have gained an advantage from such advanced warning, but with Avshar's sorcery they were themselves not hidden.

The Arshaum turned to meet Varatesh's horsemen, shaking out into battle order as they rode. They were, Viridovix saw, more orderly in their warfare than the Khamorth. The latter fought by clan and by band or family grouping within the clan, with each family patriarch or band leader a general in small. Though the Arshaum also mustered under their khagans, each clan was divided into squads of ten, companies of a hundred, and, in the large clans, regiments of a thousand. Every unit had its appropriate officer, so that commands passed quickly through the ranks and were executed with a precision that astonished the Gaul.

"They might as well be legionaries," he said to Gorgidas, half complaining, as a company of Arghun's plainsmen thundered by, broke into squads, and then re-formed. They carried out the evolution in perfect silence, taking their cues from black and white signal flags their captain carried.

The Greek grunted something in reply. He had been in more battles than he cared to remember, but always as a physician, fighting only in self-defense, relying on the legionaries for protection. The Arshaum, however well organized they were by nomad standards, had no place for such noncombatants. Even Tolui and his fellow shamans would take up bows and fight like any of their people once their magicking was done.

Thorough as usual, Gorgidas checked his equipment with great care, making sure his *gladius* was sharp, that his boiled-leather cuirass and small round shield had no weak spots, that all the straps on his horse's tackle were sound and tight. "You'll make a warrior yet," Viridovix said approvingly. He was careless in many ways, but went over his gear as exactingly as the Greek had.

"The gods forbid," Gorgidas said. "But there's no one to blame but me, should anything fail." He felt a curious tightness in his belly, half apprehension, half eagerness to have it over, one way or another—a very different feeling from the one he had known as a legionary physician. Then his chief reaction to battle had been disgust at the carnage. This twinge of anticipation made him ashamed.

When he tried to exorcise it by speaking of it aloud, Viridovix nodded knowingly. "Och, indeed and I've felt it, the blood lust, many's the time. Hotter than fever, stronger than wine, sweeter than the cleft between a woman's thighs—" He broke off, his smile going grim as he remembered Seirem and how she died. After a few seconds he went on, "And if your healing could find a cure for it, now, that'd be a finer thing nor any other I could name."

"Would it?" Gorgidas tossed his head. "Then how would those cured ever resist the outrages of wicked men?"

The Celt tugged at his mustaches. "To the crows with you, you carper! Here we've gone and chased ourselves right round the tree, so you're after saying there's need for warring, and it's me who'd fain see the end of it. Gaius Philippus, the sour auld kern, would laugh himself sick to hear us."

"You're probably right, but he'd think the argument was over the shadow of an ass. He's not much for rights or wrongs; he takes what he finds and does what he can with it. Romans are like that. I've often wondered if it's their greatest wisdom or greatest curse."

A couple of companies of Arshaum trotted ahead of the main body, to skirmish with the Khamorth and test their quality. Some of the plainsmen bet that the sight of them alone would be enough to scatter Varatesh's followers. Batbaian glowered, unsure whether to hope they were right or be angry at hearing his people maligned.

The skirmishers returned a little before nightfall; a few led horses with empty saddles, while several more men were wounded. Their comrades shot questions at them as the Arshaum set up camp. "It was strange," one said not far from Gorgidas. "We ran into two bands of Hairies, outriders like us, I suppose. The first bunch fired a few shots and then turned tail. The others, though, fought like crazy men." He scratched his head. "So who knows what to expect?"

"And a fat lot o' good all that did," Viridovix grumbled. "The omadhaun might as well be Tolui—or Gavras back in Videssos, come to that—for all the news we get from him."

In the light of the campfires, the dozen naked men were spread-eagled on the ground, as if staked out; though no ropes held them, they could not move. Some fearfully, others smiling like so many wolves, the Khamorth watched them as they lay. "See the rewards cowardice wins," Avshar said, his voice filling Varatesh's camp. He made a swift two-handed pass; his robes flapped like vulture's wings.

There was a rending sound. One of the helpless men shrieked as first one shoulder dislocated, then another; a louder cry came from another man as a thighbone ripped free from its hip-socket. Varatesh bit his lip as the screams went on. He was no stranger to using cruelty as a weapon, but not with the self-satisfied relish Avshar put into it.

The cries bubbled down to moans, but then, one by one, screams rang out again when limbs began to tear away from bodies. Blood spouted. The shrieks faded, this time for good.

"Bury this carrion," Avshar said into vast silence. "The lesson is over."

Varatesh gathered his courage to protest to the wizard-prince. "That was too much. You will only bring down hatred on us both."

Perhaps sated by the torment, Avshar chuckled, a sound that made

Varatesh want to hide. "It will encourage them," he said carelessly. "What do I care if they hate me, so long as they fear me?" He chuckled again, in gloating anticipation. "Come tomorrow, the Arshaum will envy those wretches. The sorcery is cumbersome, but very sure."

The scout was bleeding from a cut over his eye, but did not seem to notice. He rode his lathered pony up to Arghun and sketched a salute. "If they hold their pace, the main body of them should hit us in an hour or so."

The khagan nodded. "My thanks." The scout saluted again and hurried off to rejoin his company. Arghun turned to his sons and councilors. "It's of a piece with the rest of the reports we've had."

"So it is," Irnek said. "About time for me to get back to my clan. Good hunting, all." Several lesser khagans also rode away from the gathering under the standard of Bogoraz's coat.

"And you, Tolui," Arghun said. "Are you ready?"

"As ready as I was when you asked me before." The shaman smiled. He still carried his devil-mask under one arm; the day was warm and sunny, and he would have sweltered, putting it on too soon. "I can cast the spell, that I know. Whether it will do as we hope . . ." He shrugged.

Dizabul said, "I hope it fails." He mimed shooting a bow and made cut-and-thrust motions. "The slaughter will be greater if we overcome them hand-to-hand." His eyes glowed at the prospect.

"The slaughter among us, too, witling!" Arigh snapped. "Think of your own men first."

Dizabul bridled, but before the quarrel between the two brothers could flare again Arghun turned to the Videssian party and said quickly, "Well, my allies, does it suit you to fight this day?"

Skylitzes' nod was stolid, Pikridios Goudeles' glum: the chubby bureaucrat was no soldier and made no secret of it. Agathias Psoes reached over his shoulder, drew an arrow from his quiver, and set it in his bow.

Batbaian already carried a shaft nocked. "Here I hold with Dizabul," he said. His one-eyed grin was a hunting beast's snarl.

"And I as well, begging your pardon, Arigh dear," Viridovix said. Shading his eyes with his hand, he stared out over the plain, grimly eager for the first sight of a Khamorth. "Plenty of vengeance to be taken today—aye, and heads, too."

"A victory will do, whatever the means," Gorgidas said. "If we are to assail Yezd, I'd sooner see an easy one, to keep our army strong." He had to work to hold his voice steady. He could feel his pulse hammering; the lump in his throat was like some horrid tumor. He had heard many soldiers say there was no time for such pangs when the fighting started. He waited, hoping they were right.

Trumpets blared on the left; signal flags wigwagged. "They've spotted them!" Arigh exclaimed. He peered at the flags and what they showed of troop movements. "Irnek's falling back. They must have him flanked."

"Then their wing is exposed for us to nip off," his father replied. The khagan gestured to his standard-bearer, who flourished Bogoraz's caftan high overhead on its long lance. Signalmen displayed banners to swing the army west. The *naccara,* the deep-toned Arshaum war drum, thuttered out its commands. The drummer, in his constantly exposed position at the van, was one of the few nomads who protected himself with chain mail.

"Forward!" Arghun called, exhilarated by the prospect of action at last. Gorgidas flicked his horse's reins. It trotted ahead with the rest. Only Tolui and his fellow shamans held their place, making last preparations and awaiting the order to begin.

Viridovix pulled close to the Greek. "Fair useless you'll feel for a longish while," he warned. "There's a deal of shooting to be done or ever it comes to sword work." Gorgidas dipped his head impatiently. He had seen the nomads practicing with their composite bows and thought he knew what they could do.

Those moving dots—friends or foes? The Arshaum had no doubts. In one smooth motion they drew their bows to their ears, let fly, and were slammed back into their saddles, whose high cantles absorbed the force of the recoil. Riders and horses ahead crashed to the ground, dead at the hands of men whose faces they never saw.

Gorgidas' eyes went wide. Shooting at a mark was one thing, hitting moving targets from horseback at such a range something else again.

Not all the Khamorth went down; far from it. An arrow zipped past the Greek with a malignant whine, then several more. One of Psoes' troopers yelped and clutched his leg. An Arshaum tumbled from his horse. A nomad to his rear trampled him, but with a shaft through his throat he did not know it. Gorgidas abruptly understood what Viridovix had meant. He brandished his sword and shouted curses at Varatesh's men, those being his only weapons that could reach them.

The missile duel went on, both sides emptying their quivers as fast as they could. Now and again a band would gallop close to the enemy line, fire a quick volley of heavy, broad-headed arrows at their foes, and then dart away. For longer-range work they used lighter shafts with smaller, needle-sharp points, but those lacked the penetrating power of the stouter arrows.

Steppe war was fluid, nothing like the set-piece infantry battles the Romans fought. Retreat held no disgrace, but was often a ploy to lure foes to destruction. With their tighter command structure, the Arshaum had the better of the game of trap and countertrap. Time and again they would pretend to flee, only to signal flying columns to dash in behind the overbold Khamorth and cut them off.

Then the fighting turned savage, with the surrounded nomads making charge after desperate charge, trying to hack their way back to their comrades. Though it was on horseback, that was the sort of warfare Viridovix understood. He spurred toward the thickest action, and found himself facing a Khamorth bleeding from cuts on cheek and shoulder and with an arrow sunk to the fletching in his thigh.

The plainsman might have been wounded, but nothing was wrong with his sword arm. His face a snarling mask of pain, he cut at the Celt backhanded, then came back with a roundhouse slash Viridovix barely managed to beat aside.

They traded sword strokes. Viridovix' reach and long straight blade gave him an edge, but the nomad's superior horsemanship canceled it. He needed no conscious thought to twist his mount now this way, now that, by pressure of his knees, or to urge it in close when one of Viridovix' cuts left him off balance. Only the Gaul's strong arm let him recover in time to parry. The Khamorth's saber cut his trousers; he felt the flat kiss his leg.

But the plainsman's horse betrayed him in the end. An arrow sprouted in its hock with a meaty *thunk*. It screamed and reared, and for a moment its rider had to give all his attention to holding his seat. Before he could recover, Viridovix' sword tore out his throat. He toppled, horrified surprise the last expression his face would wear.

The Gaul felt none of the fierce elation he had expected, only a sense of doing a good job at something he no longer relished. "Och, well, it needs the doing, for a' that," he said. Then he stopped in dismay at his own words. "The gods beshrew me, I'm fair turned into a Roman!"

Not far away, Goudeles was fighting a Khamorth even fatter than he was. The nomad, though, knew what he was about and had the pen-pusher in trouble. He easily turned the Videssian's tentative cuts and had pinked Goudeles half a dozen times; luck was all that had kept him from dealing a disabling wound.

"Don't kiss him, Pikridios, for Phos' sake!" Lankinos Skylitzes roared. "Hack at him!" But the dour Videssian officer was hotly engaged himself, with no chance to come to Goudeles' rescue. The bureaucrat gritted his teeth as another slash got home.

Gorgidas raked his pony's flanks with his spurs and galloped past cursing horsemen toward Goudeles and his foe. He shouted to draw the Khamorth's attention from Goudeles. The plainsman glanced his way, but only for a moment; seeing a bearded face, he took the Greek for one of Varatesh's followers, come to help finish off his enemy.

He realized his mistake barely in time to counter Gorgidas' thrust. "Who are you, you flyblown sheepturd?" he bellowed in outrage, cutting at the physician's head. He was a powerful man, but Gorgidas was used to fencing with Viridovix and knocked the blow aside. Then it was easy to thrust again, arm at full extension, all the weight of his body behind it. The Khamorth fought with the edge, not the point; battle reflex had saved him the first time. His eyes went wide as Gorgidas' *gladius* punched through his boiled-leather jerkin and slid between ribs.

A rugged warrior, he cut at the Greek again, but his stroke had no strength behind it. Bright blood bubbled from his nose. A stream of it poured out of his mouth as he tried to gulp air. His curved shamshir dropped from his hand. His eyes rolled up in his head; he slumped over his horse's neck.

"Bravely done, oh, bravely!" Goudeles was shouting, all but cutting off Gorgidas' ear as he waved his saber about. The physician stared at the scarlet smear on his own sword point. The legionaries were right, it seemed: there was no time for fear, or even thought. The body simply reacted—and a man was dead.

He leaned to one side and vomited onto the blood-spattered grass.

The sour stuff was still stinging his nose when another plainsman, grimly intent on battling out of the Arshaum trap, stormed at him, scimitar smashing down in an arc of death. Though the nausea had filled his eyes with tears, the Greek brought up his shield to ward off the blow. He felt the light wood framework splinter and hurled the ruined target away. The second Khamorth had no more idea how to defend himself against the stabbing stroke than had the other, but Gorgidas' thrust was not as true. The nomad reeled away, clutching a shoulder wound.

The second time, the Greek discovered, he felt only anger that his opponent had escaped. That disturbed him worse than his earlier revulsion.

Close combat ran all along the battle line as arrows were exhausted. The fight, which had begun with the two sides facing north and south, wheeled to east and west as the right wing of each overlapped the other's left and made it give ground. If the Arshaum had gained any advantage, it was tenuous. Varatesh's outlaws, though they were rulers now, still fought with the renegade fury of men who had nothing to lose. The clans forced into alliance with them were less ferocious, but the sight of the white-robed figure on his charger behind them reminded them that retreat held more terrors than standing fast.

Viridovix cut another swordsman from the saddle, then found himself facing a Khamorth who carried a light lance in place of shamshir or bow. It was his turn to be out-reached; he did not care for it. Luckily the press was heavy; the lancer had no chance to charge and build momentum. He jabbed at Viridovix' face. The Gaul ducked, seized the shaft below the head, and dragged the Khamorth toward him.

His first stroke with his potent Gallic sword hewed through the lance. Its owner, who was tugging against him with all his strength, almost flew over his horse's tail when the shaft broke and the opposing pressure disappeared. His arms flailed wildly for balance. Viridovix slashed again. The Khamorth screamed briefly, half his face sheared away.

Batbaian was wreaking a revenge to dwarf the Celt's. He had slewed his fur cap around so one earflap hid his empty socket and he looked no different from any other Khamorth. He would strike, snakelike, and be gone before a victim knew to whom he had fallen. When three Arshaum assailed him, not recognizing him either, he lifted the cap for a moment. They drew back, knowing what that dreadful scar meant.

Arigh's chest was splashed with blood—not his own. "Ha, we begin to drive them!" he shouted excitedly. Varatesh's left was falling back, a retreat that was no feint. Here and there Khamorth pulled out of line and rode north for their lives. Others stubbornly battled on, but could not hold against the greater flexibility of their foes and the fury of the band that fought beneath the standard of Bogoraz' coat.

Then an Arshaum pitched forward with a black-feathered shaft driven clean through him. Another fell, and another; a horse crashed to the ground, an arrow in its right leg. Two more animals tumbled over it, spilling their riders. One nomad rolled free; the other was crushed beneath his pony's barrel.

Far behind the Khamorth line, Avshar plied his bow with deadly virtuosity. He had kept his quiver filled against the chance of disaster, and when it threatened he turned it back. He outranged even the nomads; his accuracy was fearsome. As its leaders died, the Arshaum advance staggered and began to ebb, like a wave running down a beach.

"That is the wizard?" Arghun said. The khagan's legs were weak, but there was nothing wrong with his arm; more than one Khamorth had fallen to his sword. As he spoke, another Arshaum lurched in the saddle, clutching at an arrow in his belly. His scrabbling hands went limp; he slid to the ground.

"That is Avshar," Gorgidas said. With a mixture of dread, hate, and an awe he loathed himself for feeling; he looked across the lines at the wizard-prince who had chosen himself as Videssos' nemesis. The tall, white-robed figure did not deign to notice him. One by one his deadly shafts went out, as if fired by some murderous machine.

"Whatever sort of sorcerer he is, he is no mean man of his hands," Arghun said with a face like iron, watching another of his men cough blood and die. "He will break us if he holds to it much longer; we cannot stand up under such archery."

For Viridovix and Batbaian, no awe mingled with their hate at the sight of Avshar; it burned hot and clean. With one accord, they spurred their ponies forward, ready to cut their way through all the Khamorth who stood between them and the sorcerer. But the Arshaum did not press the charge with them, and Varatesh's men took fresh courage from the mighty power at their back. Gaul and plainsman killed and killed again, but could not force a breakthrough by themselves.

Them Avshar seemed to recognize, for he bowed contemptuously in the saddle and gave a mocking wave as he slung his bow over an armored shoulder and rode from that part of the field.

Far away on his army's right wing, Varatesh shook his head for the hundredth time, trying to keep the blood welling from the cut on his forehead from running into his eyes. He was exhausted, snatching panting breaths on his pony, which was wounded, too. His hand trembled from his weariness; the shamshir he grasped felt heavy as lead.

And this Irnek in front of him was a very devil. Beaten at the outset when his men were outflanked, he had somehow regrouped, steadied his line, and fought back with a savagery that chilled even the longtime outlaw. One lesson Varatesh had learned: never to trust an Arshaum retreat, no matter how panic-stricken it seemed. That mistake had cost him the slash over his eye and nearly his life with it.

But it was past noon, and Irnek was not retreating any more. His riders pressed foward, probing for weaknesses and making the most of whatever they found. Lacking their enemies' discipline, the Khamorth in retreat only opened themselves to greater danger. They wavered; a few more pushes would crack them.

Varatesh bawled for a messenger, despising himself as he did so. He had thought to win this battle without help from Avshar, to free himself once and for all from the wizard's domination. Now he was on the point of losing. Having had a taste of life as Royal Khagan, he would not go back to outlawry, the best fate he could expect from failure.

The words gagged him, but he brought them out: "Ride to Avshar and tell him to let it begin."

Arghun shouted for a courier. A young Arshaum appeared at his side, face gray-brown with dust save for streaks washed clean by sweat. The khagan said, "We stand at the balance. Ride back to Tolui and tell him to let it begin."

The nomad hurried away.

"Get yourself gone, you lumpish clot," Avshar snarled. "If I waited for Varatesh's leave for my sorceries, his cause would have foundered long before this. Go on, begone, I say." The quailing Khamorth wheeled his pony and fled.

The wizard-prince forgot him before he was out of sight. The conjuration over which he labored sucked up his attention like a sponge. If the barbarian had broken into his spell-casting half an hour from now, his life would not have been enough to answer for the interruption.

Avshar drew a fat viper from a saddlebag. The snake thrashed wildly, trying to strike, but his grip behind its head was sure and inescapable. His mailed fingers tightened; bone crunched dully. He threw the broken-backed serpent, still alive, onto the small fire that smoked in front of him. The flames leaped up to engulf it.

He began a preliminary incantation, chanting in an archaic tongue and moving his hands through precise passes. Even so early in the spell, a mistake could mean disaster. He intended no mistakes.

Clouds passed across the sun. With the edges of his perception, he felt another power—a tiny one, next to his—making magic. When his chant was done, he allowed himself the luxury of laughter. A rain summons, was it? If his foes thought him so lacking in imagination as to repeat the walls of fire he had loosed against Targitaus' riders, all the better. He had nothing so trivial in mind.

As a temple went up brick by brick, so with one spell upon another was his sorcery built. He laughed again, liking the comparison. But despite his grim amusement, he did not let himself be tempted out of methodical precision for the sake of speed. Even for a wizard of his might, summoning demons was not undertaken lightly. Calling and then controlling them taxed him to the utmost; if his will slipped once, they would turn and rend him in an eyeblink of time.

He could count on the fingers of both hands the invocations he had performed in all the centuries since he first recognized the dominance of Skotos in the world. There had been the dagger-imprisoned spirit which should have drunk the accursed Scaurus' soul, but somehow failed; and a few decades before that a conjuring which did not fail at all—the fiend that slew Varahran, the last King of Kings of Makuran, in his bed and opened his land to the Yezda. Before that, it had been more than a hundred years.

His reverie vanished as the gathered power of the demon swarm he was raising heaved against his control. He restrained them harshly, sent them torment for daring to set themselves against him. Their howls of anguish rang in his mind. When he had punished them enough, he resumed the slow, careful business of preparing them for release—on his terms.

This time his laughter was full of expectant waiting. As demons went, each member of the swarm was small and weak. So is a single bee or wasp. Several hundred, all enraged together, are something else again. The Arshaum would go down as if scythed.

Avshar would have rubbed his hands together at the prospect, had they not been full of a certain powder. He cast it into the fire. The flames flared in blue, malignant violence. Fell voices cried out from the heart of the blaze, roaring, demanding. He quieted them, soothed them. "Soon," he said. "Soon."

A faint, halfhearted squib of thunder rumbled overhead—like a windy man with too many beans in him, the wizard-prince thought scornfully. Rain pattered down, a few drops here and there. The pulsing fire ignored them. It was no longer consuming wood and brush, but the force of the wizard's spirit. He felt strength drain from him, but what he had left would suffice.

He raised his hands above his head in a sinuous pass and began the hypnotically rhythmic canticle that would guide the first of the swarm to do his bidding. A shape began to flicker, deep within the leaping blue flames. It turned this way and that, blindly, until it chanced to face him. It bowed low then, recognizing its master.

Avshar dipped his head in acknowledgment, but warned in a voice like rime-covered stone, "See to it thou remembrest, aye, and thy brethren with thee."

The demon cringed.

Varatesh hardly heard the mutter of thunder in the distance; he was beating down an Arshaum's stubborn guard and finally cutting the man from the saddle. Nor had he thought much about the dark scudding clouds suddenly filling the sky—doubtless some side-effect of Avshar's wizardry. He had not made any deep inquiries into that. He did not want to know.

A raindrop splashed on his cheek, another on the palm of his left hand. The thunder came again, louder. He felt a light touch on the back of his neck and brushed at it automatically. His hand closed around something small and soft. It wriggled against his fingers.

He opened his hand. A tiny tree frog, green mottled with brown, sat frozen on his palm, its golden eyes wide with fear, the sac under its throat swelling and deflating at each quick breath.

Varatesh shouted in horrified disgust and threw the little creature as far as he could, then wiped his hands frantically on his buckskin trousers. With their cold slimy skins and thin, peeping voices, frogs housed the spirits of the dead, according to Khamorth legend. Even hearing them was bad luck; to touch one was infinitely worse, a sign he would soon die himself.

Shaken, he tried to put the evil omen out of his thoughts and concentrate on the fighting again. Then another froglet dropped from the sky, to tangle itself in the long hair of his pony's mane. Its pale legs thrashed and kicked. Yet another landed on Varatesh's knee. It hopped away before he could bring down his fist and smash it. There was another phantom touch at the side of his neck; a little frog with clinging toepads skittered wildly across his face, too fast for him to kill it. He spat and blinked, over and over. His stomach churned.

Varatesh was almost thrown from his horse when the rider on his right, who was swatting at himself like a madman, lost control of his mount and sideswiped him. "Careful, you slubberer!" he cried. The other did not seem to hear him. Still smashing away at frogs, he rode ahead with no thought for his own safety and quickly fell, easy meat for a grinning Arshaum's saber.

Too late, Varatesh understood the clouds above the field were no part of Avshar's sorcery. Frogs fell from them in streams, in torrents, in a deluge, and as they fell, chaos spread through the Khamorth ranks. Some men fled, screaming in terror. Others, like the luckless fellow who had collided with the outlaw chief, were too unstrung by the frogs' dreadful prophecy to think of their own safety—and thus helped fulfill it. And the hard cases who put aside panic and omens alike were too few to hold back the Arshaum, who stormed forward as they saw their foes in confusion.

Fury banished fright from Varatesh. He roared foul oaths, trying to rally his unmanned followers. "Stand!" he shouted. "Stand, you stoneless spunkless sheep-hearted cravens!" But they would not stand. Neither his words nor his savage sword work stemmed the growing rout. By ones and twos, by groups, by whole bands, his army streamed away north, back toward their familiar pastures, and he with them.

Viridovix howled his glee as the frogs rained down and the nomads began to waver. "Look at the little puddocks, will you now, falling from the skies!" he chortled. Several fell on him. He felt very kindly toward them and let them stay; they were safer than they would be under the horses' pounding hooves.

He rode close to Gorgidas and slapped the Greek on the back so hard that he whirled round, sword in hand, thinking himself attacked. "Sure and you're a genius, you and your puddocks!" the Gaul cried. "D'you see the whoresons flapping about like hens wi' the heads off 'em, not knowing whether to shit or go blind? They're addled for fair!"

"So it would seem," Gorgidas agreed, watching two Khamorth gallop full tilt into each other. He picked a frog off his cheek. It sprang away as he was trying to set it on top of his fur cap. "Tolui and the rest of the shamans are doing splendidly, aren't they?"

Viridovix clapped a hand to his forehead. "Is that all you'll say?" he said disgustedly. "You might as well be a dead corp, for all the relish you take from life. Where's the brag? Where's the boast? Where would Tolui and the whole lot o' he-witches be, outen your scheme to play with?"

"Oh, go howl!" Gorgidas said, but a grin stretched itself across his spare features as he watched the Khamorth lines dissolve under the froggy cloudburst like men of salt caught in the rain. *"Brekekekex!"* he shouted in delight. *"Brekekekex! Koax! Koax!"*

Viridovix looked at him strangely. "Is that what a frog's after saying in your Greek? Gi' me a good Celtic puddock any day, who'll croak his croak and ha' done."

The physician had no chance to come up with a sharp answer. Three Khamorth were riding at him and the Gaul, stout-spirited warriors sacrificing themselves to buy time for their comrades' escape. He recognized Rodak son of Papak. The onetime envoy spurred toward him, still shouting, "Varatesh!" Gorgidas had no chance to use his thrusting attack. It was all he could do to save himself from Rodak's whirlwind assault. He yelped as the Khamorth's saber scored a bleeding line down his arm.

Then Rodak's head leaped from his shoulders. As every muscle in the spouting corpse convulsed, Batbaian pushed on to the next outlaw and hewed away half his hand. With a shriek, the Khamorth jammed it under his other arm to try to stem the bleeding. He spun his horse round and rode for his life. Batbaian galloped to Viridovix' aid against the third. After his mutilation and the slaughter of his clan, mere frogs held no terror for him.

Viridovix killed his man before Batbaian reached him. The young Khamorth stared at the standards in Varatesh's army. They were in disarray, some moving in one direction, some in another, others shaking as if their bearers were taken by an ague.

"I know those clans," he said. "They cannot all be corrupt—the Lynxes, the Four Rivers clan, the Spotted Goats, the Kestrels.. . ." He spurred forward toward the Khamorth, crying, "To me! To me! Rise now against Varatesh and his filthy bandits! The Wolves!" he shouted, and followed it with the howling war cry of his clan.

A chill ran up Viridovix' spine. Only Batbaian could raise that shout now. No, there was another—had not Targitaus and he shared blood in brotherhood? He threw back his own head and howled, took up the cry himself. "The Wolves! Are you hearing me, you dung-eating mudsouls? The Wolves!" He pounded after Batbaian. Even in their confusion, heads whipped round among the Khamorth to listen.

A flood of fleeing Khamorth came up from the south, Arshaum riding in pursuit. "Irnek's turned them!" Arigh said. "He's rolling them up!"

"Aye!" said his father. "If we strike now, we can bag the lot of them." Arghun seized the lance that carried Bogoraz' coat from the standard bearer. He leveled it at the milling Khamorth, who were losing any semblance of order as the new wave of fugitives crashed through bands still fighting. "At them!" he cried. Hard on the heels of Batbaian and Viridovix, the Gray Horse Arshaum charged.

When the first frog dropped from the sky, Avshar thought it a freak of nature and crushed it under his boot. Then another one fell, and then a handful of them. A few hundred yards ahead, the sound of battle changed. The wizard-prince lifted his head, wary as an old wolf at a shift of wind.

Sensing his distraction, the demon cowering in the sorcerous fire lashed out with all its might, trying to break free from his control. Avshar staggered. "Test me, wilt thou?" he roared, gathering all his powers to hurl against the rebellious fiend. It resisted, but could not draw on the full power of its swarm; its mates were not yet entirely on the plane where it battled. He beat it back and lashed it with agony it had never imagined. With a final gesture of sublime hatred, the wizard-prince severed the connection between the swarm leader and its comrades.

Aghast, solitary in a way it had never known, the demon wailed and yammered. "Less than thou deservest, traitorous maggot!" Avshar hissed.

He readied the cantrip that would reunite the swarm with its leader and bring them through to do his bidding, but had no time to cast it. While he and the demon had fought, the battle ahead was collapsing. Khamorth galloped by, too unstrung by frogs and Arshaum to fear the wizard anymore. And the Arshaum themselves could only be seconds behind, hot for revenge against his archery.

His fists balled in fury. It all but choked him—outdone by a two-copper bit of conjuring! But he had survived too long to yield to rage's sweet temptation. He bounded atop his great black charger—no time for a spell of apportation, even if he were not spent by his earlier magics. His long-sword rasped out. Cold iron, then, and nothing else.

No, not quite. As the wizard touched spurs to the stallion's flanks, he swung his sword arm in a quick, intricate pattern. The blue flames of his balefire died; the demon within sprang free.

Avshar pointed east. "Slay me the leader of that accursed rabble, and then I give thee leave to get hence and join thy fellows once more."

The demon's claws clutched hungrily. Its slanted eyes were still filled with horror at aloneness. It mounted to the air on black, leathery bat-wings and circled above the field to seek its commanded quarry.

The wizard-prince did not watch it go. He was already galloping south, away from the fleeing Khamorth. They were a broken tool, but he had others.

Viridovix paid no attention when the druids' stamps on his sword flared to golden life. They had been gleaming gently for some time from Tolui's sorcery, and he was deep in the press, laying about him for all he was worth. He kept shouting the Wolves' war cry, though his throat was raw and his voice hoarse. Several times he had heard answering shouts that did not come from Batbaian and once saw a pair of Khamorth chopping at each other with axes. Varatesh's jerry-built power was cracking at the first defeat.

As if the name was enough to conjure the man, he spied the outlaw chief not fifty feet away, using the strength of his fine horse to force his way through the crush. Varatesh's eyes locked with his. Viridovix raised his sword in challenge. Varatesh nodded, once, and turned his mount's head. He struck one of his own men across the shoulders with the flat of his shamshir. "Make way, there! This is between the pair of us!"

They moved cautiously toward one another, each aware of his opponent's strengths. At swords afoot Viridovix would have been confident; he was a better man with the blade than Varatesh ever would be. But the nomad's lifelong rapport with his horse canceled the Gaul's advantage.

Confident in his horsemanship, Varatesh struck first, a cut at the Celt's head that Viridovix easily beat aside. The outlaw chief swung up his blade in salute. "A pity it must end this way. Had the spirits made the world but a little different, we might have been friends, you and I."

"Friends, is it?" Viridovix wheeled his horse, slashed; with liquid grace, Varatesh ducked under the stroke. Memories swam behind the Gaul's eyes until a red mist all but robbed him of vision: Varatesh kicking him in the point of the elbow to warn against escape when he was the renegade's captive; a butchered camp—oh, and one body in particular—the remembrance of Seirem smote him like a blow; a thousand blinded men stumbling along with weeping red empty sockets, tied to half a hundred left one-eyed to guide them. "Friends wi' the likes o' you, you murthering sod? The Empire's Skotos'd spit on you." He cut again, anger lending his arm fresh force. Varatesh grunted as he turned the slash. The next one got home.

Pain twisted the Khamorth's mouth, but from Viridovix' words, not the wound. "I know what you think," he said, and the Celt could not help but believe him. "Those outrages I was forced to, and the ones before as well. I loathe myself for every one. It was do as I did or die, after I was wrongly outlawed." His voice was full of desperate pleading, as though he was trying to convince himself and Viridovix both that he spoke truly.

For a moment the Gaul felt sympathy, but then his eyes grew hard and his hand tightened once more on his sword hilt. "A man flung into a dungheap can climb out and wash himself, or he can wade deeper. Think on the choice you made."

The explosive rage that made Varatesh dangerous to friend and foe alike turned his handsome features into a mask more frightening than the one Tolui wore. He showered blows on Viridovix, using his lighter, quicker blade to strike and then strike again, never giving the Celt a chance to reply. Viridovix dodged in the saddle, parrying as best he could. He felt steel cut him, but battle fever ran too high to let him know the hurt yet.

Not so his horse; it squealed and bucked when Varatesh laid open its shoulder. Viridovix flew over its head. He landed heavily on his side. As Varatesh wheeled his own beast to come round and finish the job, the

Gaul scrambled to his feet. He grabbed at his pony's reins, hoping he could mount before the Khamorth was upon him. He missed. The pony, wild with pain, ran off still leaping and kicking.

Varatesh's gore-smeared grin was a ghastly thing to see. Viridovix hefted his sword and planted his feet firmly, though facing a horseman afoot was a fight with only one likely ending.

Just as Varatesh urged his horse at the Gaul, another rider hurtled toward him out of the crowd of fighters watching the single combat. The outlaw chief whirled to face the unexpected attack, but too late. Batbaian's scimitar rose and fell. "For my father!" he cried. Blood spurted. He slashed again. "My mother!" Varatesh reeled. "Seirem!" Two cuts, forehand and back, delivered with savage force. "And for me!" Varatesh gave a bubbling scream as the sword hacked across his face, giving Batbaian exact retribution for his own disfigurement.

The renegade toppled to the ground, lay still. "Take his horse," Batbaian called to Viridovix. He hurried forward. Varatesh groaned and rolled over onto his back. Viridovix swung up his sword to finish him, but the outlaw's one-eyed dying stare transfixed him.

Varatesh's mouth worked. "Outlawed wrongly . . . not . . . my fault," he choked out. "Swear . . . Kodoman drew knife . . . first." He coughed blood and died, the dreadful insistence still set on his face.

The pony did a nervous dance step as Viridovix' unfamiliar weight swung into the saddle, but it bore him. The Celt glanced at Varatesh's corpse. "D'you suppose he was telling the truth, there at the end?"

Batbaian frowned. "I don't care. He earned what he got." He hesitated, looked for a moment as young as his years. "I'm sorry I broke into the duel."

"I'm not, lad," Viridovix said sincerely. He was starting to feel his wounds. "For all he was a cullion, the kern was as bonny a fighter as ever I faced; belike he had me there. And," he added quietly, "you gave him your reasons for it." Satisfied, Batbaian nodded.

Their chief's fall spurred on the rout of the Khamorth. They fled north, pressed hard by Arghun's forces. The khagan waved the standard over his head, urging his riders on. Flanked by his two sons, he caught up with Viridovix and Batbaian at the spearhead of the attack. "You know him, the one you brought down?" he said.

"Aye," said Batbaian; Viridovix, almost as brief, amplified: "Varatesh, it was."

Arghun's face lit with the smile of a general who sees victory assured, the smile of a man for whom war still holds joy. "No wonder they break, then! Well fought, both of you."

Viridovix grunted; Batbaian said nothing. Dizabul and even Arigh scowled at their churlishness, but the Gaul did not care. Some triumphs were too dearly won for rejoicing.

Someone was plucking at his sleeve. He turned to find Gorgidas by his side; it was like meeting someone from another world. "Still alive, are you?" he said vaguely.

The Greek's answering grin was haggard. "Through no fault of my own, I think. Wherever I get the chance hereafter, I'll stick to writing up battles instead of fighting in them—safer and less confusing, both." He grew businesslike, drawing a long strip of wool from his saddlebag. "Let me tie up your arm. That slash that got through your cuirass will have to wait until we have time to get it off you."

For the first time, Viridovix realized that the dull ache in his chest was not just exhaustion; he felt warm wetness trickling down his ribs and saw the rent in his boiled-leather armor. A flesh wound, he decided, since he had none of the shortness of breath that went with a punctured lung.

He held out his arm to Gorgidas for bandaging, then jerked it away. The druids' marks were yellow fire down the length of his sword. But the rain of frogs, having served its purpose, was slackening. "Avshar!" the Gaul shouted, looking wildly in every direction for the wizard-prince.

But when the danger came, it dropped from the skies like Tolui's frogs, hurtling down like a stooping hawk. Arghun suddenly groaned. The standard went flying from his hands and fell to the ground as he pitched forward on his horse, clawing at the crow-sized horror that clung to the back of his neck.

It was clawing too, its talons ripping through sinew and softer flesh. Its razor-sharp beak tore deeply into him; everyone close by heard bone break. Batwings overlay the khagan's shoulders like the shadow of death. His struggles lessened.

Arigh and Dizabul cried out together; no one could have said which of their swords first descended on the demon's back. But its armored integument turned their blades. It glared hatred at them through slit-pupiled eyes red as the westering sun and did not loose its hold.

Then Viridovix slashed at the creature. The druids' stamps flashed like lightning as his sword cleaved the unearthly flesh; he blinked and shook his head, half dazzled by the explosion of light. The demon shrieked, a high, thin squall of anguish. Foul-smelling ichor sprayed from it, spattering the Gaul's sword hand. He jerked it away; the stuff burned like vitriol.

Still screaming, the demon dropped off Arghun and thrashed in its death throes. In a rage born of disgust and dread, Virdovix hacked it clean in two. The wailing stopped, but each half quivered on with unnatural vitality. Then, when it was truly dead, its flesh crumbled to fine gray ash and blew away on the breeze.

"Out of my way, curse you!" Gorgidas said, pushing past the Celt and Arigh to reach Arghun's side. The khagan was slumped over his horse's back; Gorgidas sucked in a sharp, dismayed breath when he saw the gaping wound Arghun had taken. The khagan's face was gray, his eyes rolled back in his head. Gorgidas stanched the flow of blood as well as he could and groped for a pulse. He felt none.

Near panic, the physician reached into himself for the healer's trance. He felt his awareness of his surroundings, of everything but Arghun's dreadful injuries, slip away. Laying his hands on them, he sent out the healing power with all the force at his command. But there was nothing to receive it, no spark of life for it to jump to. He had felt that awful emptiness before, trying to save Quintus Glabrio when his lover was far past saving.

Slowly Gorgidas returned to himself. He looked from Arigh to Dizabul and spread his hands, wet with their father's blood. "He is gone," he told them. His voice broke and he could not go on; Arghun had treated him like a son these last few months, in gratitude for his life. This time it was a gift Gorgidas could not give him.

Dizabul and Arigh shed no tears; that was not the Arshaum way. Instead they drew their daggers and gashed their own cheeks, mourning with blood rather than water. Then, knives still in their hands, they stared at each other with sudden hard suspicion. One of them would be khagan, and Arghun had named no successor.

When Arghun's standard fell, the pursuit of the fleeing Khamorth broke down in confusion as the Arshaum reined in to find out what had happened. As they did, they followed his sons in marking his passage with their own blood. Lankinos Skylitzes unhesitatingly imitated the nomads; the rest of the Videssian embassy party mourned in their own way.

"Where did the wizard run?" Arigh called to the growing crowd of men around him. He jerked his chin northwards at the cloud of dust that marked the flight of the broken Khamorth. "If he's with that rabble, I'll chase them till I fall off the edge of the world."

Several of Irnek's men spoke to their own chieftain, who rode forward and bowed in the saddle to Arigh and Dizabul both, with nicely calculated impartiality. They eyed each other again. Irnek smiled, quickly erased it. *He's setting them against each other while they're groggy with grief,* Gorgidas realized, *to weaken the Gray Horses and advance his own Black Sheep clan.* He had thought that tall, cool Arshaum had a ready wit—the fellow maneuvered like a Videssian.

Irnek's words, though, could not have been rehearsed, not when he had just learned of Arghun's death. He said, "A giant in white mantlings on a great horse cut his way through my riders and headed south." His warriors shouted confirmation; one had been disarmed by a stroke of Avshar's broad-sword, and counted himself lucky not to have lost his head as well.

"Anthrax take the Hairies, then! Let them run," Arigh said. His wave encompassed a score of his clansmen. "Get fresh horses from camp and be after the wizard. I don't care how fast that big black stallion is—aye, I've seen it. He has no remounts, and we'll run him down, soon or late." He grinned wolfishly at the prospect.

As the riders hurried away, Dizabul rounded on his brother, angrily demanding, "Who are you, to give orders so?" One of Irnek's eyebrows might have twitched, but his features were too well schooled to give away much of what he was thinking.

"And who are you, to say I may not?" Arigh's voice was silky with danger. The Gray Horse Arshaum surreptitiously jockeyed for position, some lining up behind one brother, some behind the other. Gorgidas was dismayed to see how much support Dizabul enjoyed. He had largely recovered from the ignominy of backing Bogoraz, and many of his clanmates were more comfortable with him than with Arigh after Arghun's elder son had spent so much time in Videssos, away from the steppe.

Irnek sat quiet on his horse, weighing the balance of forces.

"A moment, gentlemen!" Pikridios Goudeles forced his way through the crowd to Arigh and Dizabul. The dapper envoy was sadly draggled, covered with blood, dust, and sweat. His voice had nothing wrong with it, though, rolling out rich and deep in the trained phrasing of the rhetorician. "The command is sensible, no matter who gives it."

He could not be as grandiloquent in the Arshaum tongue as in his own Videssian, but by now he spoke it fairly well. Agrhun's sons turned their heads to listen. He continued, "Consider who gains from your disunity at the moment of victory—only Avshar. Suppressing him is your chiefest goal; all else comes afterward. Is it not so?"

"Truth," Arigh said soberly. Dizabul still glowered, but nodded in reluctant agreement. The Gray Horse clansmen visibly relaxed. Irnek's mouth was a little tight, but he bobbed his head Goudeles' way, respecting the diplomat for his skill.

But then Batbaian spoke out: "It is *not* so!" Heads swung his way in surprise. He said, "With Varatesh dead—may the ghosts of hungry wolves gnaw his spirit's privates forever—and Avshar routed, what needs doing is setting Pardraya right once more, so their wickedness can never flourish here again." He trotted his pony a few paces north, toward the vanished Khamorth. "Are you with me, V'rid'rish?"

The Gaul started; he had not expected the question. The naked appeal on Batbaian's face tore at him, and life with Targitaus' clan, though very different from the one he had known in Gaul, had had some of the same easygoing freedom to it. Two summers before, he had been ready to desert Videssos for Namdalen, but now when he probed his feelings he found only a small temptation and a regret that it was not greater.

He shook his head sadly. "I canna, lad. Avshar's the pit o' the peach, I'm thinking, and my foeman or ever I came to the plains. I willna turn away from him the now."

Batbaian slumped like a man taking a wound. "I'll go alone, then. I have my duty, just as you think you have yours." Viridovix flinched at his choice of words. The Khamorth said, very low, "There will always be a place for you in my tents." He wheeled his horse and started to ride away.

"Wait!" Irnek called. Batbaian reined in. The Arshaum chieftain said, "Would you ride with my men at your back? With your Hai—" He choked the word off. "—ah, people in disarray, we can make you master as far east as the plains run."

Here, thought Gorgidas, was truly one with an eye toward the main chance. Batbaian might have been reading his mind, for he barked out two syllables of a laugh. "If I said yes to that, Arshaum, your men would be riding on my back, not at it. I'll not be your bellwether for you, with my ballocks cut off and a chime round my neck to lead my folk to your herding. We remember how you drove the last of us east over the Shaum a lifetime ago. You hunger for Pardraya, too, now, do you? Thank you all the same, but I'll win or fall on my own."

"Will you?" Irnek said. He was still smiling, but with his mouth only; his eyes had gone flinty. His men stirred, looking to him for orders. Batbaian hesitated, then reached for his shamshir.

But Arigh rapped out, "By the wind spirits, he does as he pleases. He's paid the price for the right." This once, Dizabul backed his brother. A mutter of agreement rose from the riders of the Gray Horse Arshaum, who knew and admired Batbaian's quality. They stared in challenge at Irnek's Black Sheep.

Irnek refused to be drawn. His laugh came, easy and natural-sounding. "A dismal state of affairs, when Arshaum are reduced to arguing over the fate of a Hairy." He no longer wasted politeness on Batbaian, but waved him away. "Go, then, if it suits you." Batbaian gave Arigh a sketched salute, Viridovix another. He trotted north. The twilight gloom swallowed him.

"Tis Royal Khagan he'll be one day, I'm thinking," Viridovix whispered to Gorgidas.

"I'd say you're right, if he lives," the Greek replied. He was remembering the wand Tolui had used to symbolize the Khamorth, and how its pieces had begun to burn. With Varatesh dead and his power shattered, civil war would run through the clans of Pardraya, one-time collaborators against their vengeful foes. Batbaian, he was sure, knew the danger he was riding into.

As darkness fell, the Arshaum ranged over the field, stripping corpses and slitting the throats of those Khamorth who still moved—and those of Arshaum who knew themselves mortally wounded and sought release from pain. The shamans, Gorgidas with them, did what they could for those less seriously hurt. The physician used the healing art on two badly injured warriors with good results, then tottered and almost fell; combined with the day's exertions, the fatigue the healer's trance brought with it left him shambling about in a weary daze.

Most corpses remained above ground, to await the services of carrion birds and the scavengers of the plains. Only Arghun and a couple of fallen subchiefs from other clans received burial. The Gray Horse Arshaum worked by firelight to dig a grave large and deep enough to hold him and his pony. Tolui cut the beast's throat at the edge of the pit, in accordance with the nomads' custom. Either Arigh or Dizabul might have done so, but neither would yield the other the privilege.

Gorgidas got back to camp as that quarrel was winding down. He collapsed by a fire with the rest of the embassy party and gnawed mechanically at a chunk of smoked meat. It must have been past midnight; the crescent moon was long set.

Arghun's sons flared at each other again, shouting furiously. "You spoiled, stupid puppy, why should you deserve the rule?"

"A fine one to talk you are, coming back after years to try and rob me—"

"Not long will they be going on like that," Viridovix said with glum certainty; he had been in faction fights of his own. "A word too many and it's out swords and at 'em!"

The Greek feared he was right. The insults were getting louder and more personal. "You'd futter a mangy sheep!" Dizabul hissed.

"No. I wouldn't risk taking your pox from it."

"And here's more trouble," Viridovix said as Irnek came striding briskly between campfires. "What's he after?"

"His own advantage," Gorgidas said.

Arghun's sons fell silent under Irnek's sardonic eye. He was older and more experienced than either of them; his simple presence was a weapon. "I trust I'm not interrupting," he said, earning a glare from Dizabul and a hard frown from Arigh.

"What is it?" Arigh snapped, with hauteur enough to make the leader of the Black Sheep pause.

Irnek, as was his way, recovered well. "I have something to tell the Gray Horse khagan," he said, "whichever of you that may be." He did not stop to savor their sputters, but went on, "As your—friend? client?—Batbaian made it clear my clan was not welcome east of the Shaum, I have decided the only proper thing for us to do is return to our lands and herds in Shaumkhiil. We've been too long away, anyhow. We leave tomorrow."

Both brothers exclaimed in dismay. Dizabul burst out, "What of your fancy promises of help?" He had reason to be disconcerted; Irnek led a good quarter of the Arshaum forces.

"What do you call this past day's work?" Irnek retorted, with some justice. "I lost nearly a hundred men killed, and twice as many wounded—help enough, I'd say, for a fight that wasn't my own in the first place." He turned on his heel and stalked away, leaving Dizabul still expostulating behind him.

"You must be a farmer, to find your land so dear," the young prince jeered. Irnek's back stiffened, but he kept walking.

"Good shot!" Arigh said, slapping his brother on the shoulder. His anger at the Black Sheep leader put the damper on the quarrel with Dizabul, at least for the moment. He shouted to Irnek, "We'll go on without you, then!" Irnek shrugged without breaking stride.

Gorgidas' head and Goudeles' came up at the same instant; their eyes met in consternation. "They don't see their danger. How do we fix it?" Gorgidas demanded.

"Do we?" Goudeles said. "Better for the Empire if we leave it alone."

Viridovix and Lankinos Skylitzes looked at them as if they had started speaking an unknown tongue. But Gorgidas said angrily, "We do! There's no justice in loading all the risk on them and having them ruined on their pastures as well. Besides, I like them."

"Amateurs," Goudeles sighed. "What do likes matter, or justice?"

Even so, he gave a few sentences of pithy advice, very much what Gorgidas had also been thinking. Their friends' eyebrows rose in sudden understanding. The pen-pusher finished, "Do you want to put it to them, or shall I?"

"I will," Gorgidas said, his knees creaking as he rose. He started to walk over to the Arshaum, then turned back to Goudeles. "Tell me, Pikridios, if justice does not matter, how are you different from Avshar?" He did not wait for an answer.

Arghun's sons were running up their light felt tents when the Greek approached. Arigh nodded in a friendly enough way, Dizabul curtly. The physician still wondered whether he had been glad or sorry to see his father saved from Bogoraz' hemlock. He would probably never know.

In time-honored Hellenic tradition, he put his business in the form of a question. "What do the two of you think Irnek will do in Shaumkhiil while we chase after Avshar?"

"Why, go back to his herds," Dizabul said before he realized the question was out of the ordinary. Arigh saw it quicker. He had been using the heavy pommel on the hilt of his dagger to hammer tent pegs; he threw the weapon down with an oath.

"The answer is, anything he pleases," he ground out. "Who'd be there to stop him?"

"We can't let him get away with that," Dizabul said fiercely. Where the fortunes of the Gray Horses were touched, they stood in perfect accord; what use to be khagan of a ruined clan?

"Would you forget why we're here, then, and what we owe Yezd? All the more, now." Arigh eyed his younger brother with comtempt. Not far away, nomads were still filling in Arghun's grave.

"N-no, but what can we do?" Dizabul said, troubled. Arigh chewed his lip.

"May I suggest something?" Gorgidas asked. Again, Arigh nodded first, Dizabul following warily. When he saw he had their consent, he went on: "This could be one time when having both of you as leaders will work for you, not against. One could go ahead and move on Yezd, while the other took part of your force back across the Shaum to your stretch of the steppe. It need not be nearly as big as Irnek's band, only enough to make him think twice about starting trouble."

The Greek watched them calculate. Whichever one held to the pursuit of Avshar would keep the greater part of the army, but the other would have the chance to solidify his position on his native ground with the rest of the clan. If they bought the scheme, he thought he knew who would pick which role—Goudeles had set it up to make each half attractive to one of them.

They came out of their study at the same time. "I'll go back," Dizabul said, while Arigh was declaring, "Come what may, I push on." They looked at each other in surprise; Gorgidas kept his face straight. The imperials knew tricks Irnek had never thought of.

After that, the haggle was over how many riders would go on, how many back to Shaumkhiil. Not all the nomads accompanying Dizabul would be Gray Horse clansmen; some of the clans that had sent out smaller contingents were also nervous about Irnek's intentions.

"I mislike giving away so many men," Arigh said to Gorgidas when agreement was finally reached, "but what choice have I?"

The physician was so tired he hardly cared what he said; it was almost like being drunk. "None, but I don't think numbers matter much. By himself Avshar outnumbers all of us." Arigh rubbed his slashed cheek, nodded somberly.

V

Swords clashed. Pressed hard, Nevrat Sviodo gave ground. Her foe slashed at her legs. She barely turned the blow with her saber and had to retreat again. The next cut came high. Again her parry was just in time. Sweat ran into her eyes. It burned. She did not have even an instant to blink it away, for her opponent was sidling forward, a nasty grin on his face.

A quick flurry of steel—an opening! Nevrat ducked a cut, stepped in close. Her wrist knew what to do then. Her foe reeled away.

He was still grinning. She scowled at him, her eyes dark and dangerous. "Curse you, Vazken, did you let me get home there? Don't try that again when you practice with me, or you'll end up bleeding for real."

Vazken placatingly spread his hands. "It's hard to make myself go all out against a woman."

"Do you think the Yezda match your courtesy?" Nevrat snapped. She suspected she had seen more combat than her partner on the drill field—scouting was a chancier business than fighting in line. She did not say so. Vazken would only have stomped off in a huff.

She also did not want to practice with him anymore. If not fully tested, how could she get better?

Seeing her cousin Artavasdos riding up was something of a relief. She had the excuse she needed to escape from Vazken without telling him to go to the ice. She greeted Artavasdos with a dazzling smile.

He had to work to return it. She realized with surprise that he was frightened. "What is it" she asked, steering him away from Vazken. One thing the sometimes stolid Vaspurakaners learned in Videssos was the joy of gossip.

Artavasdos understood that, too. He waited until Vazken was well out of earshot before he dismounted and offered her a stirrup, saying,

“Climb up behind me. I’ve been sent to fetch you. We’ll ride double into the city.”

“Fetch me?” She made no move to mount. “By whom?”

“Alypia Gavra,” her cousin said, adding, “If I don’t get you to her fast, we’re both for it.” The answer sent her scrambling onto Artavasdos’ horse. He hardly waited for her to slide behind his saddle before he sprang up, seized the reins, and sent the horse back toward the city walls at a fast trot.

“Phos!” Nevrat exclaimed. “I can’t meet the princess like this. Look at me—in these leathers I look like a Yezda. I stink like one, too. Let me stop at the barracks to change and at least sponge myself off a little.”

“No,” Artavasdos said flatly. “Speed counts for everything now.”

“You’d better be right.”

He hurried west along Middle Street. When he turned north off it, Nevrat said, “Do you know where you’re going?”

“Where I was told to,” he said. She felt like reaching forward and wrenching a better answer out of him, but with difficulty forbore. If this was a joke, she thought grimly, Thorisin’s palace would get itself a new eunuch, cousin or no.

A few minutes later, Nevrat burst out, “By Vaspur Phos’ firstborn, are you taking us to the High Temple?” The great shrine had been growing against the sky since Artavasdos left Middle Street, but Nevrat had not thought much about it—following their own version of Phos’ faith, the Vaspurakaners did not worship along with imperials. Now, though, the High Temple was too close to ignore.

Artavasdos turned in the saddle to give Nevrat a respectful look. “You’re very close. How did you guess?”

“Never mind.” She would rather have been wrong. She slid off the horse with a sigh of relief as Artavasdos tethered it outside the stucco building at the edge of the High Temple courtyard. Together, cautiously, they went to the door of the patriarchal residence. Nevrat grasped the knocker and rapped twice.

Even she had not expected Balsamon to answer himself. “Come in, my friends, come in,” he said, beaming. Nevrat felt his smile like warm sunshine; no wonder, she thought, the Videssians loved him so well.

"Where are your retainers, sir?" she asked as he led her and her cousin down a corridor.

"I have but the one," Balsamon said, "and Saborios is off on a bootless errand. Well, not quite, but more than he thinks." He laughed. Though Nevrat did not see the joke, she found herself grinning, too.

The patriarch led the two Vaspurakaners into his disreputable study. He and the young woman waiting there cleared space for them to sit. She was quite plainly dressed, but for a necklace of emeralds and mother-of-pearl; Nevrat took a moment to realize who she was.

"Your Highness," she said, and began a curtsey, but Alypia help up a hand to stop her.

"We have no time for that," she said, "and in any case, the favor I am going to ask of you I ask as a friend, not as a princess."

"Don't worry, my dear, Saborios will be bootless a while longer," Balsamon told her.

"Not even Nepos knows how long his spell will hold," Alypia retorted. Quickly, as if begrudging every word, she explained to Nevrat, "Saborios—he's my uncle's watchdog here—is off taking a pair of Balsamon's blue patriarchal boots to be redyed. So long as Nepos' magic works, he won't notice the *very* long wait he's having for them. Nor—Nepos hopes—will anyone detect that I am not back in the palace complex. But he cannot juggle the two magics forever, so we must hurry with our business here."

"Then let me ask at once what you want of me, your Highness," Nevrat said, carefully not abandoning Alypia's formal title, "and ask you why you choose to call me friend when we have never met."

Artavasdos gasped at her boldness, but Alypia nodded approvingly. "A fair question. We are, though, both friends of Marcus Aemilius Scaurus."

Her quiet statement hung in the air a moment. "So we are," Nevrat said. She studied the princess and added, "You are a good deal more than that, it seems."

Despite his role as go-between, Artavasdos looked about ready to flee. Nevrat paid no attention to him; she wanted to see how Alypia would react. Balsamon, though, spoke first: "It also seems Scaurus somehow infects everyone who knows him with his own blunt speech." Had his words been angry, Nevrat would have been as frightened as her cousin, but he sounded amused.

"Hush," Alypia told him. She turned back to Nevrat. "Yes, he and I are a good deal more than friends, as you put it. And because of that, he has been sent to what will almost surely be his death." She explained what Thorisin required for Marcus to redeem himself.

"Zemarkhos!" Nevrat exclaimed. Having traveled so long with Gagik Bagratouni's men, she knew more than she ever wanted to of the fanatic priest's pogrom against all Vaspurakaners. Anything to hurt him sent hot eagerness surging through her. But she agreed with Alypia—she did not think Scaurus had a chance against him.

When she said so, the princess sagged against the back of her couch in dismay. Nevrat abandoned her half-formed thought of telling Alypia that Marcus had wanted her, too. That might have cured an infatuation, but she was convinced Alypia felt more—and so did Scaurus, if he was willing to beard Zemarkhos for her sake.

"Tell me what to do," she said simply.

Alypia's eyes glowed, but she wasted no time on thank-yous. "To destroy Zemarkhos, I think Marcus will have to have an army at his back. His Romans and those who have joined them are in Garsavra. If you rode to tell them what has happened to him, what do you think they would do?"

Nevrat never hesitated. Give Bagratouni another chance for revenge? Give Gaius Philippus—no, it would be Minucius; Gaius Philippus was with Scaurus—the chance to save his beloved commander? "Charge for Amorion, and Phos spare anything in their way."

"Exactly what I thought," Alypia said, eager now for the first time.

Nevrat looked at her in wonder. "You would do this, in spite of your uncle's command?"

"Command? What command?" Alypia was the picture of innocence. "Balsamon, you as patriarch must be well informed of what goes on in the palaces. Has his Imperial Majesty ever ordered me not to send word to Garsavra of Marcus' dismissal?"

"Indeed not," Balsamon said blandly, though he could not keep the corners of his mouth from twitching upward.

Only because Thorisin never dreamed you would, Nevrat thought. She did not say that. What she did say was, "I think Marcus is a very lucky man, Princess, to have you care for him."

"Is he?" Alypia's voice was bitter and full of self-reproach. "His luck has an odd way of showing itself, then."

"So far," Nevrat said firmly.

"You'll go, then?"

"Of course I will. Senpat will be furious with me—"

"Oh, I hope not!" Alypia exclaimed. "I would have gone through him—"

"—because he'll be stuck here in the city," Nevrat said.

At the same time the princess was concluding, "—but with his duties here, I thought he would have trouble getting away inconspicuously."

They stared at each other and started to laugh. Nevrat flashed the thumbs-up gesture the Romans used. She was unsurprised to find Alypia knew what it meant. The princess said, "How will I ever repay you for this?"

"How else?" Nevrat said. At Alypia's puzzled look, she explained: "Invite me to the wedding, of course."

They laughed again. "By Phos, I will!" Alypia said.

"Most touching, my children," Balsamon put in. "But I suggest we bring our pleasant gathering to an end, before this poor lad jitters himself to death." He made a courteous nod toward Artavasdos, who did seem on the point of expiring. "And, even more to the point, before my *dear* colleague Saborios at last returns with my boots."

After embracing Nevrat, Alypia left first, by a back way. Then Balsamon led Nevrat and her cousin out to Artavasdos' horse. "It matters less if Saborios should happen to see you," he said. "He'll merely think me daft for consorting with heretics." One of his shaggy eyebrows rose. "Surely I've given him better reason than that." He patted Nevrat's arm and went back inside.

The two Vaspsurakaners were still close to the High Temple when a priest came by carrying a pair of blue boots. He had an upright bearing and rugged features, but his face was vaguely confused.

"Don't gape at him like that," Nevrat hissed in Artavasdos' ear. Her cousin ostentatiously looked in the other direction. He was not cut out for intrigue, Nevrat thought. But it did not matter. Past a glance any man might have sent an attractive woman, Saborios paid no attention to either of them.

Nevrat began thinking about what she had agreed to try, and also began worrying. From Garsavra to Amorion was no small journey, and many Yezda roamed between the two towns. Could the legionaries force their way through? More to the point, could they do it in time?

"The only thing to do is find out," she muttered to herself. She grinned. What better omen to start with than sounding like Scaurus?

Riding west through the lush farming country of the coastal plain, Nevrat became certain she was being followed. She could see a long way in the flatlands, and the horseman on her trail was noticeably closer than he had been when she first spotted him early that morning.

She checked her bowstring to make sure it was not frayed. If Thorisin was fool enough to send a single rider after her, he would regret it. So, even more pointedly, would the rider. Not many imperials, she thought proudly, could match her at the game of trap and ambush.

She did spare concern for Balsamon, Alypia Gavra, and her cousin Artavasdos. She wondered what had gone wrong, back in the city. Maybe Saborios had noticed something amiss in spite of the sorcerous befuddlement Nepos cast on him, or maybe Nepos had just tried keeping too many magics in the air at once, like a juggler with too many cups.

On the other hand, maybe pincers and knives had torn the truth from Artavasdos, who could not hide behind rank.

In the end, none of that mattered. What did matter was the fellow coming after her. She glanced back over her shoulder. Yes, he was closer. He had a good horse—not, Nevrat thought, that having it would help him.

A couple of mule-drawn cars, piled high with clay jugs full of berries, were coming toward her. She swerved behind them. They hid her from view as she rode off the road into the almond orchard along the verge.

One of the farmers with the carts called, "Old Krates don't like trespassers on his land."

"To the ice with him, if he begrudges me a quiet spot to squat a minute," Nevrat said. The farmers laughed and trudged on.

Nevrat walked into the orchard and tethered her horse to a tree out of sight from the roadway. She gave the beast a feed-bag so it would not betray her with a neigh. Then she took her bow and quiver and settled down to wait, well hidden by bushes, for her pursuer.

Something with too many legs crawled up under her trousers and bit her several times, just below her knee, before she managed to kill it. The bites itched. Scratching at them gave her something to do.

Here came the fellow at last. Nevrat peered through the leaves. Like her, he was riding one of the nondescript but capable horses the Videssians favored. She set an arrow in her bow, then paused, frowning. She wished she could see better from her cover. Surely no Videssian would wear a cap like that one, with three peaks and a profusion of brightly dyed ribbons hanging down in back. . . .

She rose, laughing, her hands on her hips, the bow forgotten. "Senpat, what *are* you doing here?"

"At the moment, being glad I found you," her husband replied, trotting his horse up to her. "I was afraid you'd gone off the road to give me the slip."

"I had." Nevrat's smile faded. "I thought you were one of Thorisin's men—the more so," she added, "as you told me you were staying in the city the other night when I left."

Senpat grinned at her. "The thought of sleeping alone for who knows how long grew too disheartening to bear."

Her hands went to her hips again, this time in anger. Her eyes flashed dangerously. "For that you would risk us both? Have you all of a sudden gone half-witted? The very reason I got this task was that your leaving the capital might be noticed. You were trailing me—how many imperials are after you?"

"None. My captain felt very bad when I got a letter from home bidding me return at once because my older brother had just died of snakebite. The same thing had happened to him three years ago, which is why I had Artavasdos write the letter that way. For good measure, he wrote it in Vaspurakaner, which Captain Petzeas doesn't read."

"You have no older brother," Nevrat pointed out.

"Certainly not now, poor fellow, and Petzeas has the letter to prove it." Senpat arched an elegant eyebrow. "Even if anyone who knows differently hears of it, it'll be too late to matter."

"Oh, very well," Nevrat grumbled. She could never stay annoyed at her husband for long, not when he was working so hard to charm her. And he was right—the imperials were unlikely to see through his precautions. Still: "It was a risky thing to do."

Senpat clapped a hand to his forehead. "This, from the woman who rode out alone from Khliat after Maragha? This, from the woman who, if I know her as the years have given me a right to, is itching to tangle with the Yezda or Zemarkhos or both at once?" Nevrat hoped he did not see her guilty start, but he did, and grinned. He went on, "I don't expect to keep you out of mischief, but at least I can share it with you. And besides, Scaurus is a friend of mine too."

Again Nevrat wondered whether he would say that if he knew the Roman had made a move in her direction. Probably, she thought—Marcus was at low ebb the past fall, but took a no when he heard one even so. Senpat would likely chuckle and say he could not fault the tribune's taste.

Nevrat did not intend to find out.

She said, "Come with me while I get my horse. I tied him up in the nut orchard so I could do a proper job of ambushing you."

"Hmmp. I suppose I should be honored." As they scuffed through last year's dry leaves, Senpat remarked, "Nice quiet place."

"A couple of locals told me old Krates, who I take it owns the orchard, doesn't care for intruders."

"He doesn't seem to have troubled you any while you were setting up your precious ambush." Senpat put a hand on Nevrat's shoulder. "Do you suppose he might stay away a while longer?"

She moved toward him. "Shall we find out?"

"I still say you shouldn't have shot Krates' dog," Nevrat told her husband a few days later.

By then they were almost to Garsavra, but Senpat still sounded grumpy. "You're right. I should have shot Krates, for showing up when he did."

"We've made up for it since."

"Well, so we have." Senpat peered toward the town ahead. "Why does it look different?"

"The Romans have been busy," Nevrat said. A man-high earthwork wall, faced with turf so it would not melt in the rain, surrounded Garsavra. It has been unfortified for hundreds of years, but times were changing in Videssos' westlands, and not for the better. From the direction in which she was coming, Nevrat could see two openings in the wall, one facing due north, the other east. She was dead certain a matching pair looked west and south. "They've turned the place into a big legionary camp."

"Sounds like what Gaius Philippus would do—there's nothing he likes better." Senpat chuckled. "I wonder if he had the Romans knock down half the buildings in town so he could make the streets run straight between his gates."

Nevrat shook her head. "He's not wasteful. Look at the way they made the Namdalener motte-and-bailey part of their works." She found the senior centurion too single-mindedly a soldier to be easy to like, but she was always glad they were on the same side.

The sentries at the north gate were Vaspurakaners, men from Gagik Bagratouni's band. They brightened at the approach of two of their countrymen. Still, their questions were brisk and businesslike—Roman drill working, Nevrat thought as the foot soldiers stood aside to let her and Senpat into Garsavra.

Sextus Minucius made his headquarters where Scaurus and Gaius Philippus had before him, in what had been the city governor's residence. He was a handsome young man, taller than most of the legionaries, with blue-black stubble that darkened his cheeks and chin no matter how often he shaved.

He greeted Senpat and Nevrat warmly, but with a trace of awkwardness. He had been only a simple trooper when they first attached themselves to the legion; now he outranked them. At their news, though, he abruptly became all business. His face went hard as stone.

"Gaius Philippus, too, eh?" he murmured, half to himself. He followed it with something in Latin that Nevrat could not follow. Seeing her incomprehension brought him back to the here-and-now, and to Videssian. "Sorry. It sounds like him, I said. The two of you had best wait here while I send for Bagratouni and Pakhymer. They ought to hear your story firsthand, to give me the best advice."

That last sentence killed any doubts Nevrat had about who was in charge at Garsavra. In his firm, unhesitating acceptance of duty, Minucius sounded much like Scaurus.

The orderly outside his office was a Roman. His hobnailed *caligae* clattered on marble flooring as he dashed off to fetch the officers his commander wanted.

Laon Pakhymer showed up first. Somehow that surprised Nevrat not at all. Nothing took Pakhymer by surprise—the light cavalry officer from Khatrish had a nose for trouble and a gift for exploiting it.

Minucius was pacing impatiently by the time Gagik Bagratouni arrived, though the Vaspurakaner was prompt enough. He embraced Senpat and Nevrat in turn. He had known them since he and they still held estates in Vaspurakan, before the Yezda invasions forced so many nobles from their native land.

"So," he said at last, turning to Minucius. "I am glad to see them, yes, but is this occasion enough to drag me from my quarters?" His voice was deep and deliberate, a fit match for his solid frame and strong, heavy features, the latter framed by an untrimmed beard as dark and thick as Minucius' would have been.

"Yes," the Roman said flatly. Nevrat exchanged glances with her husband; not many men could withstand Bagratouni's presence when he chose to exert it. Minucius nodded their way. "Seeing them is one thing, hearing them something else again."

Nevrat told most of the story, Senpat filling in details and adding how he had managed to get out of the city to join her. That earned him an admiring grin from Pakhymer. Nevrat saw how her husband drew himself up with pride; praise from the Khatrisher was praise from a master schemer.

When they were through, Bagratouni did what Nevrat had known he would—he slammed his fist down on the table in front of him and roared, "My men march now! Give me Zemarkhos, Phos, and I will ask for nothing more in this life!"

Minucius was the one who surprised her. He waited until Bagratouni's thundering subsided a little, then told the Vaspurakaner, "Your men march nowhere without my leave, Gagik."

Bagratouni's beard swallowed most of his dark flush of anger, but not all. "Who are you to tell me what to do? I am a *nakharar,* a lord of Vaspurakan, and I act with my retainers as I will."

"You are not in Vaspurakan," Minucius said, "and you have taken Roman service as commander of a maniple. Do you remember that, or not?"

Nevrat leaned forward, afraid Bagratouni would throw himself at the Roman. "With Zemarkhos in front of me, I remember nothing," the *nakharar* ground out. "How do you propose to stop me from slaying him, as is less than he deserves?"

"With my men, if I have to," Minucius said evenly. "There are more Romans than Vaspurakaner legionaries in Garsavra. Look at me, Gagik. Do you doubt I would use them if you disobey my orders? I value your counsel; you know that. But I will have your obedience and I will do what I must to get it."

Bagratouni studied the younger man. The silence stretched. "You would," the Vaspurakaner said wonderingly. "Very well, then, what are your orders?" He spat the last word at Minucius.

"Why, to go after Scaurus, of course," the Roman said at once. He was not as calm as he wished to seem; sweat beaded on his forehead.

"Why this game, if we want the same thing?" Bagratouni exclaimed.

"I know how you feel about the Yezda, and about Zemarkhos. I don't blame you, Gagik, but I need you to remember you go as part of my forces, not have you haring off on your own."

Laon Pakhymer spoke up. "How will the Emperor feel when *you* go haring off on your own? No different from you about Gagik, I expect."

Suddenly and disarmingly, Minucius grinned. It made him look very young indeed. "Probably not. But there are more Romans than Videssian troops in Garsavra, too, so what is he going to do about it?"

"Not bloody much, except pitch a fit." Pakhymer grinned, too, his teeth white in a scraggly beard that rode high on his cheeks to cover pockmarks. He looked delighted at the prospect.

"If you take back Amorion for him, Thorisin won't care about the wherefores," Nevrat said to Minucius.

“She’s right.” Pakhymer turned his impudent smile her way. She suspected he approved of her person more than of her idea, but having men look at her did not bother her. Rather the reverse, unless they went further than looking, and Pakhymer knew better than that.

“If the Yezda kill all of us along the way, of course, we won’t care what Thorisin thinks,” Minucius said. “I’m glad we gave Yavlak something to think about when he raided last winter—his clans won’t want any part of us.”

“You leave Yavlak to me,” Pakhymer said. “I bought an attack on the Namdaleni from him when we needed it; I expect a little gold will get him not to mind us marching through his land.”

“Videssos’ land,” Minucius said, frowning.

“Yavlak’s there, the Emperor’s not. Do you really want to risk having to fight your way through and wasting Phos knows how much time?”

Minucius bit his lip. Nevrat saw Pakhymer had found the magic word to tempt him, despite his abhorrence for dealing with the Yezda in any way but at sword’s point. He drummed his fingers, muttered again in Latin. Nevrat heard a familiar word, but could not follow the phrase.

But in the end, the Roman said, “No. If we move fast, Yavlak won’t dare try troubling us.”

Unlike Bagratouni, Pakhymer knew determination when he heard it. “You’re the boss,” he said with the casual wave he used for a salute. “Not much point to more talk, then, is there? Let’s get ready to go.” He got up and left. Bagratouni followed a moment later.

Minucius rose, too. “The Khatrisher is right. Time to get moving.”

“May I ask you something first?” Nevrat said. Minucius paused. She went on, “I thought I heard you say Marcus’ name, but I didn’t know what the rest of that meant.”

The Roman looked, of all things, embarrassed. “That’ll teach me to talk to myself. Do you really want to know?” He waited till she nodded, then said sheepishly, “I was just asking myself what Scaurus would do in this spot. Now I’m off. One thing he wouldn’t do is waste time.”

Senpat Sviodo strummed the strings of his pandoura as he rode; he guided his horse with his knees. His song and the splashing of the

Arandos River were the only music to accompany the column marching west. The Roman army, unlike its Videssian equivalent, mostly traveled in silence.

Nevrat, along with everyone else, was glad for the Arandos. The westlands' central plateau was nothing like the lush coastal lowlands. Away from running water, the sun baked the land to dust.

Her husband's song jangled to a stop. Two Khatrishers from Pakhymer's cavalry screen were riding back toward the main body of foot soldiers with a third man between them. "Yezda," Senpat said unnecessarily. The fellow was dressed in nomad leathers and carried a small round shield daubed here and there with whitewash—a truce sign.

At Minucius' signal, the buccinators trumpeted the legionaries to a halt; when they needed it, the Romans did not despise music. The Yezda rode up to him and said in loud, bad Videssian, "What you doing on land belong to mighty Yavlak?"

"Marching on it, not that it is Yavlak's," the Roman commander said. He ignored the Yezda's effort to stare him down; having outfaced Gagik Bagratouni, he was more than equal to this smaller challenge. "And if Yavlak doesn't care for it, let him recall what happened when he tried visiting Garsavra."

"He stack up your corpses like firewood," the Yezda herald blustered.

"Let him try. But tell him this—for now I have no quarrel with him. If I have to turn aside to deal with him, the only land he will claim is enough to bury him in. Now get out. I've wasted enough time on you."

Minucius nodded to the buccinators. They blew advance. The army tramped forward. The Yezda had to swing his horse into a sidestep to keep from being ground into the dirt. Scowling, he wheeled and trotted away.

"Trouble," Nevrat said, watching his angry back.

Senpat answered, "Mm, maybe not. Yavlak's no fool and he is still smarting from last winter. Besides, it will take some time for him to gather enough men to fight, even if he wants to. By the time he does, we may be past the stretch of country he holds." But as he spoke, he stowed his precious pandoura in its soft leather cover and began checking the fletching on the arrows in his quiver. Nevrat did the same.

Despite such forebodings, no trouble came that day. One reason,

Nevrat was sure, was the speed with which the legionaries moved. As they were traveling along a river, they needed to carry only iron rations; no cumbersome wagons impeded their march. Dash might have been a better word—they fairly flung themselves up the Arandos.

At the end of the first grueling day, when the legionaries were building their familiar fortified camp, Nevrat asked Minucius, "How do you go so fast? I've seen cavalry armies that would have trouble matching your pace."

"We Romans train for it from the minute we join the legions," he answered. No doubt he was tired; his face was red and wet, his voice hoarse. But he was ready for more, managing a worn grin as he went on, "We call ourselves 'mules,' you know, for all the marching we do in full kit. And by now, all these Vaspurakaners and imperials have been with us long enough to keep up."

"If I had to bet, I'd say Yavlak will lead his horsemen to where we were early this afternoon."

"I hope he stays away. But if not, let's hope you're right." Minucius looked around, as he did every minute or so. "No, you idiot!" he bellowed at a Khatrisher. "Water your damned horses downstream from camp, not up! The fornicating Arandos is muddy enough already, without them stirring up more muck for us to drink."

Despite being the only woman in camp, Nevrat shared a tent with her husband unconcerned and would have worried no more had she been among the legionaries without him. It was not just that she was as handy with weapons as most men. After all the dangers she had shared with the Romans, none of them would have annoyed her, any more than he would a sister.

The next day, she saw a few Yezda. The nomads fled at the sight of the legionaries and looked back over their shoulders in disbelief at seeing troops loyal to Videssos pushing through country they had come to think of as theirs. Never were they in numbers enough to offer combat.

Later that afternoon, a Khatrisher rear guard came galloping up to warn that a real force of nomads was approaching from behind the Romans. Minucius gave Nevrat a Roman salute, holding his clenched fist out at arm's length in front of him. She waved her hat in reply.

Horns brayed. "Form lines to the rear!" Minucius shouted. With the smoothness of endless drill, the legionaries performed the maneuver.

"Where do you want us?" Laon Pakhymer asked.

"Out front, to foul up their archery." Minucius studied the ground. "And put a few squads over there, in that little copse. The gods willing, the Yezda will be too busy with us to study it much. If your men pop out at the right time, they'll count for a lot more than their numbers." Pakhymer nodded and bawled orders in the lisping Khatrisher dialect.

As soon as he was finished, Senpat called, "Shall we ride with you?"

"I'd sooner your lady asked that," Pakhymer said, and waited for Nevrat's snort before continuing, "but aye, come ahead. Another couple of good bows won't do us any harm."

"You have a care, mistress," one of the horsemen said as Nevrat passed him. "Get in trouble, and we'll all try and save you—and we might mess ourselves up to do it." He spoke with the half-joking tone Khatrishers often used, but Nevrat knew he meant what he said.

She was warmed and irritated at the same time. "I thank you," she said "I expect I'll manage." The Khatrisher nodded and waved.

The Yezda were not far behind the scout who brought news of them. Already Nevrat saw them emerging from the dust their ponies kicked up and heard the thunder of the horses' hooves.

"You've done this before, lads," Pakhymer told his men, calm as if he were discussing carting home a sack of beans. "Pick your targets while you're shooting and help your mates when the sabers come out."

A horse's skull on a pole—Yavlak's emblem-advanced. Closer, closer . . . Nevrat drew her bow back to her ear, let fly. The string lashed across the leather bracer on her wrist. She did not wait to see if her arrow hit; she was reaching for another while the first was still descending.

Here a horse stumbled, there another shrieked like a woman in labor when it was struck. Men were shouting, too, both from wounds and to terrify their foes. Icy fear shot through Nevrat when she saw blood on her husband's face. "A graze," Senpat reassured her when she cried out. "I'll let my beard get a little fuller to hide the scar, if it bothers you."

"Don't be an idiot." In itself, that kind of minor wound was nothing. But it reminded Nevrat how easy it was to find worse, and how little anyone could do to evade the death flying through the air.

The arrow duel, though, did not last as long as in the usual nomad engagement. Yavlak seemed intent on forcing the issue. His riders bulled through the Khatrishers, who, outnumbered, were forced aside. Nevrat understood why when she yeard Yavlak yelling toward the Roman standards: "With muds and snows you us once beat! Not we gets revenge!"

Senpat's face wore a grim smile. "Does he really think so? He hasn't brought near enough men, looks like to me."

Nevrat never heard him. She was hotly embroiled with a Yezda whose arms seemed as long as an ape's. She could parry his sword strokes, but her counters did not reach him.

Then the fellow suddenly grinned and moved in to fight at closer quarters. Nevrat recognized the new light in his eyes. It was not battle fury, but simple lust; he had realized he was facing a woman. His tongue flicked over his lips in slow, deliberate obscenity.

But he was no great swordsman, not when Nevrat could get at him at last. Her saber bit between his neck and shoulder. He howled a curse as he reeled away. Nevrat never knew whether her blow finished him—battle was often like that. She had to throw up her sword just in time to turn another nomad's slash and lost track of the first.

The heat of combat lessened, at least for the Khatrishers. Yavlak flung his horsemen at the legionaries. Senpat clapped a hand to his forehead in disbelief. "He's an idiot," he shouted. "He thinks they'll break and run."

"Probably the only foot soldiers he's faced since Maragha are herders with bows and axes trying to keep his men from running off their sheep." Nevrat's hand clamped down hard on her sword hilt in delighted anticipation of the shock the nomad chief was about to get.

Watching from the flank, she saw at once that Senpat had been right; Yavlak did not have enough men to take on the legionaries. He tried, regardless. Shouting and brandishing their swords, the Yezda spurred toward the waiting lines of shields. If they could force a breach, numbers would not matter.

The horns cried out, echoing Minucius' dropped arm. With a single great cry that cut cleanly through the random yells of their foes, the Romans cast their heavy javelins at the Yezda. An instant later, another wave of spears flew. The legionaries drew their stubby thrusting swords and surged forward, peering over the tops of their semicylindrical *scuta.*

The first ranks of the Yezda were in hideous confusion. The volleys of *pila* had blunted the momentum of their charge, emptying saddles and felling horses. Yet they could not turn tail and flee, the usual nomad tactic when pressed, because their comrades behind them were still trying to push up and get in the fight. The result was a few minutes of slaughter.

Watching the legionaries swarm over the Yezda, Nevrat thought of ants. Usually the Romans operated at a disadvantage in numbers and gave better than they got. With an edge, they were terrifying. A hamstrung horse screamed. Even before it fell, two soldiers beset its rider, one from either side. He did not last long. Another Roman turned a nomad's slash with the edge of his big, heavy shield, then used its weight to push the Yezda off balance. Another legionary stabbed him in the back; boiled leather could not keep out steel.

The Yezda could not even seek to outflank their opponents. The Arandos anchored the Romans' right wing, while Pakhymer's Khatrishers covered the left. And at close quarters, even mounted the nomads were no match for the disciplined, armored veterans Minucius led. Remembering ravaged fields and burned keeps in Vaspurakan, Nevrat found only fierce delight in their predicament.

But an army of infantry cannot wreck horsemen unless they stay to fight. The Yezda the legionary advance had not caught began pulling away, first by ones and twos, then in larger groups. Then the concealed Khatrisher squadron came galloping out of ambush, emptying their quivers as fast as they could into the Yezda flank. Retreat turned to rout.

"Ride over to Minucius," Pakhymer bawled in Nevrat's ear. She started; she had not noticed him come up. "Find out how far he wants us to chase the buggers."

The Roman's answer came promptly: "Only far enough to be sure they're in no shape to re-form. I want to get moving again. This mess has cost us close to half a day."

"Not much else, though." Hardly any of the men on the ground were legionaries.

The young man inside Minucius peeped out for a moment from behind the stern commander's mask. "It did work well, didn't it? Yavlak got what anyone too eager gets." His eyes flicked to Bagratouni's men, who were grimly making certain all the downed Yezda were corpses.

"On my way back to Pakhymer, shall I stop and thank Gagik for you, for not breaking ranks in his own eagerness to get at the nomads?"

"Thank him for obeying orders?" Minucius' astonishment was perfectly real. "By the gods, no! He does what he does because I command it, not as a favor to me."

"He's right," Senpat said in their tent that night when Nevrat told him of the exchange. They were lying side by side on the bedroll, too tired after the fight for anything more, but too keyed up to sleep.

"Of course he's right." Nevrat brushed back a wet lock of hair from her cheek—washing the grime and sweat from it was the only pleasure for which she'd had the energy after the legionaries made camp. She went on, "But how did he make Bagratouni see that, after all he's suffered from the Yezda? What happened back in Garsavra means nothing now—the Romans would never turn on Gagik's men here, not in the middle of enemy-held country."

"I suppose not," Senpat half agreed, "though I wonder what would happen if Minucius gave the order. I'm glad we don't have to find out. Still, you're right; that's not what held Gagik back."

"What, then?"

"Do you really want to know what I think? I think over the last couple of years, without ever quite knowing it, Bagratouni has gone from being a *nakharar* to a—what do they call it?—a centurion, that's right. This Roman discipline digs deep into a man. I'm just glad it hasn't set its hooks too deep in us."

Nevrat thought about that. Imagining Gagik Bagratouni as a clean-shaven Roman made her smile, but she decided her husband had a point. The *nakharar* had snarled at Minucius, but in the end he obeyed. The Bagratouni she had known of old, affronted so, might well have made the legionary commander carry out his threat.

After a while, she said, "If the Romans have no hold on us, why are we here by the Arandos instead of back in the capital following the Avtokrator's orders?"

Only a snore answered her. She rolled over. A few minutes later she was asleep herself.

Yavlak had fought the Romans once before they began their drive to the west, but had learned little from his earlier defeat. The nomad chieftains further into the interior of the central plateau knew nothing of the newcomers and were foolish enough to believe they could run them off with whatever forces they scraped together on the spur of the moment.

A couple of stinging defeats taught them otherwise. Word spread quickly from one clan to the next. After that, the Yezda left them alone. In fact, the nomads fled before them, flocks and all.

"I found another abandoned camp ahead of us," Nevrat reported to Minucius at an evening council after her return from a scouting run. "The tracks leading out of it look two or three days old."

"Senseless," the Roman said. Stubble rasped as he rubbed his chin. "If they left us alone, we wouldn't go after them. You'd think they'd have noticed that by now."

"Do you miss them?" Nevrat teased.

"Not even slightly." Again she saw the amused youngster through Minucius' grave shell, but only for a moment. He went on, "I mistrust what I don't understand, though."

"It is the nomads' way," Bagratouni said. "When a strong clan comes, the weak ones move aside. They will be fighting among themselves now, over grazing land, and shifting all about in more country than we could hope to march to in a year." Somber satisfaction at the prospect filled his voice.

Laon Pakhymer's eyes lit with mock indignation. "Ha! Are you saying my noble ancestors were forced off the steppe into Khatrish, instead of being the great heroes our minstrels sing of?"

Bagratouni took him literally. "It could be so, but with the original push hundreds of miles away."

"Are we going to push the Yezda into Amorion ahead of us, then?" Minucius said slowly.

Nevrat and Senpat exchanged glances of consternation; neither had worried about that. Gagik Bagratouni's big hands curled into fists. "Better, maybe, if we do. Zemarkhos and the Yezda deserve each other. The more they fight, the easier time we have coming after."

"Normally I would agree and be grateful," Minucius said, his face troubled. "But, the gods willing, Scaurus and Gaius Philippus are also in Amorion, or getting close. We came to rescue them, after all, not to throw more calamities down on them."

With his gift for pointing out what was so obvious as to be easily overlooked, Pakhymer broke the worried silence that followed. "Well, it's a bit late to turn back, isn't it?"

Nevrat thought about the Khatrisher's wry comment the next day, when she and her husband spotted the horseman coming up along the Arandos after the legionaries. The two Vaspurakaners had rotated back to rear guard, with some of Pakhymer's men riding in front of the army.

Senpat gave a puzzled grunt as he looked back over his shoulder. "Fellow doesn't sit his horse like a nomad."

"So he doesn't," Nevrat agreed after a moment's study. The Yezda, like the Khatrishers and other folk ultimately of Khamorth stock, used very short stirrup leathers and rode with their knees drawn up. The unknown kept his legs down at his horse's side.

"There just seems to be the one of him." Senpat whistled three notes from a Vaspurakaner hunting song, then set an arrow in his bow. "Cover me—I saw him first."

Her chance to argue forestalled by that last, offhand remark, Nevrat trailed her husband at easy bowshot range as he approached the stranger. The two men talked briefly before Senpat waved an all-clear. Her bow still across her lap ready to grab, she came up.

"He's not a Yezda, Nevrat." Senpat's face bore a faintly bemused expression. "His name is Arsakes Akrounos—he's an imperial courier."

Looking at Akrounos, Nevrat Sviodo was not surprised. He had the air of unimpressive competence the job required. If he was nonplused at finding a woman on patrol, he never let on. All he said was, "I have a dispatch for your leader."

"We'll get you to him," Nevrat said.

Like most Videssians, Akrounos liked to hear himself talk. He gossiped on about this and that as he rode west between Nevrat and Senpat. Unlike many of his countrymen, he gave nothing away with his chatter, and Nevrat was sure no detail escaped his eyes as he trotted past the marching lines of legionaries.

Minucius tramped along at the front of the column. "Is he now?" he said when Senpat explained who and what Akrounos was. He stepped to one side to let the Romans pass him as he eyed the courier with scant liking. "All right, I suppose he can speak his piece."

For the first time, Akrounos looked annoyed; he was used to warmer welcomes. He rummaged in a saddlebag and produced a parchment that prominently displayed the imperial sunburst seal. With a flourish, he handed it down to Minucius.

The Roman handed it back, discomfiting him again. "Suppose you just tell me the gist. Sorry and all that, but I don't read Videssian very fast."

"Surely you can guess—" Akrounos began.

Minucius cut him off. "Why should I guess, with you here? Say what you have to say or go home."

"*What?*" Now the courier was openly scandalized; no one spoke so to imperial representatives. Mastering himself with a visible effort, he broke the seal on the document he carried. "'His Imperial Majesty Thorisin Gavras, Avtokrator of the Videssians, to Sextus Minucius, commanding my Majesty's forces at Garsavra: greetings. I regret to learn that you have forgotten your obedience to me and—'"

"The gist," Minucius said. "I haven't the time to waste on this."

Akrounos took a moment to put his thoughts in order; saying things short and clear did not come easy to Videssians. At last he said, "Return your force to Garsavra and in his mercy the Emperor will overlook your brief defection."

"I thought as much." Minucius folded his arms. "No."

Again Akrounos hesitated, expecting some further answer. When he saw he would get none, he cried, "Why such ingratitude? Did the Empire not take you in when you were homeless, feed you when you were hungry?"

The Roman frowned. Nevrat's respect for Thorisin Gavras' wits, already high, went up another notch. The argument he had given his courier to cast in Minucius' face appealed to the legionary's strong sense of duty.

But Minucius said, "We follow Scaurus first, not Gavras. And we've earned our keep with blood. Besides, your master sent my two commanders off to die alone. Where's the charity in that, Akrounos?"

The soldiers marching by growled in agreement with Minucius' words. A couple of them hefted *pila* and glowered at Akrounos. Minucius quelled them with a gesture.

Bagratouni's contingent replaced a maniple still almost wholly Roman. Akrounos called to the Vaspurakaner, "Do you, too, prefer some outland mercenary as your lord, rather than the Emperor?"

"Why not?" Bagratouni had been listening to the exchange all the while. "Did not Scaurus take us in when we were homeless, feed us when we were hungry?" His deep-set eyes gleamed as he placed the barb. Akrounos' face froze. Bagratouni nodded gravely to Minucius and walked on.

Senpat murmured in Vaspurakaner, "It would take more than Thorisin to keep Gagik from going after Yezda—and after Zemarkhos."

"But he doesn't say that," Nevrat replied in the same tongue. "He answers as a Roman centurion would—another sign you were right."

"I will take your answer back to his Imperial Majesty," Akrounos was saying to Minucius.

"Stay with us," the Roman urged. "You were lucky to come this far once by yourself. Think how slim the odds are of getting back whole."

The courier shrugged. "As may be. I have my loyalty, too, and the Emperor will need to hear the news I bring."

"Go, then," Minucius said, waving a hand in recognition of Akrounos' courage. "I am not your enemy, or Thorisin's either."

"Ha!" Akrounos turned his horse sharply and trotted east. Minucius marched double time in the opposite direction to catch up to the head of his column. He did not look back.

The legionaries marched northwest along the Ithome River after it joined the Arandos. Amorion was only about three days away. Anticipation grew among the troopers, in the Romans for the chance to rescue their tribune and in the Vaspurakaners for that reason and at the prospect of striking a blow at the hated persecutor of their people.

Just when Nevrat began to hope Zemarkhos was too busy with his theological rantings to bother about such mundane details as frontier guards, a Khatrisher scout rode back to the army bearing a helmet, saber, and bow as trophies.

"A pair of the buggers tried to jump me," he reported to Minucius. "I shot the one this junk used to belong to, but the other whoreson got away. They were imperials, not Yezda."

The Roman commander sighed. "I wish you'd picked off both of them, but you did well to get the one." The scout grinned at the praise.

"So much for surprise," Laon Pakhymer observed. "If I were you, Sextus, I'd expect attack later today."

"Even Yavlak waited to gather some of his forces," Minucius protested.

"Yavlak seeks only loot and blood," Bagratouni said. "Myself, I think Pakhymer is right. The foul, lying cur of a Zemarkhos has his men deluded into thinking Phos will lift them straight to heaven if they die doing the madman's will."

Minucius shook his head in wonder. "What idiocy." Again he reminded Nevrat of Scaurus, to whom the sectarian quarrels among Phos' worshipers meant nothing. As for herself, she had grown up with the Vaspurakaner version of the faith and never thought of changing. Some Vaspurakaners in the Empire did, to rise more quickly. Their countrymen had a word for them—traitor.

"I can't believe any soldier would be so stupid," Minucius insisted. Pakhymer and Bagratouni argued, but could not change his mind. The louder they shouted, the more he set his strong chin and looked stubborn.

Nevrat thought they were right. She wondered what would have made Marcus see reason. She caught Minucius' eye and said, "Don't let your not sharing a belief blind you into thinking it isn't real. Remember how Bagratouni and his men joined yours."

The Roman pursed his lips. Pakhymer was sharp enough to stay quiet and let him think, and to kick Bagratouni in the ankle when he would have kept on wrangling. Finally Minucius said, "We'll march with maniples abreast. That way we can shift quickly into line if we have to."

He shouted orders, at the same time swearing under his breath at the delay they would cause. Pakhymer winked at Nevrat, then startled her by saying in fair Vaspurakaner, "You have more than logic behind your words."

Minucius looked up sharply. Nevrat had not thought he knew any of her language either.

"Can't trust anyone anymore," Senpat chuckled when he rode up from patrol a few minutes later. But the amusement rode lightly on his voice, and on his face. He and Nevrat had not had to flee Zemarkhos' pogrom, but they had seen the fanatic priest's venom at Bagratouni's vanished home in Amorion before the battle of Maragha.

This time the outriders gave only brief warning. "Curse you, how many?" Minucius shouted when a Khatrisher came galloping in to cry that horsemen were chasing him.

"Didn't stop to count 'em," the scout retorted. He ignored Minucius' glare. Nevrat giggled. The freewheeling Khatrishers had a talent for getting under the Romans' skins.

"Form line!" Minucius commanded. He nodded to Laon Pakhymer. "You were right, it seems. Can your men buy us some time to deploy?"

"Hurry," Pakhymer said, waving to the rapidly approaching cloud of dust to the west. Smooth as on a parade ground, the legionaries were already moving into position. That seemed to annoy Pakhymer as much as his own soldiers' cheerful rowdiness irritated Minucius.

"Come on, come on!" Pakhymer bawled to his men. "Don't you know what a rare privilege it is to die for an officer who'll admit he was wrong?" He sent Senpat and Nevrat a languid wave better suited to some great lord. "Would you care to join the ball? The dancing will begin shortly."

Bowstrings had begun to thrum. The cavalry troop trading arrows with the Khatrishers seemed hardly more orderly than so many Yezda; they knew nothing of the intricate maneuvers Videssian military manuals taught. But they knew nothing of retreat either, though Nevrat saw how few they were compared to their foes.

"Zemarkhos!" they shouted. "Phos bless Zemarkhos!"

That war cry infuriated Gagik Bagratouni's men. They sent it back with obscene embellishments. The leader of Zemarkhos' men whipped his head around. Even fighting Roman-fashion, Bagratouni's followers were recognizable for what they were by their stocky builds and thick black beards.

"Vaspurs!" the leader howled. He swung his sword toward them.

Laon Pakhymer was a cool professional. He had his horsemen sidling out to flank Zemarkhos' irregulars, threatening them with encirclement if they did not withdraw. Neither he nor anyone else who thought only in military terms would have expected them to hurl themselves straight for the legionary line.

Because the charge was such a surprise, it succeeded better than it should have. Nevrat shot at an onrushing Videssian at point-blank range and, to her mortified disgust, missed. She ducked low, grinding her face into the coarse hair of her horse's mane. She heard his blade hiss bare inches above her head. Then he was past, still yelling Zemarkhos' name.

Once through the cavalry screen, the Videssians spurred straight for Bagratouni's men. The rest of the army did not seem to exist to them, save as an obstacle between them and their chosen prey. The volly of *pila* they took slowed them, but they came on regardless. A dying horse bowled over three Vaspurakaners and gave Zemarkhos' men a breach to pour into. They stabbed and slashed at the targets of their hatred. The Vaspurakaners fought back as savagely.

But the battle did not stay private long. The Roman maniples by Bagratouni's moved up and swung in on the sides of Zemarkhos' troop. And behind them, the Khatrisher cavalry swiftly re-formed to close off escape.

"The cork's in the bottle now!" Senpat shouted. He yelled a challenge to one of the harried band in front of him: "Here, scum, what about me? I am a prince of Vaspurakan, too!" All the Vaspurakaners styled themselves princes, for they claimed descent from the first man Phos created.

Senpat's foe fought with desperation and fanaticism. That helped even the fight, since Senpat was a better swordsman. But the Videssian never saw Nevrat, a few paces away, draw her bow. This time her aim was true. The man crumpled.

"Did you doubt me?" Senpat demanded.

"I've learned from the Romans, too. I take no chances."

"Good enough. I won't complain over unspilled blood, especially when it's mine." Senpat urged his horse ahead. Nevrat followed. She had saved arrows and she used them now to wicked effect.

At last even fanaticism could not maintain Zemarkhos' men. A remnant of them disengaged and tried to fight their way clear. A few did; more died in the attempt. The whole sharp little fight had lasted only minutes.

Minucius came up to Gagik Bagratouni. The Roman commander's walk was wobbly; a fresh dent in his helmet showed why. His wits still worked, though. "Well fought, Gagik. Let's talk to some of the prisoners, to see what's ahead for us."

The Vaspurakaner spread large hands. "Prisoners? What a pity—there don't seem to be any." His eyes dared Minucius to make something of it.

"Ah, well, we'll find out soon enough," Minucius said. He looked round for Pakhymer, who, predictably, was not far away. "Can you send your scouts out a bit further, Laon? It wouldn't do to get hit by a big band of those madmen without warning."

"I'll see to it." The cavalry leader sounded more serious than usual as he gave his orders. The rough handling Zemarkhos' irregulars gave his men in that first charge did not sit well with him, even if the Khatrishers had gained a measure of revenge.

The trumpets blared advance. The army moved ahead. Senpat finished bandaging a small cut on the side of his horse's neck. "We've done all this," he said, "and we don't even know if Scaurus ever made it to Amorion."

"I know," Nevrat said. "I keep wondering how he'd fare if he ran into some of Zemarkhos' zealots."

"He's not a Vaspurakaner," her husband pointed out.

"So he isn't. I hadn't thought of that. But even if he's got to the city, what can he hope to do?" Nevrat dug her heels into her horse's ribs. "As Minucius said, we'll find out soon enough."

VI

A catapult thumped. A stone ball bigger than a man's head hissed through the air, almost too fast for the eye to follow. It buried itself in the soft ground at the edge of the steppe. The wind blew away the puff of dust it raised.

Viridovix shook his fist at the fortress, which lay like a beast of tawny stone in the mouth of the pass that led south into Erzerum. Like fleas on the back of the beast, men scurried along the battlements. "Come out and fight, you caitiff kerns!" the Gaul shouted.

"That was a warning shot," Lankinos Skylitzes said. "At this range they could hit us if they cared to."

Pikridios Goudeles sighed. "We built too well, it seems, we and the Makuraners, the one time we managed to work together."

Gorgidas touched his saddlebag. He had written that tale down a few days before, when Goudeles told it at camp. Centuries ago the two great empires saw it was in their joint interest to keep the steppe nomads from penetrating Erzerum and erupting into their own lands. The northern passes were beyond the permanent power of either of them, but Makuran had provided the original construction money to fortify them, with Videssos contributing skilled architects and an annual subsidy to the local princelings to keep the strong points garrisoned. Now Makuran was no more and the Videssian subsidy had ceased when the Empire fell on hard times these past fifty years, but the Erzrumi still manned the forts; they warded Erzerum as well as the lands farther south.

"Show parley," Arigh ordered, and a white-painted shield went up on a lance. Trying to force one of the narrow passes would have been suicidal, and the great mountains of Erzerum, some in the distance still snow-covered though it was nearly summer, offered no other entranceways.

A postern gate opened; a horseman carrying a like truce sign and riding a big, rawboned mountain beast came toward the Arshaum. Arigh quickly chose a party to meet him: himself, Goudeles and Skylitzes—the one for his diplomatic talent, the other for his command of the Khamorth tongue, which anyone at the edge of Pardraya should know—and Tolui. At Goudeles' suggestion, he added one of Agathias Psoes' troopers who knew some Vaspurakaner; the "princes" had dealt with their northwestern neighbors before Videssos' influence reached so far, and affected some of them greatly.

"May I come, too?" Gorgidas asked.

"Always looking to find things out," Arigh said, half amused, half scornful. "Well, why not?" Viridovix asked no one's leave, but rode forward with the rest, cheerfully pretending not to see Arigh's frown.

The Erzrumi waved them to a halt at a safe distance. He looked much like a Vaspurakaner—stocky, swarthy, square-faced, and hook-nosed—but he trained his curly beard into two points. His gilded cuirass, plumed bronze helmet, and clinging trousers of fine silk proclaimed him an officer. He was within five years either way of forty.

He waved again, this time in peremptory dismissal. "Go back," he said in the plains speech; he had a queer, hissing accent. "Go back. We will crush you if you come further. I, Vakhtang, second chief of the castle of Gunib, tell you this. Are we simpletons, to open our country to murderous barbarians? No, I say. Go back, and be thankful we do not slay you all."

Arigh bridled. Goudeles said hastily, "He means less than he says. He has a Videssian style to him, though a debased one."

"Videssian, eh? There's a thought." The Arshaum's years at the imperial capital had given him a good grasp of the language. He used it now: "Why the high horse, fellow? We have no quarrel with you or yours. It's Avshar we're after, curse him."

Vakhtang's eyebrows rose to his hairline. "I know what that speech is, though I do not use it." He seemed to take a first good look at the group in front of him. In their furs and leathers, Gorgidas, Goudeles, Skylitzes, and Psoes' soldier—his name was Narbas Kios—might have been Khamorth, if odd ones. But Arigh and Tolui were something else again. And Viridovix, with his drooping mustaches, red hair spilling from under his fur cap, and pale freckled skin, was unlike any man the Erzrumi captain had seen. His careful composure deserted him. "Who *are* you people, anyway?" he blurted.

Goudeles nudged Narbas the trooper, who rode forward a couple of paces. "Make sure he understands you," the pen-pusher said. Vakhtang showed fresh surprise when Narbas spoke hesitantly in the Vaspurakaner tongue, but stifled it. He gave a regal nod.

"Good," Goudeles said. He paused; Gorgidas could see him discarding the florid phrases of Videssian rhetoric to stick with ideas Kios could put across. "Tell him Skylitzes and I are envoys of the Avtokrator of the Videssians. Tell him where the Arshaum are from, and tell him they've come all this way as our allies against Yezd. We only ask a safe-conduct through Erzerum so we can attack the Yezda in their own land. Here, give him our bona-fides, if he'll take them."

He produced the letter of authority Thorisin had given him, a bit travel-worn but still gorgeous with ink of gold and red and the sky-blue sunburst seal of the Videssian Emperors. Skylitzes found his letter as well. Holding one in each hand so he could draw no weapon, Narbas offered them to Vakhtang. The officer made a show of studying them. If he spoke no Videssian, Gorgidas was sure he could not read it, but he recognized the seals. Few men in this world would not have.

The Erzrumi gravely handed the letters back. He spoke again, this time in the throaty Vaspurakaner language. Narbas Kios translated: "Even this far north, he says, they know of Yezd, and know nothing good. They have never yet let a nomad army past their forts, but he will take what you said to the lord of Gunib."

"Tell him we thank him for his courtesy," Arigh said, and bowed from the waist in the saddle. Viridovix watched his friend with surprised respect; a roisterer in Videssos, the Arshaum was learning to be a prince.

Vakhtang returned Arigh's compliment and turned to go back to the fortress. Before he got far, Tolui rode out of the parley group and caught him up. Vakhtang spun in alarm and started to reach for his sword, but stopped after a glance at the shaman; though not in his regalia, Tolui still had a formidable presence. He put his hand on the captain's arm and spoke to him in the few words of Khamorth he had learned from Batbaian: "Not—fight you. Not—hurt you. Go through, is all. Oath."

His broken speech seemed to have as much effect on Vakhtang as Goudeles' arguments and letters both. Gorgidas saw the self-important bureaucrat redden as the officer gave Tolui what was plainly a salute, putting both clenched fists to his forehead. Then he clasped the shaman's hand before releasing it and urging his horse into a trot. The postern gate swung open to readmit him.

"Now what?" Gorgidas asked.

"We wait," Arigh said. Gorgidas and the Videssian fidgeted, but with nomad's patience Arigh sat his horse quietly, ready to wait there all day if need be. After a while the main gate of the fortress of Gunib opened a little. "They trust us—some, at least," Arigh said. "Now we do business."

Flanked by a small bodyguard of lancers in scaled mail came Vakhtang and another, older man whose gear was even richer than his. Age spots freckled the backs of his hands, Gorgidas saw as he drew close, but there was strength in him. He had the eyes of a warrior, permanently drawn tight at the corners and tracked with red. He inspected the newcomers with a thoroughness Gauis Philippus might have used.

At last he said, "I am Gashvili, Gunib's lord. Convince me, if you can, that I should give you leave to pass." His voice was dry, his heavy features unreadable.

He heard the tale they had given Vakhtang, but in more detail. He kept interrupting with questions, always searching ones. His knowledge of Pardrayan affairs was deep, but not perfect; he knew of Varatesh's rise to power and the magical aid Avshar had given him, but thought the latter a Khamorth sorcerer. When Arigh told how the wizard-prince had fled southward, Gashvili rammed fist into open palm and growled something sulfurous in his own language.

"Day before yesterday we let one through who answered to your account of him," he said when he had control of a speech the men from the plains could follow. "He claimed he was a merchant beset by bandits on the steppe. As there was just the one of him and he was no Khamorth, we had no reason to disbelieve him."

Suddenly all of Arigh's party was shouting at once. For all their hopes, for all their anticipation, they had not run Avshar to earth. He must have had some magic to make his stallion run night and day, far past the normal endurance of any horse. The beast had gained steadily on the Arshaum, tireless in the saddle though they were. Then a rainstorm covered its tracks, and they lost the trail.

"Well, whatever is your honor waiting for?" Viridovix cried. "Why are you not after calling yourself's men out to be riding with us to take the spalpeen, the which'd be worth a million years o' this sitting on the doorstoop o' nowhere." The Gaul wanted to leap down from his pony and shake sense into Gashvili.

The noble's mouth twitched in amusement. "Perhaps I shall." He turned to Arigh. "You ask me to take a heavy burden on myself. What guarantees would I have from you that it shall be as you say, and that your army will not plunder our fair valleys once you get past me here? Will you give hostages on it, to be held in Gunib as pledge against bad faith?"

"As for pledges," Arigh said at once, "I will swear my own people's oath, and any that suit you. Are you a Phos-worshiper like the Videssians? He seems not a bad god, for farmer-folk."

The Arshaum meant it as a compliment, though Skylitzes' face was scandalized. Gashvili shook his head, setting silver curls bouncing under his gilded helm. "For all the blue-robes' prating, I and most of mine hold to the old gods of sky and earth, rock and river. I am a stubborn old man, and they humor me." His tone belied the self-mockery; he was proud his people followed his lead.

"No trouble there, then," Arigh said. His manner abruptly harshened. "But what is this talk of hostages? Will you give me hostages in turn, so no man of mine will be risked without knowing that, if he dies from treachery, some Erzrumi's spirit will go with him to serve him in the next world?"

"By Tahund of the thunders, I will, and more!" Gashvili spoke with sudden hard decision. "I and all but a skeleton garrison will ride with you. With the Khamorth in disorder, the pass will be safe this year. And," he added, looking shrewdly at Arigh, "having watch-hounds along will no doubt encourage you to keep your fine promises."

"No doubt," Arigh said, so blandly that Gorgidas stared at him. This one, he thought, has nothing to fear from haughty Dizabul, however handsome Arghun's younger son might be. Still mild, Arigh went on, "You'll have to keep up with us, you know."

The fortmaster chuckled. "You may know the steppe, but credit me with some idea of my business here. We'll stick tight as burrs under your horses' tails." He rode to brush cheeks with Arigh. "We agree, then?"

"Aye. Bring on your oath."

"It is better done by night." Gashvili turned his head. "Vakhtang, go tell the men to get ready to—" But Vakhtang was already trotting back toward Gunib, waving to show all was well. Gashvili laughed out loud. "My daughter knew what she was about when she chose that one."

The Arshaum and the Gunib garrison spent the afternoon warily fraternizing. No plainsman was invited into the fortress, and Gashvili made it clear his vigilance had not relaxed. Arigh was offended at that until Goudeles reminded him, "He is going against generations of habit in treating with you at all."

Through Sklylitzes—who looked acutely uncomfortable as he translated—an Erzrumi priest, a wizened elder whose thick white beard reached his thighs, explained his people's way of binding pledges to Tolui. The shaman nodded thoughtfully when he was done, saying, "That is a strong ritual."

In a way, the Erzrumi oath-taking ceremony reminded Gorgidas of the one the Arshaum had used to pledge the Videssian party and Bogoraz of Yezd against threat to Arghun. At twilight the priest, whose name was Tzathmak, lit two rows of fires about thirty feet long and three or four feet apart. "Will he be walking through them, now?" asked Viridovix, who had heard about but not seen the Arshaum rite.

"No; the ways here are different," Goudeles said.

In striped ceremonial robe, Tzathmak led one of the fort's scavenger dogs out to the fires. Tolui joined him in his fringed shaman's regalia and mask. Together they prayed over the dog, each in his own language. Tolui called to his watching countrymen, "The beast serves as a sign of our agreement."

Normally nothing could have made the dog walk between the two crackling rows of flame, but at Tzathmak's urging it padded docilely down them. "As the dog braves the fire, so may the peace and friendship between us overcome all obstacles," Tolui said. Tzathmak spoke in his own tongue, presumably giving Gashvili's men the same message.

At the far end of the fires stood a muscular Erzrumi, naked to the waist and leaning on a tall axe not much different from the sort the Halogai used. When the dog emerged, he swung the axe up in a glittering arc, brought it whistling down. The beast died without a sound, cut cleanly in two. All the Erzrumi cried out at the good omen.

"May the same befall any man who breaks this pact!" Tolui shouted, and the Arshaum, understanding, yelled their approval, too.

Gashvili could roar when it suited him. "Tomorrow we ride!" he cried in the Khamorth tongue. Both groups yelled together then—the Arshaum raggedly, for not all of them had even a smattering of Khamorth, but with high spirits all the same.

"Effective symbolism, that, if a bit grisly," Goudeles remarked, pointing toward the sacrificed dog.

"Is that all you take it for?" Gorgidas said. "As for me, I'd sooner not chance finding out—I remember what happened to Bogoraz too well."

"Gak!" the bureaucrat said in horror. He tenderly patted his middle, as if to reassure himself no axeblade, real or sorcerous, was anywhere near.

Viridovix squinted with suspicion at the new valley shimmering in the sultry heat-haze ahead. "Sure and I wonder what'll be waiting for us here."

"Something different," Gorgidas said confidently. At the first sight of the Arshaum army's outriders, herders were rushing their flocks up into the hills and peasants dashing for the safety of their nobles' fortresses. Other men, armored cavalry, were moving together in purposeful haste.

Viridovix snorted at the Greek. "Will you harken to the Grand Druid, now? That's no foretelling at all, at all, not in this Erzerum place. Were you after saying 'twould be the same, the prophecy'd be worth the having."

"With your contrariness, you should feel right at home," the physician snapped. He clung to his patience and to the subject. "It makes perfectly good sense for every little valley here to be nothing like any of its neighbors."

"Not to me, it doesn't," Viridovix and Arigh said in the same breath. The Arshaum continued, "My folk range over a land a thousand times the size of this misbegotten jumble of rocks, but all our clans make up one people." He looked haggard. Seven separate bands of Erzrumi were with the nomads, and as overall leader he had the thankless job of keeping them from one another's throats. They used five different languages, were of four religions—to say nothing of sects—and were all passionately convinced of their own superiority.

"You have the right of it, Arigh dear," Viridovix backed him. "In my Gaul, now, I'll not deny the Eburovices, the tribe southwest o' my own Lexovii, are a mangy breed o' Celt, but forbye they're Celts. Why, hereabouts a wight canna bespeak the fellow over the hills a day's walk away, and doesna care to, either. He'd sooner slit the puir spalpeen's weasand for him."

Lankinos Skylitzes said, "We Videssians hold that Skotos confounded men's tongues in Erzerum when the natives fell away from Phos' grace by refusing to accept the orthodox faith."

"No need to haul in superstition for something with a natural cause," Gorgidas said, rolling his eyes. Seeing Skylitzes bristle, he demanded, "Well, how does your story account for the men of Mzeh riding with us? They're as orthodox as you are, but the only Videssian they have is learned off by rote for their liturgy. Otherwise not even Gashvili can follow their dialect."

The officer tugged at his beard in confusion, not used to the notion of testing ideas against facts. Finally he said, "What is this famous 'natural cause' of yours, then?"

"Two, actually." The Greek ticked them off on his fingers. "First, the land. Size means nothing. Shaumkhiil and Gaul are open countries. People and ideas move freely, so it is no wonder they aren't much different from one end to the other. But Erzerum? It's all broken up with mountains and rivers. Each valley makes a bastion, and since none of the peoples here could hope to rule the whole land, they've been able to keep their own ways and tongues without much interference."

He paused for a gulp of wine. Erzerum's vintages were rough, but better than kavass. Down in the valley, behind a covering stream, the band of cavalry was moving two by two into position at the edge of the stream. Bright banners snapped above them.

Gorgidas put the wineskin away; he would rather argue. “Where was I? Oh, yes, the second reason for Erzerum’s diversity. Simple—it’s the rubbish-heap of history. Every folk beaten by Makuran, or Videssos, or even by Vaspurakan or the peoples of Pardraya, has tried to take refuge here, and a good many pulled it off. Thus the Shnorhali, who fled the Khamorth when they entered Pardraya who knows how long ago—their remnant survives here.”

“Isn’t he the cleverest little fellow, now?” Viridovix said, beaming at the Greek. “Clear as air he’s made the muddle, the which had me stymied altogether.”

“Clear as fog, you mean,” Skylitzes said. He challenged Gorgidas: “Does your fine theory explain why the Mzeshi *are* orthodox? You brought them up, now account for them. By your rules they should have taken their doctrine from the heretic Vaspurakaners, who were the first people close to them to follow Phos, even if wrongly.”

“An interesting question,” the physician admitted. After thinking a bit, he said slowly, “I would say they are orthodox for the same reason the Vaspurakaners aren’t.”

“There you go, speaking in paradoxes again,” Skylitzes growled.

“These Greeks are made for talking circles round a body,” Viridovix put in.

“To the crows with both of you. There is no paradox. Look, Vaspurakan liked Videssos’ religion, but was afraid the influence of the Empire would come with its priests. So the ‘princes’ worked out their own form of the faith, which satisfied them and kept the Empire at arm’s length. But Vaspurakan was to the Mzeshi what Videssos was to Vaspurakan: a land with attractive ideas to borrow, but maybe risky to their freedom, too. So they decided for orthodoxy. Videssos is too far away to be dangerous to them.”

Skylitzes wore a grimace of concentration as he worked that through, but Goudeles, who had been quiet till now, said, “I like it. It makes sense. And not only does it show why the Mzeshi are orthodox and the ‘princes’ not, it also makes clear why Khatrish, Thatagush, and Namdalen keep clinging to their own pet heresies.”

“Why, so it does,” Gorgidas said. “I hadn’t thought of that. Well, a good theory should be able to cover a wide range of cases." He paused and waved back toward the varied groups of new allies. "Erzerum is a wide range of cases by itself."

Arigh said, "To me this history of yours only makes so much fancy talk. I'm just glad the one thing all these hillmen can get together on is hating Yezd."

"Right you are," Skylitzes said, and the others nodded. Though most of the Yezda had roared east against Vaspurakan and Videssos, enough raiders had pushed north to rape and loot and kill among the Erzrumi valleys that the locals, whatever tiny nation they might claim, welcomed Yezd's foes. That was the only reason Arigh could control them at all. Hitting back was too sweet a prospect to jeopardize with their own petty quarrels.

The Arshaum waved for a messenger. "Fetch me, hmm, let's see, Hamrentz of the Khakuli. Let's see what he can tell us about these horsemen ahead." The riders were still deploying along their stream; through the dust their mounts kicked up, the sun glinted off spearpoints.

Hamrentz, whose holding lay a couple of days' ride north, was a thin, gloomy man with enormous hands. He wore a mail coif, but the rest of his armor was a knee-length shirt of leather covered with bone scales. Though he spoke some Videssian, he followed the Four Prophets of Makuran and had lines from their writings tattooed on his forehead.

When Arigh put the question to him, his doleful features grew even longer; one of his verses almost disappeared in a deep fold of skin. "This is—how would you say?—the Vale of the Fellowship. So they call it here, let me say. They are no cowards. I give them so much. I have seen them fight. But to their neighbors they are the—" He used a guttural obscenity in his own language, adding an equally filthy gesture.

Arigh repeated the scurrility with a grin. It was one to fill the mouth and soothe the angry spirit. "I know that's foul," he said. "What exactly does it mean?"

"What it says, of course," Hamrentz said. "In this language, I do not know the words." He seemed offended. The rest of his answers were hardly more than grunts. "You will find out, and then you will understand," he finished cryptically, and rode off.

Arigh looked at his advisors, who shrugged one by one. Goudeles said, "You might summon one of the others."

"Why waste my time when I can see for myself? Come along, if you care to." The Arshaum raised his voice. "Narbas, to us! The further south we get, the more of these people speak Vaspurakaner."

They hoisted the truce sign and trotted down toward the stream. Behind them, several Erzrumi contingents erupted in hisses, catcalls, and the whistles some of the hillmen used for jeers. Viridovix scratched his head. "You'd think these Fellowship laddies the greatest villains left unkilled, sure and you would, the way the carry on. To see 'em, though, why, they're better-seeming soldiers than half we have wi' us."

The troops drawn up on the far side of the little river were indeed disciplined-looking, well-horsed, and well-armored in crested helms, mail shirts under surcoats, and bronze greaves. They numbered archers as well as lancers. The Arshaum scouts, not wanting to start a war by accident, were keeping a respectful distance from the border stream.

A few of the locals nocked arrows or let their horses move a couple of paces forward as Arigh's party drew close, but in the center of their line a black-bearded giant in an orange coat nodded to his companion, a younger man whose surcoat matched his. The latter blew three bright notes from a coiled horn. At once the horsemen settled back into watchful waiting.

Perhaps drawn by the action of the leaders, Viridovix ran an eye down the line. "Will you mark that, now? Pair by pair they are, matched by their coats." The others saw he was right. One pair wore light green, the next scarlet, then ocher, then the deep blue of woad; remembering a tunic of that exact shade he had once owned, the Celt ached for his lost forests.

"How quaint," Goudeles said, with the disdain he showed any non-Videssian custom. "I wonder what it might signify."

Gorgidas felt himself go hot, then cold. He was suddenly sure he understood Hamrentz's obscenity. In a way he hoped he did, in a way not; if not altogether satisfying, his life had been simple for some time now. Were he right, it might not long stay so.

He had only a moment to reflect; with a sudden toss of his head, the big man in orange spurred forward into the stream, which proved only belly-deep on his mount. Without a second thought, his comrade with the horn followed. Cries of alarm rang along the line. The big man shouted them down.

With his size and his horse's—it was one of the big-boned mountain breed—he towered over Arigh. But the Arshaum, backed by a much bigger army, met his stare with a king's haughtiness; he had learned a great deal, treating with the Erzrumi. The local gave a rumbling grunt of approval. He said something in his own language. Arigh shook his head. "Videssian?" he asked.

"No," the black-bearded chief said; it seemed the only word he knew. He tried again, this time in throaty Vaspurakaner. Narbas Kios translated: "The usual—he wants to know who we are and what in the name of Wickedness we're doing here."

"They follow the Four Prophets, then," Skylitzes said, recognizing the oath.

"In the name of Wickedness it is, with Avshar and all," Viridovix said.

"Aye." Arigh began to explain their goal. When he said "Yezd," both the locals growled; the younger one reached for the spiked mace on his hip. Thanks to Gunib and the other forts in the passes, the only nomads they had seen were Yezda raiders from the south, and thought Arigh was identifying himself as one. They laughed when Kios made them understand their mistake. "All we ask is passage and fodder," Arigh said. "You can see from the bands with my men that we did not plunder their countryside. We'll all loot to glut ourselves in Yezd."

Black-Beard jerked his chin toward the Erzrumi with the Arshaum. "I care not a turd for them. But," he admitted, "they are a sign you tell some of the truth." He could not keep a glow from his eyes, the glow that comes to any hillman's face when he thinks of the booty to be taken in the flatlands below.

He shook himself, as if awaking to business from a sweet dream. "You have given your names; let it be a trade. Know me to be Khilleu, prince of the Sworn Fellowship of the Yrmido. This is Atroklo, my—" He dropped back into his own tongue. Atroklo, who by the fuzziness of his beard could not have been far past twenty, smiled at the prince when his name was mentioned.

Gorgidas knew that smile, had felt it on his own face years—a lifetime!—ago, before he left provincial Elis for Rome and whatever it might offer. No, he thought, his life would not be the same.

Khilleu was laughing in his beard; his face was heavy-featured but open, a good face for a leader. "So you'd poke the Yezda, eh? I like that, truly I do."

Atroklo broke in in their language, his voice, surprisingly, not much lighter than his chieftain's bass. Khilleu pursed his lips judiciously and gave an indulgent wave, as if to say, "You tell it." Atroklo did, in halting Vaspurakaner: "That wizard you speak—*spoke*—of, I think he pass through here."

From the way all eyes swung toward him, he might have been a lodestone. He reddened with the almost invisible flush of a swarthy man, but plowed ahead with his story. "Four days ago we find in field a black stallion, dead, that none of us knows." He had given up on the past tense of his verbs. "It is a fine horse once, I think, but used to death. Used past death, I mean—never I see an animal so worn. A skeleton, lather long caked on sides, one hoof with no shoe and down to bloody nub. Cruel, I think then. Now I think maybe magic or desperate, or both. No tackle is with this dead horse, and next day our noble Aubolo finds two of his best beasts missing. Who thief is, he does not know then and does not know now."

"Avshar!" Arigh's companions exclaimed together; it was, Gorgidas thought, becoming a melancholy chorus. "Four days!" the Arshaum chief said bitterly. "See, we've lost another two to him. These Erzrumi can't stay with us; they only slow us down."

Khilleu had watched them closely; attitudes spoke for much, even if he could not follow their talk. He and Atroklo dropped into a low-voiced colloquy in the Yrmido tongue. The prince returned to Vaspurakaner. "I begin to believe you," he said, looking straight at Arigh. "We too have suffered from the southern jackals, more than once. I ask you two questions: Would you have the Sworn Fellowship at your side? And will our charming neighbors," he continued, irony lurking in that resonant bass, "bear with our coming?"

"As for the first, why not? One Erzrumi slows us as much as a thousand, and you look to have good men. As for the other, Hamrentz of the Khakuli said you were no cowards."

"Among other things," Atroklo guessed. His laugh and Khilleu's did not sound amused.

"Here's another argument for you, then," Sklyitzes put in. "These Arshaum here outnumber all the hillmen with us three to one."

"A point," Khilleu said. He spread his hands. "In the end, what choice have I? You have not three, but ten times my numbers. Oh, we could hold out in our keeps if we would, but stop your passage? No." Again, his chuckle was grim. "So I will leap on the snow leopard's back, hold on to its ears, and pray to the Four to petition the kindly gods not to let it turn aside for my sheep."

Atroklo blew a different call on his horn; Gorgidas watched a vein pulse at his temple. He must have played the signal for truce. The Sworn Fellowship abandoned their defensive stand at the edge of the stream and formed up into a long column.

"You will answer to me if you betray us," Khilleu warned Arigh. "Tell that to Hamrentz and the rest, too; for all your numbers, I vow it."

"No," Arigh said. "I will tell them they will answer to me."

"Spoken like a king!" Khilleu cried when Narbas translated. "I would have bid you to a feast at my keep this night for my own honor's sake, but now I see I may enjoy the evening. Bring all these here. Invite my neighbor chiefs, too; some may come." Wry mirth edged his voice. "There will be pleasures for every taste, not merely our own."

"I will eat with you outside your castle, but not in it," Arigh answered. He did not need Goudeles' hisses or Skylitzes' surreptitious wave to make him wary of the squat, square pile of masonry toward which the Yrmido chief was pointing.

Atroklo started an angry exclamation, but Khilleu cut him off. "Can't say I blame you," he told the Arshaum. "My Lio is a strong keep; if I intended mischief, I could hole up there for ten years. Outside it will be—at sunset? Good. Best your men camp here—not only, I admit, because there is good water, but also to keep as much distance between you and my people as we can."

He waited, watching Arigh narrowly, ready to judge his sincerity by how he reacted. "Till sunset," was all the nomad said. He wheeled his horse, leaving Khilleu to make the best of the economical plains style.

Hamrentz, whose respect for the Yrmido was grudging but real, agreed to banquet with them, as did Gashvili, who owned frankly that he knew nothing about them for good or ill. The other Erzrumi leaders said no, with varying degrees of horror. One, Zromi of the Redzh, took up his hundred horsemen and rode from home at the thought of the Yrmido joining the expedition. "Good riddance," Skylitzes said. "We gain more here than we lose, seeing the last of his band of thieves."

Though troopers stayed on the walls of Lio, its drawbridge came down. Retainers kept scurrying in and out of the castle, running up trestle tables and benches outside the moat. Cookfires smoked in the castle forecourt. Along with the reek of the midden, the breeze brought the savory smell of roasting mutton. Viridovix' nostrils twitched of their own accord; he patted his belly in anticipation.

But appetite did not keep him from carefully inspecting the arrangements as Arigh's party rode up through ripening fields of wheat and barley. He found himself satisfied. "If they were after mischief, now," he said, tethering his horse, "they'd put us all together in a body instead of amongst their own. Then archers on the wall could hardly be missing us, e'en in sic torchlight as this. As is, they'd be apt to shoot holes in their chiefs, the which'd win 'em no thanks, I'm thinking."

"Hardly," Gorgidas answered. He brushed a bit of lint from his embroidered tunic, wishing the grease spot on his trousers had come cleaner. He was in Videssian dress; the last thing he wanted tonight was for the Yrmido to take him for a steppe nomad.

There was courtesy, if no more, in the greeting Khilleu and Atroklo gave their guests. The two of them seemed inseparable friends. They rose together to bow the newcomers to their places. Viridovix found himself between a chunky Yrmido a few years older than he was and a lean one a few years younger. The one knew a couple of words of Khamorth, the other none. Both were politely curious about his strange looks, but went back to their wine when they found they could not understand him.

He raised his pewter mug and a serving girl filled it. He watched her hips work as she moved away. After Seirem he had vowed he would stay womanless for life, a promise easy enough to keep in the Arshaum army as it traveled across the plains. But time wore away at grief, and his body had its own demands. When a wench among the Mzeshi made her interest plain, he had not backed away. Half a night behind a haystack was a small thing; it could not erase what he had known before.

No women of quality sat with the men. Most of the Erzrumi held to that custom, perhaps borrowed from Makuran. Used to the freer ways of the nomads, Viridovix missed them. Just by being there, they livened a gathering.

Gorgidas also noted their absence and drew his own conclusions from it. There was a pair of Yrmido to either side of him, one set somber in black slashed with silver, the other gaudy in scarlet and yellow. None of them shared a language with him. He sighed, resigning himself to a long evening. The maid who served him wine smiled invitingly. His answering look was so stony that she tossed her head in disdain.

Unexpectedly, one of the men across the table spoke in accented Videssian: "May I this tongue on you practice? When I a lad was, I served two years as hired soldier in the Empire before my brother died and I his holding inherited. I Rakio am called."

"Glad to know you," Gorgidas said heartily, and gave his own name. Rakio, he judged, was in his late twenties. Neither handsome nor the reverse, his face had character to it, with a beard trimmed closer than the usual Yrmido style, a chipped tooth his smile showed, and a nose whose imperious thrust was offset by an eyebrow that kept quirking whimsically upward. Pleasant fellow, the Greek thought.

Then the food appeared, and he forgot Rakio for some time. His year on the steppe had made him all too used to lamb and goat, though it was enjoyable to have them broiled with cloves of garlic rather than hastily roasted over a dung fire. But peas, spinach, and steamed asparagus were luxuries he had almost forgotten, and after months of flat, chewy wheatcakes, real bread, still soft and steaming from the ovens, brought him close to ecstasy.

He let his belt out a notch. "That was splendid."

Rakio was grinning at him. "I once had to eat with a squad of Khamorth," the Yrmido said. "I how you feel know."

The Greek poured a small libation on the ground and raised his mug high. "To good food!" he cried, and drank. Laughing, Rakio emptied his own cup. So did Goudeles, a couple of tables away. The plump bureaucrat's ears were as sharp as his pleasure in eating.

A minstrel wandered among the feasters, accompanying his songs with the plangent notes of a pandoura. A juggler kept half a dozen daggers in the air, his hands a blur of speed. Someone tossed him a coin. He caught it without dropping a knife. Two dancers carrying torches leaped back and forth over upturned swords.

When the girl with the wine came past again, Viridovix slid an arm around her waist. She did not pull away, but smiled down at him. She put out a forefinger to stroke his fiery mustache, not the first time his coloring had drawn a woman's eye in these dark-haired lands. He nibbled at her fingertip. She snuggled closer.

Khilleu boomed something in Vaspurakaner. The men who spoke that tongue shouted agreement. Narbas Kios said to the Gaul, "He asks you not to take her away for tumbling until she's emptied her jug."

"Only fair, that." Viridovix patted the girl's rump. "Soon, my pretty," he murmured. Without a word in common, she understood him. Arigh had already contrived to disappear into the night with the buxom wench who had fetched meat to his table. Gashvili and Vakhtang were gone, too. Khilleu looked on benignly, glad his guests were contented. No Yrmido had left.

Gorgidas let his own serving wench pass by again. Rakio's eyebrows rose. "She does not you please? You would prefer another? Fatter? Thinner? Younger, perhaps? We would not you have lonely." His concern sounded real.

"My thanks, but no," the physician said. "I do not care for a woman tonight."

Rakio gave a comic shrug, as if to say the foreigner was mad, but perhaps harmlessly so. Gorgidas stared down at his hands. He knew what he wanted to say, but had no notion of how to say it without risking grave offense. Yet he was so sure. . . .

He gave up on the dilemma for the moment when another servitor brought a tray of candied fruit. But that was soon done. The thing could be avoided no longer, unless he had not the nerve to broach it at all.

He felt his heart pound as though he were a nervous youth. Through a dry mouth he said, as casually as he could, "There are many fine pairs of your men here tonight."

Rakio caught the faint emphasis on "pairs." This time the eyebrow went up like a warning flag. "Most foreigners would say that we foul vices practice." The Yrmido regarded Gorgidas with the suspicion years of outsiders' despisal had in-gained in his people.

"Why should that be?" Remembering Platon's golden words, Gorgidas gave them back as well as he was able: "If the man who loves is caught doing something ugly, he would sooner be caught by anyone, even his father, than by his lover. And because lovers, feeling this way, would do anything rather than show cowardice before each other, and would do their best to spur each other on in battle, an army of them, however small it was, might conquer the world."

It was said. With bleak courage, the Greek waited to be wrong, waited for Rakio to scorn him. The Yrmido's jaw dropped. He shut it with a snap and broke into excited speech in his own tongue. Then the men in black and silver on Gorgidas' left and the bright peacocks on his right were clasping his hand, pounding his back, pressing food and wine on him and shouting noisy toasts.

Relief washed over him like sweet rain. He disentangled himself from a bear hug, then jumped as someone he had not heard coming up behind him tapped him on the shoulder. Viridovix grinned down at him. "Friendlier they are to you than they were for me, and you such a sobersides and all."

Gorgidas nodded at the girl on the Gaul's arm, who was plainly impatient at the delay. "To each his own."

"Och, aye, and this one's mine. Are you not, my sweet colleen?" She shrugged at his words, but giggled when he nuzzled her neck. He led her away from the feast, then let her find a quiet spot for the two of them. There was a stand of apple trees just out of bowshot from the castle of Lio and in the middle of it, the Gaul discovered, a small grassy patch. He spread his cloak with a flourish; the grass was soft as any bed, and sweeter-smelling.

The girl—he thought her name was Thamar—was eager as he. They helped each other off with their clothes; she was smooth and soft and warm in his arms. They sank together to the cloak, but when he rose on knees and elbows to mount her she shook her head vehemently and let loose a torrent of incomprehensible complaint.

Finally, with gestures, she made him understand the Yrmido did not favor that style of lovemaking. "Well, whatever suits you, then," he exclaimed, spreading his hands in acquiescence. "I'm ever game for summat new."

She rode him reversed, her hands at either side of his calves. A drop of sweat fell on his thigh. It was, the Gaul thought, a different view of things. "Though indeed," he muttered to himself, "one a pederast might be finding more gladsome than I."

Then suddenly everything the Gaul had seen in the Yrmido country came together. He shouted laughter, so that Thamar looked back at him in mixed surprise and indignation. "Nay, lass, it's nought to do with you," he said, stroking her ankle.

But he was still chuckling. "Sure and I see why you're after doing it this way, is all," he said, as if she could understand his speech. "Och, that Gorgidas, the puir spalpeen! Puir like the cat that fell in the cream jar, I'm thinking. Where were we, now?" He applied himself with a will.

Gorgidas had got his hosts to grasp that he was no Videssian and told them something of how he had come to the Empire and of the customs of his lost homeland. Naturally, most of their questions centered on one area. With the contempt their neighbors had heaped on them for centuries, they found it astonishing past belief that an outsider could see them with sympathy.

The Greek spoke of the military companionships of Sparta, of Athens' more genteel ways, and at last of the Sacred Band of Thebes, whose hundred-fifty pairs of lovers had fallen to the last man against Philip of Macedon and his son, Alexander the Great.

That account brought his listeners, whose number had grown as the night wore on, close to tears. "How then?" asked Rakio, who had been interpreting. "Did they show outrage to their bodies?"

"In no way," Gorgidas answered. "When Philip saw that all of them had taken their death wounds in front, he said, 'Woe to those who think evil of such men.' "

"Ahh," said all the Yrmido when Rakio was done translating. They bent their heads in a moment of silent respect for the men almost three hundred years dead. Moved past speech himself, Gorgidas shared it with them.

After a time his unquenchable curiosity reasserted itself. He said,

"You've listened to me. May I ask you in return how your own Sworn Fellowship came to be?"

Rakio scratched his head. "Came to be? Always it was. Since before the time of Fraortish, first of the blessed Four, it was."

That, Gorgidas knew, was another way of saying forever. He sighed, but not too deeply; there were more vital things than history. He said to Rakio, "Is your Sworn Fellowship all pairs, as the Theban Scared Band was? So it would seem, but for you, from the feasters here."

"More closely look. See over there—Pidauro and Rystheu and Ypeiro. They are a three-bond—and their wives with them, it is said. Another such there is, though tonight they are on patrol in the south. And there are a fair number such as myself. 'Orphans' we are named. I no life-partner yet have, but because I am my father's eldest son, I still when I reached manhood became a member of the Fellowship."

"Ah," the Greek said, annoyed at himself—seeing Rakio alone should have answered that for him. To hide his pique, he took a long drink of wine. It sent recklessness coursing through him. He said, "Will you not take offense at a personal question from an ignorant foreigner?" Rakio smiled for him to go on. He asked, "Are you an 'orphan' because you, ah, do not care to follow all the ways of the Fellowship?"

Rakio frowned in thought, then realized what Gorgidas, as an outsider, had to be trying to say. "Do I only like women, mean you?" He translated the question into his own language. All the Yrmido hooted with glee; someone threw a crust of bread at him. "I only am slow settling down," he said unnecessarily.

"So I gather," Gorgidas said, dry as usual.

That eyebrow of Rakio's was twitching again. This time, a look of frank speculation was on the Yrmido's face. Gorgidas dipped his head, then remembered how little that gesture meant to non-Greeks. He nodded slightly. When the torches round the feasting table guttered low, he and Rakio left hand in hand.

From the top of the pass the Erzrumi called the Funnel, the Arshaum and their allies could spy in the southwestern distance the river Moush. It sparkled like a silver wire, reflecting the afternoon sun. Beyond the green fertile strip along the bank of the stream lay the dun-colored flatlands where the Yezda ruled.

The plainsmen raised a cheer to see their goal at last, but Viridovix was not sorry when they started down the southern slope of the Funnel and that bare brown terrain disappeared once more. "A worse desolation it looks than the Videssian plateau," he said, "the which I hadna thought possible."

"It's desert away from water," Goudeles admitted, "but where the land is irrigated it can be fantastically rich. You'll see that, I'd say, in the valleys of the Tutub and the Tib—they raise three crops a year there."

"I dinna believe it," the Gaul said at once. Thinking of his own land's cool lush fruitfulness, he could not imagine this bake-oven of a country outdoing it, water or no.

But Skylitzes backed his countryman, saying, "Believe as you will; it's true regardless. They call the land between the Tutub and the Tib the Hundred Cities because it can support so many people. Or could, rather; it's fallen on evil times since the Yezda came."

"Honh!" Viridovix said through his nose. He changed the subject, asking "Where might Mashiz be, once we're after sacking these Hundred Cities o' yours?"

"It might be on the far side of the moon," Goudeles said, adding mournfully, "but it's not, worse luck. The cursed town is nestled in the foothills of the mountains of Dilbat, just west of the Tutub's headwaters."

When the army camped that night, the Celt drew lines in the dirt to help him remember what he had learned. He explained his scratchings to Gorgidas, who copied them on wax with quick strokes of his stylus. "Interesting." The Greek snapped his tablet closed. He said, "I'm off to the Yrmido camp. Their customs promise to make a worthwhile digression for my history."

"Do they now?" Viridovix tried not to laugh at how transparent his friend could be. The physician had used the same excuse three nights running. Twice he had not come back till past midnight; the other time he spent the whole night with the Sworn Fellowship.

"Well, yes," Gorgidas answered seriously. "Their account of the first Yezda incursion into Erzerum, for example—confound it, what are you smirking about?"

"Me?" The Celt aimed for a look of wide-eyed innocence, an expression which did not suit his face. He gave up and chortled out loud. "Sure and it's nae history alone you're finding with the Yrmido, else you'd not be sleeping like a dead corp and wearing that fool grin the times you're awake."

"What fool grin?" Viridovix' parody made the Greek wince. He threw his hands in the air. "If you already know the answer, why ask the question?"

"Begging your pardon I am," Viridovix said quickly, seeing the alarm that always came to Gorgidas when his preference for men was mentioned by someone who did not share it. "All I meant by it was that it's strange for fair, seeing a sour omadhaun like your honor so cheery and all."

"Go howl!" From long habit, the physician searched Viridovix for the sort of killing scorn the Yrmido met from all their neighbors. He did not find it, so he relaxed; it was not as though the Gaul had just discovered the way his habits ran.

Viridovix slapped him on the back, staggering him a little. On his face was honest curiosity. "Might you be telling me now, how do you find it after a year with women?"

"After a year my way, how would you find a wench?"

The Gaul whistled. "I hadna thought of it so. I'd marry her on the spot, beshrew me if I didn't."

"I'm in no danger of *that,*" Gorgidas said, and they both laughed. There was more than one kind of truth in his words, though, the physician thought. Rakio would never come close to filling the place Quintus Glabrio had in his heart.

True, the Yrmido, like most of his countrymen, was brave to a fault, and he had the gift of laughter. But he was hopelessly provincial. Despite his travels in Videssos, he cared for nothing beyond his own valley, while for Gorgidas the whole world seemed none too big. And where Glabrio and Gorgidas had shared a common heritage, Rakio's strange syntax was the least reminder of how different his background was from the Greek's. Finally, the Yrmido openly scoffed at fidelity. "Faithfulness for women is," he had said to Gorgidas. "Men should enjoy themselves."

Enjoying himself the physician was. Let it last as long as it would; for now it was good enough.

With their speed, the Arshaum expected to swarm over the river Moush and into Yezd before its defenders were ready to receive them. There again, they reckoned without Avshar. The wizard-prince, still ahead of his enemies, had given his followers warning. The boat-bridges leading north into Erzerum had been withdrawn. Squadrons of nomad horse patrolled the Moush's southern bank. Better-drilled troops, men of Makuraner blood, guarded the river's ford with catapults.

Against the advice of all the Erzrumi commanders, Arigh tried to force one of the river-crossings in the face of the Yezda artillery and was repulsed. The stonethrowers reached across the Moush, which even his nomads' bows could not. And the catapults shot more than stones. Jugs of incendiary mix crashed among he Arshaum, splashing fire all about. Horses and men screamed; there was nearly a panic before the plainsmen drew back out of range.

Arigh shouldered the blame manfully, saying, "I should have listened. They know more of this fighting with engines than I do." He scratched at the pink, shiny scars on his cheek. "From now on I will stay with what we do best. Let the Yezda have to figure out how to meet me."

"That is a wise general speaking," said Lankinos Skylitzes, and the Arshaum's eyes lit.

He proved as good as his word, taking advantage of the plainsmen's mobility and skill at making do. Under cover of night he sent a hundred Arshaum over the widest part of the Moush, swimming with their horses and carrying arms and armor in leather sacks tied to the beasts' tails. As soon as they were across and starting to remount, the rest of their countrymen followed.

By sheer bad luck, a single Yezda spied the forerunners just as they were coming out of the river. He raised the alarm and managed to escape in the darkness. The Yezda were steppemen themselves; they reacted quickly. The fight that blew up was no less fierce for being fought half-blind. The Arshaum struggled to expand their perimeter, while their opponents battled to crush them and regain control of the riverbank before the bulk of the army could cross.

Viridovix stripped naked and splashed into the Moush just after the advance force. Some of the Arshaum hooted at him. "What good will a sword do, when you can't see what to hit?" someone called.

"As much good as a bow," he retorted, "or are your darts after having eyes of their own?"

When his pony clambered up onto the southern bank of the Moush, he let go of its neck and armed himself with frantic haste. Not long ago he would have gone to a fight sooner than to a woman, most times, but that was gone forever. Yet the Yezda ahead were obstacles between him and Avshar. For that he would kill them if he could.

He could hear them shouting ahead as he mounted his pony and spurred toward the fighting. He understood their cries, or most of them; the dialect they spoke was not that far removed from the Khamorth tongue of Pardraya.

A rider appeared ahead of him, indistinct in the starlight. "Can you bespeak me, now?" he called in the speech he had learned in Targitaus' tent.

"Aye," the other horseman said, reining in. "Who are you?"

"No friend," Viridovix said, and slashed out. The Yezda fell with a groan.

An arrow snarled past the Gaul's ear. He cursed; it had come from behind him. "Have a care there, ye muck-brained slubberers!" he roared, this time in the Arshaum language. The cry in the alien tongue drew another Yezda to him. They fenced half by guess. Viridovix took a cut on his left arm and another above his knee before a double handful of Arshaum came galloping up and the Yezda fled.

His mates were beginning to give ground all along the line. The company that had happened to be close by was big enough to face Arigh's first wave, but more and more Arshaum were emerging, dripping, from the Moush and going into action. It was not the nomad way to fight a stand-up battle against superior numbers. The Yezda scattered, saving themselves but yielding the position.

It was too dark for signal flags. The *naccara* drum boomed. Arigh's messengers rode orders up and down the line: "Hurry west for the ford!" Picking their way over unfamiliar ground, the Arshaum obeyed. Their Erzrumi allies paced them on the far side of the Moush. The heavily armored mountaineers could not cross the river as easily as the plainsmen; it was up to the Arshaum to win them safe passage.

Viridovix hoped they would take the guards at the ford by surprise, but they did not. A ring of bonfires made the space round the enemy camp bright as day. Catapult crews stood to their weapons; darts, stones, and jars of incendiary were piled high by the engines. Cavalry in ordered rows waited for the Arshaum. The firelight gleamed from their corselets and lances. No irregulars these, but seasoned troops of the same sort Videssos produced, Makuraner contingents fighting for their land's new masters.

Arigh's white grin was all there was to see of him. "This will be easy—only a couple hundred of them. We can flatten them before they get reinforced." He confidently began deploying his men.

As he was sending messengers here and there, a single figure from the enemy lines rode out past the bonfires toward the Arshaum. He loomed against the flames, tremendous and proud. Viridovix' heart gave a painful leap; he was sure that huge silhouette had to belong to Avshar. Then the horseman turned his head and the Gaul saw his strong profile. A mere man, he thought, disappointed; the wizard-prince's mantlings would have hidden his face.

The rider came closer, brandishing his spear. He shouted something, first in a language Viridovix did not understand but took to be Makuraner, then in the tongue of Vaspurakan, finally in the Yezda dialect. The Celt could follow him there: "Ho, you dogs! Does any among you dare match himself against me? I am Gusnaph, called with good reason the Feeder of Ravens, and fourteen men I have struck down in the duel. Who among you will join them?"

He rode back and forth, arrogant in his might, crying his challenge again and again. The Arshaum murmured among themselves as those who understood translated for the rest. No one seemed eager to answer Gusnaph. Aboard his great horse, armored head to foot, he might as well have been a tower of iron. He laughed scornfully and made as if to return to his own lines.

Viridovix whooped and dug his heels into his pony's flanks. "Come back, you idiot!" he heard Skylitzes yell. "He has a lance to your sword!" The Gaul did not stop. Even with a won battle, he had leaped to fight

Scaurus; had he not, the fleeting thought went by, he would still be in Gaul. But he had not hesitated then and did not now. An enemy leader slain was worth a hundred lesser men.

Gusnaph turned, swung up his lance in salute, then lowered it and thundered at the Celt. He grew bigger with terrifying quickness. The spear was fixed unerringly on Viridovix' chest, no matter which way he swerved.

At the last instant the Gaul feinted again, and again Gusnaph met the move—too well. The lancepoint darted past the Celt's shoulder as their horses slammed together in collision.

Both men were thrown. They landed heavily. Viridovix scrambled to his feet. He was faster than Gusnaph, whose armor weighed him down. His lance lay under his thrashing horse. He reached for a weapon at his belt—a shortsword, a mace, a dagger; Viridovix never knew which. The Gaul sprang forward. Gusnaph was still on one knee when his sword crashed down. The Makuraner champion fell in the dirt.

Following the custom of his own nation, Viridovix bent, chopped, and raised Gusnaph's dripping head for the rest of the enemy to see. He let out a banshee wail of triumph. There was an awful stillness on the other side of the fires.

With the resilience of the nomad breed, Viridovix' pony was on its feet and seemed unhurt, though Gusnaph's charger was screaming enough to make the Celt think it had broken a leg. The steppe animal shied from the smell of blood when he approached it with his trophy.

He set the head down. "I've no gate to nail it to, any road," he said to himself. The pony side-stepped nervously, but let him mount. He waved his sword to the Arshaum, who were erupting in a cloudburst of cheers. "Is it summat else you're waiting for, then?" he shouted.

The plainsmen advanced at the trot. Their foes hardly waited for the first arrows to come arcing out of the night, but fled, abandoning their tents, the catapults, and the ford. The first hint of morning twilight was turning the sky pale when Arigh stood on the bank of the Moush and waved to the Erzrumi to cross.

They came over band by band, the water at the ford lapping at their horses' flanks. Gorgidas crossed with the Sworn Fellowship, just behind Rakio. In his boiled leather, armed only with a *gladius*, he felt badly out of place among the armored Yrmido, but he had discovered Platon was right. He would do anything before he let his lover think him afraid.

The Yezda managed a counterattack at dawn, nomad archers fighting in the familiar style of the plains. But as they had only faced the Arshaum during the night, the Erzrumi took them by surprise. They shouted in dismay as the plainsmen's line opened out and the big mountain horses crashed down on them.

With the Yrmido, Gorgidas was at the point of the wedge. There were a few seconds of desperate confusion as the Sworn Fellowship and the rest of the Erzrumi speared Yezda out of the saddle and overbore their light mounts. Some fell on their side, too; an Yrmido just in front of the physician flew from his horse, his face bloodily pulped by a morningstar. His partner, tears steaming down his cheeks, killed the nomad who had slain him.

The Greek slashed at a Yezda. He thought he missed. It did not much matter. The advance rolled ahead.

Gashvili shouted something in Vaspurakaner to Khilleu. The lord of Gunib had a dent in his gilded helmet, but was undismayed. Khilleu, grinning, gave back an obscene gesture. "What was that?" Gorgidas asked Rakio, who was tying up a cut on the back of his hand.

"Says Gashvili, 'You damned fairies can fight.'"

"He's right," the Greek said with a burst of pride.

"Why not?" To Rakio, war came as naturally as breathing. He touched spurs to his horse, driving against the Yezda. Gorgidas' steppe pony snorted in affront when he spurred it, but followed.

Then, quite suddenly, the enemy was reeling away, each man fleeing to save himself, with no thought of holding together as a fighting force. The Arshaum and Erzrumi cheered each other till they were hoarse. The way clear before them, they pushed into Yezd.

VII

Gaius Philippus slapped at a horsefly buzzing round the head of the bony gray nag he was riding. It droned away. He growled, "I'm amazed this arse-busting chunk of buzzards' bait has enough life in it to draw flies. *Get* up, you mangy old crock! Make it to Amorion by sundown and you can rest."

He jerked on the reins. The gray gave him a reproachful look and came out of its amble for a few paces' worth of shambling trot. It blew until its skinny sides heaved, as if the exertion were too much for it. As soon as it thought it had satisfied him, it fell back into a walk. "Miserable gluepot," he said, chuckling in spite of himself.

"It's an old soldier, sure enough," Marcus said. "Be thankful it's not better—it didn't tempt the Yezda into trying to steal it."

"I should hope not!" Gaius Philippus said, taking perverse pride in his decrepit mount. "Remember that one whoreson who looked us over a couple of days ago? He fell off his pony laughing."

"As well for us," the tribune answered. "He was probably a scout for a whole band of them."

At that thought he slipped out of the bantering mood. The journey inland from Nakoleia was much worse that he had expected. The port was still in Videssian hands, but its hinterland swarmed with Yezda, who swooped down on farmers whenever they tried to work their fields. If the Empire had not kept the city supplied by sea, it could not have survived.

Most of the villages on the dirt track that led south were deserted, or nearly so. Even a couple of towns that had kept their ancient walls through the centuries of imperial peace now stood empty. The Yezda made growing or harvesting crops impossible, and so the towns, though safe from nomad siege, withered. He wondered how many had died when they were forced to open their gates, and how many managed to get away.

It occurred to him that the devastation the nomads were inflicting on the westlands had happened on a vastly greater scale long before, when the Khamorth swarmed off the edge of the steppe into Videssos' eastern provinces. He shook his head. No wonder those lands had fallen into the heresy of reckoning Skotos' power equal to that of Phos; evil incarnate must have seemed loose in the world.

A squad of horsemen came round a bend in the road, trotting briskly north. Their leader swung up an arm in warning when he caught sight of the Romans, then brought it down halfway as he recognized they were not Yezda. He rode up to inspect them. Scaurus saw that he had helmet, shortsword, and bow, but no body armor. His men were similarly equipped and mounted on a motley set of animals. The tribune had met their like on the road the day before—Zemarkhos' men.

The squad leader drew the sun-sign over his heart. Marcus and Gaius Philippus quickly imitated him; it would have been dangerous not to. "Phos with you," the Videssian said. He was in his late twenties, tall, stringy, scarred like a veteran, with disconcertingly sharp eyes.

"And with you," the tribune returned.

A tiny test had been passed; the Videssian's head moved a couple of inches up and down. He asked, "Well, strangers, what are you doing in the dominions of the Defender of the Faithful?" Having heard Zemarkhos' self-chosen title from the riders he had come across yesterday, Marcus did not blink at it.

"We're for the holy Moikheios' *panegyris* at Amorion," he said, giving the cover story he and Gaius Philippus had worked out aboard the *Seafoam*. "Maybe we can sign on as caravan guards with one of the merchants there."

The squad leader said, "That could be." He studied the tribune. "By your tongue and hair, you are no Videssian, but you do not look like a Vaspurakaner. Are you one of the Namdalener heretics?"

For once Marcus was glad of his blondness; though it marked him as a foreigner, it also showed he was not of the sort Zemarkhos' men killed on sight. He recited Phos' creed in the version the Empire used; the Namdaleni appended "On this we stake our very souls" to it, an addition which raised the hackles of Videssian theologians. Gaius Philippus followed his lead. He went through the creed haltingly, but got it right.

The horsemen relaxed and took their hands away from their weapons. "Orthodox enough," their chief said, "and no one will take it ill if you hold to that usage. Still, you'll find that many, out of respect for our lord Zemarkhos, add 'We also bless the Defender of thy true faith,' after 'decided in our favor.' As I say, it is optional, but it may make them think the better of you in Amorion."

" 'We also bless the Defender of thy true faith,' " Scaurus and Gaius Philippus repeated, as if memorizing the clause. Zemarkhos, it seemed, had a perfectly secular love of self-aggrandizement, no matter how he phrased it. The tribune kept his face blank. "Thanks for the tip," he said.

"It's nothing," the Videssian answered. "Outlanders who come to the true belief of their own accord deserve to be honored. Good luck in town—we're off to watch for Yezda thieves and raiders."

"And filthy Vaspurakaners, too," one of his men added. "Some of the stinking bastards are still skulking around, for all we can do to root 'em out."

"That's not so bad," said another. "They make better sport than bustards, or even foxes. I caught three last winter." He spoke matter-of-factly, as he might of any other game. Scaurus' twinge of regret at his hyprocrisy over the creed disappeared.

The squad leader touched a forefinger to the rim of his helmet, nodded to the Romans, and started to lead his troops away. Gaius Philippus, who had been mostly silent till then, called after him. He paused. The senior centurion said, "I was through these parts a few years ago and made some good friends at a town called Aptos. Have the Yezda got it, or Zemarkhos?"

"It's ours," the Videssian said.

"Glad to hear it." Marcus suspected Gaius Philippus was mostly worried about Nerse Phorkaina, the widow of the local noble; Phorkos had died at Maragha. She was the only woman the tribune had heard Gaius Philippus praise, but when the legionaries had wintered at Aptos the veteran did nothing at all to let her know his admiration. Fear of one sort or another, Marcus thought, found a place to root in everyone.

Amorion was no great city, even next to Garsavra, only a dusty town in the middle of the westlands' central plateau. Without the Ithome River, the place would have had no reason for being. But the only two times Marcus had seen it, it was jammed past overflowing, first by Mavrikios Gavras' army marching west toward disaster and now with the *panegyris.*

Twilight was descending when the Romans rode between the parallel rows of commercial tents outside the city. Thorisin had been right; in the crush they were just another pair of strangers. A merchant with the long rectangular face and liquid eyes of the Makuraners laughed in staged amazement at the price a Videssian offered him for his pistachioes. Half a dozen turbaned nomads from the desert south of the Sea of Salt—slender, big-nosed men with a family likeness—were packing up their incenses and quills of spice till morning. They had camels tethered back of their tent; Marcus' horse shied at the unfamiliar stink of them.

A priest dickered with a fat farmer over a mule. The rustic's respect for the blue robe was not making him drop his price any. Somehow a Namdalener merchant had found his way to Amorion with a packhorse-load of clay lamps. He was doing a brisk business. The priest bought one after the mule seller laughed in his face.

"I don't see *him* making it hot for heretics," Gaius Philippus remarked.

"Seems to me 'heretics' and 'Vaspurakaners' mean the same thing to Zemarkhos," Scaurus answered. "He's got himself and his people worked into such a froth about them that he has no time to stew over anybody else's mischief."

The senior centurion grunted thoughtfully. Caravan masters, lesser merchants, swaggering guardsmen, and bargain hunters represented a great sweep of nations, some heterodox, others outside Phos' cult altogether, yet every one of them carried on undisturbed by the clergy. But not a single Vaspurakaner was to be seen, although the land of the "princes"—as they called themselves—was not far northwest of Amorion, and although many of them had settled round the city after Yezda assaults made them flee Vaspurakan. Zemarkhos' pogroms had done their work well.

The Romans rode past a caravan leader—a tall, wide, swag-bellied man with a shaved head, great jutting prow of a nose, and drooping black mustachioes almost as splendid as Viridovix'—cursing at a muleteer for letting one of his beasts go lame. He swore magnificently, in several languages mixed to blistering effect; his voice was the bass crash of rocks thundering down a mountainside. By unspoken joint consent, Scaurus and Gaius Philippus pulled up to listen and admire.

The caravaneer spotted them out of the corner of his eye. He broke off with a shouted, "And don't let it happen again, you motherless wide-arsed pot of goat puke!" Then he put meaty hands on hips in a theatrical gesture that matched his clothes—he wore a maroon silk tunic open to the waist, baggy wool trousers dyed a brilliant blue tucked into gleaming black knee-high boots, a gold ring in his right ear, and one of silver in his left. Three of his teeth were gold, too; they sparkled when he grinned at the Romans. "You boys have a problem?"

"Only trying to remember what all you called him," Gaius Philippus said, grinning back.

"Ha! Not half what he deserves." A chuckle rumbled deep in the trader's chest. He gave the Romans a second, longer look. "You're fighters." It was not a question. With a broad-bladed dagger and stout, unsheathed cutlass on his belt, the caravaneer recognized his own breed. "I'm short a couple of outriders—are you interested? I'll take the both of you in spite of that horrible screw you're riding there, gray-hair."

"Why did you think I wanted your curses?" Gaius Philippus retorted.

"Don't blame you a bit. Well, what say? It's a goldpiece a month, all you can eat, and a guardsman's share of the profits at the end of the haul. Are you game?"

"We may be back in a day or two," Marcus said; it would not do to refuse outright, for their story's sake. "We have business to attend to in town before we can make plans."

"Well, you can paint me with piss before I tell you I'll hold the spots, but if I haven't filled 'em by then, I'll still think about you. I'll be here—between the damn Yezda and all this hooplah over the Vaspurs, things are slow. Ask for me if you don't see me; I'm Tahmasp." The Makuraner name explained his slight guttural accent and his indifference to Zemarkhos' persecution, except where it interfered with trade.

Someone bawled Tahmasp's name. "I'm coming!" he yelled back. To the Romans he said, "If I see you, I'll see you," and lumbered away.

Gaius Philippus booted his horse in the ribs. "Come on, you overgrown snail." He said to Marcus, "You know, I wouldn't half mind serving under that big-nosed bastard."

"Never a dull moment," Scaurus agreed. The centurion laughed and nodded.

At any other time of the year Amorion would have shut down with nightfall, leaving its winding, smelly streets to footpads and those few rich enough to hire link-bearers and bodyguards to hold them at bay. But during the *panegyris* of the holy Moikheios, the town's main thoroughfare blazed with torches to accomodate the night vigils, competing choirs, and processions with which the clergy celebrated their saint's festival.

"Buy some honied figs?" called a vendor with a tray slung over his shoulder. When Marcus did, the man said, "Phos and Moikheios and the Defender bless you, sir. Here, squeeze in beside me and grab yourselves a place—the big parade'll be starting before long." The Defender again, was it? The tribune frowned at the hold Zemarkhos had on Amorion. But he had an idea how to break it.

Practical as always, Gaius Philippus said, "We'd best find somewhere to stay."

"Try Souanites' inn," the fig seller said eagerly. He gave rapid directions, adding, "I'm called Leikhoudes. Mention my name for a good rate."

To make sure I get my cut, Marcus translated silently. Having no better plan, he made Leikhoudes repeat the directions, then followed them. To his surprise, they worked. "Yes, I have something, my masters," Souanites said. It proved to be piles of heaped straw in the stable with their horses at the price of a fine room, but Scaurus took it without argument. Each stall had a locking door; Souanites might see his place near empty the rest of the year, but he made the most of the *panegyris* when it came.

After they stowed their gear and saw to their animals, Gaius Philippus asked, "Do you care anything about this fool parade?"

"It might be a chance to find out what we're up against."

"Or get nailed before we're started," Gaius Philippus said gloomily, but with a sigh he followed the tribune into the street.

They took a wrong turn backtracking and were lost for a few minutes, but the noise and lights of the main street made it easy to orient themselves again. They emerged a couple of blocks down from where they had turned aside to go to Souanites' and promptly bumped into the fig seller, who had been working his way through the gathering crowd. His tray was nearly empty, he spread his hands apologetically. "I'm sorry I no longer have such a fine view to offer you."

"We owe you a favor," Marcus said. With Leikhoudes between them, he and Gaius Philippus elbowed their way to the front of the crowd. They won some black looks, but Scaurus was half a head taller than most of the men and Gaius Philippus, though of average size, did not have the aspect of one with whom it would be wise to quarrel. Leikhoudes exclaimed in delight.

They were just in time, though the first part of the procession left the Romans fiercely bored. The company of Zemarkhos' militia drew cheers from their neighbors, but looked ragged, ill-armed, and poorly drilled to Marcus. They held the Yezda off with holy zeal, not the spit and polish that made troops impressive on parade. Nor was the tribune much impressed by the marching choruses that followed. For one thing, even his insensitive ear recognized them as rank amateurs. For another, most of their hymns were in the archaic language of the liturgy, which he barely understood.

"Are they not splendid?" Leikhoudes said. "There! See, in the third row—my cousin Stasios the shoemaker!" He pointed proudly. "Ho, Stasios!"

"I've never heard any singers to match them," Scaurus said.

"Aye, but plenty to better them," Gaius Philippus added, but in Latin.

Another chorus went by, this one accompanied by pipes, horns, and drums. The din was terrific. Then came a group of Amorion's rich young men on prancing horses with manes decorated by ribbons and trappings bright with gold and silver.

The noise of the crowd turned ugly as a double handful of half-naked men in chains stumbled past, prodded along by more of Zemarkhos' irregulars with spears. The prisoners were stocky, swarthy, heavily bearded men. "Phos-cursed Vaspurakaners!" Leikhoudes screeched. "It was your sins, your beastly treacherous heresy that set the Yezda on us all!" The crowd pelted them with clods of earth, rotten fruit, and horsedung. In a transport of fury, Leikhoudes hurled the last of his figs at them.

Marcus set his jaw; beside him Gaius Philippus shifted his feet and swore under his breath. They had no hope of making a rescue; to try would get them ripped to pieces by the mob.

The growls around them turned to cheers. "Zemarkhos! His Sanctity! The Defender!" With neighbors watching, no one dared sound halfhearted.

Before the fanatic priest marched the parasol bearers who symbolized power to the Videssians, as the lictors with their rods and axes did in Rome. Marcus whistled when he counted the flowers of blue silk. Fourteen—even Thorisin Gavras was only entitled to twelve.

As if oblivious to the adulation he was getting, Zemarkhos limped down the street, looking neither right nor left. His gaunt features were horribly scarred, as were his hands and arms. Limp and scars both came from the big prick-eared hound that paced at his side.

The hound was called Vaspur, after the legendary founder of the Vaspurakaner people. Zemarkhos had named it long before Maragha, to taunt the Vaspurakaner refugees who fled to his city. Finally Gagik Bagratouni had his fill of such vilification. He caught priest and dog together in a great sack, then kicked the sack. Striking out in pain and terror, Vaspur's jaws had done the rest.

Marcus, who had been at Bagratouni's villa, had persuaded the *nakharar* to let Zemarkhos out, fearing his death as a martyr would touch off the persecution the priest had been fomenting. Maybe it would have, but looking back, the tribune did not see how things could have gone worse for the "princes." He wished he had let Vaspur finish tearing Zemarkhos' life away.

The hound paused, growling, as it padded past the Romans. The hair stood up along its back. It had been close to three years, and the beast had only taken their scent for a few minutes; could it remember? For that matter, would Zemarkhos know them again if he saw them? Scaurus suddenly wished he were a short brunet, to be less conspicuous in the crowd.

But the dog walked on, and Zemarkhos with it. The tribune let out a soft sigh of relief. The priest had been dangerous before, but now he carried an aura of brooding power that made Marcus wish he could raise his hackles like Vaspur. He did not think mere temporal authority had put that look on Zemarkhos' ruined features; something stranger and darker dwelt there. By luck, it was directed inward now, growing, feeding on the priest's fierce hate.

Still shouting, "Phos watch over the Defender," the crowd fell in behind Zemarkhos as he made his way into Amorion's central forum. They swept Scaurus and Gaius Philippus with them. More Videssians filled the edges of the square; the newcomers pushed and shoved to find places.

The spear-carrying guards forced their Vaspurakaner captives into the middle of the forum. They released the ends of the chains they held. One took a short-handled sledge from his belt and secured each prisoner by staking those free ends to the ground. A couple of the Vaspurakaners tugged at their bonds, but most simply stood, apathetic or apprehensive.

The guards moved away from them in some haste.

Zemarkhos limped toward the prisoners. Beside him, Vaspur barked and snarled, showing gleaming fangs. "Is he going to set the hound on them?" Gaius Philippus muttered in disgust. "What did they do to him?"

Marcus expected the dog to go for the prisoners in vengeance for Bagratouni's treatment of Zemarkhos. That made a twisted kind of sense. But at the priest's command it sat next to him. Zemarkhos' profile was predatory as a hunting hawk's as he focused his will on the Vaspurakaners.

He extended a long, clawlike finger in their direction. The crowd quieted. The priest quivered; Scaurus could fairly see him channeling the force that boiled within him. In a way, he thought, it was an obscene parody of the ritual healer-priests used to gather their concentration before they set to work.

But Zemarkhos did not intend to heal. "Accursed, damned, and lost be the Vaspurakaner race!" he cried, his shrill voice searing as red-hot iron. "Deceitful, evil, mad, capricious, with wickedness twice compounded! Malignant, treacherous, beastly, and obstinate in their foul heresy! Accursed, accursed, accursed!"

At every repetition, he stabbed his finger toward the captives. And at every repetition, the crowd bayed in bloodthirsty excitement, for the Vaspurakaners writhed in torment, as if lashed by barbed whips. Two or three of them screamed, but the noise was drowned in the roar of the crowd.

"Accursed be the debased creatures of Skotos!" Zemarkhos screeched, and the prisoners fell to their knees, biting their lips against anguish. "Accursed be their every rite, their every mystery, abominable and hateful to Phos! Accursed be their vile mouths, which speak in blasphemies!" And blood dripped down into the Vaspurakaners' beards.

"Accursed be these wild dogs, these serpents, these scorpions! I curse them all, to death and uttermost destruction!" With as much force as if he cast a spear, he shot his finger forward again. Their faces contorted in terror and agony, their eyes starting from their heads, the Vaspurakaners flopped about on the ground like boated fish, then subsided to twitching and finally stillness.

Only then did Zemarkhos, unwholesome triumph blazing in his eyes, stalk up to them and spurn their bodies with his foot. The crowd, fired to the religious enthusiasm that came all too readily to Videssians, shouted its approval. "Phos guard the Defender of the Faithful!" "Thus to all heretics!" "The true faith conquers!" One loud-voiced woman even cried out the imperial salutation: "Thou conquerest, Zemarkhos!"

The priest gave no sign the acclaim moved him. Urging Vaspur to his feet, he limped off toward his residence. He fixed his unblinking stare on the crowd and said harshly, "See to it you fall not into error, nor suffer your neighbor to do so."

His people, though, were used to his unbending sternness and cheered him as though he had granted them a benediction. They streamed out of the plaza, well pleased with the night's spectacle.

As they were making their way back to their meager lodgings, Gaius Philippus turned to Marcus and asked, "Are you sure you want to go through with what you planned?"

"Frankly, no." The strength of Zemarkhos' wizardry, fueled with a fanatic's zeal and a tyrant's rage, daunted the tribune. He walked some paces in silence. At last he said, "What other choice do I have, though? Would you sooner be an assassin, sneaking through the night?"

"I would," Gaius Philippus answered at once, "if I didn't think they'd catch us afterward. Or, more likely, before. But I'm glad I'm no big part of your scheme."

Marcus shrugged. "The Videssians are a subtle folk. What better to confound them with than the obvious?"

"Especially when it isn't," the veteran said.

Dawn the next day gave promise of the ferocious heat of the Videssian central plateau, the kind of heat that would quickly kill a man away from water. The horse trough in which Scaurus washed his head and arms was blood-warm.

He had no appetite for the loaf he bought from the innkeeper. Gaius Philippus finished what was left after polishing off his own. It was not, Marcus knew, that the other felt easier because he was sure of his safety. Had their roles been reversed, the unshakable centurion would not have eaten a bite less.

They stayed in the shade of the stable until early afternoon, drawing curious glances from the horseboys and the guests who came in to take their beasts.

When the shadows started to grow longer again, Marcus unpacked his full Roman military kit and donned it all—greaves, iron-studded kilt, mail shirt, helmet with high horsehair crest, scarlet cape of rank. Even in the shadows, he began to sweat at once.

Gaius Philippus, still in cloth, clambered aboard his spavined gray. He led the tribune's saddled horse after him as he emerged from the stable and leaned down to clasp hands with Scaurus. "I'll be ready at my end, not that it'll make any difference if things go wrong. The gods with you, you great bloody fool."

A good enough epitaph, Marcus thought as the senior centurion clopped away. His own progress was as leisurely as he could make it; in armor under that blazing sun he understood, not for the first time, how a lobster must feel boiled in its shell.

He collected a crowd of small boys before he got to Amorion's chief street. The youngsters had grown used to soldiers, but not ones so resplendent as he. He gave out coppers with a free hand; he wanted to attract all the notice he could. He asked, "Is Zemarkhos preaching today?"

Some of the lads perked up at mention of the priest, while others watched the tribune with blank faces; not through love alone did Zemarkhos rule Amorion. One of the boys who had smiled said, "Aye, so he is, sir. He talks in the plaza every day, he do."

"Thanks." Scaurus gave him another coin.

"Thank *you,* sir. Are you going to go listen to him? I can see, sir, you've come from far away, maybe even just to hear him? Isn't he a marvel? Have you ever run across his like?"

"That I haven't, son," the Roman said truthfully. "Yes, I'm going to listen to him. I may," he went on, "even speak with him."

The corpses of the Vaspurakaners still lay in their agonized postures in the center of the square. They did nothing to slow the furious buying and selling of the *panegyris,* which went on all around them. Two rug sellers had set up stalls across from each other, and loudly sneered at one another's merchandise. A swordsmith worked a creaking grindstone with a foot pedal as he sharpened customers' knives. A plump matron examined herself in a merchant's bronze mirror, looking for flaws in the speculum and in her makeup. She put it down with a reluctant nod; the haggling began in earnest.

Sellers of wine, nuts, roasted fowls, ale, fruit juice, figs, little spiced cakes, and a hundred other delicacies wandered through the eager crowd, crying their wares. So did strongmen sweating under the great stones they had heaved over their heads, strolling musicians, acrobats—including one who walked on his hands and had a beggar's tin cup tied to his leg—trainers with their performing dogs or talking ravens, puppeteers, and a host of other mountebanks.

And so, for all Zemarkhos' ascetic prudery, did prostitutes, drawn with the other merchants to the *panegyris'* concentration of wealth. Marcus spied Gaius Philippus, well posted at the edge of the square, talking with a tall, dark-haired woman, attractive in a stern-faced way. Perhaps she reminded him of Nerse Phorkaina, the tribune thought. She slid her dress off one shoulder for a moment to show the centurion her breasts. Startled, Marcus laughed—perhaps she didn't, too.

As the street lad promised, Zemarkhos was exhorting a good-sized gathering. Flanked by several spear-carrying guardsmen, he stood, Vaspur at his side, behind a portable rostrum. He emphasized his points by pounding it with his fists. Scaurus did not need to have heard the first part of the harangue to know what it was about.

"They are Skotos' spawn," Zemarkhos was shouting, "seeking to corrupt Phos' untarnished faith through the vile mockery of it they practice in their heretical rites. Only by their destruction may right doctrine be preserved without blemish. Aye, and by the destruction of those deluded heresy-lovers in the capital, whose mercy on the disbelievers' bodies will be justly requited with torment to their souls!"

The audience cheered him on, crying, "Death to the heretics! Zemarkhos' curse take the hypocrites! Praise the wisdom of Zemarkhos the Defender, scourge of the wicked Vaspurakaners!"

Flicking his crimson cape round him, Marcus worked his way toward Zemarkhos' podium. He cut an impressive figure; people who turned to grumble as he pushed past them muttered apologies and stepped back to let him by. Soon he stood in the second or third row, close enough to see the veins bulging at Zemarkhos' throat and on his forehead as he ranted against his chosen victims.

"Anathema to those who spring from Vaspurakan, the root-stock of every impurity!" he screamed. "May they be cast into Skotos' outer darkness for their wicked inspirer to devour! They are the worst of all mankind, howling like wild dogs against our correct faith—hardhearted, stiff-necked, vain, and insane!"

Marcus pushed his way to the very front of the audience. "Rubbish!" he shouted, as loud as he could.

He heard gasps all around him. Zemarkhos' mouth was open for his next pronouncement. It hung foolishly for a moment as the priest gaped; it had been years since anyone opposed him. Then he waved to his guards. "Kill me this blasphemous oaf." Grinning, they stepped forward to obey.

"Yes, send your dogs to do your work," the Roman jeered. "Too stupid to learn, are you? Look what happened to you when you tried that with your precious Vaspur. You're a scrawny, murderous fraud and you deserve every scar you have."

Several people near Scaurus scrambled away, afraid they might somehow be tainted by his sacrilege. Vaspur snarled. The guards, no longer grinning, hefted their spears in anger. The tribune set his hand to the hilt of his sword, but kept his eyes riveted on Zemarkhos. Confident in his own power, the priest gestured to his men again. They growled, but gave way.

"Very well, madman, let it be as you wish; you are as fit a subject as my other for the proof of Phos' power within me." Zemarkhos' eyes glittered with consuming hunger. As he measured Scaurus, his stare reminded the tribune of that of an old eagle, ready to stoop.

Then the zealot priest's eyebrows twitched, surprise returning humanity to his expression. "I know you," he rasped. "You are one of the barbarians who preferred the company of Vaspurakaners to my exposition of the truth. Your repentance will come late, but none the less certain for that."

"Of course I'd sooner have guested with them than with you. They're whole men, not twisted, venomous fanatics, 'hardhearted, stiff-necked, vain, and insane!'" Marcus quoted with insulting relish. The crowd gasped again; Zemarkhos jerked as if stung.

"'Whole men,' is it?" he returned. His stabbing finger darted at the Vaspurakaners he had slain. "There they lie, a mort of them, given over to death by Phos' just judgment."

"Horseshit. Any evil wizard could work the same, without taking Phos' mantle for himself in the bargain." The tribune sneered. "Phos' power! What nonsense! If you weren't so damned cruel, Zemarkhos, you'd be a joke, and a lame one at that. Go on, show everyone here Phos' power—if it comes through you, strike *me* dead with it."

"No need to beg," Zemarkhos said, his voice an eager whisper. "I will give you what you want." He did not move, but seemed nonetheless to grow taller behind the podium. Marcus could all but see the power he was summoning to himself. His eyes were two leaping back flames; his whole body quivered as he aimed his dart of malice.

His arm shot toward the tribune. Scaurus stumbled under the immaterial blow and wished for his *scutum* to hold up against it. His ears roared; his sight grew dark; agony filled his mind like the kiss of molten lead. He bit his lip till he tasted blood. Dimly he heard Zemarkhos' cackle of cruel, vaunting laughter.

But he held on to his sword, though he kept it in its sheath. Zemarkhos' fanatic zeal powered his magic to a strength to match any Marcus had seen since he came to Videssos, but the druids' charms were equal to it. "You'll have to do better than that," he called to Zemarkhos, and stood straight once more.

The hatred on the priest's face was frightening, making him into something hardly human. He gathered all his might within him and loosed it in a single blast of will. This time, though, the Gallic blade's ward spells were already alive and easily turned aside the thrust. Scaurus barely flinched.

The tribune stretched his mouth into a grin. "I don't think Phos is paying much attention to you," he said. "Try again—maybe he's doing something important instead."

The crowd muttered at his effrontery, but also at Zemarkhos' failure. The priest readied another curse, but Marcus saw in his eyes the beginning of doubt, sorcery's fatal foe. The third attack was the weakest; the tribune felt vague discomfort, but did not show it.

"There—do you see?" he shouted to the folk around him. "This old vulture tells lies with every breath he takes!" He forbore to mention that he would have been lying dead in the dirt without his sword's unseen protection.

"You have sold your soul to Skotos and stand under his shield!" Zemarkhos shrieked, his voice cracking. His harsh features were greasy with sweat; he panted like a soldier after an all-day battle.

That was a cry to get Scaurus mobbed, but he was ready for it. "Hear the desperate liar, grabbing at straws! Do you not teach, Zemarkhos, that Phos will beat Skotos in the end? Or are you a Balancer all of a sudden, one of those Khatrisher heretics who do not profess that good is stronger than evil?"

At another time, the expression the priest wore might have been funny. He had thrown charges of heresy past counting, but never expected to catch one, or to see his very piety discredited. "Kill him!" he started to scream to his guardsmen, but a cabbage flew out of the crowd and caught him in the side of the head, sending him sprawling off the podium. Not all of Amorion had enjoyed living under his religious tyranny.

Nor had all hated it, either; the cabbage-flinger went down with a shriek as the man in front of him whirled and stabbed him in the side.

He kicked savagely at the man he had knifed, then fell himself as the woman beside him smashed a clay water jug over his head.

"Dig up Zemarkhos' bones!" she screamed—the Videssian cry for riot. A hundred voices took up the call. A hundred more rose in horror, shouting, "Blasphemers! Heretic lovers!"

Zemarkhos scrambled to his feet. Two men rushed him, one swinging a chunk of firewood, the other barehanded. Growling horribly, Vaspur leaped for the first man's throat. He threw up his arms to protect himself. Vaspur tore them to the bone; the man dropped his club and fled, dripping blood. One of the priest's guards speared the unarmed man. He stared in amazement at the point in his belly, crumpled, and fell.

"Murderer! See the murderer!" that same woman cried. Her voice was loud and coarse as a donkey's bray and rang through the square. Before the guard could pull his pike free, she led the charge at him. He went down and did not get up. "Dig up Zemar—" Her cry was abruptly cut off as another guard reversed his spear and clubbed her with it. A moment later an uprooted paving stone dashed out his brains.

"Death to those who mock the Defender!" a wild-eyed youth shouted, and was fool enough to punch Marcus in his ironclad ribs. The tribune heard knuckles break. The young man howled. The tribune kicked him in the stomach before he could think of something worse to do; the youth folded up like a fan.

Armed, armored, and well-trained in the midst of rioting civilians, Scaurus enjoyed a tremendous edge. He swung his sword in great arcs, not so much to strike as to keep a little space around him. The sight of a yard of edged steel in the hands of someone who knew how to use it made even the most fiery zealot think twice. The tribune began slipping through the mob toward Gaius Philippus.

His worst worry was Zemarkhos' guardsmen, but the three or four of them still standing had all they could do holding the rioters back from their master. His curses now rained on the crowd that had followed him so long. But in civil strife as in battle, uproused passion went far to protect against magic. And as one intended victim after another did not drop, the priest's assurance failed him. He turned and fled, robe flapping about his shanks as he forced them into a hobbling run.

A fusillade of stones and rubbish followed him. Several missiles landed; he staggered and went to one knee. More struck the dog Vaspur. It howled and leaped as far as the chain Zemarkhos still held would let it. When the chain went taut the dog fell heavily, half-throttled.

Its snarl sent everyone close by scrambling back. The closest target for its fury was its master. Zemarkhos screamed "No!" as Vaspur sprang for him. The dog's teeth tore at his throat. The scream rose higher and shriller for a moment, then bubbled away to silence.

Zemarkhos' backers cried out in horror, but his foes raised a great hurrah. His death did nothing to end the riot. By then, everyone in the square had been hit from behind at least once and struck back blindly, keeping fights going and starting new ones. Some went through the crowd with more purpose, looking for old enemies to pay back.

The mob also began to realize no one would keep them from plundering whatever traders whose goods took their fancy. The first merchant's stall went over with a crash. Friends and foes of Zemarkhos forgot their quarrel and looted it together.

"Phos and no quarter!" bellowed a squat, brawny man in a butcher's leather apron. He rampaged through the crowd, heavy fists churning. Marcus wondered whose side he was on, and wondered if he knew himself.

Someone bludgeoned the tribune. His helmet took the worst of the blow, but he still staggered. He whirled by reflex and felt his sword bite. His attacker groaned, fell, and was trampled. He never did see the fellow.

Across the plaza, a disappointed looter cursed because all of a ring seller's best opals had already been stolen before he got a chance at them. "It's not fair!" he yelled, paying no attention to the jeweler who lay unconscious on the ground a few feet away, a thin stream of blood trickling down the side of his face.

"Cheer up," another man said. "There's bound to be better stuff in the merchants' tent city outside of town."

"You're right!" the first rioter exclaimed. "And most of those buggers are heretics or out-and-out heathens, so they must be fair game." He had been howling against Zemarkhos, but only because his brother-in-law had fallen victim to the priest. Now he filled his lungs and shouted, "Let's clean out those rich whoresons who come here just to cheat us every year!"

The cheers were like the baying of wolves. Brandishing torches and makeshift weapons, the mob streamed north through Amorion's streets, hot for loot. Most houses were slammed tight against the riot, but the tide of excitement swept more than a few men from them.

Marcus fought his way across the current toward Gaius Philippus. The veteran's *gladius* was in his scarred fist; his feet dangled outside the stirrups. Just before the tribune made it to him, a rioter tried to steal the roan he was leading. Disdaining the sword, the centurion raked out with his left foot. The nailed soles of his *caligae* shredded the Videssian's back. The man howled like a whipped dog; when he turned to run, Gaius Philippus sped him along with a well-aimed toe to the fundament.

As Scaurus mounted, the senior centurion scowled at him. He grumbled, "You could have waited a bit before you started the brawl. I might have had time for a quick one against the wall with that tart, but as soon as the ruction got going she ran off to lift whatever wasn't nailed down. Easier than friking, I suppose."

"Go howl." Marcus booted his horse forward. He took off his crested helmet and threw away his cape, trying to look as little like the man who had set Amorion aboil as he could.

It helped, but not as much as he wanted. "Pawn of Skotos!" an old bald man yelled, rushing at him with looted dagger in hand. But the tribune's horse was a trained war-beast from the imperial stables. It reared and struck out with iron-shod hooves. The man toppled, his knife flying through the air.

"This wretched slug I'm on would kill itself if it tried that," Gaius Philippus said envyingly. The gray was not at risk; one display was enough to make the rioters keep their distance. Undisturbed for the moment, the Romans rode the mob's current north.

"What now?" the senior centurion asked, shouting to be heard. "Back to Nakoleia?"

"I suppose so," Marcus said, but he still hesitated. "I do wish, though, I had a token to prove Zemarkhos dead."

"What are you going to do, go back and take his head so you can toss it at Thorisin's feet the way Avshar gave you Mavrikios'?" When Scaurus did not answer at once, Gaius Philippus turned astonished eyes on him. "By the gods, you're thinking of it!"

"Yes, I'm thinking of it," the tribune said heavily. "After all this, I'm damned if I'll leave Gavras any excuse for cheating me. I have to be sure he can't."

"He can if he wants to, anyway—that's what being Emperor is all about. All going back'll do is get you killed to no purpose." Gaius Philippus paused a moment. "Now you listen to me and see if I don't argue like some fool Greek sophist—shame Gorgidas isn't here to give me the horselaugh."

"Go on."

"All right, then. Without Zemarkhos, do you think this town can hold off the Yezda long? What'll *they* be doing? Sitting back with their thumbs up their arses? Not bloody likely. And even Thorisin can't help noticing them being here instead of that maniac in a blue robe."

"You're not wrong," Marcus had to admit. "Gavras won't thank us for giving them Amorion, though."

"Then why didn't he give *you* an army, to keep them out of it? You know the answer to that as well as I do." Gaius Philippus drew the edge of his hand across his throat. "You've done what he told you to; he can't complain over what happens next."

"Of course he can; you just showed me that yourself." But Marcus realized Gaius Philippus was right. Zemarkhos was done, and without troops the tribune could not help Amorion. "Very well, you have me. Let's get out while we can."

"Now you're talking." Gaius Philpus bullied a resentful lope out of his horse and slapped its bony flank when it tried to slack off. "Not this time, you don't." Soon he and Marcus were near the front of the mob. The centurion grinned maliciously at the rioters around them. "They'd best enjoy their loot while they can. The Yezda'll swarm down on 'em like flies on rotten meat."

"So they will." Marcus swore in sudden consternation. "And one of the ways they'll come swarming is out of the north, straight down the path we need to use."

"A pox! I hadn't thought of that. We were lucky when we got here, not seeing more than a few scattered bands." Gaius Philippus rubbed his scarred cheek. "And they'll be hot for plunder, too, when they come across us. Bad."

"Yes." Buildings were beginning to thin out as they got near the edge of town; like most cities in the once-secure Videssian westlands, Amorion had no wall. Ahead, Marcus could see the tents of wool, linen, and silk, the merchants' assembly that rose like mushrooms after a rain, only to disappear once the *panegyris* was over. "I have it!" he exclaimed, wits jogged by them. "Let's take that Tahmasp up on turning guardsman. There's booty in his caravan, aye, but only the biggest band of raiders would dare have a go at him. He'd bloody any smaller bunch."

"You've thrown a triple six!" Gaius Philippus said. "The very thing!" He bunched the thick muscles in his upper arms. "We may get to have another whack at these jackals around us, too. I wouldn't mind that one bit." Like most veteran soldiers, he loathed mobs, as much for their disorder as for their looting habits.

The tent city was already in an uproar when the Romans reached it. The first wave of rioters had come just ahead of them; they were running from one vendor to the next, snatching what they could. The buyers already there were catching the fever, too, and joining the mob. Several bodies, most of them locals, lay bleeding in the dirt.

But the mob's onset was not the only thing sowing confusion. Merchants were frantically shutting up displays, taking down tents, and loading everything onto their horses, donkeys, and camels. Some were nearly done; they must have started at first light, long before Scaurus touched off the scramble at Amorion.

"Now where was Tahmasp lurking?" Gaius Philippus growled. The Romans had counted on finding him by his main tent, which was an eye-searing saffron that had glowed even in the twilight of the night before. But it was already down.

"There, that way, I think," Marcus said pointing. "I remember that blue-and-white striped one wasn't far from him."

They rode forward. "Right you are," Gaius Philippus said, spotting the yellow canvas baled up on horseback. There was no sign of the caravan master, though traders who traveled with him were still dashing about finishing their packing.

Despite the chaos, the mob left Tahmasp's caravan alone. A good forty armored guardsmen, most of them mounted, formed a perimeter to daunt the most foolhardy rioters. Some had drawn bows, others carried spears or held sabers at the ready. They had the mongrel look of any such company, with no matching gear and men who ranged from a blond Haloga through Videssians and Makuraners to robed desert nomads and even a couple of Yezda. They were all scarred, several missing fingers or an ear, and probably four-fifths of them outlaws, but they looked like they could fight.

They bristled as the Romans approached. "Where's Tahmasp?" Marcus shouted to the man he figured for their leader, a short, dark, hatchet-faced Videssian who wore his wealth—his hands glittered with gold rings, his arms with heavy bracelets. His sword belt and scabbard were crusted with jewels, and the torque round his neck would have raised the envy of Viridovix or any Gallic chieftain. Baubles aside, he looked quick and dangerous.

"He's bloody well busy," he snapped. "What's it to you?"

Gaius Philippus spoke up, in piping falsetto: "Oh, the wicked fellow! He's got me in trouble, and my daddy's coming after him with an axe!" The guard chief's jaw dropped; several of his men doubled over in laughter. In normal tones, the centurion rasped, "Who are you, dung-heel, to keep people from him?"

The other purpled. Marcus said hastily, "He said for us to come see him if we were looking for spots in your troop. We are."

That got them a different kind of appraisal from Tahmasp's rough crew. Suddenly the gaudy little troop leader was all business. His darting black eyes inspected the puckered scar on the tribune's right forearm, his sleeveless mail shirt. "Funny gear," he muttered. He gave Gaius Philippus a hard once-over. "Well, maybe," he said. He called to the Haloga, "Go on, Njal, fetch the boss."

"What idiocy is this?" Tahmasp boomed as he came up at a heavy run. He glared at his guard chief. "This had better be good, Kamytzes. These boneheads with me this trip couldn't figure out how to put a prick where it goes, let alone—" He broke off, recognizing the Romans. "Ha! Done with your precious 'business,' are you?"

Somewhere behind Marcus, a rioter yelled as a merchant slammed a box closed on his hand. "You might say so," the tribune said.

Tahmasp's eyes glinted, but he rolled his shoulders in a massive shrug. "The fewer questions I ask, the fewer lies I get back. So you two want to join me, eh?" Receiving nods, he went on, "You've soldiered before—no, don't tell me about it; I'd sooner not know. That makes things easier. You know what orders are. Pay and all I told you about already. Steal, and we'll stomp you the first time; stomp you again, harder, and kick you out naked the next. Try and run out on us, and we'll kill you if we can. We don't like bandits planting spies."

"Fair enough," Marcus said. Gaius Philippus echoed him.

"Good." The caravaneer's bushy eyebrows went down as he frowned. "I forgot to ask—what do I call you?"

They gave their praenomens. "Never heard those before," Tahmasp said. "No matter. You, Markhos, from now on you are in Kamytzes' band. Once we are on the move, that is right flank guard. And you, Gheyus—" His Makuraner accent made the veteran's name a grunt. "—you belong to Muzaffar and left flank patrol." He pointed to a countryman of his, a tall, thin man with coal-black hair going gray at the temples and an aristocratic cast of features marred by a broken nose.

Tahmasp saw the Romans look at each other. He laughed until his big belly shook—not like so much jelly, as Balsamon's did, but like a boulder bouncing up and down. "I don't know you bastards," he pointed out. "Think I'll let you stay together and maybe plot who knows what? Not frigging likely."

He might not be a Videssian, Marcus thought, but his mind worked the same way. No help for it; taking precautions kept Tahmasp alive.

Gaius Philippus asked the caravaneer, "What's all your hurly-burly about? Seems you were going to get out even before the riot started—and 'most everybody else up here with you." As if to punctuate his words, another merchant company pulled away, the traders lashing their animals ahead. The lash fell on looters, too, driving them away with curses and yelps.

"I'd have to have my head stuffed up my backside to stay. A rider came in this morning with news of a thundering big army pushing east up the Ithome toward us. That says Yezda to me, and I'm not blockhead enough to sit still and wait for 'em."

"You called it," Scaurus said to Gaius Philippus. The approaching force had to be the nomads, he thought. Thorisin had hardly begun mobilizing when Marcus was expelled from the city; he doubted whether an imperial force could even have reached Garsavra.

"Enough of this jibber-jabber," Tahmasp declared. "We've got to get out of here fast, and standing around chinning don't help. Some of the stupid sods with me would hang around to sell a Yezda the sword he'd take their heads with the next second. Kamytzes, Muzaffar, these two are your headache now. If they give trouble, scrag 'em; we got on without 'em before, and I'll bet we can again." He turned and clumped away, shouting, "Isn't that bleeding tent down yet? Move it, you daft buggers!"

Kamytzes ordered Marcus forward with a brusque gesture. Muzaffar smiled at Gaius Philippus, his teeth white against swarthy skin. When he spoke, his voice was soft and musical: "Tell me, what do you call that steed of yours?"

"This maundering old wreck? The worst I can think of."

"A man of discernment, I see. That would seem none too good." He beckoned to the veteran to join him. "If you are one of us, you are facing the wrong way."

Tahmasp's caravan pulled out less than an hour after the Romans took service with him. Forty guards seemed an impressive force when the caravan was gathered together, but, even eked out by merchants, grooms, and servants, they were pitifully few once it stretched itself along the road. Divided into three-man squads, Kamytzes' troop patrolled its side of the long row of wagons, carts, and beasts of burden, while Muzaffar's took the other.

Marcus looked for Gaius Philippus, but could not see him.

What might have been a bad moment came just outside Amorion, when the rioters were still thick as fleas on a dog. A double handful of them attacked Scaurus and the squadmates he had been assigned, Njal the Haloga and a lean, sun-baked desert nomad who spoke no Videssian at all. The tribune heard his name was Wathiq.

Some of the looters tried to keep the guards in play while the rest went for the donkeys behind them. Against their own kind, the simple plan would have worked. But Njal, wielding his axe with a surgeon's precision, sliced off one rioter's ear and sent him running away shrieking and spurting blood. Marcus cut down another before the fellow could jump in to hamstring his horse. Wathiq turned in the saddle and shot one of the men who had run past them in the back. The rioters gave it up as a bad job and fled, while the three professionals grinned at each other.

Njal and Wathiq could talk to each other after a fashion in broken Makuraner. Through the Haloga, the tribune learned Wathiq had backed the wrong prince in a tribal feud and had to flee. Njal himself was exiled for being too poor to pay blood-price over a man he had killed. Scaurus gave out that he was a wandering mercenary down on his luck, a story the other two accepted without comment. He had no idea whether they believed him.

The Roman thought nothing of it when Tahmasp led his charges west; with enemies coming from the opposite direction, he would have gone the same way to get maneuvering room.

They camped by the Ithome. With summer's heat drawing near, the river was already low in its bed, but it would flow the year around. On the parched central plateau, that made it more precious than rubies.

Each squad of guards shared a tent; Marcus gave up the idea of any private planning with Gaius Philippus. Still, he thought, with Latin between them, their talk would be safe enough from prying ears. But when he went looking for the centurion at the cookfires, he discovered his comrade's squad had picket duty the first watch of the night. Kamytzes had given him, Wathiq, and Njal the mid-watch. From what he had seen of Tahmasp's methods, he suspected that was no accident.

The blocky caravaneer hired the best, though. His cook somehow managed a savory stew out of travelers' fare of smoked meats, shelled grain, chick-peas, and onions. The very smell of it had more substance than the thin, sorry stuff Thorisin Gavras' jailers had dished out.

The tribune settled down by a fire to enjoy the stew, but before he got the spoon to his lips, one of the other guardsmen stumbled over him. Marcus' bowl went flying. The trooper was a Videssian, thicker through the shoulders than most imperials, with a gold hoop dangling piratically from his left ear. "Sorry," he said, but his mocking grin made him out a liar.

"You clumsy—" Marcus began, but then he saw the rest of the guards watching him expectantly and understood. Any new recruit could look forward to a hazing before veterans would accept him.

His tormentor loomed over him, fists bunched in anticipation. Without standing up, the tribune hooked his foot back of the other's ankle. The Videssian went down with a roar of rage; Scaurus sprang on top of him.

"No knives!" Kamytzes shouted. "Draw one, and it's the last thing you'll do!"

The two fighters rolled in the dirt, pummeling each other. The Videssian rammed a knee at Marcus' groin. He twisted aside just enough to take it on the point of the hip. He grabbed his opponent's beard and pulled his face down into the dust. When the other tried for a like hold on him, his hand slipped off the tribune's bare chin.

"Ha!" someone exclaimed. "Some point to this shaving business after all."

The Roman saw sparks when the guard's fist smashed into his nose. Blood streamed down his face; he gulped air through his mouth. He punched the Videssian in the belly. The fellow was so muscular it was like hitting a slab of wood, but one of the tribune's blows caught him in that vulnerable spot at the pit of the stomach. The guard folded up, the fight forgotten as he struggled to breathe.

Marcus climbed to his feet, gingerly feeling his nose. There was no grate of bone, he noted with relief, but it was already swelling. His voice sounded strange as he asked Kamytzes, "Have I passed, or is there more?"

"You'll do," the little captain said. He nodded at the tribune's foe, who was finally starting to do more than gasp. "Byzos there is no lightweight."

"Too true," Scaurus agreed, touching his nose again. He helped Byzos up and was not sorry to see he had scraped a good piece of hide off the Videssian's cheek. But the guard took his hand when he offered it. The fight had been fair and was no tougher an initiation rite, the tribune decided, than the branding that sealed a man to a Roman legion.

"Pay up, chief," one of the guards said. Kamytzes, looking sour, pulled off a ring and gave it to him.

Marcus frowned, not caring to have his new commander resentful at having lost money on account of him. "If you want to get your own back," he said, "bet on my friend Gaius when his turn comes after he gets off watch."

"With his head full of gray?" Kamytzes stared. "He's an old man."

"Don't let him hear you say that," the tribune said. "Tell you what; make your bets. If you lose, I'll make them good for you—and here are your witnesses to see I said so."

"The bigger fool you, but I'm glad to take you up on it. Never turn down free money or a free woman, my father always told me, and money won't give you the clap."

When the squad rode out on picket duty, Njal said, "You'd best be richer t'an you look, outlander. T'at Kamytzes, he might almost be a Namdalener for gambling." He said something to Wathiq, who nodded vigorously and pantomimed a man rolling dice.

"I'm not worried," Marcus said, and hoped he meant it.

The watch passed without incident; only the buzz of insects and a nightjar's chuckling call broke the stillness. Videssos' constellations, still alien to the tribune after nearly four years, rolled slowly across the heavens. Making idle talk with Njal, he learned the Halogai recognized constellations altogether different from the patterns the imperials saw in the sky. Wathiq, it turned out, had another set still.

It seemed a very long time before the late-watch squad came to relieve them. They shook their heads when Scaurus asked whether they knew how Gaius Philippus had done. "We sacked out soon as our tent was up," one said for all. "Take more than a brawl to wake us, too—hate this bloody last watch of the night."

As Marcus was yawning himself, he could hardly argue. Back at the camp, the fires had died into embers; even gossipers and men who had stayed up for a last cup or two of wine were long since abed. "Come morning you'll know," Njal consoled Scaurus as they slid into their bedrolls. The tribune fell asleep in the middle of a grumble.

Tahmasp announced the dawn not with trumpets, but with a nomad-style drum whose deep, bone-jarring beat tumbled men out of bed like an earthquake. Bleary-eyed, Marcus splashed water on his face and groped for his tunic. He was still mouth-breathing; his nose felt twice its proper size.

After the sweaty closeness of the tent, the smell of wheatcakes sizzling was doubly inviting. Marcus stole one from the griddle with his dagger, then tossed it up and down till it was cool enough to hold. He devoured it, ignoring the cook's curses. It was delicious.

A nudge in the ribs made him whirl. There stood Kamytzes, looking like a fox who had just cleaned out a henhouse. The troop leader handed him a couple of pieces of silver. "I made plenty more," he said, "but this for the tip."

"Thanks." Marcus pocketed the coins. He looked round for Gaius Philippus, but Muzaffar's half of the guard troop was billeted at the far end of the camp. Turning back to Kamytzes, he asked, "How did he do it?"

"They picked a big hulking bruiser to go at him, all muscles and no sense. From the way he came swaggering over, a blind idiot would have known what he had in mind. Your friend hadn't had time to sit down to his supper yet. He made as if he didn't notice what was going on until the lout was almost on top of him. Then he spun on his heel, cold-cocked the bugger, dragged him over to the latrine trench, and dropped him in—feet first; he didn't want to drown him. After that he got his stew and ate."

Scaurus nodded; the encounter had the earmarks of the senior centurion's efficiency. "Did he say anything?" he asked Kamytzes.

"I was coming to that." The cocky officer's eyes gleamed with amusement. "After a couple of bites he looked up and said to nobody in particular, 'If anything like that happens again, I may have to get annoyed.' "

"Sounds like him. I doubt he need worry much."

"So do I." Filching a wheatcake the same way Marcus had, Kamytzes bustled away to help Tahmasp get the caravan moving.

They were on the road by an hour and a half after sunrise—not up to the standard of the legions, but good time, the tribune thought, for a private band of adventurers. Tahmasp went up and down the line of merchants who traveled with him, blasphemously urging them to keep up. "What do you think you are, a eunuch in a sedan chair?" he roared at one who was too slow to suit him. "You move like that, we'll fornicating well go on without you. See how fast you'll run with Yezda on your tail!" The trader mended his pace; the caravaneer had no more potent threat than leaving him behind.

As they had the day before, they traveled west. Marcus waved to Tahmasp as he came by on his unceasing round of inspections. "What is it?" the flamboyant caravaneer asked genially. "Kamytzes tells me you carved yourself a place," he said, chuckling, "though you'll not gain favor by making your nose as big as mine."

"As I wasn't born with it that way, I'll be as glad when it's not," the tribune retorted. Happy to find Tahmasp in a good mood, he asked when the caravan would swing north toward the Empire's ports on the coast of the Videssian Sea.

Tahmasp dug a finger in his ear to make sure he had heard correctly. Then he threw back his head and laughed till tears streamed down his leathery cheeks. "North? Who's ever said a word about north? You poor, stupid, sorry son of a whore, it's Mashiz I'm bound for, not your piss-pot ports. Mashiz!" He almost choked with glee. "I hope you enjoy the trip."

VIII

"Surrender!" Lankinos Skylitzes bawled up to the Yezda officer atop the mud-brick wall.

The Yezda put his hands on his hips and laughed. "I'd like to see you make me," he said. He spat at the Videssian, who was interpreting for Arigh.

"Och, will you hear the filthy man, now?" Viridovix said. He shook his fist at the Yezda. "Come down here and be doing that, you black-hearted omadhaun!"

"Make me," the officer repeated, still laughing. He gestured to the squad of archers beside him. They drew their double-curved bows back to their ears. The sun glinted off iron chisel-points; to Gorgidas every shaft seemed aimed straight at him. The Yezda said, "This parley is over. Pull back, or I will fire on you. Fight or not, just as you please."

To give the warning teeth, one of the nomads put an arrow in the dirt a couple of feet in front of Arigh's pony. He sat motionless, staring up at the Yezda, daring them to shoot. After a full minute, he nodded to his party and made a deliberate turn to show the town garrison his back. He and his comrades slowly rode off.

The moment they left the shade of the wall, the blasting heat of the river-plain summer hit them once more with its full power. Viridovix wore an ugly hat of woven straw to protect his fair skin from the sun, but he was red and peeling even so. The sweat that streamed down his face stung like vinegar. Armor was a chafing torment no amount of bathing could ease.

Arigh cursed in a low monotone until they were well away from the city, not wanting to give the Yezda officer the satisfaction of knowing his anger. The drawn-up lines of his army, banners moving sluggishly in the sweltering air, made a brave show. But without the siege train they did not have, assaulting a walled town with ready defenders would cost more than they could afford to lose.

"May the wind spirits blow that dog's ghost so far it never finds its way home to be reborn," Arigh burst out at last, bringing his fist down on his thigh in frustration. "It galls me past words not to watch him drown in his own blood for his insolence, crying defiance at me with his stinking couple of hundred men."

"The trouble is, he knows what he's about," Pikridios Goudeles said. "We haven't the ladders to go at the walls of this miserable, overgrown village, whatever its name is—"

"Erekh," Skylitzes put in.

"A fitting noise for a nauseating town. In any case, we don't have the ladders and we can't do much of a job making them because the only trees in this bake-oven of a country are date palms, with worthless wood. To say nothing of the fact that if we sit down in front of a city instead of staying on the move, all the Yezda garrisons hereabouts will converge on us instead of each one being pinned down to protect its own base."

"Are you a general now?" Arigh snarled, but he could not argue against the pen-pusher's logic. "This will cost us," he said darkly. When he drew closer to his assembled soldiers, he waved to the southwest and yelled, "We ride on!"

He gave the order first in the Arshaum speech for his own men, then in Videssian so Narbas Kios could translate it into Vaspurakaner for the Erzrumi. The mountaineers' ranks stirred; it would have taken a deaf man to miss their resentful mutters. Some of the Erzrumi were not muttering. Part of the Mzeshi contingent shouted their fury at the Arshaum chief and at those of their own leaders content to remain with the plainsmen.

One of their officers advanced on Arigh. Dark face suffused with rage, he roared something at the Arshaum in his own strange language, then brought himself under enough control to remember his Vaspurakaner. His accent was atrocious; Narbas Kios frowned, trying to be sure he understood. At last he said, "He calls you a man of little spirit." From the savage scowl on the Mzeshi's face, Gorgidas was sure Narbas was shading the translation. The trooper went on, "He says he came to fight, and you run away. He came for loot, and has won a few brass trinkets his own smiths would be ashamed of. He says he was tricked, and he is going home."

"Wait," Arigh said through the Videssian soldier. He went through Goudeles' arguments all but unchanged, and added, "We are still unbeaten, and Mashiz still lies ahead. That has been our goal all along; stay and help us win it."

The Mzeshi frowned in concentration. Gorgidas thought he was considering what Arigh had said, but then he loudly broke wind. His face cleared.

"Not the most eloquent reply, but one of unmistakable meaning," Goudeles remarked with diplomatic aplomb.

Smirking triumphantly, the officer trotted back to his followers and harangued them for a few minutes. They shouted their agreement, brandishing lances and swords. Their harness and chain mail jingled as they pulled away from their countrymen and started back to their mountain home. Several individual horsemen peeled away from the remaining men of Mzeh to join them.

Arigh had his impassivity back as they began to grow small against the sky. "I wonder who the next ones to give up will be," he said. Already a good third of the Erzrumi had abandoned the campaign and turned back.

Viridovix blew a long, glum breath through his mustaches. "And it all started out so simple, too," he said. Fanning out as they crossed the Tutub, the Arshaum had fallen on three or four towns before startled defenders realized an enemy was loose among the Hundred Cities. It was as easy as riding through open gates; there was next to no fighting and, in spite of Mzeshi complaints, they came away with their horses festooned with booty.

But it had not stayed easy long. Not only were the cities shut up against attack, Yezda raiders began the hit-and-run warfare they shared with the Arshaum. Two scouts were ambushed here, a forager there. The Yezda lost men, too, but they had the resources of a country to draw on. Arigh did not.

He gave his commands to the *naccara* drummer, who boomed them out for the whole army to hear. It shifted into traveling order, with what was left of the Erzrumi heavy cavalry in a long column in the center, flanked and screened by the Arshaum.

Gorgidas rode with Rakio, near the front of the Erzrumi formation. Most of the Sworn Fellowship was hurrying back to the Yrmido country; Khilleu did not relish giving up the campaign, but he did not dare leave his land unprotected when his unfriendly neighbors were going home. A fair number of "orphans" and a handful of pairs, mostly older men, stayed on.

The physician flattered himself that Rakio was still with the army for his sake. Certainly the Yrmido found no delight in the journey itself. "What strange country this is," he said. He pointed. "What is that little hill, out of the flat plain rising? Several of them I have seen here."

Gorgidas followed his pointing finger. It was truly not much of a hill, perhaps not even as tall as the walls around Videssos, but in the dead-flat river plain it stood out like a mountain, springing up so abruptly he did not think it could be natural.

Having no idea how it came about, he poised tablet and stylus before he called out the question to whoever might hear it. Skylitzes was not far away, talking with Vakhtang of Gunib. He raised his head. "It's the funeral marker for a dead town," he told the Greek. "You've seen how they build with mud brick hereabouts. They have to; it's all there is in this country. No stone here to speak of, Phos knows. The stuff is flimsy, and the people don't care for work any more than they do anywhere else. When a house or a tavern falls down, they rebuild on top of the rubble. Do it enough times, and there's your hillock. That should be plain to anyone, I'd think."

Gorgidas scowled at the officer's patronizing tone. Skylitzes let out one of his rare, short laughs. "See how it feels to get a lecture instead of giving one," he said. Ears burning, Gorgidas quickly stowed his tablet.

Rakio did not notice his lover's discomfiture; he was still complaining about the countryside. "It looks like it leprosy has. What parts are in crop seem rich enough, but there are so many patches of desert, ugly and useless both."

Overhearing him, Skylitzes said, "Those are new; blame the Yezda for them. They made them by—"

"Destroying the local irrigation works," Gorgidas interrupted. He was not about to have his self-esteem tweaked twice running. "Without the Tutub and the Tib, this whole land would be waste. It only grows where their waters reach. But the Yezda are nomads—what do they care about crops? Their herds can live on thorns and thistles, and if they starve away the farmers here, so much the better for them."

"Just what I would have said," Skylitzes said, adding, "but at twice the length."

"What are you arguing about?" Vakhtang demanded in the plains speech. When Skylitzes had translated, the Erzrumi advised Gorgidas, "Pay no attention to him. I have not known him long, but I see he bites every word to test it before he lets it out."

"Better that way than the flood of drivel Goudeles spouts," the officer said, not missing the chance to score off the man who was a political rival back in Videssos.

Vakhtang, though, favored the bureaucrat's more florid style of oratory. "Meaning can disappear with not enough words as well as from too many."

They hashed it back and forth the rest of the day as they rode through farmland and desert. It made for a good argument; there were points on both sides, but it was not important enough for anyone to take very seriously.

With empty fields all around, Gorgidas forgot he was at war. Rakio, though, knew at a glance what that emptiness meant. "They hide from us," he said. "Peasants always do. In a week come, and the fields will be full of farmers."

"No doubt you're right," the Greek sighed. It saddened him to think that to the locals he was only another invader.

"Yezda!" The peasant was short, stooped, and naked, with great staring eyes. He pointed to an artificial mound on the southern horizon, larger and better-preserved than the one Rakio had noticed a couple of days before. He rapidly opened and closed his hands several times to show that they were numerous.

Arigh frowned. "Our scouts saw nothing there this morning." He glanced at the native, who repeated his gestures. "I wish you spoke a language some one of us could follow." But the farmer had only the guttural tongue of the Hundred Cities, reduced to a patois by centuries of subjection to Makuran and the Yezda.

He smiled ingratiatingly at the Arshaum chief, pantomiming riders going up to tether their horses in the ruins. He pointed to the sun, waved it through the sky backwards. "This was yesterday?" Arigh asked. The local shrugged, not understanding. "Worth another look," Arigh decided. He ordered a halt and sent a squad of riders out to examine the hillock.

It was nearly twilight when they came back. "Nothing around there," their leader told Arigh angrily. "No tracks, no horseturds, no signs of fire, nothing."

The peasant read the scout's voice and fell to his knees in the dirt in front of Arigh. He was shaking with fear, but kept stubbornly pointing south. "What's he sniveling about?" Gorgidas asked, walking up after seeing to his pony.

"He claims there are soldiers up on that hillock there, but he lies," the Arshaum answered. "He's cost us hours with his nonsense; I ought to cut off his ears for him for that." He gestured so the native would understand. The local cringed and went flat on his belly, wailing out something in his own language.

Gorgidas scratched his head. "Why would he put himself in danger to lie to you? He has no reason to love the Yezda; see how well he lives under them." Every rib of the farmer's body was plainly visible beneath his dirty skin. "Maybe he's just trying to do you a favor." The Greek wanted to believe that; he did not like being put on the same level as the Yezda.

"Where are the warriors, then?" Arigh demanded, putting his hands on his hips. "If you tell me my scouts are going blind, you might as well cut your own throat now."

"Blind? Hardly—we'd be dead ten times over if they were. But still . . ." He eyed the peasant, who had given up moaning and was gazing at him in mute appeal. The physician's trained glance caught the faint cloudiness of an early cataract in the man's left eye. His mind made a sudden leap. "Not blind—but blinded? Magic could hide soldiers better than rubble or brush."

"That is a thought," Arigh admitted. "If I'd taken this lout—" He stirred the peasant with his foot; the fellow groaned and covered his face, expecting to die the next instant. "—more seriously, I'd have sent a shaman to smell the place out." He became the brisk commander once more. "All right, you've made your point. Get Tolui and round up a company of men, then go find out what's going on."

"Me?" the Greek said in dismay.

"You. This is your idea. Ride it or fall off. Otherwise I have no choice but to think Manure-foot here a spy, don't I?"

Arigh, Gorgidas thought, was getting uncomfortably good at making people do what he wanted. "A concealment spell?" Tolui said when the doctor found the shaman eating curded mares' milk. "You could well be right. That's not battle magic; whoever cast it could not mind if it fell apart as soon as his men burst from ambush."

He drew his tunic over his head and undid the drawstring of his trousers with a sigh. "In this weather the mask is a torment, and the robe is of thick suede. Ah, well, better by night than by day."

"Round up a company," Arigh had said, but Gorgidas had no authority over the nomads, who did not fancy taking orders from an outsider. Tolui's presence finally helped the Greek persuade a captain of a hundred to lead out his command. "A hunt for a ghost stag, is it?" the officer said sourly. He was a broken-nosed man named Karaton, whose high voice ruined the air of sullen ferocity he tried to assume.

His men grumbled as they wolfed down their food and resaddled their horses. Karaton worked off his annoyance by swearing at Gorgidas when the physician was the last one ready. Still, it was not quite dark when they rode for the mound that had once been a city.

Rakio caught up with them halfway there. He gave Gorgidas a reproachful look as he trotted up beside him. "If you go to fight, why not me tell?"

"Sorry," the physician muttered. In fact he had not thought of it; he always had to remind himself that his comrades did not share his distaste for combat. Rakio was as eager as Viridovix once had been.

The hillock was ghostly by moonlight. Atop it Gorgidas could see stretches of wall still untumbled; his mind's eye summoned up a time when all the brickwork was whole and the streets swarming with perfumed men dressed in long tunics and carrying walking sticks, with veiled women, their figures robed against strangers' glances. The place would have echoed with jangling music and loud, happy talk. It was silent now. Not even night birds sang.

Like a good soldier, Karaton automatically sent his men to surround the base of the hill, but his heart was not in it. He waved sarcastically. "Ten thousand hiding up there, at least."

"Oh, stop squeaking at me," Gorgidas snapped, wishing he had never set eyes on the peasant in the first place. He hated looking the fool. In his self-annoyance he did not notice Karaton stiffen with outrage and half draw his saber.

"Stop, both of you," Tolui said. "I must have harmony around me if the spirits are to answer my summons." There was not a word of truth in that, but it gave both men a decent excuse not to quarrel.

Karaton subsided with a growl. "Why call the spirits, shaman? A child of four could tell you this place is dead as a sheepskin coat."

"Then fetch a child of four next time and leave me in peace," Tolui said. Echoing from behind the devil-mask he wore, his voice carried an otherworldly authority. Karaton touched a finger to his forehead in apology.

Tolui drew from his saddlebag a flat, murkily transparent slab of some waxy stone, which was transfixed by a thick needle of a different stone. "Chalcedony and emery," he explained to Gorgidas. "The hardness of the emery lets a man peering through the clear chalcedony pierce most illusions."

"Give it to me," Karaton said impatiently. He squinted up to the top of the mound. "Nothing," he said—but was there doubt in his voice? Tolui took the seeing-stone back and handed it to Gorgidas. Things at the crown of the hillock seemed to jump when he put it to his eye, but steadied quickly.

"I don't know," he said at last. "There was a flicker, but . . ." He offered the stone to Tolui. "See for yourself. The toy is yours, after all; you should be able to use it best."

The shaman lifted the mask from his head and set it on his knee. He raised the stone and gazed through it for more than a minute. Gorgidas felt the backwash of his concentration as he channeled his vision to penetrate semblance and see truth.

The physician had never thought much about Tolui's power as a sorcerer. If anything, he assumed the shaman was of no great strength, as he had been second to Onogun until Bogoraz poisoned Arghun's old wizard because he favored Videssos. Since then Tolui's magic had always been adequate, but the Greek, not seeing him truly tested, went on reckoning him no more than a hedge-wizard mainly interested in herbs, roots, and petty divinations.

He abruptly realized he had misjudged the shaman. When Tolui cried, "Wind spirits, come to my aid! Blow away the cobwebs of enchantment before me!" the night seemed to hold its breath.

A howling rose above the hillock, as of a storm, but no wind buffeted Gorgidas' face. Then Karaton shouted in amazement while his men drew bows and bared swords. Like a curtain whisked away from in front of a puppet-theater's stage, the illusion of emptiness at the crest of the hill was swept aside. Half a dozen campfires blazed among the ruins, with warriors sprawled around them at their ease.

The first arrows were in the air before Karaton could give the order to shoot. A Yezda pitched forward into one of the fires; another screamed as he was hit. A different scream went up, too, this one of fury, as the pair of wizards with the enemy felt their covering glamour snatched away.

"Up and take them!" Karaton yelled. "Quick, before they get their wits about them and go for weapons and armor!"

Shouting to demoralize the Yezda further, his men drove their ponies up the steep sides of the hill, then dismounted and scrambled toward the top on foot. Gorgidas and Rakio were with them, grabbing at shrubs or chunks of brick for handholds. Looking up toward the crest, the Greek saw the campfires and running figures of the Yezda shimmer and start to fade as their sorcerers tried to bring down the veil once more. But Tolui was still working against them, and the fear and excitement of their own men and the Arshaum ate at their magic as well. The fires brightened again.

A pony thundered downhill past Gorgidas. A daredevil Yezda, seeing his only road to safety, took that mad plunge in the dark and lived to tell of it. His horse reached level ground and streaked away. "That is a rider!" Rakio exclaimed. A crash and a pair of shrieks, one human, the other from a mortally injured pony, told of a horseman who tried the plummet and failed.

Several more mounted Yezda broke out down the path they would have taken to attack the Arshaum army. Most, though, stunned by the unexpected night assault, were still throwing saddles on their beasts or groping for sabers when Karaton's men reached them.

As he gained the top of the mound, Gorgidas stumbled over an upthrust tile. An arrow splintered against masonry not far from his head. Rakio hauled him to his feet. "You crazy are?" he shouted in the Greek's ear. "Get out your sword."

"Huh? Oh, yes, of course," Gorgidas said mildly, as if being reminded of some small blunder in a classroom. Then a Yezda was in front of him, shamshir whistling at his head. He had no room for fine footwork. He parried the stroke, then another that would have gutted him. The Yezda feinted low, slashed high. Gorgidas did not feel the sting of the blade, but warm stickiness ran down the side of his neck, and he realized his ear had been cut.

He thrust at the Yezda, who blocked and fell back awkwardly, confused by the unfamiliar stroke. Gorgidas lunged. At full extension he had a much longer reach than the nomad thought possible. His *gladius* pierced the Yezda's belly. The man groaned and folded up on himself.

Most of the enemy, outnumbered two to one, drew back for a stand at a small courtyard whose ruined walls were still breast high. The Arshaum hacked at them over the bulwark and sent arrows and stones into their crowded ranks. Unable to stand that punishment for long, the Yezda surged out again and with the strength of desperation broke through their foes' lines. Karaton squalled in outrage as Yezda hurled themselves down the hillside with no thought for broken bones or anything but escape.

Only a few got that far; the Arshaum cut down the greater part of them as they fled. One of the Yezda wizards, a shaman in robes hardly less fringed than Tolui's, fell in that mad chase, a sword in his hand in place of the magic that had failed him.

The other sorcerer was made of different, and harsher, stuff. Gorgidas thought he saw motion down a narrow alleyway and called out in the Arshaum tongue, "Friend?" He got no answer. *Gladius* at the ready, he stepped into the rubble-choked lane.

A campfire flared behind him. The sudden brightness showed him that the alley was blind—and that it trapped no ordinary Yezda. For a moment the red robe and jagged tonsure meant nothing to the physician. Then ice walked up his spine as he recognized Skotos' emblems.

The wizard's face, Gorgidas thought, would have revealed his nature even in the absence of other signs. A man who knows both good and evil and with deliberate purpose chooses the latter will bear its mark. The eyes of the dark god's votary gave back the fire like a wolf's. The skin was drawn taut on his cheeks and at the corners of his mouth, pulling his lips back in a snarl of hate. But it was not directed at the Greek; he was sure the wizard wore it awake and asleep.

The physician edged forward. He saw the other had only a short dagger at his belt. "Yield," he called in Videssian and the Khamorth tongue. "I would not slay you out of hand."

As it focused on Gorgidas, the wizard's sneer tightened. His hands darted out, his lips twisted in soundless invocation. Mortal fear lent his spell force enough to strike despite the chaos of battle. Gorgidas staggered, as if clubbed from behind. His sight swam; his arms and legs would not answer; the sword fell from his hand. The air rasped harshly in his throat as he struggled to breathe. He slipped to one knee, shaking his head over and over to try to clear it.

The spell had been meant to kill; perhaps only the discipline of the healer's art gave the Greek strength of will enough to withstand it even in part. He was groping for his blade as the sorcerer came up to him. The dagger gleamed in the wizard's hand, long enough to reach a man's heart.

The wizard knelt for the killing stab, a vulpine smile stretched over his lean features. Gorgidas heard a dull thud. He thought it was the sound of the knife entering his body. But the Yezda sorcerer reeled away with a muffled grunt of pain. The power of the spell vanished as his concentration snapped.

Gorgidas sprang for the wizard, but someone hurtled by him. A sword bit with a meaty thunk. The Yezda thrashed and lay still; Gorgidas smelled his bowels let go in death.

"You crazy are," Rakio said, wiping his blade on his sleeve. It was statement this time, not question. He seized the Greek by the shoulders. "Are you too stupid not to go wandering away from help and get caught alone?"

"So it would seem. I'm new to this business of war and don't do the right thing without thinking," Gorgidas said. He drew Rakio into a brief embrace and touched his cheek. "I'm glad you were close by, to keep me from paying the price of my mistake."

"I would want you for me to do the same," the Yrmido said, "but would you be able?"

"I hope so," Gorgidas said. But that was no good answer, and he knew it. They heard an Arshaum shout not far away and rushed to his aid together.

Fewer than half the Yezda managed to get away or to hide well enough in the ruins to escape their enemies' search. The rest, but for a couple saved to question later, were cut down; the Arshaum captured a good three dozen horses. The cost was seven dead and twice that many wounded.

"That was a true lead," Karaton said to Gorgidas, the nearest thing to an apology he would give a non-Arshaum. He lay on his belly while the Greek stitched up a gash on the back of his calf. The wound was deep, but luckily ran along the muscle instead of across it; it did not hamstring him. A clean, freely bleeding cut, it did not require the healing art to mend.

Karaton did not flinch as the needle entered his flesh again and again, or even when the physician poured an antiseptic lotion of alum, verdigris, pitch, resin, vinegar, and oil into the wound. "You should have kept that wizard of theirs alive," the commander of a hundred went on, his tone perfectly conversational. "He would have been able to tell us more than these no-account warriors we have." Without liking the man, the Greek had to admire his fortitude.

"I was almost sorry for having lived through the encounter myself," he told Viridovix much later that night. The Celt was yawning, but Gorgidas was still too keyed up to sleep. Having seen the peasant who had warned them loaded with gold and sent home, he kept hashing over the fight.

“The shindy would’ve been easier for you lads, I’m thinking, were you after having me along,” Viridovix interrupted. Most times he would have heard his friend out gladly, but his eyes were heavy as two balls of stone in his head.

“Aye, no doubt you would have stomped the hill flat with one kick and saved us the trouble of fighting,” Gorgidas said tartly. “I thought you over your juvenile love for bloodletting.”

“That I am,” the Gaul said. “But for one who prides himself on the wits of him, you’ve no call to be twitting me. If it was magic you suspected, now, couldna this glaive o’ mine ha’ pierced it outen the folderol and all puir Tolui went through?”

“A plague! I should have thought of that.” Hardly anything annoyed Gorgidas worse than Viridovix coming up with something he had missed. Sitting back combing his mustaches with his fingers, the Celt looked so smug Gorgidas wanted to punch him.

“Dinna fash yoursel’ so,” he said, chuckling. “Forbye, you won and got back safe, the which was the point of it all.” He laid a large hand on the Greek’s shoulder.

Gorgidas started to shrug it away in anger, but had a better idea. He gave a rueful laugh and said, “You’re right, of course. I wasn’t very clever, was I?” Viridovix’ baffled expression made a fair revenge.

The Yezda band slashed through Arigh’s cavalry screen, poured arrows into the Erzrumi still with his army, and fled before the slower-moving mountaineers could come to grips with them. Arshaum chased the marauders through the fields. Wounded men reeled in the saddle; as Gorgidas watched, one lost his seat and crashed headlong into the trampled barley. The locals, he thought, would find the corpse small compensation for the hunger those swathes of destruction would bring come winter.

As the last of the Yezda were ridden down or got away, their pursuers returned. A couple led new horses, while more showed off swords, boots, and other bits of plunder. Even so, Viridovix clucked his tongue in distress over the skirmish. “Och, the more o’ the Hundred Cities we’re after passing, the bolder these Yezda cullions get. ’Tis nobbut a running fight the last two days, and always the Erzrumi they’re for hitting.”

"It works, too." Gloom made Pikridios Goudeles unusually forthright. Of the hillmen, all had seen enough of the lowlands, but for a couple of hundred adventurers from various clans and Gashvili's sturdy band, who still reckoned themselves bound by oath. Casualties and desertions reduced their count by a few every day.

"Tomorrow will be worse," Skylitzes said. Hard times loosened his tongue as they checked Goudeles'. "The Yezda have our measure now. They know which towns we can reach and which are safe from us. The garrisons are coming out to reinforce the bushwhackers who've dogged us all along."

Viridovix did not like the conclusion he reached. "We'll be fair nibbled to death, then, before too long. We havena the men to spare."

"We should have," Goudeles said. "But for the mischance of battle on the steppe and for the squabbles among the Arshaum themselves, we would be twice our present numbers."

Skylitzes said, "I served under Nephon Khoumnos once, and he was always saying, 'If ifs and buts were candied nuts, then everyone would be fat.'" His eyes traveled to Goudeles' belly. "Maybe he was thinking of you."

Reminding the bureaucrat of their political rivalry back in Videssos proved unwise. "Maybe," Goudeles said shortly. "I'm sure the good general's philosophy is a great consolation to him now."

Appalled silence fell. Avshar's wizardry had killed Khoumnos at Maragha. Goudeles reddened, knowing he had gone too far. He hurriedly changed the subject. "We'd also be better off if the Erzrumi had not proved summer soldiers, going home when things turned rough."

Some truth lay in that, but after his gaffe his companions were not ready to let him off so easily. "That is unjust," Gorgidas said, doubly irritated because of the implied slur on Rakio's countrymen. "They came to fight for themselves, not for us, and we've seen how the Yezda keep singling them out for special attention."

"Aye; to make them give up." Goudeles was not about to abandon his point. "But when they do, they get off easy while we pay the price of their running out. Deny it if you can." No one did.

Gorgidas' side of the argument, though, received unpleasant confirmation later that afternoon. The bodies of several Erzrumi who had been captured in a raid the week before were hung on spears in Arigh's line of march. With the time to work on them, the Yezda had used their ingenuity. Among other indignities, they had soaked their prisoners' beards in oil before setting them alight.

Arigh buried the mistreated corpses without a word. If they were meant to intimidate, they had the opposite effect. In cold anger, the Arshaum hunted down a squad of Yezda scouts and drove them straight into the lances of the mountaineers still with them. The enemy horsemen did not last long. The evening's camp held a grim satisfaction.

But the Yezda returned to the attack the next day. The iron-studded gates of one of the larger of the Hundred Cities, Dur-Sharrukin, swung open to let out a sally party, while two troops who had been shadowing the Arshaum nipped in from either flank.

They were still outnumbered and could have been badly mauled, but Arigh threw the bulk of his forces at Dur-Sharrukin's gate. If he could force an entrance, the city was his. The Yezda gate-captain saw that, too. He was, unfortunately, a man of quick action. He put a shoulder to the gate himself and screamed for his troops to help. The bar slammed into place seconds before the Arshaum got there. Much of the garrison was trapped outside, but the town was secure.

The plainsmen milled about in confusion just outside Dur-Sharrukin. In their dash for the gate they had pulled away from the Erzrumi, and the Yezda flanking attack fell on the hillmen.

Gashivili's company stopped one assault in its tracks. Used to clashing with the Khamorth at the edge of the steppe, the lord of Gunib's veterans waited till the Yezda drew close enough to be hurt by a charge and then, with nice timing, delivered a blow that brought a dozen lightly armed archers down from their horses at the first shock and sent the rest galloping away for their lives.

On the other wing the combat went less well. The free spirits who had clung with the Arshaum acknowledged no single commander. They grouped together by nation or by friendship, and each little band did as it pleased. Lacking the discipline for a united charge, they tried to fight nomad-style, and the nomads had much the better of it.

"Stay close to me," Rakio called to Gorgidas as the first arrows whipped past them. The Yrmido swung his lance down and roweled his big gelding. He thundered toward a Yezda who was restringing his bow. On a more agile mount, the other had no trouble eluding him, but his grin turned to a snarl as he saw Gorgidas bearing down on him behind Rakio.

The Greek rode a steppe pony himself and was thrusting at the Yezda as the latter snatched out his saber. A backward lean saved him from Gorgidas' sword, but another "orphan" from the Sworn Fellowship speared him out of the saddle. All the remaining Yrmido, about fifteen of them, stuck close together; even now, few of the other Erzrumi would have anything to do with them.

They cut down a couple of Yezda more and took injuries in return. One was shot in the shoulder, another wounded in the leg by a sword stroke. His foe's saber cut his horse as well. Crazed with pain, it leaped into the air and galloped wildly away, by good fortune toward Gashvili's troops. One of their rear guard rode out to the hurt warrior, helped bring his beast under control, and hurried him into the safety of their ranks.

"That is well done," Rakio said. "These men of Gunib decent fellows have themselves shown to be. Some here would let the Yezda take him."

Back at Dur-Sharrukin, the Arshaum were reversing themselves and riding to help their allies. The Yezda, seeing that their advantage would soon be gone, battled with redoubled vigor, to do all the damage they could before they had to retreat.

The Yrmido took the brunt of that whirlwind assault, and, because they were who they were, the rest of the Erzrumi did not hurry to help them. Gorgidas parried blow after blow and dealt a few of his own. "Eleleleu!" he shouted—the Greek war cry.

He wished he could use a bow; arrows flew by him, buzzing like angry wasps. He noticed his left trouser leg was torn and wet with blood and wondered foolishly if it was his.

Through the tumult he heard Viridovix' yowling battle paean. "Eleleu!" he yelled, and waved his hat to show the Celt where he was. The wild Gallic howl came again, closer this time. He thought he could hear Skylitzes' cry as well; Goudeles was apt to be noisier before a fight than during.

Rakio shouted and flung both hands up in front of his face. A little kestrel stabbed claws into the back of one wrist, then screeched and streaked away to its Yezda master. Another Yezda landed a mace just above Rakio's ear. The Yrmido slid bonelessly to the ground.

Gorgidas spurred his pony forward, as did the two or three men of the Sworn Fellowship who were not fighting for their own lives at that instant. But Rakio had got separated from them by fifty yards or so. Though Gorgidas burst between two Yezda before either could strike at him, more were between him and his lover, too many for him to overcome even had he had a demigod's strength and Viridovix' spell-wrapped blade.

He tried nonetheless, slashing wildly, all fencing art forgotten, and watched with anguish as a Yezda leaped down from his horse to strip off Rakio's mail shirt. The Yrmido stirred, tried groggily to rise. The Yezda grabbed for his sword, then saw how weak and uncertain Rakio was. He shouted for a comrade. Together they quickly lashed Rakio's hands behind him, then heaved him across the first warrior's saddlebow. Both men remounted and trotted off toward the west.

The Yezda were breaking contact wherever they could as the Arshaum drew near. Gorgidas' chase stopped as soon as it began. An arrow tore through his pony's neck. The horse foundered with a choked scream. As he had been taught, the Greek kicked free of the stirrups. The wind flew from him as he landed in the middle of yet another trampled grain field, but he was not really hurt.

Viridovix was almost thrown himself as he stormed toward Gorgidas. He was spurring his horse so hard that blood ran down its barrel. At last it could stand no more and tried to shake him off. He clung to his seat with the unthinking skill a year's waking time in the saddle had given him.

"Get on, ye auld weed!" he roared, slapping the beast's rump. He saw its ears go back and slapped it again, harder, before it could balk. Defeated, it ran. "Faster now, or it's forever a disgrace to sweet Epona you'll be," he said as he heard Gorgidas' war cry ring out again. As if the Gallic horse goddess held power in this new world, the pony leaped forward.

The Celt shouted himself, then cursed when he got no answer. "Sure and I'll kill that fancy-boy my ain self, if he's after letting the Greek come to harm, him such a fool on the battlefield and all," he panted, though he would sooner have been flayed than have Gorgidas hear him.

He hardly noticed the Yezda horseman in his path, save as an obstacle. One sword stroke sent the other's shamshir flying, a second laid open his arm. Not pausing to finish him, Viridovix galloped on.

Though the physician was in nomad leathers, the Celt recognized him from behind by the straight sword in his hand and by the set of his shoulders, a slump the self-confident Arshaum rarely assumed. "'Twill be the other way round, then," the Gaul said to himself, "and bad cess to me for thinking ill o' the spalpeen when he's nobbut a dead corp."

But when he dismounted to offer such sympathy as he could, Gorgidas blazed at him: "He's not dead, you bloody witless muttonhead. It's worse; the Yezda have him."

Having seen the grisly warning in the army's path, Viridovix knew what he meant. "No help for it but that we get him back, is there now?"

"How?" Gorgidas demanded, waving his hand toward the retreating Yezda. As was their habit, they were breaking up and fleeing every which way. "He could be anywhere." Clenching his fists in despair, the physician turned on Viridovix. "And what is this talk of 'we'? Why should you care what happens to my catamite?" He flung the word out defiantly, as if he would sooner hear it in his own mouth than the Gaul's.

Viridovix stood silent for a moment. "Why me? For one thing, I wouldna gi' over a dead dog to the Yezda for prisoner. If your twisty Greek mind must have its reasons, there's one. For another, your *friend,*" he emphasized, turning his back on the hateful word, and on his own thoughts of a few minutes before, "is a braw chap, and after deserving a better fate. And for a third," he finished quietly, "didn't I no hear you tried to chase north over Pardraya all alone, the time Varatesh took me?"

"You shame me," Gorgidas said, hanging his head. Memory of Rakio's remarks when the Yrmido had saved him came scalding back.

"Och, I didna aim to," Viridovix said. "If kicking the fool arse o' you would ha' worked the trick, it's that I'd have done, and enjoyed it the more, too."

"Go howl!" The physician could not help laughing. "You fox of a barbarian, no doubt you have the rescue planned already."

"That I don't. Your honor has made the name for being the canny one. Me, I'd sooner brawl nor think—easier and less wearing, both."

"Liar," Gorgidas said. But his wits, once the Gaul had dragged him unwilling from despondency, were working again. He said briskly, "We'll need to see Arigh for soldiers, then, and Tolui, too, I think. What better than magic for tracking someone?"

To their surprise and anger, Arigh turned them down flat when they asked him for a squad. None of their arguments would change his mind. "You've chosen a madman's errand," he declared, "and one I do not expect you to come back from. Kill yourselves if you must, but I will not order any man to follow you."

"Is that the way a friend acts?" Viridovix cried.

"It is how a chief acts," the Arshaum returned steadily. "What sort of herdsman would I be if I sought a lost sheep by sending twenty more to meet the wolves? I have all my force to think of, and that is more important than any one person. Besides, if the Erzrumi is lucky he is dead by now." He turned away to discuss the evening's campsite with two of his commanders of a hundred.

That what he said had a great deal of truth in it did not help. Gorgidas was coldly furious as he went looking for Tolui. He found the shaman and learned that Arigh had preceded him. When he put his request to Tolui, the nomad shook his head, saying, "I am ordered not to accompany you."

"Och, and what's a wee order, now?" Viridovix said airily. "They're all very well when you'd be doing what they tell you with or without, but a bit of a bother otherwise."

Tolui raised an eyebrow. "My head answers for this one." Seeing Gorgidas about to explode, he stopped him with an upraised hand. "Softly, softly. I may be able to help you yet. Do you have anything of your comrade's with you?"

From his left wrist the physician drew off a silver bracelet stamped with the images of the Four Prophets. "Handsome work," Tolui remarked. He reached behind him, took the staring devil-mask of his office from his saddlebag, and lowered it over his head. "Aid me, spirits!" he called softly, his voice remote and disembodied. "Travel the path between the possession and the man and show the way so the journey may be made in this world as well as in your country."

He cocked his head as if listening. With an annoyed toss of his head, he got out his fringed oval summoning drum. "Aid me, aid me!" he called again, more sharply, and tapped the drumhead in an intricate rhythm. Gorgidas and Viridovix started when an angry voice spoke from nowhere. Tolui laid his command on the spirit, or tried to, for it roared in protest. With drum and voice he brought it to obedience and flung out his hands to send it forth.

"They have your view of orders," he said to Viridovix.

"Honh!" The Celt waited with Gorgidas for the spirit's return. Watching the Greek's set features, all the more revealing in their effort to conceal, he knew what pictures his friend was imagining. He had his own set, and it was not hard to substitute Rakio's face for Seirem's.

Tolui repeated that odd, listening pose, then grunted in satisfaction and handed the bracelet back to Gorgidas. Accepting it, the physician was puzzled until he noticed the faint bluish glow crowning the head of the leftmost prophet. Answering the unspoken question, the shaman said, "There is your guide. As the direction of your search changes, the light will shift from figure to figure, from west to north to east to south; it will grow brighter as you near your goal."

He waved aside thanks. Gorgidas and Viridovix hurried away; the sun was low in the west, and the army slowing as it prepared to camp. Somewhere the Yezda would be doing the same, Gorgidas thought—if they had not made a special stop already.

As they rode away, someone shouted behind them. Viridovix swore—was Arigh going to stop them after all? He lay his sword across his knees. "If himself wants to make a shindy of it, I'll oblige him, indeed and I will."

Their pursuer, however, was no Arshaum, but one of the Yrmido, a quiet, solid man named Mynto. "I with come," he said in broken Vaspurakaner, of which the Greek and Celt had picked up a handful of words. He was leading a fully saddled spare horse. "For Rakio."

Viridovix smacked his forehead with the heel of his hand. "What a pair o' cullions the two of us make! We'd have had the poor wight riding pillion, and belike wrecking our horses for fair."

Gorgidas was marshaling what Vaspurakaner he knew. "Big danger," he said to Mynto. "Why you come?"

The Yrmido looked at him. "Same reason you do."

The answer was one the physician might have been as glad not to have, but there could be no arguing Mynto's right to join them. "Come, then," the physician said. Viridovix managed to swallow a grin before the Greek turned his way.

The peaks of Dilbat hid the sun. The day's vicious heat subsided a little. Night in the land of the Hundred Cities had a beauty missing from the flat, monotonous river plain by day. The sky was a great swatch of blue-black velvet, with the stars' diamonds tossed carelessly across it.

The horsemen, though, had little chance to enjoy the loveliness. Swarms of mosquitoes rose, humming venomously, from the fields and the edges of the irrigation channels to make the journey a misery. The riders slapped and cursed, slapped and cursed. Their mounts' tails switched back and forth as they did their best to whisk the bugs away. Gorgidas was reminded of the fight between Herakles and the Hydra; for every insect he mashed, two more took its place.

The mosquitoes particularly tormented Viridovix, whose face in the starlight was puffed and blotchy. "Dogmeat I'll be before long," he said sadly, waving his arms in a futile effort to frighten the biters away.

Thanks to a swollen bite over one eye, Gorgidas had to squint to see the bracelet that was steering them. "North," he said after a bit, as the blue radiance began to shift, and then, a little later, "More west again." He had no doubt the glow was stronger than it had been when they set out.

As well as they could, the three of them tried to decide what they would do when they found Rakio. More than language hindered them; much depended on how many enemies held the Yrmido and what they would be doing to him when the rescuers arrived. Viridovix made the key point: "We maun be quick. Any long fight and we're for it, and no mistake."

They skirted one Yezda camp without being spotted; the bracelet was still guiding them northwest. Soon after, a squadron of Yezda rode past them only a couple of hundred yards away. No challenges rang out; the squad leader must have taken them for countrymen. "No moon—good," Mynto whispered.

"Bloody good," Gorgidas said explosively once the Yezda were out of earshot.

He was hiding the bracelet in his sleeve to conceal its brightness when he and his companions passed the mound that marked yet another abandoned city. As they came round it they saw several fires ahead and men moving in front of them. When the physician checked the bracelet, its glow almost dazzled him. "That must be it."

"Yes." Mynto pointed. He was farsighted; they had to draw closer before the unmoving figure by one of the fires meant anything to the Greek. He caught his breath sharply. No wonder the man did not move—he was tied to a stake.

"Ready for sport, are they, the omadhauns?" Viridovix said. "We'll give them summat o' sport."

They made plans in low mutters, then almost had to scrap them at once when a sentry called a challenge from out of the darkness. "Not so much noise, there," Viridovix hissed at the Yezda in the Khamorth speech they shared, doing his best to imitate the fellow's accent. "We've a message for your captain from the khagan himself. Come fetch it, an you would; there's more stops for us after the one here."

The sentry rode forward, not especially suspicious. He was only a few feet away when he exclaimed, "You're no—" His voice cut off abruptly as Mynto hurled half a brick at his face. He went over his horse's tail.

They waited tensely to see whether the noise would disturb the Yezda in the camp. When it was clear the enemy had not noticed, Viridovix said, "Here's how we'll try it, then," and shifted into his lame Vaspurakaner, eked out with gestures, so Mynto could follow.

"That place is mine," Gorgidas protested when the Gaul came to his own role.

"No," Viridovix said firmly. "Mynto has his chain-mail coat, and I this whopping great blade and all the practice using it. Each to the task he's suited for, or the lot of us perish, and Rakio, too. Is it aye or nay?"

"Yes, damn you." Having lived his life by logic and reason, the physician wished he could forget them.

"You'll get in a lick or two, that you will," Viridovix promised as they moved in. They kept their horses to a walk, advancing as quietly as they could. The Yezda around the fires went about their business. One walked up to Rakio and slapped him across the face with the casual cruelty so common among them. Several others laughed and applauded.

Gorgidas could hear them plainly. With his comrades, he was less than fifty yards from the campfires before one of the Yezda turned his head their way—close enough for them to see his eyes go big and round and his mouth drop open in astonishment.

"Now!" Viridovix bellowed, snatching the reins of the spare horse from Mynto. Spurring their beasts, they stormed forward.

They were at a full gallop when they crashed down on the startled Yezda, shouting at the top of their lungs. In the first panic-filled moments, they must have seemed an army. The Yezda scattered before them. Men screamed as lance pierced or pounding hooves trampled. One soldier dove into a fire to escape a swing of Viridovix' sword and dashed out the other side with his coat ablaze.

Gorgidas swerved sharply toward the ponies tethered beside the camp. Viridovix had been right; already a couple of Yezda were there, clambering onto their horses. He cut them down, then rode through the rearing snorting animals, cutting lines and slashing at the horses themselves. He screeched and flapped his arms, doing everything he could to madden the beasts and make them useless to their masters.

Cries of fright turned to rage as the Yezda realized how few their attackers were. But Mynto in their midst was working a fearful slaughter, alone or not. His charger's iron-shod feet cracked ribs and split skulls; his spear killed until the clutch of a dying warrior wrenched it from his grasp. Then he pulled his saber free and, bending low in the saddle, slashed savagely at a pair of Yezda rushing toward him. One spun and fell, the other reeled away with a hand clapped to his slit nose.

In the chaos Viridovix made straight for Rakio. He sprang down from his horse beside the Yrmido. The Yezda had not really begun to enjoy themselves with their prisoner. He was bruised and battered, one eye swollen shut, a trickle of blood starting from the corner of his mouth where the last slap had landed. His mail shirt, of course, had gone for booty. His undertunic, ripped open to the waist, showed that his captors had tested their daggers' edges on his flesh.

But he was conscious, alert, and not begging to die. "Sorry your evening to disrupt," he said, moving his wrists so Viridovix could get at his bonds more easily. The Celt sliced through them and stooped to free his ankles. As he did so, a sword bit into Rakio's post just above his head.

He half rose, bringing his dagger up in the underhanded killing stroke of a man who knows steel. A Yezda shrieked, briefly.

Rakio staggered once the thongs that bound his feet were cut. When Viridovix steadied him, he turned his head and kissed the Gaul square on the mouth. "I am in your debt," he said.

Sure his face was redder than his hair, Viridovix managed to grunt, "Can ye ride?"

"It is ride or die," the Yrmido said.

Viridovix helped him onto the horse Mynto had brought and set his feet in the stirrups. Hands still too numb to hold the reins, Rakio clasped them round the horse's neck.

Viridovix seized the lead line and vaulted aboard his own pony. With a wild howl of triumph, he dug his spurs into its flanks and slapped its muzzle when it turned to bite. Neighing shrilly, it bolted forward. A Yezda leaped at Rakio to tear him from the saddle, but spied Mynto bearing down at him and thought better of it. A crackle of excited talk ran between the two Sworn Fellows.

The Gaul's screech cut through the turmoil as easily as his knife tore flesh. With a skill he had not had till he went to the steppe, Gorgidas used the reins, the pressure of his knees, and a firm voice to steer his pony through the loosed animals that plunged and kicked all around him. He pounded after his comrades.

By the time he caught up with them, Rakio was in control of his own horse and Viridovix had let the lead line go. He rode close to the Yrmido and reached out to clasp his hand. "As I said I would be, I am here," he said.

Eyes shining, Rakio nodded, but winced at the Greek's touch; his hand was still puffy from trapped blood. "Sorry," Gorgidas said, the physician's tone and the lover's inseparable in his voice. "Are you much hurt?"

"Not so much as in another hour I would have been," Rakio said lightly. "All this looks worse than it is." He reached out himself, carefully, and ruffled the Greek's hair. "You were brave to come looking for me; I know that you are no warrior born." Before Gorgidas could say anything to that, he went on, "How did you find me?"

"Your gift." Gorgidas lifted his arm to show Rakio the bracelet, its light now vanished. He explained Tolui's magic.

"You have a greater one me given," the Yrmido said. With equestrian ability Gorgidas still could not have matched, he leaned over to embrace the physician.

"Och, enough o' your spooning, the twa o' ye," Viridivox said, the memory of Rakio's kiss making him speak more gruffly than he had intended. He was far too set on women for it to have stirred him, but it had not revolted him, either, as he would have expected. He pointed back to the Yezda camp. "Pay attention behind. They're coming round, I'm thinking. Bad cess for us they're so quick about it."

The confused cries and groans of the wounded were fading in the distance, but Gorgidas could also hear purposeful orders. When he turned his head, he saw the first pursuing riders silhouetted against the campfires. He cursed himself for not doing a better job of scattering their horses.

Viridovix brought him up short. "Where was the time for it? Nought to be gained worrying now, any road."

More familiar with the ground than their quarry, the Yezda closed the gap. An arrow clattered against a stone somewhere behind them. It was a wild, wasted shot, but others would come closer before long. Viridovix bit his lips. "The sons o' pigs'll be overhauling us, the gods send 'em a bloody flux."

"Up the mound, then?" Gorgidas said unhappily. They had agreed the dead city would make a refuge at need, but had hoped they would not have to use it. "We'll be trapping ourselves there."

"I ken, I ken," the Gaul replied. "But there's no help for it, unless your honor has a better notion. Sure as sure they're running us down on the flat. In the ruins we'll make 'em work to winkle us out, at least, and maybe find a way to get off. It's a puir chance, I'm thinking, but better than none."

Having seen the Yezda caught in a similar position, Gorgidas knew just how slim the chance was, but some of them had indeed escaped. And without cover, he and his comrades could not shake off their pursuers; Viridovix was right about that, too. The physician jerked on the reins, changing his pony's direction. The others were already making for the artificial mound.

Shouts from behind said their swerve had been marked. By then they were reining in sharply, slowing their beasts to a walk as they picked their way up the steep, cluttered sides of the mound. Mynto, heaviest in his armor, dismounted and climbed on foot, leading his horse. His companions soon had to follow his example.

Rakio came up side by side with Viridovix. Fighting through brush and shattered masonry that shifted under his feet at every step, the Celt paid little attention until Rakio nudged him. He turned. Even by starlight, the puzzlement was plain on Rakio's face. "Why are you here?" he asked, softly so Gorgidas and Mynto could not overhear. "I thought you my enemy were."

Once he had untangled that, Viridovix stared at the Yrmido. "And would you be telling me whatever gave ye sic a daft notion, now?"

"You had been sleeping with Gorgidas for a year." Rakio set out what seemed to him too obvious to need explaining. "It only natural is for you to be jealous, with me taking him away from you. Why you aren't?"

All that kept the Gaul from laughing out loud was that it would draw the Yezda. "Och, what a grand ninny y'are. 'Twas nobbut sleeping in the tent of us, that and some powerful talk. A finer friend nor the Greek there couldna be, for all his griping, but the next man's arse I covet'll be the first."

"Really?" It was Rakio's turn for amusement. No matter what he knew intellectually of other peoples' ways, emotionally the Sworn Fellowship's customs were the only right and proper ones to him. "I am sorry for you."

"Why are you sorry for him?" Gorgidas asked; Rakio had forgotten to keep his voice down.

"Never you mind," Viridovix told him. "Just shut up and climb. The losels ahint us'll be here all too quick."

But when the Greek looked back to see how close the Yezda were, he watched, dumfounded, as they trotted east past the mound. From their shouts to one another, they still thought they were in hot pursuit of Rakio and his rescuers. Mynto said something in the Yrmido tongue. Rakio translated: "A good time for them to lose their wits, but why?"

The question was rhetorical, but answered nonetheless. From the top of the hillock a thin voice called, "Come join me, my friends, if you would." At first Gorgidas thought he was hearing Greek, then Videssian.

From the muffled exclamations of the others, he was sure they felt the same confusion; Viridovix gave a startled answer in his musical Celtic speech. In whatever language they heard the summons, none of them thought of disobeying, any more than they might a much-loved grandfather.

Before long they had to tether their horses and help each other with the last rugged climb to the hill's crest. The same jumble of eroded mudbrick walls and buildings Gorgidas had seen at the would-be Yezda ambush presented itself here, made worse because no fires lit it. The voice came again: "This way." They stumbled through the ruins of what might once have been the town marketplace and came at last to work that was not ancient—a lean-to of brush and sticks, propped against a half-fallen fence.

There was motion as they approached. A naked man emerged, at first on hands and knees before painfully getting to his feet. He raised his left hand in a gesture of blessing that was new to Gorgidas and Viridovix, but which Rakio and Mynto returned. "In the names of a greater Four, I welcome the four of you."

Gorgidas wondered how the hermit knew their number; his eyes were white and blind. But that wonder was small next to the physician's amazement that he could stand at all. He was the most emaciated human being the Greek had ever seen. His thighs were thinner than his knees; the skin fell in between his sharply etched ribs, or what could be seen of them behind a matted white beard. But for his blindness, his face might once have been princely; now he resembled nothing so much as a starved hawk.

While Gorgidas was taking the measure of the physical man, Viridovix penetrated at once to his essence. "A holy druid he is," the Gaul said, "or more like one nor any priest I've yet found here." Bowing to the hermit, he asked respectfully, "Was it your honor kept the Yezda from chasing us here?"

"A mere sending of phantoms," the other said. Or so the Celt understood him; watching, he did not see the holy man's lips move.

He was surprised when the hermit bowed to him in turn, then looked him full in the face with that disconcerting, empty gaze. He heard, "I have broken my rule of nonintervention in the affairs of the world for your sake; you carry too much destiny to be snuffed out in some tiny, meaningless scuffle."

They were all looking at Viridovix now, the two Yrmido in bewilderment, Gorgidas appraisingly. He could feel the truth emanating from the man. So could Viridovix, who protested, "Me? It's nobbut a puir lone Celt I am, trying to stay alive—for the which I maun thank you, now. But wish no geases on me."

Gorgidas cut in, "What destiny do you speak of?" This was no time, he thought, for Viridovix to have an uncharacteristic fit of modesty.

For the first time the hermit showed uncertainty. "That I may not—and cannot—tell you. I do not see it clearly myself, nor is the outcome certain. Other powers than mine cloud my view, and the end, for good or ill, is balanced to within a feather's weight. But without this stranger, only disaster lies ahead. Thus I chose to meddle in the ways of man once more, though this is but one of the two required pieces."

"Och, a druid indeed," Viridovix said, "saying more than he means. Is it so with your oracles, too, Greek?"

"Yes," Gorgidas said, but he caught the nervousness in the Gaul's chuckle.

Rakio spoke in the Yrmido language; with his gift of tongues, the holy man understood. Gorgidas caught only a couple of words; one was "Master," the title priests of the Four Prophets bore. The physician waited impatiently for the hermit's reply.

"I have made this hill my fortress against temptation since before the Yezda came," he said, "seeking in negation the path the sweet Four opened to a better life ahead. But I failed; my faith tottered when the murderers swept out of the west and laid waste my land and my fellow believers with no sign of vengeance being readied against them. Often I wondered why I chose to remain alive in the face of such misery; how much easier it would have been to let go my fleshly husk and enjoy bliss forever. Now at last I know why I did not."

He tottered forward to embrace Viridovix. The Celt had all he could do to keep from shying; not only was it like being hugged by a skeleton, but he did not think the holy man had washed himself since he took up his station a lifetime ago. Still worse, that confident touch told again of the holy man's certainty about his fate. He was worse afraid than in any battle, for it tore his freedom from him as death never could.

He pulled away so quickly the hermit staggered. Mynto righted the old man, glaring at the Celt. "Begging your honor's pardon," Viridovix said grudgingly. He looked to his comrades. "Should we not be off with us the now, with the Yezda so befooled and all?"

They started to agree, but the holy man quivered so hard Viridovix thought he would shake himself to pieces. He grasped the Celt's arm with unexpected strength. "You must not go! The fiends yet prowl all about, and will surely destroy you if you venture away. You must stay and wait before you try to return to your friends."

Mynto and Rakio were convinced at once. Gorgidas shrugged at Viridovix' unvoiced appeal. "Whatever else the man may be," the physician pointed out, "we've found him wizard enough to outfox the Yezda. Dare we assume he doesn't know what he's talking about?"

"Put that way, nay," the Gaul sighed, "but och, I wish we did."

Had he known the wait would stretch through four days, Gorgidas would have taken his chances on the Yezda. With Mynto there, he did not feel easy with Rakio, the more so because Rakio seemed to enjoy teasing him by playing up to his onetime lover. Nor was Viridovix, kicking against what the holy man insisted was to be his destiny, any better company. The Gaul, by turns somber and angry, either moped about in moody silence or snarled defiance at the world.

That left the hermit. Gorgidas did his best to draw the man out, but he was as faith-struck as the most fanatical Videssian priest. The Greek learned more than he really wanted to know about the cult of the Four Prophets, as much by what the hermit did not say as by what he did. Like Rakio and Mynto, he never mentioned his god or gods, reckoning the divinity too sacred to pollute with words, but he would drone on endlessly about the Prophets' attributes and aspects. Caught for once without writing materials, Gorgidas tried to remember as much as he could.

The first morning they were there, he asked the holy man his name, to have something to call him by. The hermit blinked, in that moment looking like an ordinary, perplexed mortal. "Do you know," he answered,

"I've forgotten." He did not seem to mind when Gorgidas followed Rakio's usage and called him "Master."

He refused in horror to share the field rations the Greek and his comrades had with them. With ascetic zeal, he ate only the roots and berries he grubbed from the ground himself. His water came from the one well that had not fallen in since the dead city he lived in was abandoned. It was warm, muddy, and gave all four of his guests a savage diarrhea.

"No wonder the wight's so scrawny," Viridovix said, staggering up the hill after a call of nature. "On sic meat and drink I'd be dead in a week, beshrew me if I wouldn't."

Despite everything, though, the Celt did not urge his fellows to leave before the hermit said it was safe. For the first two days, Yezda constantly trotted past the mound. One band had a red-robed sorcerer with it. Gorgidas' heart was in his mouth lest the wizard penetrate the defenses of the place, but he rode on.

When the holy man finally gave them leave to go, the physician felt he was being released from gaol. And, like a warden cautioning freed prisoners against new crimes, the hermit warned: "Ride straight for the main body of your companions and all will be well with you. Turn aside for any reason and you will meet only disaster."

"We scarcely would do anything else," Rakio remarked as the hillock grew smaller behind them. "In this flat, ugly land there precious few distractions are." Perhaps seeking one, he winked at Mynto. Gorgidas ground his teeth and pretended not to see.

Following the Arshaum army did not rate the name of tracking. War's flotsam was guide enough: unburied men and horses swelling and stinking under the merciless sun, trampled canal banks where scores of beasts had drunk, a burnt-out barn that had served as a latrine for a regiment, discarded boots, a broken bow, a stolen carpet tossed aside as too heavy to be worth carrying.

The four riders drove their horses as hard as they dared; the Arshaum, unburdened now by many allies, would be picking up the pace. They saw no Yezda, save as distant specks. "You had the right of it," Viridovix admitted to Gorgidas. "Himself knew whereof he spoke. But for the draff and all, we might be cantering in the country."

The next morning rocked their confidence in the hermit's powers. Dust warned of the approaching column before it appeared out of the south, but they were in a stretch of land gone back to desert after the Yezda wrecked the local irrigation works, and the baked brown earth offered no cover. The column swerved their way.

"Out sword!" Viridovix cried, tugging his own free. "Naught for it but to sell oursel's dear as we may."

Mynto drew his saber, a handsome weapon with gold inlays on the hilt. He patted the empty boss on the right side of his saddle and said something to Rakio. "He wishes he had his spear," Rakio translated. Irrepressible, he added an aside to Gorgidas: "It was a long one."

"Oh, a pest take Mynto and his spear, and you with them," the physician snapped. He could feel his sweat soaking into the leather grip of his *gladius*. The shortsword fit his hand as well as any surgical knife, and he was beginning to gain some skill with it. But the size of the oncoming troop only brought despair at the prospect of a hopeless fight.

He could see men in armor through the swirling dust, their lances couched and ready. What that meant escaped him until Viridovix let out a wordless yowl of glee and slammed his blade into its sheath. "Use the eyes of you, man," he called to the Greek. "Are those Yezda?"

"No, by the dog!" Along with his comrades, Gorgidas booted his horse toward the Erzrumi.

Rakio identified them. "It is Gashvili's band from Gunib."

Though he kept shouting and waving to show the mountain men he was no enemy, trepidation stirred in Viridovix. Frightful oaths had bound Gashvili to ride with the Arshaum. If he was forsaking them, would he leave witnesses to tell of it? The Gaul did not draw his sword again, but he made sure it was loose in the scabbard.

His alarm spiked when the men of Gunib almost rode him and his companions down in spite of their cries of friendship. Only as the Erzrumi finally pulled up could he see them as more than menacing figures behind their lanceheads. They were reeling in the saddle, red-eyed with fatigue; every one was filthy with the caked dust of hard travel. Scraps of grimy cloth covered fresh wounds. Clouds of flies descended to gorge on oozing serum or new blood. Most of the troopers did not bother slapping them away.

"They're beaten men," the Celt said softly, in wonder. He looked in vain for Gashvili's gilded scale-mail. "Where might your laird be?" he asked the nearest Erzrumi.

"Dead," the fellow replied after a moment, as if he had to force himself to understand the Khamorth tongue Viridovix had used.

"The gods smile on him when he meets them, then. Who leads you the now?"

Vakhtang made his way through his men toward the newcomers. He surveyed them dully. "I command," he said, but his voice held no authority. He was a million miles from the coxcomb who had come out to confront Arigh's men in front of Gunib. His two-pointed beard made an unkempt tangle down the front of his corselet, whose gilding was marred by sword stroke and smoke and blood. The jaunty feather was long gone from his helm. Out of a face haggard and sick with defeat his eyes stared, not quite focused, somewhere past Viridovix' right ear.

He was worse than beaten, the Gaul realized; he was stunned, as if clubbed. "What of your oath to Arigh?" he growled, thinking to sting the ruined man in front of him back to life. "Gone and left him in the lurch, have you now, mauger all the cantrips and fine words outside your precious castle?"

As lifelessly as before, Vakhtang said, "No. We are not forsworn." But in spite of himself, his head lifted; he met Viridovix' eyes for the first time. His voice firmed as he went on. "Arigh himself and his priest Tolui absolved us of our vow when the army began to break up."

"Tell me," Viridovix said, overriding cries of dismay from Gorgidas and then in turn from Rakio and Mynto as Vakhtang's words were rendered into Videssian and the Yrmido speech.

The story had an appalling simplicity. Yezda in numbers never before seen had come rushing up out of the south to repeat on a vastly larger scale the pincer tactics they had tried in front of Dur-Sharrukin. They were better soldiers than the Arshaum had seen before, too; a prisoner boasted that Wulghash the khagan had picked them himself.

All the same, Arigh held his own, even smashing the Yezda left wing to bits against a tributary of the Tib. "No mean general, that one," Vakhtang said, growing steadily more animated as he talked. But his face fell once more as newer memories crowded back. "Then the flames came."

Viridovix went rigid in the saddle. "What's that?" he barked. He jerked at a sudden pain in his hands. Looking down, he willed his fists open and felt his nails ease out of his flesh.

He did not need the Erzrumi's description to picture the lines of fire licking out to split apart and trap their makers' foes; Avshar had shown him the reality in Pardraya. As Vakhtang continued, though, he saw that Arigh had not had to face the full might of the spell. The noble said, "It was battle magic; our priests and shamans fought it to a standstill, in time. But it was too late to save the battle; by then our position was wrecked past repair. That was when your Arshaum gave us leave to go. The gods be thanked, we mauled the Yezda enough to make them think twice about giving chase."

"Begging your pardon, I'm thinking you saw nobbut the second team," Viridovix said. "Had himself been working the fires and not his mages—a murrain take them—only them as he wanted would ever ha' got clear."

"As may be," Vakhtang said. A few of his men bristled at the suggestion that less than Yezd's best had beaten them, but he was too worn to care. "All I hope now is to see Gunib again. I am glad we came across you; every sword will help on our way home."

Gorgidas and then Rakio finished translating; silence fell. The two of them, the Gaul, and Mynto looked at each other. Wisdom surely lay with retreat in this well-armed company, but they could not forget the hermit's warning that changing course would bring misfortune. In the end, though, that was not what shaped Viridovix' decision. He said simply, "I've come too far to turn back the now."

"And I," Gorgidas said. "For better or worse, this is my conflict, and I will know how it ends."

As nothing else had, their choice tore the lethargy from Vakhtang. "Madmen!" he cried. "It will end with an arrow through your belly and your bones baking under this cursed sun." He turned to the two Yrmido, his hands spread in entreaty, and spoke to them in the Vaspurakaner tongue.

Mynto gave a sudden, sharp nod. He and Rakio got into a low-voiced dispute; from what little Gorgidas could follow, he was echoing Vakhtang's arguments. Rakio mostly listened, indecision etched on his features. When at last he answered, Mynto's lips thinned in distress. Rakio shifted to Videssian: "I will travel south. To disregard the words of the holy hermit after he his gifts from the Four has shown strikes me as the greater madness."

When Mynto saw he could not sway his countryman, he embraced him with the tenderness any lover would give his beloved. Then he rode forward to join the men of Gunib. Vakhtang brought both fists to his forehead in grateful salute.

"I wish you the luck I do not expect you to have," he told the other three. He waved to his battered company. They started north on their lathered, blowing horses, the jingle of their harness incongruously gay.

Soon dust and distance made Mynto impossible to pick out from the men of Gunib around him. Rakio let out a small sigh. "He is a fine, bold fellow, and I him will miss," he said. His eyes danced at Gorgidas' expression.

Viridovix caught the byplay. He rounded on the Ymrido. "Is it a puss-cat y'are, to make sic sport? Finish the puir wight off or let him be."

"Will you shut up?" Gorgidas shouted, scarlet and furious.

Laughing, Rakio looked sidelong at the Gaul. "You are sure it is not jealousy?" He went on more seriously: "Should I tell Mynto all my reasons for going with you two? That only would hurt him to no purpose."

Having reduced both his companions to silence, he set out south along the trail Vakhtang's men had left. They followed. Neither met the other's eye.

IX

Money clinked in Marcus' palm. "Four and a half," Tahmasp said. "One for your month with us, the rest your fair share of the pot." Two of the goldpieces were Yezda, stamped with Yezd's leaping panther and a legend in a script the tribune could not read. The rest came from Videssos. Even in Mashiz, imperial gold was good.

Gaius Philippus stepped up to take his pay. "We'd have earned more in time served if you'd not taken the southern route," he said.

Tahmasp made a sour face. "More in profit, too." The lands between the Tutub and the Tib would have given him twice the trade his desert-skirting track yielded, but a barbarian invasion had thrown the Hundred Cities into confusion.

The caravaneer folded each Roman in turn into a beefy embrace. "You bastards sure you won't stick around till I set out again?"

"A couple of months from now?" Marcus shook his head. "Not likely."

"Not that I care a flying fart what happens to you," Tahmasp said, a frown giving his gruff words the lie, "but two men riding through the Yezda by themselves stand the same chance of coming out whole as two eggs about to be scrambled."

"Actually, I think we may do better alone," the tribune answered. "At least we won't draw nomads the way your traveling madhouse does." The Yezda had swarmed thick as flies the first two weeks out of Amorion. To ride away then would have been death, even without Tahmasp's vow of destruction to deserters.

Later they might have escaped with ease, but by then the shared dangers of three desperate fights and endless hours of picket duty and talk around campfires had welded them indissolubly to the company. It was easy to abandon strangers; not so, friends. And so, Scaurus thought, here we are in the heart of Yezd, all for loyalty's sake.

It seemed strange and not very fair.

Tahmasp pumped Gaius Philippus' hand, slapped Marcus on the back. As always, he set himself; as always, he staggered. "You have the wits of a couple of sun-addled jackasses, but good luck to you. If you live—which I doubt—maybe we'll meet again." The caravaneer turned away. To him they were finished business.

They led their horses out of the fortified warehouse into the shadows of Mashiz' afternoon. Marcus could look east and see the sun still shining brightly, but the peaks of Dilbat brought an early twilight to the city. In a way it was a blessing, for it cut the Yezda summer's heat. Yezd made Videssos' central plateau temperate by comparison.

"What now?" Gaius Philippus asked, his mind firmly on the problem of the moment. "Me, I'm for shagging out of here right away. Tahmasp is welcome to this place."

Marcus nodded slowly. More shadows than the ones cast by the mountains of Dilbat hung over Mashiz. He looked around, trying to pinpoint the source of his unease. It was not the buildings; he was sure of that much. The eye grew used to thin towers topped by onion domes, to spiral ramps instead of stairways, to pointed arches wider than the doors beneath them, and to square columns covered with geometric mosaics. Mashiz seemed fantastically strange, but Makuraner architecture was only different, not sinister.

The Yezda, but two generations off the steppe, were not builders. They had put their mark on Mashiz all the same. The tribune wondered what the sack had been like when the city fell. Every other block, it seemed, had a wrecked building, and every other structure needed repair. That air of decay, of a slow falling into ruin, was part of the problem, Scaurus thought.

But only part. A disproportionate number of ravaged buildings had been shrines of the Four Prophets; the Yezda had been as savage toward Makuran's national cult as they were to the worship of Phos. As the Romans headed for the city's market, they passed only a couple of surviving shrines. Both were small buildings that had probably once been private homes, and mean ones at that.

Further west, toward the edge of Mashiz, stood another temple once dedicated to the Four: a marvelous red granite pyramid, no doubt the

Makuraner counterpart to Phos' High Temple in Videssos. The Yezda, though, had claimed it for their own. Scored into every side, brutally obliterating the reliefs that told the story of the Four Prophets, were Skotos' twin lightningbolts. A cloud of thick brown smoke rose above the building. When the breeze shifted and sent a tag end of it their way, Marcus and Gaius Philippus both coughed at the stench.

"I know what meat that is," the senior centurion said darkly.

The people of Mashiz, Scaurus reflected, lived with that cloud every day of their lives. No wonder they were furtive, sticking to the deeper shadows of buildings as they walked along the street, looking at strangers out of the corners of their eyes, and rarely talking above a whisper. No wonder a born swaggerer like Tahmasp spent most of his time on the road.

In Mashiz, the Yezda swaggered. Afoot or on horse, they came down the middle of the road with the arrogance of conquerors and expected everyone else to stay out of their way.

The Romans saw priests of Skotos for the first time; they seemed a ghastly parody of the clergy who served Phos. Their robes were the color of drying blood—to keep the gore of their sacrifices from showing, Marcus thought grimly. Their dark god's sigil was blazoned in black on their chests; their hair was shorn into the double thunderbolt. The locals ducked aside whenever a pair of them came by; even the Yezda appeared nervous around them.

They did not speak to Scaurus, which suited him.

To his relief, something like normality reigned in the marketplace. The sights and sounds of commerce were the same wherever men gathered. He needed no knowledge of the guttural Makuraner tongue to understand that this customer thought a butcher was cheating him, or that that one was going to outhaggle a wool merchant if it took all night.

Marcus was afraid he would have to bargain by dumb show, but most of the venders knew a few words of Videssian: numbers, yes, no, and enough invective to add flavor to no. He bought hard cheese, coarse-ground flour, and a little griddle on which to cook wheatcakes. As a happy afterthought, he added a sackful of Vaspurakaner-style pastries, a rich mixture of flour, minced almonds, and ground dates, dusted with sugar.

"'Princes' balls,'" the baker said, chuckling, as he tied the neck of the sack. Marcus had heard the joke before, but his answering laugh got a couple of coppers knocked off the price.

"Anything else we need?" he asked Gaius Philippus.

"A new canteen," the centurion said. "The solder's come loose from the seam on this one, and it leaks. Maybe a patch'll do, but something, anyway. The kind of country this is, losing water could kill you in a hurry."

"Let's find a tinker, then, or a coppersmith." To Marcus' surprise, there did not seem to be any tinkers wandering through the square, nor did the baker understand the Videssian word. "Not something they have here, I gather. Oh, well, a smith it is."

The coppersmiths' district was not far from the marketplace. The baker pointed the way. "Three blocks up, two over."

The Romans heard a scuffle down a sidestreet. So did several locals, who paid no attention; if it was not happening to them, they did not want to know about it. But when Scaurus and Gaius Philippus came to the alleyway, they saw a single man, his back to a mud-brick wall, desperately wielding a cudgel against four attackers.

They looked at each other. "Shall we even up the odds?" Marcus asked. Without waiting for an answer, he sprang onto his horse. Gaius Philippus was already mounting. He had a better beast than the gray these days, a sturdy brown gelding with a white blaze between the eyes.

The robbers whirled as the drumroll of hoofbeats filled the narrow street. One fled. Another threw a dagger at the tribune, a hurried cast that went wild. Scaurus' horse ran him down. The third bravo swung a mace at Gaius Philippus, who turned the stroke with his *gladius* and then thrust it through the fellow's throat. The last of the robbers grappled with him and tried to pull him from the saddle, but their would-be victim sprang out to aid his unexpected rescuers. His club caved in the back of the bandit's skull.

Marcus rode after the footpad who had run, but the fellow escaped, vanishing in a maze of twisting alleys the tribune did not know. When he got back, the man he had saved was bending over the trampled robber, who groaned and thrashed on the ground. Pulling out a penknife, he jerked the bandit's head back and cut his throat.

Scaurus frowned at such rough-and-ready justice, but decided the robber was probably lucky not to fall into the hands of whatever passed for a constabulary among the Yezda.

The man rose, bowing low to one Roman and then to the other. He was about Marcus' age and nearly as tall as the tribune, but with a much leaner frame. His face was long and gaunt, with hollows below the cheekbones. His eyes, somber and dark, also looked out from hollows.

He bowed again, saying something in the Makuraner language. Marcus had picked up just enough of it to be able to answer that he did not understand. Without much hope, he asked, "Do you speak Videssian?"

"Yes, indeed I do." The fellow's accent was thicker than Tahmasp's, but also more cultured. "May I ask my rescuers' names?"

The Romans looked at each other, shrugged, and gave them.

"I am in your debt, sirs. I am Tabari." He said that as if they ought to know who Tabari was. Marcus tried to seem suitably impressed. Gaius Philippus grunted.

Just then, a squad of archers came dashing round the corner. Someone finally must have let the watch know a fight was going on. The leader of the Yezda saw the robber's body lying on the ground in a pool of blood and growled something to his men. They turned their bows on the Romans and Tabari.

Scaurus and Gaius Philippus froze, careful not to do anything threatening with the swords they still held. Tabari strode forward confidently. He spoke a couple of sentences in the Yezda tongue. The city guards lowered their weapons so fast that one dropped an arrow. Their commander bowed low.

"As I said, I am Tabari," said the man the Romans had rescued, turning back to them, "minister of justice to my lord the great khagan Wulghash." Suddenly his eyes no longer looked somber to Marcus. They looked dangerous. Justice, these days, meant prison to the tribune, and he had seen more of prison than he ever wanted to.

Tabari went on, "As a small token of my gratitude, let me present you at the court banquet this evening. Surely my lord Wulghash will take notice of your courage and generosity and reward you as you deserve. My own resources, I fear, are too small for that, but know you have my undying gratitude."

"Wulghash? Oh, bloody wonderful!" Gaius Philippus said in Latin.

"Surely you do us too much honor," Marcus said to Tabari, doing his best to frame a polite refusal. "We know nothing of courts or fancy manners—"

"My lord Wulghash does not insist on them, and I tell you he will be delighted to show favor to the men who saved his minister of justice, even if," Tabari's voice held irony, "they were unaware of his rank." He spoke to the Yezda underofficer, who bowed again. "Rhadzat here will take you to the palace. I would escort you myself, but I fear I have pressing business this dead dog of a robber and his confederates interrupted. I shall see you there this evening. Until then, my friends."

"Until then." Marcus and Gaius Philippus echoed him with a singular lack of enthusiasm.

Unlike the rambling Videssian palace complex, the court at Mashiz was housed in a single building. The great stone blocks from which it was built looked as if they had been ripped from the mountains' heart. Studying the smoothly weathered outwalls, Marcus guessed the palace had been a citadel before Mashiz was a city.

Once inside the outwalls, a couple of Yezda from Rhadzat's squad peeled off to lead the Romans' horses to the stables. Knowing the care the Yezda lavished on their own beasts, Scaurus was sure his would get fine treatment from them. It did nothing to ease his mind. Being away from their mounts would only make flight harder for the Romans.

Rhadzat conducted the tribune and senior centurion to the palace entrance, where a steward eyed him and them with distaste. The servitor was of Makuraner blood, slim, dark, and elegant, wearing a brocaded caftan and sandals with golden clasps. His haughty air vanished when the Yezda officer explained why they had come. Graceful as a cat, he bowed to the Romans.

He called into the palace for another servant. When the man arrived, the steward spoke to the Romans in his own tongue. Marcus shrugged and spread his hands. A ghost of the doorman's sneer returned. "You please to follow him," he said, his Videssian slow and rusty but clear enough.

Their guide knew only Makuraner and the Yezda speech. He chattered on, not caring whether they understood, as he led them up a ramp of green marble polished till it reflected the light of the torches that hung in gilded sconces every few feet along the wall. His soft-soled slippers did better on the smooth surface than the Romans' *caligae;* he giggled out loud when Gaius Philippus skidded and almost fell.

The couches in the waiting room were stuffed with down and upholstered in soft suede. The sweetmeats that the palace servitors brought came on silver trays and filled the mouth with delicate perfume. Watching shadows move across the ornate wall hangings, Marcus felt like a fly gently but irresistibly trapped in spider silk.

The room was in twilight by the time the court official returned to take the Romans away. At the entrance to the throne room he surrendered his charges to another chamberlain, an elderly Makuraner eunuch whose caftan was of almost transparent silk.

He had some Videssian. "No need for proskynesis when you present yourself before Khagan Wulghash," he said, sniffing in disapproval at his master's barbarous informality. "A bow will do. He keeps his grandfather's ways—as if a lizard-eating nomad's customs were valid." Another sniff. "He even allows his primary wife a seat beside him." A third sniff, louder than the other two.

Marcus did not pay much attention. The throne room was long and narrow; the tribune felt his shoes sinking into the thick wool of the carpet as he walked toward the distant pair of high ivory seats ahead. Without turning his head too much, he tried to spot Tabari. In the flickering torchlight, one man looked like the next.

With its moving shadows, the light of the torches did a better job showing up the reliefs on the walls behind the nobility of Yezd. Like the defaced ones on the temple that now belonged to Skotos, they were carved in a florid style that owed nothing to Videssian severity. One was a hunting scene, with some long-forgotten Makuraner king slaying a lion with a sword. The other—Marcus' eyes went wide as he recognized the regalia of the man shown kneeling before another king on horseback. Only an Avtokrator wore such garb.

Beside him, Gaius Philippus gave a tiny chuckle. "I wonder what the imperials have to say about *that* in their histories," he whispered.

A herald was coming forward from the thrones as the Romans approached them. He raised their hands above their heads—no easy feat; he was several inches shorter than Gaius Philippus—and cried out in the Makuraner and Yezda tongues. Scaurus caught his own name and the centurion's.

Applause washed over the Romans. A couple of Makuraner lords, seeing they were foreigners, cried out "Well done!" in Videssian. The tribune finally spotted Tabari, sitting close to the front. He and the other Makuraners cheered louder and longer than their Yezda counterparts. It was a heady moment, though Marcus wondered how many of the clapping men had led armies into the Empire.

The herald led them toward the thrones. The khagan sat on the right-hand one, which was higher than the other. Wulghash wore a headdress like those of the Makuraner kings remembered on the throne room walls, a high, conical crown of stiff white felt, with earflaps reaching nearly to his shoulders. A vertical row of gems ran up from edge to peak; a double band of horsehair made a diadem across the khagan's forehead.

Marcus sized Wulghash up—he had never wanted to meet the ruler of Yezd, but would not waste what chance had set before him. The khagan was swarthy, about fifty. His thick beard, cut square at the bottom, was salt-and-pepper, with salt gaining. His square features had a hard cast partly offset by tired, intelligent eyes. He was wide shouldered and well made, his middle only beginning to thicken.

"Careful," Gaius Philippus said. "He's not one to mess with." Scaurus gave a small nod; that fit his view exactly.

The herald stopped the Romans just past the end of the carpet, at a stone smoothed by thousands of feet over the centuries. They made their bows, to fresh applause. It grew even louder when Wulghash came down to clasp their hands—his own was hard, dry, and callused, more like a soldier's than a bureaucrat's—and embrace them.

"You have saved a valued member of my court, and have my friendship for it," Wulghash said. His Videssian was polished as any courtier of Thorisin's. "Allow me to present you to my senior queen, Atossa." He nodded to the woman on the lower throne.

Studying Wulghash so, the tribune had hardly noticed her. She was about the khagan's age and handsome still. She smiled and spoke in the Makuraner tongue. "She apologizes for being unable to thank you in a language you know," Wulghash translated.

Marcus returned the first compliment that popped into his mind: "Tell her she is as kind as she is beautiful." Atossa regally inclined her head. He nodded back, thoughts whirling. Here with a friendly hand on his shoulder stood Videssos' sworn enemy, the man Avshar named master. If he jerked his dagger from his belt, thrust—

He did not move. To violate Wulghash's generosity so was not in him. What point in fighting Avshar if he fell to his methods? That thought brought him closer to understanding Videssos' dualism than he had ever come.

A pipe's clear whistle cut through the court chatter. Everyone brightened. "The feast is ready," Wulghash explained, "and about time, too." He handed Atossa down from her throne; she took his arm. The Romans fell in line behind the royal couple.

The banquet hall, though merely a palace chamber, was nearly as large as the Hall of the Nineteen Couches in Videssos. Torchlight sparkled off the blue crystal and gold and silver foil of the abstract mosaic patterns on the walls. As guests of honor, Scaurus sat at Wulghash's right while Gaius Philippus was on Atossa's left.

The khagan rose to toast them. He drank wine, as did the nobles Marcus had picked as Makurani. Most of the Yezda chieftains preferred their traditional kavass. When a skin of the fermented mares' milk reached the tribune, he slurped for politeness' sake and passed it to Wulghash. The khagan wrinkled his fleshy nose and sent it on without drinking.

"There is also date wine, if you care for it," he told the Roman. Marcus declined with a shudder. He had sampled the stuff on the journey with Tahmasp. It was so sweet and syrupy as to make the cloying Videssian wine seem pleasantly dry.

Some of the food was simple nomad fare: wheatcakes, yogurt, and plain roast meat. Again, though, Wulghash liked Makuraner ways better than those of his ancestors. Enjoying grape leaves stuffed with goat and olives, an assortment of roasted songbirds, steamed and sauteed vegetables, and mutton baked in a sauce of mustard, raisins, and wine, Scaurus decided he could not fault the khagan's taste. And at sizzling rice soup he positively beamed; he had met it in a Makuraner cafe in Videssos that first magic winter night with Alypia Gavra.

The thought of her made the celebration strange and somehow unreal. After fighting the Yezda for years, what was he doing here making polite small talk with a prince whose people were destroying the land he had taken for his own? And what was Wulghash doing as that prince? He seemed anything but the monster Scaurus had pictured, and no ravening barbarian either. Plainly a capable ruler, he was as much influenced by Makuran's civilization as the great count Drax was under Videssos' spell. His presiding over the devastation the Yezda worked posed a riddle the tribune could not solve.

He got his first clue when a dispatch rider, still sweaty from his travels, brought the khagan a sheaf of messages. Wulghash read rapidly through them, growing angrier with each sheet. He growled out a stream of commands.

When the messenger interrupted with some objection or question, the khagan clapped an exasperated hand to his forehead. He wrote on the back of one of the dispatches with quick, furious strokes. Then he wet the signet ring he wore on the middle finger of his right hand in mustard sauce and stamped a smeary, yellow-brown seal on his orders. Goggling, the messenger saluted, took the parchment, and hurried away.

Wulghash, still fuming, drained his ivory rhyton at a gulp. He turned to Marcus. "I have days I think all my captains idiots, the way they panic at shadows. They've been raiding Erzerum since my grandfather's time—is it any wonder the hillmen strike back? I know the cure for that, though. Hit them three ways at once so their army breaks into all its little separate groups and they're nothing much. We've already started that; all we have to do is keep on with it. And the heads have started going up into their valleys. They'll think a long time before they stir out again."

"Heads?" the tribune echoed.

"Killed in battle, prisoners, what does it matter?" Wulghash said with ruthless unconcern. "So long as the Erzrumi recognize most of them, they serve their purpose."

The khagan slammed his fist down on the table; Atossa touched his left arm, trying to soothe him. He shook her off. "This is *my* land," he proudly declared to Scaurus, "and I intend to pass it on to my son greater than it was when I received it from my father. I have beaten Videssos; shall I let a pack of fourth-rate mountain rats get the better of me?"

"No," Marcus said, but he felt a chill of fear. Wulghash's wish was irreproachable, but the khagan did not care what steps he took to reach it. The man on that path, the tribune thought, walks at the edge of the abyss. To cover his unease, he asked, "Your son?"

As any father might, Wulghash swelled with pride. "Khobin is a fine lad—no, I cannot call him that now. He has a man's years on him, and a little son of his own. Where does the time go? He watches the northwest for me, making sure the stinking Arshaum stay on their side of the Degird. There will be trouble with them; the embassy I sent last year won no success."

Scaurus concealed the excitement that coursed through him. If the Yezda embassy had failed, perhaps the Videssian mission to the steppe tribes was faring well. He wondered how Viridovix and Gorgidas were and even spared a moment's thought for Pikridios Goudeles. The pen-pusher was a rogue, but a slick one.

Only a few drops of wine came from the silver ewer when Wulghash lifted it to refill his drinking-horn. "I need more, Harshad," he called, absentmindedly still using Videssian. A Yezda at the foot of the table looked up when he heard his name. Seeing him scratch his head, the khagan realized his mistake and repeated the request in his own language.

Grinning now, Harshad muttered a few words into his beard and moved his fingers in a quick, intricate pattern over the wine jar in front of him. It rose smoothly until it was a couple of feet above the table, then drifted toward Wulghash. Gaius Philippus had been cutting the meat from a pork rib; he looked up just as the jar floated past him. He dropped his knife.

None of the Yezda or Makuraner nobles took any special notice of the magic. A small smile on his lips, Wulghash said, "A little sorcery, that one." He pointed at Gaius Philippus' cup and spoke in a language Marcus almost thought he knew. The cup lifted, glided over to the floating ewer. The wine jar tipped and poured, then straightened as the cup was full. Wulghash gestured again. The cup returned to Gaius Philippus; the wine jar settled to the table. The khagan filled his rhyton the ordinary way.

Gaius Philippus was staring at his cup as if he expected it to get up and shoot dice with him. "Merely wine," Wulghash assured him, tasting his own. "Better than what we had, in fact. You are not very familiar with wizardry, are you?"

"More than I want to be," the veteran answered. He picked up the cup in both hands and emptied it at a gulp. "That *is* good. Could you pass me the jar for more?" He managed to laugh when Wulghash lifted the ewer with the same exaggerated care he had given the cup.

The khagan turned back to Marcus who had done his best not to show surprise at the magic. That best, apparently, was not good enough, for Wulghash said, "How is it sorcery seems so strange to you? You must have seen magecraft enough among the Videssians." His gaze was suddenly sharp; the tribune remembered he had thought the khagan's eyes intelligent the moment he saw him. Now they probed at the Roman. "But then, you have an accent I do not know and you talk with your comrade in a tongue I do not recognize—and I know a good many."

He saw the Roman's face turn wary, and said, "I do not mean to frighten you. You are my friends, I have promised you that. By all the gods and prophets, were you the Avtokrator of the Videssians you could leave my table in safety if you had that pledge." He sounded angry at himself and Scaurus both; more than anything, that made the tribune believe him.

The khagan went on, "As a friend, though, you make me wonder at you, all the more when magic startles you despite the blade you carry." This time Marcus could not help jumping. Wulghash's chuckle was dry as boots scuffing through dead leaves. "Am I a blind man, to miss the moon in the sky? Tell me of yourself, if you will, as one friend does for another."

Marcus hesitated, wondering what Wulghash might have heard of Romans from Avshar or from the spies the khagan had to have in

Videssos. The story he decided on was a drastically edited version of the truth. Saying nothing of the rest of the legionaries, he gave out that he and Gaius Philippus were from a land beyond the eastern ocean, forced to flee to these strange shores by a quarrel with a chieftain. After serving as mercenaries for Videssos, they had to flee again when Scaurus fell foul of the Emperor—he did not say how. Tahmasp's caravan, he finished truthfully, had brought them to Mashiz.

"That scoundrel," Wulghash said without rancor. "Who knows how much trade tax and customs revenue he cheats me out of every year?" He studied the tribune. "So Gavras outlawed you, did he? With his temper, you should be thankful you're still breathing."

"I know," Scaurus said, so feelingly the khagan gave that dry chuckle again.

"You have poor luck with nobles, it appears," Wulghash remarked. "Why is that?"

The tribune sensed danger in the question. As he cast about for a safe answer, Gaius Philippus came to his rescue. "Because we have a bad habit—we speak our minds. If one highborn sod's greedy as a pig at the swill trough or the next is a liverish son of a whore, we say so. Aye, it gets us in trouble, but it beats licking spit."

"Liverish, eh? Not bad," Wulghash said. As Gaius Philippus had intended, he took it to refer to Thorisin. He seemed reassured—the centurion's raspy voice and blunt features were made for candor.

The khagan looked musingly from one Roman to the other. "I know nothing of the countries beyond the eastern sea," he said. "Past Namdalen and the barbarous lands on the southern shore of the Sailors' Sea, our maps are blank. You could teach me a great deal." He went on, as his smile exposed strong yellow teeth, "And you were officers with Videssos. No doubt you will be able to tell me quite a lot about your sojourn there as well. Shall I have an apartment prepared for you here in the palace? That would be most convenient; I think we will be spending a good deal of time together over the next couple of weeks."

"We would be honored," Marcus said, and knew he had told Wulghash another lie.

To the Romans' dismay, the khagan was good as his word. He was full of questions, yet did not really subject them to a serious interrogation, asking almost as much about their homeland as about Videssos and its armies. Those questions Scaurus answered honestly, after the initial deception about the eastern ocean. Sometimes he and Gaius Philippus disagreed sharply; he came from the urban upper class, while the centurion was a product of farm and legion.

Wulghash was that rarity, a good listener. His queries always moved arguments along and convinced Scaurus afresh of his brain. His secretary Pushram, who wrote down the Romans' replies, asked no questions. He made a point of seeming bored about everything outside the khagan's court. It was a mischievous sort of boredom, for he was a skinny little brown man with outsized ears and amazingly flexible features.

Well into the second week of the Romans' presence at court, a servant came by with a tray of eggplant slices cooked in cheese and oregano. Wulghash took one. "That's excellent," he exclaimed. "Much better than usual. Here, fellow, give my friends some, too."

"Very nice," Marcus said politely, though in fact he found the eggplant bland and its sauce too sharp. Gaius Philippus, no timeserver, left his slice half-eaten.

Pushram, however, screwed up his face into a blissful expression. "Most glorious eggplant! Handsome to look upon, delicate on the tongue, full of flavor and of pleasing texture, a comestible to be esteemed for all the multifarious ways it may be prepared, each more delicious than the next. Truly a prince—no, let me say more: a khagan—among vegetables!"

Scaurus had heard fulsome flattery at the Videssian court, but nothing close to this sycophancy. "Who would want to be a king and have to put up with such tripe?" Gaius Philippus said in Latin.

After a while Wulghash rolled his eyes and went back to questioning the Romans. Pushram's paean of praise never slowed, even while he was recording Marcus' answers. Trying to find some way to shut him up, the khagan took another piece of eggplant, wrinkled his lip, and said, "I have changed my mind. This is vile."

Pushram assumed a look of loathing with a speed that amazed Scaurus. He plucked the eggplant slice from Wulghash's hand and threw it to the floor. "What a foul, noxious weed eggplant is!" he cried. "Not only is it of a bilious color, it brings no more nourishment to mankind than so much grass. Moreover, it makes me burp."

And he was off again, as ready to continue in that vein as to shower the vegetable with compliments. Marcus listened, open-mouthed. Wulghash gave Pushram a look that should have chilled any man's marrow, but the secretary's stream of abuse never faltered. "Enough!" Wulghash finally growled. "Were you not praising eggplant to the skies not two minutes ago, instead of cursing it?"

"Certainly."

"Well?" The word hung in the air like doom.

But Pushram was unruffled. "Well, what?" he said cheerfully. "I am your courtier, not the eggplant's. I have to say what pleases you, not what pleases the eggplant."

"Get out!" Wulghash roared, but he was laughing. Pushram scurried away anyhow. The khagan shook his head. "Makurani," he said, more to himself than to the Romans. "Sometimes they make me wish my grandfather had stayed on the steppe."

Marcus pointed to the plate of eggplant. "Yet you have taken on many Makuraner ways. If your grandfather was a nomad, he never would have cared for such a dish."

"My grandfather ate beetles, when he could catch them," the khagan said, and then sighed. "Too many of my chiefs think any change from the old customs wrong simply because it is change. Some of the plains ways have their point. What sense does it make to lock away women? Are they not people, too? But on the whole we were barbarians then, and for all their oiliness and foolishness the Makurani have worked out many better ways of living—and of ruling—than we ever knew. Try and tell that to an old nomad who has no thoughts past his flocks, though. Try and make him listen, or obey."

For a moment Scaurus understood him perfectly; he had lived with that feeling of being trapped between two cultures ever since the legionaries came to Videssos.

There was some sort of commotion outside the throne room. Marcus heard shouts of anger, then of fear. Nobles' heads turned as they looked to see what was wrong. A couple of eunuchs trotted toward the door. Wulghash's guards still stood impassive, but the tribune saw arm muscles bunch as hands tightened on sabers.

"Let me by, or regret it evermore!" At the sound of that voice, Marcus and Gaius Philippus were both on their feet and reaching for their swords. Crying out in alarm, the nearest guardsmen broke freeze and sprang at them.

"Stand!" Wulghash shouted, halting the Romans and his own soldiers alike. "What idiocy are you playing at?"

Scaurus was saved the trouble of finding an answer. Back at the entrance to the throne room, the last palace servitors were retreating in dread. Avshar strode down the carpet toward the twin thrones. Despite the thick, soft wool, every bootfall echoed. The muffled thuds were the only sounds in the hall, growing ever louder as he drew close.

No longer were the wizard-prince's robes an immaculate white. They swirled in filthy, dusty tatters round him. As protocol demanded, he stopped just past the edge of the carpet; his head turned from one Roman to the other. "Well, well," he said with horrible good humor, "what have we here?"

He ignored Wulghash, who said sharply, "We have a servant who does not know his master, it seems. Did you forget the respect you owe me, or is this merely more of your natural rudeness?"

Marcus looked at the khagan in surprised admiration. Wulghash showed none of the fear that paralyzed Avshar's friend and foe alike, the fear whose full weight the tribune was feeling now.

The wizard-prince stiffened angrily and gave Wulghash a long measure of his chilling stare, all the worse because his eyes were unseen. The khagan met it, something few men could have done. Fairly bursting with rage, Avshar bent in a bow whose very depth was an insult. "I pray your pardon, your Majesty," he said, but his voice held no apology. He went on, "My surprise betrayed me—seeing these two rogues here, I thought me for a moment I was back in cursed Videssos again, at the damned Avtokrator's court. Tell me, did you capture them in battle or were they taken spying?"

"Neither," Wulghash said, but his eyes slid to the Romans. He asked Avshar, "How is it you claim to have met a couple of no-account mercenaries at the Videssian court? What were they doing there, guard duty?" He still did not sound as if he believed the wizard-prince.

"No-account mercenaries? Guard duty?" Avshar threw back his head and laughed, a horrid sound that sent the nobles closest to him scrambling back in dismay. Its echoes came back cold and spectral from the high-arched roof; a nightjar perched near the top of the throne room wall woke to terror and flapped away. "Is that what they told you?" Avshar laughed again, then gave a colored but largely accurate account of Scaurus' career in Videssos, finishing, "And this other one, the short one, is his chief henchman."

"Bugger yourself," Gaius Philippus said. He stood balanced on the balls of his feet, ready to throw himself at Avshar.

Wulghash ignored the senior centurion. "Is this true?" he asked Marcus in a voice like iron.

Avshar hissed, a serpent on the point of striking. "Have a care what thou dost, Wulghash. Thou couldst yet try me too far, seeking the word of this miscreant espier to weigh it against mine own."

"Be thou still. I act as I list, with or without thy let." The khagan was as fluent as Avshar in the archaic Videssian dialect the wizard-prince often used. Maybe, Marcus thought, Avshar had taught it to him.

Wulghash asked the tribune again, "Is what he says true?"

"Most of it," Scaurus sighed. With Avshar standing there to give him away, what use in lying?

Avshar laughed once more, this time in triumph. "From his own mouth he stands convicted. Give them over to me, Wulghash. The debt I owe them is larger and older than yours. I pledge you, the insult they offered with their base falsehoods shall be requited—oh, yes, a thousand times over." He was all but purring in anticipation. At his gesture, the palace guards edged forward, expecting the khagan's order to seize the Romans.

Wulghash stopped them. "I have told you once, wizard—aye, and times enough before this—that I command here, yet always you seem to forget. Whatever story these men told, before they said a word to me they saved my minister's life. I have made them my friends."

"And so?" Avshar's whisper crawled with menace.

"A favor for a favor. I give them back their lives in exchange for

Tabari's." Wulghash turned to Scaurus and Gaius Philippus. "Get your horses. You may leave. No one will pursue you, I vow. I have called you my friends and I do not go back on my word—but you should have trusted me in full. I am no longer happy with you, friends or not. Go on; get out."

Hardly daring believe his ears, Marcus searched the khagan's face. It was stormy with disappointed anger, but he read no deceit. As Wulghash had said of himself, he was as determined in friendship as he was in enmity. "You are a man of honor," the tribune said softly.

"You do well to remind me, for I am tempted to forget." Wulghash waved brusquely for them to be gone.

"Thou dung-headed fool!" Avshar roared before the Romans could move. They froze again; any exit would take them straight past the wizard-prince.

But Avshar had nearly forgotten them in his rage. He screamed abuse at the khagan: "Thou dolt, thou clodpoll, thou idiot puling mousling with fantasies of manhood! Reeking filthy louse-bearded barbarous bastard son of a camel turd, thinkest thou to gainsay *me*? These sneaking spies are mine; get thee down on thy wormish belly and grovel in thanksgiving that I do not serve thee worse than them for thine insolence!"

White about the lips, Wulghash snapped an order in the Yezda tongue to his guards. They drew their weapons and advanced on the wizard-prince.

"Thou'lt not find it so simple to be shut of me as that," Avshar sneered. "Am I as stupid as thyself, to take no precautions against thy childish thoughts of treachery?" He spoke a single word, in Videssian or some darker speech, the trigger to a spell long prepared against this time. The khagan's guards came to a ragged halt. All at once they were looking at Avshar with the devotion a lap dog gives its mistress. "How now, O clever booby?" he chuckled.

Wulghash, though, was wise in the ways of Makuran for reasons stronger than antiquarianism. He knew why the Makuraner kings of old had ordained that men seeking audience with them should halt at a certain spot. His hand darted to a spring cunningly concealed in the arm of his throne. A six-foot slab of stone fell away beneath Avshar's feet.

But the wizard-prince did not drop into the pit below. An abrupt pass let him bestride the empty air like polished marble. Wulghash's nobles moaned; some covered their faces. The khagan's guards—no, Avshar's now—smiled at the new proof of their master's might. Those smiles made Scaurus shudder. Only the soldiers' lips moved. Their eyes stayed bright and blank.

"This farce wearies me," Avshar said. "Let there be an end to it. Look now, Wulghash, on the power thou hadst thought to oppose." Still standing easily on nothing, the wizard-prince threw back the mantlings that always veiled his face.

Even Gaius Philippus, calloused by more than half a lifetime of hard soldiering, could not hold back a groan. His cry was lost in the chorus of horror that swelled and swelled as Avshar turned toward the nobility of Yezd.

Two thoughts raced across Scaurus' mind. The first was that he had gone mad. He wished it were true. And the second was of the myth of Aurora's lover Tithonus. The goddess had begged immortality for him from Jupiter, but forgot to ask that he not grow old.

In his decrepitude, Tithonus had been turned by Jove into a grasshopper. No god had shown Avshar such kindness. Staring—he could not help but stare—the tribune tried to guess how many years had rolled over the sorcerer. He gave up; as well try to reckon how many goldpieces had gone into Phos' High Temple. Imagining such age would have been enough to make the skin prickle into gooseflesh. Seeing it, and seeing it combined with Avshar's undoubted vigor, was infinitely worse.

"Well?" Avshar said into vast silence. "I own eight and a half centuries. Eight hundred years have passed since I learned in the ruins of Skopentzana where true power lay. Which of you puny mayfly men will stand against me now?" There was no answer; there could be no answer. Smiling a lich's smile, the wizard-prince gestured to the guardsmen he had ensorceled. "I rule here. Kill me that lump of offal fouling my throne."

He spoke Videssian, but they understood. They surged toward Wulghash, sabers clenched in their fists.

The khagan was perhaps the only man in the room not paralyzed by dismay. He did not need Avshar's unmasking to know what had served him. No small wizard himself, he had divined that long ago. In his ambition he thought to use the other to exalt himself, to ride to greatness on Avshar's back. For all that arrogance, though, he always remembered tool and user might one day be reversed. And so he pressed another stud mounted on his throne. A hidden doorway swung open behind it. He darted into the tunnel it had concealed.

Avshar howled in fury; the door was secret even to him. "After him, you bunglers," he screamed to the guards, though the blunder had not been theirs.

Pushram sprang up and grappled with the leading guardsman. He was scrawny and carried nothing more deadly than a stylus, but he bought his master a few seconds with his life.

His sacrifice jerked the Romans from their daze. They both seemed to have the same thought at once—better to die fighting than in Avshar's clutches. They tore their swords free and hurled themselves at the wizard-prince's soldiers.

Avshar understood immediately. "Take them alive!" he shouted. "Their end shall not be as easy as they wish."

Sword in hand, a Makuraner noble dashed toward the thrones, rushing to the Romans' aid and to the defense of the khagan. Avshar cursed and moved his guantleted hands in savage passes. The nobleman crashed to the floor, writhing in torment. "More?" the wizard asked. There were none.

By weight of numbers, the guards forced Scaurus and Gaius Philippus away from the doorway down which Wulghash had vanished. Several rushed after the khagan. The tribune laid about him desperately, but a cleverly aimed slash caught his sword just above the hilt. It flew from his numbed fingers. Knowing how little good it would do, he snatched out his dagger and stabbed at the nearest guardsman. He felt the blade bite and heard a grunt of pain.

Avshar's order hampered his men, who took losses because of it and passed up several sure killing strokes. The Romans battled ferociously, trying to make their foes finish them. Then a guardsman sent his fist clubbing down on the back of Marcus' neck. The tribune toppled. He did not see the Yezda swarm over Gaius Philippus and finally bring him down.

An echoing shout from the secret tunnel's opening returned Scaurus to blurry consciousness. Someone screamed, then silence fell once more. A couple of minutes later, a broad-shouldered guard, staggering under the weight, came out of the doorway with a corpse on his back. It wore royal robes. Marcus had a glimpse of fleshy nose, square-cut gray beard, eyes gone set and staring—no way now to see if intelligence had been there.

Avshar's terrible grin grew wide. "Well done," he said. "Thou'lt be a captain for this day's work. What end did he make?"

As usual, the sorcerer spoke in Videssian, but the guardsman had no trouble with it. He answered in his own tongue. Avshar grimaced impatiently. "What care I that your stupid comrade fell? Incompetence punishes itself, as always. Here, give the body to these others to fling on the midden; hie yourself off to the officers' chambers, to deck yourself with something finer than those rags you wear."

The soldier said something that sounded like a protest of unworthiness. Avshar made his harsh voice as genial as he could, answering, "Nay, thou hast earned it. Hyazdat, Gandutav, take him along and fit him out." Pounding the trooper on the back, the two guards officers led him away.

More guardsmen carried off the corpse that had won him his promotion. Save for those still grasping the tribune and Gaius Philippus, only a couple were left in the throne room.

Avshar did not need them. By himself he cowed the nobility of Yezd, bold haughty Makurani and fierce Yezda alike. Men stared at their shoes, at each other, at the walls, anything to keep from meeting his eyes. He snarled at them. They went to their knees and then to their bellies in proskynesis before him. Some, mostly Makurani, performed the prostration with grace, others were slow and clumsy. But all knelt.

"And thou," Avshar said to Marcus. "I have heard thou wouldst not bend the knee before the Avtokrators. I am greater than they, for I am at once priest and lord, patriarch and Emperor. They shall know my power, and my god's—as shalt thou."

He gave the tribune no chance to refuse; at his command, the guards cast Scaurus at his feet. His boot, still smelling of lathered horse, ground cruelly into the Roman's shoulder. He suddenly asked, "What didst thou with the head of Mavrikios Gavras, when I gave it thee?"

"Buried it," Marcus answered, too startled not to respond.

“A pity; now when I take Thorisin’s, the set will remain broken. Perhaps thine shall serve in its stead. Such decisions should not be frivolously made, but then I now enjoy the leisure to choose among the interesting possibilities.”

Avshar strode over to the tribune’s sword, which still lay where it had fallen. The wizard-prince stooped to pick up the prize, but paused before his hand closed on the hilt—that blade had shown itself dangerous to his spells too many times for him to be easy about touching it. But he did not stay baffled long. He pointed to a noble. “Tabari, come you forward.”

“Aye, my lord,” the man the Romans had rescued said eagerly. He prostrated himself before the wizard. His face to the floor, he went on, “I am privileged to see you raised at last to your proper estate. Your followers here have waited long for this day.”

“As have I,” Avshar said. “As have I.” The pain behind Marcus’ eyes was not the only thing to sicken him now. Bad enough to have saved a Yezda minister. To have preserved one of Avshar’s creatures and fallen into the wizard-prince’s hand because of it mortified him past bearing.

He hardly noticed when two of the ensorceled guards hauled him to his feet. Another pair did the same with Gaius Philippus, who had also been cast down. The senior centurion struggled in their grasp, but could not break free.

Avshar was saying, “Carry this piece of rusty iron down to my workroom in the dungeons. As minister of justice, you doubtless know them well enough to find the place without difficulty.”

Tabari’s laugh was not pleasant, except to Avshar. “Oh, indeed, my lord.”

“Excellent,” he said. “I thought as much. And while you are about it, guide the guards holding these wretches”—a thumb jabbed toward the Romans—“to the block of cells adjacent. Perhaps the blade will yield up its secrets to me when housed in their flesh.”

“What a pleasant prospect,” Tabari said, killing any lingering hope Scaurus had for the permanence of his gratitude. Tabari gestured to the tribune’s captors. They dragged him away. He heard Gaius Philippus, still swearing, forced along behind him.

Avshar’s voice pursued them: “Enjoy this respite while you may, for you shall have none other, ever again.”

Tabari waved the guards down a narrow spiral ramp cut into the living rock just outside the throne room. As they descended into the bowels of the palace, a woman's shriek rang out far above. Atossa, Marcus thought dully, must have come into the court. The scream was abruptly silenced.

Gaius Philippus also recognized the cry. "Wulghash has a son," he said.

"What of it? What chance has he, when Wulghash couldn't stand against Avshar in his own palace?"

"Damn little," the veteran sighed. "For a minute, I thought he'd get away—he was ready for anything. Did you hear Avshar howl when that passage opened up? He hadn't a clue it was there."

The guards gave little doglike grunts of devotion to hear their master's name. Otherwise they did not seem to care if their prisoners talked. Wondering whether Avshar's spell had taken more of their wits than that, Marcus tensed to try to break free. Their grip tightened. Nothing wrong with their physical reactions, he saw ruefully.

They did not mind his turning his head this way and that. Several tunnels had already branched off from the ramp. Some held storerooms; from another came the rhythmic clang of a smith's hammer on hot iron. Down and down they went. More than once, they passed workers replacing burned-out torches. Even far underground, the brands burned steadily and did not fill the passageway with smoke. The Makuraner kings, Marcus thought as a puff of cool air touched his cheek, had worked out a better ventilation system than the Videssians used in their prison. He wondered how many men had compared the two.

Gaius Philippus barked laughter when he muttered that under his breath. "It's nothing to brag of." Scaurus' nod made fresh pain flare in his head.

The tribune's ears clicked before the guards finally turned down a still, lonely side corridor. "Yes, gentlemen, we are almost there," Tabari said. He had been very quiet on the long trip down, nor had the Romans cared to speak to him.

Now at last, though, Marcus turned his head to plead with Wulghash's—no, Avshar's—minister. He did not beg for his life; he had lost hope for it. Instead he said, “Take my sword and strike us down. You owe us that much, if nothing else.”

“I am the judge of my debts; no one else.” Tabari hefted the Gallic blade. Without warning, he drove it into the back of one of Gaius Philippus’ guards. The Yezda groaned and crumpled.

Gaius Philippus acted as if he had been waiting for the blow. He spun and grappled with his other captor, giving Tabari the moment he needed to wrench out the sword.

Scaurus’ guards hesitated a fatal instant. Had they shoved him away at once, they might have quickly overwhelmed Tabari and then wheeled round to retake him. As it was, he managed to thrust out a foot and trip one of them. He sprang on the fellow’s back, grabbing for his knife wrist.

The Yezda was strong as a bull. They thrashed on the ground. The tribune felt his grip failing. The guard tore his hand free. His dagger slashed along Scaurus’ ribs. Gasping, the tribune tried to seize his arm again, all the while waiting for the thrust that would end it. I made them kill me, he thought with something like triumph.

The guard snorted, as if in disdain. The weight pressing on Marcus suddenly grew heavier. He groaned and shoved desperately at the Yezda. The guard slid off, knife clattering to the floor as it slipped from his fingers. Another dagger stood in his back. Gaius Philippus pulled it out. Marcus’ nose caught the death stench of suddenly loosed bowels.

The other guards were down, too. The one Gaius Philippus had fought lay unmoving. “Bastard had a hard head, but not as hard as a stone floor,” the senior centurion said. And Tabari knelt by the last one, wiping the Gallic sword clean on the fellow’s caftan.

“You are hurt,” the Yezda minister said, pointing to the spreading red stain on Marcus’ chest. He helped the tribune shed his tunic, tore rags to try to dress the long cut that ran down from just outside Scaurus’ left nipple. The bleeding slowed but did not stop; the rough bandages began to grow soggy with blood.

“That was all an act, you cheering Avshar on up there?” Gaius Philippus demanded. He did not sound as though he believed it, and held his dagger in a knife-fighter’s crouch.

“No, not all of it,” Tabari said.

Gaius Philippus was poised to hurl himself at the minister. "Hear him out," Marcus said quickly.

Calmly, Tabari went on, "I've long favored Avshar over Wulghash; he will make Yezd mighty. But I have already said once that I judge my debts." He handed Marcus the Gallic sword. The tribune snatched at it; without it, he felt more than half unmanned.

As Scaurus struggled to his feet, Gaius Philippus snapped at Tabari, "Are you crazy, man? When that walking corpse finds out you've let us go, you'll envy what he had planned for us."

"That thought had occurred to me." One of Tabari's dark eyebrows quirked upward. "I will ask you, then, to lay me out roughly—I hope without permanent damage. If I am stunned and battered when found, everyone will think I put up the best fight I could."

"What do we do then?" Marcus said.

"Can you walk?"

Scaurus tried it. The effort it took dismayed him; he could feel blood trickling down his belly. But he said, "If I have to, I can. I'd try flying to keep out of Avshar's hands."

"Then go into the maze of tunnels down here." Tabari pointed to an opening in the rock wall. "They run farther than any man knows these days, except perhaps Wulghash, and he is dead. Maybe you will find a way free. I have no better hope to offer you."

"I think I'd sooner fly," Gaius Philippus muttered mistrustfully, eyeing the blank black hole. But there was no help for it; he realized that as fast as Marcus.

Tabari drew himself up to stiff attention. "At your service," he said, and waited.

Gaius Philippus approached him, thumped him on the shoulder. "I've never done this as a favor before," he said. In the middle of the sentence, he slammed his left fist into Tabari's belly. As the minister folded, Gaius Philippus' right hand crashed against his jaw. He slumped to the floor.

Rubbing bruised knuckles, the senior centurion opened the unconscious man's tunic and used the dagger to make a bloody scratch on his chest. "Now they'll figure we thought he was dead."

"Don't forget to cut the tunic, too," Marcus said. Gaius Philippus swore at himself and attended to it. Marcus took canteens from the dead guards—no telling how long the Romans might wander this labyrinth. He wished the Yezda had food with them. When he was finished, he saw Gaius Philippus pulling torches from the sconces set in the tunnel wall. "Why do that? All these ways should have lights ready for us to take."

"Aye, but if we do, whoever comes after us will be able to track us by it," the veteran said, and it was Scaurus' turn for chagrin. Gaius Philippus went on, "Eventually we'll have to start using the torches we come on, but by then we should be lost enough that it won't matter." The centurion's chuckle held no mirth. He strode toward the lightless tunnel entrance. Marcus reluctantly followed. The two Romans plunged in together.

The circle of light behind them shrank, then abruptly vanished as the tunnel veered to the right. Before and behind the flickering glow of the torch was impenetrable black.

Gaius Philippus led, holding the brand high. Marcus did his best to keep up. The cut along his ribs began to stiffen. He did not think he was bleeding anymore, but the wound made him slow and weak. In spite of himself, he would fall behind, into the darkness.

When he did, he saw the druids' marks on his sword glowing faintly—magic somewhere, he thought. As long as the gleam stayed dim, he refused to let it worry him.

The way branched every hundred paces or so. The Romans went now left, now right at random. At every turning they put three pebbles by the way they chose. "They'll keep us from doubling back on ourselves," Scaurus said.

"Unless we miss 'em, of course."

"Cheerful, aren't you?" Marcus thought they were deeper underground; his ears had popped again. There was no sign of pursuit behind them. They would have heard it a long way off; but for their own breathing and the faint sound of their feet on stone, the silence was absolute as the darkness.

After a while they paused to rest. They drank a couple of swallows of water. Then, feeling like ants lost in a strange burrow, they wandered on. Once, far off, they saw a lighted corridor and shied away as if it were Avshar in person.

"What's that?" Gaius Philippus said—something was scratched into the side of the tunnel.

"It's in the Videssian script," Marcus said in surprise. "Bring the light close. No, hold it to one side so shadow fills the letters. There, better." He read: " 'I, Hesaios Stenes of Resaina, dug this tunnel and wrote these words. Sharbaraz of Makuran took me in the ninth year of the Avtokrator Genesios. Phos guard the Avtokrator and me.' "

"Poor sod," Gaius Philippus said. "I wonder when this Emperor Genesios lived."

"I couldn't tell you. Alypia would know." Her name sent a wave of loneliness washing over Scaurus.

"I hope you get the chance to ask her, not that it looks likely." Gaius Philippus shook a canteen. The tribune did not need the slosh to remind him they only had so much water. A couple of days after that was gone and it would not matter whether Avshar tracked them down or not.

They pressed on. They no longer needed to mark a path. This deep in the maze, long-undisturbed dust held their footprints.

Hesaios' graffito went back to the night that had enfolded it for centuries.

The Romans' only pastime in the tunnels was talk, and they used it till they grew hoarse. Gaius Philippus' stories reached back to the days when Scaurus was a child. The veteran had first campaigned under Gaius Marius, against the Italians in the Social War and then against Sulla. "Marius was old and half-crazy by then, but even in the wreck of him you could see what a soldier he'd been. Some of his centurions had been with him in every fight since Jugurtha; they worshipped him. Of course he made most of them—till his day, landless men couldn't serve in the legions."

"I wonder if that's better," Marcus said. "With no land of their own, they're always beholden to their general, and a danger to the state."

"So say you, who grew up landed," Gaius Philippus retorted, the gut response of a man born poor. "If he can get 'em land, more power to him. What would they do without the army? Starve in the city like that Apokavkos you rescued in Videssos—and not many as bad at thieving as him."

Only women ranked with war and politics for hashing over. Despite his earlier try at sympathy, Gaius Philippus could not understand Marcus' devotion first to Helvis and then to Alypia. "Why buy a sheep if all you want is wool?"

"What do you know? You married the legions." The tribune intended that for a joke, but saw it was true. It gave him pause; he went on carefully, "A good woman halves sorrows and doubles joys." But he had the feeling he was explaining poetry to a deaf man.

He was right. Gaius Philippus said, "Doubles sorrow and halves joy, you ask me. Leaving Helvis out of the bargain—"

"Good idea," Scaurus said quickly. The abandonment was fresh enough still to ache in him every time he thought of it.

"All right. What has Alypia given you, then, that you couldn't have for silver from some tavern wench? I take it you weren't bedding her for ambition's sake?"

"*Et tu?* You sound like Thorisin." From anyone else, the blunt questions would have angered Marcus, but he knew the centurion's manner. He answered seriously. "What has she given me? Besides honest affection, which silver won't buy, her courage outdoes any man's I know of, to hold herself together through all she's endured. She's clever, and kind, and gives everything she has—wisdom, wit, heart—for those she cares about. I only hope to be able to do as much. When I'm with her, I'm at peace."

"You should write paeans," Gaius Philippus grunted. "At peace, is it? Seems to me she's brought you enough trouble for four men, let alone one."

"She's saved me some, too. If not for her, who knows what Thorisin would have done after"—he hesitated; here came the hurt again—"after the Namdaleni got away."

"Oh, aye. Kept you out of jail a few extra months—and made sure you'd be in hotter water when you did land there."

"That's not the fault of who she is; it's the fault of who she was born."

Marcus had hardly noticed the druids' marks stamped into his blade gleaming brighter, but now they were outshining Gaius Philippus' torch. "Hold up," he told the veteran. "There's magic somewhere close." They peered into the darkness, hands tight on their weapons, sure sorcery could only mean Avshar.

But there was no sign of the wizard-prince. Scratching his head, Scaurus took a few steps back the way he had come. The druids' marks grew fainter. "In front, then. Give me the lead, Gaius. The sword will turn magic from me."

They traded places. The tribune slowly moved forward, sword held before him like a shield. The glow from it grew steadily brighter, until the tunnel that had never known daylight was lit bright as noon.

In that golden light the pit ahead remained a patch of blackness. It was three times the length of a man; only a narrow stone ledge allowed passage on either side. Scaurus held his sword over the edge of the pit and looked down. The bottom was wickedly spiked; two points thrust up through the rib cage of a skeleton sprawled in ungainly death.

Gaius Philippus tapped Marcus on the shoulder. "What are you waiting for?"

"Very funny. One more step and I'll keep that fellow down there company." The tribune pointed to what was left of the victim in the pit.

Or so he thought. The senior centurion gave him a puzzled look. "What fellow? Down where? All I see is a lot of dusty floor."

"No pit? No spears set in the bottom of it? No skeleton? One of us has lost his wits." Scaurus had an inspiration. "Here—take my sword."

They both exclaimed then, Marcus because as the sword left his fingers the pit disappeared, leaving what lay ahead no different to the eye from the rest of the tunnel, Gaius Philippus for exactly the opposite reason as he took the blade. "Is it real?" he asked.

"Do you care to find out? Three steps forward and you'll know."

"Hmm. The ledge'll do fine, thanks. We see that with or without." He held out the blade to Scaurus. "You take it in your left hand, I'll hold it in my right, and we'll sidle by crab-fashion, our backs to the wall. We'll both be able to see what we're doing that way—I hope."

As the tribune touched the sword hilt, the pit jumped into visibility again. The ledge was wide enough for the Romans' feet and not much more. Some of the spikes below still gleamed brightly, reflecting the light of the sword; others had rusty points and dark-stained shafts that told their own story.

The Romans were about two thirds of the way across when Marcus stumbled. His foot slipped off the edge, toes curling on emptiness. Gaius

Philippus slammed him back against the tunnel wall with a strong forearm. The jar sent anguish through him. When he could speak again, he wheezed, "Thanks. It's real, all right."

"Thought so. Here, have a swig." Even with his sudden sideways leap to save Scaurus, the veteran had not spilled a drop of precious water. Marcus' stomach twisted at the thought of impalement.

The druids' stamps dimmed once more as the Romans put distance between themselves and the pit. Gaius Philippus returned to the lead, his torch a better light than the tribune's blade.

As the sword faded, though, excitement flared in Scaurus. He said, "The Makurani wouldn't have dug that mantrap if it didn't guard the way to something important—the escape route?"

"Maybe." With ingrained pessimism, Gaius Philippus added, "I wonder what else they used to keep unwelcome guests out."

Hope revived brought fresh anxiety. Every branching of the tunnel became a crisis; the wrong choice might mean throwing freedom away. For a while the Romans agonized over each decision. At last Gaius Philippus said, "A pox on it. The dithering doesn't help. One way or the other, we just go." That helped, some.

Scaurus lifted his head like a hunted animal tasting the wind. "Stand still," he whispered. Gaius Philippus froze. The tribune listened, then grimaced at what he heard. The corridors behind them were silent no more. Echoing strangely in the distance, now strong, now faint, came the cries of soldiers and, like the murmur of surf, the sound of trotting feet. Avshar had awakened to his loss.

The Romans did their best to make haste but, battered as they were, could not match the speed of fresh men. The noise of the pursuit grew louder with terrible speed. The Yezda were not searching haphazardly; they must have come across the fugitives' trail in the dust. Perhaps Avshar's magic had led them to it. Marcus wasted a breath cursing him.

But the wizard-prince was not master of all the secrets of the maze below the palace he now held, nor had he readied his minions for them. A dreadful scream reverberated through the tunnels, followed a moment later by two more. One of them went on and on.

The wizard-prince's minions must have probed round the edges of the pit and found at last the narrow ways by the trap. That was how Scaurus read the silence behind the Romans, a silence broken by a terrified shriek as another Yezda stepped onto deceitfully empty air and fell to his doom.

The tribune shuddered. "They're no cowards, to dare those ledges without being able to tell them from the pit."

"When they're after me, I'd sooner they *were* cravens. But they've had enough for now, sounds like." The loss of that fourth trooper must have dismayed the Yezda past the breaking point. They came no further; soon the only sounds in the tunnels were the groans of the dying men in the pit.

Neither Marcus nor Gaius Philippus said what they both feared, that their respite would not last long. Either their pursuers would find a route that dodged the mantrap, or Avshar would reveal it with his magic so they could get safely past.

When the druids' marks sparked again, the tribune at first thought that had happened and that his sword was reacting to the backwash of the wizard-prince's spell. But the light from the stamping brightened as he went farther and farther from the pit.

"What now?" Gaius Philippus grunted.

"Who knows? It started when that side tunnel joined this one, I think." Scaurus took back the lead, trying to look every way at once. It might not be a pit this time, but vitriol from a spigot in the ceiling, or a blast of fire, or . . . anything.

The uncertainty ate at him, made him start at the shift of his own shadow as he walked. He paused to rest a moment, letting his sword drag in the dust.

Light fountained from the blade, so brilliant the tribune flung up his arms to shield his eyes. The dazzling burst lasted only an instant. Marcus leaped backward, wondering what snare he had tripped. Then he saw the line of footprints stretching out ahead in the dust.

They were invisible to Gaius Philippus until he touched the hilt of the Gallic longsword. "So someone's covering his tracks by magic, is he?" the veteran said. He made a menacing motion with his dagger. "Can't you just guess who?"

"Who else but Avshar?" Marcus said bitterly. How had the wizard-prince got ahead of them? No matter, the tribune thought grimly; there he was. The Romans could not retreat, not with the Yezda in the corridors behind them. No choice but to go on. “He won’t take us unawares.”

“Or need to.” But Gaius Philippus was already moving forward. “We’ll stalk him for a change.”

As it did all through the tunnel system, the dust went thick and thin by turns, now rising in choking clouds when the Romans scuffed through it, now only a film. The light of Scaurus’ sword, though, picked out the sorcerously concealed trail even at its most indistinct.

“Branching up ahead,” Gaius Philippus said. “Which direction did the bastard go?” He spoke in a whisper; in these twisting passages, sound carried further than light.

“Left,” Marcus answered confidently. But after continuing for about another fifteen feet, the trail disappeared, Gallic magic or no. “What the—” the tribune said. He heard a sudden rush of steps behind him. Knowing he had been tricked again, he whirled with Gaius Philippus for a last round of hopeless combat.

He would remember the tableau forever—three men with upraised weapons, each motionless in astonishment. “You!” they all cried at once, and, like puppets on the same string, lowered their blades together.

“I saw you dead,” Marcus said, almost with anger in his voice.

“It was not me you saw,” Wulghash replied. The deposed khagan of Yezd wore an officer’s silk surcoat over a boiled-leather cuirass, and trousers of fine suede. Trousers and coat were filthy, as was he, but he still bore himself like a king. He went on, “I put my seeming—and my robes—on one of the traitors I slew and took his image for myself when I carried him out. In his arrogance, Avshar did not look past the surface.” The khagan spoke matter-of-factly of his sorcery; Scaurus could only imagine his haste and desperation as he had worked, not knowing whether more of the wizard-prince’s guards would fall on him before his spells were done. But Wulghash was looking at the Romans with like amazement. “How is it you walk free? I saw you taken by Avshar in truth, not seeming. You have no magic save your sword, and you had already lost that to him.”

Marcus hid the blade behind his body before he answered. Wulghash’s eyes were watering; he had known little light in the tunnels. The tribune said, “There was no magic to it.” He explained what Tabari had done.

"Gratitude is a stronger magic than most of the ones I know." Wulghash grunted. "You conjured more of it from Tabari than I, it seems, if he obeys Avshar now." Scaurus thought the minister of justice lucky he was nowhere near his khagan at that moment.

With characteristic practicality, Gaius Philippus demanded of Wulghash, "So why didn't you flee, once you were wearing another man's face?"

"I would have, but Avshar, his own Skotos eat him, saw fit to promote me for murdering myself, and to give me these gauds." The khagan patted his draggled finery. "That meant I was in his henchmen's company and could hardly up and go. Besides, the glamour I had cast was a weak one. I had no time for better, but it could have worn off at any moment. That *would* have killed me, did it happen while I was still in the palace for his slaves to spot. So when I was finally alone a moment, the best I could think of was to take to the tunnels."

He waved. "Here I am safe enough. I know these ways better than most. They must be learned on foot; masking spells hide much of them—and many traps—from sorcerous prying. Some go back to the Makuraner kings, others I set myself against an evil day; if you ride the snake, watch his fangs. And if you know where to search, there are cisterns and caches of Makuraner bread baked hard as rock to keep forever. Not fare I relish, but I can live on it."

The Romans looked at each other and at their canteens, which held a couple of swallows apiece now. How many times had they missed chances to fill them? Tone roughened by chagrin, Gaius Philippus said, "All right, you escaped Avshar. But this moles' nest must have its ways out. Why didn't you use one?"

Pride rang in Wulghash's answer: "Because I aim to take back what is mine. Aye, I know Avshar has been pickling in his own malice like a gherkin in vinegar these many hundred years, but I am no mean loremaster either. Let me but catch him unawares, and I can best him."

Marcus and Gaius Philippus glanced at each other again. "You do not believe me," the khagan said. "As may be, but with no hope at all I would still be here." His voice, his entire aspect, softened. "Whom else has Atossa to rely on?"

The Romans could not help starting. Wulghash did not miss it.

“What do you know? Tell me.” He hefted his saber as if to rip the answer from them.

“I fear she is dead,” Scaurus said, and told of the shriek from the court room that had been so suddenly cut off.

Wulghash raised the saber again. Before the tribune could lift his own blade for self-defense, the khagan slashed his own cheeks in the mourning ritual of the steppe. Blood ran into his beard and dripped in the dust at his feet.

He paid it no attention. Pushing past the Romans, he started down the corridor from which he had come. Now he made no effort to conceal his tracks; he cared nothing for magic any more. The sword in his hand was all that mattered to him. “Avshar!” he roared. “I am coming for you!”

Near mad with grief and rage, he could not have stood against the wizard-prince for an instant. Gaius Philippus realized at once the only course that might stay him. He taunted the khagan: “Aye, go on, throw yourself away, too. Then when you meet your woman in the next world you can tell her how you avenged her by getting yourself killed to no purpose.”

The jeer served where Marcus’ more reasoned tone would have failed. Wulghash whirled with catlike grace. He was close to Gaius Philippus’s age, but hardly less a warrior. “What better time to take the spider unawares in the palace than when everything is topsy-turvy after your escape?” He spat the words at the veteran, but that he argued at all showed reason still held him, if narrowly.

“Who’ll take whom unawares?” the senior centurion said with a scornful laugh. “The palace, is it? My guess is the son of a whore’s not five tunnels behind us, and his guards with him, magicking their way past the spiked pit back there.”

That reached Wulghash, though not for the reason Gaius Philippus had expected. “You came this way past the pit?” he demanded in disbelief. “How, without wizardry? That is the deadliest snare in all the tunnels.”

“We have this,” Scaurus reminded him, motioning with his sword. “It bared the trap before we fell into it—the same way it showed your footprints,” he added.

Wulghash's jaw muscles jumped. "Strong sorcery," he said. "Strong enough to draw Avshar were he blind as a cave-fish." He scowled at Gaius Philippus. "You have reason, damn you. With Avshar close by and his magic primed and ready, I cannot hope to beat him now. Best we flee, though saying so gags me."

Still scowling, he turned back to Marcus. "What point in flying, if you carry a lantern calling the huntsmen after you? Leave the sword here."

"No," the tribune said. "When he took me, Avshar feared to touch it. I will not abandon the best weapon I have, or let him put it to the test at his leisure."

"Ill was the day I met you," Wulghash said balefully, "and I would had never named you friend."

"Cut the horseshit," Gaius Philippus snapped. "If you'd never met us, you'd be dead yourself, and Avshar running your stinking country anyway."

"So forward a tongue is ripe for the cropping."

The hue and cry from the Roman's pursuers gave a sudden surge. "The wizard's men are past the pit," Marcus said to Wulghash. "You talk like Avshar; maybe you're thinking like him, too, and hoping to buy your own life from them with ours."

"By whatever gods may be, I will never deal in peace with him or his, so long as breath is in me." The khagan paused to think. He set down his saber. His hands flashed through passes; he muttered in the same archaic Videssian dialect Avshar used.

"Your magic will not touch me or my blade," Scaurus reminded him.

"I know," Wulghash said when he could speak normally. "But I can set a spell round you and it both, to befog one seeking it through sorcery. The magic does not touch you, you see; if it did, it would perish. But because of that it only befogs. It will not blind. So, my friends" he said, his tone making it an accusation to flinch from, "can you run with me, since you have proven running the greater wisdom?"

They ran.

X

"THERE IT SITS, MASHIZ ITS AIN SELF, AND DAMN ALL WE CAN DO ABOUT it," Viridovix said glumly. He peered through evening twilight toward the Yezda capital from the jumbled hills at the edge of the mountains of Dilbat.

"Aye, one glorious, sweeping charge, and it's ours," Pikridios Goudeles said in ringing tones that went poorly with his dirty buckskin tunic and bandaged shoulder. Sour laughter floated up from the edge of the Arshaum camp where the survivors of the Videssian embassy party and their few friends congregated.

Gorgidas found he could not blame the plainsmen for their bitterness toward the imperials. Despite Arigh's steadfast friendship, most of the nomads felt they had been drawn into a losing campaign for the Empire's sake. And Mashiz, so close yet utterly unattainable, symbolized their frustration.

The cloud of noxious smoke rising from the granite pyramid in the western part of the city did not hide the throng of yurts and tents and other shelters that daily grew greater as Yezd's strength flowed in to the capital. Campfires glittered like stars. At its freshest the Arshaum army would have lost to such a host. Fragmented as the plainsmen were, a determined assault would have swept them away.

The Greek wondered why it had not come. After the blows that broke the Arshaum apart, their foes seemed to have lost interest in them. Daily patrols made sure the scattered bands stayed away from Mashiz, but past that they were ignored. The Yezda even let them make contact with each other, though the mountain country was too broken and too poor for them to regroup as a single force.

"Who comes?" Prevalis Haravash's son barked nervously when an Arshum approached; things were at the point where the imperial trooper from Prista was as leery of his allies as he would have been of the enemy. Then the young sentry relaxed. "Oh, it's you, sir."

Arigh leaned against a boulder set into the side of the hill and looked from Goudeles to Viridovix to Skylitzes to Gorgidas to Agathias Psoes. He slammed a fist down on his thigh. "I don't propose living out my life as an outlaw skulking through these mountains, thinking I'm a hero because I've stolen five sheep or an ugly wench."

"What do you aim to do instead, then?" Psoes asked. The Videssian underofficer had a Roman air of directness to him.

"I don't know, the wind spirits curse it," Arigh glared at the winking field of campfires in the distance.

Skylitzes followed his gaze. He said, "If we skirt them, we can ride for the Empire."

"No," Arigh said flatly. "Even if I could jolly my men into it, I will not turn away from Mashiz while I can still strike a blow. My father's ghost would spurn me if I gave up a blood-feud so easily."

Familiar with the customs of the plains, the Videssian nodded. He tried a different tack. "You would not be abandoning your vendetta, simply getting new allies for it as you did in Erzerum. Seeking the Empire's aid would bring your soldiers round."

"That may be so, but I still will not. In Erzerum I was master of the situation. With Thorisin I would be a beggar."

Gorgidas said, "Gavras is as much Yezd's enemy as you. It's not as if you would be forgetting your fight by seeking his aid."

"No," Arigh repeated. "Thorisin has his own kingdom to rule; his concerns and mine are different. He might have reason to make peace with Yezd for now—what if the Namdaleni still hang over him, as they did last year? I am too weak to be able to take such chances. They would cost me my last freedom of action. If I had something to offer Gavras, now, something to deal with, it might be different. As is, though . . ."

He sighed. "You mean well, all of you, but mercenary captain has no more appeal to me than robber chief as a lifelong trade. What will become of my clan, with Dizabul as their khagan? I must find a way back to Shaumkhiil with my people."

His clipped Arshaum accent added to the urgency of his words. Viridovix marveled at how his friend had grown from a roistering young blood in Videssos to a farsighted chieftain over the course of a year. "Indeed and he's outgrown me," the Gaul murmured to himself in surprise. "I'd go for my revenge and be damned to what came next. Och, what a braw prince he'll make for his people, for he's ever after thinking on the good o' them all."

To Gorgidas, though, Arigh showed the doomed grandeur of a tragic hero. The physician wondered how many defeated lords had been driven into the uplands of Erzerum, vowing to return with victory. But Erzerum was a distant backwater. In Dilbat the Arshaum could only be hunted down.

"What does your shaman say of the omens?" Psoes asked. Having served so long at the edge of the steppe and on it, he was more ready than the other imperials to find value in the nomads' rites. Skylitzes frowned at him.

"He's taken them several times and got no meaning from them. Too close to *that*—" Arigh pointed at the smoking pyramid. He did not need to elaborate. Gorgidas knew the odor that rode those fumes; once he had helped carry corpses from a charred building. Arigh went on, "The very ground is full of pits beneath our feet, Tolui says."

"Heathen superstition." Skylitzes' frown deepened, but he admitted, "One could, I suppose, take that as metaphor for the reek of evil that hangs over Mashiz." He, too, recognized the stench of burned human flesh; the Videssian army used incendiary mixes fired from catapults.

"Metaphor?" Goudèles raised an eyebrow in mocking surprise. "I'd not thought a bluff soldier type like you would know a metaphor if one strolled up and bit your foot, Lankinos."

"Then whose ignorance is showing, mine or yours?"

Viridovix drew a tally mark in the air. "A hit, that." Irritated, Goudeles scowled at him. It irked the bureaucrat that Skylitzes, in his taciturn way, gave as good as he got.

A low, grating sound came from the boulder against which Arigh was leaning. Pebbles and small stones spattered around his feet. He yelped and leaped away. "What's this? Do the rocks walk in this stinking country?"

"Earthquake!" Rakio said it first, with Gorgidas, Skylitzes, and Goudeles a beat behind. But the ground was not really shaking, and no stones fell anywhere but around the gray granite boulder. Gorgidas bit back a startled exclamation. The boulder itself was quivering, as if alive.

"Meta-whatever, eh?" Arigh said triumphantly to Skylitzes. The Arshaum reached for his sword. "Seems more like an ordinary snare to me. Now to close it on the ones who set it—they aimed too well for their own good this time." His companions also drew their blades.

After that grinding beginning, the boulder moved more smoothly. "There is a path for it to run in," Rakio said, pointing. Sure enough, a shallow trench let the great stone move away from the hillside. Blackness showed behind it. "They try to befool us with a secret doorway, eh?" The Yrmido sidled forward on the balls of his feet.

Viridovix started. He remembered Lipoxais the *enaree* in doomed Targitaus' tent. The Khamorth shaman had seen fifty eyes, a door in the mountains, and two swords. The first part of the prophecy had proven such a calamity that the Gaul wanted no part of the second.

The opening in the side of the hill was almost wide enough to admit a man. "Whoever it is lurking in there, I'll cleave him to his navel," Viridovix cried. He pushed past Rakio, his sword upraised.

As he approached the moving chunk of stone, the marks stamped down the length of his blade came to golden life. " 'Ware," he called to his companions. "It's Avshar or one of his wizards."

Behind the stone, someone spoke. "I'm losing it, Scaurus. I thought I just heard that great Gallic chucklehead out there."

At the familiar rasp, Viridovix had to make a quick grab to keep from dropping his sword. He and Gorgidas traded wild stares. Then the Celt was shoving the stone out with all his strength. The physician rushed up to help him. The stone overbalanced and fell on its side. Blinking against the glare of the campfires, the two Romans and their comrade stumbled out of the tunnel.

With a whoop of joy, Viridovix flung open his arms. Gaius Philippus returned his embrace without a qualm. Marcus, though, flinched at his touch. "A wound," he explained, courteous even if both he and the senior centurion were bruised, hollow-cheeked, and filthy.

"Phos save me, it is Scaurus," Pikridios Goudeles whispered. For the first time Gorgidas could remember, he sketched the sun-circle over his heart.

The Greek hardly noticed, nor did he pay attention to Arigh shouting to his men that these were, past all expectation, friends. He needed to be no physician to see the Romans were badly battered. "What are you doing here?" he all but shouted at them as he helped ease them down by a fire.

Neither Scaurus nor Gaius Philippus tried to resist his ministrations. *"Khaire,"* the tribune said, his voice slow and tired: "Greetings." Gorgidas had to turn his head to hide tears. No one else in this world could have hailed him in Greek. It was like the tribune to do it, exhausted though he was.

Marcus looked from the physician to Viridovix, still hard pressed to understand he was seeing them. "This is a long way from the steppes," he managed at last, an inane effort but the best he had in him.

"A long way from Videssos, too," Gorgidas pointed out. He was also too taken aback to come up with anything deep.

"Is that really you, quack?" Gaius Philippus said. "You look bloody awful with a beard."

"It's better than that face-mange you're sprouting," the Greek retorted. Gaius Philippus sounded exactly as he always had; it helped Gorgidas believe the Romans were really there in front of him. He also had not lost the knack for getting under the physician's skin.

The man who had emerged from the tunnel with Scaurus and Gaius Philippus knelt by the tribune. He was a Yezd, Gorgidas saw, an officer from his gear, but dirty even by the slack standards the Greek had grown used to, and with his face bloody. He used the Empire's tongue, though, with accentless fluency. "Arshaum and Videssians, by whatever gods there be," he said angrily, looking around. Then, to Marcus: "You know these people?"

Provoked by his rough tone, Viridovix put a hand on his shoulder. "Dinna be havering at him so, you. And who might ye be, anyhow? Is it friend y'are, or gaoler?"

The Yezda knocked the Celt's hand aside and looked up at him, unafraid. "If you touch me again without my leave, you will see who I am." The warning was winter-cold. Viridovix' sword came up a couple of inches.

"He's a friend," Marcus said quickly. "He helped us escape. He's called—" He paused, not sure if Wulghash wanted to make himself known.

"Sharvesh," the khagan broke in, so smooth the hesitation was imperceptible. "I was taken when Avshar overthrew Wulghash, but I got free. I spent a while wandering the tunnels, then met these two doing the same." Scaurus admired his presence of mind; but for the name he gave, nothing he said was quite untrue.

Moreover, the news he casually tossed out made everyone forget about him. "Avshar *what*?" Skylitzes, Goudeles, and Arigh exclaimed, each louder than the next.

Wulghash told the tale, creating the impression that he had been one of his own bodyguards who failed to succumb to the wizard-prince's sorcery.

"And so Avshar has a firm grip on Mashiz," he finished. "You are his enemies, yes?" The growl that rose from his listeners was answer enough. "Good. May I beg a horse from you? I have kin to the northwest who may be endangered because of me and I would warn them while I may."

"Choose any beast we have," Arigh said at once. "I would have asked you to ride with us, but it's plain you know your own needs best."

Wulghash gave a stiff nod of thanks. As he started toward the tethered ponies, Marcus got painfully to his feet, despite Gorgidas' protests. "Ah—Sharvesh!" he called.

The khagan of Yezd was too shrewd to miss his alias. He turned and waited for the Roman to join him.

"A favor," Scaurus said, soft enough that only Wulghash could hear. "Treat Viridovix'—he's the tall man with the red hair and mustaches—treat his sword the same way you did mine, so Avshar cannot follow us by it."

"Why should I? I did not name him friend. I have no obligation to him."

"He is my friend."

"So is Thorisin Gavras, I gather, and I am no friend of *his*," Wulghash said coldly. "That argument has no weight with me. And if Avshar pursues you, he cannot come after me. That is how I would have it. No, I will not do what you ask."

"Then why should you go free now? We could hold you with us."

"Go ahead. If you think you can wring magic out of me, how can I stop you from trying?" Every line of Wulghash's body showed his contempt for anyone who would break the bond of friendship. Marcus felt his ears grow hot. After all the khagan had suffered on account of the Romans, he could not force what Wulghash did not want to give.

"Do as you please," the tribune said, and stepped aside.

A little life came into the khagan's face. "Were we to meet again one day, you and I, I could wish you were my friend as well as my friend." Intonation made his meaning clear. He bobbed his head at Scaurus and went off toward the line of horses.

When the Arshaum whose animal he picked protested, Arigh gave the man one of his own ponies as compensation. Satisfied, the nomad gave Wulghash a leg up. He had no trouble riding bareback. With a wave to Arigh, he kicked the horse into a trot and rode up the valley into the mountains.

The tribune returned to the fire; sitting proved no easier than rising had been. "Lay back," Gorgidas told him. "You've earned it."

Scaurus started to relax, then sat up again, quickly enough to wrench a gasp from him. "By the gods," he exclaimed, pointing at the tunnel-mouth, "Avshar himself may be coming out of that hole any minute."

"Ordure!" That was Gaius Philippus. "With all this, I clean forgot the shriveled he-witch. He may have half of Yezd with him, too."

Arigh weighed the choice, to move or fight. "We move," he decided.

The Arshaum broke camp with a speed that impressed even the Romans. Of course, Scaurus thought, there was a great deal less involved than with a legionary encampment—fold tents, mount horses, and travel.

They did not ride far, three or four miles through a pass, south and a bit west so that Mashiz, now northeast of them, was screened from sight by the Dilbat foothills. Though the journey was short, jouncing along on the backs of a couple of rough-gaited steppe ponies left Marcus and Gaius Philippus white-lipped.

When at last they dismounted, Scaurus' distress was so plain that Gorgidas said in peremptory tones, "Shuck off those rags. Let me see you."

No less than officers, physicians learn the voice of command; Marcus obeyed without thinking. The tribune saw Gorgidas' eyes widen slightly, but the Greek was too well schooled to reveal much. His hands moved down the length of the slash, marking Scaurus' reaction at every inch. He muttered to himself in his own tongue, "Redness and swelling, heat and pain," then spoke to Scaurus: "Your wound has inflammation in it."

"Can you give me a drug to check it? We'll be doing more riding than this, I'm sure, and I have to be able to sit a horse."

He thought Gorgidas had not heard him. The Greek sat staring into the fire. But for his deep, regular breathing, he might have been cast from bronze; his features were calm and still. Marcus had just realized he was not even blinking when he turned and laid his hands on the tribune's chest.

The grip was strong, square on the place that hurt worst. Involuntarily, Scaurus opened his mouth to cry out, but he found to his amazement that the physician's touch brought no pain. Very much the opposite, in fact; he felt anguish flowing away, to be replaced by a feeling of well-being he had not known since Avshar took him.

The Greek's fingers unerringly found the most feverish places in the cut. At each firm touch, the tribune felt pain and inflammation leave. When Gorgidas drew his hands away, Scaurus looked down at himself. The cut was still there; he would carry the mark to his grave. But it was only a pale line on his flesh, as if he had borne it for years. He bent and stretched and found he could move freely.

"You can't do that," he blurted. Gorgidas' failure to learn the Videssian healing art had been one of the things that drove him to the plains.

The physician opened his eyes. His face was drawn with fatigue, but he gave the ghost of a grin. "Obviously," he said. He turned to Gaius Philippus. "I think I can deal with you, too, if you want, though like as not you think it's manly to let all your bruises hurt."

"You must have me mixed up with Viridovix," the veteran retorted. "Come on, do what you can, and I'll be grateful. I will say, though, that healing or no healing, beard or no beard, some ways you haven't changed much."

"Good," the Greek said, spoiling the gibe.

When Gorgidas dropped into the healer's trance again, Marcus whispered to Viridovix, "Do you know how he learned the art?"

"The answer there is aye and nay both. Sure and I was there, and you might even say the cause of it all, being frozen more than a mite, but in no condition to make notes for your honor's edification, if you see what I mean. Puir tomnoddy that I was, I thought you back safe and cozy in Videssos, belike wi' six or eight bairns from that Helvis o' yours—by the looks of her, one to keep a man warm o' nights, I'm thinking."

Gaius Philippus' hiss had nothing to do with the hands that squeezed his upper arm. "Did I say summat wrong?" Viridovix asked, then studied Scaurus' face, which had gone grim. "Och, I did that. Begging your pardon, whatever it was."

"Never mind," the tribune sighed. "We have a busy year's worth of catching up to do, though."

Gorgidas came out of his trance and let Gaius Philippus go. "Tomorrow, I beg you, when I can hear it, too," he said. He was scarcely able to keep his eyes open. "For now, all I crave is rest."

After going through the same set of contortions Marcus had, Gaius Philippus gave the physician a formal legionary salute, clenched fist held straight out in front of him. "You do just as you please," he said sincerely. "By my book, you've earned the right."

The touchy Greek raised an eyebrow. "Is that so? We'll see." He waved to a young man in scale mail of a pattern Marcus did not recognize. The fellow ambled over, smiling, and put a hand on Gorgidas' shoulder. The physician said, "This is Rakio, of the Sworn Fellowship of the Yrmido. My lover." He waited for the sky to fall.

"I am pleased you gentlemen to meet," Rakio said, bowing.

"To the crows with you," Gaius Philippus growled at Gorgidas. "You'll not make me out a liar that easily." He stuck out his hand. So did Scaurus. Rakio clasped them in turn; his grip had a soldier's controlled strength. The Romans gave their own names.

"Then you are men from Gorgidas' world," Rakio exclaimed. "Much he about you has said."

"Have you, now?" Marcus asked the physician, but got no answer. Gorgidas was asleep where he sat.

Leaving Rakio to bundle Gorgidas into his bedroll, the Romans wandered through the Arshaum camp. The healing had stripped away their exhaustion as if it had never been, and moving without pain was a pleasure to be savored for its newness. In sheer animal relief, Marcus stretched till his joints creaked. "Seems Viridovix was right," he said. "A busy year indeed."

He spoke Videssian because he had been using it with Rakio. Pikridios Goudeles snapped him out of his reverie with a sardonic jab: "If you have no further profound philosophical insights to offer, you might consider taking counsel with me over our next course of action—unless, of course, you relish Yezd so much that you are enamored of the prospect of remaining here indefinitely. As for myself, I find any place, including Skotos' hell, would be preferable."

"At your service," the tribune said promptly. "With Avshar in the saddle here, the difference between one and the other isn't worth spitting on." He squatted, again feeling the delight of pain-free motion. "First, though, tell me how you got here and what your situation is."

"You still talk like an officer," Goudeles said. He started the story in his own discursive way. Seeing them with their heads together, Skylitzes joined them and boiled the essentials down to a few sentences. The bureaucrat gave him a resentful stare, but took back the conclusion almost by main force: "Arigh will not go east if alliance with Videssos means sacrificing his independence, or if he thinks the Emperor might make peace with Yezd."

"No danger of that," Scaurus said. "When I left Videssos, Gavras was planning this summer's campaign against the Yezda. And as for the other, he'll take allies on whatever terms he can get—he's not so strong himself that he can afford to sneeze at them."

"We have him, then!" Goudeles said to Skylitzes. He reached up to pound the taller man on the back. Marcus glanced at the two of them curiously. The pen-pusher caught the look. With a self-conscious smile, he said, "Once back in the city a while, I shall undoubtedly oppose the soldier's faction once more with all my heart—"

"Not much there," Skylitzes put in.

"Oh, go to the ice. Here I was about to say that spending time amongst the barbarians had changed—at least for the moment—my view of the world and Videssos' place in it, and what thanks do I get? Insults!" Goudeles rolled his eyes dramatically.

"Save your theatrics for Midwinter's Day," Skylitzes said, unperturbed. "Let's talk to Arigh. Now we have news to change his mind."

Gaius Philippus inspected the *gladius* with a critical eye. "You've taken care of it," he allowed. "A nick in the edge here, see, and another one close to the point, but nothing a little honing won't fix. Can you use it, though? There's the rub."

"Yes," Gorgidas said shortly. He still had mixed feelings about the sword and everything it stood for.

A few feet away, Viridovix was teasing Marcus. "Aren't you the one, now? Bewailing me up, down, and sideways over a romp with Komitta Rhangavve, and then caught 'twixt the sheets with her yourself. My hat's off to you, that it is." He doffed his fur cap.

The tribune gritted his teeth, resigned to getting some such reaction from the Gaul. He looked for words as his pony splashed through the headwaters of the Gharraf River, one of the Tutub's chief tributaries. Nothing much came, even though he was using Latin to keep the imperials he was traveling with from learning of his connection with Alypia. All he could say was, "It wasn't—it isn't—a romp. There's more to it than that. More than with Helvis, too, I'm finding. Looking back, I should have seen the rocks in that stream early on."

Remembering Viridovix' tomcat ways back in Videssos, he expected the Celt to chaff him harder than ever. But Viridovix sobered instead. "One o' those, is it? May you be lucky in it, then. I wasna when I had it and I dinna ken where I'll find the like again." He went on, mostly to himself, "Och, Seirem, it was no luck I brought you."

They rode east in melancholy companionship. The lay of the land was not new to Scaurus, who had come the other way with Tahmasp on a route a little south of the one Arigh was taking. The country was low, rolling, and hilly, the southern marches of the rich alluvial plain of the Hundred Cities. Towns hereabout were small and hugged tight to streambeds. Away from water, the sun blasted the hills' thin cover of grass and thornbushes to sere yellow. There was barely enough fodder to keep the horses in condition.

A scout trotted back over the rise ahead, shouting in the plains speech. Gorgidas translated for the Roman: "A band of Yezda heading our way." He listened some more. "We outnumber them, he says." Marcus grunted in relief. Arigh hardly led six hundred men. A really large company of Yezda going to join Avshar at Mashiz could have ridden over them without difficulty.

As a competent general should, Arigh made his decision quickly. Signal flags waved beside him. The Arshaum deployed from column to line of battle with an unruffled haste that reminded Scaurus of his legionaries. The riders on either flank trotted ahead to form outsweeping wings. The center lagged. Along with his own horse-archers, Arigh kept the remnant of the Erzrumi and the Videssian party there. When he noticed Scaurus studying his arrangements, he bared his teeth in a mirthless grin. "Not enough heavy-armed horsemen to do much good, but if they count for anything, it'll be here."

A messenger came streaking from the left wing, spoke briefly with the Arshaum leader, and galloped away. More flags fluttered. "They've spotted the spalpeens there," Viridovix said, reading the signal. The whole force swung leftward.

No great horseman, Marcus hoped he would be able to control his pony in a fight. Gaius Philippus must have been wrestling with the same worry, for he looked more nervous than the tribune had ever seen him just before combat. He hefted a borrowed saber uncertainly. Gorgidas had offered him his *gladius* back, but he declined, saying, "Better me than you with an unfamiliar sword." The tribune wondered if he was regretting his generosity.

They topped the rise over which the outrider had come. Partly obscured by their own dust, Scaurus saw Yezda galloping away in good order. Viridovix shouted a warning: "Dinna be fooled! It's a ploy all these horse-nomads use, to cozen their foes into thinking 'em cowards."

The pursuing Arshaum on either wing, wary of the trick, kept at a respectful distance from their opponents' main body. Already, though, the faster ponies among them were coming level with the Yezda on slow horses. They did not try to close, but swept wide, seeking to surround the Yezda.

Seeing they might succeed and bag his entire force, the Yezda leader bawled an order. With marvelous speed and skill, his men wheeled their horses and thundered back the way they had come, straight for Arigh and the center of his line. One by one, they rose high in their short-stirruped saddles to shoot.

Marcus had faced a barrage from nomadic archers at Maragha. Then he had been afoot, with no choice but to stand and take it. It had seemed to go on forever. Now he, too, was mounted, in the midst of plainsmen matching the Yezda shot for shot, and then charging the enemy at a pace that left his eyes teary from wind.

An Arshaum horse went crashing down, rolling over its luckless rider. The pony behind it slewed to avoid it, exposing its barrel to the Yezda. An instant later the second beast screamed and foundered a few feet past the first. The plainsman on it kicked free and tumbled over the rough ground, arms up to protect his head.

An arrow bit Scaurus' calf. He yelped. When he looked down, he saw a freely bleeding cut, perhaps two inches long; the head of the shaft had scored the outside of his leg as it darted past. The wound was just below the bottom of his trouser leg. The breeches, borrowed from an Arshaum, fit him well through the waist but were much too short.

Then it was sword on sword, the Yezda trying to hack their way through their foes before the latter could bring all their numbers to bear, Arigh's men battling to keep them in check. Marcus did his best to put himself in a Yezda's way, though to his moritfication the first rider he came near avoided him as easily as if he and his mount had suddenly frozen solid.

Another horseman approached. The fighting was at closer quarters now, and the going slower. The Yezda feinted, slashed. Marcus was lucky to turn the blow; he had to think about everything he did, a weakness easily fatal in combat. His answering stroke almost cut off his horse's ear. The Yezda, seeing he was up against a tyro, let a smile peek through his thick black beard.

His own swordplay, though, had more ferocity than science, and Scaurus, after beating aside a series of roundhouse slashes, felt his confidence begin to return. He could fight this way, even if only on the defensive. The Yezda's grin faded. A fresh surge of combat swept them apart.

The tribune noted with a twinge of envy how well Viridovix and

Gorgidas handled themselves on horseback. The Celt's long arm and long, straight blade made him a deadly foe; Gorgidas was less flamboyant but held his own. And there was Gaius Philippus, laying about with his saber as though born to it. Marcus wished he had more of that adaptability.

He was hotly engaged with a Yezda who was a better warrior than the first when the man suddenly wheeled to protect himself from a new threat. Too late; an Erzrumi lance pierced his small leather shield as if it were of tissue, drove deep into his midriff, and plucked him from the saddle. Not since the Namdaleni had Scaurus seen heavy horse in action; he wished Arigh had more mountaineers along.

Those Yezda who could broke out and fled westward. The Arshaum did not pursue—their road was in the opposite direction. The skirmish had cost them a double handful of men. Three times that many Yezda lay dead on the parched ground; several more howled and writhed with wounds that would kill them more slowly but no less surely.

Arigh stood over a Yezda whose guts spilled out into the dry grass. The man whimpered at every breath; he was far past saving. Arigh called Skylitzes to him. "Tell him I will give him release if he answers me truthfully." The Arshaum chief drew his dagger; the Yezda's eyes fixed on it eagerly. He nodded, his face contorted with pain. "Ask him where Avshar intends to take the army he's forming."

Skylitzes put the question into the Khamorth tongue. "Videssos," the Yezda wheezed, tears, oozing down his cheeks. He added a couple of words. "Your promise," Skylitzes translated absently. His face had gone grim, the news was what he had expected, but bad all the same.

Arigh drove his dagger through the Yezda's throat.

"Best be sure," he said, and started to put the question to another fallen enemy, but the soldier died while Skylitzes was translating it. A third try, though, confirmed the first. "Good," Arigh said. "I feel easier now—I'm not leaving Avshar behind."

The Arshaum left their foes where they had fallen. They took up the corpses of their own men and dug hasty graves for them when they came to soft ground by the side of a stream. Tolui spoke briefly as the plainsmen covered over their comrades' bodies. "What is he saying?" Marcus asked Gorgidas.

"Hmm? Just listen—no, I'm an idiot; you don't know the Arshaum tongue." The physician knuckled his eyes. "So tired," he muttered; he had helped heal three men after the skirmish. With an effort, he gathered himself. "He prays that the ghosts of their slain enemies will serve these warriors in the next world."

A thought struck Scaurus. "How strong a wizard is he?"

"Stronger than I first guessed, surely. Why?"

Without naming Wulghash, the tribune explained how his sword had been partly masked. Gorgidas dipped his head to show he understood. "Aye; Viridovix was tracked across the steppe by his blade. If Tolui can match the magic done for you, it would be no small gain to cover our trail from Avshar." His gaze sharpened. "That sounds like a potent sorcery for a chance-met guardsman to have ready to hand."

Marcus felt himself flush; he should have known better than to try to hide anything from the Greek. "I don't suppose it matters now," he said, and told Gorgidas who the sorcerer was.

The physician had a coughing fit. When he could talk again, he said, "As well you didn't name him in Arigh's hearing. He would have seen Wulghash only as the overlord of Yezd, and an enemy; he would not have spared him for rescuing you. He likes you, mind, but not enough to turn aside from his own plans for your sake."

"He's like his opposite number, then," Scaurus said. "Thorisin, too, come to think of it." He grinned lopsidedly. "Sometimes I was unhappy with Rome's republic, but having seen kings in action, I hope it lasts forever."

That evening Tolui examined the tribune's sword with minute care, then did the same for Viridovix'. "I see what has been done," he said at last, "but not how. Still, I will try to match it in my own way." He quickly donned his fringed regalia, tapped on the oval spirit-drum to summon aid to him.

Scaurus jumped when a voice spoke from nowhere; he had not seen wizardry of this sort before. More and louder drum-work enforced the shaman's command on the spirit.

But the magic in the Gaul's blade must have taken its approach as inimical, for the druids' marks suddenly blazed hot and golden. The spirit wailed. Tolui staggered and cried out urgently, but only fading, derisive laughter answered him.

With trembling hands, he lifted off his leering mask. His wide, high-cheekboned face was pale beneath its swarthiness. In a chagrined voice, he spoke briefly to Gorgidas. The Greek translated: "He says he praises the wizard who disguised your sword, Scaurus. He gave the best he had, but his magic is not subtle enough for the task."

The tribune hid his disappointment. After making sure by gestures that Tolui was all right, he said to Gorgidas, "Worth the try—we're no worse off than we were before."

"Except for the puir singed ghostie, that is," Viridovix amended wryly, sheathing his blade. "Yowled like a scalded cat, it did."

Later, Gorgidas remarked to Scaurus, "I didn't think Tolui would fail you. He's beaten two magicians at once; Wulghash must be far out of the ordinary, to succeed in putting a spell on your blade."

"Not on, exactly—*around* is closer, I think," the tribune answered. "Even Avshar didn't dare to try making a spell cling to the sword itself."

"As it should be, that," Viridovix said. "The holy druids ha' more power to 'em nor any maggoty wizard, for it's after walking with the true gods that they are." He had utter confidence in the supremacy of his Celtic wise men.

Gaius Philippus snorted. "If your mighty druids are as marvelous as all that, how did Marcus here win his Gallic blade from one of them in battle? And how is it the magic in his sword and yours fetched all of us here, you included, instead of leaving you back in your own country as a properly crafted piece of wizardry would?"

Viridovix looked down his long, straight nose at the senior centurion. "Sure, and I'd managed to forget what a poisonous beetle y'are." He leaned forward to stir up the embers of the fire they were sitting around. That done, he resumed, "For all you ken, 'twas purposed we come here."

The Gaul spoke in reflex defense of the druids, but Gorgidas broke through Gaius Philippus' derisive grunt to say, soberly, "Maybe it was. The hermit in the ruins thought so."

"What tale is this?" Marcus asked; with so much having happened on both sides, neither was caught up on all the other's doings.

The physician and Viridovix took turns telling it. While he listened, Scaurus scratched his chin. Stubble rasped his fingers. One of the first things he had done after regaining his freedom was to borrow Viridovix' razor and scrape off his beard. He kept at it, though shaving with stale grease left a lot to be desired.

When they were through, Gaius Philippus, who was also beardless again, commented: "Sounds like just another priest to me, maybe stewed in his own juice too long. He didn't say what this whacking big purpose was, did he now?"

"To my way of thinking, men make purposes, not the other way round," Gorgidas said. He challenged the veteran: "What would you aim for, given the choice?"

"Ask me a hard one." The laugh Gaius Philippus gave had nothing to do with mirth. "I want Avshar."

"Aye." Viridovix crooned the word, in his eagerness once more looking and sounding the barbarian he had almost ceased to be. "The head of him over my door."

Marcus thought the question hardly worth asking. Beyond what the wizard-prince had done to any of them, he put Videssos in mortal peril. Leaving his own scars—even leaving Alypia—out of the bargain, that alone would have turned the Roman against him forever. For all its faults, Scaurus admired his adopted homeland's tradition of benign rule; he knew how rare it was.

He was rubbing his chin again when his hand stopped cold, forgotten. Very slowly, he turned to Viridovix and asked, "How much would you give to bring him down?"

"Himself?" The Celt did not hesitate. "No price'd be too much."

"I hope you mean that. Listen . . ."

The Arshaum halted at a branching in the road. Neither path east seemed promising. The northern track ran through more of the barren scrub country with which they had already become too familiar, while the other swerved south into what was frankly desert.

Marcus and Gaius Philippus urged Arigh toward the southern route. "You'll enter Videssos sooner, for its border swings further east in the south," the tribune said. "And the Yezda will be fewer. They leave the waste to the desert nomads; there's not enough water to keep their herds alive."

"Then how will we find enough for ourselves?" Arigh asked pointedly.

"It's there, if you know where to look," Gaius Philippus said, "and Scaurus and I do. This is the way we went west with Tahmasp's caravan. Aside from the towns, that pirate knows the name of every little well, and its grandmother's, too. We're no rookies, Arigh; we kept our eyes open."

"A strange route for a caravan master," the Arshaum chief mused. "The Hundred Cities surely offered richer trade."

"Normally, yes, but the fox had wind of invaders turning them upside down." Marcus grinned. "That would have been you, I suppose."

"So it would." Arigh pondered the coincidence. "Maybe the spirits are granting us an omen. Be it so, then." Seldom indecisive long, he waved his followers down the road the Romans suggested.

The air had the smell of hot dust. The sun glared off stretches of sand. Rakio stared through slitted eyes at the baked flatlands he and his comrades were traversing. "Oh, for valleys and streams and cool green meadows!" he said plaintively. "This would be a sorrowful place to die."

"As if the where of it mattered," Viridovix said. "I'll be dead soon enough, here or someplace else." As he had since hearing Scaurus' plan, he sounded more resigned than gloomy. Fey, Gorgidas thought; the Celtic word fit.

For his part, the tribune did his best not to think about the likely fruits of his ingenuity. His role as guide helped. He quickly found the promises he and Gaius Philippus had given Arigh were easier to make than keep. Landmarks looked different from the way he remembered them. The blowing sand was part of the reason. Sometimes hundreds of yards of road disappeared under it.

Worse, he had only made the journey coming west. Seen from the opposite side, guideposts went unrecognized. Only after he had passed them and looked back was he sure of them. "A virtue of hindsight I hadn't realized," he remarked to the senior centurion after they managed to backtrack the Arshaum to the first important water hole.

At the Romans' urging, the plainsmen kept their horses in good order as they let them drink. "If you foul an oasis, the desert men will hunt you down and kill you," Scaurus warned Arigh.

The Arshaum chief was doubtful until Skylitzes said, "Think of the care your clans take with fire on the plains."

"Ahh. Yes, I see," Arigh said, making the connection. "Here fire is no risk; where will it go? But wasting or polluting water must be worth a war."

Sentries' alarms tumbled the Arshaum from their bedrolls at earliest dawn. A band of desert tribesmen was shaking itself out into loose array as it approached from the south. Most of the nomads rode light, graceful horses; a few were on camels. Some of the Arshaum ponies snorted and reared, taking the camels' unfamiliar scent.

"Will they attack without parleying?" Arigh demanded.

"I wouldn't think so, with three of us for their one," Scaurus said. Behind them, the plainsmen were scrambling to horse.

"Never trust 'em, though," Gaius Philippus added. "They turn traitor against each other for the sport of it; outsiders are prey the second they look weak. And have another care, too. Those bows don't carry far, but sometimes they poison their arrows."

Arigh nodded. "I remember that the envoys from their tribes were always at feud with each other in Videssos." He was so thoroughly a chieftain these days that Marcus had almost forgotten his years as ambassador at the imperial city.

The Arshaum gave his attention back to the newcomers. "What's this?"

The desert men had sent a party forward. They came slowly, their hands ostentatiously visible. "You know more about them than anyone else here," Arigh said to the Romans. "Come on." Accompanied by Arshaum archers, they rode out with him toward the approaching nomads.

The desert tribesmen and men from the steppe studied each other curiously. Instead of trousers and tunics, the horsemen nearing the oasis wore flowing robes of white or brown wool. Some wrapped strips of cloth round their heads, while others protected themselves from the sun with scarves of linen or silk. They were most of them lean, with long, deeply tanned faces, features of surprising delicacy, and deep-set eyes as chilly as their land was hot. A couple had waxed mustaches; most preferred a thin fringe of beard outlining the jaw.

They waited for Arigh to speak first and lose face. But the startlement they showed when he asked, "Do you know Videssian?" regained it for him.

"Aye," one of them said at last. His beard was grizzled, his face dark as old leather. The leader, Marcus guessed, as much from the way the rest of the tribesmen eyed him as from the heavy silver bracelets he wore on each wrist. "I am Shenuta of the Nufud." He waved at his men. "Who are you, to use the waters of Qatif without our leave? Your strangeness is no excuse."

Arigh named himself, then said loudly, "I am at war with Yezd. Is that excuse enough?"

It was a keen guess; Shenuta could not keep surprise off his face. He spoke rapidly in his own guttural tongue. Several of his followers exclaimed; one shook his fist at the northwest, toward Mashiz. "It is to be thought on," Shenuta admitted, his features under control again.

Arigh pressed the advantage. "We have done nothing to Qatif save drink there. Send men to see if you care to. And in exchange for its water I have a gift for you." He gave the Nufud chief his spare bow. "See the backing of horn and sinew, here and here? It will easily outrange the best you have. Make more; use them against the Yezda."

"You are the oddest-looking man I have ever seen, but you have the ways of a prince," Shenuta said. "Have you a daughter I might marry, to seal our friendship?"

"I am sorry, I do not; and if I did, the journey from my land, which lies far to the north, would not be easy." Arigh spread his hands in regret.

Shenuta bowed in the saddle. "Then let the thought be taken for the deed. I give you and yours leave to use Qatif as if it were your own. This privilege you share with but three caravan masters: Stryphnos the Videssian, who taught me this speech in return; Jandal, whose mother is of the Nufud; and Tahmasp, who won the right to all my oases from me at dice."

"Sounds like him," Gaius Philippus said with a laugh.

For the first time, Shenuta swung his gaze toward the Romans. "You know Tahmasp?" He paid particular attention to Scaurus. "I have seen yellow-haired ones in his company once or twice."

"They are of a people different from mine," the tribune answered. "My comrade here and I served only one tour as guards with him, when he was on the road to Mashiz earlier this year. This is the fastest route we know to Videssos, which is why we told our friend Arigh of it. As he said, we meant no harm to what is yours."

"That is well spoken," Shenuta said. "If I had to choose between Videssos and Yezd, I think I would choose Videssos. But I do not have to choose; neither of them will ever master the desert. Perhaps one day they will destroy each other. Then the Nufud and the other tribes of free men shall come into their own."

"Maybe so," Marcus said politely, though his thought was that the desert nomads, for all their dignified ways, were no less barbarians than the Khamorth or Arshaum. Still, the Khamorth had conquered much of Videssos once.

The Nufud leader and Arigh exchanged oaths; Shenuta swore by sun, moon, and sand. Scaurus thought the encounter was done, but as Arigh was wheeling his pony to return to the oasis, Shenuta said, "When you catch up to Tahmasp, tell him I still think his dice were flats."

"Tahmasp is still in Mashiz gathering a cargo, we thought," Gaius Philippus said. "He told us he'd be months at it."

Shenuta shrugged. "He watered his animals at the Fadak water hole south of here day before yesterday." Marcus did not know that oasis. The desert nomad went on, "He said, though, that he planned to swing more north once he was further east. Your horses look good and you are not burdened by wares; my guess would be that you will meet him soon. Do not forget my message." He bowed again to Arigh, nodded to the tribesmen with him, and rode back to the rest of the Nufud. At his shouted command, they trotted off to the south.

"Wonder what made Tahmasp pull out so quick," Gaius Philippus said. "It doesn't seem like him."

"Would you want to stay in a city Avshar had just seized?" Marcus asked.

The veteran considered, briefly. "Not a chance."

When the Arshaum left Qatif, they traveled with double patrols in case the Nufud took their oaths lightly. But, though a couple of desert nomads stayed in sight to keep a similar eye on the plainsmen, Shenuta proved a man of his word.

Marcus and Gaius Philippus gradually grew hardened to the saddle, undergoing the same toughening Viridovix, Gorgidas, and Goudeles had endured when they went to the steppe the year before. At every rest halt the senior centurion would rub his aching thighs. When the Arshaum snickered at him, he growled, "If you were on a forced march in the legions, you'd laugh from the other side of your faces, I promise you that." They paid no attention, which only annoyed him more.

After Scaurus got the plainsmen to the next oasis, he felt his confidence begin to return. And when they came upon the signs of a recently abandoned camp and a trail leading east, excitement coursed through him. "Tahmasp, sure enough!" he exclaimed, finding a scrap of yellow canvas impaled on a thornbush. Holes in the ground where pegs had been driven showed the size of the caravaneer's big tent.

Pacing it off, Arigh was impressed. "Not bad, for one not a nomad born. Few yurts are larger."

Viridovix gave Marcus a sly glance. "A good thing, I'm thinking. Once we're after having this trader to hand, now, we'll no more be at the mercy o' these Romans for directions, with them so confused and all."

So much for confidence, the tribune thought. He said, "It'll be a relief for me, too, let me tell you."

He was astonished when the mercurial Celt cried angrily, "Och, a bellyful o' these milksop answers I've had from the Greek already!" and stalked off. Viridovix stayed in his moody huff all night.

The desert wind had played with the caravan's trail, but the Arshaum clung to it. And as they gained, the signs grew clearer. The sun was sinking at their backs when they spotted Tahmasp's rear guard. They were spotted in turn; by the time they caught up with the caravan itself, it was drawn up for defense, with archers crouched behind hastily dumped bales of cloth. Merchants scrambled this way and that; Marcus heard Tahmasp's familiar bellow roaring out orders.

The tribune said to Arigh, "Let us talk with him."

"You'd better. I don't think he'd listen to me." The Arshaum chief allowed himself a dry laugh. His slanted eyes were gauging the caravan's preparations. "Looks like he knows his business. Go on, calm him down."

Unexpectedly, Pikridios Goudeles said, "If you don't mind, I'll accompany you. Perhaps I shall be able to render some assistance."

"Not with one of your long speeches," Gorgidas said in alarm, remembering the grandiloquent orations the pen-pusher had delivered on the steppe. "From what the Romans have said, I don't think this Tahmasp is one to appreciate rhetoric."

Goudeles sniffed. "Permit me to remind you that I know what I'm about. Where there's a will, there's a lawyer."

With that his comrades had to be content. Shrugging, Arigh said, "As you please." The tribune, centurion, and imperial bureaucrat urged their horses out from the Arshaum around them and walked the beasts forward until they were well within range of the caravan's bows.

No one shot at them. Scaurus called, "Tahmasp! Kamytzes!" Gaius Philippus echoed with the name of the lieutenant under whom he'd served: "Muzaffar!" They shouted their own names.

"You two, is it?" Tahmasp yelled back furiously. "Another step closer and you'll be buzzards' meat, the both of you. I told you what we do to spies."

"We weren't spies," the tribune returned. "Will you listen, or not?"

Goudeles spoke for the first time: "We'll make it worth your while." Marcus wondered at that; the Arshaum had little past horses, clothes and weapons. But the bureaucrat's self-assurance was unruffled.

Scaurus heard Kamytzes' voice raised in expostulation. Knowing the turn of the grim little Videssian's mind, he guessed Tahmasp's aide was arguing against a parley. But the numbers at Marcus' back had a logic of their own, and Tahmasp, beneath his bluster, was an eminently practical man. He yielded gruffly, but he yielded. "All right, I'm listening. Come ahead."

The Romans' former comrades-in-arms met them with icy glares as they entered the perimeter of the improvised camp. Tahmasp stumped forward, closing the last catch on a chain-mail shirt Scaurus and Gaius Philippus could both have fit into. A spiked Makuraner-style helmet sat slightly askew on his shaved head. Kamytzes hovered a couple of steps behind him, his hands near a brace of throwing-knives at his bejeweled belt.

The caravan master folded his arms across his massive chest. "Thought you'd be in Videssos by now," he accused the Romans. "Or is this more of what you call 'business'?"

"We thought you were still in Mashiz," Marcus returned. "Or

couldn't you stomach Avshar?" He hoped his guess was right. When Tahmasp's eyes shifted, he knew it was. He said, "Neither could we," and tugged his tunic over his head.

At the sight of the scar, Tahmasp pursed his lips. Several troopers who had been friendly with the Romans swore in a handful of tongues. But Tahmasp's first concern, as always, was for his caravan. "So—we have reasons for disliking the same man. But what has that to do with those robbers out there?" He jabbed a thumb at the Arshaum, a vague but threatening mass in the deepening twilight.

"That's a long story," Gaius Philippus said. "Remember why you chose not to go through the Hundred Cities on your way west?"

"Some barbarian invasion or—" The caravaneer juggled facts as neatly as he did bills of lading. "Them, eh? Don't tell me you were mixed up in that."

"Not exactly." Marcus told the story quickly, finishing, "You're heading into Videssos and so are we, but you know all the shortcuts and best roads. Show them to us and you'll have the biggest guard force any caravan ever dreamed of. The Yezda won't dare come near you."

"And if I don't . . ." Tahmasp began. His voice trailed away. The answer there was obvious. He took off his helmet and kicked it as far as he could; it flew spinning into the darkness. "What can I say but yes? Maybe your bastards'll plunder me later, but you'll sure plunder me now for a no. The pox take you, outlanders. My old granddad always told me to run screaming from anything that smelled like politics, and here you're dragging me in up to my neck."

"Not all politics are evil," Goudeles said. "Nor will you suffer for aiding us."

In his Arshaum suede and leather, with his beard untrimmed and his hair long and not very clean, the pen-pusher cut an unprepossessing figure. Tahmasp rumbled, "Who are you to make such promises, little man?"

The bureaucrat had learned on the plains to make do with what he had. When he drew himself up and declared haughtily, "Sirrah, you have the privilege of addressing Pikridios Goudeles, minister and ambassador of his Imperial Majesty Thorisin Gavras, Avtokrator of the Videssians." It did not occur to Tahmasp to doubt him.

He was not, however, a man to be overawed for long. "Why is it such a privilege, eh?"

"Fetch me a parchment, pen and ink, and some sealing wax." At the caravan master's order, one of his men brought them. The bureaucrat wrote a few quick lines. "Now, have you fire?" he asked.

"Would I be without it?" Several of Tahmasp's men carried fire-safes, to keep hot coals alive while they traveled. One of them upended his over a pile of tinder. When a small blaze sprang up, Goudeles lit the red wax' wick and let several drops fall at the foot of his parchment. He jammed his seal ring into the wax while it was still soft and handed Tahmasp the finished document.

The caravaneer squatted by the little fire. His lips moved as he read. Suddenly a grin replaced the scowl he had been wearing since the Romans and Goudeles entered his encampment. He turned to his followers and shouted, "Exemption from imperial tolls for the next three years!"

The guardsmen and merchants burst into cheers. Tahmasp enfolded Goudeles in a beefy embrace and bussed him on both cheeks. "Little man, we have a deal!"

"How delightful." The pen-pusher disentangled himself as fast as he could.

While Marcus was waving to the Arshaum that agreement had been struck, Tahmasp dug an elbow into Goudeles' ribs. Goudeles yelped. The caravaneer said craftily, "You know, it's likely I could beat the tolls anyway. Even your damned inspectors can't be everywhere."

"I daresay." Goudeles held out his hand. "Shall I take the document back, then? The penalty for smuggling is, of course, confiscation of all illegal goods and a branding for the criminals involved."

Tahmasp hastily made the parchment disappear. "No, no, no need of that. It is, as I said, a bargain."

The rest of the Videssian party, Arigh, and a few of his commanders rode up to fraternize with the caravan master and his aides; bargain or no bargain, Tahmasp was nervous about letting too many of his new-found allies near his goods. He was politic enough, however, to send several skins of wine out to the plainsmen—enough to make them happy without turning them rowdy.

Having been drinking naught but water for some time, Scaurus enjoyed the wine all the more. He was in the middle of his second cup when he exclaimed, "I almost forgot!" He went over to Tahmasp, who was simultaneously asking quetions of Viridovix—whose red hair fascinated him—and answering them from Gorgidas, who wanted to know everything there was to know about all the strange places the caravaneer had seen in his travels. Tahmasp chuckled when the tribune delivered Shenuta's message.

"So he thinks my dice are crooked, does he? He's wrong; I'd never do such a thing," the burly trader declared righteously. Then he winked. "But I'm surprised the old sand shark has a robe to call his own if he's still using the pair he had that night. Those were loaded, all right—the wrong way!"

His booming laughter filled the desert night.

XI

"THIS IS ALL MOST IRREGULAR," EVTYKHIOS KORYKOS SAID. THE *hypasteos* of Serrhes had said that several times already. Irregular or not, it was plainly too much for him. Nothing ever happened in Serrhes, a small city at the junction of the desert and the imperial westlands' central plateau. Even the Yezda passed it by; their invasion routes ran further north. All the convulsions in Videssian affairs had left it untouched and nearly forgotten.

That suited Korykos, whose chief aim was to vegetate along with his town. He stared resentfully at the rough-looking strangers who packed his office. "Irregular," he repeated. "This document grants an unprecedented exemption, and I am not certain I possess the authority to countersign it."

"You tripe-faced idiot!" Tahmasp roared. "No one gives a frike whether you countersign it or not. Just obey it and go back to gathering dust."

"Though his phrasing is crude, the good caravan master has captured the essence of the matter. The authority in question here is my own," Goudeles said smoothly. He confused the *hypasteos* more than any of the others. He looked like a barbarian, but spoke like the great noble he claimed to be.

"I also approve," Marcus put in. He bothered Korykos almost as much as Goudeles did. His speech and appearance both proclaimed him an outlander, but if he was to be believed, he was not only a general but also Goudeles' superior in the imperial chancery. And he knew so much more than Korykos about doings at the capital that there was no way to make him out a liar.

"Give us supplies and some fresh horses and send us on our way to Gavras at Videssos," Arigh said. Normally he would have scared Korykos witless. Dealing with him now was something of a relief—he did not pretend he was anything but what he seemed.

He also gave the *hypasteos* a chance to vent his suspicions and a moment of petty triumph. "The Avtokrator is not *at* Videssos," Korykos said primly. "Why are allegedly high imperial officials ignorant of such a fact?"

He did not enjoy the discomfiture he created. "Well, where is he, you worthless cretin?" Gaius Philippus barked, leaning over Korykos' desk as if about to tear the answer from him by force. Arigh was right beside him. If Thorisin had gone east against the Namdaleni, the Arshaum's hopes were ruined. This time Goudeles did not try to hold them back. He was leaning forward himself, his right hand on the hilt of his sword, an unconscious measure of how much he had changed in the past year.

"Why, at Amorion, of course," Korykos got out through white lips.

"Impossible!" Scaurus, Gaius Philippus, and Tahmasp said it together. The trader's caravan had left the place one step ahead of the Yezda.

"Oh, is it?" Korykos fumbled through the parchments on his desk. Serrhes being as slow as it was, there weren't many of them. Marcus recognized the sunburst of the imperial seal as the *hypasteos* finally found the document he was after. Holding it at arm's length, he read: "'. . . and so it is required that you send a contingent numbering one third of the garrison of your city to join ourself and our armies at Amorion. No excuse will be tolerated for failure to obey this our command.'" He looked up. "I sent off the nine men, as ordered."

"Wonderful," Gaius Philippus said. "I'm sure the Yezda thank you for the snack." Korykos blinked, wondering what he meant. The veteran sighed and gave it up.

"That definitely is Gavras—no mistaking the blunt, ugly style," Goudeles said. Skylitzes made a noise at the back of his throat, but let the bureaucrat's sneer slide.

"What's he doing in Amorion?" Marcus persisted. Aside from the Yezda, the town had been Zemarkhos', and not under imperial control at all.

The tribune had not intended the question for Korykos, but it seemed to push the harassed official over the edge. "I neither know, nor care!" he shrilled. "Go find out and leave me a peace!" With one of the spasms of energy weak men show, he grapped the toll exemption from a startled Tahmasp, scrawled his signature in large letters under Goudeles', and threw the document in the caravaneer's face. "Go on, get out, before I call the guards on you!"

Tahmasp tapped his forehead. "All eighteen you have left, eh?" Marcus said in his politest tones. Arigh sputtered laughter, adding, "Bring 'em on! The roomful of us'll clean 'em out, the three that aren't hiding already."

"Get out! Get out!" Korykos purpled with impotent fury. Skylitzes stiffened to attention and threw him an ironic salute. The *hypasteos* was still blustering when his unwelcome guests filed out, but Marcus did not miss the relief on his face as they left.

"Troglodytes!" Gorgidas exclaimed a couple of days out of Serrhes. Instead of raising houses from the soft gray stone of the area, the locals carved their homes, even their temples to Phos, into the living rock. The Greek scribbled observations whenever he passed through a village: "Because even its users do not view the technique as natural, they imitate more usual styles of construction as closely as they can. Thus one sees brickwork, shutters, lintels, even balustrades, all executed in relief to fool the eye into thinking them actually present."

The people of the rock villages reacted to the arrival of the Arshaum much as had those of Serrhes. Most slammed their doors tight and, Marcus was sure, piled their heaviest furniture behind them. The adventurous few came out to the town marketplaces to trade with Tahmasp's merchants.

The caravan master was unhappy at how slow business was. "What good does it do me to be tax-free if no one is buying?"

"What good would it do you to be rich when the Yezda swoop down on you?" Marcus retorted.

"I can't say you're wrong," Tahmasp admitted, "but I'd like it better if it didn't look so much like they already had."

His complaint held justice. As the Arshaum traveled east toward Amorion, to the eye they might have been just one more nomadic band drifting into Videssos in the wake of the imperial defenses' collapse after Maragha. At a distance, even the Yezda took them for countrymen. Small parties of horsemen passed them several times without a second glance. And to the Videssians, they seemed as frightful as the rest of the nomads. Even Goudeles' formidable eloquence was not always enough to win the locals' confidence.

"Can't hardly trust nobody these days," one grizzled village elder said when finally coaxed out of his home, a building whose fresh stonework showed an eye for defense. He hawked and spat. He spat very well, being without front teeth in his upper jaw. He went on, "We would have had trouble ourselves last year, but for dumb luck."

"How's that?" Tahmasp asked. He seemed a bit less morose than he had; the villagers were coming out to buy, once they saw nothing had happened to their leader. Women exclaimed over lengths of cloth dyed Makuraner-style in colorful stripes and argued with merchants about the quality of their bay leaves while their husbands fingered the edges of daggers and tried to get the most in exchange for debased goldpieces.

The old man spat again. "We was holding a wedding feast—my granddaughter's, in fact. Next morning when we go out to tend our herds, what do we find? Tracks to show a Yezda war party had come right close to the edge of town, then turned round and rode like Skotos was after 'em. Must've been the singing and dancing and carrying on fooled 'em into thinking we had soldiers here, and they lit out."

"A genuine use for marriage," Goudeles murmured, "something I had not previously believed possible." Having met the bureaucrat's wife, a rawboned harridan who only stopped talking to sleep, Marcus knew what prompted the remark.

The elder took it for a joke and laughed till he had to hug his skinny sides. "Hee, hee! Tell that to my missus, I will. I'll sleep in the barn for a week, but worth it, gentlemen, worth it."

"Be thankful you're after having one to rail at ye, now," Viridovix said, which perplexed the Videssian but failed to dampen his mirth, leaving both of them dissatisfied with the exchange.

The journey across the plateau country put all of Tahmasp's gifts on display. He always knew which stream bed would be dry and which had water in it, which band of herdsmen would sell or trade a few head of cattle and which run them deep into the badlands at first sight of strangers.

He also had a knack for knowing which routes would have Yezda on them and which would be clear. The Arshaum only had to fight once, and then briefly. A band of Yezda collided with Arigh's vanguard and skirmished until the rest of the plainsmen came up to help their comrades, at which point their foes abruptly lost interest in the encounter and withdrew.

Along with his other talents, the swashbuckling caravaneer was soon fluently profane in the Arshaum tongue. His huge voice and swaggering manner made the plainsmen smile, but before long they were obeying him as readily as they did Arigh, who shook his head in bemused respect. "This once I wish I could write like you do," he remarked to Gorgidas one day. "I'd take notes, I really would."

For all Tahmasp's skills, though, there was no escaping the fact the invaders were loose in the westlands. Broken bridges, the burned-out shell of a noble's estate, unplanted cropland all told the same story. And once the Arshaum traversed a battlefield where, by the wreckage still lying about, both sides had been Yezda.

As was his way, Gorgidas looked for larger meanings in what he saw. "That field shows Videssos' hope," he said when they camped for the evening. "It is the nature of evil to divide against itself, and that is its greatest weakness. Think of how Wulghash and Avshar fell out with each other instead of working together against their common enemy."

"Well said!" Lankinos Skylitzes exclaimed. "At the last great test, Phos will surely triumph."

"I didn't say that," Gorgidas answered tartly. Skylitzes' generalizations were not the sort he was after.

Gaius Philippus irritated both the Greek and the Videssian by objecting. "I wouldn't lump Avshar and Wulghash together. You ask me, they're different."

"How, when they both seek to destroy the Empire?" Skylitzes said.

"So did the Namdaleni last year—and would again if they saw the chance. Wulghash, from what I saw of him, is more like that—an enemy, aye, but not wicked for wickedness' sake, if you take my meaning. Avshar, now . . ." The senior centurion paused, shaking his head. "Avshar is something else again."

No one argued that.

Marcus said, "I think there's something wrong with your whole scheme, Gorgidas, not just with the detail of how evil Wulghash is—though I read him the same way Gaius does."

"Go on." The prospect of a lively argument drew Gordigas more than criticism bothered him.

Scaurus picked his words with care. "It strikes me that faction and mistrust are part of the nature of mankind, not of evil alone. Otherwise how would you explain the strife Videssos has seen the last few years, or for that matter, Rome, before we came here?"

When the Greek hesitated, Skylitzes gave his own people's answer: "It is Skotos, of course, seducing men toward the wrong."

That smug "of course" annoyed Gorgidas enough to make him forget for a moment how deeply the Videssians believed in their faith. He snapped, "Utter nonsense. The responsibility for evil lies in every man, not at the hand of some outside force. There would be no evil, unless men made it."

That Greek confidence in the importance of the individual was something Marcus also took for granted, but it shocked Skylitzes. Viridovix had been sitting quietly by without joining the discussion, but when he saw the imperial officer's face grow stern he tossed in one of the mordant comments that came easily to his lips these days: "Have a care there, Gordigas dear; can you no see the pile o' fagots he's building for you in his mind?"

On the steppe Skylitzes would have managed a sour smile and passed it off. Now he was back in his native land. His expression did not change. The discussion faltered and died. Sometimes, Marcus thought, the imperials were almost as uncomfortable to be around as their enemies—another argument against Gorgidas' first thesis.

The little spring bubbled out from between two rocks; a streamlet trickled away eastward. "Believe it or not, it's the rising of the Ithome," Tahmasp said. "You can follow it straight into Amorion from here."

"You're not for town with us, then?" Viridovix asked disappointedly; the flamboyant caravaneer was a man after his own heart. "Where's the sense in that, to be after coming so far and sheering off at the very end?"

"You'd starve as a merchant," Tahmasp answered. "No trader in his right mind will hit the same city twice in one year. I've kept the bargain I had forced on me; now it's time to think of my own profit again. A *panegyris* is coming up in Doxon in about two weeks. If I push, I'll make it."

Nothing anyone said would make him change his mind. When Arigh, who admired his resourcefulness, pressed him hard, he said, "Another thing is, I want out from under soldiers. Aye, your plainsmen have treated me better than I thought they would, but there'll be a big army at Amorion, and I want no part of it. To a trader, soldiers are worse than bandits, because they have the law behind 'em. Why do you think I got out of Mashiz?" The Arshaum had no reply to that.

Tahmasp pounded Gaius Philippus on the shoulder. "You're all right." He turned to Scaurus, saying, "As for you, I'm glad I don't have to bargain against you—a high mucky-muck and never let on! Well, now that I'm shut of you, I wish you luck. I have the feeling you'll need it."

"So do I," the tribune said.

He did not think Tahmasp even heard him. The caravan master was shouting orders to his guardsmen and the merchants with him. The guards, under the capable direction of Kamytzes and Muzaffar, smoothly took their places. When the merchants dawdled, Tahmasp bellowed, "Last one in line is my present to the Arshaum!" That got them moving. His big shaved head gleaming in the sun, Tahmasp burst into bawdy song as his caravan pulled away from the plainsmen, and never looked back.

"There goes a free man," Gaius Philippus said, following him with his eyes.

"Maybe so, but how long will he stay that way if Avshar wins? It's our job to keep him free," Marcus answered.

"Plenty of worse work, comes to that."

The Arshaum followed the Ithome east. It swiftly grew greater as one small tributary after another added their waters to it. By the end of their first day of travel, it was a river of respectable size, and the land through which it passed was beginning to seem familiar to the Romans.

"At this rate, we'll make Amorion in a couple of days," Scaurus remarked as they camped by the side of the stream.

"Aye, and Gavras bloody well better be glad to see us, too," Gaius Philippus said. "Seeing as how he's sitting there, he'll have a time saying we didn't get it back for him."

"I wonder." Now that their goal was so close, the tribune found himself more and more apprehensive. Had the Avtokrator pledged him only nobility, he would have felt sure of his reward. But there had been more in the bargain than that. . . . He wondered how Alypia was.

Viridovix did nothing to help his self-assurance, saying, "Sure and a king's a bad one for keeping promises, for who's to make him if he doesna care to?" Despite having heard from the Romans that Thorisin had put Komitta aside, he was also uncertain of the welcome the Emperor had waiting for him. Fretting over that took his mind off other concerns.

Morning twilight roused the Arshaum with a jolt when their sentries caught sight of a squad of strange horsemen. "Careless buggers," Gaius Philippus said, bolting down a wheatcake. "They stand out like whores at a wedding, silhouetted against the dawn that way. From any other direction, they'd be invisible."

The riders showed no sign of pulling back after they were discovered. "The cheek o' them now, looking us over bold as you please," Viridovix said. He set his Gallic helmet firmly on his head; its crest, a seven-spoked bronze wheel, glinted red as his hair in the light of the just-risen sun.

Marcus shielded his eyes with his hand to study the horsemen, who still had not moved. "I don't think that's cheek," he said at last. "I think it's confidence. They have a big force somewhere behind them, unless I miss my guess."

Gorgidas was also squinting into the sun. As he was a bit farsighted while Scaurus was the reverse, he saw more than the tribune. "They're nomads," he said worriedly. "What are the Yezda doing in strength so close to a big imperial army?"

Speculation ceased as they ran for their horses; most of the Arshaum were already mounted and hooted at them for their slowness. "Took you long enough," Arigh sniffed when they were finally in the saddle. "Let's find out what's going on."

He led a hundred riders toward the strangers: in line, not column, but advancing slowly so as not to seem an open threat. Marcus could see the horsemen ahead reaching over their shoulders for arrows, but none of them raised a bow. Two or three were in corselets of boiled leather like those of the Arshaum, but most wore chain-mail shirts.

With a raised hand, Arigh halted his men at the extreme edge of arrow range. He rode forward alone. After a few seconds, one of the waiting riders matched the gesture. When they were about eighty yards apart, the Arshaum chief shouted a Khamorth phrase he had memorized: "Who are you?" By his looks, the approaching horseman could have been a Yezda or off the Pardrayan plain.

"Who are *you*?" The answer came back in oddly accented Videssian.

Marcus had heard that lilt before. He dug his heels into his pony's sides and rode toward Arigh at a fast trot. Several Arshaum shouted for him to get back in his place. His own shout, though, was louder than theirs: "Ho, Khatrisher! Where's Pakhymer?"

The stranger had set a hand to his saber when the Roman came toward him, but snatched it away at the hail. "He's right where he belongs and nowhere else," he yelled back. "Who wants to know?" The flip answer did not bother Scaurus; most Khatrishers were like that.

"They're friends," he called to Arigh, then shouted his own name to the Khatrisher.

"Why, you lying whoreson! He's dead!"

"Dead, am I?" The tribune rode past Arigh until he was close enough to see the Khatrisher clearly. As he'd hoped, the fellow was one of Laon Pakhymer's minor officers. "Look me over—" What was the name? he had it! "—look me over, Konyos, and tell me I'm dead."

Konyos did, carefully. "Well, throw me in the chamberpot," he said. "It is you. Is that other duck still with you, the ornery one?"

"Gaius?" Marcus hid a smile. "He's back there."

"He would be," Konyos said darkly. He waved at the Arshaum. "Who are those beggars, anyway? If you're with 'em, I don't suppose they're Yezda."

"No." As Scaurus began to explain, the Arshaum and Khatrishers, seeing there would be no fighting, moved toward each other.

Konyos eyed the men from Shaumkhiil with lively interest; their wide, almost beardless faces, snub noses, and slanted eyes were all new to him. "Funny-looking bastards," he remarked without malice. "Can they fight?"

"They've come through Pardraya and Yezd."

"They can fight."

The tribune introduced Konyos to Arigh, then nearly shouted the question that was burning in him: "What is Gavras doing in Amorion?"

"You ought to know," the Kharisher said. "It's your fault."

"Huh?" That was the last answer Scaurus expected.

"What else? When Senpat and Nevrat Sviodo gave Minucius the word you'd been shipped off to give Zemarkhos what for, wild horses couldn't have held him back from piling in to help. Naturally, Pakhymer brought us along for the ride."

A lump rose in Marcus' throat, despite Konyos' breezy way with the story. More than anything else, it showed what his troops—and the Khatrishers, too—felt about him. "The legionaries are at Amorion, then?"

"I just said so, didn't I? Everything by the numbers, one-two—damn boring, if you ask me. Not that you did."

"Hmmp." That was Gaius Philippus, crowding up with Viridovix and Gorgidas to hear the news.

Konyos backtracked for them, then went on, grinning. "We had a rare old time, punching up the Arandos. We moved so hard and fast Yavlak still doesn't know what hit him."

Gaius Philippus jabbed an accusing finger at the Khatrisher. "It was your bloody army—our own bloody army!—moving on Amorion all the time?"

"Of course. Who did you think it was?"

"Never mind," the veteran said. "Oh, my aching head." Marcus wanted to cry and laugh at the same time. He and Gaius Philippus had only gone west with Tahmasp's caravan—had only ended up in Mashiz, and the tunnels under it—because they were sure that army had to be Yezda.

Konyos turned to the tribune. "Oh, one more thing—Gagik Bagratouni has a bone to pick with you."

"Me? Why? I got rid of Zemarkhos for him."

"That's just why. He wanted to do it himself, a little at a time, over days. Can't say I blame him much, either, after things I've heard. But seeing as the bugger's dead, I expect Bagratouni'll forgive you this once." The Khatrisher sobered for a moment. "We thought the two of you'd gone into a hole you'd never come out of, too. We tore Amorion apart looking for you and never found a trace." He sounded a little indignant they had survived.

"A hole we'd never come out of?" Scaurus said with a shudder of memory. "That's too close to being true—there are worse places than Amorion."

The orderly rows of eight-man leather tents behind the square, palisaded earthwork made a striking contrast with the irregular arrangements all around them: here a noble's silk pavilion; there a clump of yurts; further over, a whole forest of shelters clumped together at random, lean-to next to three or four small cotton tents next to a huge canvas arrangement that could have held a platoon.

The sentry at the entrenched gate was a dark, stocky man wearing a sleeveless mail shirt. He peered over the edge of his big semicylindrical shield at the four approaching horsemen in nomad leathers. Hefting his heavy javelin, he called, "Halt and state your business."

"Hello, Pinarius. That's not much of a good day," Marcus said in Latin, and watched the Roman legionary drop his *pilum*.

"Will you look at the puir gowk of a man, now?" Viridovix said, shaking his head sadly. "If he canna put names to the lot of us, sure and he'll be useless for telling friend from foe."

Pinarius had been about to dash away into the camp, but when he recognized Gaius Philippus he did not dare break discipline by leaving his post. Instead he shouted, "By the gods, the tribune's back, and everybody with him!" Snatching up his spear and reversing it with a flourish, he stood aside to let the newcomers enter.

Discipline did suffer then, as Romans tumbled from their tents and came rushing from their drills with sword and spear. Marcus and his comrades scrambled down from their ponies before they were pulled off.

The legionaries swarmed round them, reaching over each other to embrace them, clasp their hands, pound them on the back, simply touch them.

"Och, ye didna gi' me such a thrashing back in Gaul," Viridovix complained in mock anger. The Romans hooted at him.

For Gorgidas, who was particular about whom he touched, the tumultuous welcome was something of an ordeal. He was surprised to find Rakio at his side; the Yrmido had followed him when he left Arigh's band, but at a distance. Someone noticed the stranger. "Who's this?"

"A friend," the Greek answered.

"Good enough." From then on Rakio was pummeled with as much enthusiasm as any of the others. Unlike Gorgidas, he relished it.

"Way there! Clear aside!" Sextus Minucius came pushing through the legionaries. He made slow going of it, for the crush was very tight, but at last he stood in front of the tribune. Months of command had matured the young soldier; there was a finished look to his broad, handsome face that Scaurus had not seen before.

He snapped off a precise salute. "Returning your command to you, sir!"

Marcus shook his head. "It's not mine to take back. Gavras stripped me of it before he sent me out against Zemarkhos."

The legionaries cried out angrily. Minucius said, "We heard about that, sir. All I have to say is, we choose who leads us, and nobody else." He saluted again.

The Romans shouted again, this time in vociferous agreement. "Damn right!" "We don't tell Gavras his business; let him stay out of ours!" "Weren't for us, he'd still be sitting back in Videssos. We punched a hole in the Yezda a blind man could've walked through." And a rising chorus: "Scaurus, Scaurus, Scaurus!" Moved past words, the tribune returned the salute.

The cheers were deafening. Viridovix nudged Gaius Philippus. "You'll be noticing there's none of 'em making the welkin ring for you," he chuckled.

"There'd be something wrong if they were," the veteran replied evenly. "I'm supposed to be the cantankerous blackguard who makes the boss look good."

Fed up with soft answers, the Gaul snapped, "Aye, well, you're right for it," and felt better for earning a scowl from the senior centurion.

The non-Romans among the legionaries hung back at first to let Marcus' countrymen greet him, but they soon joined the celebration, too. Burly Vaspurakaners folded him into bear hugs, shouting a welcome in vile Latin and almost equally thick Videssian.

"So, you are safe after all," Gagik Bagratouni boomed, crushing the breath from the tribune. With his proud, heavy-boned features, thick wavy hair, and black mat of beard, the *nakharar* always reminded Scaurus of a lion. "For all we tried, we did not get here enough quickly, and thought the cursed priest had killed you."

"I'm amazed you came so close," Marcus said.

"Good information," Bagratouni said smugly. He turned, looked around, pointed. "Senpat, Nevrat—to me!"

The two shoved their way up to the *nakharar* and Scaurus. Senpat Sviodo was the only man the tribune knew who could bring off wearing the Vaspurakaners' traditional three-crowned tasseled cap; his good looks and zestful character let him get away with whatever he chose. He stamped a booted foot and shouted out the first three notes of a war song. "Hai, hai, *hai*! We thought we'd see you sooner, but rather late than not at all, as the old saw goes."

His grin was infectious; Marcus felt one stretch across his own face. He turned to Nevrat. Even if she was not his, she deserved attention. The Vaspurakaners' features were too strong for beauty in most women, but she was a fortunate exception—as with Senpat, part of that was her own nature shining through.

She would not listen to the tribune's thanks. "This was nothing—a few days' ride through friendly country to Garsavra. Not worth thinking about. What of the time we were fighting Drax' men in the first civil war, and you killed that Namdalener who had me down?"

"Oh, that. Do you remember how you paid me back?"

Howls went up from the legionaries around them. Something in Nevrat's eyes said she remembered other things as well, but mischief also sparked there. "Quite well," she said boldly.

"I'll settle this the same way, then," Marcus said. The howls got louder. The tribune said to Bagratouni, "Watch close—I'm about to kiss a married woman." He gathered Nevrat in.

"Is it well with you?" she whispered against his ear. At his nod, she murmured, "All right, then," and made the kiss a more thorough, unhurried one than he had intended. Her lips were firm and sweet against his. "If you do something, do it properly," she said when they separated.

"Maybe we should have stayed in Videssos," Senpat growled, but he was laughing, too. A tiny headshake from Nevrat told Scaurus he did not know—not, really, that there was much to know.

Bagratouni dug an elbow into the tribune's ribs. "What was I supposed to watch? That much I knew when I was twelve."

The commotion in the Roman camp sent other imperial troops—Videssians, Khatrishers, Halogai, Khamorth, a few Namdaleni—rushing up to the rampart to see what had got into the usually staid legionaries. Troopers shouted the news to friends or to the world at large.

"So much for keeping our arrival quiet," Gorgidas said.

Scaurus understood what he meant as well as what he said. "It doesn't matter," he said. "With Goudeles and Skylitzes reporting to the Emperor, he already knows who came in with the Arshaum." Before long, he was sure, a summons would be on its way.

That did not seem to have occurred to Viridovix. "At least you're after having a pledge from himself," he told Marcus. "Me he'll chop into catmeat, belike, for playing 'tween the sheets with his ladylove."

Nothing the Romans had said had convinced him that Thorisin was not only rid of Komitta Rhangavve, but heartily glad she was gone. And the tribune was wondering how much the Avtokrator's promises to him were worth. He knew Gavras as a man of his word, but he also knew how great the temptation to break it would be.

No help for that. And no matter what Thorisin intended doing, Avshar had plans, too, that were all too likely to shatter everyone else's. "We need to know more of what's going on here," the tribune said to Gaius Philippus.

"Minucius and Bagratouni are right beside you," the veteran replied. "And I've already sent a runner after Pakhymer."

"Good."

Minucius led them to the commander's tent, which stood at the center of the *via principalis,* the chief street of the camp. He stood aside to let Scaurus enter first, saying, "Looks like I'll have to get used to smaller quarters again."

The inside of the tent belied his words. But for a bedroll, a few mats, and his kit, it was bare. The kit was an ordinary legionary's; Minucius had risen from the ranks over the last couple of years. Viridovix looked around, shook his head, and said, "What do you care what space y'have? You could live in a barrel, I'm thinking, wi' room to spare."

"I don't think Erene would like that," Minucius said. "She's expecting again."

"She's back in Garsavra?" Marcus asked.

"Yes. All the women are, but for Nevrat, and she's a story to herself. We came west in a tearing hurry. We didn't drive the Yezda away, we just pushed through them. So did Gavras; the buggers are still swarming between Garsavra and here."

"That answers one thing," Gaius Philippus said. "It's not what I wanted to hear, but it's what I expected."

Laon Pakhymer arrived just as they were settling down onto the mats. He sat, too, and nodded to Scaurus and Gaius Philippus as casually as if he had seen them a couple of hours before.

"That was quick," the senior centurion said grudgingly. It was hard to be sure whether Pakhymer's slapdash style or effectiveness annoyed him more.

The Khatrisher leader knew he irritated the veteran and played on it. "We have our ways," he said airily.

"He talked with Konyos before the Roman runner got to him," Gorgidas said.

Pakhymer assumed an injured expression. "Why do I bother with my tricks, if you're going to shine a lantern on them?"

"Let's get on with it," Marcus said. The Khatrisher leaned forward, abruptly as businesslike as anyone in the tent.

Scaurus got the same picture from him as he had from the others: the legionaries and Khatrishers had made the thrust from Garsavra on their own, and when it looked like a success Thorisin had followed with the rest of the forces now at Amorion. He had not gained control of the Arandos valley, but the tribune learned that he had sent a detachment north to Nakoleia on the coast of the Videssian Sea. "Sensible," he said. "We aren't altogether cut off from the rest of the Empire here, then."

After that the talk shifted to questions of provisions, the readiness of the troops, and Gavras' plans. Sextus Minucius said, "At first I don't think he had any when he followed us here, past making sure we didn't keep Amorion for ourselves. But now there's a report Avshar's pushing through Vaspurakan toward us. If that's so, then this makes a good base to use against him."

The newly returned men exchanged glances. "Damned perambulating corpse moves too fast to suit me," Gaius Philippus said, but that was the only comment. None of them doubted the wizard-prince aimed to crush Videssos once and for all. They had seen his preparations with their own eyes; the tribune and senior centurion had his boasts and threats straight from his fleshless lips.

Pakhymer said, "There's more to the Emperor coming after us than Minucius spoke of, I think." He waited to let Scaurus and his friends supply the answer for themselves.

"Politics?" Gorgidas ventured.

The Khatrisher leader scratched his head. His version of the faith differed from the Videssians', but he was part and parcel of their world in a way the Greek, the Romans, and Viridovix could never be. He said, "Sometimes I think you people were born half-blind. See now, if you can: these past couple of years, Amorion has been in schism against the capital and its clergy, thanks to Zemarkhos. You Romans are most of you heathen, while the imperials reckon my folk one kind of heretic and Bagratouni's another. Thorisin couldn't trust any of us to set things right here; why else would he fetch Balsamon along, but to bring the schismatics back to the fold?"

"Did he?" Marcus pricked up his ears. "I hadn't heard that."

"He certainly did. The old baldhead's been preaching up a storm, too. I've listened once or twice myself; he's a lively one. Truth to tell, a few more like him and I'd think of converting to the imperials' way of looking at things—he makes you believe in the good."

"I listen, too," Bagratouni said. "Better than Zemarkhos? Yes, a thousand times. Convert? No, never. Too much the 'princes' suffer from Videssos for me ever to change the Empire's belief."

The conference limped after that. Marcus did not think even the pious Skylitzes would have dared urge his faith on the *nakharar* then. As for himself, though he did not follow Phos at all, he felt more apprehension about Videssos' ruler than all its ecclesiastics rolled together.

The next morning two Haloga guardsmen were waiting for Scaurus at the *porta praetoria*. They had learned something of legionary customs, he thought as he went out to them; the *porta praetoria* was the closest of the camp's four gates to the commander's tent. He tried to keep his mind on such trivia. The Halogai had only summoned him, not Gaius Philippus, Gordigas, or Virdovix. He was not sure that was any kind of good sign.

The northern mercenaries were sweating in the Videssian summer heat. They were big blond men, as tall as the tribune and wider through the shoulders. One wore his hair shoulder length; the other tied it back in a thick braid that fell to the small of his back. Both had swords belted at their hips, but relied more on their nation's characteristic weapon, a stout, long-handled war axe.

They nodded when they recognized him. The one with the braid said, "Ve are charged to bring you before t'Avtokrahtor." The Haloga accent was thick, but the tribune understood. He fell in between the guardsmen, who shouldered their axes and marched him away.

Several of Thorisin Gavras' officers enjoyed pavilions more impressive than his. He did not seek luxury for its own sake and in the field always lived simply. The blue pennant with the golden imperial sunburst in front of his tent said everything about his status that needed saying.

Another pair of Halogai paced in front of the tent's entranceway. They drew themselves up alertly as Marcus and his escort neared. The northerner with the queue spoke in a formal voice: "It is t'captain of t'Romans." The sentries stood aside.

Ducking under the tent flap, Scaurus fought to keep surprise off his face. Thorisin had taken his rank from him—was it his again? He got no time to wonder; up ahead the Emperor was saying impatiently, "All right, go see to it, then. I have other business to attend to now."

"Yes, sir." The officer who saluted had his back to Scaurus, but the tribune stiffened at the sound of his voice. And when Provhos Mourtzouphlos turned to leave, he stopped in his tracks, disbelief and rage chasing each other across his regular features. "You!" he cried, and went for his sword.

Marcus' hand flashed downward. One of the Halogai leaped between Mourtzouphlos and the Roman; the other seized Scaurus' wrist in an iron grasp. "Leave it in t'sheat'," he ordered, and the tribune could only obey.

Thorisin had not moved from behind the parchment-strewn folding table at which he was sitting. "Carry out your orders, Provhos," he said. "I assure you I shall deal with this one as he deserves."

The sound of that did not appeal to Scaurus, but it suited Mourtzouphlos no better. "Yes, sir," he repeated, but this time he had to choke it out. He flourished his cloak with aristocratic disdain and stalked past Marcus, snarling, "This is not done between us, you ass in a lion's skin."

All that kept the Roman from throwing himself at Mourtzouphlos was the guardsman's unbreakable grip on his arm. His fury astonished him, and the reason for it even more. He was not angry over what he had gone through himself; that was over and done. But Mourtzouphlos was also responsible for everything that had happened to Alypia these past months, and for that the tribune could not forgive him. She had already suffered too much to deserve more.

Perhaps the sight of the Emperor helped provoke Scaurus by reminding him of Alypia. Thorisin's oval face was longer than hers, and craggier, his eyes dark rather than green, but at a glance anyone would have known them for close kin.

"Take yourselves off, Bjorgolf, Harek," Gavras said to the Halogai flanking the tribune. "Eyvind and Skallagrim are outside to see to it this one doesn't try murdering me. He won't—he needs me alive. Isn't that right, outlander?" He gave Marcus a cynical stare. Nor sure if he was being baited, the tribune stood mute.

The Halogai saluted and left; they had no intention of arguing with their paymaster. Thorisin turned to a servant who was polishing a pair of boots. He flipped the man a piece of silver. "That will keep, Glykas. Go on; spend it on something." With effusive thanks, the Videssian followed the mercenaries out.

When he was gone, the Emperor grunted in satisfaction. "Now you've no one to scandalize but me by ignoring the *proskynesis.*" Marcus stayed silent. He had seen Thorisin in this playful mood once or twice before. It made him nervous; he could not read him in it. Gavras raised an eyebrow. "If you won't go on your belly, you may as well take a chair."

The tribune obeyed. Steepling his fingers, Thorisin studied him for a good minute before he spoke again. "What am I to do with you, Roman? You're like a counterfeit copper; you keep turning up."

Marcus was suddenly sick of this oblique approach; Gavras would have been more direct before he became Avtokrator. He said, "Seems to me you have two choices. Either keep our bargain or execute me."

The Emperor smiled thinly. "Are you trying to persuade me? There have been enough times I'd have liked to see your head go up on the Milestone. But I won't be the one to settle your fate now."

"Avshar." It was not a question.

"Aye." Military matters turned Thorisin serious again. "Here, see for yourself." Scaurus hitched his chair forward; Gavras turned a map of the Videssian westlands around so it was right-side up for the Roman. He pointed to the Rhamnos River at the eastern edge of Vaspurakan. "I have word by fire-beacon that the Yezda army crossed just north of Soli yesterday."

The tribune gauged distances. The wizard-prince had moved faster than he thought possible. "A week away, then. Maybe a day or two more; there's rugged country in their way as they turn southeast. Or will you meet them somewhere halfway between?"

"No; I aim to stand on the defensive." Gavras bared his teeth in a grimace of frustration; his instinct was to attack. But he went on, "After Maragha, after these rounds of civil war, this is the last army I can scrape together. If I throw it away, I—and Videssos—have nothing left. Which is another reason to keep you healthy—I can't afford a mutiny from your troops."

Marcus let the Emperor's concession of his command go as casually as Thorisin had made it. He asked, "How many men does Avshar have with him?"

"I was hoping you could tell me. It's a bigger force than mine, I think, but you know what long-distance scouting reports are worth. And the

Yezda travel with all those spare horses, which makes them seem more than they are. But you were in Mashiz; Skotos' hell, from what Goudeles says, you were in Wulghash's throne room when Avshar stole the throne out from under him. That was the first news I'd had of the usurpation. You should know more of what went on in Yezd than anyone."

"Only if you're after the view from the tunnels. I can tell you something of Avshar, if you care to hear that."

Thorisin shook his head impatiently. "I know more than I want already. Whether it's been him or Wulghash with the title of Khagan of Yezd, he's been behind things for years."

"Having met Wulghash, I'm not so sure," the tribune said. "Here's something you didn't learn from Goudeles: Wulghash isn't dead, though Avshar thinks he is." He told how the khagan and the Romans had met far below the palace.

"A good story, but what of it?" Gavras said. "Dead or fled, he's out of play, and I miss him even less if he's sharp as you say."

Marcus shrugged. "You have my news, then. If you want to hear about the Yezda, talk with Arigh. He's been fighting them all summer and he watched them build up around Mashiz."

"I'll do that. There was something solid you did, Scaurus, bringing him and his plainsmen in." The Emperor stopped, looked at the Roman with annoyance and grudged respect. "May you rot, you son of a whore, you've turned out too bloody useful to shorten. If we live, maybe we'll have to chaffer after all."

The tribune nodded. "Is Alypia well?" he asked quietly.

Thorisin's mouth tightened. "You don't make it easy for me, do you?"

"I may as well find out the worst now. What good does it do me to catch you cheerful today if you turn sour again tomorrow?"

"Mmp. Sometimes I think Mavrikios should have curbed your insolence from the start; it would have saved us trouble." The Emperor drummed his fingers on the tabletop. At last he said, "Aye, she's in fine feather. She had half the young nobles—and all the ambitious ones—dancing attendance on her at my wedding. Not that she paid heed to them."

Scaurus was not worried about her fidelity, but the rest of Gavras' sentence made him goggle like a fool. "At your what?"

"Wedding," Thorisin repeated. "High time, too; your diddling reminded me how much I need a real heir. And I'll have one, too—four days ago I got word she's pregnant."

"Congratulations," Marcus said sincerely. If Thorisin bred a successor, he might be less hindersome where Alypia was concerned. The tribune hesitated, then asked, "Er—who is she?"

"That's right, how could you know? She's Alania Vourtze—ah, you've heard of the family, I see. Aye, they're pen-pushers, right enough. It'll help put the buggers in my camp, or at least divide 'em amongst themselves. She's a quiet little thing—one of the reasons I chose her, after a few years of that shrieking jade of mine. Dear Komitta—Phos help the convent I shipped her to."

The Emperor smiled lopsidedly. "You're still close-mouthed, aren't you? You've heard a good deal more from me than you've said, that's certain." The tribune started to protest that Gavras had not wanted to listen to his news, but Thorisin brushed that aside. "Never mind. Take yourself out. And if there's one of my eparchs out there, tell him it's his turn."

Blinking in the bright sun after the dimness of the tent, Scaurus found a bureaucrat shifting from foot to foot outside the entrance. He held it open in invitation. The eparch went through with a singular lack of eagerness. Marcus heard Thorisin roar, "You blithering, bungling, incompetent ass, where's the fifty wagons of wheat you said would be here day before yesterday?"

"He hasn't mellowed altogether, I see," the tribune whispered to one of the Halogai. The guardsman rolled his eyes.

When Marcus got back to the Roman camp, he found it in an uproar, with a large crowd of legionaries gathered in front of one tent. He could see Viridovix in front of the tent, a head taller than most of them. "What's this in aid of?" he demanded. The soldiers separated to let him through.

The Gaul had driven two tent poles into the ground, then sharpened their upper ends. Each impaled a dripping head. One still bore a snarl of defiance; the expression of the other was impossible to read, as a sword stroke had sheared away most of one side of its face.

"Trophies?" Scaurus asked dryly.

Viridovix looked up. "Och, hullo, Roman darling. So they are. Set on me, the spalpeens did, without so much as a by-your-leave. Begging your pardon for the mess and all, but I'm not after having a doorway to nail 'em to."

"Or even a Milestone," the tribune said, remembering his recent conversation. He looked at the heads again. Both had belonged to swarthy men with long, unkempt beards, now soaked with blood. "Yezda."

"I'm thinking you're right, though I didna stop to ask."

"How did they get into camp?" Marcus asked.

The commotion had drawn Gaius Philippus. He turned to the onlookers. "You, you, you, and you!" he said, telling off four. "One to each gate—relieve the sentries and send them back here to be questioned. They'll take their posts back as soon as we're through with them." The senior centurion had been back only a day, but his authority was unquestioned. The legionaries saluted and hurried away.

The Roman who had admitted the would-be assassins stared in horror at Viridovix's handiwork. "I, I never thought twice about it," he stammered in response to Marcus' question. "They asked for you or the Gaul by name. It was all over camp that the Emperor had summoned you, so I told them where to find him. I thought they were friends the two of you had picked up on your travels."

"Not your fault, Vectilianus," Scaurus reassured him. He did not need to ask how the Yezda had followed Viridovix and him across the miles, but did spare a moment to wish again that he had managed to persuade Wulghash to throw his sorcerous veil over the Celt's sword—then Avshar would have had less by which to track them.

"It turned out right enough," Viridovix said, wiping his blade clean. "Here's two less o' the omadhauns to be taking the blackheart's side come the day, and he's not likely to try flunkies again with his own self so close and all."

"Closer than we thought." Marcus relayed what Thorisin had told him.

"Good. It'll soon be over then, one way or t'other." With a faint scrape of metal against metal, Viridovix ran his sword into its sheath.

It was not yet dawn the next morning when a Vaspurakaner legionary stuck his head into the tribune's tent and woke him. "There a messenger is for you outside the *porta principalis dextra*," he said, mangling his Videssian and Latin about equally. "After what happens yesterday, I no want him to let into camp."

"You did right," Scaurus mumbled. He groped for tunic and trousers. Under his breath he complained, "At least Gavras gave me a whole night's sleep." He slid the tunic over his head, splashed water on his face. Through splutters, he asked the sentry, "Whose messenger is it?"

"He say he from the imperials'—how you say?—chief priest." The Vaspurakaner spat; after Zemarkhos, he had no liking for anyone in the Videssian clerical hierarchy. "You ask me, he can wait forever."

Marcus pushed past him. A summons from Balsamon carried almost as much weight as one from the Emperor.

The *porta principalis dextra* got its name from its position as seen by the encamped legionaries. But the commander's tent was on the other side of the *via principalis;* Scaurus turned left into the camp's main way and hurried to the gate.

He recognized the blue-robed priest waiting for him, though not with any pleasure. His voice came out as a growl: "What do you want with me, Saborios?"

Balsamon's attendant priest, despite his tonsured pate, bore himself like the soldier he had been. "To bring you to my master, of course," he replied crisply. He looked Scaurus straight in the face. "Hold whatever grudge you care to. My first concern is for his Imperial Majesty."

"Bah," Marcus said, but the wind was gone from his sails. His own strong sense of duty answered too readily to that of Saborios.

The sun rose as they marched into Amorion. The town had suffered since the tribune last saw it. Many buildings bore the scars of fighting, whether in the riots Scaurus had touched off or later, when Zemarkhos' remaining fanatics had been rash enough to oppose the professional skill of the legionaries and Khatrishers.

Other buildings were simply deserted, weeds growing up at the base of walls, courtyard gates opening onto forlorn emptiness. Some of the city's finest houses stood thus. "The owners are long fled," Saborios said, following Marcus's gaze. "Some ran from your troopers, others for fear of the Yezda—or of the Emperor's justice."

A few homes had been reoccupied, by one squatter family or six. More newcomers crowded the town marketplace, which was half filled by a squalid collection of tents and crackerbox shacks. "Refugees from the tender mercy of the Yezda," Saborios explained unnecessarily.

"More will come in front of Avshar," Marcus predicted.

"I know. We have trouble feeding the ones here now. Of course, some of those will run again and even the balance a bit." Saborios spoke with the certainty of a man who had seen such things before.

Balsamon was dwelling in the cottage that had been Zemarkhos', close by the main temple of Amorion. Like most chief shrines in provincial towns, that was a smaller, clumsier copy of Phos' High Temple in Videssos. Marcus and Saborios walked in the shadow of its dome as they came up to the little building behind it. The tribune saw old bloodstains on its whitewashed walls.

Balsamon himself opened the door to greet them. "Welcome, welcome!" he said, beaming at Scaurus. "An unlooked-for guest is worth a dozen of the ordinary kind." He wore a look the tribune knew well, as if inviting him to share some secret joke.

But that droll expression was almost all that was left of the prelate Marcus had known in the capital. He had wondered at Balsamon's health then; now the patriarch was visibly failing. He had lost a great deal of flesh, so that his beloved threadbare old robe was draped in loose folds around him. His skin sagged unhealthily at his cheeks and jowls; he had to support himself by leaning against the doorpost.

Ill or not, he missed very little. He laughed at the dismay Marcus could not hide. "I'm not dead yet, my friend," he said. "I'll last as long as need be, never fear. Come in, come in. We have much to talk about, you and I."

For the life of him, Marcus could not see what that "much" was, but he stepped forward. Then he stopped and turned. As Saborios had before, he met the tribune's eye without flinching. "The Emperor knows you are here," he said steadily. "I shan't be listening at the keyhole."

Scaurus had to be satisfied with that. Balsamon moved aside to let him come in. Walking slowly and painfully, the patriarch made his way to the closest one of the three stiff-backed chairs that, but for a small table, were the only furnishings in the little room. The ascetic barrenness had to be a legacy of Zemarkhos.

Balsamon sat with a soft grunt of relief. Marcus said angrily, "What right did Thorisin have to drag you away from Videssos like this?"

"The best right of all: he is the Avtokrator, Phos' viceregent on earth," the patriarch replied. He surprised Scaurus by speaking in perfect seriousness; to the Videssians, the Emperor's power was very real. Balsamon went on, "To be exact, he ordered me here to preside over the dissolution of Zemarkhos' schism. I have attended to that with pleasure—you saw for yourself the hatred he preached."

"Yes," the tribune admitted. "But why you? Is it regular practice to send the patriarch out of the city to attend to such things?"

"The last one to leave Videssos, to my knowledge, was Pothos, three hundred fifty years ago. He was sent to Imbros to help uproot an outbreak of the Balancer heresy." Balsamon's tired eyes managed a twinkle. "I think I managed to provoke my Emperor quite a bit more than Pothos did his."

Knowing what had roused Gavras' wrath, Marcus lowered his head in embarrassment. Balsamon laughed out loud. "Phos preserve me, I've abashed the man of stone." That only served to fluster the tribune worse. The patriarch continued, "By the bye, man of stone, I have a message for you—a trifle late, as you were not in Amorion when you were expected to be, but perhaps of interest all the same."

"Go on," Scaurus said. He knew from whom he wanted the message to be, but after Balsamon's sly teasing he was not about to give the patriarch the satisfaction of showing anxiety or eagerness.

His studied composure seemed to amuse the prelate about as much as excitement would have. "I was speaking of stones, wasn't I?" Balsamon said in the allusive, elusive Videssian style. "Well, there is someone who would have me tell you that there are certain stones with which you may be familiar which that person has worn continuously since the last time you two saw each other, and that person will continue to do so until your next meeting, whenever that may be."

Let Saborios make something of that, Marcus thought; he assumed

Balsamon's attendant had his ways of knowing what was going on with his nominal master, whether he listened at keyholes or not. But the tribune only wasted a moment on Saborios. Alypia's making a token of the necklace he had given her warmed him clear through.

Seeing that Balsamon knew he understood, all he said was, "My thanks. I hope I'll be able to answer that myself."

"So does the person who entrusted it to me." The patriarch paused, as if not sure how to change the subject. Then he said, "You traveled much further than Amorion."

"I hadn't planned to, and I didn't need to," Scaurus said, still chagrined at fleeing west with Tahmasp at the very moment his men were pounding to his rescue.

"Never be certain of that too soon," Balsamon said. "One of the things I've seen, both as a priest and, before that, as a scholar seeking the world's wisdom, is that the web of affairs is always bigger than it seems to the fly struggling in one corner."

"There's a pretty picture."

"Is it not?" the patriarch said blandly. He gave that odd hesitation again, before going on, "I am given to understand that you, ah, had considerable to do with the leaders of Yezd."

"Yes." Marcus was not surprised that Balsamon had his sources of information; knowing the Videssians, he would have been startled if the prelate did not. He spoke of his encounter with Wulghash. Balsamon listened politely, but without much interest.

Once Scaurus mentioned Avshar, though, the patriarch's attitude changed. His eyes bored into the Roman's; his expression and bearing grew so intense that he and Marcus both forgot his infirmity. He snapped questions at Scaurus as he might have at some none-too-bright student in a classroom at the Videssian Academy.

When the tribune somehow dredged the name Skopentzana from his memory, Balsamon sagged back against his unyielding chair. Then Marcus could see how old and sick and tired he was. The patriarch sat still and silent so long that Scaurus thought he had fallen asleep with his eyes open, but at last he said, "Much is now explained."

"Not to me," the tribune said pointedly.

"No?" Balsamon quirked a tufted eyebrow. "Avshar was ours once, long centuries ago. Why else would he loathe Videssos so, and mock our every creation with his own?"

Marcus slowly nodded. Both the skill with which the sorcerer-prince used the language of the Empire and his antique turn of phrase argued for Videssian as his birth tongue. And thinking of the temple to Skotos in Mashiz, and of the dark-god's red-robed priesthood, Scaurus saw what the patriarch meant.

"How did Skopentzana tell you that?" he asked. "What is it, anyhow? I've never heard of it, save that once in Avshar's mouth."

"These days, Skopentzana means nothing," Balsamon said. "All that remains of it is ruins, hovels, and, in season, nomads' tents. It lies in what is now Thatagush. But when Avshar had only a man's years, the province was Bratzista, and Skopentzana the third city of the Empire, or maybe the second. Of golden sandstone it was built, and the river Algos ran singing to the gray sea, or so an ancient poet says."

"And Avshar?"

"Was its prelate. Does that really surprise you so much? It shouldn't. He was truly a prince as well, a distant cousin of the Avtokrator in the glorious days when Videssos held sway from the borders of Makuran in a grand sweep all the way to the frozen Bay of Haloga. He was highborn, he was able—one day he expected to be patriarch, and he might have been a great one."

"Ruins, Thatagush—" Marcus made a connection. "That was when the Khamorth invaded the Empire, wasn't it?"

"So it was." From the way Balsamon eyed him, perhaps he had some hope as a student after all. "A civil war weakened the frontier, and in they poured. They cast down in a decade three hundred years of patient growth and civilization. Along with so many other lesser towns, Skopentzana fell. In a way, Avshar was lucky. He lived. He made his way down the Algos to the sea, eventually he came home to Videssos the city. But the horrors he had seen and endured twisted his thoughts into a new path."

The tribune remembered what Avshar had said, that dreadful day in the courtroom at Mashiz. "He turned from Phos to Skotos then?"

His mark had just gone up again, he saw. Balsamon said, "Just so. For he reasoned that good could have no power in a world where such evil dwelt, and that the dark god was its true master. And when he reached the capital, he saw it as his duty to convert all the hierarchy to his views."

A Videssian indeed, Scaurus thought. But he said, "They're stupid views. If your house burns down, do you go live in the bushes forever after? More sensible to make the best of whatever comes and rebuild as you can."

"So say you; so say I. But Skotos' cult is like poisoned wine, sweet till the dregs. For without good, don't you see, there is no guilt; why not kill a man, force a woman, do anything for pleasure or power?"

The ultimate egotism—a heady wine indeed. In a way, it reminded Marcus of the Bacchic rites the Roman senate had banned a century before his birth. But at their wildest, the Bacchic rituals were a temporary, constrained release from the real world. Avshar would have made lawlessness a way of life.

The tribune said so, adding, "Didn't people realize that? Without rule and custom, everyone is at the mercy of the strongest and most cunning."

"So declared the synod that condemned Avshar," Balsamon said. "I have looked at the acts of that synod; they are the most frightening thing I ever read. Even after he turned toward the false he was brilliant and terrible, like a thunderbolt. His arguments against deposition are preserved. They have a vicious clarity that chills the blood to this day.

"And if," the patriarch mused, "in worshipping the dark he found a means to preserve himself to our own time and to seek to lay low the Empire that first gave him favor and then damned him—"

"Not to lay it low, but to conquer it, and rule it as he would," Scaurus broke in.

"That is worse. But it being so, much of what has passed in the intervening centuries makes better sense—just as one example, the savage behavior of the Haloga mercenary troop that crossed the Astris in the reign of Anthimos II? five hundred years ago—though I would still say Anthimos' antics had much to do with the success they enjoyed until Krispos gained the throne a few years later."

"I'm afraid I don't know those names," Marcus said. The admission saddened him. Even after so long in Videssos, he was ignorant of so much about it.

He started to say something more, but Balsamon was paying no attention. The patriarch's eyes had the distant, slightly glazed stare Scaurus had seen once before, back in Videssos. The back of the tribune's neck tingled as his hair tried to stand on end. He recognized that light trance and what it meant.

Caught up in his prophetic vision, Balsamon seemed a man trapped by nightmare. "The same," he said, voice thick with anguished protest, "it is ever the same."

He repeated that several times before he came back to himself. Marcus could not bring himself to question the patriarch; he took his leave as soon as he decently could. The day was warm, but he shivered all the way back to the legionary camp. He remembered too well what Alypia had said of the patriarch's visions: that he was cursed only to see disaster ahead. With Avshar getting closer day by day, the tribune was afraid he knew the direction it was coming from.

XII

Thorisin's scouting report was good, Marcus thought; by the campfires winking at the far edge of the plain, the Yezda had a bigger army than the one standing in their way. The westerly breeze carried their endless harsh chant to the tribune: "Avshar! Avshar! Avshar!" Deep-toned drums beat out an unceasing accompaniment, *boom*-boom, *boom*-boom, *boom*-boom.

It was a sound to raise the hackles of anyone who had fought at Maragha, bringing back memories of the terrible night when the Yezda had surrounded the imperial camp. Now, though, Gaius Philippus gave an ostentatious snort of contempt. "Let 'em pound," he said. "They'll ruin their own sleep long before mine."

Scaurus nodded. "Gavras may not like the defensive, but he knows how to use it when he has to." The Emperor had moved north and west from Amorion until he found the exact battlefield he wanted; the sloping plain whose high ground the Videssians held formed the only sizeable opening in a chain of rough hills. A few companies and a couple of light catapults plugged the smaller gaps.

Avshar had not even tried to force them. He made straight for the main imperial force. Unlike Thorisin, he sought battle.

Scouts were already skirmishing in the space between the two armies. The squeal of a wounded horse cut through the Yezda chant.

"Tomorrow," Gaius Philippus said, fiddling with the cheekpiece of the legionary helmet he had borrowed. When it suited him, he turned his back to the fire by which he had been sitting and peered into the darkness, trying to see who had won the clash. There was no way to tell.

He turned his attention to the imperial forces. After a while he sat again, a puzzled expression on his face. "Near as I can see, Gavras is doing everything right. Why don't I like it?"

"The sitting around, it is," Viridovix said at once. Even more than Thorisin's, his temper demanded action.

"That wouldn't matter, in a confident army," Gorgidas half disagreed. "With this one, though . . ." He let his voice trail away.

Marcus knew what he meant. Some units of the heterogeneous force were confident enough. The legionaries had always given the Yezda all they wanted, as had the Khatrishers who fought beside them. The Emperor's Haloga bodyguards feared no man living. And to the Arshaum, the Yezda were so many more Khamorth, to be beaten with ease. Arigh's men formed a big part of the army's cavalry screen.

But the Videssians who made up the bulk of Thorisin's men were of variable quality. Some veteran units were as good as any of the professionals who served beside them. Others, though, were garrison troops from places like Serrhes, or militiamen facing real combat for the first time. How well they would do was anyone's guess.

And in the background, unmentioned but always there, lurked the question of what deviltry Avshar had waiting. It preyed on the minds and sapped the spirits of veterans and new soldiers alike.

"Tomorrow," Scaurus muttered, and wondered if it was prayer or curse.

Cookfires flared with the dawn, giving the troops a hot meal before they took their places. Having chosen the field, the Emperor had settled his order of battle well in advance. He and the Halogai of the Imperial Guard anchored the center of his line. As the northerners marched forward, their axeheads gave back bloody reflections from the rising sun.

The legionaries were on their right, drawn up maniple by maniple, each behind its own *signum;* the wreath-encircled hands topping the standards had been freshly gilded and made a brave show in the morning light. The points of the legionaries' *pila* were like a moving forest as they advanced.

Here and there a man clung to the weapons he was used to, instead of adopting Roman-style javelins and shortsword. Viridovix, of course, kept his Gallic blade. And Zeprin the Red, shouldering his axe, might have been one with his countrymen in the Emperor's guard. But the

Haloga still did not think himself worthy of serving in their ranks and tramped instead with the rest of the legionaries.

To the left of the Imperial Guard were a couple of hundred Namdalener knights, men who still had Thorisin's trust in spite of the strife between the Duchy and Videssos. They wore conical helms with bar nasals and mail shirts that reached to their knees, and carried long lances, slashing swords, and brightly painted kite-shaped shields. The stout horses they rode were also armored, with canvas and leather and metal.

Rakio, in his own full caparison, rode over from the Roman camp to join them as the imperial force moved out. "No fear for me have," he said to Gorgidas. "I will be best fighting with men who fight as I do." He leaned down from the saddle to kiss the Greek good-bye.

The legionaries howled. Rakio straightened. "Jealous, the lot of you," he said, which raised a fresh chorus of whoops. They did not disturb the Yrmido at all; he was comfortable within his own people's standards. He waved and trotted off.

Gorgidas wished for his lover's innocent openness. Back among the legionaries, he found himself automatically falling into the old pattern of concealment. But when he looked around, he saw the grinning Romans were not so malicious after all. Maybe Rakio's nonchalance reached them, too. The Greek didn't know, or care. He accepted it gratefully.

"Pass me a whetstone, will you, someone?" he said, wanting to hone his *gladius* one last time.

Two or three legionaries offered stones; one chuckled, "The horseman thinks your blade is sharp enough." Gorgidas flinched, but it came out as camp banter, not the vicious mockery Quintus Glabrio had been forced to face a few years before. He gave back a rude gesture. The trooper laughed out loud.

Laon Pakhymer made his pony rear as he led his Khatrishers out to flank the legionaries. Marcus doffed his helmet to return the salute. "They're all right, that bunch, sloppy or no," Gaius Philippus said, echoing his thoughts.

Videssian troops, lighter-armed but more mobile than the men of Gavras' center, took their stations to either side. Some were horse-archers, others bore javelins or sabers. One of their officers brought his mount up on its hind legs, too, for no reason Scaurus could see other than high spirits. The imperials did not usually act like that; few of them gloried in war. Then he recognized Provhos Mourtzouphlos. He scowled. He did not want to grant his enemy any virtues, even courage.

Thorisin had stationed nomads at either wing of his army, outside his native soldiers. On the left were Khamorth, hired off the Pardrayan steppe. Marcus wondered if they were men who lived near the Astris, Videssos' river-boundary with the plains, or if his friends' friend Batbaian had sent them to the Empire's aid by way of Prista.

He had no such questions about the warriors on the other flank. Arigh was posted there. The Roman could hear the *naccara-drum,* at once deeper and sharper than the ones the Yezda used, through the horns and pipes that signaled the imperial force forward.

Avshar's army was moving, too, guided by the will of its chieftain. It looked to be all cavalry. The wizard-prince's tokens were at the center, opposite Videssos' gold sunburst on blue. Avshar had two huge banners. The smaller was Yezd's flag, a springing panther on a field the color of drying blood. The other's ground was of the same hue, but it took a while to recognize the device. When the imperials finally did, many of them sketched a quick circle over their hearts; it was Skotos's twin lightning bolts.

Around the wizard-prince came regiments of Makuraner lancers; their gear was between that of the Videssians and Namdaleni in weight and protective strength. A lot of them wore plumes atop their spiked helmets to make themselves seem taller.

The greater part of Avshar's power, though, resided in the Yezda proper. Scaurus had seen them in action too often to despise them for the poor order they kept trotting into battle; they combined barbarous spirit with the refined cruelty they had learned from their master. The emblems of many clans—here a green banner, there a wolf's skull, or a man's, on a pole—were held on high at irregular intervals up and down their line.

Avshar had taught them something of obedience, too; they drew to a ragged halt when Skotos' flag wagged back and forth three times. The armies were still several bowshots apart. Suspecting some sorcerous trap, Thorisin drew up his own forces. His mission was to hold, not to attack; let Avshar come to him.

A horseman emerged from the ranks of the Yezda and rode slowly into the no man's land between the two armies. Mutters ran up and down the imperial line as he grew close enough to be recognized; that terrible face could only belong to the wizard-prince himself.

He used a sorcery then, a small one, to let all the Emperor's troops hear his voice as if he stood beside them: "Curs! Swine! Last scrapings of outworn misbelief! Breathes there any among you whose blood flows hot enough to dare face me in single combat?"

"I dare!" roared Zeprin the Red, his face dark with the flush that gave him his byname. His axe upraised and his heavy chain-mail shirt jingling about him, he pushed out of the Roman line and began a lumbering rush at the wizard-prince, the object of his supreme hatred since Maragha.

"Stop him!" Marcus snapped, and several legionaries sprang after the Haloga. Alone and afoot, he stood small chance against Avshar in a fair fight, and the tribune did not think he would get one.

Avshar ignored Zeprin in any case. A Videssian horseman spurred toward the wizard-prince, crying, "Phos with me!" He drew his bow to the ear and fired.

Laughing his terrible laugh, Avshar made a quick, derisive pass. The arrow blazed for an instant, then vanished. "Summon your lying god again," the wizard-prince said. "See how much he heeds you." He gestured once more, this time in a complex series of motions. A beam of orange-red light shot from his skeletal fingers at the charging Videssian, who was now only yards away.

The soldier and his mount jerked and twisted like moths in a flame. Their charred, blackened bodies crashed to the ground at the feet of Avshar's stallion, which side-stepped daintily. The wind was thick with the smell of burned meat.

"Are there more?" Avshar said into vast silence. By then the Romans had managed to wrestle Zeprin back into their ranks. The overlord of Yezd laughed again, a sound full of doom.

Viridovix caught Scaurus' eye. The tribune nodded. If Avshar would meet them, they would never have a better chance. And at its worst, the match would be more even than the one the wizard-prince had given the brave, rash Videssian.

"Are there more?" Avshar said again. Plainly he expected no response. Scaurus filled his lungs to shout. Before he could, though, there was a stir in the very center of the Videssian army. The ranks of the Halogai divided to let a single rider through.

The tribune's throat clogged with dread. He had not thought Thorisin could be madman enough to dare his enemy's challange. He was a fine soldier, but Avshar's might was more than a man's.

But it was not the Avtokrator who advanced to face the wizard-prince, but an old man in a threadbare blue robe, riding a flop-eared mule. And from him Avshar recoiled as he would have from no living warrior. "Go back," Balsamon said; the same minor magic that let Avshar's voice ring wide was his as well. "The synod cast thee into the outer darkness of anathema an age ago. Get thee gone; Videssos has no room for thee and thy works."

Marcus stared in awe at the patriarch's back. He had seen how Balsamon, so casual and merry in private, could instantly assume the dignity his priestly office demanded. This, though, surpassed the one as much as that outdid the other. Balsamon seemed strong and stern in judgment as the great mosaic image of Phos in the dome of the High Temple in Videssos the city.

But Avshar quickly rallied. "Thou art a fool, thou dotard, to stand before me and prate of anathemas. Even aside from thy presumption here, in a year thou wouldst be dead, dead as all those purblind witlings who would not see the truth I brought them. Yet I faced them then and I face thee now. Who, then, cleaves to the more potent god?"

"One day thy span will end. Soon or late, what does it matter? Thou'lt be called to account for thy deeds and spend eternity immured in Skotos' ice with the rest of his creatures."

The wizard-prince's grim eyes burned with scorn. "Thou showest thyself as deluded as thy forefathers. We are all of us Skotos' creatures, thou, and I, and the headstrong bumpkin who sits the throne that is mine by right, and everyone else as well. Aye, in sooth man is Skotos' finest work. Of all living beings, only he truly knows evil for what it is and works it of his own free will."

He spoke as though he and Balsamon were alone, and indeed in a way they were, both being products, no matter how different, of the rigors of the Videssian theological tradition. Balsamon replied in the same fashion, seeming to seek to bring an erring colleague back to sound doctrine rather than to confront the deadliest enemy of his faith and nation.

He said, “As well argue all food is corrupt on account of a piece of bad fish. Or art thou so blind thou’dst forget there is great good as well as wickedness in the soul of every man?”

The patriarch might have meant the question as rhetorical, but Marcus thought it reached the heart of the matter. The older a man gets, the more fully he becomes himself. Avshar had been no more evil than any other man, before he read in the Khamorth invasions and the collapse of Videssos the sign of Skotos’ triumph on earth and turned to the dark god. But through his magic he had gained centuries to live with his choice and grow into it, and now . . .

Now he cursed Balsamon with a savagery worse than any his Yezda could aspire to, for the outcast always hates more fiercely than the mere enemy. His voice rose until he was screaming: “Die, then, and see what thy goodness gets thee!”

His hands twisted through the same set of passes he had used against the Videssian cavalryman. As the fiery light stabbed at Balsamon, Marcus cried out and sprang forward, Viridovix at his side. The patriarch deserved better than to fall unavenged to Avshar’s sorcery.

But Balsamon did not fall, though he slumped in the saddle as if suddenly bearing up under a heavy weight. “I deny thee and all thy works,” he said; his voice was strained but full of purpose. “While I live, thy foul sorceries shall hold no more sway on this field.”

“So thou sayest.” Avshar loosed another enchantment against the patriarch. This one had no visible emanation, but Scaurus heard Balsamon groan. Then the prelate dropped as inessential the small magic that projected his voice over the plain.

The wizard-prince rained spell after spell on him. Balsamon was not, could not be, the sorcerer to match his opponent. He lurched several times, almost toppled once. He did not try to strike back. But in defense, his will was indomitable. Like an outclassed warrior seeking only to hold his foe at bay as long as he could, he withstood or beat aside wizardry that would have devastated a stronger but less purposeful magician.

Seeing him survive in the maelstrom of sorcery, the Videssian army took up his name as a war cry, shouting it again and again until the distant hills echoed with it: "Balsamon! Balsamon! Balsamon!" And, as Marcus had seen before, the patriarch drew strength from his admirers. He straightened on his mule, his arms wide-flung, his blunt hands darting now this way, now that, as he deflected every blow Avshar aimed at him or at the imperial army as a whole.

"Och, a good fairy has hold of him," Viridovix whispered beside Scaurus. Gorgidas, well away from them, murmured a Greek word to himself: *"Enthousiasmós."* It meant exactly the same thing.

Finally, screaming in thwarted fury, Avshar gave up the assault, wheeled his horse with a brutal jerk of the reins, and stormed back to his own lines. A chorus of jeers and insults rose from the imperials. Everyone cheered as a Haloga ran out to take the reins of Balsamon's mule and lead him back to safety within the Videssian army. Exhausted but unbeaten, the patriarch waved to the soldiers around him. But Marcus could see his face. He looked like a man who had staved off defeat, not won a victory.

There was a brief lull. All along both lines, officers harangued their men, trying to whip them to fever pitch. Marcus looked inside himself for inspiring words. He did not find many. Whatever illusions he had of the glory of the battlefield were long since dust, as were those of the legionaries.

At last he raised his voice and said, "It's very simple. If we lose this one, we're ruined. There's nothing left to fall back on any more. Hang together, do what your officers order you, and don't let those bastards out there through. That's all, I guess."

He heard a few voices translating what he said into throaty Vaspurakaner for those "princes" who had never picked up Latin. He got no great applause; the legionaries had given Balsamon the cheers they had in them. He did not care. His men seemed ready and unafraid. Past that, nothing mattered.

Scaurus thought he heard thunder from a clear sky and wondered what new spellcraft Avshar was essaying. But it was not thunder. "Here we go," Gaius Philippus said as the Yezda urged their horses at Thorisin Gavras' line. The pounding of their hooves was the noise that filled the world.

Laon Pakhymer bawled an order. The Khatrishers galloped out to screen the infantry on their flank, to keep the legionaries and Halogai from having to stand against a barrage of arrows to which they could not reply. Pakhymer's troopers traded shots with the Yezda, slowing the momentum of their charge. Marcus watched horses and men fall on both sides.

The Khatrishers were gallant but outnumbered. Having done as much as he could, Pakhymer waved his disreputable hat in the air. His men, those who survived, fell back into their place in the line.

"Avshar! Avshar!" The shouts of the Yezda filled Scaurus' ears. Arrows began falling on the Romans. Somewhere behind the tribune, there was a curse and a clatter of metal as a legionary went down. Another swore as he was hit.

Thock! An arrow smacked against Marcus' *scutum*. He staggered and was glad for the multiple thicknesses of wood and leather and metal. The shaft would have torn through the light target he had carried with the Arshaum.

Pushed on by the mass behind them, the first ranks of Yezda were very close. "*Pila* at the ready!" the tribune shouted, gauging distances. He swung his sword arm high and caught the eyes of the buccinators, who raised their cornets to their lips. "Loose!" he cried; the horns blared out the command to the legionaries.

Hundreds of heavy javelins flew as one. Wounded Yezda roared; their horses screamed. The cries of dismay went on as onrushing ponies stumbled over the fallen.

Some riders blocked flung *pila* with their shields. That saved them for the moment, but when they tried to tear the spears out and throw them back, they found that the weapons' soft iron shanks had bent at impact, fouling their shields and making the *pila* useless. With guttural oaths, they discarded their suddenly worthless protection.

"Loose!" Another volley tore into the Yezda. Then the legionaries' shortswords came rasping out. Whether the Yezda fought from fear of their master or raw blood lust, they did not shrink from combat. They crashed into the Romans.

The dust their horses kicked up rolled over the legionaries in a choking cloud. Marcus sneezed and coughed. His eyes streaming, he hacked blindly at the rider in front of him. He felt the soft resistance that meant flesh. Warm wetness splashed him. He heard a groan. Whether it was man or beast he never knew.

He swiped at his face with the back of his forearm to clear his vision and quickly looked about. Here and there the Yezda had driven deep wedges into the legionaries' line, but he saw no breakthroughs. By squads and maniples, the Romans moved up to cover the points of greatest pressure. At close quarters they had the advantage, despite the horses of the Yezda. Their armor, shields, and disciplined flexibility counted for more than their foes' added reach and ability to strike from above.

Marcus saw Titus Pullo engage a Yezda, yelling and taunting and turning slash after slash with his *scutum*. While the underofficer's furious enemy thought of nothing but slaying him, one of Pullo's troopers ducked down unseen and plunged his sword into the belly of the Yezda's pony. It foundered with a coughing squeal; Pullo killed the man who had ridden it.

"That's right, get him when he's down," Lucius Vorenus laughed. He dueled with an unhorsed Yezda; his *gladius* flicked out in the short stabs the Roman fencing masters taught. Mere ferocity could not withstand such deadly science for long. The Yezda reeled away, clutching at himself; Scaurus smelled the latrine odor that meant a punctured gut.

Pullo was already battling another horseman. He and Vorenus might have buried their feud, but he was not about to let his comrade get ahead of him.

A Yezda thrust his lance at Zeprin the Red, who twisted aside with a supple ease that belied the thickness of his body. He sent his axe crashing down between the eyes of the barbarian's pony. Brains spattered everyone nearby, and the horse collapsed as if it had rammed a stone wall. A second stroke dealt with its rider.

Axes rose and fell continuously on the legionaries' left, where Thorisin's Haloga guardsmen were taking a heavy toll of Avshar's finest troops. But the Makuraner lancers who opposed them fought with dash and courage themselves, and fresh northerners had to keep pressing forward to take the places of those who had fallen.

"Tighten up there!" Marcus yelled. "Help them out!" He led a maniple leftward to make sure no gap opened between the Halogai and his own troops. In an army made up of units fighting nation by nation, that danger was always there. Drax' Namdaleni had taught him that, to his cost, at the Sangarios.

Though under no man's order, Viridovix moved with the tribune. He was glad to go to the aid of the Halogai. They were more somber by nature than his own Celtic folk, but came closer to reminding him of them than any other people of this world.

A Makuraner tried to hit him over the head with a broken spear-shaft. He ducked and countered; the horseman's damascened corselet kept the edge from his vitals. His mount kicked at the Gaul, who nimbly skipped away.

The two men looked at each other for a moment, both breathing hard. Under the Makuraner's plumed helm, his swarthy face was greasy with sweat, though his mustaches, waxed stiff, still swept out fiercely like horns. Viridovix' own whiskers were limp and sodden. Warily, his eye on the Gaul, the Makuraner swigged from a wineskin. He raised it in salute to Viridovix, then turned his horse in another direction.

"May you come through safe," Viridovix called after him. He had no idea whether the Makuraner heard him, or understood Videssian if he did.

A fresh Yezda surge almost sent Marcus hurrying back with his maniple to relieve the pressure on the rest of the legionaries, but Gaius Philippus and Gagik Bagratouni battled the nomads to a standstill. Bagratouni's Vaspurakaners, men driven from their homeland by the Yezda, fought the invaders now with a dour ferocity and a disregard for consequences that horrified Gaius Philippus.

The senior centurion had to wince, watching one of the "princes" and Yezda stab each other and fall together, locked in a death embrace. "Idiots!" he shouted, though Bagratouni's men showed no sign of listening. "Don't waste yourselves! One for one's no bargain with these buggers!

"You!" he rasped, spotting a foot soldier who seemed not to know where his place was. The fellow turned his head. "Oh, you," Gaius Philippus said in a different tone.

Gorgidas did not answer. Just then a Roman lurched by, clutching at a slash on the inside of his arm that was spurting bright blood. "Stop!"

the physician shouted, and the legionary, trained to obedience, stood still. Gorgidas tore a long strip of cloth from the hem of the soldier's tunic, pressed the edges of the wound together, and bound it tightly. "Go to the rear," he said. "You can't fight any more with that."

When the legionary tried to protest, the Greek argued him down. "Do as I tell you; as you are now, you're more trouble protecting than you're worth. The Yezda won't come pouring through because you've gone." The soldier stumbled away. Gorgidas hoped the bandage would hold the bleeding; that arm had been cut to the bone.

He unsheathed his *gladius,* which he had put away to tend to the injured Roman. Then he jerked in alarm as someone twisted it out of his hand. "Steady, there," Gaius Philippus said. "I think I want this back after all."

"Fine time," Gorgidas said indignantly. "What am I supposed to defend myself with?"

"Let us worry about that," the veteran answered, grunting in satisfaction at the familiar heft of his old sword. "From what I've seen, you're more use to us as a doctor than you'd ever be as a legionary. It's not bad you know how and all, but stick to what you're best at."

The Greek considered, then dipped his head in agreement, saying, "Give me the blade you've been carrying, though. It's better than nothing."

Gaius Philippus had already turned away from him; the fight was picking up again. "Come on, Minucius!" he roared. "I need another two squads here!"

Even as he shouted, a couple of Yezda burst through the struggling line of soldiers. The centurion caught a saber slash on his *scutum,* then grappled with the nomad, tearing him from the saddle and hurling him to the ground. He sprang at the other warrior and drove his *gladius* into the small of the Yezda's back before his victim knew he was there.

But the first Yezda had only been slightly stunned. He scrambled up and leaped at Gaius Philippus. Gorgidas tackled him from behind. He seized the nomad's sword wrist in both hands and held his grip as they rolled on the ground. His wiry strength kept his foe from tearing free until Gaius Philippus, working carefully so as to miss him, thrust through the Yezda's throat.

"Bravely done," the senior centurion said, helping the Greek to his feet. "But why didn't you stab him with your dagger?"

"I forgot I had it," Gorgidas said in a small voice.

"Amateurs!" Gaius Philippus turned the word into a curse. "Try not to kill yourself with this, all right?" he said, handing Gorgidas the blade he had asked for. The Greek was spared further embarrassment when the veteran ordered the reinforcements from Minucius into the line to shore up the weak spot that had let the Yezda through.

The presence on the legionaries eased as deep-voiced horns brayed to the left of Thorisin Gavras' center. His Namdaleni rumbled forward, shouting what might be the only battle cry they could share with the Videssians: "Phos with us!" At first the weight of their armor and of the big horses they rode gave their advance an all but irresistible impetus. Avshar's Makuraners slowed but could not stop them; in tight fighting the Yezda, on ponies and lightly armed, went down like winnowed barley.

Had there been more Namdaleni, they might have torn the battle open. As it was, the Yezda swarmed round their flanks and poured arrows into them. Not even their mail coats or their horses' protective trappings were wholly proof against that withering fire. Their progress slowed.

But in bringing the knights to a standstill, the Yezda thinned their own line. Seeing an opening in front of him, Provhos Moutzouphlos stormed through it with the headlong dash that had first made Thorisin notice him. Shooting and chopping, he led a company of Videssian horsemen as reckless as himself clean into the enemy's rear.

Again, if the rest of the imperials had matched his troopers' quality, they could have split the Yezda in two and rolled up their right wing. The Yezda knew it, too; their cries grew frantic. The legionaries cheered, not knowing what had happened but sure it meant no good for their foes.

Yet despite the cheers, despite Mourtzouphlos' pleading and his oaths, the other Videssians hung back a few seconds too long. The Yezda repaired the breach, and then Mourtzouphlos was trapped, not they.

He turned his company straight for Avshar, but that way was blocked—too many Yezda and Makurani, all headed straight for him. His shout rose above the battlefield din: "Back to our own, lads!" Those who made it—maybe half the number who had plunged into the breach—burst out between the Namdaleni and Halogai, having hacked their way through a third of the Yezda army.

Along with the rest of Gavras' forces, Marcus was yelling himself hoarse at the exploit—until he recognized Mourtzouphlos. "I will be damned," he said to no one in particular. "Something to the popinjay after all." As it had before, the thought grated.

In the heart of the Yezda battle array, Avshar seethed with frustration. He felt all his designs, all his long-nursed plans tottering. For the hundredth time he gave Balsamon his curses, hurling another spell at the patriarch of Videssos.

It hurt; he could sense Balsamon's anguish. That was sweet, but not sweet enough. Eventually, he knew, he would shatter the patriarch like a dropped pot—but when? Ordinarily Balsamon could not have withstood the first blast of his sorcery, but this, worse luck, was no ordinary time. In his desperation he had somehow screwed himself up to such a pitch that he was still resisting. Even without Avshar's assaults, the effort that took would kill him in a couple of days, but the wizard-prince could not wait so long.

Being unable to use his magic frightened Avshar as nothing else had. Without it he was just another warlord, dependent on his wit and his soldiers to gain his triumph—or to lose. The imperials showed no sign of giving way; if anything, they seemed steadier than his barbarous levies. The Yezda were bold enough when they scented victory, but quick as any nomads to melt away if checked.

The wizard-prince ground his teeth. Why, he had almost been in the hand-to-hand himself, when that Videssian maniac sliced his men like cheese. He wished Mourtzouphlos *had* reached him; even without his sorceries, he would have given the wretch a bitter death for his daring.

Suddenly Avshar threw back his head and laughed. Several horses around him shied; he paid no notice. "What a dolt I am!" he exclaimed. "If the bridge has fallen into the stream, I can swim across just the same."

He stared over the grappling lines of soldiers, measuring what he had to do. Even for him it would not be easy, but it was within his power. Laughing again, he reached for a black-fletched arrow and set it to his bow.

The moan that went up from the Videssian center was so loud and deep that Marcus thought the Emperor had fallen. But Thorisin's sunburst standard still flew, and the tribune saw him under it on his bay charger, urging his troops on. In his gilded parade armor, coronet, cape, and red boots, he was unmistakable.

The Halogai were holding well, and the left wing, if anything, was still advancing. Where was the trouble, then? Scaurus used his inches to peer about. There was some confusion a bit behind the Avtokrator, several imperials huddled around a riderless mule—

The tribune did not realize he had groaned aloud until Viridovix said, "Where is it you're hit, man?"

"Not me," Scaurus said impatiently. "Balsamon's down."

"Och, a pox!"

Marcus grabbed one of his Romans by the arm. "Find Gorgidas and get him over there," he ordered, pointing. Almost certainly, Videssian healers were already tending to the patriarch, but he did not overlook the one-in-a-thousand chance that they were all dead or out of action. The legionary dashed away.

Gorgidas went to Balsamon's aid at the dead run. He did not know the patriarch as Scaurus did and cared nothing for him as a religious leader; Gorgidas was no Phos-worshiper. But any man with the spiritual strength and will to bring Avshar's sorcery to a standstill was too precious to lose to a chance-fired dart—for such the Greek assumed it was.

Scaurus had been right in thinking the healer-priests would be doing their best for the prelate. They stared suspiciously at Gorgidas as he came puffing up, then eased in manner as they recognized him for one who shared their skill, even if a foreigner. "The good god bless you for your concern," one said, sketching Phos' sun-circle over his heart, "but you are too late. You would have been too late the instant he was hit."

"Let me see him," the physician said. He pushed through the imperials; with their near-miraculous gift, they knew far less of simple medicine than he had learned. Perhaps the training he had scorned since coming to the Empire and finding the higher art would serve him now.

A glance at Balsamon, though, showed him the Videssian healer-priest was right. The patriarch lay awkwardly crumpled on his left side. His face wore an unsurprised expression, but his eyes were set and empty; a thin trickle of blood ran from the corner of his mouth and fouled his beard. His chest did not rise or fall. The shaft that had struck him down was buried almost to the feathers, a few digits to the left of his breastbone. Gorgidas knelt to take his wrist, but knew he would find no pulse.

The physician looked toward the battle line. He knew the power of nomad bows, but it would have taken a prodigious shot to reach this far. Then he stiffened. Viridovix had told tales of such archery—and of arrows feathered with black. Anyone who thought of Avshar as sorcerer alone made the fatal mistake of forgetting what a warrior he was.

The reverse also held . . . and now the imperials' shield had been snatched away. Springing to his feet in alarm, Gorgidas cried to the men around him, "Are any of you wizards as well as healers?"

Several nodded. The Greek had time to say, "Then look to yourself, for Avshar is—" He never got "unleashed" out of his mouth. All but one of the healer-priests who were also sorcerers toppled as if bludgeoned. Some got out gasps or choked screams; others simply fell, horror on their faces, their mouths twisted in agony.

The last healer, stronger than his fellows, stood swaying a good two minutes, a fox cub facing a dragon. Tears streamed down his cheeks; after a moment they were tears of blood. He pounded his temples with his fists, as if to relieve unbearable pressure inside his head. Then his eyes rolled up, and he dropped beside Balsamon's corpse.

Wizards went down one by one all along the Videssian line, broken under Avshar's savage onslaught. A couple of the mightiest held on to life and sanity, but that was as much as they could do; they had no strength to ward the army.

Gorgidas felt the tide of battle turning. Suddenly the imperials were uncertain and afraid, the Yezda full of fresh courage. The Greek drew the shortsword Gaius Philippus had given him and ran for the front line. The veteran had been wrong; it looked like he was going to have some fighting to do after all.

Had Avshar been a cat, he would have purred. He rested his bow on his knee, watching consternation spread through the Videssian army like ink through clear water or black clouds across the sun. He ground another sorcerer between the millstones of his wizardry and felt the man's spirit fade and die. It was easy, without Balsamon. He patted the bow affectionately.

"For thy gifts, Skotos, I give thee thanks," he whispered. He thought for a moment, considering what to do next. Magic could only win so much more for him now. As long as he kept up the killing pressure against the sorcerers who still opposed him, he was limited to minor spells on the side. But if he let them go to work some greater cantation, they might somehow find a way to block it. Battle magic, even his battle magic, was tricky.

Let it be the smaller sorceries, then, he decided. They would be enough to panic the imperials, who would surely see them as the forerunners of worse. And that would give his soldiers the battle; already they were pushing forward, sensing their enemies' discomfiture.

The wizard-prince put away his bow and drew his long, straight sword. He wanted no doubt about who was going to cut down Thorisin Gavras. With Emperor—two Emperors!—and patriarch fallen to his hand, Videssos would learn who its rightful master was. He briefly regretted not having Balsamon to sacrifice to his god on the altar of the High Temple in the capital, but no help for that.

His eyes gleamed. There would be plenty of victims.

Being at the forefront of the fighting, Marcus sensed the advantage slipping away from the imperials even before the shift became obvious to Gorgidas. The center held steady, and far off on the right wing Arigh was crumpling the Yezda facing him. But the Videssians themselves wavered as the news of Balsamon's fall spread; it was as though some of their heart had gone with him.

The tribune wished Mourtzouphlos was back where he belonged. Thanks to his own vainglory, the noble was not cast down by the loss of the patriarch, and could have inspired regiments of wobblers by his example. His reckless dash through the Yezda line, though, left him in the middle of troops who needed no incentive.

As he had at Maragha, Scaurus marveled at the steadfastness of the Halogai. They bore a burden worse than the legionaries', for the main force of Avshar's Makuraner lancers concentrated on them and on the Emperor they protected. Yet they stood firm against the armored horsemen, their axes working methodically, as if they were hewing timber rather than men. Whenever one went down, another tramped forward to take his place.

They sang as they fought, a slow chant in their own tongue that reminded the tribune of waves breaking on a rocky, windswept beach. The music had to be strong to reach him so; he was half baked in his cuirass, his face a dusty mask runneled by sweat. And this flat, hot plain had never known the touch of the ocean and never would.

Thinking such thoughts, Marcus was almost cut down by a Yezda's saber. He jerked his head away at the last possible instant. Viridovix clucked reproachfully. "There's better times nor this for smelling the pretty flowers, Roman dear."

"You're right," the tribune admitted. Then they both failed to give the battle their full attention; the druids' stamps on their blades came to flaming life at the same time. "Avshar!" Marcus exclaimed. A couple of hundred yards to the rear, Gorgidas was yelling his futile warning.

Cries of fright rose from the imperials as the wizard-prince smashed their magicians like worms under his feet. Through the alarm and the din of battle, Scaurus heard Thorisin Gavras shouting, "Stand fast! Stand fast!" The Emperor did not sound panicked, or even much upset. From his voice, it might have been an order in a parade-ground drill.

His coolness helped bring the army back to itself. Seeing their leader unfazed, the soldiers borrowed courage from him and fought back. Again the Yezda were checked.

Viridovix glanced at his sword. The druids' marks were still glowing, and getting brighter. He shook his head gloomily. "Let 'em be brave whilst they can, puir sods. There's worse coming, sure and there is."

At first Marcus thought the buzzing that filled his head was a product of his exhaustion. Then the Haloga next to him broke off his song to growl something foul and slap at himself. A moment later another did the same, and a legionary, and yet another Haloga.

The imperial guard wiped his hand on his tunic. He noticed Scaurus looking at him. "Damned flies," he said with a sour grin. "Vorse t'an arrows, I t'ink sometimes."

The tribune nodded; bugs were always one of the small torments of the field. He had not been bitten himself, but he could see the big black flies droning around as they darted from one victim to the next.

Their bites were almost impossible to ignore, as a Roman found to his misfortune. Stung unexpectedly in a tender spot, he could not stop the reflex that made him clap his hand to it. The Yezda he was facing, untroubled by the cloud of insects, sworded him down.

Since the flies did not harass Scaurus, he took some time to realize how rare his protection was. Hardly an imperial was not swatting frantically or trying with all his might not to because he was locked in a fight for his life. And all their opponents shared the immunity that one nomad had enjoyed.

When the tribune recognized that, he knew with grim clarity where the blame lay. Avshar had worked grander magics, he thought, but hardly a more devilish one. The flies were hard enough for Thorisin's men to take; they robbed them of their concentration and gave their Yezda foes an edge. That first legionary was far from the only soldier to pay dearly for a second's involuntary lapse.

But the effect on the Videssian army's animals was ten times worse. There is no way to school a horse against a pain striking out of nowhere. Beast after beast squealed and reared or ran wild, leaving its rider, even if unstung himself, easy meat for a Yezda on a pony under control.

Thrown into sudden confusion, the imperials began to waver again. This time Thorisin had trouble steadying them. It was all he could do to keep his seat; his bay was bucking and plunging like any other fly-tormented beast.

He would not let himself be tossed. As he forced the stallion to yield to his will, he kept up the shouts of encouragement he had been giving all along: "Come on, you bastards, will you let a few bugs bugger you? Tomorrow you can scratch; today's for fighting!"

His cheers and similar words from a score of stubborn officers here and there along the line helped, but it was as if the Videssians were battling in the midst of a sandstorm blowing full in their faces. Each Yezda thrust was harder to contain, and those thrusts came ever more often.

Belong long, Scaurus thought as he cut at a nomad, the Yezda would find a gap or force one, and that would end everything.

But Avshar did not see anything that looked like victory. He had thought to sweep everything before him, and he was not succeeding in that aim. True, the imperials were giving ground on the wings, but not much, and their center remained unbudged. In that part of the field his plague of flies was failing. Gavras' infantry had the resolve to fight on despite them, and the horses of the Namdaleni were so heavily caparisoned that the biting insects could hardly reach their hides.

The wizard-prince clenched his jagged teeth as he watched his foes hold yet another attack. He had labored more than half a century to forge this latest weapon; he would *not* let it turn in his hand. His war on Videssos had cost too many years, too many defeats, for him to bear another. If for once his magic was stretched too thin, raw force would have to serve.

He turned to the messenger beside him. "Fetch me Nogruz and Kaykaus." The Makuraner generals came quickly. Nogruz, had things gone differently in his grandfather's time, might have been King of Kings of Makuran, but he bowed his head to Avshar. He was proud, able, and ruthless, a better servant even than Varatesh, the wizard-prince thought, and Kaykaus almost his match.

Avshar pointed at the sunburst standard still proudly flying to mark Thorisin Gavras' station. "Gather your men together—you see your target. We will shatter their best." He drew his sword. "I shall head the charge myself."

A slow smile lit Nogruz's lean, aquiline features. "I will guard your side," he said.

"And I." That was Kaykaus, though ragged bandages wrapped his shoulder and thigh. The great nobles of Makuran had a tradition of enmity with the Empire older than Avshar's vendetta. Any tool that came to hand, the wizard-prince thought, and made his preparations.

The Halogai roared in derision when the horsemen they had been fighting all day drew back, but they were too battle-wise to go lumbering in pursuit. Foot soldiers who chased cavalry asked to be cut off and slaughtered. Instead they leaned on their axes and rested, crushing flies, gulping wine or water from canteens, binding up wounds, and fanning at themselves to cool down before the battle began again.

Marcus stood with them, panting and wishing he could shed his mail shirt. As often happened in hard fighting, he had picked up several small wounds without knowing it: his cheek, his right forearm—cutting across an old scar—and on his right thigh just above his knee. When he noticed them, they began to hurt. He also realized that he stank.

Viridovix looked out at the enemy. "Bad cess for us, they're not through at all, at all," he sighed, wiping sweat from his face. Sunburn and exertion combined to make him as florid as Zeprin the Red.

He rubbed dirt in the palm of his hand, spat, rubbed again, then tested his sword grip. "Och, better."

The Makurani formed themselves into a great wedge aimed straight at the heart of Thorisin's army. There were more of them than Scaurus had thought. He mouthed an oath that was part prayer, part curse, when he saw the double lightning-bolt banner move to the point of the wedge.

The Emperor's standard came forward, too, and Gavras with it. This fight he would lead from the front. "The last throw of the dice," Marcus said to no one in particular.

A trumpet wailed in a minor key. The Makuraners shouted Avshar's name. Those who still had unshattered lances swung them down. The rest brandished sabers or shook their fists.

The Halogai and legionaries tensed to receive the charge. Far to the right, Scaurus heard Gaius Philippus bellowing orders and had a moment to feel glad the veteran was still in action. Then that mournful trumpet cried again, and Avshar's horsemen thundered toward the imperial army's center.

Scaurus' mouth went drier even than the day's thirsty work called for. He had faced cavalry charges before, and never wanted to see another. The greatest and most frightening difference between the Roman and Videssian arts of war was the stirrup and what it did for cavalry. Here the horse was the killing force, not the foot.

Brave as a terrier, Laon Pakhymer tried to lead his light-armed Khatrishers in a spoiling attack on the wedge, but the Yezda with whom they were already hotly engaged would not be shaken off. Pakhymer had to pull back quickly to keep his regiment from getting surrounded.

The Namdalener countercharge was something else again. The islanders' commander, a big burly man named Hovsa whom Scaurus barely knew, had no intention of receiving Avshar's assault with his own knights motionless; the momentum of their chargers was as important a weapon as their lanceheads. They slammed through the Yezda who darted out to bar their path and crashed into the right side of the Makuraner wedge close to its apex.

The noise of the collision was like an earthquake in an ironmonger's shop. The Namdaleni drove deep into the ranks of their opponents, thrusting Makurani from the saddle, overbearing their horses, and hewing them down with great, sweeping swordstrokes.

Provhos Mourtzouphlos unhesitatingly threw the survivors of his daredevil band after the knights from the Duchy. He despised and distrusted them, but he was too good a soldier not to see what needed doing.

The islanders and Videssians staggered the wedge and shoved it leftward. But the Makurani, no matter the leader they served, were warriors in their own right. They fought back ferociously, using their greater numbers to contain the imperial horse while their attack went home near the join of the legionaries and Halogai.

The first few ranks of infantry tumbled like ninepins, spitted on lances or ridden down by the Makurani, a fate Marcus barely escaped. He was spun off his feet; an iron-shod hoof thudded into the ground an inch from his face, flinging dirt in his eyes. He stabbed blindly upward. His blade pierced flesh, though it was almost ripped from his fingers. The wounded horse squealed. Its rider cried out in alarm and then in pain as the beast fell on top of him.

The tribune gained his feet, slashing wildly in all directions. He was not the only one to have got a blow in; there were horses with empty saddles and unhorsed lancers trying to rise and to keep from being trampled by their own comrades.

A few feet from him, a legionary was using a hoarded *pilum* to fend off a Makuraner. With his last strength, a dying Haloga hamstrung the lancer's horse. As it toppled, the Roman trooper drove his spear through the Makuraner's neck.

It could not have been more than twenty paces back to where the imperial foot was fighting to hold a battered line, but it seemed as many miles. Scaurus and the legionary fought back to back as they worked their way through the press. A Makuraner raked the tribune with a spurred heel. He yelped and hit the man in the face with the crossguard of his blade, being too nearly crushed for anything else.

A stone, thrown or perhaps kicked up by a horse, rang off the side of his helmet. He lurched and almost went down again, but then hard hands were pulling him and his companion away from the enemy and inside the imperials' shield-wall.

Though the Romans and Halogai were still being pushed back, they did not give way to panic. They knew they were done for if they broke. *Gladii* and *pila* thrust out between big *scuta* with drilled precision. The Halogai were not singing anymore, but they kept chopping away with axes and broadswords, overhand now to get the most benefit from their round wooden shields. Where the fighting was fiercest, they and the Romans were inextricably mixed—any man standing after the Makuraner charge helped his mates without looking to see if they were blond or swarthy.

They had blunted the point of Avshar's wedge, but were no more able than the Namdaleni and Videssians to stop it. The wizard-prince cut down trooper after trooper. The sight of his eyes blazing in that ancient face chilled the blood of the boldest and left them easy meat, but he would have been deadly without the fear he created. His charger, a trained war-horse, shattered shields and bones with its hooves, while he swung his long heavy sword like a schoolmaster's switch.

His men followed him from fear, not affection, but they followed. The distance between Skotos' bloody banner and the imperial sunburst narrowed. Little by little, the wizard-prince forced his attack back in the direction from which it had been pushed. "First thy brother, Gavras, then thy priest—now thee, and Videssos with thee!" he cried.

The Emperor brandished his lance in defiance and urged his mount toward Avshar, but the big bay could not get through the tight-packed, struggling foot soldiers ahead.

He was not the only one seeking the wizard-prince. Marcus sidled along the line, now managing one step, now two or three, now having to stand and fight. He bawled Avshar's name over and over, but his voice was lost in the cries around him.

Viridovix was not far away, though the impact of the charge had swept him and the tribune apart. He had his own war cry. It meant nothing to the troopers by him, but he did not care. "Seirem!" he shouted. "For Seirem!"

A pair of Makurani who had lost their horses came at him. He parried one saber cut, then turned the next with his shield. The Makurani moved to take him from either side. His head swiveled as he desperately looked for a way to deal with one before the other could kill him.

Then one of them collapsed with a groan, hamstrung from behind. Viridovix sprang at the other. They slashed at each other, curved sword ringing against straight. The Gaul was stronger and quicker. He beat down the Makuraner's guard and felled him with a stroke that half severed his head.

He whirled to make sure of the other Makuraner, but that one was down for good, the legionary who had dealt with him already fighting someone else. He was in trouble, too, for he had no shield. Viridovix rushed to his aid. Together they managed to force the enemy horseman back among his comrades.

"Indeed and I thank you," the Gaul said. " 'Twas a rare nasty spot, that."

"Think nothing of it," answered his rescuer, a spare man of about his own age with a beard going white. "Even Herakles can't fight two, as the saying goes."

"Och, tha daft kern of a Greek, what're you doing here? Tend to your wounded."

"Someone else would be tending your corpse if I had been," Gorgidas retorted with a toss of his head.

Having no ready response, Viridovix ducked down to strip a fallen Makuraner of his shield, then handed it to Gorgidas. It was a horseman's target, small, round, and faced with boiled leather—not much for a foot soldier, but better than nothing. The Greek had a moment to grunt his thanks before the struggle picked up again.

Moving crab-fashion, Marcus had worked to within thirty feet or so of Avshar. In the crush, the wizard-prince gave no sign of knowing he was there; Wulghash's glamour still veiled his sword. It was all hard fighting now. The lancers at the thin end of the Makuraner wedge were the pick of the army; getting past each one was a fresh challenge, with finesse as important as brute strength.

Or so the tribune thought. But then, quite suddenly, several horses went crashing down. Makurani on Avshar's left, the opposite side from Scaurus, shouting in alarm. Above their cries he heard someone bellowing like a wild bull. Roaring in berserker fury, his axe hewing a swathe of death ahead of him, Zeprin the Red hurled himself toward Avshar.

Only one rider was left between him and the wizard-prince—a noble in silvered corselet and gilded helm. He cut at Zeprin. Marcus saw the blow land, but the Haloga took no notice of it. He swung his axe in a glittering arc. The noble stared in disbelieving horror at the spouting stump of his wrist. The next stroke caved in his cuirass and pitched him from his horse, dead.

"Kaykaus!" the Makurani cried; a name, the tribune thought.

Zeprin cared not at all. With another incoherent yell, he rushed on Avshar, his gore-splattered axe upraised.

It was too late for the wizard-prince to twist and meet him weapon to weapon, but Avshar was truly the greatest sorcerer of the age. Without letting go of any of his own spells, he flawlessly executed the complex magic that had slain the Videssian who met him in single combat. Fiery light stabbed again from his fingers.

But the Haloga, though he staggered, did not fall in flames. His battle-madness and thirst for vengeance proofed him against sorcery. He recovered; his axe rose and fell. Avshar met the blow with his sword, but could do no more than turn it slightly. Instead of splitting his skull, it fell square on his charger's neck.

The beast was dead before its legs went out from under it. Seeing it go down, the imperials raised a mighty cheer. "Avshar is fallen!" a legionary bleeding from a slashed cheek screamed in Scaurus' ear.

The tribune shouted too, hoarsely. The cry stuck in his throat when the wizard-prince kicked free of the stirrups, lit rolling, and gained his feet before Zeprin could finish him.

The Haloga rushed at him. Marcus scrambled to help, but they were already fighting before he could get close. Zeprin's first wild stroke met only air. Full of insane strength, he sent his axe whistling in another deadly arc. Avshar parried, though the force of the cut nearly tore his blade from his hand.

Yet he was laughing, in spite of his fearful plight. "If thou'dst kill a man, wilting," he mocked, "it should be done so—and so—and so!" Each slash went home almost faster than the eye could follow. Blood spurted after every one. Any of them would have dropped a normal warrior, especially the last, a frightful cut to the side of Zeprin's neck.

In his berserker rage, the Haloga did not seem to feel them. He waded ahead once more, and this time Avshar bellowed in pain and fury as the axe lopped the little finger from his left hand as neatly as if it had been on the block. He bunched the hand into a fist to stanch the flow of blood.

After that he fought silently, but with no less ferocity. He dealt three blows for every slash of Zeprin's, and most of his landed; the Haloga had forgotten defense. His arm drawn back for another chop at the wizard-prince, Zeprin paused in sudden confusion. A torrent of blood streamed from his mouth and nose. His madly staring eyes clouded; the axe slipped from his fingers. His armor clattering about him, he swayed and fell.

"Is there another?" Avshar cried, waving his sword on high and setting his booted foot on Zeprin's neck in token of victory. He strode forward, confident no imperial would dare face him. Then he halted in his tracks, his fleshless face contorted in angry surprise. "Thou!" he hissed.

"Me." Winded and afraid, Scaurus had breath but for the one word. He was so tired he could hardly hold up his shield. Unlike the time so long ago in the Hall of the Nineteen Couches, Avshar had no buckler. This time the Roman cared nothing for chivalry. He hefted his sword. "No farther," he said.

He thought with dread that Avshar would try to overwhelm him at the first onset, but the wizard-prince hung back, letting the tribune gather himself. Of course, Scaurus realized—he wonders where I've sprung from, for he didn't sense my blade. He risked turning his head to look for Viridovix, but could not find the Gaul.

Avshar's hesitation lasted no more than a handful of heartbeats. When he did advance on the Roman, he moved more warily then he had against Zeprin. Having crossed swords with Marcus before, he knew the tribune was no spitfire seeking only to attack—and he had a healthy respect for the Gallic longsword.

The first clash of arms showed Scaurus he was in over his head. He was close to exhaustion, while Avshar drew from a seemingly unending well of strength. The tribune took blow after blow on his *scutum;* Avshar's keen blade bit into the bronze facing of the shield and chewed at the wood beneath. The wizard-prince easily evaded or beat aside the thrusts he managed in reply.

They dueled alone. No Makurani came to Avshar's aid; had he been a different sort of commander, Marcus would not have lasted long. But the imperials as well as his own men feared the wizard-prince. None of them had the courage to join the Roman against him. As if the two sides were both reproaching themselves, they fought each other harder than ever.

To Gorgidas, who was directly in back of the tribune, Marcus seemed like Aias battling Hektor in the *Iliad*—outmatched, baffled, but too mulish to yield an inch except by dying. The Greek shoved Viridovix in the back. "By the gods, hurry! He can't hold him off forever."

"Ha' care, tha sot!" Viridovix yelped, wriggling like a snake to evade a Makuraner's slash. "Is it trying to get me killed y'are?" His backhand reply caught his foe in the right shoulder. The Makuraner dropped his saber and started to run. A Haloga guardsman cut him nearly in half from behind.

"Hurry!" Gorgidas insisted again. He stabbed at the lancer who loomed in front of him, pinked the rider's horse. Its flailing hooves proved as dangerous as the Makuraner's long spear. The Greek skipped back just in time.

Up ahead, Marcus was still on his feet, though he blearily wondered how. Avshar played with him as a kitten toys with a mouse, giving torment but holding off the blow that would end it. Every so often he would inflict another gash and smile his carnivore smile. "Escape me now, an thou canst!" he gloated in high good humor. He relished victory over the tribune almost as much as if it had been Gavras and was in no hurry to end his pleasure.

Not all the blood on his robes and cuirass came from his amputated finger; even a mouse can have fangs. But his injuries were of no importance, while Marcus bled in a score of places.

After some endless time the wizard-prince exclaimed, "Let the farce be done at last," and leaped at Scaurus. His armored shoulder slammed against the Roman's shield and bowled him over.

As he had been trained, Marcus kept the *scutum* between his enemy and himself. Avshar's sword came smashing down. The tribune felt boards split under that crushing impact. The next stroke, he knew, would be aimed with cunning, not blind blood lust. He waited for the steel to enter his flesh.

Then he heard the wizard-prince cry out in wrath and turn from him to meet a new foe. At the same time, the druids' stamps on the tribune's sword flashed so brilliantly that he screwed his eyes shut, dazzled by the explosion of light. Above him, Viridovix' blade was another brand of flame. The Gaul roared, "Here, you murthering omadhaun, use your sword on an upright man."

He traded savage cuts with Avshar, driving the wizard-prince from Scaurus. That was not what the tribune had intended. "Wait!" he shouted, getting to one knee and then to his feet.

But Viridovix would not wait. With Avshar in front of him at last, his rage consumed him, just as Zeprin's had. The plans he and Scaurus had made for this moment were swept away by a red torrent of fury. To wound, to maim, to kill . . . had Avshar been unarmed, Viridovix would have thrown his sword aside to rend him with his hands.

If Gaius Philippus had taught Marcus anything, it was to keep his wits about him in combat. He rushed after the Gaul, whose wild onslaught had forced Avshar back a dozen paces. At every step he took, his sword and Viridovix' glowed brighter. The magic raging in his blade seemed to lend him fresh vigor, as if he was becoming a conduit through which some force larger than himself might flow.

The hammerstrokes Viridovix aimed at the wizard-prince bespoke the same sudden rush of strength. But Avshar, indomitable as a mountain, was yielding ground no more. His bodily power and swordsmanship matched the Gaul's, and in force of will he was superior.

Nor did his spells falter as he fought. He maintained his hold over the wizards in the imperial army, and his plague of flies still tormented his foes and their horses. Thorisin Gavras' beast, maddened by scores of bites, squealed and bucked and would advance no further in spite of the Emperor's curses and his spurs.

At last Avshar's men began to move to help him. One closed with Scaurus, a solidly built warrior who cut at the Roman's legs. To Marcus he was an obstacle, no more. The tribune parried, countered in a similar low line. His point tore open the Makuraner's thigh just below his mail shirt. The man gasped, stumbled, and fell, grabbing at his leg. Marcus raced past him.

Avshar's deadly eyes flicked to the tribune. "Come ahead, then," he said, shifting his stance slightly. "Both of you together do not suffice against me."

Marcus stopped short. The wizard-prince's withering laugh flayed him. The tribune's sword darted forth. Avshar's moved to beat it aside, but Scaurus had not thrust at him. Instead, quite gently, his blade touched Viridovix'.

The fabric of the world seemed to stretch very tight. The pounding of the tribune's heart was louder than all the Yezda drums. Never since the Celtic blades brought the Romans to Videssos had he hazarded the ultimate magic in them. Viridovix' sea-green eyes were wide and staring. He had agreed to Scaurus' plan, but it daunted him now. Who could tell to what strange land the druids' magic would sweep them next?

The same thought screamed in Scaurus' mind, but if he took Avshar with him he did not care. His greatest fear was that the spells which had been woven to ward Gaul would not protect Videssos. Yet the Empire was now truly his homeland, and Viridovix' long service for it argued that he, too, held it dear.

The wait between hope and dread could only have lasted for an instant. Avshar was still twisting to redirect his lunge when a torrent of golden flame leaped from his opponents' swords. Feeling the power of the unleashed sorcery, he sprang backward, throwing his own blade aside to shape passes with both hands. His mouth worked soundlessly as he raced through a spell to defend himself against the druids' charms.

Scaurus looked for the flame to form a great glowing dome, as it had in the blood-soaked Gallic clearing four years before—a dome to carry away Avshar, the flower of his army, and, all too likely, the tribune and Viridovix as well. But in Gaul no opposing magic had been operating. Here the power released from the two swords was hardly enough to contain the chiefest of Videssos' enemies; their sorcerous fire surrounded him in light but went no further.

The wizard-prince gave a trapped wolf's howl. Determined to the end, he hurled his strongest magics one after the other against the force that held him, striving to break free. The barrier heaved and billowed like a ship's sail in contrary winds. Two or three times it faded almost to transparency, but when Avshar tried to step through it back into his own world he found he was still restrained.

Men from both armies cried out in terror at the sudden outburst of sorcery. Many averted their eyes, either from the fierce glare or out of awe and fear of the unknown.

That was not Gorgidas' way. He wished he could take notes as he watched the flickering ring of light slowly tighten around Avshar. When the wizard-prince's desperate spells left him visible, he seemed surrounded by a swirling gray mist. Then the light flared to an intolerable peak of brilliance and abruptly winked out. Peering through green-purple afterimages, the Greek saw it had taken Avshar with it.

"I wonder where he went," he muttered to himself, and tossed his head in annoyance at another question he would never have answered.

He had been some yards away; Scaurus saw and heard much more, though he never spoke of it afterward, not even to Viridovix. That was no mist inside the barrier, it was snow, not falling but driven horizontally by a roaring gale whose sound was enough to freeze the heart. The wizard-prince's feet skidded on ice, a flat, black, glistening sheet; somehow Marcus was sure it was miles thick.

Avshar's voice rose to a frightened wail, as if he recognized where he was. And in the instant when the ring of light flashed brightest, Scaurus thought he heard another voice, slow, deep, and eternally hungry, begin to speak. He was forever glad he had not caught enough to be certain.

He wished the wizard-prince joy of the master he had chosen.

XIII

A GREAT SILENCE HELD THE CENTER OF THE FIELD. MEN ON BOTH sides stood with lowered weapons, stunned at what they had seen. The din of combat on either flank seemed irrelevant. Marcus and Viridovix looked at each other, dazed by the force they had called up and finding it hard to believe they had not been swept away with Avshar.

Then one of the wizard-prince's flies bit Scaurus on the back of the neck. Now that they were no longer under sorcerous control, his sword did not protect against them. The sudden pain and his automatic slap made victory real to him.

Across the line, the Makuraners began swatting at themselves, too. One of them caught the tribune's eye: a lanky, blade-nosed warrior who sat his horse with the inborn arrogance of a great noble. He smiled and nodded, as if to a friend. "We are all well rid of that one," he said, only a faint guttural rasp flavoring his Videssian.

Trumpets blared behind Scaurus. He heard Thorisin Gavras cry, "Drive them now, drive them! They'll be quaking in their corselets without the stinking he-witch to do their dirty work for 'em!"

The tribune's hand tightened on his sword. A last push against a demoralized enemy . . .

The Makuraner's smile grew wider and less pleasant, and Marcus felt a chill of foreboding. "Do you think we will run off?" the fellow said. "We are taking this fight; now it will be for ourselves instead of for a master who ruled us only because of his might."

He called to his lancers in their own language. They yelled back eagerly, clapping their hands and clashing swords and shields together. Their cry became a swelling chorus: "Nogruz! Nogruz!"

"Och, it's another round for the shindy, I'm thinking," Viridovix said softly.

"Come over to us," the Makuraner noble urged. "Neither of you is an imperial by blood. Would you not sooner serve the winners?"

Marcus could see the ambition blazing from him like fire. No wonder this Nogruz had followed Avshar—he would not shrink from anything that looked to be to his advantage. The tribune shook his head; Viridovix answered with a contemptuous snort.

"A pity," Nogruz said, shouting to make himself heard over the yells of his men. "Then I will kill you if I can."

He spurred his horse forward. He was too close to the Roman and Gaul to build up the full, terrifying momentum on which heavy cavalry depended, but so clever with his lance that he almost skewered Marcus as the tribune sprang away. Viridovix slashed from the other side, but Nogruz was as good with his shields as he was with his spear and turned the blow. More Makurani rumbled after him, and the battle began again.

"Out of my way!" Thorisin Gavras shouted impatiently, pushing his charger through the ranks of the Halogai. He nearly rode Gorgidas down when the Greek did not scramble out of his path quickly enough. Then he was face to face with Nogruz, his gilded armor and the Makuraner's silvered corselet both battered and grimy. "I'd sooner have killed the wizard, but you'll do," he said.

Both master horsemen, they probed at each other with their lances. Thorisin closed first, ducking under a thrust and booting his big bay at Nogruz. He threw his lance aside and yanked out his saber, sent it whistling down in a vicious stroke. Nogruz dropped his own lance and took the cut on his mailed sleeve. His mouth twisted in pain beneath his waxed mustaches, but he bought the time he needed to draw his sword as he twisted away from the Emperor's backhand pass.

Marcus only got glimpses of their single combat, as he was battling for life himself. He did see the brief sequence when a Makuraner came storming at Gavras from the flank. One of the Emperor's Haloga guardsmen shattered his lance and cut him from his horse with two thunderous strokes of the axe. A moment later another of Nogruz' followers killed the northerner, but did not interfere in the duel.

Nogruz's desperate use of his sword arm to meet Thorisin's attack left it numb and slow, and the noble found himself in constant danger.

The imperials roared and the Makurani groaned when his sword flew from his hand.

The Emperor's next cut was meant to kill. Nogruz ducked away, not quite far enough. The blow laid his cheek open to the teeth. He reeled in the saddle. Then his men did rush up to protect him and bore him back into their ranks before Gavras could strike again.

"They *must* break now!" Thorisin cried, brandishing his red-smeared saber. He urged his foot soldiers to another push at their foes. The Makurani, though, were tough as steel. They had been fighting Videssos for fifty generations and did not need leadership to keep on; it was in their blood.

Marcus was listening to find out what was happening on either side of the deadlocked center, and misliking what he heard. The noise he had dismissed as unimportant in the aftermath of Avshar's fall was vital again, and it showed a Yezda win in the making on the left. Even before Mourtzouphlos pulled out of line, that had been the weakest part of the imperial army; the Videssians there did not have enough plainsmen to screen them from the savage archery of the nomads who fought under Avshar's banner.

From the direction of the shouts, the Videssian left was already sagging badly. If it broke, or even if its flank was dislodged from the hill country that anchored it, the Yezda would have a free road to the imperials' rear. Scaurus' guts knotted at the thought. That was how Maragha turned into a catastrophe.

The tribune looked around for Viridovix. Having risked the unthinkable once made it less so in a second crisis. Were all the Makurani to vanish as Avshar had, the tide of battle would surely turn. . . .

But the Gaul was nowhere to be seen; a thicket of Makuraners on horseback and tall Halogai had got between him and Marcus. The Roman set out toward where he thought Viridovix had to be, but the going was as slow and hard as it had been when he was inching his way toward Avshar.

A mounted man pounded him on the shoulder from the side. He whirled and thrust, thinking he was under attack. Thorisin Gavras knocked his point away. The Emperor wore a fierce, harried expression.

"I wish I'd put the damned Arshaum over there," he said, pointing with his saber.

"Then you'd only have the same problem on the other wing."

"Maybe so, but they're grinding us on the left, and there's nothing I can do about it—all the reserves are in." Gavras was clutching his sword hilt tight enough to whiten his knuckles. He scowled. "Phos, I thought they'd scatter once you did in the wizard. And if I know you, you've had it planned for weeks, too."

With what he hoped was a suitably modest shrug, the tribune answered, "It worked better than I expected. I was afraid I'd go with him."

A messenger on a lathered, blowing horse forced his way up to Thorisin before he could reply. Marcus and a Haloga drove away an enemy lancer; the tribune wounded the Makuraner's mount, but the fellow escaped anyhow. When the Roman turned back, Gavras' face was as set as if it had been carved from marble.

"Bad news?" Marcus asked. Like Nogruz, he had to shout to be heard over the clash of weapons; the panting, oaths, and war cries of the fighting men; the pounding of horses' hooves and the beasts' squeals; and the moans and shrieks of the hurt.

"You might say so," Gavras answered in a dead voice. He pointed over the Makuraner line. "The lookouts in the hills have spotted a dust cloud heading this way—cavalry, from the speed they're making. They aren't ours." He glanced at the sun, which had slipped startlingly far into the west. "We might have hung on till dark saved us. Now . . ."

Marcus finished the sentence for himself. If the Makurani and Yezda had reinforcements coming, everything was over. Thorisin could not hold against them and could not retreat without turning his own flank.

"Make them earn it," the tribune said.

"Aye. What else is there to do?" The Emperor's eyes still held bleak courage, but a rising despair lay under it. "All for nothing," he said, so softly Scaurus could hardly make out his words. "The Yezda gobble the westlands, fresh civil war over what's left to us . . . even though you routed him, Roman, it seems Avshar wins at last."

Still more quietly, he went on, "And Phos preserve Alania and my child, for no one else will."

He spoke, Marcus thought, like Cincinnatus or one of the other heroes from the legendary days of the earliest Republic, putting the concerns of the state ahead of those of his family. But that spirit had not saved some of those heroes from disaster, and the tribune failed to see how it would here, either.

Hot fighting was an anodyne; he threw himself into it, to have no time to think of what was coming. He spied Viridovix for a moment and laughed bitterly—he was where the tribune had been not long before, probably searching for him as he had for the Celt. He struggled back in the direction he had come, but a knot of horsemen blocked his path.

"*Skhēsómetha?*" someone asked at his elbow: "Will we hold?"

His answer, to his surprise, also came out in Greek: "*Ou tón*—On my oath, no."

Gorgidas drew in a long, hissing breath of dismay. He was sadly draggled, his helmet jammed down over one ear; sweat, dust, and blood matted his beard; his cheeks were hollow with exhaustion. The target Viridovix had given him was all but hacked to flinders.

He nodded leftward and dropped into Latin to ask, "It's there, isn't it?" The noise from that part of the field was very bad. The Yezda had bent the imperials back a long way. They knew a building victory and whooped as if it were already won.

But Scaurus had to answer, "Worse than that." A head taller than the Greek, he could see over the fighting and make out that fatal onrushing cloud of dust himself. He told Gorgidas what it meant.

Too weary to curse, Gorgidas felt his shoulders sag as though someone had loaded him down with a sack of wet sand. "Not much sense in any of this after all, is there?" he said. The thought saddened him. As physician and historian, he searched for patterns to give meaning to what went on around him. All the events of the last several years, each of no great importance by itself, had come together to produce Avshar's downfall, unexpected but perfectly just. And now a relative handful of men from the west, thanks only to their untimely arrival, would rob that downfall of its significance and produce exactly the same result as if the wizard-prince still lived. Where was the right there? he wondered, and found no answer.

Yells of fear and dismay said that imperials up and down the line were spotting the approaching army. "Hold your ground!" Thorisin Gavras' shout was urgent, but he did not show his troops the hopelessness he had revealed to Scaurus. "Running won't help—you'll be caught from behind! The best chance we have is to stand fast!" The sensible advice, the kind an underofficer might give his squad, kept the soldiers steadier than any showy exhortations.

Marcus could see the banners of Yezd through the roiling dust. He felt no worse; he had known who those warriors were. Some of their countrymen spied them, too, and were waving them forward.

Lanceheads swung down as the newcomers went into a gallop. Makurani, the tribune thought dully—they would tear through the imperial line like a rockslide smashing a plank fence.

The noise of their impact was like the end of the world: the thud of body against body, horse against horse; the racket of weapons clashing and snapping; screams of terror, and others of pain. But the enemy was crying out, not the imperials; the attack crashed into their unprotected rear.

Marcus simply stood, rigid with astonishment. Then the new battle cry echoing over the field reached his ears, and he started yelling like one possessed. The newcomers were shouting, "Wulghash!"

Grinning a crazy man's grin, Gorgidas cried, "It fits! It fits!" He hugged Scaurus, danced three steps from an obscene dance, and leaped in the air in sheer high spirits. The tribune, bemused, drove off a dismounted warrior who made for the Greek while he was temporarily deranged.

If Gorgidas' pattern was completed, that of the men who had followed Avshar shattered into ruin. Chaos ripped through their ranks at the sound of the khagan's name. Some took up the cry themselves. Others, Yezda and Makurani both, had joined the wizard-prince in preference to Wulghash—or feared he would think so. They set upon men who had been their comrades until a moment before, hewing them down lest they be assailed in turn.

With fratricide loose among them, they could not hope to conquer the bewildered imperials, or even stand against them. Seeing the enemy's disarray, Thorisin Gavras went over to the attack. The Videssians' pipes and trumpets relayed his commands: "Press ahead, strike hard! This time they break!"

And break they did, unstrung at last. As nomads will, the Yezda galloped off in all directions, like spattered quicksilver. Once they were seen to be running, the pursuit was not fierce; the imperials were at the end of their tether, and Thorisin only too aware of how readily the nomads could flock back together. He let them go.

Instead he swung his forces in against Nogruz' Makurani. Less able to flee than the Yezda, they had no choices but fighting or surrender—and, having been beset from behind out of the blue, few would risk the latter. Battling with reckless desperation, they hurled the imperials back time after time.

But the troops who shouted Wulghash's name fought with an anger that made them a match for the countrymen now their foes. The khagan headed them. Older than most of his men, he was still a formidable warrior, making up with experience the little he had lost in strength. Too, his own rage propelled him as he hammered through his opponents.

Nogruz met him in the center of his riven force. The Makuraner noble's head was bandaged, but he had his wits back, and the full use of his right arm. They availed him nothing. Wulghash rained blows on him with a heavy, six-flanged mace, smashing his shield and shattering the sword in his hand. A final stroke crushed his skull.

When Nogruz went down, his followers saw at last that their game was over. They began shedding their proud, plumed helmets and giving up, though a few chose to fight to the end. More yielded to the imperials than to Wulghash's followers. Accepting the surrender of a nobleman who kept his arrogance even in defeat, Marcus thought he, too, would sooner take his chances with an out-and-out enemy than with an overlord he had renounced.

The tribune did not see any mistreatment of the soldiers who had submitted to Wulghash. It was as if he had no time for them, for good or ill. He prowled through their disheartened ranks, his eyes darting this way and that.

He was so intent on his search that he reached the imperials' line without noticing it, only drawing up in surprise when he saw he was face to face with foot soldiers. The Halogai and legionaries paid him no special attention, except when one asked if he wanted to surrender. He angrily shook his head.

Scaurus called a greeting, his voice a dusty croak. Wulghash's head whipped around. His broad nostrils flared in surprise. "You!" he said. "You turn up in the oddest places."

"So, if your Highness will pardon me, do you." Talking hurt; the tribune reached for his canteen. To his disgust, it was dry.

The khagan of Yezd grunted. "No trouble raising men against Avshar, or following his tracks, though we had to forage like so many dogs for the scraps his army—my army!—left." Wulghash's scowl was black. "And for what?" he said bitterly. "Aye, he's beaten here, but what of it? He's escaped me. One way or another, he'll be back to start his bloodsucking all over again."

"Not this time." In as few words as he could, Marcus told Wulghash of the wizard-prince's annihilation. He had to work to convince the khagan that Avshar had not simply gotten away through his own magic. When Wulghash finally believed him, he dismounted and embraced the tribune. His forearms were thick and muscled, like a wrestler's.

Only scattered fighting was left; most of Nogruz' men were either prisoners or down. Scaurus looked around to take stock. He spotted Viridovix not far away; even coated with dust, his fiery locks were hard to miss. The Gaul was relieving a captive of his gold-chased saber and knife. He waved in reply to the tribune's hoarse shout.

"Where might you ha' been?" he asked, prodding the dejected Makuraner along ahead of him as he ambled over. "Sure and I thought there we'd have to be swording it again, and you off doing a skulk." The twinkle in his eye took any sting from his words.

He glanced curiously at Wulgash. "And who's this stone-faced spalpeen?"

"We've met," the khagan said coldly, looking him up and down. "I remember your loose tongue."

The Gaul bristled and hefted his captive's sword. Several of Wulghash's men growled; one pointed a lance at Viridovix. Wulghash did not move, but shifted his weight to be ready for whatever happened.

Marcus said quickly, "Let be." He told Viridovix who the khagan was, and Wulghash of the Celt's part in beating Avshar. "We've fought the same foe; we shouldn't quarrel among ourselves."

"All right," the two men said in the same grudging tone. Startled, they both smiled. Wulghash stuck out his hand. Viridovix put the saber in his belt and took it, though the result was as much a trial of strength as a clasp.

"Touching," Thorisin Gavras said dryly. He showed no concern at riding up to the very edge of the Makuraner line. A fly flew in front of his face. He stared at it cross-eyed, then waved it away. "Surely the priests would approve of making a late enemy into a friend."

There was no mistaking him; the setting sun shone dazzlingly off his corselet and the gold circlet on his brow. Wulghash licked his lips hungrily. He had a good many retainers behind him. . . . "If I gave the word," he murmured, "*you* would be the late enemy."

The Emperor's eyebrows came down like storm clouds. "Who's this arrogant bastard?" he demanded of Scaurus, unconsciously imitating Viridovix. Wulghash scowled back; he did not care for being insulted to his face twice running.

The tribune did not answer at once. Instead he said testily, "*Will* someone give me a drink of water?" Thorisin blinked. Viridovix was first with a canteen. It held wine, not water. Marcus drained it. "Thanks," he breathed, sounding like himself again. He turned back to the Avtokrator, who was barely holding his temper. "Your Majesty, I present Wulghash, khagen of Yezd."

Thorisin sat straighter on his horse. All at once, the Halogai behind him were alert again, instead of tiredly slapping one another on the back and exclaiming over what a hard fight it had been. Scaurus could read the Emperor's mind; Gavras was thinking what Wulghash had a moment before, what the tribune had in the throne room at Mashiz—one quick blow, *now*. . . .

"You wouldn't have won your battle without him," Marcus said.

"What has that to do with anything?" Thorisin replied, but he gave no order.

Wulghash had followed Gavras' thought as readily as the Roman. His guards were as loyal as Thorisin's; they had chosen him when he was a fugitive and followed him across hundreds of miles to restore him to his throne. He lifted his mace, not to attack but in plain warning. "Move on me and thou't not enjoy it long, even an thou slayest me," he promised the Emperor.

"Save your 'thous' for Avshar," Thorisin said. He was still taking the measure of the khagan's horsemen, weighing the chances.

"Avshar is gone," Marcus said. "Without him setting Yezd against Videssos, can the two of you find a way to live in peace?"

Wulghash and Gavras both looked at him in surprise; the thought did not seem to have occurred to either of them. The moment for violence slipped away. Thorisin let out a harsh chuckle. "You hear the strangest notions from him," he said to Wulghash. "Something to it, maybe."

"Maybe," Wulghash said. He turned his back on the Emperor to remount his horse. Once he was aboard it, he went on, "We will camp for the night. If we are not assailed, we will not be the ones to start the fighting."

"Agreed." Thorisin spoke with abrupt decision. "I will send someone come morning, behind a shield of truce, to see what terms we can reach. Should we fail . . ." He stopped. Again the tribune could think along with him.

So could Wulghash. He grinned sourly. "You'll try to rip my gizzard out," he finished.

Thorisin laughed. Here, at least, was one who did not misunderstand him.

The khagan pointed at Scaurus. "Send *him;* no one else. No, I take that back—send his friend, too, the tough, stocky one. I can read a lie on him, where this one's too smooth by half." The tale Marcus had spun in Mashiz was not forgotten, then.

"Why them?" the Emperor said, not relishing Wulghash's demand. "I have real diplomats at hand—"

"Who sucked in tedium with their mothers' milk," Wulghash interrupted. "I haven't time to waste listening to their wind. Besides, that pair rescued me and let me go free out of their comrades' camp, knowing full well who I was. I trust them—somewhat—not to play me false." He gave Thorisin a measuring stare. "Can it be you do not feel the same?"

Challenged, Gavras yielded. "As you wish, then." Because he was at bottom a just man, he added, "All in all, they've served Videssos well—as has this outlander here." He nodded at Viridovix. "Ridding the world of Avshar outweighs anything else I can think of."

The Gaul had been unwontedly quiet since the Emperor came up, not wanting to draw notice to himself. At last he saw that Thorisin really did not hold a grudge against him. He beamed in relief, saying, "Sure and your honor is a fine gentleman."

"As may be. What I am is bloody tired." With that, no one in earshot could disagree. Thorisin turned to Scaurus. "See me in the morning for your instructions. Between now and then I intend to sleep for a week."

"Aye, sir," the tribune said, saluting. "By your leave . . ." At the Emperor's nod, he and Viridovix took their leave. Along the way they picked up Gorgidas, who was doubly worn with fighting and healing. After waiting for him to help a last wounded Haloga, they steered him back toward the main body of legionaries, holding him upright when he stumbled from fatigue. He muttered incoherent thanks.

"Och, Scaurus, what'll you and himself do if Gaius Philippus is after getting himself killed?" Viridovix asked. "Wouldn't that bugger up your plans for fair?"

"Phos, yes," Marcus said, surprising himself by swearing by the Videssian god. He could not imagine Gaius Philippus dying in battle; the veteran seemed indestructible. Apprehension seized him.

His heart leaped when he heard the familiar parade-ground rasp: "Form up there, you jounce-brained lugs! You think this is a fornicating picnic, just because the scrap's over for a while? Form up, the gods curse your lazy good-for-nothing bungling!"

Gorgidas roused a bit from his stupor. "Some things don't change," he said.

Darkness was swiftly falling; the Roman, Greek, and Gaul were almost on top of Gaius Philippus before he recognized them. When he did, he shouted, "All right, let's have a cheer for our tribune now—beat Avshar singlehanded, he did!"

The roar went up. "I like that," Viridovix said indignantly. "There for my health, I suppose I was."

Marcus laid a hand on his shoulder. "We both know better."

So, in fact, did Gaius Philippus. He came up to the Gaul and said in some embarrassment, "I hope you understand that was for the sake of the troops. I know nothing would have worked without your having the backbone to go through with the scheme."

"Honh! A likely tale." Viridovix tried to sound gruff, but could not help being mollified by the rare apology from the senior centurion.

It seemed the legionaries had left camp weeks ago, not half a day. Great holes were torn in their ranks; Scaurus mourned each Italian face he would never see again. With Vorenus slain on the field, Titus Pullo trudged back to the Roman ditch and earthwork like a man stunned. Their rivalry was done at last. Pinarius, the trooper who had challenged Marcus and his friends when they returned to Amorion, was dead, too, and his brother beside him, along with so many more.

And Sextus Minucius was hobbling on a stick, his right thigh tightly bound up, his face set with pain and pale from loss of blood. Having seen more battlefield injuries than he liked to remember, Marcus was not sure the young Roman would walk straight again. Maybe Gorgidas' healing would help, he thought. Still, Minucius was luckier than not—his Erene was no widow.

If anything, the Videssians and Vaspurakaners who had joined the legionaries suffered worse than the Romans, being not quite so skilled at infantry fighting. Scaurus felt a stab of guilt walking past Phostis Apokavkos' corpse; had he left the Videssian in the city slum where he found him, Apokavkos might eventually have made a successful thief.

Gagik Bagratouni limped from a wound much like Minucius'. Two "princes" were dragging his second-in-command, Mesrop Anhoghin, in a litter close behind him. Perhaps mercifully, Anhoghin was unconscious; sticky redness soaked through the bandages wrapped round his belly.

Bagratouni gave Scaurus a grave nod. "We beat them," was all he said; the victory had been too narrow for exultation.

As the legionaries began filing into camp, Laon Pakhymer led the tattered remnant of his Khatrishers up to the palisade. "May we bivouac with you?" he called to Marcus. He looked from his own men to the Romans and sadly shook his head. "There's room for the lot of us."

"Too true," Marcus said. "Of course; come ahead." He made sure an adequate guard had been detailed to watch the legionaries' prisoners, then stumbled into his tent, started to undo his armor, and fell asleep still wearing one greave.

Seeing Gaius Philippus carrying a white-painted shield on a spearshaft, Pikridios Goudeles raised a sardonic eyebrow. "First Scaurus usurps my proper function, and now you?" he said.

The veteran grunted. "You're welcome to it. I'm no diplomat, with or without any damned olive branch."

Goudeles frowned at the Roman idiom, then caught it. "Blame your honest face," he chuckled. His own features were once more as they had been at the capital; he had trimmed his hair and beard, and also shed his Arshaum leathers for a short-sleeved green robe of brocaded silk. But he was wearing his saber and kept glancing proudly at the dressing that covered an arrow wound on his arm—pen-pusher or no, he had been in the previous day's fighting.

"Let's get on with it," Marcus said, hefting his own shield of truce. His head was buzzing with Thorisin's commands, and the most urgent of them had been to reach an agreement quickly.

Several Halogai and Videssians saluted the tribune as he walked out of the imperial camp; they knew what he had done. Provhos Mourtzouphlos, though, turned his back. Marcus sighed. "It's wrong to wish someone on your own side had been killed in action, but—"

"Why?" Gaius Philippus asked bluntly. "He's a worse enemy than a whole clan of Yezda."

Vultures and carrion crows flapped into the air, screeching harsh protests, as the Romans went through the battleground. Wild dogs and foxes scuttled out of their path. Flies, Avshar's and others, swarmed over the littered corpses. Those were already beginning to swell and stink under the late summer sun.

Makuraner sentries, apparently forewarned to expect Scaurus and Gaius Philippus, led them to Wulghash. On their way, they took them through the entire camp, which was even more sprawled and disorderly than the one they had left not long before.

The tribune caught his breath sharply when they rounded a last corner and approached Wulghash's pavilion. In front of it stood a long row of heads, sixty or seventy of them. Some still wore the gilded or silvered helms of high officers.

"I don't see Tabari," Marcus said.

"You were looking for him, too, eh? Let's hope he had sense or luck enough to stay in Mashiz."

One head still seemed to be trying to say something. Scaurus wondered uneasily if awareness could linger for a few seconds after the axe came down.

Gaius Philippus' thoughts went in another direction. He said, "I was wondering why we hadn't been shown any prisoners. Now I know. With the dangerous ones shortened, Wulghash drafted the rest to fill out his army."

Marcus smacked his fist into his palm, annoyed he had not made the connection himself. It fit what he knew of Wulghash's bold, ruthless character. Following the logic a step further, he said, "Then he'll be looking to bring the scattered Yezda back under his command, too."

The words were hardly out of his mouth when a double handful of nomads rode by on their ponies. They scowled, recognizing the Romans' gear. Marcus was also frowning. "Something else we were meant to see, I think."

"Aye. Just what Gavras is afraid of, too."

The tribune's suspicion that the show had been planned grew sharper when the guides, who had disappeared into Wulghash's tent, chose that moment to emerge and beckon the Romans forward. One of the Makurani held the gray felt flap wide so they could enter.

The tent held no regal finery; its furnishings were an incongruous blend of the ornate Makuraner and spare Yezda styles—whatever had been easy to scrape up, Marcus guessed. The only exception was the large quantity of sorcerer's gear—codices, a cube of rose crystal, several elaborately sealed jars, an assortment of knives with handles that looked unpleasantly like flesh, and other oddments—now heaped carelessly in a corner.

Wulghash saw the tribune glance that way. "Useless preparations, as it turned out," he remarked.

"Like the performance you put on for us out there?" Marcus asked politely.

The khagan was unfazed. "It showed what I intended. I am not as weak as Gavras thinks—and I grow stronger by the hour."

"No doubt," Gaius Philippus nodded. He and Scaurus had agreed that he should deliver Thorisin's ultimatum. "That's why the Emperor gives you three days to begin withdrawing to Yezd. After that the truce is over, and he will attack without warning."

The senior centurion's bluntness made Wulghash's wide, fleshy nostrils flare with anger. "Does he? Will he?" he cried. "If that's what he meant by talking, let him come today, and I will speak a language he understands." He tugged his saber halfway out of its scabbard.

"You'd lose," Marcus said. "We were holding—barely, I grant, but holding—against the whole army Avshar had mustered, and you don't have much more than the core left. We'd trounce you. Why shouldn't you go home? This is not your country and never was. You have your own throne again—see to your land, and your hold on it."

The khagan looked so grim Marcus was afraid he would not be able to hold his temper. The trouble, he knew, was that Wulghash was as eager to conquer Videssos as Avshar had been. He had to be burning like vitriol inside because his charge, instead of ruining the wizard-prince, had only saved the imperial forces.

But he had been a ruler for many years, and learned realism. His bluster aside, Thorisin could crush him if willing to pay the butcher's bill. He breathed heavily for close to a minute, not trusting himself to speak, then finally ground out, "Has Gavras any other little, ah, requests for me?"

Again it was Gaius Philippus who answered. "Only one. Since all the nomads, not only from this latest invasion but from years gone by, too, have come to Videssos without his leave, he bids you order them back to Yezd and keep them there from now on."

Scaurus waited for Wulghash to explode again. Instead he threw back his head and laughed in the Romans' faces. "Then he may as well bid me tie all the winds up in a sack and keep them in the sky. The nomads in Videssos are beyond my control, or that of any other man. They go as they will; I cannot *make* them do anything."

As that was exactly what the tribune had thought when Thorisin gave him the instruction, he had no good answer ready. Wulghash went on, "For that matter, I would not recall the nomads if I could. Though they are of my blood, I have no use for them, save sometimes in battle. You've seen who backs me—Makurani. Civilized men.

"The nomads spread strife wherever they go. They plunder, they kill, they ruin farms, wreck trade, empty cities, and drain my coffers. When some of the clan chiefs wanted to harry the Empire instead of Yezd, I helped them on their way and sent more after them. Good riddance, I say. Had they all gone, my rule would have been ten times easier."

Marcus was suddenly reminded of the Romans after they had conquered Greece—captured by their captors in art, in literature, in luxury, in their entire way of life. Wulghash was much the same. His people had been barbarians, but he seized on the higher culture of Makuran with a convert's zeal.

The khagan had another reason to resent the folk from whom he had sprung. His hands bunched into fists, and he glowered down at the sleeping-mats on the ground as he paced between them. He said, "And the Yezda chose Avshar over me, followed him, worshiped him." That rankled yet, Scaurus thought. "It was not just his magic; he and they suited each other, with their taste for blood. So, since you serve Gavras, tell him he is welcome to the nomads he has. I do not want them back."

After his outburst, there did not seem to be much room for discussion. "We'll take your words back to the Emperor," Marcus promised in a formal voice, "and tell him of your determination."

"Can't say I blame you, either, looking at things from your side," Gaius Philippus added.

Wulghash softly pounded him on the shoulder in gratitude. "I said to Gavras' face you were an honest man."

"Won't stop me from cutting you up a few days from now, if I have to," the veteran answered stolidly. "Like your Makurani, I know which side I'm on."

"Be it so, then," the khagan said.

"He won't commit himself to getting the nomads out, eh?" Thorisin asked.

"No," Scaurus replied. "He disowns them. If anything, I think he hates them worse than you do. And in justice," he went on, and saw the Emperor roll his eyes at the phrase, "I don't see what he could do. Yavlak and the other clan-chiefs are their own law. They wouldn't heed his commands any more than yours, and he hasn't the power to compel them."

"I know that," Gavras said placidly. If he was angry at Wulghash's rejection of his demand, he hid it well. In fact, he looked pleased with himself, in a foxy way. "I wanted to hear them denied from his own lips."

Marcus tugged at his ear, not following whatever the Emperor had in mind. Beside him, Gaius Philippus shrugged almost invisibly.

"Never mind," Thorisin said. "Just make sure you see me tomorrow morning before you go off and haggle with him again. Now get out. I have more people to see than the two of you." He did sound in good spirits, Marcus thought.

The Romans bowed and left. Scaurus heard Thorisin shouting for his steward: "Glykas! Come here, damn it, I need you. Fetch me Mourtzouphlos and Arigh the Arshaum." A little pause. "No, you lazy lackwit, I don't know where they are. Find them, or find another job."

The Makuraner sentry spat at Marcus' feet when he and Gaius Philippus came up to Wulghash's encampment. The tribune thought he was about to be attacked in spite of the shield of truce he was carrying. He got ready to throw it away and go for his sword.

"Expected as much," Gaius Philippus said. He had also shifted into a fighting stance. Scaurus nodded.

But having relieved his feelings, the sentry haughtily turned his back and led the Romans to the khagan's tent. This time they went straight there. Wulghash's troopers shook fists as they passed. Someone threw a lump of horsedung. It smacked against Gaius Philippus' upraised truce shield, staining the smooth white paint.

Wulghash was outside the pavilion, talking with his bodyguards. One of them pointed to the Romans. The khagan rumbled something deep in his throat. He jerked his chin at Gaius Philippus' shield. "A fitting symbol for a broken peace," he growled.

"As far as Thorisin is concerned, the truce still holds," Marcus answered. "Have you been assailed here?"

"Spare me the protests of innocence, at least," Wulghash said. "I'd sooner believe in a virgin whore. You know as well as I what Gavras did in the dead of night—sent out his Videssians and those vicious savages from Shaumkhiil to harry my warriors in their scattered camps. Hundreds must have died."

"I repeat: Were you and yours attacked here?"

Scaurus' monotone made the khagan look up sharply. "No," he said, his own voice suddenly wary.

"Then I submit to you that the peace between you and the Emperor has not been breached. You told us yesterday that you had no use for the Yezda, that you could not force them to obey you, and that you did not want them. In that case, Thorisin has every right to deal with them as he sees fit. Or do you only claim them as yours when you gain some advantage from it?"

Wulghash flushed all the way up to the balding crown of his head. "I was speaking," he said tightly, "of the Yezda already in Videssos."

"That doesn't do it," Gaius Philippus said. "You were the one complaining how the buggers with Avshar kissed his boot instead of yours. Now you want 'em back. All right. The way I see it, Gavras has the right to stop you if he can. They weren't part of the deal. And as for this," he glanced at the shield of truce, "your soldier flung the horseturd."

Marcus put in, "Thorisin could have attacked you here instead of the Yezda, but he held off. He isn't interested in destroying you—"

"Because it would cost him too dear."

"As may be. It would cost you more; he is stronger than you now. And while he is stronger, he intends to see you gone from Videssos. I warn you, he is deadly serious over his ultimatum. If he sees no movement from you come day after tomorrow, he'll move on you with everything he has. And there are fresh troops just in from Garsavra."

The last was bluff, but Thorisin had set the groundwork for it by lighting several hundred extra campfires the night before. Wulghash bit his lip, examining Gaius Philippus closely. But the senior centurion revealed nothing, for the khagan had slightly misread his man. Gaius Philippus would always say what he thought, but a team of fifty horses could not have dragged a stratagem from him.

Recalling what Wulghash had told him when they were just out of the tunnels below Mashiz, Marcus said, "I would also wish we were friends as well as what my people call guest-friends." Wulghash took his meaning, and he went on, "As a friend, I would say your best course lies in retiring. You cannot succeed against Thorisin here and you need to reestablish yourself in Yezd."

"I don't think the two of us will ever be friends, whatever we might want," the khagan answered steadily. "For now, worse luck, I fear you are right, but I am not done with Videssos yet. Defend it if you can, but it is old and worn. One good push—"

"I've heard Namdaleni talk the same way, but we survived them." Scaurus thought back to Drax the opportunist, and hotheaded Soteric. Remembering her brother reminded him of Helvis and how she had scorned him for calling the Videssians *we*. He shrugged, which made Wulghash scratch his head. He was content with his choice.

The Yezda khagan was not one to leave a point quickly. "If not in my day, then in my son's," he said.

"How is Khobin?" Marcus asked, dredging the name up from Wulghash's use of it in the palace banquet hall.

"Alive and well, last I heard," Wulghash said gruffly. But his eyes narrowed, and his left eyebrow rose a fraction of an inch; the tribune knew he had gained a point. Wulghash's chuckle had a grim edge to it. "The hired killers Avshar sent out botched their job. They weren't his best; he must have thought Khobin not worth worrying about."

"I'm glad, and glad he was wrong."

"And I," the khagan answered. "He's a likely youngster."

"That's all very well, but it grows no barley," Gaius Philippus said, dragging them back to the issue at hand. "What do you propose doing about pulling out?"

Wulghash grunted, but Gaius Philippus' forthrightness had made him ask for the veteran. "If I had my choice, I would fight," the khagan said. "But the choice is not mine—and Gavras, it seems," he added wryly, "will not let me seize it. So . . . I will withdraw." He spat that out as if it tasted bad.

Scaurus could not help letting out a slow, quiet breath of relief. "The Emperor pledges that you will not be harassed as long as you are retiring in peace."

"Big of him," Wulghash muttered. He seemed surprised and not very happy to see the Romans still in front of him; he must have looked on them as symbols of his failure to hold his ground. "You have what you want, don't you? If you do, we're finished. Go away."

As they walked back to the imperial camp, Gaius Philippus said darkly, "I don't know about you, but I'm sick and tired of everyone telling me, 'Go.' Next time someone tries it, he'll know just where to go, I promise."

"You'd never make an ambassador," Marcus said.

"Good."

That evening, though, having heard their report, Pikridios Goudeles disagreed with the tribune. "You should be proud of yourselves," he told the Romans. "For amateurs, you did very well. Thorisin's unhappy because he can't slaughter Wulghash; Wulghash is disgusted because he has to go home. And after all, what is diplomacy," he paused to hone his epigram, "but the art of leaving everyone dissatisfied?"

Sullenly, Wulghash withdrew toward the west. Gavras sent out a company of Videssian horsemen to make sure he really was retreating, much as Shenuta had kept a close eye on the Arshaum when they were passing through his territory.

A couple of days later, after it became clear the khagan was pulling back, Gaius Philippus startled Marcus by requesting leave for the first time since the tribune had known him. "It's yours, of course," Marcus said at once. "Do you mind my asking why?"

The veteran, usually so direct, looked uncomfortable. "Thought I'd borrow a horse from the Khatrishers, do a bit of riding out. Sight-seeing, you might say."

"Sight-seeing?" Gaius Philippus made the most unlikely tourist Scaurus could imagine. "What on earth does this miserable plain have worth seeing?"

"Places we've been before," the senior centurion said vaguely. He shifted from foot to foot like a small boy who needs to be excused. "I might get up to Aptos, for instance."

"Why would anyone want to go to—" Marcus began, and then shut up with a snap. If Gaius Philippus had finally worked up the nerve to court Nerse Phorkaina, that was his business. The tribune did say, "Take care of yourself. There probably are still Yezda prowling the road."

"Stragglers I'm not afraid of, but Avshar's army went through there. That does worry me." The veteran rode out a couple of hours later, sitting his borrowed horse without grace but managing it with the same matter-of-fact competence he displayed in nearly everything he did.

"After his sweetling, is he?" Viridovix asked, watching the Roman trot past the burial parties busy at their noisome work.

"Yes, though I doubt he'd admit it on the rack."

Instead of laughing at the centurion, Viridovix sighed heavily and said, "Och, I hope he finds her hale and all to bring back. E'en a great gowk like him deserves a touch o' happiness, for all his face'd crack to show it."

Gorgidas spoke in Greek. Marcus translated for Viridovix: " 'Count no man happy before his end,' " Solon's famous warning to Croesus the Lydian king. The physician continued tartly, "The mere presence of the object of one's infatuation does not guarantee delight, let me assure you."

The tribune and the Gaul carefully looked elsewhere. Rakio had not returned to the legionary camp after the battle, save to get his gear. Having taken up with one of the Namdalener knights, he left Gorgidas without a good-bye or a backward glance.

"Don't stand there mooning on my account," the Greek snapped. "I knew he was fickle when we started; to give him his due, he never pretended otherwise. My pride isn't badly stung, or my heart. It's the better matches that leave the lasting sorrow."

"Aye." That was Scaurus and Viridovix together, softly. For a few seconds each of the three men was lost in his thoughts, Gorgidas remembering Quintus Glabrio; Viridovix, Seirem; and Marcus, Alypia and Helvis both.

Where nothing else would have, the thought that his second love might go as the first had almost kept him from pressing Thorisin on their bargain. His combat injuries were healing. But when he touched it unexpectedly, the wound Helvis had dealt pained him as much as it had when it was fresh. He flinched from opening himself to the risk of such hurt again.

Well, what are you going to do, then? he asked himself angrily—hide under a rock the rest of your life so the rain can't find you?

The answer inside him was quiet, but very firm.

No.

The Emperor's Haloga guardsmen were used to the tribune asking for an audience with their master. They saluted with clenched fists over their hearts; one ducked into the imperial tent to find out how long a wait Scaurus would have. "Yust a few minutes," he promised as he reemerged.

Actually it was closer to half an hour. Marcus made small talk with the Halogai, swapping stories and comparing scabs. Apprehension tightened his belly like an ill-digested meal.

Glykas the steward stuck his head out and peered round, blinking in the bright sunshine, till he spied the Roman. "He'll see you now," he said. Scaurus walked forward on legs suddenly leaden.

Thorisin looked up from the stack of papers he so despised. With Videssos' enemies bested for the moment, he had to start paying attention to the business of running the Empire again. He shoved the parchments to one side with a grunt of relief, waited for Marcus to bow, and overlooked, as usual, the tribune's omitting the prostration. "What now?" he asked in a neutral voice.

"Perhaps—" Marcus began, and was mortified to have the word come out as a nervous croak. He steadied himself and tried again: "Perhaps it might be better if we talked under the rose." Gavras frowned; the tribune flushed, realizing he had rendered the Latin phrase literally. He explained.

"'Under the rose,' eh? I rather like that," the Emperor said. He dismissed Glykas, then turned back to Scaurus, his expression watchful now. "And so?" he prompted, folding his arms across his chest. Even in the ordinary linen tunic and baggy wool breeches he was wearing, he radiated authority. He'd had three years to grow into the imperial office, and it fit him.

Marcus felt his power, though he was not so intimidated as a Videssian would have been. He took a deep breath, then, as if to beat back his trepidation, and plunged straight ahead. "As we agreed in Videssos, I'd like you to think about me as a husband for your niece—if Alypia wishes it, of course."

The Emperor steepled his fingers, making Scaurus wait. "Did we have such an agreement?" he asked lazily. "As I recall, there were no witnesses."

"You know we did!" the tribune yelped, appalled. Denial was the last tack he had foreseen Gavras taking. "Phos heard you, if no one else."

"You win nothing with me for using the good god's name; I know you for a heathen," Thorisin jeered. But he went on musingly, "To be just, you never tried that trick, either. Don't tell me so stubborn a one as you has actually changed his mind?"

The squabbling among Phos' sects still struck Marcus as insane, and he had no idea how to pick the true creed—if there was one—from the baying pack. But after his experience on the field, he could no longer ignore the Empire's faith. "I may have," he said, as honest a reply as he could find.

"Hrmmp. Most men in your shoes would come see me festooned with enough icons to turn a lance, or singing hymns, if they had the voice for it."

The tribune shrugged.

"Hrmmp," Thorisin repeated. He pulled at his beard. "You don't make it easy, do you?" He gave a short snort of laughter. "I wonder how many times I've said that, eh, Roman?" He grinned as if they were conspirators.

Marcus shrugged again. The Emperor was drifting into that unfathomable sportive mood of his. Marcus realized that any response he made might be wrong. He cast about for arguments to prove to Gavras that he was no danger to him, but stood mute.

Gavras slammed the palms of his hands down, hard. His papers jumped; one rolled-up scroll fell off the desk. His voice came muffled from behind it as he leaned over to pick up the parchment. "Well, all right, go ahead and ask her."

Triggered by the silence breaking, Marcus gabbled, "As a foreigner, I'd be no threat to the throne because the people would never accept—" He was nearly through the sentence before his brain registered what his ears had heard. "Ask her?" he whispered. The Avtokrator had not invited him to sit, but he sank into the nearest chair. It was that or the floor; his knees would not hold him up.

Tossing the scroll back onto the desktop, Thorisin ignored the breach of protocol. "I said so, didn't I? After Zemarkhos, Avshar—Avshar!—and even a peace of sorts with Yezd, I could hardly refuse you. And besides—" He turned serious in an instant. "—if you know anything about me, you'd best know this: I keep my bargains."

"Then the argument was a sham, and you were going to say yes to me all along?"

The sly grin came back to Gavras' face. "What if I was?"

"Why, you miserable bastard!"

"Who's a bastard, you cross-eyed midwife's mistake?" Thorisin roared back. They were both laughing now, Marcus mostly in relief. The Emperor found a jug of wine, shook it to see how much it held—enough to suit him. He uncorked it, gulped, put the stopper back, and tossed it to Scaurus. As the tribune was drinking, he went on. "Admit it, your heart would've stopped if I'd told you aye straight out."

Marcus started to say something, swallowed wrong, and sputtered and choked, spraying wine every which way. Thorisin pounded him on the back. "Thanks," he wheezed.

He stood and clasped the Emperor's hand, which was as hard and callused as his own. "My heart?" he said. "This would be the first time you'd ever shown a counterfeit copper's worth of care for my health if that were true."

"So it would," Gavras said calmly, unashamed at being caught out. "Would it make you feel better if I admitted I was enjoying every second of the charade?"

Marcus took another drink, this time successfully. "Nothing," he said, "could make me feel better than I do now."

The imperial army was breaking camp, shaking itself into marching order for the return to the capital, and Gaius Philippus had not returned. "No need for you to come with us," Arigh told Scaurus. "My lads'll find him, never fear." He rode at the head of a company of Arshaum.

"Me, I'd bet on us," Laon Pakhymer said; he had a band of his own horsemen behind him. "The old hardcase's ghost would haunt us for spite if we didn't do everything we could for him." The Khatrisher would head into dangerous country after Gaius Philippus before letting on that he liked him.

Marcus paid no attention to either of them, but methodically saddled his horse. He mounted, then turned from one man to the other. "Let's go."

They trotted through the battlefield. The stench of the unburied horses and Yezda was beginning to fade; scavengers had reduced many of them to bare bones. Raw mounds of earth topped the mass graves of the fallen imperial soldiers. Broken weapons and bits of harness were starting to get dusty; whatever was worth looting had long since been taken.

Behind the search party, someone let out a yowl. Scaurus turned to see Viridovix galloping after them. "Why did ye no tell me you were for chasing down t'auld man?" he complained to the tribune once he had caught up. Mischief gleamed in his eyes. "Och, what a show—himself in love. Strange as a wolf growing cabbages, I warrant."

"Maybe so, but I'd be careful twitting him over it," Marcus advised.

"That I ken."

Stretches of ground pocked with hoofprints showed where Avshar's camp, and Wulghash's, had lain. Not far past them, a Khatrisher scout whooped and pointed. Marcus peered ahead, but his eyes were not good enough to pick out the rider the scout had spotted before the fellow went to earth, letting his horse run free. The search party hurried ahead, but short of firing the scrubby brush by the side of the road or sending in dogs, no one was going to find the suspicious traveler in a hurry.

But when he heard his name shouted, Gaius Philippus cautiously emerged from cover. Recognizing Scaurus, Viridovix, and then Pakhymer, he lowered his *gladius*.

"What's all this about?" he growled. "Where I come from, they don't send this many out after parricides."

"A vice of yours we hadn't known," Laon Pakhymer said, drawing a glare. It did not bother him, which only annoyed Gaius Philippus more. "And you'll pay for that pony if it's come to any harm," the Khatrisher added; three of his troopers and a couple of Arshaum were chasing the beast down.

Marcus cut through the senior centurion's obscenities to explain why they had gone searching for him. Gaius Philippus relaxed, a little. "It's nice of you, I'm sure, but sooner or later I'd have turned up."

"Not a bad brag," Arigh said, which touched him off all over again. Scaurus did not think he had been boasting. If anyone could travel the westlands alone, it was Gaius Philippus.

After his curses ran down, he reclaimed his horse and headed back with the search party, still grumbling that they had wasted their time. Both to distract him and out of curiosity, Marcus asked, "Did you manage to get all the way up to Aptos?"

"Said I was going to, didn't I?"

"And?"

"Not a whole lot left of the town," Gaius Philippus said, frowning. "The Yezda did go through with Avshar, and wrecked the place. The keep held out, though, and Nerse was able to save a lot of the townsfolk. Some others got away to the hills. If there's a calm spell, they can rebuild."

"Nerse, you say? Ho, now we come down to it," Viridovix exclaimed.

Gaius Philippus tensed; his face went hard and suspicious. Marcus wanted to kick the Celt and waited helplessly for him to come out with some crudity—here as nowhere else, Gaius Philippus was vulnerable.

But Viridovix, who had known loss of his own, was not out to wound. He asked only, "And will you be needing groomsmen, too, like Scaurus here?"

Even that simple, friendly question was almost too much. The senior centurion answered in a low-voiced growl. "No." He turned to Marcus. "Groomsmen, eh? Nice going—you pulled it off. I hope I'll be one of them."

"You'd better be." Gaius Philippus' smile was such an obvious false front that the tribune asked gently, "She turned you down?"

"What?" The veteran looked at him in surprise. "No. I never asked her."

That was too much for Viridovix. "You didna ask her?" he howled, clapping a hand to his forehead. "Are y'unhinged? You went gallivanting on up a couple days' ride, likely near got yoursel' killed a time or two . . ."

He paused, but Gaius Philippus' bleak expression neither confirmed nor denied. "And you stopped in for a mug o' wine and a how-do-ye-do, then took off again? Och, the waste of it, man, the waste! If it were me, now—"

"Shut up," the senior centurion said with such cold anger that the Gaul actually did. "If it were you, you'd've talked her ear off and made her love every minute of it. Well, I haven't your tongue, loose at both ends, and I haven't anything much to offer her, either. She's a landed noble, and what am I? A mercenary who owns a sword and a mail shirt and precious little else." He glanced toward Pakhymer. "I had to hit up Laon here for a horse to make the trip."

Viridovix did not reply in words, merely pointed at Scaurus. Gaius Philippus turned brick red, but said stubbornly, "He's him; I'm me."

"Honh!" Viridovix said. Only the warning in Gaius Philipus' eyes kept him from going further.

The sad thing, Marcus thought, was that the veteran was right; he had grown too set in his ways to know how to change even when he wanted to. "You got there and back all right; that's what counts." He bobbed his head at Arigh. "Let's head back."

"Took you long enough," the Arshaum said. Like Pakhymer, he had waited halfway between boredom and irritation while the Romans and Viridovix talked, for they still favored Latin among themselves.

Everyone rode in silence for some time. They were nearly back to camp when Gaius Philippus said, "You know, Celt, you might have something after all. Maybe one of these days I'll get back to Aptos again and do the talking I should have done this time."

"Sure and you will," Viridovix said consolingly, but Marcus heard the melancholy edge to his voice. Gaius Philippus had no trouble making plans when he was moving directly away from his goal. Carrying them out was something else.

Thorisin Gavras had not known of the search party. Only a rear guard was left at the campsite, a garrison to hold the gap in the hills against Yezda raiders. But the main body of troops had hardly traveled a mile; Scaurus could still see companies of men and horses through the inevitable cloud of dust they kicked up.

"Let's race it!" Pakhymer shouted, spurring his pony ahead. "First one to the baggage train collects a silverpiece from everybody else!" He had given himself a head start, but his lead did not last long; an Arshaum shot past him almost before the wager was out of his mouth.

Galloping along in the middle of the laughing, shouting pack, Marcus knew he was going to lose his money. He did not care. Ahead lay Amorion, and beyond it Videssos the city. He was going home.

XIV

LAST NIGHT'S RAIN STILL DRIPPED FROM OVERHANGING EAVES AND trickled out of drainpipes, but the storm had finally blown through the capital. The day was clear and brisk, more like early spring than autumn.

"About time," Marcus said, eyeing the bright sunshine and crisp-edged shadows with relief. "If we'd had to put things off again, I think I would have screamed."

Taso Vones reached up to pat him on the shoulder. "Now, now," he said. "The people are entitled to their spectacle. A wedding procession isn't nearly as much fun if you have to get wet to watch it."

Nepos the priest shook a finger at the Khatrisher diplomat. "You have a cynical view of the world, friend Taso." He did his best to sound reproachful but his plump face was made for mirth, and he could not help smiling.

"I, cynical? Not at all, sir; merely realistic." Vones drew himself up, the caricature of affronted dignity. "If you want cynicism, look to this one." He pointed Scaurus' way. "Why else would he have chosen you for a groomsman, if not to get at least one Videssian into the party?"

"Oh, go howl, Taso," Marcus said, nettled. "I chose him because he's a friend. Besides, there's Goudeles over there, and Lemmokheir. And Skylitzes would be here, too, if he were up to it." Among other battle wounds, the dour imperial officer had suffered a broken thigh when his horse was killed and crushed him beneath it. He was mending, but could hardly hobble yet, even with two canes.

Still, as it did more often than not, Vones' sly needling held a germ of truth. Almost all the men gathered together in the little antechamber off the Grand Courtroom were not Videssians. Their various versions of finery gave them a curiously mismatched look.

Gaius Philippus was in full military gear, from hobnailed *caligae* to crested helm; his scarlet cape of rank hung from his shoulders. Marcus wished he could remember everything the veteran had called some officious chamberlain who tried to persuade him to don Videssian ceremonial raiment.

Viridovix wore a burnished corselet. Below it, a pair of baggy Videssian trousers made a fair substitute for the tighter breeches his own nation favored. His head was bare, the better to display his ruddy locks, which he had washed with lime-water until they stood up stiff as a lion's mane. "Gi' the lassies summat to look at," he was saying to Gorgidas.

For the occasion, the Greek had chosen his own people's garb, a knee-length chiton of white wool. Scaurus suspected the simple garment had originally been a blanket.

"Better than my skinny shanks, at least," Gorgidas said to Viridovix. He sighed. "You don't have to worry about drafts, either."

"You'd never get away with that thin sheet on the steppe," Arigh said. "Everything would freeze off at the first blizzard, and you'd sing soprano like any other eunuch." The Arshaum chief wore rawhide boots, leather trousers, a shirt of fine soft suede, and a wolfskin jacket. Marcus was gladder to have him in the wedding party than Arigh was to be there. He had hoped to sail for Prista with his men to start back to Shaumkhiil, but the onset of the stormy season had stooped shipping across the Videssian Sea until spring.

Senpat Sviodo was telling Gagik Bagratouni a joke in their own language. The *nakharar* threw back his head and bellowed laughter at the punch line. His wicker helmet, a traditional Vaspurakaner headgear, fell to the floor. He stooped to retrieve it, hardly favoring his injured leg. Senpat, as usual, preferred the three-crowned tasseled cap that looked dumpy on most of his countrymen.

Nepos, of course, was in the blue robe of the Videssian priesthood. Beside him stood Laon Pakhymer. The cavalry commander wore Videssian-style clothes, but not of a sort to gladden a protocol officer's heart. For reasons only he knew, he had chosen to dress like a street ruffian, with tights of a brilliant, bilious green surmounted by a linen shirt with enormous puffed sleeves tied tight at the wrists.

That left only Goudeles, Leimmokheir, and Taso Vones among the groomsmen in formal robes that reached to their ankles. And no one would have mistaken Taso for an imperial, not with his vast, bushy beard. Taron Leimmokheir was shaggy, too, but the admiral's thick gray hair and somber countenance were well-known in the city.

A eunuch steward stuck his head into the room. "Take your places, my lords, if you would be so kind. We are about to begin."

Marcus started to go to the head of the line that was forming and almost fell over. His own ceremonial robes were no lighter than Gaius Philippus' armor, and harder to move in. Gold and silver threads shot all through the maroon samite only added to its weight, as did the pearls and precious stones at the collar, over his breast, and running down along his sleeves. His wide gold belt, ornamented with more rubies, sapphires, amethysts, and delicate enamelwork, weighed more than the sword belt he was used to.

The steward sniffed at his slowness and paused to make sure everyone was in proper position. Turning his back, he said, "This way. Just as we rehearsed it," he added reassuringly.

No Videssian courtier in his right mind left anything to chance at an imperial function; the tribune had the plan of the procession down almost as thoroughly as Roman infantry drill. The thick, pleated silk of his robe rustled as he followed the eunuch.

He was glad of the weight of the material as soon as he stepped outside. The breeze had a raw edge to it. Behind him he heard teeth chattering, Arigh's chuckle, and Gorgidas' hissed retort: "Go ahead, amuse yourself. I hope you get heatstroke in the High Temple." Arigh laughed louder.

"Och, I ken this courtyard," Viridovix said. "We fought here to put Gavras on the throne and cast what-was-his-name, the young Sphrantzes, off it."

And rescued Alypia from Ortaias' uncle Vardanes, Marcus remembered, and drove Avshar out of the city. Had it really been more than two years ago? It seemed yesterday.

The bronze doors of the Grand Courtroom, which were covered with a profusion of magnificent reliefs, opened noiselessly. They had taken damage when the legionaries forced them that day, but the skilled Videssian artisans' repairs were all but unnoticeable.

First through the doors was another eunuch to direct traffic. Behind him came a dozen parasol bearers, markers of the presence of the Emperor. Thorisin Gavras wore a robe even more gorgeous than Scaurus'; only the toes of his red boots peeped from under its bejeweled hem. The imperial crown, a low dome encrusted with still more precious stones, gleamed golden on his head. Only the sword at the Emperor's belt detracted from his splendor; it was the much-battered saber he always carried.

A platoon of Videssian nobles followed Gavras, bureaucrats and soldiers together for once. Marcus spotted Provhos Mourtzouphlos, who looked as though he had an extraordinarily bad taste in his mouth. His robe was of a green that managed to outdo Pakhymer's tights.

The eye kept coming back to it, in disbelief and horrid fascination. Marcus heard Gaius Philippus mutter, "Now I know what color a hangover is." He wondered if Mourtzouphlos had chosen the dreadful thing as a silent protest against the wedding. If he was reduced to such petty gestures, his enmity was safe to ignore.

Under the watchful gaze of its chamberlain, the imperial party took its place some yards ahead of Scaurus and his comrades. He promptly forgot about it, for still another steward was leading Alypia Gavra and her attendant ladies into place between the two groups.

Her gown was of soft white silk, with silver threads running through it and snowy lace at the cuffs; it seemed spun from moonlight. A silver circlet confined her sleek brown hair.

She smiled and touched her throat as she walked by Marcus. The necklace she wore, of gold, emeralds, and mother-of-pearl, was not of a piece with the rest of her costume, but neither of them would have exchanged it for one that was.

He smiled back, wishing he could say something to her. Since returning to the city, he had only seen her once or twice, under the most formal circumstances. It had been easier when they were surreptitious lovers than properly affianced. But Thorisin had warned, "No more scandal," and they thought it wiser to obey. There was not much waiting left.

"Straighten your collar, will you, Pikridios!" shrilled Goudeles' wife, Tribonia. She was a tall, angular, sallow woman whose deep blue dress suited neither her figure nor her complexion. As the bureaucrat fumbled to fix the imaginary flaw, she complained to anyone who would listen, "Do you see how he takes no pains with himself? The most lazy, slovenly man . . ." The tribune, who knew Goudeles to be a fastidious dandy, wondered whether he had married her for money or position. It could hardly have been love.

Irrepressible, Nevrat Sviodo made a comic shrug behind Tribonia's back, then grinned triumphantly at Marcus. He nodded back, very glad his mistaken advances the year before had not cost him a friend, or rather, two.

Nevrat was the only non-Videssian in Alypia's party. Senpat said, "Some of the highborn ladies were scandalized when the princess chose her."

"I notice no one has withdrawn," Scaurus said.

An honor guard of Halogai and Romans fell in at the procession's head; another company took its place to the rear. Palace servitors formed a line on either side. Seeing everything ready at last, Thorisin's steward blew a sharp note on a pitch pipe. He strutted forward to set the pace, as if the day had been planned to celebrate him alone.

The wide pathways through the gardens of the palace compound had few spectators along them: a gardener, a cook, a mason and his wife and children, a squad of soldiers. As soon as the procession reached the forum of Palamas, all that changed. If twin sets of streamers had not kept the chosen path open, there would have been no pushing through the sea of humanity jamming the square.

Thorisin's iron-lunged herald cried out, "Rejoice in the wedding of the Princess Alypia Gavra and the Yposevastos Scaurus! Rejoice! Rejoice!" The herald's accent made the tribune's name come out as "Skavros," which did not sound too very alien to the ears of the city populace. The imposing title the Emperor had conferred on him—its significance, more or less, was "second minister," which could mean anything or nothing—also made him less obviously foreign.

One of the servants pressed a small but heavy sack into his hands. As he had been instructed, he tossed goldpieces into the crowd, now right, now left. Up ahead, the Emperor was doing the same. So were the servitors, but their sacks were filled with silver.

The sidewalks of Middle Street were also packed tight with cheering onlookers. Marcus did not flatter himself that the hurrahs were for him. The city folk, fickle and restless, applauded any spectacle, and this one was doubly delightful because of the prospect of largesse.

"Rejoice! Rejoice!" At slow march, the procession passed the three-story red granite government office building. Marcus looked at it fondly, large and ugly though it was. Had he not happened to meet Alypia coming out of it last Midwinter's Day, he would not be here now.

"Rejoice!" The herald turned north about a quarter mile past the government offices. Once off Middle Street, the crowds were thinner. With every step, Phos' High Temple dominated more of the skyline; soon it *was* the skyline. The gilded globes topping its four spires shone bright as the sun they symbolized.

The walled courtyard around the High Temple was as crowded as the plaza of Palamas had been. The palace servitors threw out great handfuls of money; tradition required them to empty their sacks. The canny Videssians knew that perfectly well and thronged to where the pickings were best.

The honor guard deployed at the foot of the broad stairway leading up to the High Temple. Already waiting on the stairs were all the surviving Romans hale enough to stand. Their arms shot up in salute as Marcus approached.

The nobles and officials in Thorisin's party peeled away from the Avtokrator to take their places on the steps, forming an aisleway through which he, the bride, the groom, and their attendants could pass. "Step smartly now!" urged the chamberlain in charge of Scaurus and his companions. The tribune hurried forward. Alypia, her ladies, and Thorisin were waiting for him and the groomsmen to catch up. The Emperor between them, he and Alypia started up the stairs. Behind them, pair by pair, came the groomsmen with the princess' attendants on their arms.

At the top of the stairs, flanked by lesser priests on either side, stood the new patriarch of Videssos, his hands raised in benediction. Scaurus felt a small shock every time he saw the tall, middle-aged man wearing the robe of cloth-of-gold and blue. "It seems wrong, not having Balsamon up there," he said.

Alypia nodded. "He was as much a part of the city as the Silver Gate."

"This Sebeos will make a sound patriarch," Thorisin said, a trifle irritably; the choice of Balsamon's successor had been in essence his. As custom demanded, he had submitted three names to a synod of high-ranking clerics, who selected the former prelate of Kypas, a port city in the westlands.

"Of course he's able," Alypia said at once. "He'll have trouble, though, making himself as loved as Balsamon—he was like a favorite uncle for all Videssos. And—" She stopped abruptly. To say what Balsamon had meant to her would only remind Thorisin of complications now past. She had too much sense for that.

They spoke in low voices, for they were approaching the High Temple. As they drew near, Marcus saw that Sebeos looked decidedly anxious himself. So he might, the tribune thought—hardly in place a month, he was conducting his first great ceremony under the Emperor's eye. Not all patriarchs reigned as long as Balsamon.

When Sebeos stayed frozen a few seconds longer than he should, one of his attendant priests leaned over to whisper in his ear. "Saborios knows his job," Scaurus murmured to Thorisin, who smiled. His clerical watchdog slid smoothly back into place.

Cued, Sebeos stepped forward to meet the wedding party, saying, "May the good god send his blessings down on this union, as his sun gives the whole world light and warmth." He had a mellow baritone, far more impressive than Balsamon's scratchy tenor—and far less interesting.

With Alypia, and Thorisin, Marcus followed the patriarch in sketching Phos' sun-sign. The ritual gesture still felt unnatural, but he performed it perfectly; he had practiced.

Sebeos bowed, turned, and led the way into the High Temple. The outside of the great building had a heavy impressiveness to it, with its walls of unadorned stucco, small windows, and massive buttresses to support the weight of the central dome and the smaller half-domes around it. For the interior Scaurus had his memories, as well as more recent ones of the shrine at Garsavra, which aped its greater model. He discovered how little they were worth the moment he set foot inside.

He could have overlooked the luxury of the seats that ranged out from the altar under the dome in each of the cardinal directions, their polished oak and sandalwood and ebony and glistening mother-of-pearl, the more easily because they were filled by notables not important enough to join the wedding party. The colonnades faced with moss agate were lovely, but the Grand Courtroom had their match in multicolored marble.

The interior walls reproduced the heavens, east and west mimicking sunrise and sunset with sheets of bloodstone, rose quartz, and rhodochrosite rising to meet the white marble and turquoise that covered the northern and southern walls down to their bases. They had their own splendor, but they also served to lead the eye up to the central dome; and before that all comparison failed.

The soft beams of light coming through the arched windows that pierced its base seemed to disembody it, to leave it floating above the High Temple. They reflected from gold and silver foil like shining milk and butter.

They also played off the golden tesserae in the dome mosaic itself; the sparkle shifted at every step Scaurus took. And that shifting field of gold was only the surround of the great image of Phos that looked down from on high on his worshipers, his long, bearded face stern in judgment. Beneath that awesome countenance, with its omniscient eyes that seemed to bore into his soul, the tribune could not help feeling the power of the Videssian faith and could only hope to be recorded as acceptable in the sealed book Phos bore in his left hand. The god depicted in the dome would give him justice, but no mercy.

He must have missed a step without noticing, for Alypia whispered, "It affects everyone so." That, he saw, was true. Even the imperials who worshipped in the High Temple daily kept glancing up at the dome, as if to reassure themselves that the Phos there was not singling them out for their sins.

A choir in a vestibule behind the northern seats burst into song, hymning Phos' praises in the archaic liturgical language Marcus still could only half follow. He thought how different Videssian marriage customs were from those of Rome. In Rome, while ceremonies, of course, usually accompanied a marriage, what made it valid was the intent of its partners to be married; the ceremonies themselves were not necessary. To the Videssians, the religious rites *were* the marriage.

As Scaurus, Alypia, and Thorisin passed the inmost row of seats, the

Empress Alania stood and joined her husband. Because of her pregnancy, she had not walked in the wedding procession, but come ahead in a sedan chair. The Avtokrator would not risk her health, though in her flowing formal robes the child she was carrying did not show. She had olive skin and jet-black hair like Komitta Rhangavve's, but her face was round and kindly; her eyes, her best feature, were dark, calm pools. Thorisin, Marcus thought, had chosen wisely.

Then the tribune had no time for such trivial ruminations, for the wedding party had reached the holy table in front of the ivory patriarchal throne. The Emperor and Empress stepped back a pace. As he had been drilled, Marcus took Alypia's right hand in his left and laid them on the altartop; the polished silver was cool beneath his fingertips. Smiling, Alypia squeezed his hand. He gently returned the pressure.

From the other side of the holy table, Sebeos said softly, "Look at me." Marcus saw the patriarch take a deep breath. Until that moment he had held his own nerves under tight control, but suddenly he heard everything through the pounding of his heart.

The choir fell silent. Sebeos intoned the creed with which the Videssians began every religious service: "We bless thee, Phos, Lord with the right and good mind, by thy grace our protector, watchful beforehand that the great test of life may be decided in our favor."

Marcus and Alypia echoed the prayer together. He did not stumble. Having decided at last to acknowledge Phos' faith, he was determined to do so properly.

The High Temple filled with murmurs as the faithful also repeated the creed. A couple of high Namdalener officers ended it with their own nation's addition: "On this we stake our very souls." Their neighbors frowned at the heresy.

Sebeos also frowned, but carried on after a glance at the Emperor told him Thorisin did not want to make an issue of it. Again the prayers were in the old-fashioned liturgical tongue, as were Scaurus' memorized responses. He knew in a general way that he was asking Phos' blessing for himself, for his wife to be, and for the family they were founding.

He gave all the correct replies, though sometimes so quietly that only those closest to him could hear. Alypia squeezed his fingers again, encouraging him. Her own responses rang out firmly. Usually she was more outgoing in private than in large gatherings, but she was determined to make this day an exception.

Finishing the prayers, Sebeos returned to contemporary Videssian. He launched into a homily on the virtues that went into a successful marriage which was so perfectly conventional that Marcus found himself anticipating what the patriarch would say three sentences before it came. Respect, trust, affection, forbearance—everything was in its place, correct, orderly, and unmemorable.

In Latin, Viridovix whispered loudly, "Och, there's a man could make sex dull."

Marcus had all he could do not to explode. He wished for Balsamon, who would have taken the same theme and turned it into something worth hearing.

Eventually, Sebeos noticed the Emperor tapping his foot on the marble floor. He finished in haste: "These virtues, if diligently adhered to, are sure to guarantee domestic felicity."

Then, his manner changing, he asked Alypia and Scaurus, "Are the two of you prepared to cleave to these virtues together, and to each other, so long as you both may live?"

Marcus made his voice carry: "Yes."

This time Alypia's answer came soft: "Oh, yes."

As they spoke the binding words, Thorisin stepped forward to place a wreath of myrtle and roses on the tribune's head, while Alania did the same for Alypia.

"Behold them decked in the crowns of marriage!" Sebeos cried. "It is accomplished!"

While the spectators burst into applause, Scaurus slipped a ring onto the index finger of Alypia's left hand. That again followed the Videssian way; the Romans preferred the third finger of the same hand, believing a nerve connected it directly to the heart. The ring, however, was of his own choosing—gold, with an emerald set in a circle of mother-of-pearl. Alypia had not seen it before. She threw her arms around his neck.

"Kiss her, tha twit!" Viridovix whooped.

That had not been part of the ceremony as rehearsed; the tribune glanced at Thorisin to see if it fell within the bounds of custom. The

Emperor was grinning. Marcus took that for permission. The cheers got louder. There were bawdy shouts of advice, of the same sort he had heard—and called—at weddings back in Mediolanum. Human nature did not change, and a good thing, too, he thought.

He felt Alypia tense slightly; some of the shouts must have touched memories she would sooner have left buried. Shaking her head in annoyance, she made a brave face of it. "This is us, as it should be," she said when he tried to comfort her. "It's all right now."

The crowds had thinned when the wedding party emerged from the High Temple for the return procession to the feast laid out in the Hall of the Nineteen Couches. The palace servitors bore freshly filled bags, bigger than the ones from which they had thrown coins on the way to the High Temple, but the city folk were much less interested in these; they held only nuts and figs, symbols of fertility.

Full circle, Marcus thought as he walked through the smoothly polished bronze doors of the Hall of the Nineteen Couches. He had met Alypia here the Romans' first evening in Videssos the city, along with so many others. He was lucky Avshar had not killed him that very night.

As tradition decreed, he and Alypia shared a single cup of wine; a serving maid hovered near them with a silver ewer to make sure it never emptied. Others were quite able to take care of such matters on their own—Gawtruz, the fat, bald ambassador from Thatagush, had somehow managed to filch an ewer for himself. "Haw! Congratulations I you give!" he shouted in broken Videssian. He found it useful to play the drunken barbarian, but in fact he was no one's fool and could use the imperial tongue without accent and with great polish when he chose.

A fried prawn in one hand, Thorisin Gavras used the other to pound on a tabletop until he had everyone's attention. He pointed to another table, in a corner close to the kitchen doors, which was piled high with gifts. "My turn to add to those," he said.

There was a polite spatter of applause and a few raucous cheers from celebrants already tipsy. Gavras waited for quiet to return. "I've already honored the groom with the rank of yposevastos, but you can't eat rank, though I sometimes think that in the city we breathe it." Inevitably, a joke from the Emperor won laughter.

Thorisin went on, "To live on, I grant him the estates in the westlands forfeited to the crown by the traitor and rebel Baanes Onomagoulos and grant him leave to settle on those estates the men of his command, so he and they may have the means to defend Videssos in the future as they have in the past."

In the near future, Marcus thought; Onomagoulos' lands were near Garsavra, on the edge of Yezda-infested territory. A rich gift but a dangerous one—Thorisin's style through and through. And the Emperor had also granted him what every Roman general sought, land for his troops.

Filled with pride, he bowed nearly double. He whispered to Alypia, "You put him up to that last part." Having studied Videssos' past, she had seen that the Empire's troubles began when it weakened the population of farmer-soldiers settled on the countryside.

She shook her head. "My uncle makes his own decisions, always." Her eyes sparkled. "I think this was a very good one."

So, apparently, did most of the Videssians, who crowded up to Scaurus to congratulate him all over again—and perhaps to reappraise one grown suddenly powerful among them. If they thought less of him because he was not of their blood, they were careful not to show it.

But Provhos Mourtzouphlos was bold enough to shout, "This accursed foreigner doesn't deserve the honors you're giving him!"

Thorisin's voice grew cold. "When your services match his, Provhos, you may question me. Until then, hold your tongue." The hotheaded young noble, true to his own principles, stamped out of the Hall.

That was the only incident marring the day's festivities, though Marcus had an anxious moment when Thorisin steered him over to the gifts table and said, "I suppose you can explain this."

"This" was an exquisite ivory statuette of a standing warrior, perhaps a foot tall, carved in the ebullient, rococo style of Makuran. The sword the warrior brandished was of gold; his eyes were twin sapphires. "It's from Wulghash," the tribune said lamely.

"I know that. First damned wedding present ever delivered behind shield of truce, I'd wager." The Emperor seemed more amused than anything else; Scaurus relaxed.

"Here's fine silk," Gavras said, running an appreciative hand along a bolt of the smooth lustrous fabric, which was dyed a deep purple-red. "A rich gift. May I ask who it came from?"

"Tahmasp," Marcus said.

Thorisin raised an eyebrow at the exotic name, then placed it. "Oh, that caravaneer you traveled with. How did he find out you were getting harnessed?"

"No idea," the tribune said, but nothing Tahmasp did could surprise him anymore. The surprise was the throwing knife next to the silk. That was from Kamytzes, and Marcus had thought the caravan guard captain utterly without sentiment.

After the Emperor let him go, Marcus returned to Alypia's side. A clavier on a little raised platform tinkled away, accompanied by flutes and a couple of men sawing away at viols of different sizes. The music was soft and innocuous; the tribune, who cared little for such things, hardly noticed it.

It mightily annoyed Senpat Sviodo, though. He slipped a servant a few coppers and gave him the password to the legionary barracks so the sentries would not take him for a thief. The man trotted away, coming back shortly with the Vaspurakaner's pandoura. "Ha! Well done," Senpat said, and tipped him again.

He sprang onto the platform. Startled, the musicians came to a ragged halt. "Enough of this pap!" Senpat cried. "My lords and ladies, here's a tune to suit a celebration!" His fingers struck a ringing chord. Heads turned, as if drawn by a lodestone. He sang in a clear, strong tenor, stamping out the rhythm with a booted foot.

Not many could follow the song, which was in the Vaspurakaner tongue, but no one could stand still with that wild music ringing through the Hall. Before long, the feasters were spinning in several concentric rings, one going one way, the next the other. They raised their hands to clap out the beat with Senpat.

Alypia's foot was tapping. "Come on," she said, touching Marcus' sleeve. He hung back, having no taste or skill for dancing. But he yielded to her disappointed look and let himself be steered into the outer ring.

"You don't get away that easy!" Gaius Philippus said. The treacherous senior centurion was in the next ring in; when he whirled past the tribune, he reached out and tugged him and Alypia toward the center.

Other dancers, laughing and clapping, pulled them further in, at last shoving them into the open space in the center of the rings, where Viridovix had been dancing alone. "Sure and it's yours," the Gaul said, easing back into the inner ring.

Scaurus felt like a man condemned to speak after Balsamon. Viridovix' Celtic dance, performed with gusto, had drawn every man's—and woman's—eye. It was nothing like the dances of the Empire, for he held his upper body motionless and kept his hands always on his hips. But his steps and leaps were at the same time so intricate and so athletic that they vividly displayed his skill.

The tribune kicked and capered, sometimes with the tune but more often not. Even with Alypia slim and graceful beside him, he knew he was cutting a sorry figure. But he soon realized it did not matter. As the bridegroom, he was supposed to be in the center. Past that, no one cared.

Senpat Sviodo finished with a virtuoso flourish, shouted "Hai!" and leaped off the platform to a storm of applause, his pandoura high over his head. Panting a little, Marcus made his escape.

Senpat's talent and his striking good looks drew a flock of admiring ladies to him. He flirted outrageously with all his new conquests and went no further with any; Scaurus saw him tip his wife a wink. Nevrat stood back easily, watching him enjoy himself.

Viridovix, Marcus thought, should also be getting some attention after his exhibition. The Gaul, though, was nowhere to be seen.

He came back through a side door a few minutes later, followed not quite discreetly enough by a noblewoman adjusting her gown. The tribune frowned; come to think of it, this was not the first time Viridovix had disappeared.

The Gaul must have caught Scaurus' expression from across the Hall. He weaved toward him. "Sure and you're right," he said in Latin as he drew near. "I'm a pig, no mistake." Only then did Marcus notice how drunk he was.

Viridovix' eyes filled with tears. "Here my sweet Seirem is dead, and me rutting like a stoat wi' Evdoxia and—och, the shame of it, I never found out t'other one's name!"

"Easy, there." Marcus set his hand on the Gaul's shoulder.

"Aye, tha can speak so, having a fine lass to wife and all. Me, I ken how lucky y'are. This hole-and-corner friking is a cruel mock, but what other way is there o' finding again what I lost?"

"What troubles him?" Alypia asked. She had not been able to follow the conversation, but the Celt's woe was plain without words. At Viridovix' nod, Scaurus quickly explained.

She considered the problem seriously, as if it were some historical dilemma. Finally she said, "The trouble, I think, is the confusion between what's called lovemaking and actual love. There's no faster road to a woman's heart than the one that starts between her legs, but many surer ones."

"Summat o' wisdom in that," Viridovix said after owlish pondering. He turned to Marcus, drunkenly serious. "A treasure she is. Do be caring for her."

"Shall I put him to bed, Scaurus?" Gorgidas appeared at the tribune's elbow, as usual where he was needed.

"Aye, I'll go with ye." Viridovix spoke for himself, then bowed to Alypia with great dignity. "My lady, I'll take myself off the now, and bad cess to me for being such an oaf as to put a gloom on your wedding day."

"Nonsense," she said crisply. "Lightening sorrows should always be in season, and too seldom is. I remember." Her voice went soft, her eyes far away. Marcus slipped an arm around her.

She shivered and came back to herself. "Don't fret over me. I'm fine, truly." She spoke quietly, but with something of the same briskness she had used toward Viridovix. When Scaurus still hesitated, she went on, "If you must have it, one proof we're right for each other is that you noticed I was low. And here's another." She kissed him, which brought a huzza from the feasters. "There. Do you believe me now?"

The best answer he could find was kissing her back. It seemed to be the right one.

Some wedding guests were still singing raucously in the darkness outside the secluded palace building the imperial family used as its own. No one followed Marcus and Alypia in, though, but Thorisin and Alania, and they went off to their own rooms at once.

The tribune swung open the door to the suite he and Alypia would live in until they left the city to take up the estate the Emperor had granted him. Servants had already come and gone, only minutes before;

a sweating silver wine jar rested in a basin of crushed ice, with the customary one cup beside it. The bedcovers, silken sheets and soft furs, were turned down. A single lamp burned on the table by the bed.

Alypia suddenly let out a squeak. "What are you doing? Put me down!"

Marcus did, inside the chamber. Grinning, he said, "I've followed Videssian ways all through this wedding. No complaints—it's only fitting. But that was one of mine. A bride should be carried across the threshold."

"Oh. Well, all right. You might have warned me."

"Sorry." He looked and sounded so contrite that Alypia burst out laughing.

Relieved, Marcus shut and barred the door. He started to laugh, too. "What is it, husband?" Alypia asked. She used the word with the proud possessiveness new brides have. "Or should I say, proved husband?" she asked mischievously, pantomiming him lifting her.

"Not proved by that," he answered. "I was just thinking, though, that that was the first time I've locked a door behind us without worrying that someone was going to kick it down."

"For which Phos be praised," Alypia said at once. Her laugh was a little nervous. "It's also, you will note, a stouter door."

"So it is, though I hadn't planned to talk about it all night."

"Nor I." She glanced at the ewer of wine. "Do you want much more of that? It's a kindly notion, but I think another cup would only put me to sleep."

"Can't have that," Marcus agreed gravely. "I drank enough at the feast, too, I think."

He took off the fragrant wedding-wreath and started to toss it to one side. "Don't do that!" Alypia exclaimed. "They go on the headposts of the bed, for luck." She took his marriage-crown from him and hung it on the nearer post, then removed hers and climbed onto the bed to set it on the other.

The tribune stepped forward and joined her. She hugged him fiercely, whispering, "Oh, Marcus, we came through everything! I love you."

He had time to say, "And I you," before their lips met.

The thick ceremonial robes hampered their embrace nearly as much as armor would have, but the fastenings were easier for Scaurus to undo. "Hurry," Alypia said as he began to pay attention to his own robe. "It's chilly here alone."

But she frowned when he shrugged the robe back from his shoulders. "That one is new," she said, running her finger down the long scar on his chest.

"It's the one I took in Mashiz. It would be worse, but Gorgidas healed it."

"Yes, I remember your saying so. It's in front, like any honorable wound. But it surprised me, and I want to get used to you again."

"There'll be years for that now." He gathered her in.

She held him tightly. "Yes. Oh, yes."

He blew out the lamp.

Gaius Philippus splashed through a puddle in the forum of Palamas. "Getting on toward spring. These last three storms only dropped rain, no new snow for a while now."

Marcus nodded. He bought a little fried squid, ate it, and licked his fingers clean. "I wish I could talk you into going to the westlands."

"How many times have we been through that?" the senior centurion said patiently. "You want to go live on a farm, fine, go' ahead. Me, I was raised on one—and I got out just as fast as I could."

"It wouldn't be like that," Scaurus protested. "You'd have the land to do what you want with, not some tiny plot you couldn't help starving on."

"So I'd bore myself to death instead. Is that better? No, I'm happy with the slot Gavras offered me. At least as infantry drillmaster I'll know what I'm doing. Don't worry over me; I won't forget my Latin. A good solid Roman cadre'll be staying in the city with me." That was true; while most of the legionaries eagerly accepted farms on the estate the Emperor had granted Marcus, a couple of dozen preferred more active duty. Thorisin was glad to keep them on so they could train Videssian foot soldiers up to their standard.

"The job counts for something," Gaius Philippus insisted. "The lot of you will lose your edge out there, too busy with the crops and the beasts and the brats to bother with drill. You won't hand it down to your sons, and it'll be lost for good unless the imperials remember—and with me teaching, they will. I'm no scribbler like Gorgidas; what better monument can I leave behind?"

"Anyone who lives through your exercises remembers them forever," Marcus assured him. He grunted, mostly in pleasure. The tribune went on, "All right, you've argued me down again. But we won't stop being soldiers ourselves, either, not with the Yezda for neighbors. Still, the main thing is that I'm selfish. I'll miss having you at my right hand—and plain miss you, come to that."

"Well, by the gods"—the veteran had no truck with Phos—"it's not as if we'll never see each other again. Come trouble, first thing Thorisin'll do is call up the Romans. And if the Yezda give *you* trouble, we'll come down from the capital to hold the line or push Yavlak further up the plateau.

"Besides, not wanting to farm doesn't mean I won't visit. I'll be by every so often, guzzling your wine and pinching your wenches for as long as you can stand me. And who knows? One of these days I may get over to Aptos again, and you'd be the perfect jumping-off point for that."

"Of course." Over the winter, Gaius Philippus had talked repeatedly of courting Nerse Phorkaina. Scaurus did not believe he would ever get around to it on his own. He frowned a little. From the friendly reception she had given the veteran the previous fall, he thought she might be interested. Maybe a message telling her to make a discreet first move might help. He filed the idea away, to act on when he found the time.

Here and there green leaf buds were appearing on the trees in the palace compound. The first hopeful new grass had begun to poke through the dead, muddy, yellow-brown growth of the previous year.

Gaius Philippus left to argue with an armorer over the proper balance of a dagger. Marcus went on to the imperial family's private residence. The cherry trees surrounding the brick building were still bare-branched; soon they would be full of fragrant pink blossoms.

Rather absently, Scaurus returned the salute of the guardsmen at the door. His eyes were on the crates and boxes and bundles piled outside: furnishings and household goods ready to ship to his new home when the dirt roads in the westlands dried enough. Years of army life had got him used to making do with very little; the thought of owning so much was daunting.

The hallway smelled faintly of sour milk. The midwives had ushered Pharos Gavras into the world a month early, but he was strong and healthy, even if he did look like a bald, pink, wizened monkey. Marcus cringed, remembering the hangover he'd had after Thorisin celebrated the birth of his heir.

Alypia's voice was raised in exasperation. "What exactly do you mean by that, then?" she demanded.

"Not what you're reading into it, that's certain!" The reply was equally bad-tempered.

The tribune looked in at the open study door. Like the rest of the suite, the room was sparsely furnished; bare, in fact, but for a couch and a writing table in front of it. The rest had already been packed.

"Softly, softly. The two of you will have the eunuchs running for cover, or more likely the sentries running this way to pry you from each other's throats."

Alypia and Gorgidas looked simultaneously shamefaced and defiant. The secretary sitting between them looked harassed. Scaurus saw he had written only a few lines, and scratched out several of those. Gorgidas said, "Now I understand the myth of Sisyphos. The rock he had to push up the hill was a translation, and I'm surprised it didn't crush him when it fell back."

Then the Greek had to explain Sisyphos to Alypia, who scribbled a note that might appear one day in her own history. "Though who can tell when that will be done?" she said to Marcus. "Another reason for coming back to Videssos often—how am I to write without the documents to check, the people to ask questions of?"

Before he could answer, she had turned back to Gorgidas. Scaurus was used to that; the long labor of turning the Greek's work into something a Videssian audience might want to read had left them thick as thieves. Alypia sighed. "It's a fine line we walk. If we're too literal, what you've written makes no sense in my language, but when we stray too far the other way, we lose the essence of what you've said. *Eis kórakas,*" she added: "To the crows with it," a Greek curse that made both the tribune and Gorgidas laugh in surprise.

The physician's irritability collapsed. "What business do I have grumbling? When I started writing, I thought I would be the only one ever to read this mess, save maybe Marcus. Who else could? To have it published—"

"It deserves to be," Alypia said firmly. "First as an eyewitness account, and second because it's history as history should be done—you see past events to the causes behind them."

"I try," Gorgidas said. "The part we're fighting through now, you understand, I didn't see for myself; I have it from Viridovix. Here, Scaurus, be useful." He thrust a parchment at the Roman. "How would *you* render this bit into Videssian?"

"Me?" Marcus said, alarmed; most of his efforts in that direction had not been well received. "Which part?" Gorgidas showed him the disputed passage. Hoping he remembered what a couple of Greek verbs meant, he said, "How about, 'Some clans backed Varatesh because they hated Targitaus, more because they feared Avshar'?"

"That's not bad," Gorgidas said. "It keeps the contrast I was drawing." Alypia pursed her lips judiciously and nodded.

"Let me have it again, please," the secretary said, and wrote it down.

Gorgidas and Alypia combined to tear Scaurus' next suggestion to pieces.

A little later, after more wrangling, Gorgidas said, "Enough for now. Maybe it'll go better, looked at fresh." His nod to Alypia was close to a seated bow. He told her, "If you like, I'd count it a privilege to search out the manuscripts you need and send them on to you at your new home. That can't take the place of your own inquiries, of course, but it might help some."

"A bargain," she said with the same quick decisiveness Thorisin might have shown. A warm smile and a word of thanks softened the resemblance.

The Greek rose to take his leave. "You'll be busy, doing your research, and some for Alypia, and healing, too," Marcus remarked as he walked to the entranceway with him.

"Physicians are supposed to be busy. As for running down the odd book for your wife, that's the least I can do, wouldn't you say? Not only for the favor she's shown me, but also because I've learned a great deal from her."

Scaurus thought the Greek could give no greater praise, but Gorgidas amazed him by murmuring, "Pity she has no sister." He barked laughter at the tribune's expression. "Not everything that happened on the steppe got written down. I can manage, after a fashion, and I'd like a son one day." As if on cue, a thin cry floated down the hall from the nursery.

One of the sentries outside must have told a dirty story. Scaurus heard chuckles, and then Viridovix saying, "Get on wi' your bragging, now. You're after reminding me o' the flea that humped the she-wolf and told her, 'Sure and I hope I've not hurt you, my dear.' "

More laughter; beside the tribune, Gorgidas let out a strangled snort. The guardsman said, "Did you come here to insult me, or do you have some honest reason?"

"Och, I like that," the Gaul exclaimed, as if cut to the quick. "But aye, I'm for Scaurus, if he's to home."

"I'm here." Marcus stepped out of the hallway into the watery sunshine.

"It's himself himself," Viridovix cried. He waved at the piled boxes and chests. "Sure and you must've emptied out all the palaces, and the High Temple, too. Me, I could carry what I'll bring with me on my back."

"Remember, though, mules carry an uncommon lot," Gorgidas said. "And if Thorisin hadn't set you up on your own estate, half the nobles in town would have clubbed together to buy you one and get you away from their wives."

The Gaul shrugged. "T'other half married ugly lasses, puir spalpeens." Gorgidas threw his hands in the air, defeated. The guards laughed so hard they had to hold each other up. Viridovix had not been able to take Alypia's advice to heart; his philanderings were notorious all over the city. But he was so good-natured through them that he had somehow kept from making any mortal enemies, male or female.

Marcus said, "Did you come here to insult me, or do you have some honest reason?"

"What an unco wicked man y'are, t'stand in there and spy on me.

But you're right, I do." To the sentries' disappointment, he dropped into Latin. "Now we're for it and about to be going and all, I'd fain thank you for talking the Gavras into granting me land for my own self, and not just a chunk I'd have from you."

"Oh, that," Marcus said in the same tongue. "Forget it; the other way embarrassed me as much as it did you. Thorisin just sees all of us as one band and, since he's mostly dealt with me, he didn't think to do otherwise this time. Not," he added, "that you ever took orders from me."

"Forbye, you never tried to give 'em, and I'll thank you for that, too." Viridovix drew himself up with lonely pride. "Still and all, I'm not sorry to be on my own. I wouldna have Gaius Philippus say he was right all along, and the only Celt here a Roman gillie."

"Are you still fighting that idiot war?" Gorgidas said in disgust. "Haven't you found enough new ways here to satisfy your barbarian craving for gore?"

"Let him be," Marcus said. "We all remember, as best we can. It helps us hang together."

"Aye," Viridovix said. "You Romans now, you're the lucky ones, wi' sic a mort o' ye here. Belike even your grandsons'll recall a word or two o' Latin. And the Greek has his histories for keepsake. So I'll remember, too, and a pox on anyone for saying I shouldna bother." He looked pointedly at Gorgidas.

"Oh, very well," the physician said with bad grace. He fumed for a few seconds, then smiled lopsidedly. "I'm always annoyed when you outargue me. Those droopy red whiskers make me forget the brain behind them." Shaking his head, he strode off.

"Here, wait!" Viridovix shouted. "We'll hash it out further over a stoup o' the grape." He trotted after Gorgidas.

The guardsmen might not have been able to follow the conversation, but they recognized the tone. "Remind me of my dog and cat, they do," one said to Scaurus.

"You have it," the tribune said.

He went back into the imperial residence, walking past the portrait of the ancient Emperor Laskaris, whose harsh peasant face gave him more the look of a veteran underofficer than a ruler. The bloodstain marring the lower part of the picture was one of the few reminders of the desperate fighting against Onomagoulos' assassins two years before. Most of the damage had been made good, but Laskaris' image was impossible to clean and too precious to throw away.

The secretary came out of Scaurus' doorway. Alypia's voice pursued him: "I'd like a fair copy of that tomorrow, Artanas, if you can have it by then."

Artanas' shoulders heaved in a silent sigh. "I'll do my best, your Highness." He sighed again, bowed to the tribune, and hurried off, tucking his case of pens into his tunic.

"I shouldn't drive him so hard," Alypia said when Marcus joined her inside. "But I want to do as much as I can before we leave for the westlands." She gave a rueful laugh. "Not that I can accomplish much, with three quarters of my things stowed away where I can't get at them."

The tribune had learned she complained only over minor upsets; she did not let frets get in the way of dealing with real problems. Knowing that, he should have changed the subject. Because he was still adjusting to her, though, he said anxiously, "I hope it won't be too strange for you, away from Videssos the city."

She looked at him with mixed fondness and exasperation. "Strange? It'll be more like going home. Have you forgotten I grew up on a country holding not very far from the one we're taking? I never thought I'd see the city until my father led the revolt that cast out Strobilos Sphrantzes. No, you needn't fear for me on that score."

Flustered because he *had* forgotten, Marcus said, "All right," so unconvincingly that Alypia could not help laughing.

"It really is all right," she assured him. "This is the happy ending the romances write about, the one we all know doesn't happen in real life. But we have it, you and I—the villain overthrown, you with the acclaim you deserve, and the two of us together, as we should be. Is any of that bad?"

He laughed himself. "No," he said, "especially the last," and kissed her. He was telling the truth; his previous experience reminded him how lucky he was. One sign was the absence of the grinding fights that had punctuated his time with Helvis. But that was only the most obvious mark of a greater tranquility. Not the least reason for it, he knew, was his learning from earlier mistakes.

Yet there was no denying the part Alypia played in their contentment together. By not trying to make him over, he thought, she left him free to change for himself instead of being frozen behind a defensive shell.

The proof of her success—and perhaps of his own—was that they cared for each other more as time went by, where before happiness had steadily leaked away once passion cooled.

That was not to say he and Alypia did not have differences. She had just shown one, with her talk of happy endings. He thought the imperial religion, with its emphasis on the battles between good and evil, had much to do with that.

Scaurus had come to terms with Phos himself, but he still felt the influence of his Stoic upbringing. Endings *were* for romances, which did not have to worry about what came after them. In the real world trouble followed trouble without cease; there was only one ending, and that predetermined.

But many roads led toward it. "Call this a good beginning," he said, and Alypia did not argue.

(1967)

1979–1983

(1985)

PHOTO: © M. C. VALADA

HARRY TURTLEDOVE is the award-winning author of the alternate-history works *The Man with the Iron Heart; Guns of the South; How Few Remain* (winner of the Sidewise Award for Best Novel); the Worldwar saga: *In the Balance, Tilting the Balance, Upsetting the Balance,* and *Striking the Balance;* the Colonization books: *Second Contact, Down to Earth,* and *Aftershocks;* the Great War epics: *American Front, Walk in Hell,* and *Breakthroughs;* the American Empire novels: *Blood & Iron, The Center Cannot Hold,* and *Victorious Opposition;* and the Settling Accounts series: *Return Engagement, Drive to the East, The Grapple,* and *In at the Death.* Turtledove is married to fellow novelist Laura Frankos. They have three daughters: Alison, Rachel, and Rebecca.